PRAISE FO

"Mr. Goodkind's compelling prose weaves a magic spell over readers." —*Romantic Times BOOKreviews*

"Makes an indelible impact." —*Publishers Weekly*

"Outstanding . . . Characters who actually behave like adults. Highly recommended." —*The San Diego Union-Tribune*

"Few writers have Goodkind's power of creation . . . a phenomenal piece of imaginative writing, exhaustive in its scope and riveting in its detail." —*Publishing News*

"Goodkind's greatest triumph: the ability to introduce immediately identifiable characters. His heroes, like us, are not perfect. Instead, each is flawed in ways that strengthen, rather than weaken their impact. You'll find no two-dimensional oafs here. In fact, at times you'll think you're looking at your own reflection." —*SFX*

Books by Terry Goodkind

Wizard's First Rule
Stone of Tears
Blood of the Fold
Temple of the Winds
Soul of the Fire
Faith of the Fallen
The Pillars of Creation
Naked Empire
Debt of Bones
Chainfire
Phantom
Confessor
The Law of Nines
The Omen Machine
The Third Kingdom
Severed Souls
The First Confessor
Warheart
Nest
The Girl in the Moon
Death's Mistress
Shroud of Eternity
Siege of Stone

Blood of the Fold

TERRY GOODKIND

A TOM DOHERTY ASSOCIATES BOOK
NEW YORK

BLOOD OF THE FOLD

Edited by James Frenkel
Map by Terry Goodkind

A Tor Book
Published by Tom Doherty Associates
175 Fifth Avenue
New York, NY 10010

www.tor-forge.com

Tor® is a registered trademark of Macmillan Publishing Group, LLC.

ISBN 978-1-250-80662-8

Our books may be purchased in bulk for promotional, educational, or business use. Please contact your local bookseller or the Macmillan Corporate and Premium Sales Department at 1-800-221-7945, extension 5442, or by email at MacmillanSpecialMarkets@macmillan.com.

First Edition: October 1996
First International Mass Market Edition: April 1997
First U.S. Mass Marked Edition: August 1997

To Ann Hansen,
the light in the darkness

ACKNOWLEDGMENTS

Many thanks, as ever, to all those who have helped: my editor, James Frenkel, for the adept way he keeps raising the bar; my British editor, Caroline Oakley, and the good people at Orion for their devotion to excellence; James Minz for the great line; Linda Quinton and the sales and marketing staff at Tor for their passion and triumphs; Tom Doherty, for his faith, the knowledge of which keeps me working hard; Kevin Murphy for the award-winning cover art; Jeri for her forbearance; and I thank the spirit of Richard and Kahlan, who continue to inspire me.

Blood of the Fold

CHAPTER 1

AT THE EXACT SAME instant, the six women suddenly awoke, the lingering sound of their screams echoing around the cramped officer's cabin. In the darkness, Sister Ulicia could hear the others gasping to catch their breath. She swallowed, trying to slow her own panting, and immediately winced at the raw pain in her throat. She could feel wetness on her eyelids, but her lips were so dry she had to lick them, for fear they would crack and bleed.

Someone was banging on the door. She was aware of his shouts only as a dull drone in her head. She didn't bother trying to focus on the words or their meaning; the man was inconsequential.

Lifting a trembling hand toward the center of the coal black quarters, she released a flow of her Han, the essence of life and spirit, directing a point of heat into the oil lamp she knew to be hanging on the low beam. Its wick obediently sprang to flame, releasing a sinuous line of soot that traced the lamp's slow, to-and-fro sway as the ship rolled in the sea.

The other women, all of them naked, as was she, were sitting up as well, their eyes fixed on the feeble, yellow glow, as if seeking from it salvation, or perhaps reassurance that they were still alive and there was light to be seen. A tear rolled down Ulicia's cheek, too, at the sight of the flame. The blackness had been suffocating, like a great weight of damp, black earth shoveled over her.

Her bedding was sodden and cold with sweat, but even without the sweat, everything was always wet in the salt air, to say nothing of the spray that sporadically drenched the deck and trickled into everything below. She couldn't remember what it was like to feel dry clothes or bedding against her. She hated this ship, its interminable damp, its foul smells, and the constant rolling and pitching that turned her stomach. At least she was alive to hate the ship. Gingerly, she swallowed back the taste of bile.

Ulicia wiped her fingers at the warm wetness over her eyes and held out her hand; her fingertips glistened with blood. As if emboldened by her example, some of the others cautiously did the same. Each of them had bloody scratches on their eyelids, eyebrows, and cheeks from trying desperately, but futilely, to claw their eyes open, to wake themselves from the snare of sleep, in a vain attempt to escape the dream that was not a dream.

Ulicia struggled to clear the fog from her mind. It must have been a simple nightmare.

She forced herself to look away from the flame, at the other women. Sister Tovi hunched in a lower bunk opposite, the thick rolls of flesh at her sides seeming to sag in sympathy with the morose expression on her wrinkled face as she watched the lamp. Sister Cecilia's habitually tidy, curly gray hair stood out in disarray, her incessant smile replaced by an ashen mask of fear as she stared up from the lower bunk next to Tovi. Leaning forward a bit, Ulicia glanced at the bunk above. Sister Armina, not nearly as old as Tovi or Cecilia, but closer to Ulicia's age and still attractive, appeared haggard. With shaking fingers, the usually staid Armina wiped the blood from her eyelids.

Across the confining walkway, in the bunks above Tovi and Cecilia, sat the two youngest and most self-possessed Sisters. Ragged scratches marred the flawless skin of Sister Nicci's cheeks. Strands of her blond hair stuck to the tears, sweat, and blood on her face. Sister Merissa, equally beautiful, clutched a blanket to her naked breast, not in modesty, but in shuddering dread. Her long, dark hair was a tangled mat.

The others were older, and adeptly wielded power tempered in the forge of experience, but both Nicci and Merissa were possessed of rare, innate, dark talents—a deft touch that no amount of experience could invoke. Astute beyond their years, neither was beguiled by Cecilia or Tovi's kindly smiles or gentle affectations. Though young and self-assured, they both knew that Cecilia, Tovi, Armina, and especially Ulicia herself were capable of taking them both apart, piece by piece, if they so chose. Still, that did not diminish their mastery; in their own right, they were two of the most formidable women ever to have drawn breath. But it was for their singular resolve to prevail that the Keeper had selected them.

Seeing these women she knew so well in such a state was unnerving, but it was the sight of Merissa's unbridled terror that really shook Ulicia. She had never known a Sister as composed, as unemotional, as implacable, as merciless, as Merissa. Sister Merissa had a heart of black ice.

Ulicia had known Merissa for close to 170 years, and in all that time she could not recall having ever seen her cry. She was sobbing now.

Sister Ulicia was first horrified and then disgusted to see the others in a condition of such abject weakness, but then her revulsion turned to silent satisfaction; in fact it pleased her; she drew strength from the sight. She was their leader, and stronger than they.

The man was still banging at the door, wanting to know what the trouble was, what the screaming was all about. She unleashed her anger toward the door. "Leave us! If you are needed you will be summoned!"

The sailor's muffled curses faded away as he retreated down the passageway. The only sound, other than the creak of timbers as the ship yawed when struck abeam by a heavy sea, was the sobbing.

"Stop your sniveling, Merissa," Ulicia snapped.

Merissa's dark eyes, still glazed with fear, focused on her. "It's never been like that before." Tovi and Cecilia nodded their agreement. "I've done his bidding. Why has he done this? I have not failed him."

"Had we failed him," Ulicia said, "we would be there, with Sister Liliana."

Armina started. "You saw her, too? She was—"

"I saw her," Ulicia said, masking her own horror with an even tone.

Sister Nicci drew a twisted skein of sodden blond hair back off her face. Gathering composure smoothed her voice. "Sister Liliana failed the Master."

Sister Merissa, the glaze in her eyes ebbing, flashed a look of cool disdain. "She is paying the price of failure." The crisp edge in her own tone thickened like winter's frost on a window. "Forever." Merissa almost never let emotion touch her smooth features, but it touched her face now as her brows drew together in a murderous scowl. "She countermanded your orders, Sister Ulicia, and the Keeper's. She ruined our plans. This is her fault."

Liliana had indeed failed the Keeper. They wouldn't all be on this cursed ship if it weren't for Sister Liliana. Ulicia's face heated at the thought of that woman's arrogance. Liliana had thought to have the glory to herself. She had gotten what she deserved. Even so, Ulicia swallowed at the memory of having seen Liliana's torment, and didn't even notice the pain of her raw throat this time.

"But what of us?" Cecilia asked. Her smile returned, apologetic, rather than merry. "Must we do as this . . . man says?"

Ulicia wiped a hand across her face. They had no time to hesitate, if this was real, if what she had seen had really happened. It must be nothing more than a simple nightmare; no one but the Keeper had ever before come to her in the dream that was not a dream. Yes, it had to be just a nightmare. Ulicia watched a roach crawl into the chamber pot. Her gaze suddenly rose.

"This man? You did not see the Keeper? You saw a man?"

Cecilia quailed. "Jagang."

Tovi raised her hand toward her lips to kiss her ring finger—an ancient gesture beseeching the Creator's protection. It was an old habit, begun the first morning of a novice's training. Each of them had learned to do it every morning, without fail, upon arising, and in times of tribulation. Tovi had probably done it by rote countless thousands of times, as had they all. A Sister of the Light was symbolically betrothed to the Creator, and His will. Kissing the ring finger was a ritual renewal of that betrothal.

There was no telling what the act of kissing that finger would do, now, in view of their betrayal. Superstition had it that it was death for one who had pledged her soul to the Keeper—a Sister of the Dark—to kiss that finger. While it was unclear whether it truly would invoke the Creator's wrath, there was no doubt it would invoke the Keeper's. When her hand was halfway to her lips, Tovi realized what she was about to do and snatched it away.

"You all saw Jagang?" Ulicia regarded each in turn, and each nodded. A small flame of hope still flickered in her. "So you saw the emperor. That means nothing." She leaned toward Tovi. "Did you hear him say anything?"

Tovi drew the coverlet up to her chin. "We were all there, as we always are when the Keeper seeks us. We sat in the semicircle, naked, as we always do. But it was Jagang who came, not the Master."

A soft sob came from Armina in the bunk above. "Silence!" Ulicia returned her attention to the shivering Tovi. "But what did he say? What were his words?"

Tovi's gaze sought the floor. "He said our souls were his now. He said we were his now, and we lived only at his whim. He said we must come to him at once, or we would envy Sister Liliana's fate." She looked up, into Ulicia's eyes. "He said we would regret it if we made him wait." Tears flooded her eyes. "And then he gave me a taste of what it would mean to displease him."

Ulicia's flesh had gone cold, and she realized that she, too, had drawn her sheet up. She pushed it back into her lap with an effort. "Armina?" Soft confirmation came from above. "Cecilia?" Cecilia nodded. Ulicia looked to the two in the upper bunk opposite. The composure they had worked so hard to bring back seemed to have settled in. "Well? Did you two hear the same words?"

"Yes," Nicci said.

"The exact same," Merissa said without emotion. "Liliana has brought this upon us."

"Perhaps the Keeper is displeased with us," Cecilia offered, "and has given us to the emperor so we may serve him as a way of earning back our place of favor."

Merissa's back stiffened. Her eyes were a window into her frozen heart. "I have given my soul oath to the Keeper. If we must serve this vulgar beast in order to return to our Master's graces, then I will serve. I will lick this man's feet, if I must."

Ulicia remembered Jagang, just before he had departed the semicircle in the dream that was not a dream, commanding Merissa to stand. He had then casually reached out, grabbed her right breast in his powerful fingers, and squeezed until her knees buckled. Ulicia glanced at Merissa's breast, now, and saw lurid bruises there.

Merissa made no effort to cover herself as her serene expression settled on Ulicia's eyes. "The emperor said we would regret it, if we made him wait."

Ulicia, too, had heard the same instructions. Jagang had displayed what bordered on contempt for the Keeper. How was he able to supplant the Keeper in the dream that was not a dream? He had—that was all that mattered. It had happened to all of them. It had not been a mere dream.

Tingling dread thickened in the pit of her stomach as the small flame of hope extinguished. She, too, had been given a taste of what disobedience would mean. The blood that was crusting over her eyes reminded her of how much she had wanted to escape that lesson. It had been real, and they all knew it. They had no choice. There wasn't a moment to lose. A cold bead of sweat trickled down between her breasts. If they were late . . .

Ulicia bounded out of bed.

"Turn this ship around!" she shrieked as she flung open the door. "Turn it around at once!"

No one was in the passageway. She sprang up the companionway, screaming as she went. The others raced after her, pounding on cabin doors as they followed. Ulicia didn't bother with the doors; it was the helmsman who pointed the ship where it was going and commanded the deckhands to the sails.

Ulicia heaved open the hatch door to be greeted by murky light; dawn was not yet upon them. Leaden clouds seethed above the dark cauldron of the sea. Luminous foam frothed just beyond the rail as the ship slid down a towering wave, making it seem they were plunging into an inky chasm. The other Sisters poured from the hatchway behind her out onto the spray-swept deck.

"Turn this ship around!" she screamed to the barefoot sailors who turned in mute surprise.

Ulicia growled a curse and raced aft, toward the tiller. The five Sisters followed on her heels as she dashed across the pitching deck. Hands gripping the lapels of his coat, the helmsman stretched his neck to see what the trouble was. Lantern light came through the opening at his feet, showing the faces of the four men manning the tiller. Sailors gathered near the bearded helmsman, and stood gawking at the six women.

Ulicia gulped air trying to catch her breath. "What's the matter with you slack-jawed idiots? Didn't you hear me? I said to turn this ship around!"

Suddenly, she fathomed the reason for the stares: the six of them were naked. Merissa stepped up beside her, standing tall and aloof, as if she were dressed in a gown that covered her from neck to deck.

One of the leering deckhands spoke as his gaze played over the younger woman. "Well, well. Looks like the ladies have come out to play."

Cool and unattainable, Merissa regarded his lecherous grin with unruffled authority. "What's mine is mine, and not anyone else's, even to look upon, unless I decide it is so. Remove your eyes from my flesh at once, or have them removed."

Had the man the gift, and Ulicia's mastery of it, he would have been able to sense the air about Merissa cracking ominously with power. These men knew them only as wealthy nobility wanting passage to strange and distant places; they didn't know who, or what, the six women really were. Captain Blake knew them as Sisters of the Light, but Ulicia had ordered him to keep that knowledge from his men.

The man mocked Merissa with a lecherous expression and obscene thrusts of his hips. "Don't be standoffish, lass. You wouldn't of come out here like that unless you had in mind the same as us."

The air sizzled around Merissa. Blood blossomed at the crotch of the man's trousers. He squealed as he looked up with eyes gone wild. Lightning glinted off the long knife at his belt as he yanked it free. Yelling an oath of retribution, he staggered ahead with lethal intent.

A distant smile touched Merissa's full lips. "You filthy scum," she murmured to herself. "I deliver you into the cold embrace of my Master."

His flesh burst apart as if he were a rotten melon whacked with a stick. A concussion of air driven by the power of the gift slammed him over the rail. A bloody trail traced his course across the planks. With scarcely a splash, the black water swallowed the body. The other men, near to a dozen, stood wide-eyed and still as statues.

"You will all keep your eyes on our faces," Merissa hissed, "and off everything else."

The men nodded, too appalled to voice their consent. One man's gaze involuntarily flicked down at her body, as if her speaking aloud what was forbidden to look upon had made the impulse to view it impossible to control. In ragged terror, he began to apologize, but a focused line of power as sharp as a battle axe sliced across his eyes. He tumbled out over the rail as had the first.

"Merissa," Ulicia said softly, "that will be quite enough. I think they've learned their lesson."

Eyes of ice, distant behind the haze of Han, turned to her. "I will not have their eyes taking what does not belong to them."

Ulicia lifted an eyebrow. "We need them to get back. You do remember our urgency, don't you?"

Merissa glanced at the men, as if surveying bugs beneath her boots. "Of course, Sister. We must return at once."

Ulicia turned to see that Captain Blake had just arrived and was standing behind them, his mouth agape.

"Turn this ship around, Captain," Ulicia said. "At once."

His tongue darted out to wet his lips as his gaze skipped among the women's eyes. "Now you're wanting to go back? Why?"

Ulicia lifted a finger in his direction. "You were paid well, Captain, to take us where we want to go, when we want to go. I told you before that questions were not part of the bargain, and I also promised you that I would separate you from your hide if you violated any part of that bargain. If you test me you will find that I am not nearly as indulgent as Merissa here; I don't grant a quick death. Now, turn this ship around!"

Captain Blake leaped into action. He straightened his coat and glared at his men. "Back to it, you sluggards!" He gestured to the helmsman. "Mister Dempsey, bring 'er about." The man seemed to be still frozen in shock. "Right bloody now, Mister Dempsey!"

Snatching his scruffy hat from his head, Captain Blake bowed to Ulicia, careful not to let his gaze stray from her eyes. "As you wish, Sister. Back around the great barrier, to the Old World."

"Set a direct course, Captain. Time is of the essence."

He squashed his hat in a fist. "Direct course! We can't be sailing through the great barrier!" He immediately softened his tone. "It's not possible. We'll all be killed."

Ulicia pressed a hand over the burning pang in her stomach. "The great barrier is down, Captain. It is no longer a hindrance to us. Set a direct course."

He rung his hat. "The great barrier is down? That's impossible. What makes you think . . ."

She leaned toward him. "Again, you would question me?"

"No, Sister. No, of course not. If you say the barrier is down, then it is. Though I don't understand how what cannot happen has happened, I know it's not my place to question. A direct course it is." He wiped his hat across his mouth. "Merciful Creator protect us," he muttered, turning to the helmsman, anxious to retreat from her glare. "Hard a-starboard, Mister Dempsey!"

The man glanced down at the men on the tiller. "Hard a-starboard, boys!" He carefully raised his eyes and asked, "Are you sure about this, Captain?"

"Don't argue with me or I'll let you swim back!"

"Aye, Captain. Get to the lines!" he shouted at men already slipping some lines and hauling in on others. "Prepare to come about!"

Ulicia surveyed the men glancing nervously over their shoulders. "Sisters of the Light have eyes in the backs of their heads, gentlemen. See that yours look nowhere else, or it will be the last thing you see in this life." Men nodded before bending to their tasks.

Back in their crowded cabin, Tovi wrapped her shivering bulk in her coverlet. "It's been quite a while since I had strapping young men leering at me." She glanced to Nicci and Merissa. "Enjoy the admiration while you're still worthy of it."

Merissa pulled her shift from the chest at the end of the cabin. "It wasn't you they were leering at."

A motherly smile wrinkled Cecilia's face. "We know that, Sister. I think what Sister Tovi means is that now that we're away from the spell of the Palace of the Prophets, we will age like everyone else. You won't have the years to enjoy your looks that we've had."

Merissa straightened. "When we earn back our place of honor with the Master, I will be able to keep what I have."

Tovi stared off with a rare, dangerous look. "And I want back what I once had."

Armina slumped down on a bunk. "This is Liliana's fault. If not for her, we wouldn't have had to leave the palace and its spell. If not for her, the Keeper wouldn't have given Jagang dominion over us. We wouldn't have lost the Master's favor."

They were all silent for a moment. Squeezing around and past one another, they all went about pulling on their undergarments, while trying to avoid elbows.

Merissa drew her shift over her head. "I intend to do whatever is necessary to serve, and regain the Master's favor. I intend to have my reward for my oath." She glanced to Tovi. "I intend to remain young."

"We all want the same thing, Sister," Cecilia said as she stuffed her arms through the sleeves of her simple, brown kirtle. "But the Keeper wishes us to serve this man, Jagang, for now."

"Does he?" Ulicia asked.

Merissa squatted as she sorted through the clothes in the chest, and pulled out her crimson dress. "Why else would we have been given to this man?"

Ulicia lifted an eyebrow. "Given? You think so? I think it's more than that; I think Emperor Jagang is acting of his own volition."

The others halted at their dressing and looked up. "You think he could defy the Keeper?" Nicci asked. "For his own ambitions?"

With a finger, Ulicia tapped the side of Nicci's head. "Think. The Keeper failed to come to us in the dream that is not a dream; that has never happened before. Ever. Instead comes Jagang. Even if the Keeper were displeased with us, and wanted us to serve penance under Jagang, don't you suppose he would have come to us himself and ordered it, to show us his displeasure? I don't think this is the Keeper's doing. I think it is Jagang's."

Armina snatched up her blue dress. It was a shade lighter than Ulicia's, but no less elaborate. "It is still Liliana who has brought this upon us!"

A small smile touched Ulicia's lips. "Has she? Liliana was greedy. I think the Keeper thought to use that greed, but she failed him." The smile vanished. "It is not Sister Liliana who brought this upon us."

Nicci's hand paused as she drew the cord tight at the bodice of her black dress. "Of course. The boy."

"Boy?" Ulicia slowly shook her head. "No 'boy' could have brought down the barrier. No mere boy could have brought to ruin the plans we have worked so hard for, all these years. We all know what he is, about the prophecies."

Ulicia looked at each Sister in turn. "We are in a very dangerous position. We must work to gain back the Keeper's power in this world, or else when Jagang is finished with us he will kill us, and we will find ourselves in the underworld, and no longer of use to the Master. If that happens, then the Keeper surely will be displeased, and he will make what Jagang showed us seem a lover's embrace."

The ship creaked and groaned as they all considered her words. They were racing back to serve a man who would use them, and then discard them without a thought, much less a reward, yet none of them were prepared to even consider defying him.

"Boy or not, he has caused all this." The muscles in Merissa's jaw tightened. "And to think, I had him in my grasp, we all did. We should have taken him when we had the chance."

"Liliana, too, thought to take him, to have his power for herself," Ulicia said, "but she was reckless and ended up with that cursed sword of his through her heart. We must be smarter than she; then we will have his power, and the Keeper his soul."

Armina wiped a tear from her lower eyelid. "But in the meantime, there must be some way we can avoid having to return—"

"And how long do you think we could remain awake?" Ulicia snapped. "Sooner or later we would fall asleep. Then what? Jagang has already shown us he has the power to reach out to us, wherever we are."

Merissa returned to fastening the buttons at the bodice of her crimson dress. "We will do what we must, for now, but that does not mean we can't use our heads."

Ulicia's brows drew together in thought. She looked up with a wry smile. "Emperor Jagang may believe he has us where he wants us, but we've lived a long time. Perhaps, if we use our heads, and our experience, we will not be quite as cowed as he thinks?"

Malevolence gleamed in Tovi's eyes. "Yes," she hissed, "we have indeed lived a long time, and we've learned to bring a few wild boars to ground, and gut them while they squeal."

Nicci smoothed the gathers in the skirt of her black dress. "Gutting pigs is all well and good, but Emperor Jagang is our plight, and not its cause. Nor is it advantageous to waste our anger on Liliana; she was simply a greedy fool. It is the one who truly brought this trouble upon us who must be made to suffer."

"Wisely put, Sister," Ulicia said.

Merissa absently touched her breast where it was bruised. "I will bathe in that young man's blood." Her eyes went out of focus, opening again the window to her black heart. "While he watches."

Ulicia's fists tightened as she nodded in agreement. "It is he, the

Seeker, who has brought this upon us. I vow he will pay with his gift, his life, and his soul."

CHAPTER 2

RICHARD HAD JUST TAKEN a spoonful of hot spice soup when he heard the deep, menacing growl. He frowned over at Gratch. The gar's hooded eyes glowed, lit from within by cold green fire as he glared toward the gloom among the columns at the base of the expansive steps. His leathery lips drew back in a snarl, exposing prodigious fangs. Richard realized he still had a mouthful of soup, and swallowed.

Gratch's guttural growl grew, deep in his throat, sounding like a moldy old castle's massive dungeon door being opened for the first time in a hundred years.

Richard glanced to Mistress Sanderholt's wide, brown eyes. Mistress Sanderholt, the head cook at the Confessors' Palace, was still uneasy about Gratch, and not entirely confident in Richard's assurances that the gar was harmless. The ominous growl wasn't helping.

She had brought Richard out a loaf of freshly baked bread and a bowl of savory spice soup, intending to sit on the steps with him and talk about Kahlan, only to discover that the gar had arrived a short time before. Despite her trepidation over the gar, Richard had managed to convince her to join him on the steps.

Gratch had been keenly interested at the mention of Kahlan's name; he had a lock of her hair that Richard had given him hanging on a thong around his neck, along with the dragon's tooth.

Richard had told Gratch that he and Kahlan were in love, and she wanted to be Gratch's friend, just as Richard was, and so the inquisitive gar had sat down to listen, but just as Richard had tasted the soup, and before Mistress Sanderholt had been able to begin, Gratch's mood had suddenly changed. He looked savagely intent, now, on something that Richard couldn't see.

"Why is he doing that?" Mistress Sanderholt whispered.

"I'm not sure," Richard admitted. He brightened his smile and shrugged offhandedly when the creases in her brow deepened. "He must just see a rabbit or something. Gars have exceptional eyesight, even in the dark, and they're excellent hunters." Her concerned expression didn't ease, so he went on. "He doesn't eat people. He would never hurt anyone," he reassured her. "It's all right, Mistress Sanderholt, really, it is."

Richard glanced up at the sinister-looking, snarling face. "Gratch," he whispered out of the side of his mouth, "stop growling. You're scaring her."

"Richard," she said as she leaned closer, "gars are dangerous beasts. They are not pets. Gars can't be trusted."

"Gratch isn't a pet, he's my friend. I've known him since he was a pup, since he was half my size. He's as gentle as a kitten."

An unconvincing smile twitched onto Mistress Sanderholt's face. "If you say so, Richard." Dismay suddenly widened her eyes. "He doesn't understand anything I'm saying, does he?"

"It's hard to tell," Richard confided. "Sometimes he understands more than I think possible."

Gratch appeared oblivious of them as they talked. He was frozen in concentration, seeming to have either the scent or the sight of something he didn't like. Richard thought he had seen Gratch growling like that one time before, but he couldn't place where or when. He tried to recall the occasion, but the mental image kept slipping away, just out of grasp. The harder he tried, the more elusive the shadowy memory became.

"Gratch?" He clutched the gar's powerful arm. "Gratch, what is it?"

Stone still, Gratch didn't react to the touch. As he had grown, the glow in his green eyes had intensified, but never before to this ferocity. They were glowing brightly.

Richard scanned the shadows below, where those green eyes were fixed, but saw nothing out of the ordinary. There were no people among the columns, or along the wall of the palace grounds. It must be a rabbit, he decided at last; Gratch loved rabbit.

Dawn was just beginning to reveal wisps of purple and pink clouds above the brightening horizon, leaving but a few of the brightest stars to glimmer in the western sky. With the faint first light came a gentle breeze, unusually warm for winter, that ruffled the fur of the huge beast and billowed open Richard's black mriswith cape.

When he had been in the Old World with the Sisters of the Light, Richard had gone into the Hagen Woods, where lurked the mriswith—vile creatures looking like men half melted into a reptilian nightmare. After he had fought and killed one of the mriswith, he had discovered the astonishing thing its cape could do; it had the ability to blend with its background so perfectly, so flawlessly, that it made the mriswith, or Richard when he concentrated while wearing the cape, seem invisible. It also prevented anyone with the gift from sensing them, or him. For some reason, though, Richard's own gift allowed him to sense the presence of the mriswith. That ability—to sense the danger despite its cloak of magic—had saved his life.

Richard found it difficult to focus on Gratch's growling at rabbits in the shadows. The anguish, the numb misery, of believing that his beloved, Kahlan, had been executed, had evaporated in a heart-pounding instant the day before when he had discovered she was alive. He felt blind joy that she was safe, and exultant at having spent the night alone with her in a strange place between worlds. His mind was in song this beautiful morning, and he found himself smiling without even realizing it. Not even Gratch's annoying fixation with a rabbit could dampen his mood.

Richard did find the guttural sound distracting, though, and obviously Mistress Sanderholt found it alarming; she sat woodenly on the edge of a step beside him, clutching her wool shawl tight. "Quiet, Gratch. You just had a whole leg of mutton and half a loaf of bread. You couldn't be that hungry already."

Although Gratch's attention remained riveted, his growling lessened to a rumbling deep in his throat, as if he was absently trying to comply.

Richard directed a brief glance once more toward the city. His plan had been to find a horse and hurry on his way to catch up with

Kahlan and his grandfather and old friend, Zedd. Besides being impatient to see Kahlan, he dearly missed Zedd; it had been three months since he had seen him, but it seemed years. Zedd was a wizard of the First Order, and there was much that Richard, in light of his discoveries about himself, needed to talk to him about, but then Mistress Sanderholt had brought out the soup and freshly baked bread. Good mood or not, he had been famished.

Richard glanced back, past the white elegance of the Confessors' Palace, up at the immense, imposing Wizard's Keep embedded in the steep mountainside, its soaring walls of dark stone, its ramparts, bastions, towers, connecting passageways, and bridges, all looking like a sinister encrustation growing from the stone, somehow looking alive, as if it were peering down at him from above. A wide ribbon of road wound its way up from the city toward the dark walls, crossing a bridge that looked thin and delicate, but only because of the distance, before passing under a spiked dropgate and being swallowed into the dark maw of the Keep. There had to be thousands of rooms in the Keep, if there was one. Richard snugged his cape closer under the cold, stony gaze of that place, and looked away.

This was the palace, the city, where Kahlan had grown up, where she had lived most of her life until the previous summer when she had crossed the boundary to Westland in search of Zedd, and had come across Richard, too.

The Wizard's Keep was where Zedd had grown up and lived prior to leaving the Midlands, before Richard was born. Kahlan had told him stories about how she had spent much of her time in the Keep, studying, but she had never made the place sound in the least bit sinister. Hard against the mountain, the Keep looked baleful to him now.

Richard's smile returned at the thought of how Kahlan must have looked when she was a little girl, a Confessor in training, strolling the halls of this palace, walking the corridors of the Keep, among wizards, and out among the people of this city.

But Aydindril had fallen under the blight of the Imperial Order, and was no longer a free city, no longer the seat of power in the Midlands.

Zedd had produced one of his wizard's tricks—magic—to make everyone think they had witnessed Kahlan's beheading, allowing them to flee Aydindril, while everyone here thought she was dead.

No one would chase after them now. Mistress Sanderholt had known Kahlan since she was born, and was delirious with relief when Richard told her that Kahlan was safe and well.

The smile touched his lips again. "What was Kahlan like when she was little?"

She stared off, a smile on her lips as well. "She was always serious, but as precious a child as I've ever seen, who grew to be a stalwart and beautiful woman. She was a child not only touched by magic, but also of a special character.

"None of the Confessors were surprised by her accession to Mother Confessor, and all were pleased because her way was to facilitate agreement, not to dominate, though if someone wrongly opposed her they'd find her cast with as much iron as any Mother Confessor ever born. I've never known a Confessor with her passion for the people of the Midlands. I've always felt honored to know her." Drifting into memories, she laughed faintly, a sound not nearly as frail as the rest of her appeared. "Even one time when I swatted her bottom after I discovered she had made off with a just roasted duck without asking."

Richard grinned at the prospect of hearing a story about Kahlan misbehaving. "Punishing a Confessor, even a young one, didn't give you pause?"

"No," she scoffed. "Had I pampered her, her mother would have turned me out. We were expected to treat her respectfully, but fairly."

"Did she cry?" he asked, before he took a big bite of bread. It was delicious, coarse ground wheat with a hint of molasses.

"No. She looked surprised. She believed she had done no wrong, and started explaining. Apparently a woman with two young ones almost Kahlan's age had been waiting outside the palace for someone she thought would be gullible. As Kahlan started for the Wizard's Keep, the woman approached her with a sad story, telling her that she needed gold to feed her youngsters. Kahlan told her to wait, and then took her my roasted duck, reasoning that it was food the woman needed, not gold. Kahlan sat the children down—" With a bandaged hand, she pointed off to her left. "—around that side over there, and fed them the duck. The woman was furious, and started yelling, accusing Kahlan of being selfish with all the palace's gold.

"As Kahlan was telling me this story, a patrol of the Home

Guard came into the kitchen dragging the woman and her two young ones along. Apparently, as the woman had been railing at Kahlan the Guard had come upon the scene. About this time Kahlan's mother showed up in the kitchen wanting to know what the trouble was. Kahlan told her story, and the woman fell to pieces at being in the custody of the Home Guard, and worse, at finding herself before the Mother Confessor herself.

"Kahlan's mother listened to her story, and to the woman's, and then told Kahlan that if you chose to help someone then they became your responsibility, and it was your duty to see the help through until they were back on their own feet. Kahlan spent the next day on Kings Row, with the Home Guard dragging the woman behind, going from one palace to another, looking for one that was in need of help. She wasn't having much luck; they all knew the woman was a sot.

"I felt guilty about giving Kahlan a swat before at least hearing her reasons for taking my roasted duck. I had a friend, a stern woman in charge of the cooks at one of the palaces, and so I rushed over and convinced her to accept the woman into her employ when Kahlan brought her around. I never told Kahlan what I'd done. The woman worked there a long time, but she never again came near the Confessors' Palace. Her youngest grew up to join the Home Guard. Last summer he was wounded when the D'Harans captured Aydindril, and died a week later."

Richard, too, had fought D'Hara, and in the end had killed its ruler, Darken Rahl. Though he still couldn't help feeling a twinge of regret at being sired by that evil man, he no longer felt the guilt of being his son. He knew that the crimes of the father didn't pass on to the child, and it certainly wasn't his mother's fault she had been raped by Darken Rahl. His stepfather loved Richard's mother no less for it, nor did he show Richard any less love for not having been his own blood. Richard would not have loved his stepfather any less had he known George Cypher was not his real father.

Richard was a wizard, too, he now knew. The gift, the force of magic within him called Han, had been passed down from two lines of wizards: Zedd, his grandfather on his mother's side, and Darken Rahl, his father. That combination had spawned in him magic no wizard had possessed in thousands of years—not only Additive but also Subtractive Magic. Richard knew precious little about being a wizard, or about magic, but Zedd would help him learn, help him control the gift and use it to aid people.

Richard swallowed the bread he had been chewing. "That sounds like the Kahlan I know."

Mistress Sanderholt shook her head ruefully. "She always felt a deep responsibility for the people of the Midlands. I know it hurt her to her very soul to have them turn against her for the promise of gold."

"Not all did that, I'd bet," Richard said. "But that's why you mustn't tell anyone she's still alive. In order to keep Kahlan safe, and protect her, no one must know the truth."

"You know you have my promise, Richard. But I expect they've forgotten about her by now. I expect that if they don't get the gold they were promised, they'll soon be rioting."

"So that's why all those people are gathered outside the Confessors' Palace?"

She nodded. "They now believe they're entitled to it, because someone from the Imperial Order said that they were to have it. Though the man who promised it is now dead, it's as if once his words were spoken aloud, the gold magically became theirs. If the Imperial Order doesn't soon begin handing out the gold in the treasury, I imagine it won't be long before those people in the streets decide to storm the palace and take it."

"Maybe the promise was only made as a diversion, and the troops of the Order intended all along to keep the gold for themselves, as plunder, and will defend the palace."

"Perhaps you're right." She stared off. "Come to think of it, I don't even know what I'm still doing here. I'm of no mind to see the Order set up quarters in the palace. I'm of no mind to end up working for them. Maybe I should leave, and see if I couldn't find a place to work where people are still free of that lot. It seems so strange to think of doing that, though; the palace has been my home for most of my life."

Richard looked away from the white splendor of the Confessors' Palace, out over the city again. Should he flee, too, and leave the ancestral home of the Confessors, and the wizards, to the Imperial Order? But how could he do anything about it? Besides, the Order's troops were probably searching for him. Best if he slipped away while they were still confused and disorganized after the death of their council. He didn't know what Mistress Sanderholt should do, but he should be going before the Order found him. He needed to get to Kahlan and Zedd.

Gratch's growl deepened into a primal rumble that rattled Richard's bones, and brought him out of his thoughts. The gar rose smoothly to his feet. Richard scanned the area below again, but saw nothing. The Confessors' Palace sat on a hill, with a commanding view of Aydindril, and from his vantage point he could see that there were troops beyond the walls, in the streets of the city, but none were close to the three of them in the secluded side courtyard outside the kitchen entrance. There was nothing alive in sight where Gratch was watching.

Richard stood, his fingers briefly finding reassurance on the hilt of his sword. He was bigger than most men, but the gar towered over him. Though little more than a youngster, for a gar, Gratch stood close to seven feet, Richard guessing his weight at half again his own. Gratch had another foot to grow, maybe more; Richard was far from an expert on short-tailed gars—he had not seen that many, and the ones he had seen had been trying to kill him at the time. Richard, in fact, had killed Gratch's mother, in self-defense, and had inadvertently ended up adopting the little orphan. Over time, they had become fast friends.

Muscles under the pink skin of the powerfully built beast's stomach and chest knotted in rippling bulges. He stood still and tensed, his claws poised out to his sides, his hairy ears perked toward things unseen. Even in taking prey when he was hungry, Gratch had never displayed this level of intent ferocity. Richard felt the hackles on the back of his neck rising.

He wished he could remember when or where it was he had seen Gratch growling like this. He finally put aside his pleasant thoughts of Kahlan and, with mounting urgency, focused his attention.

Mistress Sanderholt stood beside him, peering nervously from Gratch to where he was looking. Thin and frail-looking, she was not a timid woman by any means, but had her hands not been bandaged, he thought she would be wringing them; she looked as if she wanted to.

Richard suddenly felt quite exposed on the open, wide sweep of steps. His keen gray eyes scrutinized the murky shadows and concealed places among the columns, walls, and assortment of elegant belvederes spread across the lower parts of the palace grounds.

Sparkling snow lifted on an occasional ripple of wind, but nothing else moved. He stared so hard it made his eyes hurt, but he saw nothing alive, no sign of any threat.

Though he saw nothing, Richard began to feel a burgeoning sense of danger—not a simple reaction from seeing Gratch so riled, but welling up from within himself, from his Han, welling from the depths of his chest, coursing into the fibers of his muscles, drawing them tight and ready. The magic within had become another sense that often warned him when his other senses did not. He realized that that was what was warning him now.

An urge to run, before it was too late, gnawed deep in his gut. He needed to get to Kahlan; he didn't want to get tangled in any trouble. He could find a horse, and just go. Better yet, he could run, now, and find a horse later.

Gratch's wings unfolded as he crouched in a menacing posture, ready to launch into the air. His lips drew back further, vapor hissing from between his fangs as the growl deepened, vibrating the air.

The flesh on Richard's arms tingled. His breathing quickened as the palpable sense of danger coalesced into points of threat.

"Mistress Sanderholt," he said as his gaze skipped from one long shadow to another, "why don't you go inside. I'll come in and talk to you after—"

His words caught in his throat as he saw a brief movement down among the white columns—a shimmer to the air, like the heat rippling the air above a fire. He stared, trying to decide if he had really seen it, or just imagined it. He frantically tried to think of what it could be, if indeed he had seen something. It could have been a wisp of snow carried on a brief gust of wind. He didn't see anything as he squinted in concentration. It was probably nothing more than the snow in the wind, he tried to assure himself.

Abruptly, the manifest realization welled up within him, like cold black water surging up through a rift in river ice—Richard remembered when it was he had heard Gratch growl like that. The fine hairs on the back of his neck stood out like icy needles in his flesh. His hand found the wire-wound hilt of his sword.

"Go," he whispered urgently to Mistress Sanderholt. "Now."

Without hesitation, she dashed up the steps and made for the distant kitchen entrance behind him as the ring of steel announced the arrival of the Sword of Truth in the crisp dawn air.

How was it possible for them to be here? It wasn't possible, yet he was sure of it; he could feel them.

"Dance with me, Death. I am ready," Richard murmured, already in a trance of wrath from the magic coursing into him from the Sword of Truth. The words were not his, but came from the sword's magic, from the spirits of those who had used the weapon before him. With the words came an instinctive understanding of their meaning: it was a morning prayer, meant to say that you could die this day, so you should strive to do your best while you still lived.

From the echo of other voices within came the realization that the same words also meant something altogether different: they were a battle cry.

With a roar, Gratch shot into the air, his wings lifting him after only one bounding stride. Snow swirled, curling into the air under him, stirred up by the powerful strokes of his wings that also billowed open Richard's mriswith cape.

Even before he could see them materialize out of the winter air, Richard could sense their presence. He could see them in his mind even though he couldn't yet see them with his eyes.

Howling in fury, Gratch descended in a streak toward the base of the steps. Near the columns, just as the gar reached them, they began to become visible—scales and claws and capes, white against the white snow. White as pure as a child's prayer.

Mriswith.

CHAPTER 3

THE MRISWITH REACTED TO the threat, materializing as they flung themselves at the gar. The sword's magic, its rage, inundated Richard with its full fury as he saw his friend being attacked. He bounded down the steps, toward the erupting battle.

Howls assailed his ears as Gratch tore into the mriswith. In the heat of combat they were now visible. Against the white of stone and snow, they were difficult to distinguish clearly, but Richard could see them well enough; there were close to ten as near as he could tell in all the confusion. Under their capes, they wore simple hides as white as the rest of them. Richard had seen them black before, but he knew the mriswith could appear to be the color of their surroundings. Taut, smooth skin covered their heads down to their necks, where it began welting up into tight, interlocking scales. Lipless mouths spread to reveal small, needle-sharp teeth. In the fists of their webbed claws, they gripped the cross-members of three-bladed knives. Beady eyes, intense with loathing, fixed on the raging gar.

With fluid speed, they swept around the dark form in their midst, their white capes billowing behind as they skimmed across the snow, some tumbling under the attack, or spinning out of reach, just escaping the gar's powerful arms. With brutal efficiency, the gar caught others on claws, ripping them open, throwing a shock of blood across the snow.

So intent were they on Gratch that Richard descended upon their backs unopposed. He had never fought more than one mriswith at a time, and that had been a formidable ordeal, but with the fury of the magic pounding through him he thought only of helping Gratch. Before they had a chance to turn to the new threat, Richard cut down two. Shrill death howls sundered the dawn air, the sound needle-sharp and painful in his ears.

Richard sensed others behind him, back toward the palace. He spun just in time to see three more abruptly appear. They were racing to join the fight, with only Mistress Sanderholt in their way. She cried out at finding her escape route blocked by the advancing creatures. She turned and ran ahead of them. Richard could see that she was going to lose the race, and he was too far away to make it in time.

With a backhanded swing of his sword, Richard slashed open a scaled form that turned on him. "Gratch!" he cried out. "Gratch!"

Twisting the head off a mriswith, Gratch looked up. Richard pointed with his sword.

"Gratch! Protect her!"

Gratch instantly grasped the nature of Mistress Sanderholt's peril. Flinging aside the limp, headless carcass, he bounded into the air. Richard ducked. Swift strokes of the gar's leathery wings lifted him over Richard's head and up the steps.

Reaching down, Gratch snatched the woman up in his furry arms. Her feet jerked off the ground and over the sweeping knives of the mriswith. Spreading his wings wide, Gratch banked before the woman's weight could cost him his momentum, swooped down beyond the mriswith, and then, with a powerful stroke, broke his descent to set Mistress Sanderholt on the ground. Without pause, he sprang back into the fray and, deftly avoiding the flashing knives, struck out with his claws and fangs.

Richard spun back to the three mriswith at the base of the steps. Losing himself to the sword's rage, he became one with the magic and the spirits of those who had wielded the sword before him. Everything moved with the slow elegance of a dance—the dance with death. The three mriswith came at him, whirling with cold grace, an onslaught of flashing blades. Pivoting, they split rank, skimming up the steps to go around him. With detached efficiency, Richard caught the lone creature on the point of his blade.

To his surprise, the other two cried out, "No!"

Astonished, Richard froze. He hadn't known that mriswith could speak. They paused on the steps, holding him in beady, snakelike gazes. They had almost made it past him on their way up the steps, toward Gratch. Intent on the gar, he surmised, they wanted most to get past him.

Richard bolted up the steps, blocking their way. Again they split ranks, one going to each side. Richard feinted at the one to his left, and then reeled to strike out at the other. His sword shattered the triple blades in one of its claws. Without pause, the mriswith spun, evading the killing thrust of Richard's blade, but as the creature came around, closing the distance to deliver its own strike, he drew his sword back, slicing across its neck. With a howl, the mriswith toppled to the ground, writhing, spilling blood across the snow.

Before Richard could turn to the other, it crashed into him from behind. The two of them tumbled down the steps. His sword and one of the three-bladed knives clattered across the stone at the bottom, skittering out of reach, and disappeared under the snow.

They rolled over, each trying to gain the advantage. With its scaled arms constricting around his chest, the wiry beast tried to muscle Richard onto his stomach. He could feel fetid breath on the back of his neck. Though he couldn't see his sword, he could feel its magic, and knew exactly where it lay. He tried to lunge for it, but the mriswith's weight hobbled him. He tried to drag himself, but the snow-slicked stone denied him enough purchase. The sword remained out of reach.

Powered by his anger, Richard staggered to his feet. Still clutching him with both scaled arms, the mriswith slithered a leg around his. Richard crashed face-first to the ground, the weight of the mriswith on his back driving the wind from his lungs. The mriswith's second knife hovered inches from his face.

Grunting with effort, Richard pushed himself up with one arm and with the other hand seized the wrist that held the knife. In one smooth, mighty movement, he heaved the mriswith back, ducked under the arm, and, as he came back up, wrenched it around one full turn. Bone popped. With his other hand, Richard brought his belt knife to the creature's chest. The mriswith, cape and all, flushed to a sickening, weak greenish color.

"Who sent you!" When it didn't answer, Richard twisted its arm, pinning it behind the beast's back. "Who sent you!"

The mriswith sagged. "The dreamssss walker," it hissed.

"Who's the dream walker? Why are you here?"

Waves of waxy yellow suffused the mriswith. Its eyes widened as it struggled anew to escape. "Greeneyesss!"

A sudden blow slammed Richard back. A flash of dark fur snatched the mriswith. Claws yanked its head back. Fangs sank into its neck. A powerful jerk ripped the throat away. Startled, Richard gasped for air.

Before he could catch his breath, the gar, his green eyes wild, lunged at him. Richard threw his arms up as the huge beast smashed into him. The knife flew from his hand. The sheer size of the gar was smothering, his awesome strength overpowering. Richard might as well have been trying to hold back a mountain that was falling on him. Dripping fangs drove for his face.

"Gratch!" He snatched fistfuls of fur. "Gratch! It's me, Richard!" The snarling face drew back a bit. Vapor huffed out with each breath, reeking of the putrid stench of mriswith blood. The glowing green eyes blinked. Richard stroked the heaving chest. "It's all right, Gratch. It's over. Calm down."

The iron-hard muscles of the arms that held him slackened. The snarl wrinkled into a grin. Tears welling in his eyes, Gratch crushed Richard to his chest.

"Grrratch luuug Raaaach aaarg."

Patting the gar's back, Richard struggled to get air into his lungs. "I love you too, Gratch."

Gratch, the green gleam back in his eyes, held Richard out for a critical inspection, as if to assure himself that his friend was intact. He let out a purling gurgle that bespoke his relief, whether at finding Richard safe or at having stopped before tearing him apart, Richard wasn't sure, but he did know that he, too, was relieved that it was over. His muscles, the fear, anger, and fury of the fight abruptly gone from them, throbbed with a dull ache.

Richard took a deep breath. Just surviving the sudden attack gave him a heady feeling, but he was unsettled by the mutability of Gratch's usual gentle disposition into such deadly ferocity. He glanced around at the startling amount of foul-smelling gore spilled across the snow. Gratch hadn't done it all. As he put down the last vestige of the magic's anger, it struck him that perhaps

Gratch saw him in a similar light. Just as Richard, Gratch had risen to the threat.

"Gratch, you knew they were here, didn't you?"

Gratch nodded enthusiastically, adding a bit of a growl to make his point. It occurred to Richard that when he had last seen Gratch growling with such vehemence, outside the Hagen Woods, it must have been because he sensed the presence of the mriswith.

The Sisters of the Light had told him that occasionally the mriswith strayed from the Hagen Woods, and that no one, not Sisters of the Light—sorceresses—or even wizards, had been able to perceive their presence, or had ever survived an encounter with them. Richard had been able to sense them because he was the first in near to three thousand years to be born with both sides of the gift. So how did Gratch know they were there?

"Gratch, could you see them?" Gratch pointed to a few of the carcasses, as if to point them out for Richard. "No, I can see them now. I mean before, when I was talking to Mistress Sanderholt and you were growling. Could you see them then?" Gratch shook his head. "Could you hear them, or smell them?" Gratch frowned in thought, his ears twitching, and then shook his head again. "Then how did you know they were there, before we could see them?"

Eyebrows as big as axe handles drew together as the huge beast frowned down at Richard. He shrugged, looking perplexed about his failure to come up with a satisfactory answer.

"You mean that before you could see them, you could feel them? Something inside just told you they were there?"

Gratch grinned and nodded, happy that Richard seemed to understand. That was similar to how Richard knew they were there; before he could see them, he could sense them, see them in his mind. But Gratch didn't have the gift. How could he do it?

Perhaps it was just because animals could sense things before people could. Wolves commonly knew you were there before you knew they were. Usually, the only time you knew a deer was in a thicket was when it bolted, having sensed you long before you saw it. Animals generally had keener senses than people, and predators some of the keenest. Gratch was certainly a predator. That sense seemed to have served him better than Richard's magic had him.

Mistress Sanderholt, having come down to the bottom of the steps, laid a bandaged hand on Gratch's furry arm. "Gratch . . . thank you." She turned to Richard, lowering her voice. "I thought he was going to kill me, too," she confided. She glanced at several of the torn bodies. "I've seen gars do that to people. When he snatched me up like that, I thought sure he was going to kill me. But I was wrong; he's different." She peered back up at Gratch. "You saved my life. Thank you."

Gratch's smile showed the full length of his bloody fangs. The sight made her gasp.

Richard glanced up at the sinister-looking, grinning face. "Stop smiling, Gratch. You're scaring her again."

His mouth turned down, his lips covering his prodigious, wickedly sharp fangs. His wrinkled features melted into a sulk. Gratch viewed himself as lovable, and seemed to think it only natural that everyone else would, too.

Mistress Sanderholt stroked the side of Gratch's arm. "It's all right. His smile is heartfelt, and handsome in its own way. I'm just not . . . used to it, that's all."

Gratch smiled at Mistress Sanderholt again, adding a sudden, spirited flapping of his wings. Unable to help herself, Mistress Sanderholt lurched back a step. She was just coming to understand that this gar was different from those that were always a threat to people, but her instincts still ruled that understanding. Gratch made for the woman, to give her a hug. Richard was sure she would die of fright before she realized the gar's benign intent, so he put a restraining arm in front of Gratch.

"He likes you, Mistress Sanderholt. He just wanted to give you a hug, that's all. But I think your thanks are enough."

She quickly regained her composure. "Nonsense." Smiling warmly, she held her arms out. "I'd like a hug, Gratch."

Gratch gurgled with glee and scooped her up. Under his breath, Richard cautioned Gratch to be gentle. Mistress Sanderholt let out a muffled, helpless giggle. Once back on the ground, she squirmed her bony frame straight in her dress and awkwardly drew her shawl up on her shoulders. She beamed warmly.

"You're right, Richard. He's no pet. He's a friend."

Gratch nodded enthusiastically, his ears twitching as he flapped his leathery wings again.

Richard pulled a white cape, one that was nearly clean, off a nearby mriswith. He asked Mistress Sanderholt's indulgence, and when she granted it, stood her before an oak door to a small, low-roofed stone building. He draped the cape around her shoulders and drew the hood up over her head.

"I want you to concentrate," he told her. "Concentrate on the brown of the door behind you. Hold the cape together under your chin, and close your eyes if it will help you focus. Imagine you're one with the door, that you're the same color."

She frowned up at him. "Why am I to do this?"

"I want to see if you can appear invisible like they were."

"Invisible!"

Richard smiled his encouragement. "Just give it a try?"

She let out a breath and finally nodded. Her eyes slowly closed. Her breathing evened and slowed. Nothing happened. Richard waited a while longer, but still, nothing happened. The cape remained white, not a stitch of it turning brown. She finally opened her eyes.

"Did I become invisible?" she asked, sounding as if she were afraid she had.

"No," Richard admitted.

"I didn't think so. But how did those vile snake men make themselves invisible?" She shrugged the cape off her shoulders and shuddered in revulsion. "And what made you think I could do it?"

"They're called mriswith. It's their capes that enable them to do it, so I thought that maybe you could, too." She regarded him with a dubious expression. "Here, let me show you."

Richard took her place before the door and drew up the hood of his mriswith cape. Flipping the cape closed, he set his mind to the task. In the space of a breath, the cape became the exact same color as what she saw behind him. Richard knew that the magic of the cape, apparently with the aid of his own, somehow enveloped the exposed parts of him, too, so that he seemed to disappear.

When he moved from in front of the door, the cape transfigured to continually match what she saw behind; as he stepped in front of the white stone, the pallid blocks and shadowed joints appeared to slip across him, mimicking the background as if she truly were looking through him. Richard knew from experience that even if the background was complex, it made no difference; the cape could match anything behind him.

As Richard moved away, Mistress Sanderholt continued to stare at the door, where she had last seen him. Gratch's eyes, however, never left him. Menace gathered in those green eyes as the gar followed Richard's movements. A growl rose in the gar's throat.

Richard let his concentration relax. The background colors sloughed from the cape, letting it return to black as he pushed the hood back. "It's still me, Gratch."

Mistress Sanderholt started, jerking around to discover him in his new location. Gratch's growl trailed off, and his expression slackened, at first to confusion, and then to a grin. He rumbled with a low gurgle of a laugh at the new game.

"Richard," Mistress Sanderholt stammered, "how did you do that? How did you make yourself invisible?"

"It's the cape. It doesn't really make me invisible, but somehow it can change color to match the background, so it tricks the eye. I guess it takes magic to make the cape work, and you don't have any, but I was born with the gift so it works for me." Richard glanced around at the fallen mriswith. "I think it best if we burned these capes, lest they fall into the wrong hands."

Richard told Gratch to fetch the capes at the top of the steps while he bent to gather up the ones below.

"Richard, do you think it could be . . . dangerous to use the cape from one of those evil creatures?"

"Dangerous?" Richard straightened and scratched the back of his neck. "I don't see how. All it does is change color. You know, the way some frogs and salamanders can change color to match whatever they're sitting on, like a rock, or a log, or a leaf."

She helped him, as best she could with her bandaged hands, wrap the capes into a bundle. "I've seen those frogs. I've always thought it one of the Creator's wonders that they could do that." She smiled up at him. "Perhaps the Creator is blessing you with the same wonder, because you have the gift. Praise be to Him; His blessing helped save us."

As Gratch held out the rest of the capes, one at a time, so she could add them to the bundle, anxiety tightened like arms around Richard's chest. He glanced up at the gar.

"Gratch, you don't sense any more mriswith anywhere, do you?"

The gar handed the last cape to Mistress Sanderholt and then peered off into the distance, searching intently. Finally, he shook his head. Richard sighed in relief.

"Before you killed the last mriswi th, it said the dreamwalker saw them. Do you have any idea what direction they came from, Gratch?"

Gratch again slowly turned around, scrutinizing the surroundings. For a dead silent moment, his attention fixed on the Wizard's Keep, but at last moved on. Finally, he shrugged, looking apologetic.

Richard scanned the city of Aydindril, studying the Imperial Order troops he could see below. They were made up of men of many nations, he had been told, but he recognized the chain mail, armor, and dark leather worn by most: D'Harans.

Richard knotted the last of the loose ends around the capes, drawing them into a tight bundle, and then tossed the lot on the ground. "What happened to your hands?"

She held them out, turning them over. The wrap of white cloth was discolored with dried smears of meat drippings, sauces, and oils, and smudged with ash and soot from the fires. "They pulled off my fingernails with tongs to make me give witness against the Mother Confessor . . . against Kahlan."

"And did you?" When she looked away, Richard flushed at realizing how his question must have sounded. "I'm sorry, that came out wrong. Of course no one would expect you to defy their demands under torture. The truth doesn't matter to people like that. Kahlan wouldn't believe you betrayed her."

She shrugged with one shoulder as she lowered her hands. "I wouldn't say the things they wanted me to say about her. She understood, just as you said. Kahlan herself ordered me to testify against her to keep them from doing more. Still, it was misery itself to speak such lies."

"I was born with the gift, but I don't know how to use it, or I'd see what I could do about helping you. I'm sorry." He winced in sympathy. "Is the pain beginning to ease, at least?"

"With the Imperial Order in possession of Aydindril, I'm afraid the pain has only begun."

"Was it the D'Harans who did this to you?"

"No. It was a Keltish wizard who ordered it. When Kahlan escaped, she killed him. Most of the Order's troops in Aydindril are D'Harans, though."

"How have they treated the people of the city?"

She rubbed her bandaged hands on her arms, as if chilled in the winter air. Richard almost put his cape around her shoulders but, thinking better of it, helped her pull her shawl up, instead.

"Though D'Hara conquered Aydindril, autumn past, and their troops were brutal about the fighting, since they put down all opposition and took the city they have not been so cruel, so long as their orders are followed. Perhaps they simply saw more value in having their prize intact."

"That could be, I suppose. What of the Keep? Have they taken that, too?"

She glanced over her shoulder, up the mountain. "I'm not sure, but I don't think so; the Keep is protected by spells, and from what I am told, the D'Haran troops fear magic."

Richard rubbed his chin in thought. "What happened after the war with D'Hara ended?"

"Apparently, the D'Harans, among others, made pacts with the Imperial Order. Slowly, the Keltans took charge, with the D'Harans remaining most of the muscle but acquiescing in the ruling of the city. Keltans don't fear magic the way D'Harans do. Prince Fyren, of Kelton, and that Keltish wizard commanded the council. With the prince, the wizard, and the council now dead, I'm not sure exactly who is in charge. The D'Harans, I would guess, which leaves us still at the mercy of the Imperial Order.

"With the Mother Confessor and the wizards gone, I fear our fate. I know she had to flee or be murdered, but yet . . ."

Her voice trailed off, so he finished for her. "Since the Midlands was forged and Aydindril founded to be its heart, none but a Mother Confessor has ruled here."

"You know the history?"

"Kahlan told me some of it. She's heartsick to have had to abandon Aydindril, but I assure you, we will not let the Order have Aydindril any more than we will let them have the Midlands."

Mistress Sanderholt looked away in resignation. "What was, is no more. In time, the Order will rewrite the history of this place, and the Midlands will be forgotten.

"Richard, I know you are anxious to be off to join her. Find a place to live your lives in peace and freedom. Don't become bitter at what was lost. When you reach her, tell her that although there were people who cheered at what they thought was her execution, many more were desolate at hearing she was dead. In the weeks since she fled I've seen thc side she didn't see. Just as anywhere, there are evil, greedy people here, but there are good people, too, who will always remember her. Though we be subjects of the Imperial Order, now, as long as we live, the memory of the Midlands will live on in our hearts."

"Thank you, Mistress Sanderholt. I know she'll be heartened to hear that not everyone turned against her and the Midlands. But don't give up hope. As long as the Midlands lives on in our hearts, there is hope. We will prevail."

She smiled, but in the depths of her eyes he could see for the first time into the core of her despair. She didn't believe him. Life under the Order, brief as it had been, had been brutal enough to extinguish even the spark of hope; that was why she hadn't bothered to leave Aydindril. Where was there to go?

Richard retrieved his sword from the snow and wiped its gleaming blade clean on a mriswith's hide clothes. He drove the sword home into its scabbard.

They both turned at the sound of nervous whispers to see a crowd of kitchen workers gathered near the top of the steps, staring incredulously at the carnage in the snow, and at Gratch. One man had picked up one of the three-bladed knives, and was turning it over, examining it. Fearing to come down the steps, near Gratch, he insistently motioned for Mistress Sanderholt's attention. She gestured irritably, urging him to come to her.

He appeared to be hunched more from a life of hard labor than from age, though his thinning hair was graying. He descended the steps with a rolling gait as if carrying a heavy sack of grain on his rounded shoulders. He bobbed a quick bow of deference to Mistress Sanderholt as his gaze flicked from her, to the bodies, to Gratch, to Richard, and back again to her.

"What is it, Hank?"

"Trouble, Mistress Sanderholt."

"I'm a little busy, at the moment, with trouble of my own. Can't all you people pull bread from the ovens without me there?"

His head bobbed. "Yes, Mistress Sanderholt. But this is trouble about—" He glared at a reeking mriswith carcass lying nearby. "—about these things."

Richard straightened. "What about them?"

Hank glanced to the sword at his hip, and then diverted his eyes. "I think it was . . ." When he looked up at Gratch, and the gar smiled, the man lost his voice.

"Hank, look at me." Richard waited until he complied. "The gar won't hurt you. These things are called mriswith. Gratch and I are the ones who killed them. Now tell me about the trouble."

He scrubbed the palms of his hands on his wool trousers. "I looked at their knives, at those three blades they have. That appears to be what did it." His expression darkened. "The news is spreading on a near panic. People have been killed. Thing is, no one saw what done it. Those killed all had their bellies slit open by something with three blades."

With an anguished sigh, Richard wiped a hand across his face. "That's the way mriswith kill; they disembowel their victims, and you can't even see them coming. Where were these people killed?"

"All over the city, at about the same time, right at first light. From what I heard, I reckon it had to be separate killers. By the number of these mriswith things I'd wager I'm right. The dead mark lines, like the spokes of a wheel, all leading here.

"They killed whoever was in their way: men, women, even horses. The troops are in an uproar, as some of their men got it, too, and the rest seem to think its an attack of some sort. One of these mriswith things went right through the crowd gathered out in the street. The bastard didn't bother to step around, just slashed his way right through the middle." Hank cast a sorrowful glance to Mistress Sanderholt. "One came through the palace. Killed a maid, two guards, and Jocelyn."

Mistress Sanderholt gasped and covered her mouth with a bandaged hand. Her eyes slid closed as she whispered a prayer.

"I'm sorry, Mistress Sanderholt, but I don't think Jocelyn suffered; I got to her right away, and she was already gone."

"Anyone else of the kitchen staff?"

"Just Jocelyn. She was on an errand, not in the kitchens."

Gratch silently eyed Richard as he glanced up the mountain, at the stone walls. The snow above was flushed pink in the dawn light. He pursed his lips in frustration as he looked out over the city again, bile raising in his throat.

"Hank."

"Sir?"

Richard turned back. "I want you to get some men. Carry the mriswith out in front of the palace and line them up along the grand entrance. Get it done now, before they freeze solid." The muscles in his jaw stood out as he ground his teeth. "Put the loose heads on pikes. Line them up nice and neat, on each side, so that anyone entering the palace has to walk between them."

Hank cleared his throat, as if about to protest, but then he glanced to the sword at Richard's hip and instead said, "At once, sir." He bobbed his head to Mistress Sanderholt and rushed to the palace to get help.

"The mriswith must have magic. Maybe the fear of it will at least keep the D'Harans from the palace for a while."

Worry lines creased her brow. "Richard, as you say, apparently these creatures had magic. Can anyone but you see these snake men when they're sneaking up, changing color?"

Richard shook his head. "From what I've been told, only my unique magic can sense them. But obviously Gratch can, too."

"The Imperial Order preaches on the evil of magic, and those who have it. What if this dream walker sent the mriswith to kill those with magic?"

"Sounds reasonable. What's your point?"

Her expression grave, she watched him for a long moment. "Your grandfather, Zedd, has magic, as does Kahlan."

Goose bumps tingled up his arms at hearing her voice his own thoughts aloud. "I know, but I may have an idea. For now, I must do something about what's going on here; about the Order."

"What can you hope to accomplish?" She took a breath and softened her tone. "I mean no offense, Richard. Though you have the gift, you are ignorant of its use. You are not a wizard; you can be of no help here. Flee, while you can."

"Where! If the mriswith can reach me here, they can reach me anywhere. There is no place to hide for long." He looked away, feeling his face heat. "I know I'm no wizard."

"Then what—"

He turned a raptor's glare on her. "Kahlan, as the Mother Confessor, in the name of the Midlands, has committed the Midlands to war against the Order, against its tyranny. The Order's cause is to exterminate all magic and rule all people. If we do not fight, all free people, and all those with magic, will be murdered or enslaved. There can be no peace for the Midlands, for any land, for any free people, until the Imperial Order is crushed."

"Richard, there are too many here. What can you hope to accomplish, alone?"

He was tired of being surprised and never knowing what was coming after him next. He was tired of being held prisoner, of being tortured, of being trained, of being lied to, of being used. Of seeing helpless people slaughtered. He had to do something.

Though he was no wizard, he knew wizards. Zedd was only a few weeks away, to the southwest. Zedd would understand the need to rid Aydindril of the Imperial Order, and of protecting the Wizard's Keep. If the Order destroyed that magic, who knew what would be lost for all time?

If need be, there were others, at the Palace of the Prophets in the Old World, who might be willing, and able, to help. Warren was his friend, and although not fully trained, he was a wizard, and knew about magic. More than Richard, anyway.

Sister Verna, too, would help him. The Sisters were sorceresses and had the gift, though not as powerfully as a wizard. He trusted none but Sister Verna, though. Except, perhaps, Prelate Annalina. He didn't like the way she kept information from him, and bent the truth to serve her needs, but it had not been out of malevolence; she had done what she had to out of concern for the living. Yes, Ann might help him.

And then there was Nathan, the prophet. Nathan, living under the palace's spell for most of his life, was close to a thousand years old. Richard couldn't even imagine what that man knew. He had known that Richard was a war wizard, the first to be born in thousands of years, and helped him to understand and accept its meaning. Nathan had helped him before, and Richard was reasonably sure he would again; Nathan was a Rahl, Richard's ancestor.

Desperate thoughts churned through his mind. "The aggressor makes the rules. Somehow, I must change them."

"What are you going to do?"

Richard glared out at the city. "I must do something they don't expect." He ran his fingers over the raised, gold wire spelling out the word TRUTH on the hilt of the sword, and at the same time felt the seething texture of its magic. "I wear the Sword of Truth, conferred on me by a real wizard. I have a duty. I am the Seeker." In a haze of simmering rage that rose at the thought of the people murdered by the mriswith, he whispered to himself, "I vow to give this dream walker nightmares."

CHAPTER 4

"MY ARMS DO BE itching like ants," Lunetta complained. "It be powerful here."

Tobias Brogan glanced back over his shoulder. Scraps and patches of tattered, faded cloth fluttered in the faint light as Lunetta scratched herself. Amid the ranks of men bedecked with gleaming armor and mail, draped with crimson capes, her squat form hunched atop her horse looked as if it peered out from a rag pile. Her plump cheeks dimpled with a gap-toothed grin as she chortled to herself and scratched again.

Brogan's mouth twisted in disgust, and he turned away, knuckling his wiry mustache as his gaze again passed over the Wizard's Keep up on the mountainside. The dark gray stone walls caught the first weak rays of the winter sun that blushed the snow on the higher slopes. His mouth tightened further.

"Magic, I say, my lord general," Lunetta insisted. "There be magic here. Powerful magic." She prattled on, grumbling about the way it made her skin crawl.

"Be silent, you old hag. Even a half-wit wouldn't need your filthy talent to know that Aydindril seethes with the taint of magic."

Feral eyes gleamed from under her fleshy brows. "This be different from any you have seen before," she said in a voice too thin for the rest of her. "Different from any I have ever felt before. And some be to the southwest, too, not just here." She scratched her forearms more vigorously as she cackled again.

Brogan glowered past the throngs of people hurrying down the street, casting a critical eye at the exquisite palaces lining the wide thoroughfare called, he had been informed, Kings Row. The palaces were meant to impress the viewer with the wealth, might, and spirit of the people they represented. Each structure vied for attention with towering columns, elaborate ornamentation, and flamboyant sweeps of windows, roofs, and decorated entablatures. To Tobias Brogan, they looked like nothing more than stone peacocks: an ostentatious waste if ever he had seen one.

On a distant rise lay the sprawling Confessors' Palace, its stone columns and spires unmatched by the elegance of Kings Row, and somehow whiter than the snow around it, as if trying to mask the profanity of its existence with the illusion of purity. Brogan's stare probed the recesses of that sanctuary of wickedness, the shrine to magic's power over the pious, as his bony fingers idly caressed the leather trophy case at his belt.

"My lord general," Lunetta pressed, leaning forward, "did you hear what I said—"

Brogan twisted around, his polished boots creaking against the stirrup leather in the cold. "Galtero!"

Eyes like black ice shone from under the brow of a polished helmet beneath a horsehair plume dyed crimson to match the soldiers' capes. He held his reins easily in one gauntleted hand as he swayed in his saddle with the fluid grace of a mountain lion. "Lord General?"

"If my sister can't keep quiet when ordered to"—he shot her a glare— "gag her."

Lunetta darted an uneasy glance at the broad-shouldered man riding beside her, at his polished-to-perfection armor and mail, at his well-honed weapons. She opened her mouth to protest, but as she returned her gaze to those icy eyes she closed it again, and instead scratched her arms. "Forgive me, Lord General Brogan," she murmured as she bowed her head deferentially toward her brother.

Galtero aggressively sidestepped his horse closer to Lunetta, his powerful gray gelding jostling her bay mare. "Silence, *streganicha.*"

Her cheeks colored at the affront, and her eyes, for an instant, flashed with menace, but just as quickly it was gone, and she seemed to wilt into her tattered rags as her eyes lowered in submission.

"I not be a witch," she whispered to herself.

A brow lifted over one cold eye, causing her to sag further, and she fell silent for good.

Galtero was a good man; the fact that Lunetta was sister to Lord General Brogan would count for nothing if the order were ever given. She was *streganicha*, one tainted by evil. Given the word, Galtero or any of the other men would spill her lifeblood without a moment's hesitation or regret.

That she was Brogan's kin only hardened him to his duty. She served as a constant reminder of the Keeper's ability to strike out at the righteous, and blight even the finest of families.

Seven years after Lunetta's birth, the Creator had balanced the injustice and Tobias had been born, born to counter what the Keeper had corrupted; but it had been too late for their mother, who had already begun to slip into the arms of madness. From the time he was eight, when the disrepute had delivered his father into an early grave and his mother had finally and fully nestled into the bosom of madness, Tobias had been burdened with the duty of ruling the gift his sister possessed, lest it rule her. At that age Lunetta had doted on him, and he had used that love to convince her to listen only to the Creator's wishes, and to guide her in moral conduct, the way the men of the king's circle had schooled him. Lunetta had always needed, in fact embraced, guidance. She was a helpless soul trapped by a curse that was beyond her ability to expunge or her power to escape.

Through ruthless effort, he had cleansed the ignominy of having one with the gift born into his family. It had taken most of his life, but Tobias had returned honor to the family name. He had shown them all; he had turned the stigma to his advantage, and had become the most exalted among the exalted.

Tobias Brogan loved his sister—loved her enough to slit her throat himself, if need be, to free her from the Keeper's tendrils, from the torment of his taint, if it ever slipped the bounds of control. She would live only so long as she was useful, only so long as she helped them root out evil, root out banelings. For now, she fought the scourge snatching at her soul, and she was useful.

He realized she didn't look like much, swathed in scraps of different-colored cloth—it was the one thing that brought her pleasure and kept her content, having different colors draped around her, her "pretties" she called them—but the Keeper had invested Lunetta with rare talent and strength. Through tenacious effort, Tobias had expropriated it.

That was the flaw in the Keeper's creation—the flaw in anything the Keeper created: it could be used as a tool by the pious, if they were astute enough. The Creator always provided weapons to fight profanity, if one only looked for them and had the wisdom, the sheer audacity, to use them. That was what impressed him about the Imperial Order; they were shrewd enough to understand this, and resourceful enough to use magic as a tool to seek out profanity and destroy it.

As he did, the Order used *streganicha*, and apparently valued and trusted them. He didn't like it, though, that they were allowed to roam free and unguarded to bring information and proposals, but if they ever turned against the cause, well, he always kept Lunetta nearby.

Still, he didn't like being so close to evil. It repulsed him, sister or not.

Dawn was just breaking and the streets were already crowded with people. In abundance, too, were soldiers of different lands, each patrolling the grounds of their own palaces, and others, mostly D'Haran, patrolling the city. Many of the troops looked ill at ease, as if they anticipated an attack at any moment. Brogan had been assured that they had everything well in hand. Never one to take on faith anything he was told, he had sent out his own patrols the night before, and they had confirmed that there were no Midland insurgents anywhere near Aydindril.

Brogan always favored arriving when least expected, and in greater numbers than expected, just in case he had to take matters into his own hands. He had brought a full fist—five hundred men—into the city, but if there proved to be trouble, he could always bring his main force into Aydindril. His main force had proven themselves quite capable of crushing any insurrection.

Had the D'Harans not been allies, the indications of their numbers would have been alarming. Though Brogan had well-founded faith in his men's abilities, only the vain fought battles when the odds were even, much less long; the Creator didn't hold the vain in kind regard.

Lifting a hand, Tobias slowed the horses, lest they trample a squad of D'Haran foot soldiers crossing before the column. He thought it untoward of them to be winged out in a battle formation, similar to his own flying wedge, as they crossed the main thoroughfare, but perhaps the D'Harans, charged with the task of patrolling a vanquished city, were reduced to frightening footpads and cutpurses with a show of might.

The D'Harans, weapons to hand and looking to be in an ill mood, swept gazes over the column of cavalry bearing down on them, apparently looking for any sign of threat. Brogan thought it rather odd that they carried their weapons unsheathed. A cautious lot, the D'Harans.

Unconcerned with what they saw, they didn't hurry their pace. Brogan smiled; lesser men would have stepped up their stride. Their weapons, mostly swords and battle-axes, were neither embellished nor fancy, and that in itself made them look all the more impressive. They were weapons carried because they had proven brutally effective, and not for flash.

Outnumbered well over twentyfold, the men in dark leather and mail regarded all the polished metal with indifference. Polish and precision often displayed nothing more than conceit, and although in this case they were a reflection of Brogan's discipline, a display of deadly attention to detail, the D'Haran's probably didn't know that. Where he and his men were better known, a glimpse of their crimson capes was enough to make strong men blanch, and the glint off their polished armor was enough to make an enemy break and run.

When they had come across the Rang'Shada Mountains from Nicobarese, Brogan had met with one of the Order's armies, made up of men of many nations, but mostly D'Hara, and had been impressed with the D'Haran's general, Riggs, who had accepted counsel with interest and attention. Brogan, in fact, had been so impressed with the man that he had left some of his own troops with him to help in the conquest of the Midlands. The Order had been on its way to bring the heathen city of Ebinissia, the Crown city of Galea, to heel under the Order. The Creator willing, they had succeeded.

Brogan had learned that D'Harans didn't hold much favor with magic, and that pleased him. That they also feared magic disgusted him. Magic was the Keeper's conduit into the world of man. The Creator was to be feared. Magic, the Keeper's witchery, was to be expunged. Until the boundary had been brought down the past spring, D'Hara had been cordoned off from the Midlands for generations, so in large part D'Hara and its people were still an unknown to Brogan, a vast new territory in need of enlightenment and, possibly, purification.

Darken Rahl, the leader of D'Hara, had brought the boundary down, allowing his troops to sweep into the Midlands and capture Aydindril, among other cities. If he had been more interested in confining himself to the affairs of man, Rahl might have seized all of the Midlands before they could raise armies against him, but he had been more interested in pursuing magic, and that had been his undoing. Once Darken Rahl was dead, assassinated by a pretender to the throne, as Brogan had heard it told, the D'Haran troops had joined with the Imperial Order in its cause.

There was no longer a place in the world for the ancient, dying religion called magic. The Imperial Order was upon the world, now; the Creator's glory would guide man. Tobias Brogan's prayers had been answered, and every day he thanked the Creator for placing him in the world at this time, when he could be at the center of it all, to see the blasphemy of magic vanquished, to lead the righteous in the final battle. This was the making of history, and he was part of it.

The Creator, in fact, had recently come to Tobias in his dreams, to tell him how pleased He was with his efforts. He didn't reveal this to any of his men; that might be seen as presumptuous. To be honored by the Creator was satisfaction enough. Of course he had told Lunetta, and she had been awed; after all, it wasn't often the Creator chose to speak directly to one of His children.

Brogan squeezed his legs around his horse to pick up the pace as he watched the D'Harans move on down a side street. None turned to see if they were to be followed or challenged, but only a fool would take that for complacency; Brogan was no fool. The throng parted for the column, giving them a wide path as they proceeded down Kings Row. Brogan recognized some of the uniforms of soldiers at various palaces: Sandarians, Jarians, and

Keltans. He saw no Galeans; the Order must have been successful in their task at Galea's crown city of Ebinissia.

At last Brogan saw troops from his homeland. With an impatient wave he signaled a squad forward. Their capes, crimson to announce who they were, billowed out behind as they charged past the swordsmen, lancers, standard-bearers, and finally Brogan. Accompanied by the racket of iron shoes on stone, the horsemen charged right up the vast steps of the Nicobarese Palace. It was an edifice as garish as any of the others, with tapered, fluted columns of rare white-veined brown marble, a difficult-to-obtain stone quarried from the mountains in eastern Nicobarese. The profligacy galled him.

The regular soldiers guarding the palace stumbled back at the sight of the men on horseback and flinched into shaky salutes. The squad of horsemen herded them back farther, opening a wide corridor for the lord general.

At the top of the steps, between statues of soldiers atop rearing stallions carved from buff-colored stone, Brogan dismounted. He tossed the reins to one of the ashen-faced Palace Guard as he smiled out at the city, his eyes settling on the Confessors' Palace. Today Tobias Brogan was in a good mood. Lately, such moods were becoming increasingly rare. He drew a deep breath of the dawn air: the dawn of a new day.

The man who had taken the reins bowed as Brogan turned back. "Long live the king."

Brogan straightened his cape. "A little late for that."

The man cleared his throat, working up the courage. "Sir?"

"The king," Brogan said, as he knuckled his mustache, "turned out to be more than all of us who loved him thought. He burned for his sins. Now, see to my horse." He gestured to another guard. "You—go tell the cooks I'm hungry. I don't want to be kept waiting."

The guard backed away, bowing, as Brogan glanced up at the man still on horseback. "Galtero." The man stepped his horse closer, his crimson cape limp in the still air. "Take half the men, and bring her to me. I'm going to break fast, and then I will judge her."

With a gentle touch, his bony fingers absently stroked the case at his belt. Soon he would add the prize of prizes to his collection. He smiled grimly at the thought, the smile tightening the old scar at the corner of his mouth, but not touching his dark eyes. The glory of moral redress would be his.

"Lunetta." She was staring at the Confessors' Palace, her motley patches of tattered cloth drawn tight to her as she idly scratched her forearms. "Lunetta!"

She flinched, hearing him at last. "Yes, Lord General?"

He flipped his crimson cape back over his shoulder and straightened his sash of rank. "Come, break fast with me. We'll have a talk. I'll tell you about the dream I had last night."

Her eyes widened with excitement. "Another one, my lord general? Yes, I should like very much to hear about it. You honor me."

"Indeed." She followed as he marched through the tall brass-bound double doors, into the Nicobarese palace. "We have matters to discuss. You will listen attentively, won't you, Lunetta?"

She shuffled along at his heels. "Yes, my lord general. Always."

He paused at a window with a heavy blue drape. Drawing his dress knife, he sliced a good-sized piece from the side, including a strip of edging with gold tassels. Licking her lips, Lunetta rocked from side to side, shifting her weight from one foot to the other as she waited.

Brogan smiled. "A pretty for you, Lunetta."

Eyes glistening, she clutched it excitedly to herself before holding it in one place, then another, searching for the perfect spot to add it to the others. She giggled with glee. "Thank you, Lord General. It be beautiful."

He marched off, Lunetta scurrying to follow behind. Portraits of royalty hung from the rich paneling, and underfoot sumptuous carpets ran into the distance. Gold-leafed frames surrounded round-topped doors to either side. Gilt-edged mirrors reflected the passing flash of crimson.

A servant in brown-and-white livery bowed his way into the hall, holding out his arm to indicate the direction to the dining hall before scuttling along, looking sideways to be sure he kept himself clear of harm, and bowing every few steps.

Tobias Brogan was not a man who had ever frightened anyone with his size, but the servants, staff, Palace Guard, and partially dressed officials who charged into the hall to see what was causing such a fuss all paled at the sight of him—at seeing the lord general himself, the man who commanded the Blood of the Fold.

At his word banelings burned for their sins—whether they be beggars or soldiers, lords or ladies, or even kings.

CHAPTER 5

SISTER VERNA STOOD TRANSFIXED by the flames, their depths loosing transient whorls of glittering colors and shimmering rays alive with swaying movement, fingers twisting in a dance, luring in air that flapped their clothes in passing, and casting forth heat that would have driven them all back, if not for their shields. The huge bloodred sun hung half emerged at the horizon, at last abating the glory of the fire that had consumed the bodies. A few of the Sisters around her still sobbed softly, but Sister Verna had drained all the tears she had to give.

Well over one hundred boys and young men stood in a ring around the fire, with twice as many Sisters of the Light and novices circled inside them. Except for one Sister and one boy symbolically standing watch over the palace, and of course the one Sister who had become deranged and was locked in an empty, shielded room for her own good, all were on the hill above Tanimura watching the flames leap skyward. Even with this many people standing together, each was touched by profound loneliness, and stood withdrawn in introspection and prayer. As prescribed, no one spoke at the funeral rite.

Sister Verna's back hurt from standing ward all night over the bodies. Through the hours of darkness they had all stood, praying, and maintaining the linked shield over the corpses in symbolic protection of the revered. At least it was a relief to be away from the incessant drumming down in the city.

At first light the shield had been dropped and each had sent forth a flow of her Han into the pyre, igniting it. Fire, fed by magic, had raced through the stacked logs and the two heavily shrouded bodies, one short and squat, the other tall and powerfully built, creating an inferno of divine power.

They had had to search the vaults for guidance as no one living had ever participated in the ceremony; it had not been performed in almost eight hundred years—791, to be precise: the last time a prelate had died.

As they had learned in the old books, only the Prelate was to have her soul released to the Creator's protection in the sacred funeral rite, but in this case the Sisters had all voted to grant the same privilege to the one who had struggled so valiantly to save her. The books had said that dispensation from the exclusion could only be granted by unanimous consent. It had taken heated persuasion to make it so.

By custom, as the sun finally and fully gained the horizon, washing the fire with the complete spectacle of the Creator's own light, the flow of Han was withdrawn. Their power recalled, the pyre collapsed, leaving only a stain of ash and a few charred logs to mark the site of the ceremony on the green hilltop. Smoke curled upward, dissipating into the silent, brightening day.

Grayish white ashes were all that was left in the world of the living of Prelate Annalina, and the prophet Nathan. It was done.

Without words, Sisters began drifting away, some in solitude, others placing a comforting arm around the shoulder of a boy or a novice. Like lost souls, they meandered down the hill toward the city, and the Palace of the Prophets, going to a home without a mother. As Sister Verna kissed her ring finger, she guessed that with the prophet also dead, they were in a way without a father as well.

She folded her fingers together over her stomach as she absently watched the others walking off into the distance. She had never had the chance to make her peace with the Prelate before she had died. The woman had used her, humiliated her, and allowed her to be abased for doing her duty and following orders. Though all Sisters served the Creator, and she knew that what the Prelate had done must have been for a greater good, it hurt that the Prelate had exploited that fidelity. It made her feel a fool.

Because Prelate Annalina had been injured in the attack by Ulicia, a Sister of the Dark, and had since remained unconscious for near to three weeks prior to her death, Sister Verna had never had a chance to talk to her. Only Nathan had attended the Prelate, trying tirelessly to heal her, but in the end he had failed. It was cruel fate that took his life, too. Though Nathan had always seemed vigorous to her, the strain must have been too much for him; he had, after all, been near to one thousand years old. She guessed he had aged in the twenty-odd years she had been away seeking Richard and finally bringing him to the palace.

Sister Verna smiled at the memory of Richard; she missed him, too. He had vexed her to the limits of her tolerance, but he, too, had been a victim of the Prelate's plans, although he seemed to have understood and accepted the things she had done and had not held any ill feelings toward her.

She felt a pang of heartache at the thought that Richard's love, Kahlan, had probably died in the climax of that terrible prophecy. She hoped it wasn't so. The Prelate had been a resolute woman, and had orchestrated events in the lives of a great many people. Sister Verna hoped it had truly been done for the good of the Creator's children, and not simply for the Prelate's own ambitions.

"You look angry, Sister Verna."

She turned to see young Warren standing with his hands in the opposite, silver brocade sleeves of his deep violet robes. She glanced around and realized that the two of them were alone on the hillside; the others, long gone, were dark specks in the distance.

"Perhaps I am, Warren."

"What are you angry about, Sister?"

With the palms of her hands, she smoothed her dark skirt at her hips. "Maybe I'm just angry with myself." She sought to change the subject as she straightened her light blue shawl. "You're so young, in your studies I mean, that I'm still having trouble getting used to seeing you without a Rada'Han."

As if she had reminded him, his fingers stroked his neck where the collar had been for most of his life. "Young for those living under the spell at the palace, perhaps, but hardly young for those in the outside world—I am one hundred and fifty seven, Sister.

But I do appreciate that you took my collar off." He took his fingers from his neck and brushed back a lock of curly blond hair. "It seems like the whole world has been turned upside down in the last few months."

She chuckled. "I miss Richard, too."

An easy grin brightened his face. "Really? He was a rare person, wasn't he? I can hardly believe that he was able to prevent the Keeper from escaping the underworld, but he had to have stopped the spirit of his father, and returned the Stone of Tears to its rightful place, or we would all have been swallowed by the dead. To tell the truth, I was in a cold sweat the whole of winter solstice."

Sister Verna nodded, as if to add emphasis to her sincerity. "The things you helped teach him must have been valuable. You did well, too, Warren." She studied his gentle smile for a moment, noticing how little it had changed over all the years. "I'm glad you decided to remain at the palace for a time, even though you have your collar off. We are without a prophet, it would seem."

He looked to the stain of ashes. "Most of my life I've studied the prophecies down in the vaults, and I never knew that some were given by a prophet still living, much less at the palace. I wish they had told me. I wish they had let me talk to him, learn from him. Now the chance is lost."

"Nathan was a dangerous man, an enigma who none of us could ever fully understand or trust, but maybe it was wrong of them to prevent you from visiting him. Know that in time, when you learned more, the Sisters would have allowed it, if not required it."

He glanced away. "But now the chance has been lost."

"Warren, now that you have the collar off, I know you're anxious to go out into the world, but you've said that you intend to stay at the palace, at least for a time, to study. The palace is without a prophet, now. I think you should consider the fact that your gift manifests itself strongly in that area. You could someday be a prophet."

A gentle breeze rippled his robes as he looked out over the green hills toward the palace. "Not only my gift, but my interest, my hopes, have always involved the prophecies. I've only recently begun to understand them in a way that no one else does, but understanding them is different than giving them."

"It takes time, Warren. Why, when Nathan was your age, I'm

sure he was no more advanced in prophecy than you. If you stayed and continued to study, I believe that in four or five hundred years you might be a prophet as great as Nathan."

He was silent for a time. "But there's a whole world out there. I've heard there are books at the Wizard's Keep in Aydindril, and other places, too. Richard said there are sure to be many at the People's Palace in D'Hara. I want to learn, and there may be things to know that can't be found here."

Sister Verna rolled her shoulders to ease their ache. "The Palace of the Prophets is spelled, Warren. If you leave, you will age the same as those outside. Look at what's happened to me in a scant twenty-odd years away from it; even though we were born only a year apart you still look as if you should be thinking of marriage, and I look as if I should be preparing to bounce a grandchild on my knee. Now that I'm back, I will age by the palace's time again, but what has been lost cannot be recovered."

Warren averted his eyes. "I think you see more wrinkles than are there, Sister Verna."

She smiled in spite of herself. "Did you know, Warren, that I was once smitten with you?"

He was so astonished he stumbled back a step. "Me? You can't be serious. When?"

"Oh, it was a long time ago. Well over a hundred years, I would suppose. You were so scholarly and intelligent, with all that curly blond hair. And those blue eyes made my heart race."

"Sister Verna!"

She couldn't hold back a chuckle as his face went crimson. "It was long ago, Warren, and I was young, as were you. It was a fleeting infatuation." Her smile ghosted away. "Now you seem a child to me, and I look old enough to be your mother. Being away from the palace has aged me in more ways than one.

"Out there, you will have a few brief decades to learn what you could before you grow old and die. Here, you would have the time to learn and perhaps become a prophet. Books from those places could always be borrowed, and brought here for study.

"You're the closest thing we have to a prophet. With the Prelate and Nathan dead, you may know more about the prophecies than anyone alive, now. We need you, Warren."

He turned to the sunlight shimmering off the spires and roofs of the palace. "I'll think on it, Sister."

"That's all I ask, Warren."

With a sigh, he turned back. "What now? Who do you think will be chosen as the new prelate?"

They had learned through their research of the funeral rite that the process of selecting a new prelate was quite involved. Warren would know of it; few knew the books in the vaults as well as he.

She shrugged. "The post requires vast experience and knowledge. That means it would have to be one of the older Sisters. Leoma Marsick would be a likely candidate, or Philippa, or Dulcinia. Sister Maren, of course, would be a top nominee. There are any number of qualified Sisters; I could name at least thirty, though I doubt that more than a dozen truly have a serious chance to become prelate."

He absently rubbed the side of his nose with a finger. "I suppose you're right."

Sister Verna had no doubt that Sisters were already maneuvering to place themselves in contention, if not at the top of the list, with the less venerated choosing their champion and forming rank to back her, doing their best to see to it that she was selected, and hoping to be awarded a position of influence if their favorite became the new prelate. As the field of candidates narrowed, the more influential Sisters who hadn't yet chosen sides would be courted until they were won over to one or another of the leading Sisters. It was a momentous decision, one that would affect the palace for hundreds of years to come. It would likely be a bitter battle.

Sister Verna sighed. "I don't look forward to the struggle, but I guess that the selection process must be rigorous, so that the strongest will become prelate. It could drag on for a long time; we could be without a prelate for months, maybe a year."

"Who are you going to support, Sister?"

She barked a laugh. "Me! You're only seeing the wrinkles again, Warren. They don't change the fact that I'm one of the younger Sisters. I have no influence among those who would count."

"Well, I think you had better try to get some influence." He leaned closer, lowering his voice even though there was no one around. "The six Sisters of the Dark who escaped on that ship, remember?"

She looked to his blue eyes and frowned. "What does that have to do with who will become prelate?"

Warren twisted the robes at his stomach into a violet knot. "Who's to say there were only six. What if there's another at the palace? Or another dozen? Or hundred? Sister Verna, you're the only Sister I trust to be a true Sister of the Light. You must do something to insure that a Sister of the Dark doesn't become prelate."

She glanced to the palace in the distance. "I told you, I'm one of the younger Sisters. My word holds no sway, and the others know that the Sisters of the Dark all escaped."

Warren looked away, trying to smooth out the wrinkles in his robes. Suddenly, he turned back, suspicion creasing his brow.

"You think I'm right, don't you. You think there are still Sisters of the Dark at the palace."

She met his intense eyes with a placid expression. "While I don't think it entirely out of the realm of possibility, there is no reason to believe it is so, and beyond that, it is only one of a great many matters that must be taken into consideration when—"

"Don't give me that double-talk that comes so easily to Sisters. This is important."

Sister Verna stiffened. "You are a student, Warren, speaking to a Sister of the Light; show the proper respect."

"I'm not being disrespectful, Sister. Richard helped me to see that I must stand up for myself and for what I believe. Besides, you're the one who took my collar off, and as you said, we're the same age; you are not my elder."

"You are still a student who—"

"Who you yourself said probably knows more about the prophecies than anyone else. In that, Sister, you are my student. I admit that you know more than I about a great many things, like the use of Han, but I know more than you about some things. Part of the reason you took the Rada'Han from around my neck is because you know it's wrong to hold someone captive. I respect you as a Sister, and for the good you do, and for the knowledge you have, but I am no longer a captive of the Sisters. You have earned my respect, Sister, not my submission."

She studied his blue eyes for a long moment. "Who would have known what was under that collar." At last, she nodded. "You're right, Warren; I suspect there are others at the palace who have given a soul oath to the Keeper himself."

"Others." Warren searched her eyes. "You didn't say Sisters, you said others. You mean young wizards, too, don't you?"

"Have you so soon forgotten Jedidiah?"

He paled a little. "No, I haven't forgotten Jedidiah."

"As you said, where there is one, there could be others. Some of the young men at the palace could be sworn to the Keeper, too."

He hunched closer to her as he knotted his robes again. "Sister Verna, what are we going do about it? We can't allow a Sister of the Dark to become prelate; it would be a disaster. We must be sure one of them doesn't become prelate."

"And how would we know if she was sworn to the Keeper? Worse, what could we do about it? They have command of Subtractive Magic; we don't. Even if we could find out who they are, we couldn't do anything about it. It would be like reaching into a sack and grabbing a viper by its tail."

Warren paled. "I never thought of that."

Sister Verna clasped her hands. "We'll think of something. Perhaps the Creator will guide us."

"Maybe we could get Richard to return and help us, like he did with those six Sisters of the Dark. At least we've seen the last of those six. They'll never show their faces again. Richard put the fear of the Creator in them, and sent them running."

"And in the process, the Prelate was hurt, and later died, along with Nathan," she reminded him. "Death walks with that man."

"Not because he brings it," Warren protested. "Richard is a war wizard; he fights for what's right, to help people. If he hadn't done as he did, the Prelate and Nathan would have only been the beginning of all the death and destruction."

She squeezed his arm; her tone softened. "Of course you're right; we all owe Richard a great debt. But needing him and finding him are two different things. My wrinkles attest to that." Sister Verna let her hand drop. "I don't think we can count on anyone but each other. We'll think of something."

Warren fixed her with a dark expression. "We had better; the prophecies hold ominous portent about the next prelate's reign."

Back in the city of Tanimura, they were once again surrounded by the incessant sound of drums coming from various directions; a booming, low-pitched, steady cadence that seemed to vibrate deep in her chest. It was unnerving and, she supposed, meant to be.

The drummers and their guards had arrived three days before the prelate's death, and in short order had set up their huge kettledrums at various stations around the city. Once they had started the slow, steady beat, it had not stopped, day or night. Men took shifts at the drums so that they never ceased, even for a moment.

The pervasive sound had slowly set the people's nerves on edge, making everyone irritable and short-tempered, as if doom itself were lurking in the shadows, just out of sight, waiting to pounce. Instead of the usual shouting, talking, laughing, and music, a backdrop of eerie quiet added to the brooding mood.

At the outskirts of the city, the indigent people who had erected lean-to shelters cowered in them, instead of engaging in conversation, hawking small items, washing clothes in buckets, or cooking on small fires as they usually did. Shopkeepers stood in doorways or at simple plank tables set up to display their goods, their arms folded and scowls on their faces. Men pulling carts bent somberly to their tasks. People needing goods made their purchases quickly, making no more than a perfunctory examination of the wares. Children kept a hand clutched to their mother's skirts as their eyes darted about. Men whom she had seen playing at dice or other games in the past huddled against walls.

In the distance, at the Palace of the Prophets, a single bell tolled every few minutes, as it had all the night before and would until the sun set, announcing to all that the Prelate was dead. The drums, however, had nothing to do with the Prelate's death; manned by soldiers, they announced the impending arrival of the emperor.

Sister Verna met the troubled eyes of people she passed. She touched the heads of the scores who approached, seeking solace, and offered the Creator's blessing. "I only remember kings," she said to Warren, "not this Imperial Order. Who is this emperor?"

"His name is Jagang. Ten, maybe fifteen years ago, the Imperial Order started swallowing up the kingdoms, joining them together under its rule." With one finger, he rubbed his temple in thought, "I spent most of my time in the vaults studying, you understand, so I'm not sure of all the details, but from what I gather, they swiftly came to dominate the Old World, joining it all under their rule. The emperor hasn't ever caused any trouble, though. At least not way up here in Tanimura. He stays out of palace business, and expects us to stay out of his."

"Why is he coming here?"

Warren shrugged. "I don't know. Perhaps just to visit this part of his empire."

After conferring the Creator's blessing on a gaunt woman, Sister Verna stepped around a trail of fresh horse dung as she resumed walking. "Well, I wish he would hurry up and get here so that infernal drumming would cease. They've been at it four days now; his arrival must be imminent."

Warren glanced around before speaking. "The palace guards are Imperial Order troops. As a courtesy, the emperor provides them, since he allows no men at arms but his own. Anyway, I talked to one of the guards, and he told me that the drums are only meant to announce that the emperor is coming, not that he will be here soon. He said that when the emperor visited Breaston, the drums sounded for nearly six months beforehand."

"Six months! You mean we must endure this racket for months!"

Warren hitched up his robes and stepped over a puddle. "Not necessarily. He could arrive in months, or tomorrow. He doesn't deign to announce when he will arrive, only that he will."

Sister Verna scowled. "Well, if he doesn't arrive soon, the Sisters will see to it that those infernal drums stop."

"That would be fine by me. But this emperor sounds like someone not to be treated casually. I've heard that he has an army more vast than any ever assembled." He gave her a meaningful look. "And that includes the great war that separated the Old World from the New."

Her eyes narrowed. "Why would he need such an army, if he has already seized all of the old kingdoms? Sounds to me like it's just idle talk of soldiers. Soldiers always like to boast."

Warren shrugged. "The guards told me they've seen it with their own eyes. They said that when the Order masses, they cover the ground in every direction as far as the eye can see. What do you think the palace will make of it when he comes here?"

"Bah. The palace has no interest in politics."

Warren grinned. "You never were one to be intimidated."

"Our business is with the Creator's wishes, not an emperor's, that's all. The palace will remain long after he is gone."

After walking in silence for a time, Warren cleared his throat. "You know, way back, when we hadn't been here long, and you were still a novice . . . well, I was enamored of you."

Sister Verna stared over incredulously. "Now you're mocking me."

"No, it's true." His face reddened. "I thought your curly brown hair was the most beautiful I'd ever seen. You were smarter than the others, and commanded your Han with sureness. I thought there was no one your equal. I wanted to ask you to study with me."

"Why didn't you?"

He shrugged. "You were always so sure of yourself, so confident. I never was." He brushed his hair back self-consciously. "Besides, you were interested in Jedidiah. I was nothing to compare to him. I always thought you would just laugh."

She realized she was smoothing back her hair, and let her arm fall. "Well, perhaps I would have."

She thought better of the slight. "People can be foolish when they are young." A woman with a young child approached and fell to her knees before them. Verna paused to bestow the Creator's blessing on them. As the woman thanked her and then hurried away, Sister Verna turned to Warren. "You could go away for twenty years or so, to study those books you are so interested in, and catch up in age with me. We'd look the same age again. Then you could ask to hold my hand . . . like I wanted you to, back then."

They both looked up at the sound of someone calling out to them. Through the throng of shuffling people, she saw one of the Palace Guard waving his arm to get their attention.

"Isn't that Kevin Andellmere?" She asked.

Warren nodded. "I wonder what he's so stirred up about?"

A breathless Swordsman Andellmere vaulted over a small boy and stumbled to a halt before them. "Sister Verna! Good! I've found you at last. They want you. At the palace. Right now."

"Who wants me? What about?"

He gulped air and tried to talk at the same time. "The Sisters want you. Sister Leoma grabbed me by my ear and told me to go find you and bring you back. She said that if I was slow about it, I'd rue the day my mother bore me. There must be trouble."

"What kind of trouble?"

He threw his hands up. "When I asked, she gave me that look

Sisters give that can melt a man's bones, and told me it was Sister business and none of mine."

Sister Verna let out a tired sigh. "I guess we best return with you, then, or they'll skin you and use your hide for a flag."

The young soldier blanched, as if he believed her.

CHAPTER 6

ON THE ARCHED STONE bridge that led over the River Kern to Halsband Island and the Palace of the Prophets, Sisters Philippa, Dulcinia, and Maren stood in a row, shoulder to shoulder, like three hawks watching their dinner approach. They clutched their hands impatiently at their waists. The sun at their backs cast their faces in shadow, but Sister Verna could still make out the scowls. Warren walked onto the bridge with her as Swordsman Andellmere, his duty accomplished, hurried off in another direction.

Gray-haired Sister Dulcinia, her jaw set, leaned closer as Sister Verna came to a stop before her. "Where have you been! You've kept everyone waiting."

The drums in the city kept up their beat in the background, like the slow drip of rain. Sister Verna put them from her mind.

"I've been for a walk, reflecting on the future of the palace, and the Creator's work. What with Prelate Annalina's ashes hardly cold yet, I didn't suspect the backbiting was to begin so soon."

Sister Dulcinia leaned even closer, her penetrating blue eyes taking on a dangerous gleam. "Don't you dare get impudent with us, Sister Verna, or you will quickly find yourself a novice again. Now that you have returned to life at the palace, you had better begin bethinking its ways, and start showing your superiors the proper respect."

Sister Dulcinia returned her back to straight, as if retracting claws, now that the threat had been delivered. She expected no argument. Sister Maren, a stocky woman with muscles like a woodsman, and a tongue to match, smiled with satisfaction. Tall, dark, Sister Philippa, her prominent cheekbones and narrow jaw giving her an exotic look, kept her dark eyes on Sister Verna, watching from behind an expressionless mask.

"Superiors?" Sister Verna said. "We are all equal in the Creator's eyes."

"Equal!" Sister Maren sniffed irritably. "An interesting concept. If we were to call an assembly of review to consider the matter of your contentious attitude, you would find out just how equal you are, and would likely find yourself once again doing chores with the rest of my novices, only this time you wouldn't have Richard here to intercede and get you out of it!"

"Really, Sister Maren?" Sister Verna lifted an eyebrow. "Is that so." Warren inched behind her, into her shadow. "I seem to recall, and correct me if I'm mistaken, that the last time I 'got out of it,' you said it was because you had prayed to the Creator and it had come to you that I would best serve Him if I were returned to Sister. Now you say it was Richard's doing. Am I mistaken in my recollection?"

"*You* would question *me*?" Sister Maren pressed her hands together so tightly that her knuckles turned white. "I was punishing insolent novices two hundred years before you were born! How dare you—"

"You've now told two versions of the same event. Since both can't be true, that means that one would have to be untrue. Yes? It would seem you have been caught in a lie, Sister Maren. I would think that you, of all people, would work to keep herself from falling into the habit of lying. The Sisters of the Light hold honesty in high regard, and abhor lying—even more than they abhor irreverence. And what penance has my superior, the headmistress of the novices, prescribed for herself to make amends for lying?"

"My, my," Sister Dulcinia said with a smirk. "Such boldness. Were I you, Sister Verna, and thinking of placing myself in contention for prelate, as you seem to be doing, I would get that presumptuous notion right out of my head. When Sister Leoma was through with you, there wouldn't be enough left for her to pick her teeth with."

Sister Verna returned the smirk. "So, Sister Dulcinia, you intend to back Sister Leoma, yes? Or are you just trying to conjure a task to get her out of your way while you seek the post?"

Sister Philippa spoke up in a quiet, authoritative voice. "Enough. We have more important matters to attend. Let's get this sham over with so we can get on with the selection process."

Sister Verna planted her fists on her hips. "And just what sham would that be?"

Sister Philippa turned gracefully toward the palace, her simple but elegant yellow robe flowing behind. "Follow us, Sister Verna. You have delayed us long enough. You are the last, and then we can be on with our business. We will take up the matter of your insolence at a another time."

The other two Sisters fell in beside her as she glided off over the bridge. Sister Verna and Warren exchanged a questioning look, and then started after them.

Warren slowed his pace, letting the three Sisters lengthen their lead to a dozen paces. With a frown, he leaned close so he could whisper without them hearing.

"Sister Verna, I sometimes think you could make a sunny day angry with you! It's been so peaceful around here for the last twenty years that I had forgotten how much trouble that tongue of yours could cause. Why do you do this? Do you just enjoy making trouble to no good end?"

He rolled his eyes at her withering scowl and changed the subject. "What do you suppose those three are doing together? I thought they would be adversaries."

Sister Verna glanced to the three Sisters, to make sure they couldn't hear. "If you want to put a knife in the back of your opponent, so to speak, you must first get close enough."

In the heart of the palace, before the thick walnut doors to the great hall, the three sisters came to such an abrupt halt that Sister Verna and Warren almost ran up onto their heels. The three turned. Sister Philippa put the fingertips of one hand to Warren's chest and forced him back a step.

She lifted one, long, graceful finger to his face, letting it hover an inch from his nose as she fixed him with a cold glare. "This is Sister business." She glanced to his bare neck. "And after the new prelate, whoever she may be, is installed, you will have to have a Rada'Han put back around your neck if you wish to remain at the Palace of the Prophets. We will not abide boys who cannot be properly controlled."

Sister Verna anchored an unseen hand on the small of Warren's back to keep him from retreating. "I took his collar off under my authority as a Sister of the Light. The commitment has been made on behalf of the palace; it will not be reversed."

Sister Philippa's dark gaze slid to her. "We will discuss this matter later, at an appropriate time."

"Let's be finished with this," Sister Dulcinia said, "we need to be on with more important business."

Sister Philippa nodded. "Come with us, Sister Verna."

Warren stood hunched, looking lost, as one of the Sisters used her Han to cast open the heavy doors, allowing the three to march through. Not wanting to look like a scolded puppy following them in, Sister Verna quickened her pace to walk beside them instead. Sister Dulcinia let out a noisy breath. Sister Maren invoked one of her famous looks, with which unfortunate novices were so familiar, but she didn't voice a protest. Sister Philippa showed the slightest hint of a smile. Anyone watching might have thought that it had been at her direction that Sister Verna walked beside them.

At the inner edge of the low ceiling, between white columns with gold capitals carved to portray curled oak leaves, they came to a halt where Sister Leoma waited with her back to them. She was about Sister Verna's size; her shock of straight white hair, tied loosely with a single golden ribbon, hung halfway down her back. She wore a modest brown dress that cleared the floor by a scant inch.

Beyond, the great hall opened into a vast chamber capped with a huge vaulted ceiling. Stained-glass windows behind the upper balcony cast colored light across the ribbed dome painted with the figures of Sisters, attired in the old style of robes, surrounding a glowing figure meant to represent the Creator. His arms outstretched, he looked to be extending his affection to the Sisters, all of whom, in turn, had their arms extended tenderly toward him.

At the ornate stone railings of the two-tiered balconies ringing the room, Sisters and novices stood silently gazing down. Around the polished, zigzag-patterned floor stood Sisters: those, Sister Verna noted, mostly older and of higher status. Sporadic coughs echoed around the huge room, but no one spoke.

In the center of the room, beneath the figure representing the Creator, stood a single, waist-high, white, fluted column bathed in a faint glow of light. The light had no apparent source. The ring of Sisters stood well back from the column and its obscure shroud of illumination, giving it as much room as possible, as well they should, if the glow was what Sister Verna suspected. A small object, she couldn't tell what, sat atop the flat-topped column.

Sister Leoma turned. "Ah. Glad to have you join us, Sister."

"Is that what I think it is?" Sister Verna asked.

A slight smile crooked the creases lining Sister Leoma's face. "If you are thinking it's a light web, then it is. Not half of us, I would venture, have the talent, or power, to spin one. Quite remarkable, don't you think?"

Sister Verna squinted, trying to tell what sat on the column. "I've never seen that pedestal before, not in here anyway. What is it? Where did it come from?"

Sister Philippa stared at the white pillar in the center of the room. Her arrogant demeanor had vanished. "When we came back from the funeral, it was here, waiting."

Sister Verna glanced back to the pedestal. "What's atop it?"

Sister Leoma clasped her hands. "It's the Prelate's ring—her ring of office."

"The Prelate's ring! What in Creation is it doing there?"

Sister Philippa lifted an eyebrow. "What indeed."

Sister Verna could just detect a hint of disquiet in those dark eyes. "Well what is—"

"Just go and try to pick it up," Sister Dulcinia said. "Not that you will succeed, of course," she added under her breath.

"We don't know what it's doing here," Sister Leoma said, her voice taking on a more familiar, Sister-to-Sister, intonation. "When we came back, it was here. We've tried to examine it, but we can't get close. In view of the peculiar nature of the shield, we reasoned that before we proceed, it would be wise to see if there are any of us who could get near, and maybe discern the purpose. We've all tried to approach, but none can. You are the last to endeavor to reach it."

Sister Verna drew up her shawl. "What happens when you try to approach?"

Sisters Dulcinia and Maren looked away. Sister Philippa held Sister Verna's gaze. "It is not pleasant. Not pleasant at all."

Sister Verna wasn't surprised by that. It surprised her only that no one had been hurt. "It borders on criminal behavior to ignite a light shield and leave it where some innocent could accidentally walk into it."

"Not likely," Sister Leoma said. "Not considering where it is, anyway. The cleaning staff found it. They were wise enough to stay away."

It was ominous in the extreme that none of the Sisters had been able to break the shield to get to the ring, as Sister Verna was positive they had attempted. It would be a significant accomplishment if one of them could demonstrate that she had the power to recover the Prelate's ring, on her own.

She glanced over at Sister Leoma. "Have you tried linking webs, to drain the shield?"

Sister Leoma shook her head. "We decided that first, each would be given a chance, on the theory that it might be a shield keyed to an individual Sister. We don't know what could possibly be the purpose of that, but if true, and it is a defensive shield, then linking and trying to drain its power could very well destroy what is being protected. You're the only one who hasn't tried." She let out a tired sigh. "We even brought Sister Simona up here."

Sister Verna lowered her voice in the sudden silence. "Is she any better?"

Sister Leoma stared up at the painting of the Creator. "She still hears voices, and last night, while we were up on the hill, had another of her deranged dreams."

"Go and see if you can retrieve the ring so we can get back to the selection process," Sister Dulcinia said. She shot a forbidding look at Sister Philippa and Leoma, as if to say there had been enough talking. Sister Philippa noted the look without expression or comment. Sister Maren glanced impatiently to the soft glow under which sat the object of their desire.

Sister Leoma gestured with a gnarled hand toward the white

column. "Verna, dear, bring us the ring, if you are able. We have palace business to get back to. If you are not able, well then, we will be forced to use a link to drain the shield and attempt to retrieve the Prelate's ring. Go now, child."

Sister Verna took a deep breath, deciding not to make an issue of being called "child" by another Sister, a peer, and started off across the polished floor, her footfalls echoing around the vast room the only sound except the muted, distant beat of drums. Sister Leoma was an elder, she supposed, and due a certain amount of deference. She glanced up toward the balconies and saw her friends, Sisters Amelia, Phoebe, and Janet, offering her weak smiles. Sister Verna set her jaw and marched onward.

She couldn't imagine what the Prelate's ring would be doing under such a dangerous shield, a shield of light. Something was wrong. Her breath quickened at the thought that it might be the doing of a Sister of the Dark. One of them might have keyed the shield to her, suspecting she knew too much. Her pace slowed a bit. If that were true, and it was a trick to eliminate her, she very well could be incinerated without so much as a hint of warning.

Only the sound of her footsteps echoed in her ears as she felt the outer bounds of the web. She could see the glint off the gold ring. Muscles tense, she expected something unpleasant, as the others had obviously experienced, but she felt only warmth, like a summer sun. Slowly, step by step, she proceeded, but it grew no hotter.

By the few, small gasps she heard, she knew that none of the others had gotten this far. She also knew that that didn't mean she would be able to go all the way, or to escape. Through the soft white glow, she could see the Sisters beyond, their eyes wide as they watched.

And then, as if in the hazy light of a dream, she was standing before the pedestal. The light at the center of the shield had become bright enough that she couldn't make out the faces of those beyond.

The Prelate's gold ring sat on a folded piece of parchment sealed closed with red wax imprinted with the sunburst pattern from the ring. Writing was partially visible underneath the ring. Sliding the ring to the side, she turned the parchment with one finger so she could read it.

If you wish to escape this web alive, put the ring on the third finger of your left hand, kiss it, then break the seal and read my words inside to the other Sisters, it said, and was signed, *Prelate Annalina Aldurren.*

Sister Verna stared at the words. They seemed to stare back, waiting. She didn't know what to do. She recognized the Prelate's handwriting all too well, but realized it could be a forgery. If it was a Dark Sister's trick, especially one with a flare for the dramatic, following the instructions could kill her. If it wasn't, then not following them could. She stood frozen a moment, trying to come up with alternatives. None would come to mind.

Sister Verna reached out and picked up the ring. Gasps of surprise came from the darkness beyond. She turned the ring over in her fingers, inspecting the sunburst pattern and the wear of age. It was warm to the touch, as if heated from an inner source. It looked like the Prelate's ring, and a feeling in her gut told her it was. She glanced down at the words on the parchment again.

If you wish to escape this web alive, put the ring on the third finger of your left hand, kiss it, then break the seal and read my words inside to the other Sisters.

—Prelate Annalina Aldurren

Sister Verna, her breath coming shallow and labored, slipped the ring onto the third finger of her left hand. She brought the hand to her lips and kissed the ring as she said a silent prayer to the Creator seeking guidance and strength. She flinched as a beam shot from the figure of the Creator above her, bathing her in a bright shaft of light. The air about her fairly hummed. There were short, clipped screams and squeals from the Sisters around the room, but in the light as she was, she could not see them.

Sister Verna lifted the parchment in her trembling fingers. The air hummed more intensely. She wanted to run, but broke the wax seal instead. The shaft of light coming from the image of the Creator above intensified to blinding brilliance.

Sister Verna unfolded the parchment and looked up, though she couldn't see the faces around her. "Upon penalty of death, I am directed to read this letter."

No one made a sound, so she looked down at the neatly scribed words. "It says, 'Know all those assembled, and those not here, my last command.' "

Sister Verna paused and swallowed as Sisters gasped.

" 'These are trying times, and the palace can ill afford a protracted battle to succeed me. I will not allow it. I am exercising my prerogative as Prelate, as set down in palace canon, to name my successor. She stands before you, wearing the ring of her office. The Sister reading this is now Prelate. The Sisters of the Light will obey her. All will obey her.

" 'The spell I have left over the ring was drawn with the aid and guidance of the Creator himself. Defy my bidding at your peril.

" 'To the new Prelate, you are charged to serve and protect the Palace of the Prophets and all it stands for. May the Light cradle and guide you always.

"'In my own hand, before I pass from this life into the gentle hands of the Creator—Prelate Annalina Aldurren.' "

With a boom that shook the ground beneath her feet, the beam of light, and the glow around her, extinguished.

Verna Sauventreen let the hand holding the letter fall to her side as she looked up into the circle of stunned faces. The vast hall filled with a soft rustle as the Sisters of the Light began going to a knee and bowing their heads to their new prelate.

"This can't be," she whispered to herself.

As she shuffled across the polished floor, she let the letter slip from her fingers. Sisters cautiously scurried in behind to snatch it up, to read for themselves the last words of Prelate Annalina Aldurren.

The four Sisters came to their feet as she approached. Sister Maren's fine, sandy hair framed an ashen face. Sister Dulcinia's blue eyes were wide, and her face red. Sister Philippa's usually placid expression was now a picture of consternation.

Sister Leoma's wrinkled cheeks spread in a kindly smile. "You will be in need of advice and guidance, Sis . . . Prelate." Her smile was spoiled by the way she swallowed involuntarily. "We will be available to help in any way we can. Please consider us at your disposal. We are here to serve. . . ."

"Thank you," Verna said in a weak voice as she started out again, her feet seeming to move of their own accord.

Warren waited outside. She pushed the doors closed and stood in a daze before the young, blond-headed wizard. Warren went to a knee in a deep bow.

"Prelate." He glanced up with a grin. "I was listening at the door," he explained.

"Don't call me that." Her own voice sounded hollow to her.

"Why not? It's who you are, now." His grin grew. "This is—"

She turned and started away, her mind at last beginning to function again. "Come with me."

"Where are we going?"

Verna crossed her lips with a finger and over her shoulder shot him a scowl that snapped his mouth shut. Warren scurried to catch up with her as she marched off. Once beside her, he lengthened his stride to keep pace as she proceeded out of the Palace of the Prophets. Whenever he looked as if he might open his mouth again, she crossed her lips with the finger. He at last sighed, stuffed his hands in the opposite sleeves of his robes, and set his gaze ahead as he strode along beside her.

Novices and young men outside the palace, who had heard the riot of bells proclaiming the new prelate named, saw the ring and bowed. Verna kept her eyes ahead as she passed them. The guards on the bridge over the River Kern bowed as she crossed.

Once over the river, she descended to the bank and walked along the path through the rushes. Warren hurried to keep up with her as she passed the small docks, all empty now, the boats out on the river with their fishermen casting nets or dragging lines as they rowed slowly upriver. They would soon be returning to sell their fish at the market in the city.

A ways upriver from the Palace of the Prophets, at a deserted, flat patch of ground near an outcropping of rock around which the water gurgled and splashed, she came to a halt. Scowling into the swirling water, she planted her fists on her hips.

"I swear, if that meddlesome old woman wasn't dead, I'd strangle her with my bare hands."

"What are you talking about?" Warren asked.

"The Prelate. If she weren't in the hands of the Creator right now, I'd have mine around her throat."

Warren chuckled. "That would be quite the sight, Prelate."

"Don't call me that!"

Warren frowned. "But that's who you are now: the Prelate."

She snatched his robes at each shoulder in her fists. "Warren, you have to help me. You have to get me out of this."

"What! But this is wonderful! Verna, you're Prelate now."

"No. I can't be. Warren, you know all the books down in the vaults, you've studied palace law—you have to find something to get me out of this. There has to be a way. You can find something in the books that will prevent this."

"Prevent it? It's done. And besides, this is the best thing that could happen." He cocked his head to the side. "Why did you bring me way down here?"

She released his robes. "Warren, think. Why was the Prelate killed?"

"She was killed by Sister Ulicia, one of the Sisters of the Dark. She was killed because she fought their evil."

"No, Warren, I said think. She was killed because one day, in her office, she told me that she knew about the Sisters of the Dark. Sister Ulicia was one of her administrators, and she overheard the Prelate voice her knowledge." She leaned toward him. "The room was shielded, I made sure of it, but what I didn't realize at the time is that the Sisters of the Dark might be able to use Subtractive Magic. Sister Ulicia heard right through the shield, and came back to kill the Prelate. Out here, we could see if anyone is close enough to hear us talk, there's no corner for them to be hiding around." She nodded toward the babbling water. "And the water masks the sound of our voices."

Warren glanced nervously about. "I see what you mean. But Prelate, water can sometimes carry sounds quite a distance."

"I said stop calling me that. With the sounds of the day all about, and if we speak softly, the water will mask our voices. We can't risk talking about any of this in the palace. If we must discuss any of this, we must always go out into the country, where we can see if anyone is close. Now, I need you to find a way for me to be removed from the post of Prelate."

Warren sighed out in exasperation. "Stop saying that. You're qualified to be Prelate, perhaps more qualified than any of the other Sisters; besides experience, the Prelate must be one with exceptional power." He looked away when she lifted an eyebrow. "I have unlimited access to anything in the vaults. I've read the reports." His gaze returned. "When you captured Richard, the other two Sisters died, and in so doing passed their power on to you. You have the power, the Han, of three Sisters."

"That is scarcely the only requirement, Warren."

He leaned forward. "As I said, I've unlimited access to the books. I know the requirements. There is nothing that would disqualify you; you fit all the requirements. You should be elated to be Prelate. This is the best thing that could happen."

Sister Verna sighed. "Have you lost your wits along with your collar? What possible reason would I have for wanting to be Prelate?"

"Now we can ferret out the Sisters of the Dark." Warren smiled confidentially. "You will have the authority to do what must be done." His blue eyes sparkled. "Like I said, this is the best possible thing that could happen."

She threw her hands up. "Warren, my becoming Prelate is the worst possible thing that could happen. The mantle of authority is as restricting as the collar you're so happy to be rid of."

Warren frowned. "What do you mean?"

She smoothed back her curly brown hair. "Warren, the Prelate is a prisoner of her authority. Did you often see Prelate Annalina? No. And why not? Because she was in her office, overseeing the administration of the Palace of the Prophets. She had a thousand things to attend to, a thousand questions that demanded her attention, hundreds of Sisters and young men that needed to be overseen, including the constant dilemma of Nathan. You don't know the kind of trouble that man could cause. He had to be kept under constant guard.

"The Prelate can never drop in to visit a Sister, or a young man in training; they would be in a panic, wondering what they had done wrong, what the Prelate had been told about them. The Prelate's conversations can never be casual, they are always charged with the perception of hidden meaning. It's not because she wants it that way—it's simply that she holds a position of sweeping authority and no one can ever forget that.

"When she ventures out of her complex she is immediately surrounded by the pomp and ceremony of her office. If she goes to the dining hall to have dinner, no one has the courage to carry on with their conversation; everyone sits silently and watches her, hoping she won't look their way or, worse yet, ask them to join her at her table."

Warren wilted a little. "I never thought about it that way."

"If your suspicions about the Sisters of the Dark are true, and I'm not saying they are, then being Prelate would hinder my discovering who they are."

"It didn't hinder Prelate Annalina."

"Do you know that? Maybe if she wasn't Prelate she would have discovered them ages ago, when she would have been able to do something about it. She might have been able to eradicate them before they began killing our boys and stealing their Han, and became so powerful. As it was, her discovery came too late, and only resulted in her death."

"But they may fear your knowledge and reveal themselves in some way."

"If there are Sisters of the Dark in the palace, then they know of my involvement in discovering the six who escaped, and if anything, they will be glad to have me be Prelate so as to tie my hands and keep me out of the way."

Warren touched a finger to his lip. "But, it must be of some help to have you be Prelate."

"It will only prove a hindrance in stopping the Sisters of the Dark. Warren, you have to help me. You know the books; there must be something that can get me out of this."

"Prelate—"

"Stop calling me that!"

Warren winced in frustration. "But that's who you are. I can call you no less."

She sighed. "The Prelate, Prelate Annalina, asked her friends to call her Ann. If I am the Prelate now, then I ask you to address me as Verna."

Warren thought it over with a frown. "Well . . . I guess we are friends."

"Warren, we are more than friends; you are the only one I can trust. There is no one else, now."

He nodded. "Verna, then." He twisted his mouth as he thought. "Verna, you're right: I know the books. I know the requirements, and you fit them all. You're young, for a Prelate, but only by precedent; there's no prohibition in law about age. More than that, you have the Han of three Sisters. There is no Sister, no Sister of the Light, anyway, who is your equal. That in itself makes you more than qualified; power, the command of Han, is a prime consideration to be Prelate."

"Warren, there has to be something. Think."

His blue eyes reflected the depth of his knowledge, and regret. "Verna, I know the books. They're explicit. Once lawfully named, they specifically forbid the Prelate from abandoning her duty. Only in death may she cede the calling. Short of Annalina Aldurren coming back to life, and reclaiming her office, there is no way for you to disqualify yourself, or to resign. You are Prelate."

Verna could think of no solution. She was trapped. "That woman has been twisting my life for as long as I can remember. She keyed that spell to me, I know she did. She trapped me into this. I wish I could strangle her!"

Warren laid a gentle hand to her arm. "Verna, would you ever allow a Sister of the Dark to become Prelate?"

"Of course not."

"Do you think Ann would?"

"No, but I don't see—"

"Verna, you said you can trust none but me. Think of Ann. She was trapped, too. She couldn't allow the chance of one of them becoming Prelate. She was dying. She did the only thing she could. She could trust no one but you."

Verna stared into his eyes as his words echoed in her mind, and then she slumped down on a smooth, dark rock beside the water. Her face sank into her hands. "Dear Creator," she whispered, "am I this selfish?"

Warren sat down beside her. "Selfish? Stubborn, at times, but never selfish."

"Oh Warren, she must have been so lonely. At least she had Nathan there with her. . . . at the end."

Warren nodded. After a moment, he glanced over at her. "We're in a lot of trouble, aren't we, Verna."

"A whole palace full of it, Warren, all wrapped up nice and neat with a gold ring."

CHAPTER 7

RICHARD COVERED HIS MOUTH as he yawned. He was so tired from not getting any sleep the night before, or much, for that matter, in the last two weeks, to say nothing of the fight with the mriswith, that it was a struggle to put one foot in front of the other. The smells ran from foul to fragrant and back again seemingly every few paces as he progressed through the convoluted maze of streets, staying close to the buildings and out of the thickest of the commotion while trying his best to follow the directions Mistress Sanderholt had given him. He hoped he wasn't lost.

Always knowing where he was, and how he was going to get to where he was going, was a matter of honor for a guide, but since Richard had been a woods guide, he guessed it could be pardoned if he did become lost in a great city. Besides, he was no longer a woods guide, nor did he expect he would ever be one again.

He knew where the sun was, though, and no matter what the streets and buildings did in their efforts to confuse him with their teeming thoroughfares, dark alleys, and warrens of narrow, twisting side streets among ancient, windowless buildings laid out to no design, southeast was still southeast. He simply used taller buildings as landmarks, instead of monarch trees or prominent terrain, and tried not to worry about the exact streets he was supposed to follow.

Richard was weaving his way through the throngs of people, past shabbily dressed hawkers with pots of dried roots, baskets of pigeons, fish, and eels, charcoal makers pushing carts and calling out the price in song, past cheesemongers outfitted in crisp red-and-yellow livery, butcher shops with pig, sheep, and stag carcasses hung on spike racks, salt sellers offering different grades and textures, shopkeepers selling breads, pies and pastries, poultry, spices, sacks of grain, barrels of wines and ale, and a hundred other items displayed in windows or on tables outside shops, and past people inspecting the wares, chatting, and complaining about the prices, when he realized the flutter in his gut was a warning—he was being followed.

Suddenly wide awake, he turned and saw a crush of faces, but none he recognized. He held his black cape over his sword so as not to draw attention to himself. At least the ever-present soldiers didn't seem particularly interested in him, although some of the D'Harans looked up when he passed near, as if they could sense something, but couldn't place its source. Richard hurried his steps.

The flutter was so faint that he thought maybe those who followed weren't close enough for him to see them. But then, how was he to know who it was? It could be any of the faces he saw. He glanced at the rooftops, but didn't see the one he knew was following him, and instead checked the direction of the sunlight to help keep his bearings.

He paused near a corner building to watch the people flowing up and down the street, looking for anyone watching him, anyone who looked out of place, or unusual, but saw nothing alarming.

"Honey cake, m'lord?"

Richard turned to a small girl in a too-big coat standing behind a rickety little table. He guessed her to be ten or twelve, but he wasn't good at guessing young girls' ages. "What was that?"

She swept a hand over the wares on her table. "Honey cake? My grandmamma makes them. They're right good, I can tell you, and only a penny. Would you buy one, please, m'lord? You won't be sorry."

On the ground behind the girl, a stocky old woman in a tattered wrap of brown blanket sat on a board placed over the snow. She grinned up at him. Richard only half smiled back as he probed his inner flutter, trying to determine what he was sensing, trying to determine the nature of the foreboding. The girl and old woman smiled hopefully, and waited.

Richard glanced up the street again and then, letting a long cloud of his breath stream away in the light breeze, fished around in his pocket. He had had precious little to eat in his two-week run to Aydindril, and was still weak. All he had was silver and gold from the Palace of the Prophets. He doubted his pack, back at the Confessors' Palace, had any pennies in it, either.

"I'm not a lord," he said as he put all but a silver back into his pocket.

The girl pointed at his sword. "Anyone with a fine sword the likes of that must be a lord, surely."

The old woman had stopped smiling. With her eyes fixed on his sword, she rose to her feet.

Richard hastily pulled his cape across the hilt and the silver- and gold-worked scabbard, and handed the girl the coin. She stared at it in her palm.

"I've not enough small money to make change for this much, m'lord. Bless me, I don't even know how much small money it would take. I've never held a silver coin before."

"I told you, I'm not a lord." He smiled when she looked up. "My name's Richard. Tell you what, why don't you just keep the coin and consider the extra as payment in advance, then whenever I pass this way again, well, you can give me another of your honey cakes for the bargain, until the silver is used up."

"Oh, m'lord . . . I mean Richard, thank you."

Beaming, the girl handed the coin to her grandmamma. The old woman inspected the silver coin with a critical eye as she turned it in her fingers. "I've not seen marks like these before. You must have traveled a long way."

The woman would have no way of knowing where the coin was from; the Old and New Worlds had been separated for the last three thousand years. "I have. The silver is real enough, though."

She gazed up with blue eyes that looked as if the years had washed out nearly all the color. "Taken or given, m'lord?" When Richard's brow creased, she gestured. "That sword of yours, m'lord. Did you take it, or was it given to you."

Richard held her gaze, at last understanding. The Seeker was meant to be appointed by a wizard, but since Zedd had fled the

Midlands many years past, the sword had become a prize among those who could afford it, or those who could steal it. Pretend Seekers had given the Sword of Truth a nefarious reputation, and were not to be trusted; they used the sword's magic for selfish reasons, and not as it had been intended by those who had invested their magic in the blade. Richard was the first in decades to have been named Seeker of Truth by a wizard. Richard understood the magic, its terrible power and responsibility. He was the true Seeker.

"It was given by one of the First Order. I was named," he said cryptically.

She clutched the blanket to her buxom chest. "A Seeker," she breathed through the gaps where teeth belonged. "The spirits be praised. A real Seeker."

The little girl, not understanding the conversation, peered at the coin in her grandmamma's hand, and then handed Richard the biggest honey cake on the table. He accepted it with a smile.

The old woman leaned over the table a bit and lowered her voice. "You've come to rid us of the vermin?"

"Something like that." He took a bite of the honey cake. He smiled down at the girl again. "It's as good as you promised."

She grinned. "Told you so. Grandmamma makes the best honey cakes on Stentor Street."

Stentor Street. At least he had managed to find the correct street. Past the market on Stentor Street, Mistress Sanderholt had said. He winked at the girl while he chewed. "What vermin?" he asked the old woman.

"My son," the old woman said as her eyes flicked down, indicating the girl, "and her mother, they've deserted us to stay near the palace, waiting for the gold promised. I told them to work, but they say I'm old and foolish in my ways, that they can be given more than they could earn, if they just wait there for what's owed them."

"How do they reason it's 'owed them'?"

She shrugged. "Because someone from the palace said so. Said they were entitled to it. Said all the people were. Some, like those two, believe it; it appeals to my son's lazy ways. The young are lazy nowadays. So they sit and wait, to be given, to be taken care of, instead of seeing to their own needs. They fight over who should be given the gold first. Some of the weak and old have been killed in those fights.

"Meanwhile, fewer work, and so the prices keep going up. We can hardly afford enough bread, now." Her face set into a bitter expression. "All because of a foolish lust for gold. My son had work, for Chalmer the baker, but now he waits to be handed gold, instead of working, and she grows more hungry." She glanced out of the corner of her eye at the girl, and smiled kindly. "She works, though. Helps me make my cakes, she does, so we can feed ourselves. I won't let her roam the streets, like many of the young do, now."

She looked up again with a somber expression. "Them's the vermin: them who take what little we can earn or make with our hands so as to promise it right back to us, expecting us to be thankful at their kind hearts; them who tempt good people to be lazy so they can rule us like they do sheep at a trough; them who took our freedom and our ways. Even a foolish old woman like me knows that lazy people don't think for themselves; they only think about themselves. I don't know what the world's coming to."

When she finally seemed to have run out of breath, he gestured to the coin in her fist as he swallowed the mouthful of honey cake. Richard gave her a meaningful look. "I'd appreciate it, for now, if you would forget about what my sword looks like."

She bobbed her head knowingly. "Anything. Anything for you, m'lord. The good spirits be with you. And give the vermin a wack for me."

Richard moved up the street a ways, and sat a moment on a barrel beside an alleyway to take a bite of his honey cake. It was good, but he wasn't really paying much attention to the taste, and it didn't do anything to quell the apprehensive feeling in his stomach. It wasn't the same feeling as when he sensed the mriswith, he realized; it was more the feeling he had always gotten when someone's eyes were on him, and the fine hairs at the base of his neck stiffened. That was what he felt—someone watching him, someone watching and following. He scanned the faces, but didn't see anyone who looked as if they were interested in him.

Licking the honey off his fingers, he wove his way across the street, around horses pulling carts and wagons, and between the crush of people going about their business. At times, it was like trying to swim upriver. The din, the jangling of tack, the thud of hooves, the rattle of cargo in wagons, the creak of axles, the crunch of the compacted snow, the shouting of the hawkers, the cries of hucksters, and the buzz of talking, some in a singsong or a chatter of languages he didn't understand, was unnerving. Richard was used to the silence of his woods, where the wind in the trees or water rushing over rocks was the most sound he ever heard. Though he had often gone into Hartland, it was hardly more than a small town, and nothing to compare to the cities, like this one, that he had seen since he left home.

Richard missed his woods. Kahlan had promised him that she would return there with him one day for a visit. He smiled to himself as he thought about the beautiful places he would take her—the overlooks, the falls, the hidden mountain passes. He smiled more at the thought of how astonished she would be, and at how happy they would be together. He grinned at the memory of her special smile, the one she gave no one but him.

He missed Kahlan more than he could ever miss his woods. He wanted to get to her as fast as he could. Soon, he would, but first he had a few things to do in Aydindril.

At the sound of shouting he looked up and realized that in his daydreaming he hadn't been paying any attention to where he was going, and a column of soldiers was about to trample him. The commander cursed as he drew his men to a sudden halt.

"Do you be blind! What kind of fool walks under a column of horsemen!"

Richard glanced around. The people had all moved away from the soldiers, and seemed to be trying their best to look as if they had never had any intention of venturing anywhere near the center of the street. They worked at pretending the soldiers didn't exist. Most looked as if they wanted to become invisible.

Richard peered up at the man who had yelled at him, and briefly gave thought to becoming invisible himself before there was trouble and someone was hurt, but the Wizard's Second Rule came to mind: the greatest harm can result from the best intentions. He had learned that when you mixed in magic, the results could be disastrous. Magic was dangerous and had to be used carefully. He quickly decided that a simple apology would be prudent, and would work best.

"Sorry. I guess I wasn't looking where I was going. Forgive me."

He didn't recall having ever seen soldiers like these, all atop mounts standing in neat, precise rows. Each grim-faced soldier's armor was blinding in the sunlight. Besides the impeccably polished armor, their swords, knives, and lances glinted in the sunlight. Each man wore a crimson cape draped in exact fashion over the flank of his white horse. They looked to Richard like men about to pass in review before a great king.

The man who had yelled glared down from under the brim of a gleaming helmet topped with a red horsehair plume. He held the reins to his powerful gray gelding easily in one gauntleted hand as he leaned over.

"Get out of our way, half-wit, or we'll trample you and be done with it."

Richard recognized the man's accent; it was the same as Adie's. He didn't know what land Adie was from, but these men had to be from the same place.

Richard shrugged as he took a step back. "I said I was sorry. I didn't know there was such urgent business about."

"Fighting the Keeper always be urgent business."

Richard took another step back. "Can't argue with you about that. I'm sure he's shivering in a corner right now, waiting for you to come vanquish him, so you best be on with it, then."

The man's dark eyes shone like ice. Richard tried not to let his wince show. He wished he could learn not to be flip. He guessed it was a result of his size.

Richard had never liked fighting. As he had grown, he had become the target of others wanting to prove themselves. Before he had been given the Sword of Truth, and it had taught him the need of sometimes releasing the anger he had always kept under tight control, he had learned that he could use a smile and humor to smooth the feelings of agitated foes, and disarm those simply wanting to start a fight. Richard knew his own strength, but that confidence had lent his easy humor a tendency to become flippant. Sometimes it seemed as if he just couldn't help himself; his mouth simply moved before he thought.

"You have a bold tongue. Maybe you be one beguiled by the Keeper."

"I assure you, sir, you and I fight the same foe."

"The Keeper's minions lurk behind arrogance."

Just as Richard was thinking that he didn't need any trouble, and it was time to make a quick retreat, the man made to dismount. At the same instant, powerful hands grabbed him. Two huge men. one at each shoulder, lifted him from his feet.

"On your way, dandy," the one at his right shoulder said to the horseman. "This one is none of your concern." Richard tried to twist his head around, but he could only manage to see the brown leather of D'Haran uniforms on the men who held him from behind.

The soldier froze with his foot just out of the stirrup. "We be on the same side, brother. This one needs to be questioned—by us—and then to learn some humility. We will—"

"I said, be off!"

Richard opened his mouth to say something. Immediately, the heavily muscled arm of the D'Haran at his right came out from under a thick, dark brown, wool cape. As a massive hand clamped over his mouth, Richard saw a band of gold-colored metal just above the elbow, its razor-sharp projections glinting in the sunlight. The bands were deadly weapons used to rip open an opponent in close combat. Richard nearly choked on his own tongue.

Most D'Haran soldiers were big, but these two were well beyond merely big. Worse, they were not simply regular D'Haran soldiers; Richard had seen men like these before, with bands just above their elbows. They were Darken Rahl's personal guards. Darken Rahl almost always had two men like these with him.

The two men lifted Richard easily in their fists; he was as helpless as a stick doll. In his two-week race to Aydindril, to get to Kahlan, he had not only had little food, but little sleep. The fight with the mriswith, only hours before, had drained nearly all the energy he had left, but his fright brought a reserve of strength to his muscles. Against these two, it was not enough.

The man on the horse started swinging his leg over its flanks again, to dismount. "I told you, this one be ours. We intend to question him. If he serves the Keeper, he will confess."

The D'Haran at Richard's left shoulder growled in a menacing voice. "Come down here, and I'll lop off your head and use it to play a game of bowls. We've been looking for this one, and he's ours, now. When we're done with him, you can question his corpse all you want."

Frozen half off his horse, the man glared down at the D'Harans. "I told you, brother, we be on the same side. We both fight the Keeper's evil. There be no need for us to fight one another."

"If you want to argue, then do it with your sword. If not, be off!"

The near to two hundred horsemen watched the two D'Harans, showing no emotion, especially not fear. There were, after all, only two D'Harans—not an arduous challenge, despite the men's size. At least a fool might think so. Richard had seen D'Haran troops everywhere in the city. It was possible that at the first sign of trouble, they could show up in short order.

The horseman didn't seem too concerned about other D'Harans, though. "There be only two of you, brother. Not good odds."

The one at Richard's left glanced casually down the line of horsemen, turned his head, and spat. "You're right, dandy. Egan, here, will stand aside to make the odds more even while I deal with you and your fancy men. But be sure of yourself, 'brother,' 'cause if your foot touches the ground, by my word, you die first."

Eyes of ice, still and cold, appraised the two a moment, and then the man in the polished armor and crimson cape, grumbling a curse in a foreign tongue, let his weight drop back down in his saddle. "We have important matters that demand our attention. This one be a waste of our time. He be yours."

With a wave of his arm, the column of horsemen charged up the street, narrowly missing trampling Richard and his two captors. Richard tried, but the two holding him were too strong, and he couldn't get his hand to his sword as they carried him off. He scanned the rooftops, but saw nothing.

All the people around averted their eyes, wanting nothing to do with the trouble at hand. As the two huge D'Harans dragged Richard from the center of the street, people scattered out of the way as if they had eyes in the back of their heads. Over the noise of the city, his muffled, angry cries were lost. Try as he might, he couldn't get a hand near a weapon. His boots skimmed across the snow, his feet working in vain for purchase.

Richard struggled, but before he had time to try to think what do next, they pulled him into a narrow, dark passageway between an inn and another shuttered building.

Deep in the passageway, in the murky shadows, four dark, cloaked figures waited.

CHAPTER 8

GENTLY, THE TWO HUGE D'Harans set Richard down. As his feet found the ground, his hand found the hilt of his sword. The two men spread their feet in a relaxed manner and clasped their hands behind their backs. From the shadowed end of the passageway the four cloaked figures started toward him.

Deciding escape was preferable to a fight, Richard didn't draw his sword, but instead dove to the side. He rolled through the snow and sprang to his feet. His back smacked up against the cold brick wall. Panting, he flung his mriswith cape around himself. In a heartbeat the cape changed color to match the wall, and he vanished.

It would be an easy matter to slip away while hidden by the cape. Better to escape than to fight. As soon as he caught his breath.

The four marched forward, their dark capes billowing open as they came into the light. Dark brown leather the same color as the D'Harans' uniforms covered their shapely forms from ground to neck. A yellow star between the cusps of a crescent emblazoned the leather outfits at each woman's stomach.

The recognition of that yellow star and crescent was like a flash of lightning in Richard's mind. Too many times to count, his face, wet with his own blood, had laid against that emblem. Out of reflex he froze, drawing neither sword, nor breath. For a panic filled instant he saw only the symbol he knew all too well.

Mord-Sith.

The woman in the lead pushed back her hood, letting her long blond hair, plaited in a single thick braid, fall free. Her blue eyes searched the wall where he stood.

"Lord Rahl? Lord Rahl, where . . ."

Richard blinked. "Cara?"

Just as he slackened his concentration, allowing his cape to return to black, and her eyes found him, the sky fell in.

With a roar, a flap of wings, and a flash of fangs, Gratch plummeted to the ground. The two men had swords to hand almost instantly, but they were not as fast as the Mord-Sith. Before the men's blades had cleared their scabbards, the women had their Agiel in their fists. Though an Agiel appeared to be nothing more than a thin, red leather rod, Richard knew them to be weapons of awesome power. Richard had been "trained" with an Agiel.

Richard heaved himself at the gar, knocking him to the far wall before the two men and four women could reach him. Gratch slung him aside in his desire to get at the threat.

"Stop! All of you, stop!" The six people and one gar froze at the sound of his shriek. Richard didn't know who would win the fight, but he didn't want to find out. He snatched the instant he had before they might decide to move again and sprang in front of Gratch. With his back to the gar, he held his hands out to each side. "Gratch is my friend. He only wants to protect me. Stay where you are, and he won't hurt you."

Gratch's furry arm circled around Richard's middle and drew him back against the taut, pink skin of his chest and stomach. The passageway resounded with a growl that, while affectionate, at the same time carried a rumble of threat for the others.

"Lord Rahl," Cara said in a smooth voice as the two men sheathed their swords, "we are here to protect you, too."

Richard eased the arm away. "It's all right, Gratch. I know them. You did good, just like I asked, but it's all right, now. Just calm down."

Gratch let out a purling rumble that echoed off the walls rising up like a narrow, dark canyon. Richard knew it as a sound of satisfaction.

He had told Gratch to follow him, either high in the air, or flying from rooftop to rooftop, but to stay out of sight unless there was trouble. Gratch had indeed done a good job; Richard hadn't seen a sign of him until he dropped down on them.

"Cara, what are you doing here?"

Cara reverently touched his arm, seeming surprised at finding it solid. She jabbed a finger at his shoulder, and then broke into a grin.

"Not even Darken Rahl himself could become invisible. He could command beasts, but he could not become invisible."

"I don't command Gratch; he's my friend. And I don't exactly become . . . Cara, what are you doing here?"

She looked perplexed at the question. "Protecting you."

Richard pointed at the two men. "And them? They said they were going to kill me."

The two men stood rooted like twin oaks. "Lord Rahl," one said, "we would die before we let harm touch you."

"We had almost caught up with you when you walked into those fancy horsemen," Cara said. "I told Egan and Ulic to get you out of there without any fighting, or you could be hurt. If those men thought we were trying to rescue you, they might have tried to kill you. We didn't want to take a chance with your life."

Richard glanced to the two, great, blond-headed men. The dark leather straps, plates, and belts of their uniforms were molded to fit like a second skin over the prominent contours of their muscles. Incised in the leather at the center of their chests was an ornate letter R, and beneath that, two crossed swords. One of them, Richard wasn't sure if it was Egan or Ulic, echoed the truth of what Cara had said. Since Cara and the other Mord-Sith had helped him in D'Hara two weeks before, making it possible for him to defeat Darken Rahl, he was inclined to believe her.

Richard hadn't anticipated their choice when he had declared the Mord-Sith free from the shackles of their discipline; having their freedom, they chose to be his guardians, and were fiercely protective of him. There didn't seem to be anything he could do to change their minds.

One of the other women spoke Cara's name in caution and nodded toward the opening into the street. People slowed as they passed, peering in, looking them over. A glare from the two men as they turned put speed into the onlookers' steps, and turned their eyes away.

Cara grasped Richard's arm above the elbow. "It isn't safe here—yet. Come with us, Lord Rahl."

Not waiting for his answer, or cooperation, she pulled him into the shadows at the back of the passageway. Richard gestured silently to reassure Gratch. Lifting the bottom of a loose shutter, Cara stuffed him ahead of her through the opening. The window they entered was the only one in a room appointed with a dusty table holding three candles, several benches, and one chair. To the side sat a pile of their gear.

Gratch managed to fold his wings and squeeze through, too. He stood close to Richard, quietly watching the others. They, in turn, having been told that he was Richard's friend, didn't seem concerned at having a hulking gar eyeing them from a few feet away.

"Cara, what *are* you doing here?"

She frowned as if he were thick. "I told you, we came to protect you." A mischievous smile crooked the corners of her mouth. "Seems we arrived just in time. Master Rahl must devote himself to being the magic against magic, a task you are more suited to, and let us be the steel against steel." She held her hand out to the other three women. "We didn't have time for introductions at the palace. These are my sisters of the Agiel: Hally, Berdine, and Raina."

In the flickering candlelight, Richard studied the three faces. He had been in a terrible rush at the time and recalled only Cara; she was the one who had spoken for them, and he had held a knife to her throat until she convinced him she was telling the truth. Like Cara, Hally was blond, blue-eyed, and tall. Berdine and Raina were a bit shorter, blue-eyed Berdine with a loose braid of wavy brown hair, and Raina with dark hair, and eyes that seemed to be examining his soul for every nuance of strength, weakness, and character—an idiosyncratic, piercing scrutiny unique to Mord-Sith. Somehow, Raina's dark eyes made the penetrating judgment seem more incisive.

Richard didn't shy from their gazes. "You were among those who saw me safely through the palace?" They nodded. "Then you have my eternal gratitude. What of the others?"

"The others remained at the palace in case you returned before we found you," Cara said. "Commander General Trimack insisted

Ulic and Egan would come, too, since they are among the personal bodyguards to the Master Rahl. We left within an hour after you did, trying to catch you." She shook her head in wonder. "We wasted no time, and you gained almost a day on us."

Richard tugged straight the baldric holding his sword. "I was in a hurry."

Cara shrugged. "You are the Master Rahl. Nothing you do could surprise us."

Richard thought she had looked very surprised indeed when she saw him become invisible, but he didn't say it, in view of his new-found restraint on his flip tongue.

He glanced around at the dimly lit, dusty room. "What are you doing in this place?"

Cara pulled off her gloves and tossed them on the table. "We intended to use it as a base while we looked for you. We've only been here a short time. We chose this spot because it's close to the D'Haran headquarters."

"I was told they're in a large building beyond the market."

"They are," Hally said. "We checked."

Richard searched her piercing blue eyes. "I was on my way there when you found me. I guess it wouldn't hurt to have you along." He loosened the mriswith cape at his throat and scratched the back of his neck. "How did you manage to find me in a city of this size?"

The two men stood without showing emotion, but eyebrows went up on the women.

"You are the Master Rahl," Cara said, seeming to think that would be explanation enough.

Richard planted his fists on his hips. "So?"

"The bond," Berdine said. She looked perplexed at the blank expression on his face. "We are bonded to the Master Rahl."

"I don't understand what that means. What does it have to do with finding me?"

Looks passed among the women. Cara cocked her head to the side. "You are Lord Rahl, the Master of D'Hara. We are D'Harans. How can you not understand?"

Richard wiped his hair back off his forehead as he let out an exasperated breath. "I was raised in Westland, two boundaries away from D'Hara. I never knew anything about D'Hara, much less Darken Rahl, until the boundaries came down. I didn't even know Darken Rahl was my father until just a few months ago." He glanced away from their bewildered expressions. "He raped my mother, and she fled to Westland before I was born, before the boundaries went up. Darken Rahl never knew I existed, or that I was his son, until he died. I don't know anything about being Master Rahl."

The two men stood as they had, showing no emotion. The four Mord-Sith stared at him a long moment, the candle flame adding a point of light to the corner of their eyes as they seemed to study his soul again. He wondered if they were regretting their oath of loyalty to him.

Richard felt awkward laying out his ancestry to the scrutiny of people he didn't really know. "You still haven't explained how you managed to find me."

As Berdine took off her cape and tossed it atop their gear, Cara laid a hand on his shoulder, urging him to sit in the chair. By the way its loose joints swayed under his weight, he wasn't sure it would hold him, but it did. She glanced up at the two men. "Maybe you could better explain the bond to him, since you feel it most strongly. Ulic?"

Ulic shifted his weight. "Where should I begin?"

Cara started to say something, but Richard cut her off. "I have important things to do, and I don't have a great deal of time. Just tell me the important parts. Tell me about this bond."

Ulic nodded. "I will tell you as we are taught."

Richard gestured toward a bench, indicating he wanted Ulic to sit. It made him uncomfortable having the man tower over him like some mountain with arms. Checking over his shoulder, Richard saw that Gratch was contentedly licking his fur, but keeping his glowing green eyes on the people. Richard smiled reassuringly. Gratch hadn't been around that many people, and Richard wanted him to be comfortable, in view of what he planned. The gar's face wrinkled into a smile, but his ears were perked as he listened. Richard wished he knew for sure how much Gratch could understand.

Ulic pulled up a bench and sat. "Long ago—"

"How long," Richard interrupted.

Ulic rubbed a thumb along the bone handle of the knife at his belt as he contemplated the question. His deep voice seemed as if it might smother the candle flames. "Long ago . . . in the beginning times of D'Hara. I believe several thousand years ago."

"So what took place in these beginning times?"

"Well, that was where the bond originated. In the beginning times, the first Master Rahl cast his power, his magic, over the D'Haran people, in order to protect us."

Richard lifted an eyebrow. "You mean in order to rule you."

Ulic shook his head. "It was a covenant. The House of Rahl"—he tapped the ornate letter R incised in the leather over his chest—"would be the magic, and the D'Haran people would be the steel. We protect him and he, in turn, protects us. We were bonded."

"Why would a wizard need the protection of steel? Wizards have magic."

Ulic's leather uniform creaked as he put an elbow to his knee and leaned in with a sobering expression. "You have magic. Has it always protected you? You cannot always remain awake, or always see who is behind you, or conjure magic fast enough if the numbers are great. Even those with magic will die if someone slits their throat. You need us."

Richard conceded the point. "So, what does this bond have to do with me?"

"Well, the covenant, the magic, links the people of D'Hara to the Master Rahl. When the Master Rahl dies, the bond can be passed on to his gifted heir." Ulic shrugged. "The bond is the magic of that link. All D'Harans feel it. We understand it from birth. We recognize the Master Rahl by the bond. When the Master Rahl is near we can feel his presence. That's how we found you. When we're close enough we can sense you."

Richard gripped the arms of the chair as he leaned forward. "You mean to tell me that all D'Harans can sense me, and know where I am?"

"No. There's more to it." Ulic stuffed a finger under a leather plate to scratch his shoulder while he tried to think of how to explain.

Berdine put a foot on the bench beside Ulic and leaned forward on an elbow, coming to his rescue. Her thick, brown braid fell forward over her shoulder. "You see, first of all, we must recognize the new Master Rahl. By that I mean we must recognize and accept his rule in a formal manner. This acquiescence is not formal in the sense of ceremony, but more in the sense of an understanding and acceptance within our hearts. It does not have to be an acceptance we desire, and in the past, with us, anyway, it was not, but acceptance is implicit, nonetheless."

"You mean you must believe."

All the faces staring at him brightened.

"Yes. That's a good way to express it," Egan put in. "Once we acquiesce to his dominion, and as long as the Master Rahl lives, we are bonded to him. When he dies, the new Lord Rahl takes his place, and we are then bonded to him. At least that's the way it's supposed to work. This time, something went wrong, and Darken Rahl, or his spirit, somehow maintained a part of himself in this world."

Richard straightened in his chair. "The gateway. The boxes in the Garden of Life are a gateway to the underworld, and one was left opened. When I came back, two weeks ago, I closed it, sending Darken Rahl back to the underworld for good."

Ulic's muscles bulked as he rubbed his palms together. "When Darken Rahl died at the beginning of winter, and you spoke outside the palace, many of the D'Harans there believed you were the new Lord Rahl. Some did not. Some still held on to their loyalty, their bond, to Darken Rahl. It must have been because of this gateway you said was opened. It's never happened that way before, that I heard of, anyway.

"When you returned to the palace, and defeated Darken Rahl's spirit with the use of your gift, you also defeated the rebel officers who denounced you. In banishing Darken Rahl's spirit, you broke the bond he still held over some of them, and convinced the rest at the palace of your authority as Master Rahl. They are loyal, now. The whole palace is. They are all bonded to you."

"As it should be," Raina said with finality. "You have the gift; you are a wizard. You are the magic against magic, and the D'Harans, your people, are the steel against steel."

Richard looked up into her dark eyes. "I know less about this bond, this steel against steel and magic against magic business, than I know about being a wizard, and I know next to nothing about being a wizard. I don't know how to use magic."

The women stared for a moment, and then laughed as if he had made a joke and they wanted him to think they were amused.

"I'm not joking. I don't know how to use my gift."

Hally clapped him on the back of his shoulder and pointed at

Gratch. "You command the beasts, just as Darken Rahl did. We cannot command beasts. You even talk to him. A gar!"

"You don't understand. I saved him when he was a pup. I raised him, that's all. We became friends. It's not magic."

Hally clapped his shoulder again. "It may not seem magic to you, Lord Rahl, but none of us could do it."

"But—"

"We saw you become invisible today." Cara said. She wasn't laughing anymore. "Are you going to tell us that was not magic?"

"Well yes, I guess it was magic, but not in the way you think. You just don't understand—"

Cara's eyebrow lifted. "Lord Rahl, to you it is understandable, because you have the gift. To us, it is magic. Surely, you would not suggest that any of us could do it?"

Richard wiped a hand across his face. "No, you couldn't do it. But still, it's not what you think."

Raina's dark eyes fixed on his with that look that Mord-Sith flashed when they expected compliance, and no argument; a steely gaze that seemed to paralyze his tongue. Though he was no longer the captive of a Mord-Sith, and these women were trying to help him, the look still gave him pause.

"Lord Rahl," she said in a soft voice that filled the quiet room, "at the People's Palace, you fought the spirit of Darken Rahl. You, a mere man, fought the spirit of a powerful wizard come back from the underworld, from the world of the dead, to destroy us all. He had no corporeal existence; he was a spirit, animate only through magic. You could only battle such a demon with magic of your own.

"During the battle, you sent lightning, driven by magic, racing through the palace to destroy the rebel leaders who opposed you and wished Darken Rahl to triumph. Everyone at the palace not bonded to you already became so that day. None of us, in our whole lives, has ever seen the like of the magic crackling through the palace that day."

She leaned toward him, still gripping him in her dark gaze, the passion in her voice cutting through the stillness. "That was magic, Lord Rahl. We were all about to be destroyed, to be swallowed into the world of the dead. You saved us. You kept your part of the covenant; you were the magic against magic. You are the Master Rahl. We would lay down our lives for you."

Richard realized that his left hand was tightly gripping the hilt of his sword. He could feel the raised gold letters of the word TRUTH biting into his flesh.

He managed to disengage himself from Raina's gaze to take in the rest of them. "All you say is true, but it's not so simple as you believe. There's more to it. I don't want you to think I was able to do the things I did because I knew how. It just happened. Darken Rahl studied his whole life to be a wizard, to use magic. I know almost nothing about it. You place too much faith in me."

Cara shrugged. "We understand; you have more to learn about magic. This is good. It is always good to learn more. You will serve us better as you learn more."

"No, you don't understand. . . ."

She placed a reassuring hand on his shoulder. "No matter how much you know, there will always be more; no one knows everything. This does not change anything. You are the Master Rahl. We are bonded to you." She squeezed his shoulder. "Even if any of us wanted to change it, we could not."

Suddenly, Richard felt calm. He didn't really want to talk them out of this; he could use their help, their loyalty. "You've helped me before, maybe even saved my neck out there in the street, but I just don't want you to have more faith in me than is justified. I don't want to deceive you. I want you to follow me because what we do is right, not because of a bond forged with magic. That's slavery."

"Lord Rahl," Raina said, her voice unsteady for the first time, "we were bonded to Darken Rahl. We had no more choice in that than we do now. He took us from our homes when we were young, trained us, and used us to—"

Richard stood, putting his fingertips to her lips. "I know. It's all right. You're free now."

Cara gripped his shirt and drew his face close to hers. "Don't you see? Even though many of us hated Darken Rahl, we were compelled to serve; we were bonded. That was slavery.

"If you don't know everything, that's not important to us. We are bonded to you as the Master Rahl, regardless. For the first time in any of our lives, it is not a burden. If the bond were not there, we would chose to do the same; that is not slavery."

"We don't know anything about your magic," Hally said, "but we can help you learn what it means to be Lord Rahl." The irony of her spreading smile softened her blue eyes, letting the women behind the appellation of Mord-Sith show through. "It is, after all, the purpose of Mord-Sith to train, to teach." The smile faded as her expression turned serious. "It doesn't matter to us if you have more steps in the journey; we won't abandon you for it."

Richard raked his fingers though his hair. He was touched by the things they said, but their blind devotion somehow troubled him. "As long as you understand that I'm not the wizard you thought. I know a little about some magic, like my sword, but I don't know much about using my gift. I used what came forth from within me without understanding it or being able to control it, and the good spirits helped me." He paused a moment as he looked into the depths of their waiting eyes. "Denna is with them."

The four women smiled, each in her own private way. They had known Denna, known that she had trained him, and that he had killed her in order to escape. In so doing, he freed her of her bond to Darken Rahl, and what she had become, but at a cost that would always haunt him, even if her spirit was now at peace; he had had to turn the Sword of Truth white, and end her life with that side of the magic—through its love and forgiveness.

"What could be better than having the good spirits on our side," Cara said in a quiet tone that seemed to speak for them all. "It's good to know that Denna is with them."

Richard turned away from their eyes in an effort to also turn away from his haunting memories. He brushed the dust off his pants and changed the subject.

"Well, as the Seeker of Truth, I was on my way to see whoever is in charge of the D'Harans here in Aydindril. I have something important to do, and I need to hurry. I didn't know anything about this bond, but I do know about being Seeker. I guess it can't hurt to have all of you along."

Berdine shook her head of wavy brown hair. "It's fortunate we found him in time." The other three muttered their agreement.

Richard looked from one face to another. "Why is it fortunate?"

"Because," Cara said, "they don't yet know you as the Master Rahl."

"I told you, I'm the Seeker. That's more important than being the Master Rahl. Don't forget, as the Seeker, I killed the last Master Rahl. But now that you've told me about this bond, I intend to tell the D'Haran command that I'm also the new Lord

Rahl, and demand their allegiance. It will certainly make what I have planned easier."

Berdine barked a laugh. "We had no idea how lucky we were to catch you in time."

Raina brushed her dark bangs back as she glanced to her sister of the Agiel. "I shudder to think how close we came to losing him."

"What are you talking about? They're D'Harans. I thought they would be able to sense me, with this bond thing."

"We told you," Ulic said, "first we must recognize and accept the Master Rahl's rule in a formal manner. You have not done that with these men. Also, the bond isn't the same in all of us."

Richard threw his hands up. "First you tell me that they will follow me, and now you tell me they won't?"

"You have to bond them to you, Lord Rahl," Cara said. She sighed. "If you can. General Reibisch's blood isn't pure."

Richard frowned. "What does that mean?"

"Lord Rahl," Egan said as he came forward, "in the beginning times, when the first Master Rahl cast the web, bonding us, D'Hara was not as it is today. D'Hara was a land, within a larger land, much the same as the Midlands are made up of different lands."

Richard suddenly remembered the story Kahlan told him the night he met her. As they had sat shivering by a fire in the shelter of a wayward pine, after they had had the wits frightened out of them by an encounter with a gar, she had told him some of the history of the world beyond his home of Westland.

Richard stared off into a dark corner as he recalled the story. "Darken Rahl's grandfather, Panis, the Master of D'Hara, set about joining all the lands together under his rule. He swallowed up all the lands, all the kingdoms, making it one, making it all D'Hara."

"That's right," Egan said. "Not all the people who now call themselves D'Haran are descendants of the first D'Harans—those who were bonded. Some have a bit of true D'Haran blood, some have more, and in some, like Ulic and I, it is pure. Some have no true D'Haran blood; they do not feel the bond.

"Darken Rahl and his father before him gathered those to them who were of like mind—those who lusted for power. Many of those D'Harans were not pure of blood, but pure of ambition."

"Commander General Trimack, at the palace, and the men of the First File—" Richard gestured to Ulic and Egan. "—and Master Rahl's personal bodyguards, must be pure D'Haran?"

Ulic nodded. "Darken Rahl, like his father before him, would trust none but those of pure blood to guard him. He used those of mixed blood, or those without the bond at all, to fight the wars away from the heart of D'Hara, and to conquer other lands."

Richard stroked his lower lip with a finger as he thought. "What of the man in charge of the D'Haran troops, here, in Aydindril. What's his name?"

"General Reibisch," Berdine said. "He is of mixed blood, and so it will not be as easy, but if you can make him recognize you as the Master Rahl, he has enough D'Haran blood to be bonded. When a commander is bonded, many of his men become so at the same time, because they trust in their commanders; they will believe as he. If you can bond General Reibisch, then you will have control of the forces in Aydindril. Even though some of the men have no true D'Haran blood, they are loyal to their leaders, and will still be bonded, in a manner of speaking."

"Then I've got to do something to convince this General Reibisch that I'm the new Master Rahl."

Cara grinned wickedly. "That's why you need us. We've brought you something, from Commander General Trimack." She gestured to Hally. "Show him."

Hally unfastened the top buttons of her leather outfit and pulled a long pouch from between her breasts. With a proud smile, she handed it to Richard. He extracted the scroll inside, inspecting the symbol of a skull with crossed swords under it impressed into the gold-colored wax.

"What's this?"

"Commander General Trimack wanted to help you," Hally said. With the gleam of a smile still in her eyes she put a finger to the wax. "This is the personal seal of the commander general of the First File. The document is in his own hand. He wrote it while I stood waiting, and then told me to give it to you. It declares you to be the new Master Rahl, and says that the First File and all the troops and field generals in D'Hara recognize you as such, are bonded, and stand ready to defend your ascension to power with their lives. It threatens undying vengeance against any who stand against you."

Richard's gaze rose to her blue eyes. "Hally, I could kiss you."

Her smile vanished in an instant. "Lord Rahl, you have declared us free. We no longer have to submit . . ." She snapped her mouth closed as her face went scarlet, as did the other women's. Hally bowed her head and fixed her sight on the floor. Her voice came in a submissive whisper. "Forgive me, Lord Rahl. If you wish that of us, we of course offer ourselves willingly."

With his fingertips, Richard lifted her chin. "Hally, it was just a figure of speech. As you told me, though you are bonded, this time you are not slaves. I am not just the Master Rahl, I am also the Seeker of Truth. I hope to have you come to follow me because the cause is just. That is what I wish you to be bound to, not me. You need never fear I will revoke your freedom."

Hally swallowed. "Thank you, Lord Rahl."

Richard waved the scroll. "Now, let's go let this General Reibisch meet the new Master Rahl, so I can get on with what I need to do."

Berdine laid a restraining hand to his arm. "Lord Rahl, the words of the commander general are meant to be an aid. They, in themselves, will not bond these troops to you."

Richard put his fists on his hips. "You four have a bad habit of dangling something in front of my face, and then snatching it away. What else do I need to do? Some fancy magic?"

The four nodded as if he had finally guessed their plan.

"What!" Richard leaned toward them. "You mean this general will want me to perform some magic trick to prove myself?"

Ill at ease, Cara shrugged. "Lord Rahl, these are just words on paper. They are meant to back you, to be of help, not to perform the task for you. At the palace in D'Hara the word of the commander general is law, only you outrank him, but in the field it is not so. Here, General Reibisch is the law. You must convince him that you outrank him.

"These men will not be easily won over. The Master Rahl must be seen as a figure of awesome power and strength. They must be overwhelmed in order to invoke the bond, just as the troops at the palace were when you set the walls alive with lightning. As you said, they must believe. To believe, it will take more than words on paper. General Trimack's letter is meant to be part of it, but it can't be all."

"Magic," Richard muttered as he slumped down in the rickety

chair. He scrubbed his face, trying to think through the haze of fatigue. He was the Seeker, appointed by a wizard, a position of power and responsibility; the Seeker was a law unto himself. He had planned to do this as the Seeker. He could still do it as Seeker. He knew about being the Seeker.

Still, if the D'Harans in Aydindril were loyal to him . . .

Through the weariness, one thought was clear: he had to make sure Kahlan was safe. He had to use his head, not just his heart. He couldn't just run off after her, ignoring what was happening, not if he wanted to truly make sure she was safe. He needed to do this. He needed to win over the D'Harans.

Richard shot to his feet. "Did you bring your red leather outfits?" A Mord-Sith's blood-red leather clothes were worn when they were of a mind to dispense discipline; red didn't show blood. When a Mord-Sith wore her red leather, it was a statement that she expected there to be a lot of blood, and everyone knew it wasn't going to be hers.

Hally smiled a sly smile as she folded her arms over her breasts. "A Mord-Sith goes nowhere without her red outfit."

Cara batted her eyes expectantly. "You have thought of something, Lord Rahl?"

"Yes." Richard gave her a smooth smile. "They need to see power and strength? They want a show of awesome magic? We'll give them magic. We'll overwhelm them." He held up a cautious finger. "But you must do as I say. I don't want anyone hurt. I didn't free you just to have you get killed."

Hally fixed him with an iron gaze. "Mord-Sith do not die in bed, old and toothless."

In those blue eyes, Richard saw a shadow of the madness that had twisted these women into remorseless weapons. He had endured some of what had been done to them; he knew what it was to live with that madness. He held her gaze and, with a soft voice, sought to soften the iron he saw. "If you get yourselves killed, Hally, then who will protect me?"

"If we must lay down our lives, then we do; otherwise there will be no Lord Rahl to protect." An unexpected smile softened Hally's eyes, bringing a little light to the shadows. "We want Lord Rahl to die in bed, old and toothless. What are we to do?"

A shadow of doubt passed across his thoughts. Was his ambition twisted by that same madness? No. He had no choice. This would save lives, not cost them.

"You four put on your red leather. We'll wait outside while you change. When you're done, I'll explain."

Hally snatched his shirt as he turned to leave. "Now that we have found you, we're not letting you out of our sight. You will remain here while we change. You may turn your back, if you wish."

With a sigh, Richard turned his back and folded his arms. The two men stood watching. Richard frowned and motioned for them to turn around, too. Gratch tilted his head with a puzzled look. Shrugging, he turned his back, mimicking Richard.

"We're glad you have decided to bond these men to you, Lord Rahl," Cara said. He could hear them pulling things out of their packs. "You will be much safer with a whole army protecting you. After you have bonded them, we will all leave at once for D'Hara, where you will be safe."

"We're not going to D'Hara," Richard said over his shoulder. "I have important matters that must be attended to. I have plans."

"Plans, Lord Rahl?" He could almost feel Raina's breath on the back of his neck as she peeled off her brown leather. "What plans?"

"What kind of plans would the Master Rahl have? I plan to conquer the world."

CHAPTER 9

THERE WAS NO NEED to force their way through the crowds; they drove a wave of panic before them the way the sight of wolves drove a herd of sheep. People screamed as they scattered. Mothers gathered up children in their arms while running, men fell face-first into the snow as they scrambled to get away, peddlers abandoned their wares in a mad dash for their lives, and shop doors to each side slammed shut.

The panic, Richard thought, was a good sign. At least they wouldn't be ignored. Of course, it was hard to ignore a seven-foot gar walking through a city in broad daylight. Richard suspected that Gratch was having the time of his life. Not sharing his innocent view of the task at hand, the rest of them wore grim expressions as they marched down the center of the street.

Gratch walked behind Richard, Ulic and Egan in front, Cara and Berdine at his left, and Hally and Raina to the right. It was no chance order. Ulic and Egan had insisted that they were to be to each side, as they were Lord Rahl's bodyguards. The women didn't think much of that idea, and argued that they would be the last line of defense around Lord Rahl. Gratch hadn't cared where he walked as long as he was close to Richard.

Richard had been forced to raise his voice to bring a halt to the argument. He had told them that Ulic and Egan would be in front to clear the way if need be, the Mord-Sith would protect each side, and Gratch would be at his back, since the gar could see over them all. Everyone had seemed satisfied, thinking they had received the stations that would prove the best protection for Lord Rahl.

Ulic and Egan's capes were pushed back over their shoulders, baring the bands with sharpened projections worn above their elbows, but they carried their swords sheathed at their belts. The four women, covered from neck to toes in closely tailored bloodred leather displaying the yellow star and crescent of the Mord-Sith at their stomachs, carried their Agiel in fists swathed with armor-backed, red leather gloves.

Richard knew all too well the pain it caused to hold an Agiel. Just as the Agiel Denna had trained him with, and had given him, hurt whenever he held it, it was not possible for these women to hold their own Agiel without its magic causing them pain. The pain, Richard knew, was excruciating, but Mord-Sith were trained to endure pain, and they stubbornly prided themselves in their ability to tolerate it.

Richard had tried to convince them to give up their Agiel, but they would not. He could order it, he supposed, but to do so would be to withdraw the freedom he had granted them, and he was loath to do that. If they were to give up their Agiel, it was for them to do. Somehow, he didn't think they would. Having carried the Sword of Truth as long as he had, Richard could understand how wishes could be at variance with principles; he hated the sword, and wanted to be rid of it, of the things he did with it, of what it did to him; but at every turn, he had fought to keep it.

A good fifty or sixty troops milled about outside the square, two-story building occupied by the D'Haran command. Only six, up on the entrance landing, appeared to be formally posted. Without slowing, Richard and his small company cut a straight line through the knot of men and toward the steps. The men all stumbled back out of the way, shock registering on their faces as they took in the odd sight.

They didn't panic the way the people in the market had, but most moved back to make way. Glares from the four women moved the rest back as efficiently as bared steel. Some of the men gripped the hilts of their swords as they took a few steps in retreat.

"Make way for Lord Rahl!" Ulic called out. In disorder, the soldiers stumbled back farther. Confused, but not willing to take a chance, a few bowed.

In a private cocoon of concentration, Richard watched it all from under the hood of his mriswith cape.

Before anyone had the presence of mind to stop or question them, they were through the crowd of soldiers and climbing the dozen steps to the simple ironbound door. At the top, one of the guards, a man about Richard's size, decided he wasn't sure they should be allowed in. He stepped in front of the door.

"You will wait—"

"Make way for Lord Rahl, you fool!" Egan growled without slowing.

The guard's eyes fixed on the armbands. "What . . . ?"

Still not slowing, Egan backhanded the man, knocking him aside. The guard toppled off the landing. Two of the others jumped off to get out of the way, and the other three opened the door, backing through.

Richard winced. He had told them all, even Gratch, that he didn't want anyone hurt unless it was necessary. He worried about what each of them might imagine was necessary.

Inside, soldiers, having heard the commotion outside, rushed toward them from halls dimly lit with a few lamps. Seeing Ulic and Egan, and the gold bands above their elbows, they drew no weapons, but they didn't look to be far from doing so. A menacing growl from Gratch slowed them. The sight of the Mord-Sith in their red leather stopped them.

"General Reibisch" was all Ulic said.

A few of the men moved forward.

"Lord Rahl to see General Reibisch," Egan said with quiet authority. "Where is he?"

Suspicious, the men stared, but didn't speak. A husky officer on the right, fists on his hips and a glare on his pockmarked face, pushed through his men.

"What's this about?"

He took an aggressive step forward, one too many, and lifted a threatening finger toward them. In a blink, Raina had her Agiel on his shoulder, dropping him to his knees. She canted it up, pressing the tip into the nerve at the side of his neck. His shriek echoed through the halls. The rest of the men flinched back.

"You answer questions," Raina said in the unmistakable, smoldering tone of a Mord-Sith in complete control, "you don't ask them." The man's whole body convulsed as he screamed. Raina leaned toward him, her red leather creaking. "I grant you but one more chance. Where is General Reibisch?"

His arm jerked up, waggling uncontrollably, but still managing to point in the general direction of the central of three halls. "Door . . . end . . . hall."

Raina withdrew her Agiel. "Thank you." The man collapsed like a puppet whose strings had been cut. Richard didn't spare any of his concentration to wince in sympathy. As much pain as an Agiel could give, Raina hadn't used it to kill; he would recover, but the other men stared wide-eyed as he writhed in the lingering agony. "Bow to the Master Rahl," she hissed. "All of you."

"Master Rahl?" one panicked voice asked.

Hally lifted a hand toward Richard. "Master Rahl."

The men stared in consternation. Raina snapped her fingers and pointed at the floor. They dropped to their knees. Before they had time to think, Richard and his company were off down the hall, their boot strikes on the wide-planked wood floor reverberating off the walls. Some of the men, drawing swords, followed.

At the end of the hall, Ulic flung open the door to a large high-ceilinged room that had been stripped of decoration. Here and there, hints of the former blue color scheme showed through the utilitarian whitewash. Gratch, bringing up the rear, had to bend to fit through the doorway. Richard ignored the worry in his gut that they were sliding down into a viper pit.

Inside the room they were greeted by three formidable ranks of D'Haran soldiers, all with battle-axes or swords to hand. It was a solid wall of grim faces, muscle, and steel. Behind the soldiers was a long table before a wall of unadorned windows looking out on a snowy courtyard. Above the far courtyard wall, Richard could see the spires of the Confessors' Palace, and above it, on the mountain, the Wizard's Keep.

A row of austere-looking men sat behind the table watching the intruders. On their upper arms partially veiled by sleeves of chain mail were neat scars that Richard presumed denoted rank. The row of men certainly had the demeanor of officers; their eyes shined with confidence and indignation.

The man in the center tipped his chair back and folded his muscular arms, arms with more scars than the others. His curly rust-colored beard covered part of an old white scar that ran from his left temple to his jaw. His heavy eyebrows drew down with displeasure.

Hally glared at the soldiers. "We are here to see General Reibisch. Move out of our way, or be moved."

The captain of the guards reached for her. "You will—"

Hally clouted the side of his skull with an armor-backed glove. Egan swept his elbow up to slash the captain's shoulder. In mid-recoil, Egan snatched the captain by the hair, bent his neck back over a knee, and gripped his windpipe.

"If you wish to die, speak."

The captain pressed his lips together so hard they turned white. Angry curses rose from the other men as they pressed forward. Agiel rose in warning.

"Let them through," the bearded man behind the table said.

The men moved back, allowing only enough room for them to squeeze through. The women to each side brandished their Agiel, and the soldiers yielded more room. Egan dropped the captain. He knelt on his good arm and knees as he coughed and gasped for his breath. Behind, the doorway and hall beyond filled with more men, all armed.

The man with the rust-colored beard let the front legs of his chair thump down. He folded his hands atop a scattering of papers between stacks laid out neatly to each side.

"What's your business?"

Hally stepped forward between Ulic and Egan. "You are General Reibisch?" The bearded man nodded. Hally inclined her head to him. It was a slight bow; Richard had never seen a Mord-Sith grant more, even to a queen. "We bring a message from Commander General Trimack of the First File. Darken Rahl is dead, and his spirit has been banished to the underworld by the new Master Rahl."

He lifted an eyebrow. "Is that so?"

She drew the scroll from its pouch and handed it to him. He inspected the seal briefly before breaking it with a thumb. He tipped his chair back once more while he unfurled the letter, and his grayish green eyes flicked from side to side as he read. At last he let the chair thump down again.

"And it took all of you to bring me a message?"

Hally planted her armored knuckles on the table and leaned toward him. "We bring you not only the message, General Reibisch, we also bring you Lord Rahl."

"Is that so. And where is this Lord Rahl of yours?"

Hally flashed her best Mord-Sith expression, looking as if she didn't expect to be asked again. "He stands before you now."

Reibisch glanced past her to the company of strangers, his eyes momentarily taking in the gar. Hally straightened, holding her arm out toward Richard.

"May I present Lord Rahl, the Master of D'Hara and all its people."

Men whispered, passing her words back to those in the hall. Puzzled, General Reibisch gestured toward the women.

"One of you, is claiming to be Lord Rahl?"

"Don't be a fool," Cara said. She held a hand out toward Richard. "This is Lord Rahl."

The general's brow drew together in a scowl. "I don't know what kind of game this is, but my patience is just about . . ."

Richard pushed back the hood of his mriswith cape and let his concentration relax. Before the eyes of the general and all his men, Richard appeared to materialize out of the air.

Soldiers all around gasped. Some fell back. Some dropped to their knees in deep bows.

"I," Richard said in a quiet voice, "am Lord Rahl."

There was a moment of dead silence, and then General Reibisch burst into laughter as he slapped a hand to the table. He threw his head back and roared. Some of the men snickered with him, but by the way their eyes moved, it was clear they didn't know why they were joining in, only that they thought it best they did.

His laughter dying out, General Reibisch rose to his feet. "Quite a trick, young man. But I've seen a lot of tricks since I've been stationed in Aydindril. Why, I one day had a man entertain me by having birds fly out of his trousers." The scowl returned. "For a moment, I almost believed you, but a trick doesn't make you Lord Rahl. Maybe in Trimack's eyes, but not in mine. I don't bow down to street-corner magicians."

Richard stood stone still, the focus of all eyes, while he frantically tried to think of what to do next. He hadn't expected laughter. He couldn't think of any other magic he could use, and this man didn't seem to know real magic from a trick, anyway. Unable to come up with a better idea at the moment, Richard sought to at least make his voice sound confident.

"I am Richard Rahl, son of Darken Rahl. He is dead. I am now Lord Rahl. If you wish to continue to serve in your post, you will bow down and recognize me. If not, then I will replace you."

Chuckling once more, General Reibisch hooked a thumb behind his belt. "Perform another trick, and if I judge it worthy, I'll give you and your troupe a coin before I send you on your way. I'm inclined to give you one for your temerity, if nothing else."

The soldiers moved closer, the mood shifting with them to an edge of menace.

"Lord Rahl does not do 'tricks,'" Hally snapped.

Reibisch put his meaty hands on the table as he leaned toward her. "Your outfits are quite convincing, but you shouldn't play at being a Mord-Sith, young lady. If one of them ever got her hands on you, she would not take kindly to your pretense; they take their profession seriously."

Hally drove her Agiel down on his hand. With a shriek, General Reibisch leapt back, his face a picture of shock. He pulled a knife.

Gratch's growl rattled the windowpanes. His green eyes glowed as he bared his fangs. His wings spread with a snap, like sails in a gale. Men backed away, cocking arms that held weapons.

Inwardly, Richard groaned. Things were rapidly spinning out of control. He wished he had done a better job of thinking this through, but he had been sure that appearing invisible would awe the D'Harans into believing. He should have at least given thought to an escape plan. He didn't know how they were going to get out of the building alive. Even if they managed, it might be at great cost; it could be a bloodbath. He didn't want that. He had only started into this Master Rahl business to prevent people from being hurt, not to cause it. Shouts rose around him.

Almost before he realized what he was doing, Richard drew his sword. The unique ring of steel filled the room. The sword's magic surged into him, rising to his defense, inundating him with its fury. It was like being hit by a furnace blast that burned to the bone. He knew the feeling well, and urged it onward; there was no choice. Storms of rage erupted within. He let the spirits of those who had used the magic before soar with him on the winds of wrath.

Reibisch slashed the air with his knife. "Kill the frauds!"

As the general leapt over the table toward Richard, the room suddenly resounded with a peal of thundering noise. Shards of glass filled the air, refracting light in glittering flashes.

Richard ducked into a crouch as Gratch bounded over him. Pieces of window mullions spiraled over their heads. Officers behind the table pitched forward, many cut by the glass. Dumbfounded, Richard realized the windows were exploding inward.

Blurs of color streaked through the rain of glass. Shadows and light in midair crashed to ground. Startled, through the sword's rage, Richard felt them.

Mriswith.

They became solid as they hit the floor.

The room burst into battle. Richard saw flashes of red, streaks of fur, and sweeping arcs of steel. An officer smashed face-first atop the table, blood splashing across papers. Ulic heaved two men back. Egan hurled another two over the table.

Richard ignored the tumult around him as he seized the calm center within. The cacophony faded away as he touched cold steel to his forehead, silently beseeching his blade to be true this day.

He saw only the mriswith, felt only them. With every fiber of his being, he wanted nothing else.

The closest sprang up, its back to him. With a scream of fury, Richard unleashed the wrath of the Sword of Truth. The tip whistled as it came around, the blade found its mark: the magic had its taste of blood. Headless, the mriswith collapsed, its three-bladed knives clattering across the floor.

Richard whirled to the lizardlike creature at his other side. Hally leapt between them, into his way. Still turning, he used his momentum to shoulder her aside as he swept his sword around, cleaving the second mriswith before the head of the first had hit the ground. Reeking blood misted the air.

Richard spun ahead. In the grip of fury, he was one with the blade, with its spirits, with its magic. He was, as the ancient prophecies in High D'Haran had named him, as he had named himself, *fuer grissa ost drauka*: the bringer of death. Anything less would mean his friends' deaths, but he was beyond reasoned thought. He was lost in need.

Though the third mriswith was dark brown, the color of the leather, Richard still picked it out as it darted through the men. With a mighty thrust, he drove his sword home between its shoulder blades. The mriswith's death howl shuddered in the air.

Men froze at the sound, and the room fell silent.

Grunting with effort, and with rage, Richard heaved the mriswith aside. The lifeless carcass slid off the blade and across the floor, slamming into a table leg. The leg snapped, and the corner of the table collapsed under a flutter of papers.

Teeth gritted, Richard swept his sword back around to the man standing just beyond where the mriswith had been a moment before. The point halted at his throat, rock steady and dripping blood. The magic raged out of control, craving for more in its hunger to eliminate the threat.

The Seeker's deadly glare met General Reibisch's eyes. Those eyes saw for the first time who stood before him. The magic dancing in Richard's eyes was unmistakable; to see it was to see the sun, to feel its heat, to know it without question.

No one made a sound, but even if they had, Richard wouldn't have heard it; his entire focus was on the man at the point of his sword, at the point of his vengeance. Richard had leapt headlong over the edge of lethal commitment into a cauldron of seething magic, and returning was an agonizing struggle.

General Reibisch went to his knees and gazed up the length of the blade into Richard's hawklike glare. His voice filled the ringing silence.

"Master Rahl guide us. Master Rahl teach us. Master Rahl protect us. In your light we thrive. In your mercy we are sheltered. In your wisdom we are humbled. We live only to serve. Our lives are yours."

They weren't false words to save his own life, they were the reverent words of a man who had seen something he truly hadn't expected.

Richard had chanted those same words countless times at devotions. For two hours each morning and afternoon everyone at the People's Palace in D'Hara went to a devotion square when the bell tolled and, bowing forehead to the ground, chanted those same words. Richard, as commanded, had said those same words the first time he had met Darken Rahl.

Looking down at the general, now, and hearing those same words, Richard was repulsed, and yet another part of him was relieved at the same time.

"Lord Rahl," Reibisch whispered, "you saved my life. You saved all our lives. Thank you."

Richard knew that if he were to try to use the Sword of Truth against him now, it wouldn't touch his flesh. In his heart, Richard knew this man was no longer a threat, or his enemy. The sword, unless he turned it white and used the love and forgiveness of the magic, couldn't harm anyone who was not a threat. The wrath, though, responded not to reason, and denying it the attempt was agony. Richard finally exerted his dominion over the rage and drove the Sword of Truth into its scabbard, driving back the magic, the anger, at the same time.

It had ended as swiftly as it had begun. To Richard, it almost seemed an unexpected dream, a twitch of violence, and it was over.

Across the sloping tabletop lay a dead officer, his blood running down the incline of polished wood. Glass littered the floor, along with scattered papers and stinking mriswith blood. The roomful of soldiers, and those in the hall, were on their knees. Their eyes, too, had seen the unequivocal.

"Is everyone else all right?" Richard realized his voice was hoarse from screaming. "Is anyone else hurt?"

Silence echoed in the room. A few of the men were nursing injuries that looked painful, but not life-threatening. Ulic and Egan, both panting, both with their swords still in their scabbards, both with bloody knuckles, were standing among the men on their knees. They had been at the People's Palace; their eyes had already seen.

Gratch folded his wings and grinned. At least there was one, Richard thought, who was bonded through friendship. Four dead mriswith lay sprawled on the floor; Gratch had killed one, and Richard three, fortunately before they were able to kill anyone else. It could have easily been much worse. Cara drew a hank of hair back from her face, while Berdine brushed glass fragments off her head, and Raina released her grip on a soldier's arm, letting him slump forward to catch his breath.

Richard glanced past the severed torso of a mriswith on the floor. Hally, her red leather standing out in sharp contrast to her blond hair, stood stooped with her arms folded across her abdomen. Her Agiel dangled from its chain at her wrist. Her face was ashen.

As Richard looked down, a tingle of icy dread flushed across his flesh. Her red leather had hidden what he now saw; she was standing in a pool of blood. Her blood.

He vaulted the mriswith and caught her in his arms.

"Hally!" Richard took up her weight and lowered her to the floor. "Dear spirits, what happened?" Before the words were out of his mouth, he knew; that was the way mriswith killed. The other three women were there, kneeling behind him as he put her head in his lap. Gratch squatted beside him.

Her blue eyes fixed on his. "Lord Rahl . . ."

"Oh, Hally, I'm so sorry. I should never have let you—"

"No . . . listen. I was foolishly distracted . . . and he was quick . . . but still . . . as he slashed me . . . I captured his magic. For an instant . . . before you killed him . . . it was mine."

If magic was used against them, Mord-Sith could take control of it, leaving an opponent helpless. That was how Denna had captured him.

"Ah, Hally, I'm so sorry I wasn't fast enough."

"It was the gift."

"What?"

"His magic was as yours . . . the gift."

His hand stroked her cold brow, forcing him to keep his eyes on hers, and not look down. "The gift? Thank you for the warning, Hally. I'm in your debt."

She gripped his shirt with a bloody hand. "Thank you, Lord Rahl . . . for my freedom." She struggled to take a shallow breath. "As brief as it was . . . it was worth . . . the price." She looked to her sisters of the Agiel. "Protect him. . . ."

With a sickening wheeze, the air left her lungs for the last time. Her sightless eyes stared up at him.

Richard drew her limp body to himself as he wept, a despairing response at being powerless to undo what had happened. Gratch put a claw tenderly to her back, and Cara a hand to his.

"I didn't want any of you to die. Dear spirits, I didn't."

Raina squeezed his shoulder. "We know, Lord Rahl. That is why we must protect you."

Richard gently laid Hally to the floor, bending over her, not wanting the others to see the ghastly wound she had taken. A searching glance revealed a mriswith cape close by. He turned to a nearby soldier instead.

"Give me your cloak."

The man yanked his cloak off as if it were on fire. Richard closed Hally's eyes and then covered her with the cloak as he fought back the urge to be sick.

"We'll give her a proper D'Haran funeral, Lord Rahl." General Reibisch, standing beside him, gestured toward the table. "Along with Edwards."

Richard squeezed his eyes closed and said a prayer to the good spirits to watch over Hally's sprit, and then he stood.

"After the devotion."

The general squinted one eye. "Lord Rahl?"

"She fought for me. She died trying to protect me. Before she's put to rest, I want her spirit to see that it was to a purpose. This afternoon, after the devotion, Hally and your man will be put to rest."

Cara leaned close and whispered. "Lord Rahl, full devotions are done in D'Hara, but not in the field. In the field, one reflection, as General Reibisch has done, is customary."

General Reibisch nodded apologetically. Richard's gaze swept the room. All eyes were on him. Beyond the faces, splashes of mriswith blood stained the whitewash. He brought his steely gaze back to the general.

"I don't care what you have done in the past. This day there will be a full devotion, here, in Aydindril. Tomorrow, you may go back to the custom. Today, all D'Harans in and around the city will do a full devotion."

The general's fingers fidgeted at his beard. "Lord Rahl, there are a great many troops in the area. They must all be notified and—"

"I'm not interested in excuses, General Reibisch. A difficult path lies ahead. If you cannot accomplish this task, then do not expect me to have faith that you can accomplish the rest."

General Reibisch cast a quick look over his shoulder at the officers, as if to say he was about to give his word, and commit them to it as well. He turned back to Richard and clapped a fist over his heart. "On my word as a soldier in the service of D'Hara, the steel against steel, it will be as Lord Rahl commands. This afternoon all D'Harans will be honored to do a full devotion to the new Master Rahl."

The general glanced at the mriswith under the corner of the table. "I've never heard of a Master Rahl fighting steel against steel beside his men. It was as if the spirits themselves guided your hand." He cleared his throat. "If I may, Lord Rahl, may I ask what difficult path it is that lies ahead?"

Richard studied the man's scarred face. "I am a war wizard. I fight with everything I have—magic, and steel."

"And my question, Lord Rahl?"

"I just answered your question, General Reibisch."

A slight smile tightened the corner of the general's mouth.

Involuntarily, Richard glanced down at Hally. The cloak couldn't cover everything that had been rent from her. Kahlan would have even less of a chance against a mriswith. Again, he thought he might be sick.

"Know that she died in the way she wished, Lord Rahl," Cara said in soft condolence. "As Mord-Sith."

In his mind's eye he tried to picture the smile he had known for only a few hours. He could not. His mind would show him only the horrific wound he had seen for but a few seconds.

Richard tightened his fists against the nausea and turned a glare on the three remaining Mord-Sith. "By the spirits, I intend to see you all die in bed, toothless and old. Get used to the idea!"

CHAPTER 10

TOBIAS BROGAN KNUCKLED HIS mustache as he glanced out of the corner of his eye at Lunetta. When she returned the slightest of nods, his mouth twisted with a sour expression. His rare good mood had evaporated. The man was telling the truth, Lunetta didn't make mistakes about this kind of thing, yet Brogan knew it wasn't the truth. He knew better.

He redirected his gaze to the man standing before him on the other side of a table long enough to banquet seventy people, and willed a polite smile to his lips.

"Thank you. You have been a great help."

The man peered suspiciously at the soldiers in polished armor to each side of him. "That's all you want to know? You have me dragged all the way over here, just to ask me what everyone knows? I could have told your men if they would have asked."

Brogan forced himself to hold the smile. "I apologize for the inconvenience. You have been of service to the Creator, and to me." The smile escaped his control. "You may go."

The man didn't miss the look in Brogan's eyes. He bobbed a bow and scurried for the door.

Brogan tapped the side of his thumb on the case at his belt and glanced impatiently to Lunetta. "Are you sure?"

Lunetta, in her element, returned a serene gaze. "He be telling the truth, Lord General, as were the others." She knew her craft, filthy as it was, and when practicing it possessed a confident air. It annoyed him.

He slammed a fist to the table. "It not be the truth!"

He could almost see the Keeper in her placid eyes as she watched him. "I not say it *be* the truth, Lord General, only that he be telling what he believes to be the truth."

Tobias harrumphed. He knew the truth of that. He hadn't spent his life hunting evil without learning some of its tricks. He knew magic. The quarry was so close he could almost smell it.

The late-afternoon sun spilled through a slit in the heavy gold drapes, splashing a glowing line of light across a gilded chair leg, the ornate royal blue flowered carpet, and up over the corner of the long, lustrous tabletop. The midday meal had long ago been put in abeyance while he pressed on, and yet he was no further along the path than when he had started. Frustration gnawed in his gut.

Galtero usually displayed a talent for bringing in witnesses who could provide proper information, but so far this lot had proved useless. He wondered what Galtero had found out; the city was in turmoil over something, and Tobias Brogan didn't like it when people were in an uproar, unless he and his men were the cause. Turmoil could be a powerful weapon, but he didn't like unknowns. Surely, Galtero must have returned long ago.

Tobias leaned back in his diamond-tufted leather chair and addressed one of the crimson-caped soldiers guarding the door. "Ettore, is Galtero back yet?"

"No, Lord General."

Ettore was young, and anxious to make his mark against evil, but he was a good man: shrewd, loyal, and not afraid to be ruthless when dealing with the Keeper's own. One day he would be among the best of the baneling hunters. Tobias knuckled his aching back. "How many more witnesses do we have?"

"Two, Lord General."

He wound his hand impatiently. "Bring in the next, then."

While Ettore slipped through the door, Tobias squinted past the slash of sunlight, to his sister standing against the wall. "You were sure, Lunetta, weren't you?"

She stared as she clutched her tattered rags to herself. "Yes, Lord General."

He sighed as the door opened and the guard led in a thin woman who didn't look to be any too happy. Tobias put on his most polite smile; a wise hunter didn't let his quarry catch a glimpse of fangs.

The woman jerked her elbow from Ettore's grip. "What's this about? I was taken against my will and have been locked in a room all day. What right have you to take a person against their will!"

Tobias smiled apologetically. "There must be some misunderstanding. I am sorry. You see, we only wanted to ask a few questions of people who we judged to be reliable. Why, most of the people on the street wouldn't know up from down. You seemed an intelligent woman, that's all, and—"

She leaned over the table toward him. "And so you locked me in a room? Is that what the Blood of the Fold does to people they judge reliable? From what I hear, the Blood doesn't bother with questions, they simply act on rumor, as long as it results in a fresh grave."

Brogan could feel his cheek twitch, but he held the smile. "You hear wrong, madam. The Blood of the Fold only be interested in the truth. We serve the Creator and his will, no less than a woman of your character. Now, would you mind answering a few questions? And then we will see you safely home."

"See me home now. This is a free city. No palace has the right to drag people in to question them, not in Aydindril. I've no obligation to answer any of your questions!"

Brogan widened his smile as he forced a small shrug. "Quite right, madam. We've no right at all, and didn't mean to imply one. We are only seeking the assistance of honest, humble folk. If you would simply help us get to the bottom of a few, simple matters, you could be on your way with our heartfelt appreciation."

She scowled a moment and then rolled her bony shoulders to straighten her wool shawl. "If it will get me back home, then get on with it. What do you want to know?"

Tobias rearranged himself in his chair so as to cover a quick glance at Lunetta, to make sure she was paying attention. "You see, madam, the Midlands has been torn asunder by war since spring last, and we seek to know if the Keeper's minions have a hand in the strife now shadowing the lands. Have any of the council members spoken against the Creator?"

"They're dead."

"Yes, I've heard that, but the Blood of the Fold doesn't put stock in rumor. We must have solid evidence, such as the word of a witness."

"Last night I saw their bodies in the council chambers."

"Is that so? Well, that is powerful evidence. At last we hear the truth from an honorable person who was a witness. You see, you are already of assistance. Who killed them?"

"I didn't see the killing done."

"Did you ever hear any councilor preach against the Creator's peace?"

"They railed against the peace of the Midland alliance, and as far as I'm concerned that's the same thing, though they didn't put it in those terms. They tried to make it seem as if black were white, and white black."

Tobias lifted an eyebrow, trying to act interested. "Those who serve the Keeper use such tactics: trying to make you think doing evil be right." He lifted his hand in a vague gesture. "Was there any land in particular that wished to break the peace of the alliance?"

The woman stood with her back straight and stiff as she looked down her nose at him. "They all, including yours, seemed equally ready to cast the world into slavery under the Imperial Order."

"Slavery? I have heard that the Imperial Order seeks only to unite the lands and bring man to his rightful place in the world, under the guidance of the Creator."

"Then you heard wrong. They seek only to hear whatever lie suits their purpose, and their purpose is conquest and domination."

"I've not heard that side of it. This be valuable news." He leaned back in his chair, crossed one leg over the other, and folded his hands in his lap. "And while all this plotting and insurrection was taking place in the council chambers, where was the Mother Confessor?"

She faltered for an instant. "Away on Confessor business."

"I see. But she did return?"

"Yes."

"And when she came back, did she try to stop this insurrection? Did she try to hold the Midlands together?"

The woman's eyes narrowed. "Of course she did, and you know what they did to her for it. Don't pretend you don't."

A casual glance in the direction of the window showed Lunetta's eyes focused on the woman. "Well, I've heard every sort of rumor. If you saw the events with your own eyes, then it would be powerful evidence. Did you witness any of these events, madam?"

"I saw the Mother Confessor's execution, if that's what you mean."

Tobias leaned forward on his elbows and steepled his fingers. "Yes, that was what I feared. And she is dead, then?"

Her nostrils flared. "Why are you so interested in the details?"

Tobias widened his eyes. "Madam, the Midlands has been united under the Confessors, and a Mother Confessor, for three thousand years. We have all prospered and had a good deal of peace under Aydindril's rule. When the war with D'Hara started up after the boundary went down, I feared for the Midlands—"

"Then why didn't you come to our aid?"

"Though I wished to lend my aid, the king forbade the Blood of the Fold from interfering. I objected, of course, but he was, after all, our king. Nicobarese suffered under his rule. As it turns out, he had darker intentions for our people, and apparently, as you have said, his councilors were ready to cast us into slavery. Once the king was exposed for what he truly was, a baneling, and paid the price, I at once brought our men across the mountains, to Aydindril, to place them at the disposal of the Midlands, the council, and the Mother Confessor.

"When I arrive, what do I find but D'Haran troops everywhere, yet they are said to no longer be at war with us. I hear the Imperial Order has come to the rescue of the Midlands. On my journey, and since my arrival, I have heard all sorts of rumors—that the Midlands has fallen, that the Midlands is rallying, that the councilors are dead, that they are alive and in hiding, that the Keltans seized control of the Midlands, that the D'Harans have, that the Imperial Order has, that the Confessors are all dead, that the wizards are all dead, that the Mother Confessor is dead, that all of them are alive. What am I to believe?

"If the Mother Confessor were alive, we could help her, protect her. We are a poor land, but we wish to be of aid to the Midlands, if we can."

Her shoulders relaxed a bit. "Some of what you've heard is true. In the war with D'Hara all the Confessors, except the Mother Confessor, were killed. The wizards died, too. Since then, Darken Rahl died, and the D'Harans threw their lot in with the Imperial

Order, as did Kelton, among others. The Mother Confessor returned and tried to hold the Midlands together. For her trouble the seditious pretenders to the council had her executed."

He shook his head. "This is sad news. I had hoped the rumors false. We need her." Brogan wet his tongue. "You're quite sure she was killed in the execution? Perhaps you're mistaken. She is, after all, a creature of magic. She might have escaped in a confusion of smoke, or some such. Perhaps she still lives."

The woman fixed a glare on him. "The Mother Confessor is dead."

"But I have heard rumors that she was seen alive . . . across the Kern River."

"Idle rumors of fools. She is dead. I myself saw her beheaded."

Brogan stroked a finger across the smooth scar at the side of his mouth as he watched the woman. "I also heard a report that she had fled in the other direction: to the southwest. Surely there is hope?"

"Not true. I will say it for the last time, I saw her beheaded. She did not escape. The Mother Confessor is dead. If you wish to be of aid to the Midlands, then you will do what you can to join the Midlands together once more."

Tobias studied her grim face for a moment. "Yes, yes, you're quite right. This is all very troubling news, but it be good at last to have a reliable witness to shed light on the truth. I thank you, madam, you have been more help than you can know. I will see what I can do to put my troops to the best advantage."

"The best advantage would be to help expunge the Imperial Order from Aydindril and then the Midlands."

"You think them so wicked?"

She lifted her bandaged hands toward him. "They tore off my fingernails to make me speak lies."

"How ghastly. And what lies did they wish you to speak?"

"That black was white, and white black. As do the Blood."

Brogan smiled, feigning amusement at her wit.

"You have been a great help, madam. You are loyal to the Midlands, and for that you have my gratitude, but I am sorry you feel the way you do about the Blood of the Fold. Perhaps you, too, shouldn't listen to rumors. They be only that.

"I don't want to inconvenience you any longer. Good day."

She upbraided him with a fiery scowl before storming off.

Under other circumstances her reluctance to be forthright would have cost her much more than her fingernails, but Brogan had pursued dangerous quarry before, and he knew that discretion now would reward him later. The prize was worth enduring her mocking tone. Even without her cooperation, he had gotten something very valuable from her this day, something she didn't know she had given, and that was his design: that the hunted wouldn't know he had picked up the scent.

Tobias allowed himself, at last, to meet Lunetta's gleaming gaze.

"She tells lies, my lord general. She tells mostly the truth, to mask them, but she tells lies."

Galtero had indeed brought him a treasure.

Tobias leaned forward. He wanted to hear Lunetta say it, to hear her voice his suspicions aloud—to put the confirmation of her talent to it. "Which be lies?"

"Two be lies she guards like the royal treasury."

He smacked his lips. "Which two?"

Lunetta smiled a sly smile. "First, she be lying when she said that the Mother Confessor be dead."

Tobias slapped a hand to the table. "I knew it! When she said it, I knew it be a lie!" He closed his eyes and swallowed as he offered a prayer to the Creator. "And the other?"

"She be lying when she said that the Mother Confessor did not flee. She knows that the Mother Confessor be alive, and that she ran to the southwest. All the rest she told be true."

Tobias's good mood was back. He rubbed his hands together, feeling the warmth it brought. The hunter's luck was with him. He had the scent.

"Did you hear what I said, Lord General?"

"What? Yes, I heard you. She's alive, and to the southwest. You did well, Lunetta. The Creator will be pleased with you when I tell him of your aid."

"I mean about how all the rest be the truth."

He frowned. "What are you talking about?"

Lunetta drew her scraps of cloth up tight. "She said that the council of dead men be made up of seditious pretenders. True. That the Imperial Order seeks only to hear whatever lies suit their purpose, and their purpose be conquest and domination. True. That they tore off her fingernails to make her speak lies. True.

That the Blood acts on rumor, as long as the result be a fresh grave. True."

Brogan shot to his feet. "The Blood of the Fold fights evil! How dare you suggest otherwise, you filthy *streganicha*!"

She winced as she bit her lower lip. "I do not say it be the truth, Lord General, only that it be the truth as she sees it."

He tugged his sash straight. He didn't want to spoil his triumph with Lunetta's prattle. "She sees it wrong, and you know it." He thrust a finger at her. "I've spent more time than you've a right to, more time than you be worth, to see that you understand the nature of good and evil."

Lunetta stared at the floor. "Yes, my lord general, you have spent more time than I be worth. Forgive me. They be her words, not mine."

Brogan finally withdrew his glare and took the case from his belt. He set it down, giving it a nudge with a thumb to make it straight with the edge of the table as he sat once more. He put Lunetta's insolence from his mind as he contemplated his next move.

He was about to call for dinner when he remembered that there was one more witness waiting. He had found what he had sought, there was no need for further questioning . . . but it was always wise to be thorough.

"Ettore, bring in the next witness."

Brogan glared at Lunetta as she faded back against the wall. She had done well, but then she had spoiled it by provoking him. Though he knew it was the evil in her that bubbled up whenever she did right, it galled him that she didn't try harder to suppress its influence. Maybe he had been too kind to her of late; in a weak moment, wanting to share his joy, he had given her a pretty. Perhaps she took that to mean that he would let her get away with insolence. He would not.

Tobias ordered himself in his chair and folded his hands on the table, thinking again about his triumph, thinking about the prize of prizes. There was no need to force a smile this time.

He was a bit startled to look up and see a young girl glide into the room ahead of the two guards. The old coat she wore dragged the ground. Behind the girl, between the guards, a squat old woman in a tattered wrap of brown blanket limped along with a rolling gait.

When the group came to a halt before the table, the girl smiled at him. "You've a very nice warm home, m'lord. We've enjoyed our day here. May we return your hospitality?"

The old woman added a smile of her own.

"I'm pleased you have had a chance to get warm, and would be grateful if you and your . . ." He lifted a questioning eyebrow.

"Grandmamma," the girl said.

"Yes, grandmamma. I would be grateful if you and your grandmamma would answer a few questions, that's all."

"Ahh," the old woman said. "Questions, is it? Questions can be dangerous, m'lord."

"Dangerous?" Tobias rubbed two fingers over the furrows on his forehead. "I seek only the truth, madam. If you answer honestly, no harm will come to you. You have my word."

She grinned, showing the gaps where teeth were missing. "I meant for you, m'lord." She cackled softly to herself, then leaned toward him with a grim expression. "You might not like the answers, or pay heed to them."

Tobias waved off her concern. "You let me worry about that."

She straightened, smiling again. "If you wish, m'lord." She scratched the side of her nose. "What are your questions, then?"

Tobias leaned back, studying the woman's waiting eyes. "The Midlands has been in turmoil, of late, and we want to know if the Keeper's minions have a hand in the strife shadowing the lands. Have you heard any of the council members speak against the Creator?"

"Councilors rarely come down to the market to discuss theology with old ladies, m'lord, nor would I suppose any would be so foolish as to publicly reveal any underworld connections, had they any."

"Well, what have you heard about what they have had to say?"

She lifted an eyebrow. "You wish to hear rumors from Stentor Street, m'lord? State which sort of rumor it is you would like to hear, and I can tell you one to fit your needs."

Tobias drummed his fingers on the table. "I am not interested in rumor, madam, simply the truth."

She nodded. "Of course you are, m'lord, and you shall have it. Sometimes, people can be interested in the most foolish of things."

He cleared his throat in annoyance. "I've heard any number of rumors already, and don't need any more. I need to know the truth of what has been going on in Aydindril. Why, I've even heard that the council has been executed, as well as the Mother Confessor."

Her narrow-eyed smile returned. "Then why wouldn't a man of your high status simply stop by the palace as he rode in, and ask to see the council? That would make more sense than dragging in all sort of people who would have no direct knowledge, and asking them. The truth would be better discerned with your own eyes, m'lord."

Brogan pressed his lips together. "I wasn't here when the rumors say the Mother Confessor was executed."

"Ahh, so it's the Mother Confessor you're interested in, then. Why didn't you simply say so, instead of going all round about? I heard that she was beheaded, but I didn't see it. My granddaughter saw it though, didn't you my dear?"

The little girl nodded. "Yes, m'lord, saw it myself, I did. Chopped her head right off, they did."

Brogan made a show of sighing. "That was what I feared. She is dead, then."

The girl shook her head. "Didn't say that, m'lord. I said I saw them chop off her head." She looked right into his eyes and smiled.

"What do you mean by that?" Brogan shot a glare up at the old woman. "What does she mean by that?"

"What she says, m'lord. Aydindril has always been a city with a strong undercurrent of magic, but it has been fairly crackling with it, of late. Where magic is involved, you can't always trust your eyes alone. Though she is young, this one is smart enough to know that much. A man of your profession would know it, too."

"Crackling with magic? That portends evil. What do you know about the Keeper's minions?"

"Terrible, they are, m'lord. But magic is, in itself, not evil; it exists without guile of its own."

Brogan's fists tightened. "Magic is the Keeper's taint."

She cackled again. "That would be like saying that the shiny silver knife at your belt is the Keeper's taint. If used to menace or harm an innocent, then the holder of the knife is evil. But if, for instance, it is used to defend life against a fanatical lunatic, no matter his high standing, then the holder of the knife is good. The knife is neither, because each can use it."

Her eyes seemed to go out of focus, and her voice lowered to a hiss. "But if used for retribution, magic is vengeance incarnate."

"Well then, in your view, is this magic you say is about in the city being used for good, or evil?"

"For both, m'lord. This is, after all, the home of the Wizard's Keep, and a seat of power. Confessors have ruled here for thousands of years, as well as wizards. Power draws power. Conflict is afoot. Scaled creatures, called mriswith, have begun to appear out of the very air, and gut any innocent in their way. An ominous omen, if ever there was one. Other magic lurks to snatch the rash, or unwary. Why, the very night is alive with magic carried on the gossamer wings of dreams."

She peered at him with one faded blue eye as she went on. "A child who is fascinated with fire could easily be incinerated here. Such a child would be well advised to be very careful, and leave at the first opportunity, before he inadvertently puts his hand into a flame.

"Why, people are even pulled off the street, to have their words filtered through a sieve of magic."

Brogan leaned forward with a smoldering expression. "And what do you know about magic, madam?"

"An equivocal question, m'lord. Could you be more explicit?"

Tobias paused for a moment, trying to pick the nettles out of her ramblings. He had dealt with her kind before, and he realized she was gulling him off the subject, off the trail.

He brought back his polite smile. "Well, for instance, your granddaughter says she saw the Mother Confessor beheaded, but that that doesn't mean she be dead. You say magic can make it so. I'm intrigued by such a statement. While it's true that I know magic can occasionally fool people, I've only heard of it working small deceptions. Could you explain how death could be revoked?"

"Revoke death? The Keeper has such power."

Brogan pressed forward against the table. "Are you saying the Keeper himself brought her back to life?"

She cackled. "No, m'lord. You are so persistent in what you want that you do not pay attention, and hear only what you want to hear. You specifically asked how death could be revoked. The Keeper can revoke death. At least, I'm assuming he can because he is the ruler of the dead, holds power over life and death, so it's only natural to believe that—"

"Is she alive or not!"

The old woman blinked at him. "How would I know that, m'lord?"

Brogan ground his teeth. "You said that just because people saw her beheaded, that doesn't mean she be dead."

"Oh, back to that, are we? Well, magic can perform such a ruse, but that does not mean it did. I said only that it could. Then you went off scent asking about death being revoked. Quite a separate issue, m'lord."

"How, woman! How can magic accomplish such high deception!"

She snugged the tattered blanket up around her shoulders.

"A death spell, m'lord."

Brogan glanced to Lunetta. Her beady eyes were fixed on the old woman, and she was scratching her arms.

"A death spell. And what, exactly, is a death spell?"

"Well, I've never seen one executed, so to speak—" She chuckled at her own joke. "—so I can't give you proper witness, but I can tell you what I've been told, if you've a wish to hear secondhand knowledge."

Brogan spoke through clenched teeth. "Tell me."

"Seeing a death, comprehending it, is something we all recognize at a spiritual level. It's this seeing of a body with its soul, or spirit, departed, that we recognize as death. A death spell can mimic a real death by making people believe they have seen a death, that they have seen the body without its soul, and so make them viscerally accept the event as true."

She shook her head as if she found the matter both amazing and scandalizing. "Very dangerous, it is. It requires invoking the aid of the spirits to hold the person's spirit while the web is cast. If anything goes wrong, the subject's spirit would be cast helpless into the underworld—a very unpleasant way to die. If everything goes right, and if the spirits return that which they have preserved, I am told it will work, and the person will live, but those seeing it will think them dead. Very chancy, though. While I've heard of it, I've never heard of it actually being attempted, so it may be nothing more than hearsay."

Brogan sat quietly moving the pieces of information around in his mind, pulling together things he had learned this day, and things he had learned in the past, searching for the right fit. It must have been a trick done to escape justice, but not one she could have accomplished without accomplices.

The old woman put a hand to the girl's shoulder and started shuffling off. "Thank you for the warmth, m'lord, but I grow tired of your haphazard questions, and I've better things to do."

"Who could perform a death spell?"

The old woman halted. Her washed-out blue eyes lit up with a dangerous cast. "Only a wizard, m'lord. Only a wizard of immense power and great knowledge."

Brogan fixed her with a dangerous look of his own. "And are there any wizards here, in Aydindril?"

Her slow smile made her faded eyes gleam. She reached into a pocket under the blanket and tossed a coin on the table, where it spun in lazy circles before finally toppling over before him. Brogan picked up the silver coin, squinting at the strike.

"I asked a question, old woman. I expect an answer."

"You hold it, m'lord."

"I've never seen a coin like this. What's this image on it? It looks to be a grand structure of some sort."

"Oh it is, m'lord," she hissed. "It's the spawn of salvation and doom, of wizards and magic: the Palace of the Prophets."

"Never heard of it. What is this Palace of the Prophets?"

The old woman smiled a private smile. "Ask your sorceress, m'lord." She turned again to leave.

Brogan shot to his feet. "No one gave you permission to leave, you toothless old hag!"

She peered back over her shoulder. "It's the liver, m'lord."

Brogan blinked. "What?"

"I've a taste for raw liver, m'lord. I believe that's what makes the teeth fall out, over time."

Just then, Galtero appeared, squeezing past the woman and girl as they went through the doorway. He saluted with fingertips to bowed forehead. "Lord General, I have a report."

"Yes, yes, in a moment."

"But—"

Brogan held up a silencing finger to Galtero as he turned to Lunetta. "Well?"

"Every word true, Lord General. She be like a water bug, skimming the surface of the water, touching only the tips of her feet to it, but everything she said be true. She knows much more than she tells, but what she tells be true."

Brogan waggled his hand impatiently for Ettore to come forward. The man stiffened to attention before the table as his crimson cape swished around his legs. "Lord General?"

Brogan's eyes narrowed. "I think we may have a baneling on our hands. How would you like to prove yourself worthy of the cape you wear?"

"Yes, Lord General, very much."

"Before she gets out of the building, take her into custody. She be under suspicion of being a baneling."

"What of the girl, Lord General?"

"Weren't you watching, Ettore? She will no doubt prove to be the baneling's familiar. Besides, we don't want her out in the street crying out that her 'grandmamma' is being held by the Blood of the Fold. The other, the cook, would be missed, and that could bring troublemakers down around us, but this pair won't be missed from the street. They be ours, now."

"Yes, Lord General. I will see to it at once."

"I will want to question her as soon as possible. The girl, too." Brogan held up a cautionary finger. "They had better be ready to answer truthfully any question I ask."

Ettore's youthful face bent into a gruesome grin. "They will confess when you come to them, Lord General. By the Creator, they will be ready to confess."

"Very good, lad, now be off, before they gain the street."

As Ettore dashed through the door, Galtero stepped impatiently forward, but waited silently before the table.

Brogan sank down into the chair, his voice distant. "Galtero, you did your usual, thorough, good job; the witnesses you brought me proved up to my standards."

Tobias Brogan slid the silver coin aside, unfastened the leather straps on the case, and dumped his trophies into a pile on the table. With tender care he spread them out, touching the once living flesh. Each was a desiccated nipple—the left nipple, the one closest to the baneling's evil heart—with enough skin to include the tattooed name. They represented only a fraction of the banelings he had uncovered: the most important of the important; the most vile of the Keeper's fiends.

As he replaced the booty one at a time, he read the name of each baneling he had put to the torch. He remembered each chase, and capture, and inquisition. Flames of anger flared up at remembering the unholy crimes to which each had finally confessed. He remembered justice being done each time.

But he had yet to win the prize of prizes: the Mother Confessor.

"Galtero," he said in a soft, stony voice, "I have her trail. Get the men together. We will leave at once."

"I think you had better hear what I have to say, first, Lord General."

CHAPTER 11

"IT BE THE D'HARANS, Lord General."

After replacing the last of his trophies, Brogan flipped the lid shut on his case and looked up into Galtero's dark eyes. "What about the D'Harans?"

"Early today, I knew something be afoot when they started gathering. That be what had the people in such turmoil."

"Gathering?"

Galtero nodded. "Around the Confessors' Palace, Lord General. At midafternoon they all started chanting."

Astonished, Tobias leaned toward his colonel. "Chanting? Do you remember their words?"

Galtero hooked a thumb behind his weapons belt. "It went on for two full hours; it would be hard to forget it after hearing it that many times. The D'Harans bowed down, forehead to the ground, and all chanted the same words: 'Master Rahl guide us. Master Rahl teach us. Master Rahl protect us. In your light we thrive. In your mercy we be sheltered. In your wisdom we be humbled. We live only to serve. Our lives be yours.' "

Brogan tapped a finger on the table. "And all the D'Harans did this? How many are there?"

"Every one of them, Lord General, and there be more than we thought. They filled the square outside the palace, overflowed into the parks and plazas, and then the streets all around. You could not walk among them, they be packed in so tight, as if all wanted to be as close to the Confessors' Palace as they could get. To my count, there be near to two hundred thousand in the city, with most gathered around the palace. While it went on, the others be in a near panic, not knowing what be happening.

"I rode out into the country, and there were a great many more who did not come into the city. They, too, wherever they be, bowed forehead to the ground and chanted along with their brothers in the city. I rode hard, to cover as much ground as possible and see all I could, and I did not see even one D'Haran who not be bowed down chanting. You could hear their voices from the hills and passes around the city. None paid any heed to us as we scouted."

Brogan closed his mouth. "Then he must be here, this Master Rahl."

Galtero shifted his weight to his other foot. "He be here, Lord General. While the D'Harans chanted, the whole time they chanted, he stood atop the steps of the grand entrance and watched. Every man was bowed to him, as if he be the Creator Himself."

Brogan's mouth twisted in disgust. "I always suspected the D'Harans were heathens. Imagine, praying to a mere man. What happened then?"

Galtero looked tired; he had been riding hard all day. "When it ended, they all leaped into the air, cheering and whooping for a good long time, as if they had just been delivered from the Keeper's grasp. I was able to ride two miles around the back of the crowd while the shouting and acclaim went on. Finally, the men made way as two bodies were carried into the square, and all went silent. A pyre was thrown up and set ablaze. The whole time, until the bodies were ash and the ash at last taken to be buried, this Master Rahl stood on the steps and watched."

"Did you get a good look at him?"

Galtero shook his head. "The men were packed tight together, and I feared to force my way closer lest they set upon me for interrupting their ceremony."

Brogan rubbed his case with the side of a thumb as he stared off in thought. "Of course. I wouldn't expect you to throw your life away just to try to see what the man looks like."

Galtero hesitated a moment. "You will see him yourself soon enough, Lord General. You have been invited to the palace."

Brogan looked up. "I don't have time for pleasantries. We must be off after the Mother Confessor."

Galtero drew a paper from his pocket and handed it over. "I returned just as a big group of D'Haran soldiers were about to enter our palace. I stopped them and asked what they wanted, and they gave me this."

Brogan unfolded the paper, and read the hasty scrawl. *Lord Rahl invites all dignitaries, diplomats, and officials of all lands to the Confessors' Palace, at once.* He crumbled the paper in his fist. "I don't take audiences, I give them. And, as I said, I don't have time for pleasantries."

Galtero lifted a thumb toward the street. "I reasoned as much, and told the soldiers who gave it to me that I would pass the invitation along, but that we be busy with other matters, and I didn't know if anyone from the Nicobarese Palace would have time to attend.

"He said that Lord Rahl wanted everyone there, and we had better find the time."

Brogan waved off the threat. "No one is going to cause trouble, here in Aydindril, because we don't attend a social affair to meet a new tribal leader."

"Lord General, Kings Row be shoulder to shoulder with D'Haran soldiers. Every palace on the Row be surrounded, along with city administration buildings. The man who gave me the paper said he be here to 'escort' us to the Confessors' Palace. He said that if we are not out there soon, they would come in and get us. He had ten thousand troops standing behind him, watching me, as he said it.

"These men are not shopkeepers and farmers playing at being soldier for a few months; these be professional warriors, and they look very determined.

"I have faith in the Blood of the Fold to go against these men, if we could get to our main force, but we brought only a fist of the

Fold with us into the city. Five hundred are not near enough men to fight our way out. We would not make it twenty yards before every one of us would be cut down."

Brogan glanced at Lunetta, standing against the wall. She was stroking and smoothing her colored patches, not paying any attention to the discussion. They might have only five hundred men in the city, but they also had Lunetta.

He didn't know what this Lord Rahl's game was, but it didn't really matter; D'Hara was aligned with, and took orders from, the Imperial Order. It was probably just an attempt to put himself in higher standing within the Order. There were always those who wanted power, but didn't want to concern themselves with the moral imperative that went along with it.

"Very well. It will be dark soon, anyway. We will go to this ceremony, smile at the new Master Rahl, drink his wine, eat his food, and make him welcome. At dawn we leave Aydindril to the Imperial Order and be off after the Mother Confessor." He gestured to his sister. "Lunetta, come with us."

"And how will you find her?" Lunetta scratched her arm. "The Mother Confessor, Lord General, how will you find her?"

Tobias pushed his chair back and stood. "She be to the southwest. We have more than enough men to search. We will find her."

"Really?" Lunetta still displayed a streak of insolence from having used her power. "Tell me how you will know her."

"She be the Mother Confessor! How could we not know her, you stupid *streganicha*!"

One brow arched as her feral gaze rose to meet his eyes. "The Mother Confessor be dead. How can you see a dead person walking?"

"She not be dead. The cook knows the truth of that; you said so yourself. The Mother Confessor be alive, and we will have her."

"If what the old woman say be true, and a death spell was cast, then what would be its purpose? Tell Lunetta."

Tobias frowned. "To make people think she was killed so she could escape."

Lunetta smiled a sly smile. "And why is it they did not see her escape? For the same reason you will not find her."

"Stop talking your magic jabber and tell me what you be talking about."

"Lord General, if there be such a thing as a death spell, and it be used on the Mother Confessor, then it would only make sense that the magic would hide her identity. It would explain how she escaped; no one recognized her because of the magic around her. For the same reason, you will not recognize her either."

"Can you break it, break the spell?" Tobias stammered.

Lunetta chuckled. "Lord General, I never heard of such magic before. I know nothing about it."

Tobias realized his sister was right. "You know about magic. Tell me how we can know her."

Lunetta shook her head. "Lord General, I do not know how to see the strands of a wizard's web that was cast for the express purpose of hiding. I tell you only what would make sense, and that be that if such a spell were used to hide her, then we, too, would not recognize her."

He lifted a finger toward her. "You have magic. You know a way to show us the truth."

"Lord General, the old woman said that only a wizard could cast a death spell. If a wizard cast such a web, then to unravel it we must be able to see the strands of his web. I do not know how to see the truth through the magic's deception."

Tobias rubbed his chin as he thought it over. "See through the deception. But how?"

"A moth be caught in a spider's web because he cannot see the strands. We be caught in this web, the same as those who saw her beheading, because we cannot see its strands. I do not know how we can."

"Wizard," he murmured to himself. He gestured to the silver coin on the table. "When I asked her if there be a wizard here in Aydindril, she showed me that coin with a building on it."

"The Palace of the Prophets."

The name brought his head up. "Yes, that be what she called it. She said to ask you what it be. How do you know of it? Where did you hear about this Palace of the Prophets?"

Lunetta shrank back into herself and looked away. "Just after you be born, Mamma told me about it. It be a place where sorceresses—"

"Streganicha," he corrected.

She paused a moment. "It be a place where *streganicha* train men to be wizards."

"Then it be a house of evil." She stood stooped and stiff as he looked down at the coin. "What would Mamma know about such an evil place?"

"Mamma be dead, Tobias, leave her be," she whispered.

He shot her a withering scowl. "We will talk about this later." He straightened his sash of rank and ordered his silver-embroidered gray coat before picking up his crimson cape. "The old woman must have meant that there be a wizard in Aydindril who was trained at this house of evil." He redirected his attention to Galtero. "Fortunately, Ettore is holding her for further questioning. That old woman has a lot more to tell us; I can feel it in my bones."

Galtero nodded. "We better be off for the Confessors' Palace, Lord General."

Brogan flung his cape over his shoulders. "We will stop to see Ettore on our way out."

A fire had been well stoked and was roaring when the three of them entered the small room to check on Ettore and his two charges. Ettore was stripped to the waist, his lean muscles coated with a sheen of sweat. Several razors gleamed from their place atop the mantle, along with an assortment of sharpened spikes. The ends of iron rods were fanned out across the hearth. Their other ends glowed orange in the flames.

The old woman cowered in the far corner, and put a protective arm around the girl, who hid her face in the brown blanket.

"Has she given you any trouble?" Brogan asked.

Ettore flashed his familiar grin. "Her arrogant attitude vanished as soon as she found out we don't suffer insolence. That be the way with banelings; they give way when faced with the Creator's might."

"The three of us have to go out for a while. The rest of the fist will remain here at the palace, in case you need assistance." Brogan glanced to the iron rods glowing in the fire. "When I get back I want her confession. I don't care about the girl, but the old woman had better still be alive and anxious to give it."

Ettore touched his fingers to his forehead as he bowed. "By the

Creator, it shall be as you command, Lord General. She will confess all the crimes she has performed for the Keeper."

"Good. I have more questions, and I will have the answers."

"I'll answer no more of your questions," the old woman said.

Ettore curled his lip as he scowled over his shoulder. The old woman shrank back farther into the dark corner. "You'll break that oath before this night be over, you old hag. You'll be begging to answer questions when you see what I do to your little evil one. You get to watch her go first, so you can think about what be coming when it be your turn."

The little girl squealed and burrowed deeper into the old woman's blanket.

Lunetta stared at the pair in the corner as she slowly scratched her arm. "Do you wish me to stay and attend Ettore, Lord General? I think it be best if I did."

"No. I want you to come with me tonight." He glanced up at Galtero. "You did well, bringing me this one."

Galtero shook his head. "I never would have noticed her, had she not tried to sell me honey cakes. Something about her made me suspicious."

Brogan shrugged. "That be the way with banelings; they be drawn to the Blood of the Fold like moths to a flame. They be bold because they have faith in their evil master." He glanced again to the woman cringing in the corner. "But they all lose their spines when facing justice from the Blood of the Fold. This one will be a small trophy, but the Creator will be served by it."

CHAPTER 12

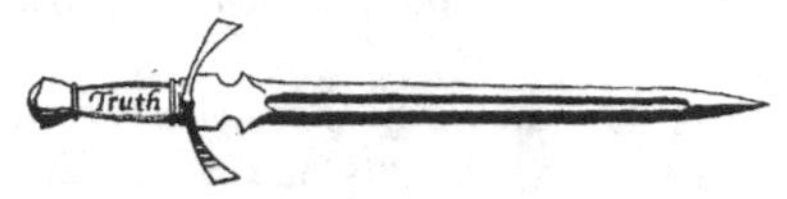

"STOP IT," TOBIAS GROWLED. "People will think you have fleas."

On a wide street lined with majestic maple trees to each side, their bare thicket of branches laced together overhead, dignitaries and officials from different lands stepped from fancy coaches to meander the remaining distance to the Confessors' Palace. D'Haran troops stood like banks at the edge of the trickling river of arriving guests.

"I cannot help it, Lord General," Lunetta complained as she scratched. "Ever since we arrived in Aydindril my arms be itching. I have never felt it like this before."

People joining the flow stared openly at Lunetta. Her tattered rags made her stand out like a leper at a coronation. She seemed oblivious of the mocking stares. More likely, she thought them looks of admiration. She had, on any number of occasions, begged off donning any of the dresses Tobias offered her, saying that none were the match of her pretties. Since they seemed to keep her mind occupied, and off the Keeper's taint, he never went so far as to insist she wear something else, and besides, he thought it blasphemy to make one touched by evil look appealing.

The arriving men were dressed in their finest robes, coats, or furs. Though some wore ornate swords, Tobias was sure they were only decoration and doubted that a one of them had ever been drawn in fear, much less anger. As an occasional wrap billowed open, he could see that the women were attired in elegant, layered gowns, the setting sun glinting off the jewels at their necks, wrists, and fingers. It would appear they were all so excited to be invited to the Confessors' Palace to meet the new Lord Rahl that they had not elicited a threat from the D'Haran soldiers. By their smiles and chatter, they all seem anxious to ingratiate themselves with the new Lord Rahl.

Tobias ground his teeth. "If you don't stop scratching, I'll tie your hands behind your back."

Lunetta dropped her hands to her sides and stopped with a gasp. Tobias and Galtero looked up to see bodies impaled on poles to each side of the promenade ahead. As the three of them approached, he realized they weren't men, but scaled creatures only the Keeper could have conceived. As they proceeded, a stink enveloped them, as thick as a bog mist, making them fear to draw a breath lest it blacken their lungs.

Some of the poles held only heads, some held whole bodies, and others parts of bodies. All appeared to have been killed in a brutal battle. Some of the beasts had been ripped open, and several were cleaved completely in two, their innards hanging frozen from what was left of them.

It was like stepping through a monument to evil, through the gates to the underworld.

The other guests covered their noses as best they could with whatever they had handy. A few of the finely dressed women sank to the ground in a swoon; attendants rushed to their aid, fanning them with handkerchiefs or rubbing a bit of snow on their foreheads. Some of the people stared in astonishment while others shuddered so violently that Tobias could hear their teeth rattling. By the time they had run the gauntlet of sights and smells, everyone around them was in a state of either high anxiety or open alarm. Tobias, having often walked among evil, regarded his fellow guests with disgust.

When a shaken diplomat asked, one of the D'Harans to the side explained that the creatures had attacked the city, and Lord Rahl had slain them. The mood of the guests brightened. As they moved on, their voices became exuberant as they chatted about the honor of meeting such a man as the new Lord Rahl, the

Master of all of D'Hara. Effervescent chuckles drifted on the chilling air.

Galtero leaned close. "While I was out earlier, before all the chanting, and the soldiers around the city were still talkative, they told me to be wary, that there had been attacks by unseen creatures, and a number of their men, as well as people on the streets, had been killed."

Tobias remembered the old woman telling him that scaled creatures, he couldn't recall what she had called them, had begun to appear out of the air to gut anyone in their way. Lunetta had said that the woman's words were true. These must be the creatures.

"How convenient of Lord Rahl to arrive just in time to slay the creatures and save the city."

"Mriswith," Lunetta said.

"What?"

"The woman said that the creatures be called mriswith."

Tobias nodded. "Yes, I believe you're right: mriswith."

White columns towered outside the entrance to the palace. The ranks of soldiers to each side funneled them through white, carved doors spread wide, and into a grand hall lit with windows of pale blue glass set between polished white marble columns topped with gold capitals. Tobias Brogan could feel himself being sucked into the belly of evil. The other guests, had a one of them known better, would be shuddering at the living monument to profanity that surrounded them, instead of dead carcasses.

After a journey through elegant halls and chambers with enough granite and marble to build a mountain, they at last passed through tall mahogany doors to enter an enormous chamber capped with a huge dome. Ornate frescoes of men and women swept across the ceiling overlooking the assembly. Round windows around the lower edge of the dome let in the waning light and revealed clouds gathering in a darkening sky. Across the room, on a semicircular dais, the chairs behind the resplendent, carved desk sat empty.

Arched openings around the room covered stairways up to colonnaded balconies edged with sinuous, polished mahogany railings. The balconies were filled with people, he noticed—not finely dressed nobility like those on the main floor, but common working people. The other guests noticed, too, and cast disapproving glances up at the riffraff in the shadows behind the railings. The people crowded there stood back from the railings, as if seeking obscurity in the darkness, lest any of them should be recognized and called to account for daring to be at so grand a function. It was customary for a great man to be introduced to the people in authority first, before letting himself be known to ordinary people.

Ignoring the audience in the balcony, the guests spread out across the patterned marble floor, keeping distance between themselves and the two Blood of the Fold, and trying to make it seem accidental, rather than by intention that they avoided the two. They looked about expectantly for their host while bending to whisper among themselves. Dressed as finely as they were they almost looked to be part of the ornate carvings and decoration; none betrayed being awed by the grandeur of the Confessors' Palace. Tobias guessed that most were frequent visitors. Though he had never been to Aydindril before, he knew sycophants when he saw them; his own king had been surrounded by enough of them.

Lunetta stayed close to his side, only mildly interested in the imposing architecture around her. She took no notice of the people who stared at her, though there were fewer of those now; they were more interested in each other and in the prospect of finally meeting Lord Rahl than in worrying about an odd woman standing between two crimson-caped Blood of the Fold. Galtero's gaze swept the expansive room, ignoring the opulence and, instead, taking constant appraisal of the people, the soldiers, and the exits. The swords he and Tobias wore were not decoration.

Despite his revulsion, Tobias couldn't help marveling at where he stood. This was the spot from where the Mother Confessors and wizards had pulled the strings of the Midlands. This was where the council, for thousands of years, had stood for unity while preserving and protecting magic. This was the spot from which the Keeper's tendrils spread forth.

That unity was shattered now. Magic had lost its grip on man, lost its protection. The age of magic was ended. The Midlands was ended. Soon, the palace would be filled with crimson capes, and only the Blood of the Fold would be seated at the dais. Tobias smiled; events were moving inexorably toward a providential end.

A man and woman drifted near, purposefully, Tobias thought.

The woman, with a pile of black hair and wispy curls hanging down around her painted face, leaned casually toward him. "Imagine, we are invited here, and they don't even have anything to eat." She smoothed the lace at the bosom of her yellow dress, a polite smile coming to her impossibly red lips as she waited for him to speak. He didn't, and she went on. "Seems very vulgar not to offer so much as a drop of wine, don't you think, considering that we've come on such short notice and all? I hope he doesn't expect we will accept his invitation again after treating us so boorishly."

Tobias clasped his hands behind his back. "Do you know Lord Rahl?"

"I may have met him before; I don't recall." She brushed a speck, which he couldn't see, from her bare shoulder, affording the jewels on her fingers, which even someone across the room would have been able to see, the opportunity to glitter before his eyes. "I'm invited to so many of these affairs here at the palace that I have difficulty remembering all the people who strive to meet me. After all, Duke Lumholtz and I would appear to find ourselves in a position of leadership, what with Prince Fyren having been murdered."

Her red lips plumped into a simper. "I do know that I've never met any of the Blood of the Fold here before. After all, the council has always viewed the Blood as officious, not that I'm saying I would agree, mind you, but they have forbade them from practicing their . . . 'craft' anywhere outside their homeland. Of course we would seem to be without a council, now. Quite ghastly, their being killed like they were, right here, and while they were deliberating the future course of the Midlands. What brings you here, sir?"

Tobias glanced past her to see soldiers closing the doors. He knuckled his mustache as he started wandering toward the dais. "I was 'invited,' the same as you."

Duchess Lumholtz strolled with him. "I hear that the Blood are held in high esteem by the Imperial Order."

The man with her, dressed in a gold-braided blue coat and displaying the carriage of authority, listened with strained indifference as he worked at appearing to have his attention elsewhere. By his dark hair and heavy brow Tobias had already guessed him as Keltish. The Keltans had been quick to align themselves with the

Order, and possessively guarded their high status among them. They also knew that the Imperial Order respected the opinion of the Blood of the Fold.

"I am surprised, madam, that you hear anything, as much as you talk."

Her face flushed as red as her lips. Tobias was spared her predictable, indignant retort when the crowd noticed a commotion across the room. He was not tall enough to see over the turned heads, so he waited patiently, knowing that in all likelihood Lord Rahl would take to the raised dais. He had placed himself carefully for that probability: close enough to be able to make an appraisal, but not so close as to stand out. Unlike the other guests, he knew this was no social function. This would likely be a stormy night; and if there was lightning, he didn't want to be the tallest tree. Tobias Brogan, unlike the fluttering fools about him, knew when prudence was warranted.

Across the room, people hurriedly tried to make way for an echelon of D'Haran soldiers wedging them aside to clear a path. A massive rank of pikemen followed, peeling off in pairs to form an ironclad corridor free of guests. The echelon deployed before the dais, a grim protective wedge of D'Haran muscle and steel. The swift precision was impressive. High-ranking D'Haran officers marched up the corridor to stand beside the dais. Over the top of Lunetta's head, Tobias met Galtero's icy gaze. No social function indeed.

The crowd buzzed in nervous anticipation as they waited to see what was to come next. By the whispers Tobias could overhear, this was well beyond precedent in the Confessors' Palace. Red-faced dignitaries murmured their indignation to one another over what they considered an intolerable use of armed force in the council chambers, where diplomatic negotiation was the rule.

Brogan had no tolerance for diplomacy; blood worked better, and left a more lasting impression. He was getting the impression that Lord Rahl understood this, too, unlike the sea of obsequious faces crowding the floor.

Tobias knew what this Lord Rahl wanted. It was only to be expected; after all, the D'Harans had shouldered most of the load for the Imperial Order. In the mountains he had met a force that had been mostly D'Haran, on their way to Ebinissia. The D'Harans had taken Aydindril, seen to keeping order, and then let the

Imperial Order have dominion over it. In the name of the Order they had put their flesh against the steel of rebels, yet others, such as Keltans, like Duke Lumholtz, had held the positions of power and handed down the orders, expecting the D'Harans to fall on the points of enemy blades.

Lord Rahl no doubt intended to lay claim to a place of high rank among the Imperial Order, and was going to coerce the gathered representatives into acceding. Tobias almost wished there had been food offered, so that he could watch all the scheming officials choke on it when the new Lord Rahl made his demands.

The two D'Harans who entered next were so huge that Tobias could see their approach over the heads of the crowd. When they came into full view, and he could see their leather armor, chain mail, and sharpened bands above their elbows, Galtero whispered to him over Lunetta's head. "I've seen those two before."

"Where?" Tobias whispered back.

Galtero shook his head as he watched the men. "Out on the street somewhere."

Tobias turned back, and to his astonishment saw three women in red leather following the two huge D'Harans. From the reports Tobias had heard, they could be nothing other than Mord-Sith. Mord-Sith had a reputation for being wholly unhealthy to those with magic who opposed them. Tobias had once sought to acquire the services of one of these women, but had been told that they served only the Master of D'Hara, and were not indulgent of anyone making offers of any kind. As he had heard it told, they could not be bought for any price.

If the Mord-Sith made the crowd edgy, what came next made them gasp. Mouths dropped at the sight of a monstrous beast, one with claws, fangs, and wings. Even Tobias stiffened at the sight of a gar. Short-tailed gars were wildly aggressive, bloodthirsty brutes that would eat anything living. Since the boundary had fallen the past spring, gars had caused the Blood of the Fold no small amount of trouble. For the moment, this beast walked calmly behind the three women. When Tobias checked that his sword was clear in its scabbard, he noticed Galtero doing the same.

"Please, Lord General," Lunetta whined, "I want to leave, now." She was furiously scratching her arms.

Brogan gripped her upper arm and drew her close, whispering through clenched teeth. "You pay attention to this Lord Rahl, or I'll find I have no further use for you. Do you understand? And stop that scratching!"

Her eyes watered as he twisted her arm. "Yes, Lord General."

"You pay attention to what he says."

She nodded as the two huge D'Harans took places at either end of the dais. The three women in red leather stepped up between them, leaving a place in the center empty, probably for Lord Rahl when he arrived, at last. The gar towered behind the chairs.

The blond-headed Mord-Sith near the center of the dais looked around the room with a penetrating blue-eyed gaze that commanded silence.

"People of the Midlands," she said, lifting an introductory arm to the empty air above the desk, "I present Lord Rahl."

A shadow formed in the air. A black cloak appeared suddenly, and as it was thrown wide, there, standing atop the dais, was a man.

Those near the front fell back in alarm. A scattering of people cried out in terror. Some called for the Creator's protection, others beseeched the spirits to intercede on their behalf, and some fell to their knees. While many stood in mute shock, a few of the decorative swords were drawn for the first time in fear. When a D'Haran in the front of the echelon calmly warned in a low, icy voice to sheath the weapons, they were reluctantly returned to scabbards.

Lunetta was scratching frantically as she gazed up at the man, but Brogan didn't stop her this time; even he could feel his skin crawling with the evil of magic.

The man atop the desk waited patiently for the crowd to become silent, and then spoke in a quiet voice.

"I am Richard Rahl, called by the D'Harans Lord Rahl. Other peoples have other titles by which I am known. Prophecies given in the dim past, before the Midlands was born, have placed appellation upon me." He stepped down off the desk to stand between the Mord-Sith. "But it is the future I come before you to address."

Though not as large as the two D'Harans standing at each end of the curved desk, he was a big man, tall and muscular, and surprisingly young. His clothes, black cloak and high boots, dark trousers, and plain shirt, were unassuming, more so for one called "Lord." Though it was hard to miss the gleam of a silver-and-gold scabbard at his hip, he looked to be nothing so much as a simple woodsman. Tobias thought, too, that the man looked tired, as if he bore a mountain of responsibility on his shoulders.

Tobias was hardly a stranger to combat, and knew by the grace with which this young man carried himself, by the easy way the baldric lay across his shoulder and by the way the sword moved with him at his hip, that he was not a man to be taken lightly. The sword was not there for decoration; it was a weapon. He looked to be a man who had made a great many desperate decisions of late, and had lived through them all. For all his outward, humble appearance, he had an inexplicable air of authority about him, and a bearing that commanded attention.

Already, many of the women in the room had recovered their composure and were beginning to flash him private smiles as they batted their lashes, falling into their well-practiced habits of ingratiating themselves with those wielding power. Even if the man were not ruggedly handsome, they would have done the same, but perhaps with less sincerity. Lord Rahl either didn't notice their warming demeanor, or chose not to.

But it was his eyes that interested Tobias Brogan; eyes were the mark of a man's nature, and the one thing that rarely deceived him. When this man's steely gaze settled on people, some stepped back without realizing it, some froze, and others fidgeted. When those eyes turned in his direction, and the gaze settled on him for the first time, Tobias took a measure of Lord Rahl's heart and soul.

That brief look was all he needed: this was a very dangerous man.

Though he was young and ill at ease being the center of all eyes, this was a man who would fight with a vengeance. Tobias had seen eyes like this before. This was a man who would jump headlong over a cliff to come after you.

"I know him," Galtero whispered.

"What? How?"

"Earlier today, when I was picking up witnesses, I came across this man. I was going to bring him to you for questioning, but those two big guards showed up and carried him off."

"Unfortunate. It would have been . . ."

The hush of the room caused Tobias to look up. Lord Rahl was staring at him. It was like looking into the penetrating, gray-eyed glare of a raptor.

Lord Rahl's eyes shifted to Lunetta. She stood frozen in the light of his gaze. Surprisingly, a small smile came to his lips.

"Of all the women at the ball," Lord Rahl said to her, "your dress is the prettiest."

Lunetta beamed. Tobias almost laughed out loud; Lord Rahl had just delivered a cutting message to the others in the room: their social status counted for nothing with him. Tobias was suddenly beginning to enjoy himself. Perhaps the Order would not be so poorly served with a man like this among their leaders.

"The Imperial Order," Lord Rahl began, "believes that the time has come for the world to be united under a common canon: theirs. They say that magic is responsible for all man's failings, misfortunes, and troubles. They claim all evil to be the external influence of magic. They say the time has come for magic to pass from the world."

Some in the room murmured their agreement, some grumbled their skepticism, but most stood mute.

Lord Rahl laid an arm across the top of the largest chair—the one in the center. "In order for their vision to be complete, and in light of their self-proclaimed divine cause, they will suffer the sovereignty of no land. They wish for all to be brought under their influence, and to go forward into the future as one people: subjects of the Imperial Order."

He paused for a moment as he met the gaze of many in the crowd. "Magic is not a fount of evil. This is merely an excuse for their actions as they ascend to supremacy."

Whispering swept back through the room, and low undertones of arguments boiled up. Duchess Lumholtz strode forward, commanding attention. She smiled at Lord Rahl before bowing her head.

"Lord Rahl, what you say is all very interesting, but the Blood of the Fold here—" She flicked her hand in the direction of Tobias and at the same time cast him an icy glare. "—say that all magic is spewed forth by the Keeper."

Brogan neither said anything, nor moved. Lord Rahl didn't look in his direction, but instead kept his gaze on the duchess.

"A child, come anew into the world, is magic. Would you call that evil?"

Lifting an imperious hand, she quieted the crowd at her back. "The Blood of the Fold preaches that magic is created by the Keeper himself, and thereby can only be evil incarnate."

From various areas around the floor and up in the balcony, people shouted their agreement. This time it was Lord Rahl who lifted a hand, bringing them to silence.

"The Keeper is the destroyer, the bane of light and life, the breath of death. As I hear it told, it is the Creator, through his power and majesty, who brings all things to be." Almost as one, the crowd shouted that it was true.

"In that case," Lord Rahl said, "to believe that magic springs from the Keeper is blasphemy. Could the Keeper create a newborn child? To ascribe the power to create, which is the sole domain of the Creator, to the Keeper, is to grant to the Keeper that which is chaste, and only the Creator's. The Keeper cannot create. To hold such a profane belief could only be heresy."

Silence fell like a pall over the room. Lord Rahl cocked his head to the duchess. "Did you step forward, my lady, to confess to being a heretic? Or simply to accuse another of heresy for personal gain?"

With a face once again as red as her tight lips, she took several steps back to her husband's side. The duke, his own face no longer calm, shook a finger at Lord Rahl.

"Tricks with words will not change the fact that the Imperial Order fights the Keeper's evil, and has come to unite us against him. They wish only for all people to prosper together. Magic will deny that right to mankind. I am Keltish, and proud of it, but it is time to move beyond fragmented and frail lands standing alone. We have had extensive talks with the Order, and they have proven themselves a civilized and decent lot, interested in joining all lands in peace."

"A noble ideal," Lord Rahl answered in a quiet tone, "one you already had in the unity of the Midlands, yet you threw it away for avarice."

"The Imperial Order is different. It offers true strength, and true, lasting peace."

Lord Rahl fixed the duke with a glare. "Graveyards rarely breach a peace." He turned his glare on the crowd. "Not long ago, an army of the Order swept through the heart of the Midlands, seeking to bring others into their fold. Many joined, and swelled their force. A D'Haran general named Riggs led them, along with officers of several lands, and was assisted by a wizard Slagle, of Keltish blood.

"Well over one hundred thousand strong, they bore down on Ebinissia, the Crown city of Galea. The Imperial Order bade the people of Ebinissia join them and become subjects of the Order. When called upon to oppose aggression against the Midlands, the people of Ebinissia bravely did so; they refused to abandon their commitment to unity and a common defense that was the Midlands."

The duke opened his mouth to speak but, for the first time, Lord Rahl's voice became menacing in tone and cut off his words.

"The Galean army defended the city to the last man. The wizard used his power to rent the city walls and the Imperial Order poured in. Once the greatly outnumbered Galean defenders had been eliminated, the Imperial Order did not occupy the city, but instead went through it like a pack of howling animals—raping, torturing, and butchering helpless people."

Lord Rahl, his jaw clenched tight, leaned across the desk, and pointed a finger at Duke Lumholtz. "The Order slaughtered every living person in Ebinissia: the old, the young, the newborn. They impaled defenseless, pregnant women in order to kill both mother and unborn child."

His face red with rage, he slammed his fist to the desk. Everyone jumped. "With that act, the Imperial Order put the lie to anything they say! They have lost the right to tell anyone anything about what is right, and what is wicked. They are without virtue. They come for one reason and one reason only: to vanquish and subjugate. They slaughtered the people of Ebinissia to show others what they had to offer anyone who fails to submit.

"They will not be halted by borders or by reason. Men with the blood of babes on their blades have no ethics. Don't you dare stand there and try to tell me otherwise; the Imperial Order is beyond defense. They have shown the fangs behind their smile, and by the spirits they have lost the right to offer words and have them taken as truth!"

Taking a calming breath, Lord Rahl straightened. "Both those innocents at the points of blades and those at the hilts forfeited much that day. The ones at the points forfeited their lives. The ones at the hilt forfeited their humanity and their right to be heard, much less believed. They have cast themselves and any who join them as my enemy."

"And who were these troops?" Someone else asked. "Many were D'Haran, by your own admission. You lead the D'Harans, by your own admission. When the boundary came down last spring, the D'Harans swept in and committed atrocities much the same as you recount. Though Aydindril was spared that cruelty, many other cities and towns suffered the same fate as Ebinissia, but at the hands of D'Hara. Now you ask us to believe you? You are no better."

Lord Rahl nodded. "What you say about D'Hara is true. D'Hara was led by my father, Darken Rahl, who was a stranger to me. He did not raise me, or teach me his ways. What he wanted was much the same as the Imperial Order wants: to conquer all lands, and rule all people. Where the Order is a monolithic cause, his was a personal quest. Besides using brute force to obtain his ends, he also used magic, much the same as the Order.

"I stand against everything Darken Rahl stood for. He would stop at no evil act to have his way. He tortured and killed countless innocent people, and suppressed magic, so that it could not be used against him, the same as the Order would do."

"Then you're the same as he."

Lord Rahl shook his head. "No, I am not. I do not lust to rule. I take up the sword only because I have the ability to help oppose oppression. I fought on the side of the Midlands against my father. In the end, I killed him for his crimes. When he used his vile magic to return from the underworld, I used magic to stop him and send his spirit back to the Keeper. I used magic again to close a doorway the Keeper was using to send his minions into this world."

Brogan ground his teeth. He knew from experience that banelings often tried to hide their true nature by regaling you with stories of how valiantly they had fought the Keeper and his minions. He had heard enough of these spurious accounts to recognize them as diversions from the actual evil in the person's heart. The Keeper's followers were often too cowardly to show their true nature, and so hid behind such boasts and concocted tales.

In fact, he would have arrived in Aydindril sooner had he not come across so many pockets of perversion after he had left Nicobarese. Villages and towns, where everyone appeared to be living pious lives, turned out to be riddled with wickedness. When some of the more strident defenders of their virtue were put to a proper questioning they finally confessed their blasphemy. When put to a proper questioning, the names of *streganicha* and banelings who lived in the neighborhood, and had seduced them to evil with the use of magic, had rolled off their tongues.

The only solution had been purification. Whole villages and towns had needed to be put to the torch. Not even a signpost to the Keeper's lairs remained. The Blood of the Fold had done the Creator's work, but it had taken time and effort.

Seething, Brogan returned his attention to Lord Rahl's words.

"I take up this challenge only because the sword has been thrust into my hand. I ask that you not judge me by who my father was, but by what I do. I do not slaughter innocent, defenseless people. The Imperial Order does. Until I violate the trust of honest people, I have the right to be granted honest judgment.

"I cannot stand by and watch evil men triumph; I will fight with everything I have, including magic. If you side with these murders, you will find no mercy under my sword."

"All we want is peace," someone shouted.

Lord Rahl nodded. "I, too, wish nothing more than that there were peace, and I could go home to my beloved woods and lead a simple life, but I can't, any more than we can go back to the simple innocence of our childhood. Responsibility has been thrust upon me. Turning your back on innocents in need of help makes you the attacker's accomplice. It is in the name of the innocent and defenseless that I take up the sword, and fight this battle."

Lord Rahl returned his arm to the center chair. "This is the chair of the Mother Confessor. For thousands of years the Mother Confessors have ruled the Midlands with a benevolent hand, struggling to hold the lands together, to have all the people of the Midlands live as neighbors in peace, and to let them tend to their own affairs without fear of outside force." He let his gaze roam the eyes watching him. "The council sought to break the unity and peace for which this room, this palace, and this city, stand, and of which you speak so longingly. They unanimously condemned her to death and had her executed."

Lord Rahl slowly drew his sword and laid the weapon at the front edge of the desk, where all could see it. "I told you I am known by different titles. I am also known as the Seeker of Truth, named so by the First Wizard. I carry the Sword of Truth by right. Last night I executed the council for their treason.

"You are the representatives of the lands of the Midlands. The Mother Confessor offered you the chance to stand together, and you turned your backs on that offer, and on her."

A man beyond Tobias's view broke the icy silence. "Not all of us approved of the action the council took. Many of us wish the Midlands to stand. The Midlands will be joined yet again and made stronger for the struggle."

Many in the crowd voiced their agreement, vowing to do their best to bring unity again. Others remained silent.

"It is too late for that. You have had your chance. The Mother Confessor suffered your bickering and intractability." Lord Rahl slammed his sword back into its scabbard. "I will not."

"What are you talking about?" Duke Lumholtz asked, irritation embrittling his tone. "You're from D'Hara. You've no right to tell us how the Midlands will function. The Midlands is our affair."

Lord Rahl stood statue still as he directed his soft, but commanding voice to the crowd. "There is no Midlands. I dissolve it, here and now. From now on, each land is on its own."

"The Midlands is not your toy!"

"Nor is it Kelton's," Lord Rahl said. "It was the design of Kelton to rule the Midlands."

"How dare you accuse us of . . ."

Lord Rahl held up his hand, bidding silence. "You are no more rapacious than some of the others. Many of you were anxious to have the Mother Confessors and wizards out of your hair so you could carve up the spoils."

Lunetta tugged on his arm. "True," she whispered. Brogan silenced her with an icy look.

"The Midlands will not tolerate this interference in our business," another voice called out.

"I am not here to discuss the governing of the Midlands. I have just told you, the Midlands is dissolved." Lord Rahl regarded the crowd with a glare of such deadly commitment that Tobias had to remind himself to take another breath. "I am here to dictate the terms of your surrender."

The crowd flinched as one. Angry shouts erupted and built until the room roared. Red-faced men swore oaths as they shook their fists.

Duke Lumholtz shouted everyone to silence and then turned back to the dais. "I don't know what foolish ideas you've gotten into your head, young man, but the Imperial Order is in charge of this city. Many have come to reasonable agreements with them. The Midlands will be preserved, will stand united through the Order, and will never surrender to the likes of D'Hara!"

When the crowd surged toward Lord Rahl, red rods appeared in the Mord-Sith's hands, the echelon of soldiers drew steel, pikes came down, and the gar's wings snapped open. The beast snarled, its fangs dripping and its green eyes glowing. Lord Rahl stood like a granite wall. The crowd halted and then receded.

Lord Rahl's whole body took on the same tight, dangerous demeanor as his glare. "You were offered a chance to preserve the Midlands, and you failed. D'Hara has been liberated from the fist of the Imperial Order and holds Aydindril."

"You only think you hold Aydindril," the Duke said. "We have troops here, as do a great many of the lands, and we're not about to let the city fall."

"A little late for that, too." Lord Rahl held out a hand. "May I introduce General Reibisch, the commander of all D'Haran forces in this sector."

The general, a muscular man with a rust-colored beard and combat scars, stepped up onto the dais, clapping a fist to his heart in salute to Lord Rahl before turning to the people. "My troops command, and surround, Aydindril. My men have been sitting on this city for months now. We are finally free of the grip of the Order, and are once again D'Harans, lead by Master Rahl.

"D'Haran troops don't like sitting around. If any of you would like a fight, I, personally, would welcome it, though Lord Rahl has commanded that we not be the ones to start the killing, but if called to defend ourselves, the spirits know we will finish it. I'm bored nearly to death with the tedium of occupation, and I'd much rather have something more interesting to do, something I'm very good at.

"Each of your lands has detachments of troops stationed to guard your palaces. In my professional judgment, if all of you decided to contest the city with the troops you have at hand, and did it in an organized fashion, it would take a day, maybe two, for us to rout them. When it was done, we would have no more troubles. Once battle is at hand, D'Harans don't take prisoners."

The general stepped back with a bow to Lord Rahl.

Everyone started talking at once, some angrily shaking their fists and shouting to be heard. Lord Rahl thrust his hand into the air.

"Silence!" It came almost instantly, and he went on. "I have invited you here to hear what I have to say. After you have decided to surrender to D'Hara, then I will be interested in what you have to say. Not before!

"The Imperial Order wishes to rule all of D'Hara and all of the Midlands. They have lost D'Hara; I rule D'Hara. They have lost Aydindril; D'Hara rules Aydindril.

"You had a chance at unity, and you squandered it. That chance has passed into history. You now have but two choices. Your first is to choose to side with the Imperial Order. They will rule with an iron fist. You will have no say, and no rights. All magic will be exterminated, except the magic with which they dominate you. If you live, your lives will be a dark struggle without the spark of hope for freedom. You will be their slaves.

"Your other choice is to surrender to D'Hara. You will follow the law of D'Hara. Once you are one with us, you will have a say in those laws. We have no desire to extinguish the diversity that is the Midlands. You will have the right to the fruits of your labor and the right to trade and flourish, as long as you work within the larger context of law and the rights of others. Magic will be protected, and your children will be born into a world of freedom, where anything is possible.

"And once the Imperial Order is exterminated, there will be peace. True peace.

"There will be a price: your sovereignty. While you will be allowed to maintain your own lands and cultures, you will not be allowed to have standing armies. The only men at arms will be those common to all, under the banner of D'Hara. This will not be a council of independent lands; your surrender is mandatory. Surrender is the price each land will pay for peace, and the proof of your commitment to it.

"Much as you all paid a tribute to Aydindril, no land, no people, will bear all the burden of freedom; all lands, all people, will pay a tax sufficient to see to the common defense, and no more. All will pay equally; none will be favored."

The room erupted with protests, with most claiming it would be robbery of what was theirs. Lord Rahl silenced them with nothing more than his glare.

"Nothing gained without cost is valued. I was reminded of that fact only today. We buried her this morning. Freedom has a cost, and all will bear it, so that all will value and preserve it."

The people up in the balcony broke out in near riot, protesting that they were promised gold, that it was theirs, and that they could not afford to pay any tax. Chanting began, demanding the gold be turned over to them. Once more, Lord Rahl held up a hand, commanding silence.

"The man who promised you gold for nothing is dead. Dig him up and complain to him, if you wish. The men who will fight for your freedom will require provisions, and our troops will not steal them. Those of you who can provide food and services will be paid a fair price for your labor and goods. All will participate in attaining freedom and peace, if not with service under arms, then at minimum with a tax to support our troops.

"All, no matter their means, must have an investment in their freedom, and will pay their part. This principle is law, and inviolate.

"If you do not wish to comply, then leave Aydindril and go to the Imperial Order. You are free to demand gold of them, as it was they who made the promise; I will not keep it for them.

"You are free to choose: with us, or against us. If you are with us, then you will help us. Think carefully before you decide to leave, for if you leave, and decide later that you would rather not suffer the Order any longer, then you will pay double the tax for a period of ten years in order to earn your way back."

The crowd in the balconies gasped. A woman on the floor, near the front, spoke up in a distraught voice.

"What if we choose neither? It is against our principles to fight. We want to be left alone to go about our lives. What if we choose not to fight, to simply go about our business?"

"Do you arrogantly believe that we want to fight—you are somehow better because you wish not to? Should you enjoy the freedom to live by the same principles you refuse to help us defend?"

"You can contribute in other ways without taking up a sword, but contribute you must. You can help tend the wounded, you can help the families of men gone to fight, you can help build and maintain roads to get supplies to them; there are any number of ways you can help, but you will help. You will pay the tax, the same as everyone else. There will be no bystanders.

"If you choose not to surrender, you will stand alone. The Order intends to conquer all people and lands. Because there is no other way to stop them, I can intend no less. Sooner or later, you will be ruled by one of us. Pray it is not the Order.

"Those lands that choose not to surrender to us will be placed under blockade and isolated until we have time to invade and conquer you, or the Order does. None of our people will be allowed to trade with you, under penalty of prosecution for treason, and you will not be allowed to transport trade or travel through our land.

"The opportunity of surrender I give now carries incentives: you will be able to join us without prejudice or sanctions. Once this peaceful offer to surrender has expired, and it becomes necessary to conquer you, you will be conquered, and you will surrender, but the terms will be harsh. Every one of your people will pay triple the tax for a period of thirty years. It wouldn't be fair to punish future generations for the actions of this. Neighboring lands will prosper and grow, while you do not, burdened as you will be with higher costs to your surrender. Your land will eventually recover, but you will probably not live long enough to see it.

"Be warned: I intend to wipe the butchers called the Imperial Order from the face of the land. If you do more than try to stand aside, and are foolish enough to join with them, then you cast your fate with theirs; no mercy will be granted."

"You can't get away with this," an anonymous voice in the crowd called out. "We'll stop you."

"The Midlands is fragmented, and cannot be made whole again, or I would instead join with you. What is past, is past, and cannot be returned.

"The spirit of the Midlands will live on with those of us who honor its purpose. The Mother Confessor committed the Midlands to war without mercy against the tyranny of the Imperial Order. Honor her command and the ideals of the Midlands in the only way that will succeed: surrender to D'Hara. If you join with the

Imperial Order, then you stand against everything the Midlands represented.

"A force of Galean soldiers, led by the queen of Galea herself, hunted down the butchers of Ebinissia, and killed them to a man. She has shown us all that the Imperial Order is vincible.

"I am engaged to wed the queen of Galea, Kahlan Amnell, and join her people to mine, and thereby show all that I will not stand for the crimes committed, even if they were committed by D'Haran troops. Galea and D'Hara will be the first to join in the new union, through Galea's surrender to D'Hara. My marriage to her will show all that it will be a union made of mutual respect, demonstrating that it can be done without blood conquest or the lust for power, and instead for strength and a hope of a new and better life. She, no less than I, intends to annihilate the Imperial Order. She has proven her heart with cold steel."

The crowd, both those on the main floor, and those in the balconies, started crying out questions and demands.

Lord Rahl shouted them down. "Enough!" The people grudgingly fell silent once more. "I have heard all I intend to hear. I have told you the way it will be. Do not mistakenly think I will tolerate the way you behaved as nations of the Midlands. I will not. Until you surrender, you are all potential enemies, and will be treated as such. Your troops will at once surrender their weapons, one way or another, and will not be allowed to leave the custody of the D'Haran troops now surrounding your palaces.

"Each of you will send a small delegation to your homeland to convey my message as I have told it to you today. Don't think to try my patience; delay could cost you everything. And do not think to wile me out of special conditions—there will be none. Each land, whether large or small, will be treated the same, and must surrender. If you choose to surrender, we welcome you with open arms, and expect you to contribute to the whole." He looked to the balconies. "You, too, have been charged with a responsibility: contribute to our survival, or leave the city.

"I am not pretending it will be easy; we stand against a foe without conscience. The creatures on the poles outside were sent against us. Consider their fate, while you think on my words.

"If you choose to join with the Imperial Order, then I pray the spirits will be kinder to you in the afterlife than I will be in this.

"You may go."

CHAPTER 13

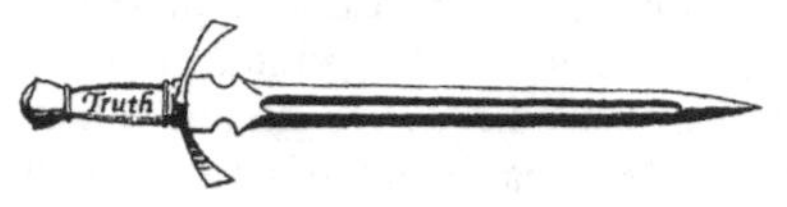

THE GUARDS CROSSED THEIR pikes before the door. "Lord Rahl wishes to speak with you."

None of the other guests remained in the room; Brogan had held back to the last in order to see if any would seek a private audience with Lord Rahl. Most had left in great haste, but a few had lingered, as Brogan had thought they would. Their polite inquiries were turned away by the guards. The balconies, too, had been emptied.

Brogan and Galtero, with Lunetta between, crossed the expanse of marble to the dais, accompanied by their footsteps echoing around the dome, along with the metallic clatter of the armor from the guards behind them. Lamplight cast a warm glow in the immense, ornate, stone room. Lord Rahl leaned back in the chair to the side of the Mother Confessor's chair and watched them come.

Most of the D'Haran soldiers had been dismissed, along with the guests. General Reibisch stood to the side of the dais, his face grim. The two huge guards to the ends, and the three Mord-Sith beside Lord Rahl watched, too, with the silent intensity of coiled vipers. The gar towered behind the chairs, watching with glowing green eyes as they came to a halt before the desk.

"You may go," General Reibisch said to the remaining soldiers. After clapping a fist to their hearts, they departed. After Lord Rahl had watched the tall double doors close, he looked to Galtero, Brogan, and then let his gaze settle on Lunetta.

"Welcome. I am Richard. What is your name?"

"Lunetta, Lord Rahl." She giggled as she performed an unpracticed curtsy.

Lord Rahl's gaze shifted to Galtero, and Galtero shifted his weight to his other foot. "I apologize, Lord Rahl, for nearly trampling you, today."

"Apology accepted." Lord Rahl smiled to himself. "See how easy that was?"

Galtero said nothing. Lord Rahl at last turned to Brogan, his expression now serious.

"Lord General Brogan, I want to know why you have been abducting people."

Tobias spread his hands. "Abducting people? Lord Rahl, we have done no such thing, nor would we."

"I doubt you are a man who tolerates evasive answers, General Brogan. We have that in common."

Tobias cleared his throat. "Lord Rahl, there must be some misunderstanding. When we arrived here in Aydindril in order to offer our assistance to the cause of peace, we found the city be in disarray and matters of authority in a state of confusion. We invited a few people to our palace in order to help determine what dangers be about, nothing more."

Lord Rahl leaned forward. "About the only thing you were interested in was the execution of the Mother Confessor. Why would that be?"

Tobias shrugged. "Lord Rahl, you must realize that my whole life the Mother Confessor be the figure of authority in the Midlands. To come to find she may have been executed disturbs me greatly."

"Nearly half the city witnessed the execution, and could have told you so. Why did you think it necessary to abduct people off the street to question them about it?"

"Well, people sometimes have different versions of events when asked separately—they remember events in different ways."

"An execution is an execution. What is there to remember differently?"

"Well, from across a square, how could you tell who it was being led to the block? Only a few people near the front could have seen her face, and many of those would not know the face as hers even if they did see it." Lord Rahl's eyes weren't losing their dangerous set, so he quickly went on. "You see, Lord Rahl, I had been hoping that the whole thing might have been a deception."

"Deception? The people assembled saw the Mother Confessor beheaded," Lord Rahl stated flatly.

"Sometimes people see what they think they will see. It be my hope that they did not really see the Mother Confessor executed, but perhaps just a show so that she could escape. At least that be my hope. The Mother Confessor stands for peace. It would be a great symbol of hope for the people if the Mother Confessor were still alive. We need her. I was going to offer her my protection, if she be alive."

"Put the hope from your mind, and dedicate yourself to the future."

"But surely, Lord Rahl, you must have heard the rumors of her escape?"

"I have heard no such rumors. And did you know the Mother Confessor?"

Brogan let an agreeable smile come to his lips. "Oh, yes, Lord Rahl. Quite well, in fact. She visited Nicobarese on any number of occasions, as we be a valued member of the Midlands."

"Really?" Lord Rahl's face was unreadable as he looked down from behind the desk. "What did she look like?"

"She was . . . well, she had . . ." Tobias frowned. He had met her but, strangely, he suddenly realized he couldn't recall what she looked like. "Well, she is difficult to describe, and I am not good with that sort of thing."

"What was her name?"

"Her name?"

"Yes, her name. You said you knew her well. What was her name?"

"Well, it was . . ."

Tobias frowned again. How could this be? He was chasing a woman who was the scourge of the pious, the symbol of the magic's suppression of the devout, a woman he hungered to judge and punish more than any of the Keeper's other disciples, and suddenly he couldn't remember what she looked like, or even her name. Confusion tumbled through his thoughts as he struggled to bring her looks to mind.

Suddenly, it came to him: the death spell. Lunetta had said that in order for it to work he probably wouldn't recognize her. It hadn't occurred to him that the spell would erase even her name, but that had to be the explanation.

Tobias shrugged as he smiled. "I'm sorry, Lord Rahl, but with the things you had to say tonight my mind seems to be in a scramble." He chuckled as he tapped the side of his forehead. "I guess I'm getting old and addled. Forgive me."

"You abduct people off the street to question them about the Mother Confessor because you are hoping to find her alive so you can protect her, yet you can't recall what she looks like, or even her name? I hope you can appreciate, General, that from my side of the desk, 'addled' would be a lenient representation. I must insist that, like her name, you forget this foolish, ill-advised quest and put your mind to the matter of the future of your people."

Brogan could feel his cheek twitch as he spread his hands again. "But Lord Rahl, don't you see? If the Mother Confessor were to be discovered alive, then it would be a great aid to you in your efforts. If she lives, and you could convince her of your sincerity and the necessity of your plan, she would be an invaluable aid to you. If she went along with your demands, then it would carry great weight with the people of the Midlands. Despite what it would appear because of the unfortunate actions of the council, which in all honesty set my blood to boiling, many in the Midlands greatly respect her, and would be swayed by her endorsement. It might even be possible, if you were to convince her to marry you—as a matter of political convenience, of course."

"I am committed to wed the queen of Galea."

"Even so, if she were alive, she could help you." Brogan stroked the scar at the side of his mouth as he fixed his eyes on the man behind the desk. "Do you think it possible, Lord Rahl, that she be alive?"

"I was not here at the time, but I am told that perhaps thousands of people saw her beheaded. They think she is dead. While I admit that were she alive she would be an invaluable help as my ally, that is not the point. The point is, are you able to offer me one good reason why all those people are wrong?"

"Well, no, but I think—"

Lord Rahl slammed a fist to the desk. Even the two huge guards jumped. "I've had enough of this! Do you think I am stupid enough to be diverted from the cause of peace by this speculation? Do you think I will grant you some special privilege because you would think to offer me suggestions to win over the people of the Midlands? I told you, there are no special favors! You will be treated the same as every other land!"

Tobias licked his lips. "Of course, Lord Rahl. That wasn't my intention—"

"If you continue on with this quest to find a woman whom thousands saw beheaded, at the expense of your charge to chart the future course of your land, then you are going to end up on the point of my sword."

Tobias bowed. "Of course, Lord Rahl. We will leave at once for our homeland with your message."

"You are doing no such thing. You are going to remain right here."

"But, I must deliver your message to the king."

"Your king is dead." Lord Rahl cocked an eyebrow. "Or did you mean that you were going to go chasing his shadow, too, in the belief that he might be hiding out with the Mother Confessor?"

Lunetta chuckled. Brogan darted her a glance and the laugh cut off abruptly. Brogan realized his smile had vanished. He managed to bring a hint of it back.

"A new king will no doubt be named. That is the way of our land: to be led by a king. It was to him, the new king, that I was going to take the message, Lord Rahl."

"Since any king that was named would no doubt be your puppet, the journey is unnecessary. You will remain at your palace until you decide to accept my terms, and surrender."

Brogan's smile widened. "As you wish, Lord Rahl."

He began to draw his knife from the sheath at his belt. Instantly, one of the Mord-Sith had a red rod an inch from his face. He froze.

Looking up into her blue eyes, he feared to move. "A custom of my land, Lord Rahl. I meant no threat. I was going to surrender my knife to you, to show my intent to comply with your wishes and remain at the palace. It be a way of giving my word, a symbol of my sincerity. Would you permit me?"

The woman didn't take her blue eyes from his. "It's all right, Berdine," Lord Rahl said to the woman.

She withdrew, but only with great reluctance, and a venomous glare. Brogan slowly pulled the knife free and gently placed it, handle first, on the edge of the desk. Lord Rahl took the knife and set it aside.

"Thank you, General." Brogan held his hand out, palm up. "What's this?"

"The custom, Lord Rahl. In my land, the custom is that when you ceremonially surrender your knife, in order to avoid dishonor the person you surrender it to gives you a coin in return, silver for silver, as a symbolic act of goodwill and peace."

Lord Rahl, his eyes never leaving Brogan, considered it a moment, and at last leaned back and drew a silver coin from his pocket. He slid it across the desk. Brogan reached up, took the coin, and then slipped it into his coat pocket, but not before he saw the strike: the Palace of the Prophets.

Tobias bowed. "Thank you for honoring my customs, Lord Rahl. If there is nothing else, then I will retire to consider your words."

"As a matter of fact, there is one more thing. I heard that the Blood of the Fold holds no favor with magic." He leaned a little closer. "So why is it you have a sorceress with you?"

Brogan looked over at the squat figure beside him. "Lunetta? Why, she be my sister, Lord Rahl. She travels with me everywhere. I love her dearly, gift and all. If I were you, I would not put great weight to the words of Duchess Lumholtz. She be Keltish, and I hear they be thick with the Order."

"I have heard it elsewhere, too, from those who are not Keltish."

Brogan shrugged. He wished he could get his hands on that cook so he could cut out her wagging tongue.

"You have asked to be judged by your actions, and not by what others say of you. Would you deny me the same? What you hear is beyond my control, but my sister has the gift, and I would not have it otherwise."

Lord Rahl leaned back in his chair, his eyes as penetrating as ever. "There were Blood of the Fold among the Imperial Order's army that butchered those at Ebinissia."

"As well as D'Harans." Brogan lifted an eyebrow. "Those who attacked Ebinissia are all dead. The offer you made tonight is to be a fresh start, is it not? Everyone given the opportunity to make the commitment to your offer of peace?"

Lord Rahl nodded slowly. "It is. One last thing, General. I have fought the Keeper's minions, and I will continue to do so. In doing battle with them, I have discovered that they don't need shadows to conceal them. They can be the last person you would expect, and worse, can do the Keeper's bidding without even realizing they are doing so."

Brogan bowed his head. "I, too, have heard it is so."

"Make sure the shadow you chase is not the one you cast."

Brogan frowned. He had heard a great many things from Lord Rahl that he did not like, but this was the first he did not understand. "I am very sure of the evil I pursue, Lord Rahl. Fear not for my safety."

Brogan began to turn away, but then halted and looked over his shoulder. "And may I offer my congratulations to you on your engagement to the Galean queen. . . . I do believe I am becoming addled. I can't seem to keep names in my head. Forgive me. What was her name?"

"Queen Kahlan Amnell."

Brogan bowed. "Of course. Kahlan Amnell. I will not forget it again."

CHAPTER 14

RICHARD STARED AT THE tall mahogany door after it had closed. It was refreshing to see a person with such a guileless nature that she would come to the Confessors' Palace, among so many important, finely dressed people, wearing an outfit made of tattered patches of different-colored cloth. Everyone must have thought her mad. Richard looked down at his simple, filthy clothes. He wondered if they thought him mad, too. Maybe he was.

"Lord Rahl," Cara asked, "how did you know she was a sorceress?"

"She was shrouded in her Han. Couldn't you see it in her eyes?"

Her red leather creaked as she leaned a hip against the desk beside him. "We would know a woman to be a sorceress if she tried to use her power on us, but not before. What is Han?"

Richard wiped a hand across his face as he yawned. "Her inner power—the force of life. Her magic."

Cara shrugged. "You have magic, so you could see it. We could not."

His thumb stroked the hilt of his sword as he answered with an absent grunt.

Over time, without realizing it, he had come to an awareness of the aspect of magic in a person—if they were using their magic, he could usually see it in their eyes. Though singular to each person, or perhaps the specific nature of their magic, there was a commonality Richard could recognize. Maybe, as Cara said, it was because he had the gift, or maybe it was simply the experience of having seen the distinctive, timeless look in the eyes of so many people with magic: Kahlan, Adie the bone woman, Shota the witch woman, Du Chaillu the spirit woman of the Baka Ban Mana, Darken Rahl, Sister Verna, Prelate Annalina, and countless other Sisters of the Light.

The Sisters of the Light were sorceresses, and he had often seen the unique glaze of distant intensity in their eyes when they were joined with their Han. Sometimes, when they were enveloped in a shroud of magic, he could almost see the air about them crackle. There were Sisters who seemed to radiate an aura of such power that when they walked past him the fine hairs at the back of his neck stood on end.

Richard had seen that same look in Lunetta's eyes; she had been shrouded in her Han. What he didn't know was why—why she would be standing there, doing nothing, yet touching her Han. Sorceresses usually didn't let their Han envelop them unless it was to a purpose, the same way he usually didn't draw his sword and its attendant magic without a reason. Maybe it simply pleased her childlike temper, the way those patches of colored cloth did. Richard didn't think so.

What concerned him was that it could have been that Lunetta was trying to ascertain if he was telling the truth. He didn't know enough about magic to know for sure if that was possible, but sorceresses often seemed somehow to know if he was being truthful, making it seem that every time he told a lie it couldn't have been any more obvious to them had his hair suddenly burst into flames. He hadn't wanted to take a chance, and had been careful not to be caught in a lie in front of Lunetta, especially about Kahlan being dead.

Brogan had certainly been interested in the Mother Confessor. Richard wished he could believe he was telling the truth; what he had said made enough sense. Maybe it was just his concern for Kahlan's safety that made him suspicious of everything.

"That man looks like trouble waiting to find a roost," he said aloud without intending to.

"Would you like us to clip his wings, Lord Rahl?" Berdine flicked her Agiel on the end of the chain at her wrist and caught it in her fist. She cocked an eyebrow. "Maybe something a little lower?" The other two Mord-Sith chuckled.

"No," Richard said in a tired voice. "I've given my word. I've asked them all to do something unprecedented, something that will forever change their lives. I have to do as I said I would, and give them all the chance to see that this is right, that it's for the common good, the best chance for peace."

Gratch yawned, showing his fangs, and sat down on the floor behind Richard's chair. Richard hoped the gar wasn't as tired as he was. Ulic and Egan seemed to ignore the conversation; they stood, relaxed, with their hands clasped behind their backs. They seemed to be a match for some of the pillars around the room. Their eyes were not relaxed, however; they constantly surveyed the columns, corners, and alcoves, watching, even though the huge room was empty except for the eight of them around the ornate dais.

With a meaty thumb, General Reibisch idly burnished the bulbous gold base of a lamp at the edge of the dais. "Lord Rahl, did you mean what you said about the men not taking what they've won?"

Richard looked to the general's troubled eyes. "Yes. That's the way of our enemies, and not ours. We fight for freedom, not plunder."

The general averted his eyes as he nodded his assent.

"Do you have something to say about that, General?"

"No, Lord Rahl."

Richard flopped back in his chair. "General Reibisch, I've been a woods guide since I was old enough to be trusted; I've never had to command an army before. I'll be the first to admit that I don't know much about the position I find myself in. I could use your help."

"My help? What sort of help, Lord Rahl?"

"I could use your experience. I would appreciate it if you expressed your opinion instead of holding it back and saying 'Yes, Lord Rahl.' I may not agree with you, and I may get angry, but I'll never punish you for telling me what you think. If you disobey my orders, I'll replace you, but you're free to say what you think of them. That's one of the things we're fighting for."

The general clasped his hands behind his back. The muscles of his arms glistened under the chain mail, and Richard could see, too, under the rings of metal, the white scars of his rank. "D'Haran troops have a custom of plundering those we defeat. The men expect it."

"Past leaders may have tolerated it, or even encouraged it, but I will not."

His sigh was comment enough to understand. "As you wish, Lord Rahl."

Richard rubbed his temples. He had a headache from lack of sleep. "Don't you understand? This isn't about conquering lands and taking things from others; this is about fighting oppression."

The general rested a boot on the gilded rung of a chair and hooked a thumb behind his wide belt. "I don't see much difference. From my experience, the Master Rahl always thinks he knows best, and always wants to rule the world. You are your father's son. War is war. Reasons make no difference to us; we fight because we are told to, same as those on the other side. Reasons mean little to a man swinging his sword, trying to keep his head."

Richard slammed a fist to the desk. Gratch's glowing green eyes became alert. In his peripheral vision, Richard could see red leather move protectively closer.

"The men who went after the butchers of Ebinissia had a reason! That reason, and not plunder, was what sustained them and gave them the strength they needed in order to prevail. They were a detachment of five thousand Galean recruits who had never before been in battle, and yet they defeated General Riggs and his army of over fifty thousand men."

General Reibisch's heavy brow drew together. "Recruits? Surely you're mistaken, Lord Rahl. I knew Riggs; he was an experienced soldier. Those were battle-hardened troops. I've received reports from the sights of those battles; they are grisly in the detail of what happened to those men as they tried to fight their way out of the mountains. They could only have been annihilated in such a fashion by an overwhelming force."

"Then I guess Riggs wasn't as experienced a soldier as he needed to be. While you have secondhand reports, I heard the story from an unimpeachable source who was there to see it done. Five thousand men, boys, really, came upon Ebinissia after Riggs and his men were finished butchering the women and children. Those recruits pursued Riggs, and took his army down. When it was finished, less than a thousand of those young men were left standing, but not Riggs nor a single one of his force was left alive."

Richard left unsaid that without Kahlan there to teach them what needed to be done, and lead them into the first battles, directing them in the forge of combat, those recruits probably would have been ground into carrion within a day. At the same time he knew it was their commitment to see the job done that gave them the courage to listen to her, and to go up against impossible odds.

"That is the power of motivation, General. That is what men can do when they have a powerful reason, a righteous cause."

A sour expression puckered his scarred face. "D'Harans have been fighting most of their lives, and know what they're about. War is about killing; you kill them before they can kill you, that's all. Whoever wins is the one who was right.

"Reasons are the spoils of victory. When you've destroyed the enemy, then your leaders write down the reasons in books, and give moving speeches about them. If you've done your job, then there aren't any of the enemy left to dispute your leader's reasons. At least not until the next war."

Richard raked his fingers through his hair. What was he doing? What did he think he could accomplish if those fighting on his own side didn't believe in what he was trying to do?

Overhead, across the plastered ceiling of the dome, the painted figure of Magda Searus, the first Mother Confessor, Kahlan had told him, and her wizard, Merritt, looked down on him. In disapproval, it seemed.

"General, what I was trying to do tonight, talking to those people, was about trying to stop the killing. I'm trying to make it possible for peace and freedom to have a chance to take root for good.

"I know it sounds a paradox, but don't you see? If we behave with honor, then all those lands with integrity, who want peace and freedom, will join us. When they see we fight to stop the fighting, and not simply to conquer and dominate, or for plunder, they will be on our side, and the forces of peace will be invincible.

"For now, the aggressor makes the rules, and our only choice is to fight or submit, but . . ."

He sighed in frustration as he thumped his head back against the chair. He closed his eyes; he couldn't bear to meet the gaze of the wizard Merritt overhead. Merritt looked as if he were about to launch into a lecture on the folly of presumption.

He had just publicly declared his intention to rule the world, and for reasons his own followers thought were empty talk. He was suddenly beginning to feel hopelessly foolish. He was just a woods guide turned Seeker, not a ruler. Just because he had the gift he was starting to think he could make a difference. Gift. He didn't even know how to use his gift.

How could he be so arrogant as to think this would work? He was so tired he couldn't think straight. He couldn't remember the last time he had slept.

He didn't want to rule anyone, he just wanted it all to stop so he could be with Kahlan and live his life without any fighting. The night before with her had been bliss. That was all he wanted.

General Reibisch cleared his throat. "I've never fought for anything before, any reason, I mean, other than my bond. Maybe it's time I tried it your way."

Richard came off the back of the chair and frowned at the man. "Are you just saying that because you think that's what I want to hear?"

"Well," the general said as he picked with a thumbnail at the carvings of acorns along the edge of the desk, "the spirits know no one would believe this, but soldiers want peace more than most people, I'd expect. We just don't dare to dream about it because we see so much killing that we get to thinking it can't ever end, and if you dwell on it, you'll get soft, and getting soft gets you killed. If you act like you're keen for a fight, it gives your enemies pause, lest they give you a reason. Like the paradox you spoke of.

"Seeing all that fighting and killing makes you wonder if there's anything to you but doing as you're bidden, and killing people. Makes you wonder if you're some kind of monster, good for nothing else. Maybe that's what happened to those men who attacked Ebinissia; maybe they just finally gave in to the voice in their head.

"Maybe, like you say, if we can do this, the killing would finally stop." He pressed back a long splinter he had worked loose. "I guess a soldier always hopes that once he kills all the people who want to kill him, then he can try laying down his sword. The spirits know that no one hates fighting more than many of those who have to do it." He let out a long sigh. "Ahh, but no one would believe that."

Richard smiled. "I believe it."

The general glanced up. "It's rare to find someone who understands the true cost of killing. Most either glorify or are repelled by it, never feeling the pain of infliction and the agony of responsibility. You're good at killing. I'm glad you don't relish it."

Richard's gaze left the general, and sought the consoling gloom of the shadows among the arches between marble columns. As he had told the assembled representatives, he was named in prophecy; in one of the oldest prophecies, in High D'Haran, he was called *fuer grissa ost drauka*: the bringer of death. He was thrice named: the one who could bring the place of the dead and the world of the living together by tearing the veil to the underworld; the one who brought the spirits of the dead forth, which he did when he used the magic of his sword and danced with death; and in its most base meaning, one who kills.

Berdine clapped Richard on the back, jarring his teeth and breaking the uncomfortable silence. "You didn't tell us you had found yourself a bride. I hope you plan on a bath before the wedding night, or she'll turn you out." The three women laughed.

Richard was surprised to find he had the energy to grin. "I'm not the only one who smells like a horse."

"If there's nothing else, Lord Rahl, I'd best see to a number of matters." General Reibisch straightened and scratched his rust-colored beard. "Just how many people do you expect there are we'll have to kill to have this peace you speak of?" He smiled crookedly. "So I can know how much farther there is to go before I don't have to have guards watch my back when I lie down for a snooze."

Richard shared a long look with the man. "Maybe they'll come to their senses and surrender, and we won't have to fight."

General Reibisch grunted a cynical laugh. "If you don't mind, I think I'll have the men sharpen their swords, just in case." He peered up. "Do you know how many lands there are in the Midlands?"

Richard thought it over a moment. "As a matter of fact, I don't.

Not all the lands are large enough to be represented in Aydindril, but many of those are still large enough to have men at arms. The queen will know. She'll join us soon, and be able to help."

Tiny specks of lamplight danced off his chain mail. "I'll start sweeps through the Palace Guard forces at once, tonight, before they have a chance to organize. Maybe it'll be nice and peaceful that way. I expect that before the night's over, though, at least one of the guard forces will try to bolt."

"Make sure there are enough men around the Nicobarese Palace. I don't want Lord General Brogan leaving the city. I don't trust that man, but I've given my word that he will have the same chance as all the rest."

"I'll see to it."

"And General, have the men be careful of his sister, Lunetta." Richard felt an odd sympathy for Tobias Brogan's sister, for her innocent-seeming heart. He liked her eyes. He steeled himself. "If they come out of their palace, intending to leave, have plenty of archers at strategic locations and in range. If she uses magic, don't take any chances by delay."

Richard already hated this. He had never had to commit men to a battle in which people could easily be hurt, or killed. He remembered what the Prelate had once told him: wizards had to use people to do what must be done.

General Reibisch eyed the silent Ulic and Egan, the gar, and the three women. He spoke to them past Richard. "A thousand men will be wide awake and a shout away, if you need them."

Cara's expression sobered after the general had gone. "You must sleep, Lord Rahl. As Mord-Sith, I know when a man is exhausted and about to fall over. You can make your plans to conquer the world tomorrow, after you have rested."

Richard shook his head. "Not yet. I have to write her a letter, first."

Berdine leaned against the desk beside Cara and folded her arms. "A love letter to your bride?"

Richard pulled open a drawer. "Something like that."

Berdine put on a coy smile. "Maybe we can help. We will tell you the proper things to say to keep her heart pounding and forget you need a bath."

Raina joined her sisters of the Agiel against the desk, adding an impish laugh that sparkled in her dark eyes. "We will give you lessons in being a proper mate. You and your queen will be happy to have us around for advice."

"And you had better listen to us," Berdine cautioned, "or we will teach her how to make you dance to her tune."

Richard tapped Berdine's leg, urging her to move aside so he could get at the drawers behind her. He found paper in the bottom one. "Why don't you go get some sleep," he said absently as he searched for a pen and ink. "You were riding hard, too, trying to catch me, and couldn't have gotten much more sleep than I did."

Cara turned her nose up in mock indignation. "We will stand watch while you sleep. Women are stronger than men."

Richard remembered Denna telling him that very thing, only she hadn't been playful when she said it. These three never let their guard down when anyone was around; he was the only one they trusted when they wanted to practice their social graces. He thought they needed a lot of practice. Maybe that was why they wouldn't give up their Agiel; they had never been anything but Mord-Sith, and were afraid they wouldn't be able to do it.

Cara leaned over, looking in the empty drawer before he pushed it shut. She flicked her blond braid back over her shoulder. "She must care greatly for you, Lord Rahl, if she is willing to surrender her land to you. I don't know if I would do such a thing for a man, even if he was one such as you. He would have to be the one to surrender to me."

Richard made her scoot aside, and at last found pens and ink in a drawer he would have opened first had she not been in the way. "You're right, she cares greatly for me. But as to surrendering her land, well, I haven't told her that part, yet."

Cara's arms unfolded. "You mean to say that you have yet to demand her surrender, as you have done tonight with the others?"

Richard wiggled the stopper from the ink bottle. "That's one reason I must write this letter at once, to explain my plan to her. Why don't you three be quiet, and let me write?"

Raina, a look of true concern in her dark eyes, squatted beside his chair. "What if she calls off the wedding? Queens are proud; she may not wish to do such a thing."

A ripple of worry surged through his gut. It was worse than that. These women didn't really understand what he was asking Kahlan to do. He was not asking a queen to surrender her land; he was asking the Mother Confessor to surrender all of the Midlands.

"She is as committed to defeating the Imperial Order as am I. She has fought with determination that would make a Mord-Sith blanch. She wishes the killing to stop as much as do I. She loves me, and will understand the benevolence of what I'm asking."

Raina sighed. "Well, if she doesn't, we will protect you."

Richard fixed her with such a deadly glare that she rocked back on her heels as if he had struck her. "Don't you ever, ever, even think of harming Kahlan. You will protect her the same as you would me, or you can leave right now and join the ranks of my enemies. You are to hold her life as dear as mine. Swear it on your bond to me. Swear it!"

Raina swallowed. "I swear it, Lord Rahl."

He glared at the other two women. "Swear it."

"I swear it, Lord Rahl," they said together.

He looked to Ulic and Egan.

"I swear it, Lord Rahl," they said as one.

He let slip his belligerent tone. "All right, then."

Richard placed the paper on the desk before himself and tried to think. Everyone thought she was dead; this was the only way. They couldn't let people know she was alive, or someone might try to finish what the council had thought they had accomplished. She would understand if he could just explain it properly.

Richard could feel the figure of Magda Searus, overhead, glaring down at him. He feared to look up, lest her wizard, Merritt, send down a bolt of lightning to punish him for what he was doing.

Kahlan had to believe him. She had told him once that she would die to protect him, if necessary, in order to save the Midlands, that she would do anything. Anything.

Cara sat back on her hands. "Is the queen pretty?" Her mischievous smile returned. "What does she look like? She won't try to make us wear dresses once you're married, will she? We'll obey her, but Mord-Sith don't wear dresses."

Richard sighed inwardly. They were only trying to lighten the mood by acting mischievous. He wondered how many people these "mischievous" women had killed. He reprimanded himself; that wasn't fair, especially coming from the bringer of death. One of them had died this very day trying to protect him. Poor Hally never had a chance against a mriswith.

Neither would Kahlan.

He had to help her. This was the only thing he could think of, and every minute that passed could be a minute too late. He had to hurry. He tried to think of what to say. He couldn't let it out that Queen Kahlan was really the Mother Confessor. If the letter fell into the wrong hands . . .

Richard looked up when he heard the door squeak open. "Berdine, where do you think you're going?"

"To find a bed of my own. We will take turns standing watch over you." She put one hand on a hip, and with the other spun the Agiel on the chain at her wrist. "Control yourself, Lord Rahl. You will have a new bride in your bed soon enough. You can wait until then."

Richard couldn't help smiling. He liked Berdine's wry sense of humor. "General Reibisch said there were a thousand men standing guard, there is no need—"

Berdine winked. "Lord Rahl, I know you like me the best, but stop thinking about my behind as I walk, and write your letter."

Richard tapped the glass-handled pen against a tooth as the door closed.

Cara's brow wrinkled in a frown. "Lord Rahl, do you think that the queen will be jealous of us?"

"Why should she be jealous?" he mumbled as he scratched the back of his neck. "She has no reason."

"Well, don't you think we're attractive?"

Richard blinked up at her. He pointed at the door. "Both of you, go stand by the doors and make sure no one can get in here to kill your Lord Rahl. If you're quiet, like Egan and Ulic here, and let me write this letter, you may remain on this side of the door, if not, then you will guard from the other side."

They rolled their eyes, but both had smiles as they headed across the room, apparently enjoying the fact that their nettling had finally gotten a reaction from him. He guessed Mord-Sith must be hungry for playful banter, it was something they got precious little of, but he had more important things on his mind.

Richard stared at the blank piece of paper and tried to think through the haze of weariness. Gratch put a furry paw on his leg and snuggled against his side as Richard dipped the pen in the ink bottle.

My Dearest Queen, he began with one hand, while patting the paw in his lap with the other.

CHAPTER 15

TOBIAS SCANNED THE SNOWY darkness as they slogged through the deepening drifts. "Are you sure you did as I instructed?"

"Yes, my lord general. I told you, they be spelled."

Behind, the lights of the Confessors' Palace and the surrounding buildings of the city's center had long ago faded into the swirling snowstorm that had swept down out of the mountains while they had been inside listening to Lord Rahl deliver his absurd demands to the representatives of the Midlands.

"Then where are they? If you lose them and they freeze to death out here, I will be more than displeased with you, Lunetta."

"I know where they be, Lord General," she insisted. "I will not lose them." She stopped and lifted her nose, sniffing the air. "This way."

Tobias and Galtero looked at each other and frowned, then turned to follow her as she scurried off into the darkness behind Kings Row. Occasionally he could just make out the dark shapes of the palaces looming in the storm. They provided ghosts of lights and guidance in the directionless void of falling snow.

In the distance he could hear the passing clank of armor. It sounded like more men than a simple patrol. Before the night was out, the D'Harans would probably make a move to consolidate their grip on Aydindril. That's what he would do if he were in their place: strike before your opponents have time to digest their options. Well, no matter, he wasn't planning on staying.

Tobias blew the snow from his mustache. "You were listening to him, weren't you?"

"Yes, Lord General, but I told you, I could not tell."

"He be no different than anyone else. You must not have been paying attention. I knew you weren't paying attention. You were scratching your arms and you weren't paying attention."

Lunetta cast him a quick look over her shoulder. "He be different. I do not know why, but he be different. I have never felt magic like his before. I could not tell if he be telling every word true, or every word a lie, but I think he be telling it true." She shook her head to herself in wonder. "I can get past blocks. I always can get past blocks. Any kind: air, water, earth, fire, ice, any kind. Even spirit. But his . . . ?"

Tobias smiled absently. It didn't matter. He didn't need her filthy taint to tell. He knew.

She mumbled on about the strange aspects of Lord Rahl's magic, and how she wanted away from it, away from this place, and how it made her skin itch like never before. He only half listened. She would have her wish to be away from Aydindril after he took care of a few matters.

"What are you sniffing at?" he growled.

"Midden, my lord general. Kitchen midden."

Tobias gripped a fistful of her colored rags. "Midden? You left them at a midden heap?"

She grinned as she waddled along. "Yes, Lord General. You said you didn't want people around. I not be familiar with the city, and did not know a safe place I could send them, but I saw the midden heap on our way to the Confessors' Palace. No one will be there in the night."

Midden heap. Tobias harrumphed. "Loony Lunetta," he muttered.

She lost a stride. "Please Tobias, do not call me—"

"Then where are they!"

She lifted her arm, pointing, and hurried her step. "This way, Lord General. You will see. This way. Not far."

He thought about it as he trudged through the drifts. It made sense. It did make sense; a midden heap was the perfect justice.

"Lunetta, you be telling me the truth about Lord Rahl, aren't you? If you lie to me about this, I will never forgive you."

She stopped and looked up at him. Tears welled in her eyes as she clutched her colored rags. "Yes, my lord general. Please. I be telling the truth. I tried everything. I tried my best."

Tobias stared at her a long moment as a tear ran down her plump cheek. It didn't matter; he knew.

He flicked his hand impatiently. "All right then, get going. You better not have lost them."

Suddenly beaming, she wiped her cheek, turned back to the way she had been going, and darted off. "This way, Lord General. You will see. I know where they be."

Sighing, Tobias started after her again. The snow was piling up, and at the rate it was coming down it looked like it was going to be a bad one. No matter, things were turning his way. Lord Rahl was a fool if he thought Lord General Tobias Brogan of the Blood of the Fold was going to surrender like a baneling under hot iron.

Lunetta was pointing. "Over here, Lord General. They be here."

Even with the wind howling at their backs, Tobias could smell the midden heap before he could see it. He shook the snow off his crimson cape when they reached the dark hump lit by the faint lights from palaces beyond the wall in the distance. The snow melted off in places as it fell on the steaming heap, leaving much of its dark shape devoid of even the pretense of purity.

He put his fists on his hips. "So? Where are they?"

Lunetta moved close to his side, hiding herself in his lee from the wind-driven snow. "Stand here, Lord General. They will come to you."

He looked down and saw a well trodden path. "A circle spell?"

She cackled softly as she pulled some scraps up around her red cheeks against the cold. "Yes, Lord General. You said you did not want them to get away, or you would be angry with me. I did not want you to be angry with Lunetta, so I cast them a circle spell. They cannot get away, now, no matter how fast they go."

Tobias smiled. Yes, the day was ending well after all. It had provided obstacles, but with the Creator's guidance he would overcome them. Now matters were in his command. Lord Rahl was going to find out that no one dictated to the Blood of the Fold.

Emerging from the darkness, he first saw the swish of her yellow skirts as her wrap was pulled open by a gust. Duchess Lumholtz, the duke a half step behind and to her side, trod purposefully toward him. When she saw who was standing beside the path, a glower darkened her painted face. She tugged closed her snow-encrusted wrap.

Tobias greeted her with a broad smile. "We meet again. A good evening to you, madam." He tilted his head in a slight nod. "And to you, too, Duke Lumholtz."

The duchess sniffed her disapproval and lifted her nose. The duke eyed them with a stern glare, as if he were placing a barrier he defied them to cross. Both marched past without a word, and off into the darkness. Tobias chuckled.

"You see, my lord general? As I promised, they wait for you."

Tobias hooked both thumbs in his belt as he straightened his shoulders, letting his crimson cape billow open in the wind. There was no need to pursue the pair.

"You did well, Lunetta," he murmured.

Before long, the yellow of her skirts appeared again. This time, when she saw Tobias, Galtero, and Lunetta standing beside her well-trodden path, a look of shock drew up her eyebrows. She really was an attractive woman, despite the superfluous paint: not girlish at all, though still young, but mature of face and figure, ripe with the proud poise of full womanhood.

With deliberate menace the duke rested a steady hand on the hilt of his sword as the pair approached. Though ornate, the duke's sword, Tobias knew, was, like Lord Rahl's, not mere decoration. Kelton made some of the best steel in the Midlands, and all Keltans, especially nobility, prided themselves on knowing well its use.

"General Bro—"

"*Lord* General, madam."

She looked down her nose at him. "Lord General Brogan, we are on our way home to our palace. I suggest you stop following us, and return to yours. It's a foul night to be out."

From beside him, Galtero watched the lace at her bosom rise

and fall in ire. When she noticed, she snatched her wrap closed. The duke noticed, too, and leaned toward Galtero.

"Keep your eyes off my wife, sir, or I'll cut you to pieces and feed you to my hounds."

Galtero, a treacherous smile spreading on his lips, looked up at the taller man, but said nothing.

The duchess huffed. "Good night, General."

The pair marched off again to make another circuit of the midden heap, thoroughly convinced they were headed toward their destination, straight as an arrow flies, but in the haze of a circle spell they went nowhere except around and around. He could have stopped them the first time, but he relished the consternation in their eyes as they tried to grasp how he could repeatedly show up ahead of them. Their spelled minds would be able to make no sense of it.

The next time by, their faces went as white as the snow, before flushing to red. The duchess stomped to a halt and, fists on her hips, scowled at him. Tobias watched the white lace right in front of his face lift and fall with the heat of her indignation.

"Look here, you greasy little nick, how dare you—"

Brogan's jaw locked rigid. With a grunt of rage, he snatched the white lace in both fists and ripped the front of her dress down to her waist.

Lunetta's hand lifted, accompanied by a short incantation, and the duke, his sword halfway out of its scabbard, stopped, rigid and unmoving, as if turned to stone. Only his eyes moved, to see the duchess cry out as Galtero pinned both her arms behind her back, rendering her as immobile and helpless as he, though without the use of magic. Her back arched as Galtero twisted her arms in his powerful grip. Her nipples stood out stiff in the cold wind.

Since he had forfeited his knife, Brogan drew his sword instead. "What did you call me, you filthy little whore?"

"Nothing." In the clutch of panic, she threw her head from side to side, her black curls whipping across her face. "Nothing!"

"My, my, lost your spine so easily?"

"What do you want?" she panted. "I'm no baneling! Leave me go! I'm no baneling!"

"Of course you be no baneling. You be too pompous to be a baneling, but that makes you no less despicable. Or useful."

"Then it's him you want? Yes, the duke. He's the baneling. Leave me go, and I'll recount his crimes."

Brogan spoke through clenched teeth. "The Creator does not be served by false, self-serving confessions. But you will serve him, nonetheless." His cheek twitched with a grim smile. "You will serve the Creator through me; you'll do my bidding."

"I'll do no such—" She cried out as Galtero tightened his grip. "Yes all right," she gasped. "Anything. Just don't hurt me. Tell me what you want, and I'll do it."

She tried unsuccessfully to back away as he put his face within inches of hers. "You will do as I tell you," he said through gritted teeth.

Her voice was choked with terror. "Yes. All right. You have my word."

He sneered derisively. "I wouldn't take the word of a whore like you: one who would sell anything, betray any principle. You will do my bidding because you have no choice."

He backed away, pinched her left nipple between his thumb and the knuckle of his first finger, and stretched it out. As she wailed, her eyes opened wide. Brogan brought the sword up and, with a sawing cut, sliced off the nipple. Her scream drowned out the howl of the wind.

Brogan placed the severed nipple in Lunetta's upturned palm. Her stubby fingers closed around it as her eyes closed in a shroud of magic. Soft sounds of an ancient incantation melded with the wind and the sound of the duchess's shivering shrieks. Galtero held her weight as the wind wheeled around them.

Lunetta's chanting rose in pitch as she tilted her head up to the inky sky. With her eyes shut tight, she summoned the spell around herself and the woman before her. The wind seemed to pull the words forth as Lunetta conjured in her *streganicha* tongue.

"From earth to sky, from leaves to roots,
from fire to ice, and soul's own fruits.
From light to dark, from wind to water,
I claim this spirit and Creator's daughter.
Till the heart's blood boils or the bones be ash,
till the tallow be dust and death's teeth gnash,
this one be mine.
I cast her gnomon into a sunless glen,

and pull this soul beyond its umbra's ken.
Till her tasks be done and the worms be fed,
till the flesh be dust and the soul has fled,
this one be mine."

Lunetta's voice lowered to a throaty chant. *"Cock's hen, spiders ten, bezoar then, I make a thrall stew. Ox gall, castor and caul, I make a chattel brew. . . ."*

Her words drifted away and were lost in the wind, but her squat body bobbed as she went on, shaking her empty hand over the woman's head, and the other, with the chunk of flesh, over her own heart.

The duchess shuddered as tendrils of magic coiled around her, snaking into her flesh. She convulsed as its fangs sank into her very soul.

Galtero had all he could do to hold her, until at last, she went limp in his grip. Despite the wind, there seemed a sudden silence.

Lunetta opened her hand. "She be mine to bid. I pass my right to you." She placed the now desiccated knob of flesh in Brogan's upturned palm. "She be yours, now, my lord general."

Brogan closed the shriveled knot in his fist. The duchess hung glassy-eyed by her arms behind her back. Her legs held her weight, but she shook with pain and cold. Blood oozed from her wound.

Brogan tightened his fist. "Stop that shivering!"

She looked into his eyes, and her glazed expression faded. She became still. "Yes, my lord general."

Brogan gestured to his sister. "Heal her."

Galtero watched with a glint of lust in his dark eyes as Lunetta cupped both hands around the woman's injured breast. Duke Lumholtz, too, watched with eyes nearly bulging out of their sockets. Lunetta's eyes closed again as she wove more magic, casting a soft spell. Blood trickled from between Lunetta's fingers until the woman's flesh began drawing together in the healing.

Brogan's mind drifted as he waited. The Creator did indeed watch over his own. A day that had started with him at the brink of the greatest of triumphs was brought nearly to ruin, but in the end he had proven that those who kept the Creator's cause in their hearts could prevail. Lord Rahl was going to find out just what happened to those who worshiped the Keeper, and the Imperial Order was going to find out just how valuable the lord general of the Blood of the Fold was to them. Galtero, too, had proven his worth this day; the man was entitled to a trifle for his efforts.

Lunetta used the duchess's wrap to wipe off the blood, and then withdrew to reveal a perfectly whole breast, as flawless as the other, except it had no nipple. Brogan had that, now.

Lunetta motioned toward the duke. "Am I to do him, too, Lord General? Do you wish to have them both?"

"No." Brogan lifted a hand with a dismissive wave. "No, I only need her. But he will play his part in my plan."

Brogan fixed his glare on the duke's panicked eyes. "This be a dangerous city. As Lord Rahl told us today, there be dangerous creatures about, attacking innocent citizens who have no chance against them. Shocking. If only Lord Rahl were here to protect the duke from such an attack."

"I will to see to it at once, Lord General," Galtero said.

"No, I can take care of this. I thought you might like to 'entertain' the duchess here, while I see to the duke."

Galtero drew teeth across his lower lip as he gazed at the duchess. "Yes, Lord General, very much. Thank you." He tossed Brogan his knife. "You will need this. The soldiers told me that the creatures disemboweled their victims with a three-bladed knife. You will need to make three slices to duplicate the effect."

Brogan thanked his colonel. He could always count on Galtero's thoroughness. The woman's eyes moved back and forth between the three of them, but she said nothing.

"Would you like me to compel her to cooperate?"

A gruesome grin spread on Galtero's usually stony face. "And what would be the purpose of that, Lord General? Better if she learned another lesson this night."

Brogan nodded. "As you wish, then." He looked to the duchess. "My dear, I do not bid this of you. You are free to express your own true feelings about it to Galtero here."

She cried out when Galtero swept an arm around her waist. "Why don't we go over there, in the darkness. I would not want to offend your delicate sensibilities, Duchess, by allowing you to see what be happening to your husband."

"You can't!" she cried out. "I'll freeze in the snow! I must do my lord general's bidding. I'll freeze!"

Galtero patted her bottom. "Oh, you won't freeze. The midden will be warm under you."

She shrieked and tried to pull away, but Galtero already had a good grip on her. He tightened his other fist in her hair.

"She be a lovely creature, Galtero; see that that beauty isn't marred. And don't be long; she yet has bidding to do for me. She will have to wear less paint," he said with a smirk, "but since she has such talent with it, at least she can paint herself a nipple where her real one be missing.

"When I be finished with the duke here, and you be finished with her, then Lunetta has another spell to cast over her. A very special spell. A very rare and powerful spell."

Lunetta stroked her pretties as she watched his eyes. She knew what he wanted. "Then I will need something of his, something he has touched."

Brogan patted his pocket. "He accommodated us with a coin."

Lunetta nodded. "That will do."

The duchess shrieked and flailed her arms as Galtero began dragging her off into the darkness.

Brogan turned and waggled the knife in front of the tall Keltan's wild eyes. "And now, Duke Lumholtz, on to your part in the Creator's plan."

CHAPTER 16

WITH GRATCH LOOMING OVER his shoulder, watching, Richard dribbled the red wax in a long puddle across the folded letter. He hastily set the candle and wax aside and picked up his sword, rolling the handle into the wax, making an impression of the hilt with its braided gold wire that spelled out the word TRUTH. He was satisfied with the results; Kahlan and Zedd would know the letter really was his.

Egan and Ulic were sitting at the ends of the long, curved desk, watching the empty room as if an army were about to storm the dais. His two, huge guards preferred to stand. He was sure they must be tired and had insisted they sit. They said standing left them more prepared to react in the event of trouble. Richard had told them that he thought the thousand men outside, guarding, would probably raise a sufficient racket if there were an attack that the two would notice, even from a seated position, and still have time to get up out of their chairs and draw their swords. It was then that they had reluctantly sat down.

Cara and Raina stood beside the doors. When he had told them that they were welcome to sit, too, they had dismissed the suggestion with haughty sniffs, and had said that they were stronger than Egan and Ulic, and would stand. Richard had been in the middle of writing his letter and hadn't wanted to argue with them, so he had said that since they looked tired and slow, he was ordering them to stand so they would have sufficient time to come to his defense in case there was an attack. They were standing now, scowling at him, but he had caught glimpses of them smiling to each other, apparently pleased with the way they had been able to draw him into their game.

Darken Rahl had given the Mord-Sith clearly delineated bounds: master and slave. Richard wondered if they were testing their limits with him, trying to find where the slack ended. Maybe they were simply gleeful to be able, for the first time, to act as they wished, on whim if they wanted.

Richard also considered the possibility that their game was a test to try to ascertain if he was mad. Mord-Sith were nothing if not accomplished at testing. It troubled him that they might think him mad. This was the only way; they had to see that.

Richard hoped Gratch wasn't as tired as the rest of them. The gar had only just joined him that morning, so Richard didn't know how much sleep he had gotten, but his glowing green eyes looked bright and alert. Gars hunted mostly at night, so perhaps that explained his wakefulness. Whatever it was, Richard hoped it was true that Gratch wasn't tired, and not simply his hope.

Richard patted the furry arm. "Gratch, come with me."

The gar came to his feet, stretched his wings along with one leg, and followed Richard across the expanse of floor to one of the covered stairways up to the balcony. His four guards instantly came alert when Richard started off. He gestured for them to stay where they were. Egan and Ulic did; the two women did not, but instead followed him at a distance.

Only the two lamps at the bottom of the covered stairway were lit, leaving the rest a gloomy tunnel. At the top, it opened onto a broad balcony, one side edged with a sinuous mahogany railing overlooking the main floor, and the other bordered by the bottom rim of the dome. Above a low, white marble ledger, round windows half again as tall as he were spaced evenly around the enormous room. Richard looked out one of the windows to a snowy night. Snow. That could be trouble.

At the bottom the window was latched with a brass lever, and to the center of each side it was hinged on massive pins. He tested the lever and found it pivoted smoothly.

Richard turned back to his friend. "Gratch, I want you to listen to me very carefully. This is important."

Gratch nodded in earnest concentration. The two Mord-Sith watched from the shadows near the top of the stairway.

Richard reached out and stroked the long lock of hair hanging on a leather thong around Gratch's neck along with the dragon's tooth. "This is a lock of Kahlan's hair." Gratch nodded that he understood. "Gratch, she's in danger." Gratch frowned. "You and I are the only ones who can see the mriswith coming." Gratch growled and covered his eyes with his claws, peeking out between—his sign for the mriswith.

Richard nodded. "That's right. Gratch, she has no way to see them coming, like you and I do. If they go after her, she won't see them coming. They'll kill her."

An uneasy, purling whine rose from Gratch's throat. His face brightened. He held out the lock of Kahlan's hair, and then thumped his massive chest.

Richard couldn't help laughing in wonder at the gar's ability to grasp what he wanted. "You guessed what I was thinking, Gratch. I would go to her myself, to protect her, but that would take too much time, and she might be in danger right now. You're big, but you're not big enough to carry me. The only thing we can do is to have you go to her, and protect her."

Gratch nodded his willingness with a grin that bared his fangs. He seemed to suddenly realize what that meant, and threw his arms around Richard.

"Grrratch luuug Raaaach aaarg."

Richard patted the gar's back. "I love you too, Gratch." He had sent Gratch away once before in order to save the gar's life, but Gratch hadn't understood. He had told Gratch he would never do that again.

He hugged the gar tight before pushing back. "Gratch, listen to me." The glowing green eyes were watering up. "Gratch, Kahlan loves you as I do. She wants you to be with us the same as I do, the same way you want me to be with you. I want all of us to be together. I'm going to wait here and I want you to go protect her and bring her back." He smiled and stroked Gratch's shoulder. "Then we'll all be together."

Gratch's prominent eyebrows drew into a dubious frown.

"Then when we're all together, you won't have just one friend, but you'll have both of us. And my grandfather, Zedd, too. He'll love having you around. You'll like him, too." Gratch was looking a bit more enthusiastic. "You'll have lots of friends to wrestle with you."

Before the gar could pounce on him, Richard held him at arm's length. There was little in life that Gratch loved as much as wrestling. "Gratch, I can't have fun wrestling with you, now, when I'm worried about the people I love. You understand, don't you? Would you want to have fun wrestling with someone else if I were in danger and needed you?"

Gratch considered it a moment, and then shook his head. Richard hugged him again. When they parted, Gratch spread his wings with a spirited flap.

"Gratch, can you fly in the snow?" Gratch nodded. "At night?" The gar nodded again, showing fangs behind his smile.

"All right, now, you listen to me, so you'll be able to find her. I taught you directions: north and south and like that. You know directions. Good. Kahlan is to the southwest." Richard pointed southwest, but Gratch beat him to it. Richard laughed. "Good. She's to the southwest. She's going away from us, on her way to a city. She thought I was going to catch up with her and go to the city with her, but I can't. I must wait here. She has to come back here.

"She's with other people. There's an old man with white hair with her; he's my friend, my grandfather, Zedd. There are other people with her, too, many of them soldiers. A lot of people. Do you understand?"

Gratch gave a sad frown.

Richard rubbed his forehead, trying to think through his weariness for a way to explain it.

"Like tonight," Cara said from across the balcony. "Like when you were talking to all the people tonight."

"Yes! Like that, Gratch." He pointed at the main floor, circling his finger around. "All the people in here tonight, when I was talking to them? About that many people will be with her."

Gratch at last grunted that he understood. Richard patted his friend's chest in relief. He held out the letter.

"You have to take her this letter so that she'll understand why she has to come back here. It explains everything to her. It's very important that she gets this letter. Do you understand?" Gratch snatched up the letter in a claw.

Richard raked back his hair. "No, that won't do. You can't carry it like that. You may need your claws, or you may drop it and lose it. Besides, it'll get all wet in the snow and she won't be able to read it." His voice trailed off as he tried to think of a way for Gratch to carry the letter.

"Lord Rahl."

He turned and Raina tossed him something through the dim light. When he caught it, he realized it was the leather pouch that had carried General Trimack's letter all the way from the People's Palace in D'Hara.

Richard grinned. "Thanks, Raina."

Smirking, she shook her head. Richard put his letter, his hopes, everyone's hopes, in the leather pouch and hung its thong around Gratch's neck. Gratch gurgled with pleasure at the new addition to his collection before again studying the lock of Kahlan's hair.

"Gratch, it's possible that for some reason she may not be with all those people. I have no way of telling what may happen between now and when you reach her. It may be hard to find her."

He watched Gratch stroking the lock of hair. Richard had seen Gratch catch a flutter mouse in midair on a moonless night. He would be able to find people on the ground, but he still had to have a way to know which people were the right ones.

"Gratch, you haven't ever seen her before, but she has long hair like this, not many women do, and I told her all about you. She won't be afraid when she sees you, and she'll call you by name. That's how you can know it's really her: she'll know your name."

Satisfied at last with all his instructions, Gratch flapped his wings and bounced on the balls of his feet, eager to be off so he could bring Kahlan back to Richard. Richard swung the window open. The snow howled in. One last time, the two friends hugged.

"She's been running away from here for two weeks, and will continue on until you reach her. It may take you a while to catch her, many days, so don't get discouraged. And be careful, Gratch; I don't want you to get hurt. I want you back here with me so I can wrestle with you, you big furry beast."

Gratch giggled, a fearsome yet happy noise, then climbed up on the ledge. "Grrratch luuug Raaaach aaarg."

Richard waved. "I love you, Gratch. Be careful. Safe journey."

Gratch waved back, and then bounded out into the night. Richard stood watching the cold blackness, even though the gar had disappeared almost instantly. Richard felt a sudden, hollow emptiness. Though he was surrounded by people, it wasn't the same. They were there only because they were bonded to him, and not because they really believed in him or in what he was doing.

Kahlan had been fleeing for two weeks, and it would probably take the gar at least another week, maybe two, to finally catch her. Richard couldn't imagine it taking less than a month or more for Gratch to find Kahlan and Zedd, and for all of them to return to Aydindril. It could be closer to two months.

He already had a knot in his gut, anxious for his friends to be back with him. They had been parted too long. He wanted this lonesome feeling to end, and only their presence could banish it.

After closing the window, he turned back to the room. The two Mord-Sith were standing right behind him.

"Gratch really is your friend," Cara said.

Richard only nodded, not wanting to test the lump in his throat.

Cara glanced at Raina before speaking to him. "Lord Rahl, we have been discussing this matter, and have decided that it would be best if you were in D'Hara, where you will be safe. We can leave an army here to guard your queen when she arrives and escort her back to D'Hara to be with you."

"I've already told you, I must remain here. The Imperial Order wants to conquer the world. I'm a wizard, and must stand against that."

"You said you didn't know how to use your gift. You said you knew nothing about how to wield magic."

"I don't, but my grandfather, Zedd, does. I have to stay here until he arrives, then he can teach me what I need to know so I can fight the Order and keep them from taking over the world."

Cara dismissed the matter with a wave of her hand. "Someone always wants to rule those they don't already rule. From the safety of D'Hara you can direct your war against the Order. When the representatives from the palaces return from their homelands to offer their surrender, then the Midlands will be yours. You will rule the world, and without having to be in harm's view. Once the lands surrender, then the Imperial Order will be finished."

Richard started for the stairway. "You don't understand.

There's more to it than that. Somehow, the Imperial Order has infiltrated the New World, and has gained allies."

"New World?" Cara asked as she and Raina started after him. "What is the New World?"

"Westland, where I'm from, the Midlands, and D'Hara make up the New World."

"They make up all the world," Cara said with finality.

"Spoken like a fish in a pond," Richard said, sliding his hand lightly down the silken smooth railing as he descended the stairs. "You think that's all there is to the world? Just the pond you see? That it all just ends at an ocean, or mountain range, or desert, or something?"

"Only the spirits know." Cara stopped at the bottom of the steps and cocked her head. "What do you think? That there are other lands beyond these? Other ponds?" She swept her Agiel around in a circle. "Out there, somewhere?"

Richard threw his hands up. "I don't know. But I do know that to the south is the Old World."

Raina folded her arms. "To the south is a barren waste."

Richard started across the expanse of floor. "Embedded in the wasteland was a place called the Valley of the Lost, and running through it, from ocean to ocean, a barrier called the Towers of Perdition. The towers were set in place three thousand years ago by wizards with unimaginable power. The spells of those towers have prevented almost anyone from crossing for the last three thousand years, and so the Old World beyond was forgotten in time."

Cara flashed a skeptical frown as their boot-strikes echoed around the dome. "How do you know this?"

"I was there, in the Old World, at the Palace of the Prophets, in a great city called Tanimura."

"Truly?" Raina asked. Richard nodded. She added a frown to Cara's. "And if no one can get through, then how did you?"

"It's a long story, but basically these women, the Sisters of the Light, took me there. We could cross because we have the gift, but not strong enough to draw the destructive power of the spells. No one else could get through, and so the Old and New Worlds remained separated by the towers and their spells.

"Now the barrier between the Old and New World has fallen.

No one is safe. The Imperial Order is from the Old World. It's a long way, but they will come, and we must be prepared."

Cara eyed him suspiciously. "And if this barrier has been in place for three thousand years, how did this come to happen, now?"

Richard cleared his throat as they followed him up onto the dais. "Well, I guess it's my fault. I destroyed the towers' spells. They no longer stand as a barrier. The wasteland has been restored to the green meadowland it once was."

The two women appraised him silently. Cara leaned past him to speak to Raina. "And he says he doesn't know how to use magic."

Raina shifted her gaze to Richard. "So, what you are saying is that you have caused this war. You made it possible."

"No. Look, it's a long story." Richard raked back his hair. "Even before the barrier was down they were gaining allies here and had started their war. Ebinissia was destroyed before the barrier came down. But now there's nothing to hold them back, or slow them down. Don't underestimate them. They use wizards and sorceresses. They wish to destroy all magic."

"They wish to destroy all magic, yet they use magic themselves? Lord Rahl, that makes no sense," Cara scoffed.

"You want me to be the magic against magic. Why?" He pointed to the men on either end of the dais. "Because they can only be the steel against steel. It often takes magic to destroy magic."

Richard gestured, his finger including the two women. "You have magic. And to what purpose? To counter magic. As Mord-Sith, you are able to appropriate the magic of another and turn it against them. It's the same with them. They use magic to help them destroy magic, just as Darken Rahl used you to torture and kill those with magic who opposed him.

"You have magic; the Order will want to destroy you. I have magic; they'll want to destroy me. All D'Haran's have magic, through the bond; eventually the Order will see that and decide to exterminate the taint. Sooner or later, they'll come to crush D'Hara, just as they would crush the Midlands."

"The D'Haran troops will crush them, instead," Ulic said over his shoulder, as if stating with confidence that the sun would set this day as it always did.

Richard shot a glare at the man's back. "Until I came along,

D'Harans joined with them, and in their name annihilated Ebinissia. The D'Harans here, in Aydindril, followed the commands of the Imperial Order."

His four guards fell silent. Cara stared at the ground before her feet as Raina let out a disheartened sigh.

"In the confusion of the war," Cara said at last, as if thinking aloud, "some of our troops out in the field would have felt the bond break, just as some of those at the palace did when you killed Darken Rahl. They would be like lost souls without a new Master Rahl to take up their bond. They may have simply joined with someone who would give them direction, take up the place of the bond. Now they have their bond back. We have a Master Rahl."

Richard slumped down in the Mother Confessor's chair. "That's what I'm hoping."

"All the more reason to return to D'Hara," Raina said. "We must protect you so you can continue to be the Master Rahl and our people will not join with the Imperial Order. If you are killed, and the bond is broken, then the army will once again turn to the Order for direction. Better to leave the Midlands to their own battles. It is not your job to save them from themselves."

"Everyone in the Midlands, then, will fall under the sword of the Imperial Order," Richard said in a soft voice. "They will be be treated as you were treated by Darken Rahl. No one will ever again be free. We can't let that happen as long as there's any chance we can stop them. It must be done now, before they gain any more of a foothold here in the Midlands."

Cara rolled her eyes. "The spirits save us from a man with a just cause. It is not up to you to lead them."

"If I don't, then in the end everyone will live under one rule: the Order's," Richard said. "All people will be their chattel, for all time; tyrants don't tire of tyranny."

The room rang with silence. Richard thumped his head against the chair back. He was so tired he didn't think he could keep his eyes open much longer. He didn't know why he was bothering to try to convince them; they didn't seem to understand, or care about, what it was he was trying to do.

Cara leaned against the desk and wiped a hand across her face. "We don't want to lose you, Lord Rahl. We don't want to go back to the way things were." She sounded on the verge of tears. "We like being able to do simple things, like make a joke, and laugh. We could never do such things before. We always lived in fear that if we said the wrong thing we would be beaten, or worse. Now that we have seen another way, we don't want to go back to that. If you throw your life away for the Midlands, then we will."

"Cara . . . all of you . . . listen to me. If I don't do this, then in the end that's what will happen. Can't you see that? If I don't unite the lands under a strong rule, under a just law and leadership, then the Order will take everything, one chunk at a time. If the Midlands fall under their shadow, then that shadow will steal across D'Hara, too, and in the end all the world will fall into darkness. I don't do this because I want to, but because I can see that I have a chance to accomplish the task. If I don't try, there will be no place for me to hide; they will find me, and kill me.

"I don't want to conquer and rule people; I just want to live a quiet life. I want to have a family and live in peace.

"That's why I must show the lands of the Midlands that we're strong and will sanction no favoritism or bickering, that we're not going to be lands in an alliance, standing as one only when it's expedient, but that we truly are one. They must be confident we will stand for what's right so that they'll feel secure joining us, so they will know that there's a place for them with us, and so that they'll be heartened by knowing that they will not have to fight alone if they wish to fight for freedom. We must be a powerful force they will trust in. Trust in enough to join."

The room fell into an icy silence. Richard closed his eyes as he laid his head back against the chair. They thought him mad. It was no use. He was simply going to have to order them to do the things he needed, and stop worrying about if they liked it or not, much less cared.

Cara finally spoke. "Lord Rahl." He opened his eyes to see her standing with her arms folded and a grim expression on her face. "I will not change your child's swaddling clothes, nor bathe it, nor burp it, nor make foolish sounds to it."

Richard closed his eyes and laid his head back against the chair again as he chuckled to himself. He remembered the time when he was back home, before all this started, and the midwife had come in a lather for Zedd. Elayne Seaton, a young woman not a whole lot older than Richard, was having her first child, and it was not going well. The midwife had spoken in hushed tones as she turned her broad back to Richard and leaned toward Zedd.

Before Richard knew Zedd was his grandfather, he only knew him as his best friend. At the time Richard hadn't known Zedd was a wizard, nor did anyone else; everyone simply knew him as old Zedd, the cloud reader, a man of considerable knowledge about the most ordinary and the most peculiar of things—about rare herbs and human ailments, about healing and where rain clouds had traveled from, about where to dig a well and when to start digging a grave—and he knew about childbirth.

Richard knew Elayne. She taught him to dance so that he might ask a girl at the midsummer festival for a turn. Richard had wanted to learn, until faced with the prospect of actually holding a woman in his arms; he was afraid he might break her or something, he wasn't sure what, but everyone always told him he was strong and had to take care not to hurt people. When he changed his mind and tried to beg off, Elayne laughed and swept him up in her arms and started twirling him about while humming a merry tune.

Richard didn't know much about the business of birthing babies, but from what he had heard he had no desire to go anywhere near Elayne's house while it was going on. He headed for the door, intending on a walk in the opposite direction from trouble.

Zedd snatched up his bag of herbs and potions, grabbed Richard's sleeve, and said, "Come with me, my boy. I may need you." Richard insisted he could be of no help, but when Zedd had his mind set on something he could make stone seem malleable by comparison. As Zedd shoved him out the door, he said, "You never know, Richard, you might even learn something."

Elayne's husband, Henry, was off with a crew cutting ice for the inns and, because of the weather, hadn't returned yet from his deliveries to nearby towns. There were several women in the house, but they were all in with Elayne. Zedd told Richard to make himself busy tending the fire and heating some water, and that he was likely to be a while.

Richard sat in the cold kitchen, sweat running down his scalp, while he listened to the most horrifying screams he had ever heard. There were muffled words of comfort from the midwife and the other women, but mostly there were the screams. He stoked the fire, melting snow in a big kettle to give himself an excuse to go outside. He told himself that Elayne and Henry might need more wood, what with a new baby and all, so he cut and chopped a good-sized pile. It did no good; he could still hear Elayne's screams. It wasn't the way they put voice to pain, but the way they were seared with panic that made Richard's heart hammer.

Richard knew Elayne was going to die. A midwife wouldn't have come for Zedd unless there was serious trouble. Richard had never seen a dead person; he didn't want the first to be Elayne. He remembered her laughter when she had taught him to dance. His face had been red the whole time, but she pretended not to notice.

And then, while he sat at the table, staring off, thinking the world was a very terrible place indeed, there was a last scream, more agonizing than the rest, that sent a shiver down his spine. It died out in forlorn misery. He squeezed his eyes shut, in the dragging silence, damming in the tears.

Digging a grave in the frozen ground was going to be near to impossible, but he promised himself that he would do it for Elayne. He didn't want them to keep her frozen body in the undertakers' shed until spring. He was strong. He would do it if it took him a month. She had taught him to dance.

The door to the bedroom squeaked opened, and Zedd shuffled out carrying something. "Richard, come here." He handed over a gory mess with tiny arms and legs. "Wash him gently."

"What? How do I do that?" Richard stammered.

"In warm water!" Zedd bellowed. "Bags, my boy, you did heat water, didn't you?" Richard pointed with his chin. "Not too hot, now. Just lukewarm. Then swaddle him in those blankets and bring him back into the bedroom."

"But Zedd . . . the women. They should do it. Not me! Dear spirits, can't the women do it?"

Zedd, his white hair in disarray, peered at him with one eye. "If I wanted the women to do it, my boy, I wouldn't have asked you, now would I?"

In a flurry of robes, he was off. The door to the bedroom banged closed. Richard was afraid to move for fear he would crush the little thing. It was so tiny he could hardly believe it was real. And then something happened—Richard began to grin. This was a person, a spirit, new to the world. He was beholding magic.

When he took the bathed and blanketed marvel into the bedroom, he was moved to tears to see that Elayne was very much alive. His trembling legs were hardly able to hold him.

"Elayne, you sure can dance" was the only thing he could think to say. "How did you manage to do such a wondrous thing?" The women around the bed stared at him as if he were daft.

Elayne smiled through her exhaustion. "Someday you can teach Bradley to dance, bright eyes." She held her hands out. Her grin grew as Richard gently put her child into her arms.

"Well, my boy, seems you figured it out after all." Zedd lifted an eyebrow. "Learn anything?"

Bradley must be ten by now, and called him Uncle Richard.

As he listened to the quiet, returning from the memories, Richard thought about what Cara had said.

"Yes, you will," he told her at last in a gentle tone. "Even if I have to command it, you will. I want you to feel the wonder of a new life, a new spirit, in your arms, so that you can feel magic other than that Agiel at your wrist. You will bathe him, and swaddle him, and burp him, so that you will know your tender care is needed in this world, and that I would trust my own child in that care. You will make foolish sounds to him, so that you can laugh with joy at the hope for the future, and perhaps forget that you have killed people in the past.

"If you can understand none of the rest, I hope you can understand at least this much of my reasons for what I must do."

He relaxed back in the chair, letting his muscles slacken for the first time in hours. The hush seemed to hum around him. He thought about Kahlan, and let his mind drift.

Cara whispered through tight lips and tears: a soft sound almost lost in the huge room and its tomblike silence, "If you get yourself killed trying to rule the world, I will personally break every bone in your body."

Richard felt his cheeks tighten with a smile. The darkness behind his eyelids swirled with dark plumes of color.

He was acutely aware of the chair around him: the Mother Confessor's chair, Kahlan's chair. From it she had ruled the Midlands alliance. He could feel the eyes of the first Mother Confessor and her wizard glaring down at him as he sat in the hallowed place after having demanded the surrender of the Midlands and the end of an alliance that they had forged to be the foundation for an everlasting peace.

He had came into this war fighting for the cause of the Midlands. He now commanded his former enemy, and had placed his sword at the throats of his allies.

In one day, he had turned the world upside down.

Richard knew he was breaking the alliance for the right reasons, but he agonized about what Kahlan was going to think. She loved him, and would understand, he told himself. She had to.

Dear spirits, what was Zedd going to think?

His arms rested heavily where Kahlan's had. He imagined her arms around him, now, as they had been the night before in that place between worlds. He didn't think he had ever been that happy in his whole life, or felt so loved.

He thought he could hear someone telling him he should find a bed, but he was already asleep.

CHAPTER 17

DESPITE RETURNING TO FIND several thousand brutish D'Haran troops surrounding his palace, Tobias was in a good mood. Things were turning out splendidly—not the way he had originally planned that morning, but splendidly nonetheless. The D'Harans made no effort to hinder his entrance, but warned him that he had better not come out again that night.

Their effrontery was galling, but he was more interested in the old woman Ettore was preparing than in the D'Harans' lack of protocol. He had questions and was impatient for the answers. She would be ready to give them by now; Ettore was well practiced at his craft. Even though this was the first time he had been trusted to handle the preparations for a questioning without a more experienced brother overseeing his hand, that hand had already proven to be talented and steady at the task. Ettore was more than ready for the responsibility.

Tobias shook the snow from his cape onto the ruby and gold carpet, not bothering to clean his boots before he marched across the spotless anteroom toward the corridors leading to the stairs. The wide halls were lit by cut-glass lamps hung before polished silver reflectors that sent wavering rays of light dancing over the gilt woodwork. Crimson-caped guards patrolling the palace touched fingertips to their foreheads as they bowed. Tobias didn't trouble himself with returning the salutes.

With Galtero and Lunetta right behind, he took the steps two at a time. While the walls on the main level were trimmed with ornate paneling adorned with portraits of Nicobarese royalty and decorated tapestries depicting their fabled, largely fictitious exploits, the walls on the lower level were simple stone block, cold to the eye as well as the touch. The room he was headed for, though, would be warm.

As he knuckled his mustache, he winced at the ache in his bones. The cold seemed to make his joints ache more of late. He admonished himself to be more concerned with the Creator's work and less with such mundane matters. The Creator had blessed him with more than a good amount of help this night; it must not be wasted.

On the upper levels the halls had been well guarded by the men of the fist, but downstairs the drab corridors were empty; there was no way into or out of the palace from the lower levels. Galtero, ever watchful, eyed the length of the hall outside the door to the questioning room. Lunetta waited patiently with a smile. Tobias had told her she had done well, especially with the last spell, and she was a glowing reflection of his good graces.

Tobias stepped into the room and came face-to-face with Ettore's familiar, wide grin.

The eyes, however, were filmed with death.

Tobias froze.

Ettore was hanging by a cord tied to either end of an iron pin driven through his ears. His feet dangled just clear of a dark, coagulated puddle.

There was a neat slice from a razor all the way around the middle of his neck. Below that, every inch of him had been skinned. Pale strips of it lay to the side in an oozing heap.

An incision just below the rib cage gaped open. On the floor in front of his gently swinging body lay his liver.

It had a few bites out of each side. The bites on one side were edged with irregular tears left by larger teeth; on the other side were those of small, orderly teeth.

Brogan spun with a wail of rage and backhanded Lunetta with his fist. She crashed to the wall beside the fireplace and slid to the floor.

"This be your fault, *streganicha*! This be your fault! You should have stayed here and attended Ettore!"

Brogan stood, fists at his side, glaring at the skinned body of one of his Blood of the Fold. If Ettore wasn't dead, Brogan would have killed him himself, with his bare hands if need be, for letting that old hag escape justice. To let a baneling escape was inexcusable. A true baneling hunter would kill the evil one before he died, no matter what it took. Ettore's mocking grin incensed him.

Brogan struck the cold face. "You have failed us, Ettore. You are discharged with dishonor from the Fold. Your name will be expunged from the roster."

Lunetta cowered against the wall, holding her bloody cheek. "I told you that I should stay and attend him. I told you."

Brogan glowered down at her. "Don't give me your filthy excuses, *streganicha*. If you knew how much trouble the old hag was going to be, then you should have stayed."

"But I told you I should." She wiped tears from her eyes. "You made me come with you."

He ignored her and turned to his colonel. "Get the horses," he hissed through gritted teeth.

He should kill her. Right now. He should slit her throat and be done with it. He was sick of her vile taint. This night it had cost him valuable information. The old woman, he was now sure, would have been a trove of information. If not for his loathsome sister, he would have had it.

"How many horses, Lord General?" Galtero whispered.

Brogan watched his sister staggering to her feet, regaining her composure as she cleaned blood from her cheek. He should kill her. This very moment.

"Three," Brogan growled.

Galtero extracted a cudgel from the interrogation tools before he glided through the door, silent as a shadow, and vanished down the hall. The guards obviously hadn't seen her, although with banelings that didn't necessarily mean anything, but it was always possible the old woman could still be around. Galtero didn't need to be told that if she were found she was to be taken alive.

Impetuous vengeance with a sword would gain no benefit. If she were found, she would be taken alive, and questioned. If she were found, she would pay the price of her profanity, but she would tell all she knew, first.

If she were found. He looked to his sister. "Do you sense her anywhere near?"

Lunetta shook her head. She wasn't scratching her arms. Even if there weren't a couple thousand D'Haran troops around the palace, with the storm raging as it was it would be impossible to track anyone. Besides, as much as he wanted the old woman, Brogan had a quarry of greater profanity to go after. And then there was the matter of Lord Rahl. If Galtero found the old woman, fine, but if not, they couldn't spare the time for a difficult, and most likely fruitless, hunt. Banelings were hardly a rarity; there would always be another. The lord general of the Blood of the Fold had more important work to see to: the Creator's work.

Lunetta hobbled to Brogan's side and slipped an arm around his waist. She stroked his heaving chest.

"It be late, Tobias," she cooed intimately. "Come to bed. You have had a hard day doing the Creator's work. Let Lunetta make you feel better. You will be pleased, I promise." He said nothing. "Galtero had his pleasure, let Lunetta give you yours. I will do a glamour for you," she offered. "Please, Tobias?"

He considered it only a moment. "There be no time. We must leave at once. I hope you have learned a lesson this night, Lunetta. I won't tolerate your misbehaving again."

Her head bobbed. "Yes, my lord general. I will try to do better. I will do better. You will see."

He led her up out of the lower levels to the room where he had talked to the witnesses. Guards stood before the door. Inside, from the long table, he picked up his trophy case and strapped it to his belt. He started for the door, but turned back. The silver coin he had left on the table, the one the old woman had given him, was gone. He looked to a guard.

"I don't suppose anyone came in here tonight, after I left?"

"No, Lord General," the stiff guard replied. "Not a soul."

Brogan grunted to himself. She had been here. She had taken back her coin so as to leave him a message. On his way out he didn't bother to question any of the other guards; they, too, would have seen nothing. The old woman and her little familiar were gone. He put them from his mind and focused on the things that needed doing.

Brogan wound his way through the corridors to the rear of the palace, where it was a short crossing of open ground to the stables. Galtero would know to gather the things they needed for a journey, and would have three of the strongest horses saddled. There were sure to be D'Harans all around the palace, but with the darkness and wind-driven snow, he was sure it would be possible for him and Lunetta to make it to the stables.

Brogan said nothing to the men; if he was to go after the Mother Confessor, it could only be the three of them. With the storm, three might be able to slip away, but the whole fist would not. That many men would surely be seen and confronted, there would be a battle, and they would probably all be killed. The Blood of the Fold were fierce fighters, but they were no match for the D'Harans' numbers. Worse, from what he had seen the D'Harans were no strangers to battle. Better to simply leave the men here as a diversion. They couldn't betray what they didn't know.

Brogan cracked open the thick oak door and peered out into the night. He saw only swirling snow lit by the dim light coming from a few of the second-floor rear windows. He would have extinguished the lamps, but he needed the little light they provided in order to find the unfamiliar stables in the storm.

"Stay close to me. If we're confronted by soldiers they will try to prevent us from leaving. We can't allow that. We must be off after the Mother Confessor."

"But, Lord General—"

"Be quiet," Brogan snapped. "If they try to stop us, you had better get us through. Understand?"

"If there be many, I can only—"

“Don’t test me, Lunetta. You said you would do better. I’m giving you that chance. Don’t fail me again.”

She pulled her pretties close. “Yes, Lord General.”

Brogan blew out the lamp just inside the hall and then pulled Lunetta through the doorway out into the blizzard, wading with her into the drifts. Galtero would have the horses saddled by now. They had only to make it to the horses. In this snow, the D’Harans wouldn’t have time to see them coming or to stop them once they were on horseback. The dark rise of the stable buildings drew closer.

Out of the snow, shapes began appearing—soldiers. When they saw him they called out to their fellows and at the same time drew steel. Their voices didn’t carry far in the howling wind, but they carried enough to collect a swarm of big men.

They were all around. “Lunetta, do something.”

She cocked an arm with fingers clawed as she began summoning a spell, but the men didn’t hesitate. They ran forward with weapons raised. He flinched as an arrow zipped past his cheek. The Creator had provided a gust of wind that carried the shaft wide, sparing him. Lunetta ducked as arrows ripped past.

Seeing men rushing toward him from all directions, Tobias drew his sword. He thought to make it back to the palace, but that way, too, was blocked. There were too many. Lunetta was so busy trying to ward off the arrows that she couldn’t call a spell to protect them. She squealed in fright.

Just as suddenly as the arrows had started, they stopped. Tobias heard screams carried on the wind. He snatched Lunetta’s arm and sprang through the deep drifts, hoping to make the stables. Galtero would be there.

Several men moved to block him. The one closest cried out as a shadow passed in front of him. The man tumbled face-first into the snow. Tobias watched in confusion as the other men began swinging swords at the gusts of wind.

The wind cut them down without mercy.

Tobias stumbled to a halt, blinking at what he was seeing. D’Harans all around him were dropping. Shrieks lifted on the howling wind. He saw snow stained red. He saw men fall in their tracks, spilling their guts.

Tobias licked his lips, afraid to move lest the wind take him, too. His gaze darted in every direction as he tried to make sense of what was happening, tried to see the attackers.

"Dear Creator," he called out, "spare me! I do your work!"

Men were converging on the stable yard from every direction, and they were being brought down as fast as they came. Well over a hundred corpses already littered the snowy field. He had never seen men slain with such speed or brutality.

Tobias crouched down, and was startled to realize that the twirling gusts were moving deliberately.

They were alive. He began to make them out. White-caped men slipped all around him, attacking the D'Haran soldiers with swift and deadly grace. Not one of the D'Harans tried to flee; they all came on fiercely, but none managed to engage the enemy before they were quickly dispatched.

The night fell silent but for the wind. Before there was time to run, it was over. The ground was cluttered with a jumble of still, dark shapes. Tobias turned all about, but saw none left alive. Already, the snow was beginning to drift over the bodies. In another hour they would vanish under the white fury.

The caped men skimmed fluidly through the snow, graceful and slithery, moving as if they were made of wind. As they came toward him, his sword slipped from his numb fingers. Tobias wanted to call out to Lunetta to strike them down with a spell, but as they came into the light, his voice failed him.

They were not men.

Scales the color of the snowy night undulated over rippling muscles. Smooth skin sheathed earless, hairless, blunt heads set with beady eyes. The beasts wore only simple hide clothes beneath capes that billowed and flapped in the wind, and in each clawed hand they gripped blood-slicked three-bladed knives.

They were the creatures he had seen impaled on the poles outside the Confessors' Palace—the creatures Lord Rahl had killed: mriswith. Having seen them slaughter all these experienced soldiers, Tobias couldn't imagine how Lord Rahl, or anyone, could have bested one, much less the number he had seen.

One of the creatures skulked toward him, watching with unblinking eyes. It glided to a stop, not ten feet away.

"Leave," the mriswith hissed.

"What?" Tobias stammered.

"Leave." It slashed the air with its clawlike knife, a quick gesture, graceful with murderous mastery. "Esssscape."

"Why? Why would you do this? Why do you want us to escape?"

The lipless mouth slit widened, mimicking a gruesome grin. "The dreamssss walker wants you to esssscape. Go now, before more skin walkerssss come. Go."

"But . . ."

With a scaled arm, the mriswith drew its cape against the wind, turned, and vanished into the blowing snow. Tobias peered into the night, but the wind had gone vacant and lifeless.

Why would such vile creatures want to help him? Why would they kill his enemies? Why would they want him to escape?

Comprehension came over him in a loving, warm rush. The Creator had sent them. Of course. How could he have been so blind? Lord Rahl had said he killed the mriswith. Lord Rahl fought for the Keeper. If the mriswith were evil creatures Lord Rahl would fight on their side, not against them.

The mriswith had said the dream walker sent them. The Creator came to Tobias in his dreams. That had to be it; the Creator had sent them.

"Lunetta." Tobias turned to her. She was cowering behind him. "The Creator comes to me in my dreams. That was what they were trying to tell me when they said the one from my dreams had sent them. Lunetta, the Creator sent them to help protect me."

Lunetta's eyes widened. "The Creator Himself has intervened on your behalf to thwart the Keeper's plans. The Creator Himself watches over you. He must have great things planned for you, Tobias."

Tobias retrieved his sword from under the snow and straightened with a smile. "Indeed. I have kept His wishes above all else, and so He has protected me. Hurry, we must do as His messengers have told us. We must be off to do the Creator's work."

As he trudged through the snow, winding his way among the bodies, he looked up to see a dark shape suddenly leap before him, blocking his path.

"Well, well, Lord General, going someplace?" A menacing grin came to the face. "Do you wish to cast a spell on me, sorceress?"

Tobias still had his sword in his hand, but he knew he wouldn't be quick enough.

He flinched at the sound of a bone-jarring thunk. The one before him pitched face-first into the snow at his feet. Tobias looked up to see Galtero standing with the cudgel above the unconscious figure.

"Galtero, you have earned your rank this night."

The Creator had just given him a priceless prize, showing him, again, that nothing was out of the reach of the pious. Thankfully, Galtero had the presence of mind to use the cudgel, and not a blade.

He saw blood from the blow, but he saw the breath of life, too. "My, my, but this be turning out to be quite the good night. Lunetta, you have some work to do on behalf of the Creator before you heal this one."

Lunetta bent beside the still form, pressing her fingers into the blood-matted, wavy, brown hair. "Perhaps I ought to do a healing first. Galtero be stronger than he thinks."

"That, my dear sister, would not be advisable, at least not from what I have heard. The healing can wait." He glanced to his colonel and gestured to the stables. "Are the horses ready?"

"Yes, Lord General, as soon as you are."

Tobias drew the knife Galtero had given him. "We must hurry, Lunetta. The messenger told us we must escape." He squatted down and rolled the unconscious figure over. "And then we be off after the Mother Confessor."

Lunetta leaned close, peering at him. "But Lord General, I told you, the wizard's web hides her identity from us. We cannot see the strands of a web like that. We will not know her."

A grin tightened the scar at the side of Tobias Brogan's mouth.

"Oh, but I have seen the strands of the web. The Mother Confessor's name be Kahlan Amnell."

CHAPTER 18

AS SHE HAD FEARED, she was a prisoner. She flipped another page over after making the appropriate entry in the ledger book. A prisoner of the highest station, a prisoner behind a paper lock, but a prisoner nevertheless.

Verna yawned as she scanned the next page, checking the records of palace expenses. Each report required her approval and had to be initialed to show that the Prelate herself had certified the expenses. Why it was necessary was a mystery to her, but having only held the office for a few days she was loath to declare it a waste of her time, only to have Sister Leoma, or Dulcinia, or Philippa divert their eyes and explain under their breath, so as not to cause the Prelate embarrassment, why it was indeed necessary, and go on in great detail to explicate the dire consequences of not doing such a simple thing that would require hardly any effort on her part, but would be of such benefit to others.

She could anticipate the reaction should she declare she was not going to bother to check the tallies: *Why, Prelate, if the people didn't fear that the Prelate herself was concerned enough to be watching their work orders, they would be emboldened to gouge the palace. The Sisters would be thought wasteful fools without an ounce of sense. And then, on the other side, if the work orders weren't paid while waiting the Prelate's directive, the poor workers' families would go hungry. You wouldn't want those children to go hungry, would you, simply because you didn't want to pay them the courtesy of approving payment for their hard work already done? Just because you don't wish to glance at the report and go to the trouble of initialing it? Would you really want them to think the Prelate so callous?*

Verna sighed as she skimmed the report of expenses for the stables: hay and grain, the farrier, the tack upkeep, replacement of lost tack, repair to the stable after a stallion staved in a stall, and repair needed after several horses apparently panicked in the night, broke down a fence, and bolted off into the countryside. She was going to have to have a talk to the stable personnel and insist they keep better order under their roof. She jammed the pen in the ink bottle, sighed again, and initialed the bottom of the page.

As she turned the stable tallies over on top of the pile of other tallies she had already perused, initialed, and entered in the ledger, someone knocked softly at the door. She pulled another paper from the stack of reports yet to be worked, a lengthy reckoning from the butcher, and started scanning down the figures. She had had no idea how expensive it was to run the Palace of the Prophets.

The soft knock came again. Probably Sister Dulcinia or Phoebe wanting to bring in another stack of reports. She was not initialing as fast as they could bring them in. How did Prelate Annalina manage to get it all done? Verna hoped it wasn't Sister Leoma, come again to bring to her attention news of some calamity the Prelate had caused by an unthinking action or comment. Maybe they would think her too busy and go away if she didn't answer.

Along with her old friend, Phoebe, Verna had named Sister Dulcinia to be one of her administrators. It only made sense to have a Sister of Dulcinia's experience at hand. It also allowed Verna to keep an eye on the woman. Dulcinia herself had requested the job, citing her "knowledge of palace business."

Having Sister Leoma and Philippa as "trusted advisors" was at least useful in keeping them in sight, too. She didn't trust them. For that matter, she didn't trust any of them; she couldn't afford to. Verna had to admit, though, that they had proven themselves willing advisors who always scrupulously kept the best interest of the Prelate and the palace uppermost in their advice. It vexed her that she could find no fault in their counsel.

The knock came again, polite, but insistent.

"Yes! What is it?"

The thick door opened enough to admit Warren's head of curly blond hair. He grinned when he saw the scowl on her face. Verna could see Dulcinia craning her neck to see past him, checking the Prelate's progress on the stacks of paper. Warren let himself the rest of the way in.

He peered about in the somber room, scrutinizing the work done on it. After the losing battle her predecessor had had with the Sisters of the Dark, the office had been left in ruins. A crew of workmen had hurriedly repaired it, putting it back to order as quickly as possible so that the new Prelate wouldn't be inconvenienced for long. Verna knew the cost; she had seen the expense tally.

Warren strolled up to the opposite side of the heavy walnut table. "Good evening, Verna. You look to be hard at work. Important palace business, I presume, to be up this late."

Her lips pressed into a thin line. Before she was able to launch into a tirade, Dulcinia took the opportunity, before closing the door behind the visitor, to poke her head in.

"I've just finished ordering the day's reports, Prelate. Would you like to have them now? You must be near to finished with the others."

Verna flashed a villainous grin as she crooked her finger at her aide. Sister Dulcinia flinched at the smirk. Her penetrating blue eyes swept the room, lingering on Warren, before she entered, brushing back her gray hair in a submissive gesture.

"May I be of assistance, Prelate?"

Verna folded her hands on the table. "Why, yes, Sister, you may. Your experience would be valuable in this matter." Verna lifted a report off the pile. "I would like you to immediately go on a mission to the stables. It seems we have trouble there, and a bit of a mystery."

Sister Dulcinia brightened. "Trouble, Prelate?"

"Yes. It would seem there are some horses missing."

Sister Dulcinia leaned forward a bit, lowering her voice in that tolerant manner of hers. "If I remember the report you speak of, Prelate, the horses were frightened by something in the night and bolted. They've simply not turned up yet, that's all."

"I know that, Sister. I would like Master Finch to explain how it is that horses that broke down his fence were able to run off, and not be found."

"Prelate?"

Verna lifted her eyebrows in mock wonder. "We live on an island, do we not? How is it that the horses are no longer on the island? No guard saw them gallop across a bridge. At least I've seen no report of it. This time of year the fishermen are out on the river day and night, eeling, yet none saw any horses swimming to the mainland. So where are they?"

"Well, I'm sure they simply bolted, Prelate. Perhaps . . ."

Verna smiled indulgently. "Perhaps Master Finch sold them, and just said they ran off in order to cover their loss."

Sister Dulcinia straightened. "Surely, Prelate, you would not want to accuse—"

Verna slapped a hand to the table and shot to her feet. "Tack is also missing. Did the tack also bolt in the night! Or did the horses decide to put it on themselves and go for a jaunt!"

Sister Dulcinia blanched. "I . . . well, I . . . I'll see—"

"You go down to the stables right now and tell Master Finch that if he doesn't find the palace's horses by the time I decide to inquire of the matter again, their cost will come out of his pay and the tack out of his hide!"

Sister Dulcinia bobbed a quick bow and scurried from the room. When the door banged closed, Warren chuckled.

"Seems you're falling right into the job, Verna."

"Don't you start with me, Warren!"

The grin left his face. "Verna, calm down. It's just a couple of horses. The man will find them. It's not worth you getting yourself in a state of tears over."

Verna blinked at him. She touched her fingers to her cheek and felt that they were indeed wet. She let out a tired groan and flopped down in her chair.

"I'm sorry, Warren. I don't know what's come over me. I guess I'm just tired and frustrated."

"Verna, I've never seen you like this, letting a matter like some silly pieces of paper get you so worked up."

"Warren, look at this!" She snatched up the report. "I'm a prisoner in here, approving the cost of hauling away manure! Do you have any idea how much manure those horses produce? Or how much food they eat, just to make all that manure?"

"Well, no, I guess I would have to admit that . . ."

She pulled the next report off the stack. "Butter—"

"Butter?"

"Yes, butter." Verna scanned the report. "Seems it went rancid and we had to buy ten peck to replace it. I'm to consider this and determine if the dairyman has asked a fair price and is to be retained in the future."

"It must be important to have these matters checked."

Verna picked up the next paper. "Masons. Masons to fix the roof over the dining hall that leaks. And slate. A lightning bolt broke the slate, they say, and near to a square had to be torn off and replaced. Took ten men two weeks, it says here. I'm to decide if that was timely, and approve payment."

"Well, if people do work, they've a right to be paid, haven't they?"

She rubbed a finger on the gold, sunburst-patterned ring. "I thought that if I ever had the power, there would be changes in the way the Sisters do the Creator's work. But this is all I do, Warren: look at reports. I've been in here day and night reading the most mundane of things until my eyes glaze over."

"It must be important, Verna."

"Important?" She selected another report with exaggerated reverence. "Let's see . . . seems two of our 'young men' got drunk and set fire to an inn . . . the fire was put out . . . the inn sustained quite a bit of damage . . . they would like the palace to reimburse them." She set the report aside. "I'm going to have a long, loud talk with those two."

"Seems the right decision, Verna."

She selected another report. "And what have we here? A seamstress accounting. Dressmaking for the novices." Verna picked up another. "Salt. Three kinds."

"But Verna—"

She plucked another. "And this one?" She waved the paper with mock solemnity. "Grave digging."

"What?"

"Two gravediggers. They want to be paid for their work." She scanned the tally. "And I might add that they think highly of their skill, by the price they're asking."

"Look, Verna, I think you've been cooped up in here too long and need a little fresh air. Why don't we go for a walk."

"A walk? Warren, I don't have time—"

"Prelate, you've been sitting in here too long. You need a little activity." He canted his head while rolling his eyes in an exaggerated gesture toward the door. "How about it?"

Verna glanced toward the door. If Sister Dulcinia did as she was told, then only Sister Phoebe would be in the outer office. Phoebe was her friend. She reminded herself that she could trust no one.

"Well . . . yes, I guess I would like a bit of a walk."

Warren marched around the desk and lifted her by the arm. "Oh, good, then. Shall we go?"

Verna pulled her arm away from his grip and shot him a murderous glare. She gritted her teeth as she spoke in a singsong voice. "Why yes, why don't we."

At the sound of the door, Sister Phoebe hastily stood to bow. "Prelate . . . do you need something? Perhaps a bit of soup? Some tea?"

"Phoebe, I've told you a dozen times now that you don't need to bow every time you lay eyes on me."

Phoebe bowed again. "Yes, Prelate." Her round face flushed red. "I mean . . . I'm sorry, Prelate. Forgive me."

Verna gathered her patience with a sigh. "Sister Phoebe, we've known each other since we were novices. How many times were we sent to the kitchens together to scrub pots for . . . ?" Verna glanced to Warren. "Well, I can't remember for what, but the point is that we're old friends. Please try to remember that?"

Phoebe's cheeks plumped with a smile. "Of course . . . Verna." She winced at calling the Prelate "Verna" even if it was under order.

Out in the hall Warren asked why they were sent to scrub pots.

"I said I don't remember," she snapped as she glanced back down the empty hall. "What's this about?"

Warren shrugged. "Just a walk." He checked the hall himself, and then flashed her another meaningful look. "I thought that maybe the Prelate would like to visit Sister Simona."

Verna missed a step. Sister Simona had been in a deranged state for weeks—something about dreams—and had been kept in a shielded room so she couldn't hurt herself, or some innocent.

Warren leaned close and whispered. "I went to visit her earlier."

"Why?"

Warren jabbed his finger up and down, pointing at the floor. The vaults. He meant the vaults. She frowned at him.

"And how was poor Simona?"

Warren checked the corridor to the right and left when they reached an intersection, then looked behind again. "They wouldn't let me see her," he whispered.

Outside, the rain roared in a downpour. Verna pulled her shawl over her head and dove into the deluge, dancing over puddles, trying to tiptoe across the steppingstones set in the soggy grass. Yellow light from windows flickered in the pools of standing water. The guards at the gates to the Prelate's compound bowed as she and Warren trotted by, making for a covered walkway.

Inside, under the low roof, she shook the water from her shawl and draped it across her shoulders as the two of them caught their breath. Warren shook rain from his robes. The walkway's arched sides were protected only by open lattice thick with vines, but the rain wasn't driven by wind, so it was dry enough. She peered into the darkness, but couldn't see anyone. It was quite a ways to the next building: the squat infirmary.

Verna slumped down on a stone bench. Warren had been ready to be off, but when she sat, he did, too. It was cold and the heat of him right next to her felt good. The pungent smell of rain and wet dirt was refreshing after being inside for so long. Verna was not used to being inside so much. She liked the out-of-doors, thought the ground made a fine bed, the trees and fields a fine office, but that part of her life was over now. There was a garden just outside the Prelate's office, but she hadn't had time to put her head out to see it.

In the distance, the incessant drums thundered on, like the heartbeat of doom.

"I used my Han," he said at last. "I don't feel the presence of anyone else near."

"And you can feel the presence of one with Subtractive Magic, yes?" she whispered.

He glanced up in the dark. "I never thought of that."

"What's this about, Warren?"

"Do you think we're alone?"

"How should I know?" she snapped.

He looked around again and swallowed. "Well, I've been doing a lot of reading lately." He pointed again toward the vaults. "I just thought we should go see Sister Simona."

"You already said that. You still haven't told me why."

"Some of the things I've been reading have been about dreams," he said cryptically.

She tried to gaze into his eyes, but she could only see the dark shape of him. "Simona has been having dreams."

His thigh was pressed against hers. He was shaking with the cold. At least she thought it was the cold. Before she realized what she was doing, she had put her arm around him and pulled his head to her shoulder.

"Verna," he stammered, "I feel so alone. I'm afraid to talk to anyone. I feel like everyone's watching me. I'm afraid everyone is going to ask me what I'm studying, and why, and under whose orders. I've only seen you once in three days, and there's no one else I can talk to."

She patted his back. "I know, Warren. I've wanted to talk to you, too, but I've been so busy. There's so much work to do."

"Maybe they're giving you work to keep you occupied and out of their hair while they go about . . . business."

Verna shook her head in the murk. "Maybe. I'm afraid, too, Warren. I don't know how to be Prelate. I'm afraid I'll bring the Palace of the Prophets to ruin if I don't do the things that need to be done. I'm afraid to say no to Leoma, Philippa, Dulcinia, and Maren. They're trying to advise me in how to be Prelate, and if they really are on our side, then their advice is true. If I don't take it, I could be making a big mistake. If the Prelate makes a mistake everyone pays for it. If they aren't on our side, well, the things they ask me to do don't seem as if they could cause any harm. How much ruin can reading reports cause?"

"Unless it's to keep you distracted from something important."

She stroked his back again before pushing away. "I know. I'll try to go for more 'walks' with you. I think the fresh air is doing me good."

Warren squeezed her hand. "I'm glad, Verna." He stood and straightened his dark robes. "Let's go see how Simona is faring."

The infirmary was one of the smaller buildings on Halsband

Island. The Sisters could heal many common injuries with the aid of their Han, and illnesses beyond the power of their gift usually ended all too quickly in death, so mostly the infirmary housed a few elderly and feeble of the staff who had spent their lives in their work at the Palace of the Prophets, and now had no one to care for them. It also was where the insane were confined. The gift was of limited use for sickness of the mind.

Near the door, Verna sent her Han into a lamp and carried it with her as they moved through the simple painted corridors toward where Warren said Simona was confined. Only a few of the rooms were occupied, their residents sending snores, wheezes, and coughs echoing through the dim halls.

When they reached the end of the corridor that housed the old and feeble, they had to pass through a series of three flimsy doors, each shielded with powerful webs of varied composition. Shields, however, might be broken by those with the gift, even the insane. The fourth door was iron, with a massive bolt protected by an intricate shield designed to deflect attempts to open it from the other side with the use of magic; the more force applied, the tighter the bolt held. It had been set in place by three Sisters, and so could not be broken by one on the other side.

Two guards came to attention when she and Warren rounded the corner. They bowed their heads, but didn't move away from the door. Warren greeted them pleasantly and motioned with a flit of his hand for them to lift the bolt.

"Sorry, son, but no one is allowed in."

Her fiery eyes fixed on the guard, Verna pushed Warren aside. "Is that right, 'son'?" He nodded confidently. "And who gave those orders?"

"My commander, Sister. I don't know who gave the orders to him, but it had to be a Sister of some authority."

Scowling, she thrust the sunburst ring in front of his face. "More authority than this?"

His eyes widened. "No, Prelate. Of course not. Forgive me, I didn't recognize you."

"How many are behind this door?"

The bolt sent a clang echoing down the hall. "Just the one Sister, Prelate."

"Are there any Sisters attending her?"

"No. They've gone for the night."

Once on the other side and out of earshot, Warren chuckled. "I guess you've found some use for that ring, at last."

Verna slowed to a puzzled stop. "Warren, how do you suppose the ring came to be on that pedestal after the funeral?"

Warren's grin held, but barely. "Well, let's see . . ." The grin finally vanished. "I don't know. What do you think?"

She shook her head. "It had a light shield around it. Not many can spin such a web. If, as you say, Prelate Annalina trusted no one but me, then who did she trust to put the ring there, and spin such a web around it?"

"I can't imagine." Warren hiked his damp robes up on his shoulders. "Could she have spun the web herself?"

Verna lifted an eyebrow. "From her funeral pyre?"

"No, I mean could she have spun it, and then had someone else just put it there. You know, like investing a stick with a spell, so that someone else can light a lamp with it. I've seen Sisters do that so the staff can light the lamps without having to carry around a candle dripping hot wax on their fingers, or the floor."

Verna raised the lamp higher to look into his eyes. "Warren, that's brilliant."

He smiled. The smile faded. "The question remains: who?"

She lowered the lamp. "Maybe one of the staff she trusted. Someone without the gift so she wouldn't have to worry about them being . . ." She glanced back up the dark, empty hall. "You know what I mean." He nodded that he did as she started out. "I'll have to look into it."

Flashes of light were coming from under the door to Sister Simona's room: silent little flickers of lightning licking out through the gap under the door. The shield sparkled when the crackles of light managed to reach it, dissipating the power with counterforces, grounding the magic with an opposite. Sister Simona was trying to break the shield.

Since Sister Simona was deranged, that was to be expected. The question was, why wasn't it working? Verna recognized the shield around the door as a simple one used to keep young wizards confined when they were being mulish.

Verna opened herself to her Han and stepped through the shield. Warren followed as she knocked. The flickers of light coming from under the door cut off.

"Simona? It's Verna Sauventreen. You remember me, don't you, dear? May I come in?"

No answer came, so Verna turned the knob and eased the door open. She held the lamp out before herself, sending its yellowy glimmers ahead to break the darkness within. The room was empty but for a tray with a pitcher, bread, and fruit, a pallet, a chamber pot, and a filthy little woman cowering in the corner.

"Leave me be, demon!" she shrieked.

"Simona, It's all right. It's only me, Verna, and my friend, Warren. Don't be afraid."

Simona blinked in the light, as if it were the sun just risen. Verna set the lamp behind, so as not to blind the woman.

Simona peered up. "Verna?"

"That's right."

Simona kissed her ring finger a dozen times, gushing thanks and blessings on the Creator. She scurried across the floor on her hands and knees to snatch up the hem of Verna's dress, kissing it, too, over and over.

"Oh, thank you for coming." She scrambled to her feet. "Hurry! We must escape!"

Verna grasped the small woman's shoulders and sat her down on her sleeping pallet. With a gentle hand she smoothed back the shock of gray hair.

Her hand froze.

Simona had a collar around her neck. That was why she wasn't able to break the shield. Verna had never seen a Sister wearing a Rada'Han. She had seen hundreds of boys and young men wearing one, but never a Sister. The sight of it turned her stomach. She had been taught that in the dim past, Rada'Han had been put around the necks of Sisters who had lost their minds. Having one with the gift afflicted with insanity was like loosing lightning in a crowded market square. They had to be controlled. But still . . .

"Simona, you are safe. You're in the palace, under the watchful eye of the Creator. No harm will come to you."

Simona broke into tears. "I must flee. Please, let me go. I must flee."

"Why must you flee, my dear?"

The woman wiped tears from the dirt on her face. "He comes."

"Who?"

"The one from my dreams. The dream walker."

"Who is this dream walker?"

Simona shrank back. "The Keeper."

Verna paused. "This dream walker is the Keeper?"

She nodded so hard Verna thought her neck might come unhinged. "Sometimes. Sometimes, he's the Creator."

Warren leaned in. "What?"

Simona flinched. "Is it you? Are you the one?"

"I'm Warren, Sister. A student, that's all."

Simona touched a finger to her cracked lips. "You should run, too, then. He comes. He wants those with the gift."

"The one in your dreams?" Verna asked. Simona nodded furiously. "What does he do in your dreams?"

"Torments me. Hurts me. He . . ." She kissed her ring finger frantically, beseeching the Creator's protection. "He tells me I must forsake my oath. He tells me to do things. He's a demon. Sometimes he pretends to be the Creator, to trick me, but I know it's him. I know. He's a demon."

Verna hugged the frightened woman. "It's just a nightmare, Simona. It's not real. Try to see that."

Simona almost shook her head right out of its skin. "No! It's a dream, but real. He comes! We must run!"

Verna smiled sympathetically. "What makes you think that?"

"Told me, he did. He comes."

"Don't you see, dear? That was just in the dream, not when you're awake. It's not real."

"The dreams are real. When I'm awake, I know, too."

"You're awake now. Do you know now, dear?" Simona nodded. "How do you know, when you're awake, if he isn't there in your head to tell you, like when you dream?"

"I can hear his alert." She looked from Verna's face to Warren's, and back again. "I'm not crazy. I'm not. Can't you hear the drums?"

"Yes, Sister, we hear the drums." Warren smiled. "But that's not your dream. It's just the drums announcing the impending arrival of the emperor."

Simona touched a finger to her lip again. "Emperor?"

"Yes," Warren comforted, "the emperor of the Old World. He's coming for a visit, that's all. That's what the drums are."

Her brow creased in worry. "Emperor?"

"Yes," Warren said. "Emperor Jagang."

With a wild shriek Simona leapt into a corner. She screamed as if she were being stabbed. Her hands flailed. Verna rushed to her, trying to catch her arms and calm her.

"Simona, you're safe with us. What is it?"

"That's him!" she screamed. "Jagang! That's the dream walker's name! Let me go! Please let me go before he comes!"

Simona tore away, careering around the room, sending flashes of lightning flicking everywhere. It raked the paint off the walls like glowing claws. Verna and Warren tried to calm her, tried to catch her, tried to stop her. When Simona could find no way from the room, she began bashing her head against the wall. Simona was a small woman, but she seemed to have the strength of ten men.

In the end, and with great reluctance, Verna was forced to use the Rada'Han to gain control.

Warren healed Simona's bleeding forehead after they had quieted her. Verna remembered a spell she had been taught to use on boys newly come to the palace, when they were having nightmares from being taken from their parents, a spell to calm fears and let the frightened child sleep a dreamless sleep. Verna clasped the Rada'Han between her hands and sent a flow of her Han into Simona. At last, her breathing slowed, she went limp, and she slept. Verna hoped it was a dreamless sleep.

Shaken, Verna leaned against the door after she closed it on the dark room. "Did you find out what you wanted to know?"

Warren swallowed. "I'm afraid so."

That wasn't the answer Verna had expected. He didn't offer anything more. "Well?"

"Well, I'm not so sure Sister Simona is insane. Not in the conventional sense, anyway." He picked at the braiding on the sleeve of his robe. "I'll need to do more reading. It could be nothing. The books are complex. I'll let you know what I find."

Verna kissed her finger, but felt the still unfamiliar touch of the Prelate's ring under her lips. "Dear Creator," she prayed aloud, "keep this foolish young man safe, for I may snatch his head bald and then strangle him with my bare hands."

Warren rolled his eyes. "Look, Verna—"

"Prelate," she corrected.

Warren sighed and at last nodded. "I guess I should tell you, but understand that this is a very old and obscure fork. The prophecies are clogged with false forks. This is doubly tainted, because of its age, and its rarity. That makes it suspect even if it weren't for the rest of it. There are crossovers and backfalls galore in tomes this old, and I can't verify them without months of work. Some of the links are occluded by triple forks. Back-tracing a triple fork squares false forks on the branches, and if any of them are tripled, well then, the enigma created by the geometric progressions you encounter because of the—"

Verna put a hand to his forearm to silence him. "Warren, I know all that. I understand the degrees of progression and regression as they relate to random variables in bifurcations of a triple fork."

Warren flicked his hand. "Yes of course. I forget what a good student you were. I'm sorry. I guess I'm just rambling."

"Out with it, Warren. What did Simona say that makes you think she may not be insane, 'in the conventional sense'?"

"This dream walker she mentioned. In two of the oldest books there are a few references to 'dream walker.' These books are in bad shape, hardly more than dust, but the thing that worries me is that because the books are so old, the mention of dream walker might only seem rare to us because we have only two of the texts, when in fact it might not be rare at all for back then. Most of the books from that time were lost."

"How old?"

"Over three thousand years."

Verna lifted an eyebrow. "From the time of the great war?" Warren confirmed it was so. "What about the dream walker?"

"Well, it's hard to understand. When they mention it, it's not so much a person, as a weapon."

"A weapon? What kind of weapon?"

"I don't know. The context is not exactly that of an object, either, but more of an entity, though it could be a person."

"Maybe it's meant in the way that a person who is so good at something, like a blade master, that they are often described, with respect, or reverence, as a weapon?"

Warren lifted a finger. "That's it. A very good way to describe it, Verna."

"What do the books say this weapon did with this skill?"

Warren sighed. "I don't know. But I do know that the dream

walker had something to do with the Towers of Perdition that finally cut the Old and New Worlds apart and kept them separated for the last three thousand years."

"You mean the dream walkers built the towers?"

Warren leaned closer. "No. I think the towers were built to stop them."

Verna stiffened. "Richard destroyed the towers," she said aloud, not intending to. "What else?"

"That's all I know, so far. Even what I've told you is largely conjecture. We don't know much about books from the time of the war. For all I know, it could simply be tales, and not real."

Verna rolled her eyes to the door behind her. "What I saw in there looked real to me."

Warren grimaced. "Me, too."

"What did you mean about her not being insane 'in the conventional sense'?"

"I don't think Sister Simona is having deranged dreams and imagining things; I think something real happened and that's what made her the way we see her. The books allude to instances where this 'blade master' of sorts slipped, and left the subject unable to separate their dreams from reality, as if their mind can't fully wake from the nightmares, or slip from the world around them when they sleep."

"That sounds like insanity to me, not being able to distinguish what's real from what's not."

Warren turned his palm up. A flame ignited just above the flesh. "What is reality? I imagined there was a flame, and my 'dream' became reality. My wakeful intellect governs what I do."

She pulled on a brown curl as she thought out loud. "Just as the veil separates the world of the living from the world of the dead, there is a barrier in our minds that separates reality from the imagination, from dreams. Through discipline and our force of will we control what is reality for us."

She looked up suddenly. "Dear Creator, that barrier in our minds is what keeps us from using our Han when we sleep. If there were no barrier, then the person would have no intellectual control of their Han while they sleep."

Warren nodded. "We have control of our Han. When we imagine, it can become real. But the conscious imagination is overlaid with the limitations of the intellect." He leaned toward her, his blue eyes intense. "The sleeping imagination has virtually none of these limitations. A dream walker can bend reality. Those with the gift can bring it to be."

"Weapon indeed," she whispered.

She took Warren's arm and started down the hall. As frightening as the unknown was, it was a comfort to have at least one friend to help. Her head swirled with a confusion of doubts and questions. She was the Prelate now, it was up to her to find some answers before trouble visited the palace.

"Who died?" Warren asked at last.

"The Prelate and Nathan," Verna said absently, because that was where her thoughts were.

"No, they had the funeral rite. I mean besides them."

Verna came back from her mind travels. "Besides the Prelate and Nathan? No one. No one has died in quite a while."

The lamplight danced in his blue eyes. "Then why did the palace hire the services of gravediggers?"

CHAPTER 19

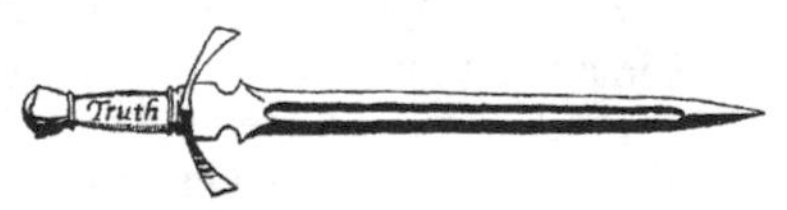

RICHARD SWUNG HIS LEG over his horse's flanks, landed on the trampled snow of the stable yard, and tossed the reins to a waiting soldier as the company of two hundred soldiers galloped in behind him. He patted his footsore horse's neck while a tired Ulic and Egan dismounted right behind. The still, cold, late-day air steamed with drifting clouds of breath of man and horse alike. The silent men were frustrated and discouraged; Richard was angry.

He pulled off a thickly padded glove and scratched the four

days' growth of beard as he yawned. He was tired, dirty, and hungry, but mostly he was angry. The trackers he had taken with him were good men, General Reibisch had told him, and Richard had no cause to dispute the general's word, but as good as they were, they were not good enough. Richard was a keen tracker, too, and several times he had found telltales the others had missed, but two days of fierce blizzard made the job impossible and in the end they had failed.

It shouldn't have been necessary in the first place, but he had let himself be duped. His first minor challenge as a leader, and he had botched it. He should never have trusted the man. Why was he always thinking people would see the side of reason and do the right thing? Why did he always think that people had good in them and, if allowed the chance, it would come to the surface?

As they slogged through the snow toward the palace, its white walls and spires mellowing to a dusky gray in the evening twilight, he asked Ulic and Egan to go find General Reibisch and to inquire about any other disasters that might have transpired while he was gone. The Keep watched him from the gloom in the shadows of the mountains, the snow a dark, moody, steel blue shawl drawn around its granite shoulders.

Richard found Mistress Sanderholt busy with her covey of workers in the din of the kitchen and asked if it would be possible for her to find him and his two big guards something to eat, a chunk of dry bread, some leftover soup, anything. She saw that he was in no mood for conversation and offered a silent squeeze of his arm as she told him to put his feet up while she saw to it. He headed for a quiet study not far from the kitchens to sit for a rest while he waited for the others to return.

Coming around the corner to the study doorway, Berdine stepped in front of him. She was wearing her red leather. "And just where have you been?" she asked in an icy Mord-Sith tone.

"Chasing phantoms in the mountains. Didn't Cara and Raina tell you where I was going?"

"*You* did not tell me." Her hard blue eyes didn't budge from his gaze. "That is what counts. You will not wander off again without telling me where you are going. Do you understand?"

Richard felt a chill run through his marrow. There was no mistaking who was speaking: not Berdine, the woman, but

Mistress Berdine, a Mord-Sith. And it was not a question; it was a threat.

Richard gave himself a mental shake. He was just tired and she had been worried about the Lord Rahl. He was imagining things. What was the matter with him? He had probably given her a fright when she woke to discover he had taken off after Brogan and his sorcerous sister. She had an odd sense of humor, maybe this was her idea of a joke. He forced a toothy grin, and thought to lighten her concern.

"Berdine, you know I like you the best. I thought of nothing the whole time but your smiling blue eyes."

Richard took a step toward the door. Her Agiel came up in her fist. She planted its tip against the far side of the doorframe, blocking his way. He had never seen Berdine unmask such a sinister countenance.

"I asked you a question. I expect an answer. Don't make me ask again."

This time there was no excusing her tone or her actions. The Agiel was right in front of his face, and it wasn't there casually. He was seeing for the first time her true Mord-Sith persona, the personality her victims had seen, the core character of her vicious indoctrination—and he didn't like it. For an instant, he saw through the eyes of those forsaken victims she had had at the end of her Agiel. No one died an easy death as the captive of a Mord-Sith, and none but he had ever survived the ordeal.

He suddenly viewed his faith in these women with regret, and felt the sting of disappointment in his trust of them.

Instead of a chill, it was the heat of anger that surged through his bones this time. He realized he was about to do something he might regret, and immediately took control of his temper, but he could feel the rage powering in his glare.

"Berdine, I had to go after Brogan as soon as I found out he had escaped, if I was to have any chance to find him. I told Cara and Raina where I was going and at their insistence took Ulic and Egan with me. You were asleep. I saw no need to wake you."

Still she did not move. "You were needed here. We have many trackers and soldiers. We have only one leader." The tip of her Agiel swept around, stopping before his eyes. "Don't disappoint me again."

It took all his willpower not to reach out and break her arm.

She withdrew her Agiel, along with her blistering glower, and stalked away.

Inside the small, darkly paneled room, he hurled his heavy hide mantle at the wall beside the narrow fireplace. How could he be so naive? They were vipers with fangs, and he had allowed them to drape themselves around his neck. He was surrounded by strangers. No, not strangers. He knew what Mord-Sith were; he knew some of the things the D'Harans had done; he knew some of the things the representatives of some of the lands here had done; yet he was foolish enough to believe they could do right if given the chance.

He leaned a hand on the window frame and stared out on the darkening, mountainous landscape as he let the warmth from the low, crackling fire soak in. In the distance the Wizard's Keep looked down on him. He missed Gratch. He missed Kahlan. Dear spirits, he wanted to hold her in his arms.

Maybe he should give this whole thing up. He could find someplace in the Hartland Woods where they would never be found. The two of them could just vanish and let the rest of the world fend for itself. Why should he care—they didn't.

Zedd, I need you here to help me.

Richard saw light creep across the room toward him when the door opened. He looked over his shoulder to see Cara standing in the doorway. Raina was just behind. Both wore their brown leather outfits and mischievous smiles. He was not amused.

"Lord Rahl, glad to see your handsome hide back in one piece." With a smirk, she tossed her blond braid back over her shoulder. "Did you miss us? I hope you will not—"

"Get out."

Her playful smile withered. "What?"

He rounded on her. "I said get out. Or did you come to threaten me with an Agiel? I don't want to look at your Mord-Sith faces right now. Get out!"

Cara swallowed. "We will not be far, if you need us," she said in a small voice. She looked as if he had slapped her. She turned and ushered Raina away with her.

When they had gone, Richard slumped down in a tufted leather chair behind a small, dark, glossy table with claw-foot legs. The smoky, acrid smell from the hearth told him it was oak, a choice he would have made himself for such a cold night. He pushed the lamp to the side near the wall where hung a grouping of small paintings of country scenes. The largest was no bigger than his hand, yet each still managed to portray grand, sweeping vistas. He stared at their peaceful views, wishing life could be as simple as it looked in the idyllic paintings.

He was brought out of his thoughts when Ulic and Egan appeared with General Reibisch at the door.

The general clapped a fist over his heart. "Lord Rahl, I'm relieved to see you've returned safely. Did you have any success?"

Richard shook his head. "The men you sent with me were as good as your word, but the conditions were impossible. We managed to track them for a ways, but they went up Stentor Street, into the center of the city. Once they did that, there was no way to tell which direction they took. Probably to the northeast, back to Nicobarese, but we swept a circle of the entire city anyway in case they went another direction, and could find no trace of them. A meticulous search of all the possibilities took quite a while and allowed the storm ample time to cover their trail."

The general grunted as he thought. "We questioned the ones they left behind at their palace. None knew where Brogan went."

"They could be lying."

Reibisch's thumb stroked the scar on the side of his face. "Take my word, they didn't know where he went."

Richard didn't want to know the details of what had been done on his behalf. "From the signs at the beginning we were able to discern that there were only three—undoubtedly Lord General Brogan, his sister, and that other one."

"Well, if he didn't take his men, then it would appear he was simply running. You probably scared the wits out of him, and he just bolted for his life."

Richard tapped a finger to the table. "Maybe. But I wish I knew where he went, just to be sure."

The general shrugged. "Why didn't you put a tracer cloud on him, or use your magic to follow his trail? That's what Darken Rahl did when he wanted to follow someone."

Richard knew that all too well. He knew what a tracer cloud was, from its unfavorable end. This had all started when Darken Rahl had hooked a tracer cloud to him so he could come and collect him at his leisure in order to recover the Book of Counted Shadows. Zedd had stood Richard up on his wizard's rock to unhook the cloud. Though he had felt the magic flowing through himself, Richard didn't know how it worked. He had also seen Zedd use some of his magic dust to cover their trail, to keep Darken Rahl from following, but he didn't know how that worked, either.

Richard didn't really want to shake General Reibisch's faith in him by admitting he didn't know the first thing about magic; he wasn't feeling very comfortable with his allies at the moment.

"You can't hook a tracer cloud to someone when there's a sky full of storm clouds. You couldn't tell which was yours, in order to follow it. Lunetta, Brogan's sister, is a sorceress; she would use magic to obscure their trail."

"That's a shame." The general scratched his beard, apparently believing the bluff. "Well, magic's not my specialty. We have you for that business."

Richard changed the subject. "How is everything going here?"

The general grinned wickedly. "There isn't a sword in the city that isn't ours. Some of them didn't like it, but once the alternatives were clearly explained, they all went along without a fight."

Well, there was that much. "The Blood of the Fold at the Nicobarese Palace, too?"

"They'll be having to eat with their fingers. We didn't let them keep so much as a spoon."

Richard rubbed his eyes. "Good. You've done well, General. What about the mriswith? Have there been any more attacks?"

"Not since that first bloody night. It's been real quiet. Why, I've even slept better than I have for weeks. Since you took over, I've not even had any of those dreams."

Richard looked up. "Dreams? What sort of dreams?"

"Well . . ." The general scratched his head of rust-colored hair. "That's odd. I don't really remember them, now. I was having these dreams that troubled me greatly, but since you came I haven't had them. You know how it is with dreams, after a while they fade and you can't remember them."

"I guess." This whole thing was beginning to feel like a dream: a bad dream. Richard wished that was all it was. "How many men did we lose when the mriswith attacked?"

"Just shy of three hundred."

Richard stroked his forehead as he felt his stomach lurch. "I didn't think there were that many bodies. I wouldn't have thought it was that many."

"Well, that includes the others."

Richard took his hand away from his face. "Others? What others?"

General Reibisch pointed through the window. "The ones up there. Nearly eighty men on the road up by the Wizard's Keep were cut down, too."

Richard swung around and looked out the window. Only the silhouette of the Keep was visible against the deep violet sky. Would the mriswith be trying to get into the Keep? Dear spirits, if they were, what could he do about it? Kahlan told him that the Keep was protected by powerful spells, but he didn't know if the webs could hold back creatures like the mriswith. Why would they want to get into the Keep?

He told himself not to let his imagination run away with him; the mriswith had killed soldiers and other people all over the city. Zedd would be back in a few weeks and would know what to do. Weeks? No, it would likely be more than a month, maybe two. Could he wait that long?

Maybe he should go have a look. But that could be foolish, too. The Keep was a place of powerful magic, and he knew nothing about magic, except that it was dangerous. He would just be asking for more trouble. He had enough trouble. Still, maybe he should have a look for himself. That might be best.

"Your dinner's here," Ulic said.

Richard turned back. "What? Oh, thanks."

Mistress Sanderholt had a silver tray loaded with steaming vegetable stew, black bread slathered with butter, spiced eggs, herbed rice with brown cream, lamb chops, pears with white sauce, and a mug of honeyed tea.

With a friendly wink, she set down the tray. "Eat all your dinner, it will do you good, and then rest well, Richard."

The only night he had spent at the Confessors' Palace he had slept in the council chambers, in Kahlan's chair. "Where?"

She shrugged, "Well, you could stay in—" She paused, catching herself. "You could stay in the Mother Confessor's room. It's the finest room in the palace."

That was where he and Kahlan were to have spent their wedding night. "I wouldn't feel right about that, just now. Is there another bed I could use?"

Mistress Sanderholt gestured with a bandaged hand. The bandages were less bulky now, and cleaner. "Up that wing, at the end, take to the right and there is a row of guest rooms. We have no guests right now, so you can have your pick."

"Where are the Mord . . . Where are Cara and her two friends sleeping?"

She made a wry face and pointed in the opposite direction. "I directed them to the servant quarters. They share a room there."

The farther the better, as far as he was concerned. "That's good of you, Mistress Sanderholt. I'll take one of the guest rooms, then."

She elbowed Ulic. "What would you big boys like to eat?"

"What do you have?" Egan asked, with a rare show of enthusiasm.

She cocked an eyebrow. "Why don't you two come to the kitchen and choose for yourselves?" She saw the glance to Richard. "It's just a short distance. You won't be far from your charge."

Richard threw the sides of his black mriswith cape back over the arms of the chair. He waved for them to go as he took a spoonful of the vegetable stew and a swig of the tea. General Reibisch clapped a fist to his heart and bid him a good night. Richard acknowledged the salute with a flourish of brown bread.

CHAPTER 20

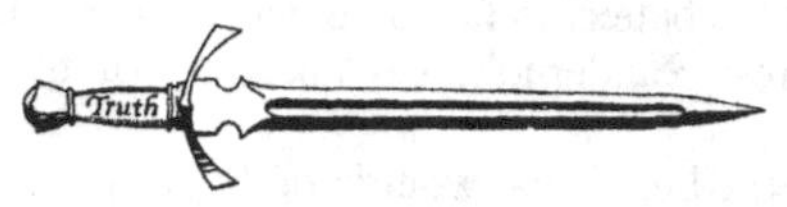

IT WAS A RELIEF to be alone at last. He was weary of people standing ready to jump should he command it. Though he had tried to put the soldiers at ease, they had been apprehensive about having him along, seeming to fear he would strike them down with magic should they fail to find Brogan's trail. Even when they couldn't and he had told them that he understood, it didn't put them at ease. Only near the end had they relaxed a bit, but they still watched him constantly in case he should whisper an order they might miss. It unnerved Richard to be surrounded by people who held him in such awe.

His mind churned with troubled thoughts as he downed the stew. Even if he wasn't half starved it could have tasted no better; it wasn't freshly made, but had simmered for a good long time, bestowing on it the rich melding of flavors that no ingredient but time could add.

When he looked up from his mug of tea, Berdine was filling the doorway. His muscles tensed. Before he could tell her to go away, she spoke.

"Duchess Lumholtz of Kelton is here to speak with the Lord Rahl."

Richard sucked a piece of the stew from between two teeth as he locked his eyes on Berdine. "I'm not interested in seeing petitioners."

Berdine's advance was halted by the table. She flicked her wavy brown braid back over her shoulder. "You will see her."

Richard's fingertips stroked the familiar nicks and scratches on the hickory handle on his knife at his belt. "The terms of surrender are not open to discussion."

Berdine planted her knuckles on the table and leaned toward him. Her Agiel, at the end of the fine chain at her wrist, rolled around her hand. Her blue eyes were cold fire. "You will see her."

Richard could feel his face heating. "I've given my answer. You will get no other."

She didn't back away. "And I have given my word that you would see her. You *will* speak with her."

"The only thing I will hear from Kelton's representative is unconditional surrender."

"And that is what you shall hear." The melodious voice came from a silhouette just beyond the doorway. "If you will agree to hear me out. I have not come to make any threats, Lord Rahl."

In her soft, humble tone, Richard could hear the hesitancy of fear. It evoked a pang of sympathy.

"Show the lady in—" His glare returned to Berdine. "—and then shut the door behind yourself on your way to bed." He left no doubt in his tone that it was a command, and he would brook no violation.

Showing no emotion, Berdine went to the door and held her arm out in invitation. When the duchess stepped into the warm glow of the firelight, Richard rose to his feet. Berdine cast him a blank glance and then shut the door, but he hardly noticed.

"Please, Duchess Lumholtz, come in."

"Thank you for seeing me, Lord Rahl."

He stood mute a moment, gazing at her soft brown eyes, her curvaceous red lips, and her thick mane of black hair, ringlets of it framing her flawless, glowing face. Richard knew that in the Midlands the length of a woman's hair denoted her social standing. This woman's long, luxurious hair bespoke a standing of high order. The only hair he had seen that was longer was a queen's, and beyond that, the Mother Confessor's.

Dizzy, he drew breath, and suddenly remembered his manners. "Here, let me get you a chair."

He didn't remember the duchess looking like this, possessing such pure, captivating elegance, but then, he hadn't been standing this close. He remembered her as ostentatious, with unnecessary glitter and paint, and a dress not at all simple and delicate, like the one she wore now, of simple, supple, rose-colored silk flowing easily over the contours of her form, complementing her voluptuous shape, cinched just below her breasts.

Richard groaned when he remembered their last encounter. "Duchess, I'm sorry I said such cruel things to you in the council chambers. Can you ever forgive me? I should have listened; you were only trying to warn me about General Brogan."

At the mention of the name, he thought he saw a flash of fright in her eyes, but it was gone so quickly he wasn't sure. "It is I, Lord Rahl, who should beg forgiveness. It was unpardonable of me to interrupt you before the assembled representatives."

Richard shook his head. "You were only trying to warn me about that man, and as it turns out, you were right. I wish I had listened to you."

"It was wrong of me to express my opinion in the manner I did." A demure smile graced her features. "Only the most gallant of men would try to make it seem otherwise."

Richard blushed at her calling him gallant. His heart was thumping so hard he feared she would be able to see the veins in his neck throb. For some reason, he imagined his lips brushing back the loose wisp of downy hair hanging free in front of her exquisite ear. Pulling his gaze from her face was almost painful.

A small voice of warning was sounding in the back of his mind, but it was being drowned out in the roar of a river's flood of warm sensations. In one hand, he snatched the twin to his tufted chair and spun it around in front of the table, holding it out for her.

"You are most kind," the duchess stammered. "Forgive me, please, if my voice is less than steady. It's been a trying few days." As she moved in front of the chair, her eyes tilted up to meet his again. "And I'm just a little nervous. I've never been in the presence of such a great man as yourself, Lord Rahl."

Richard blinked, unable to leave her gaze when he thought he had tried. "I'm just a woods guide a long way from home."

She laughed, a soft silky sound that turned the room into a cozy, pleasant place. "You are the Seeker. You are the Master of D'Hara." Her expression slipped from amusement to reverence. "You may one day rule the world."

Richard reacted with a wincing shrug. "I don't want to rule anything, it's just that . . ." He thought he must sound a fool. "Won't you sit down, please, my lady?"

Her smile returned, radiant, warm, and of such tender charm that he found himself frozen in its glow. He could feel the sweet warmth of her breath on his face.

Her gaze lingered. "Forgive me for being so forward, Lord Rahl, but you must know your eyes drive women mad with longing. I'd venture you broke the heart of every woman in the council chambers. The queen of Galea is an extremely fortunate woman."

Richard's brow furrowed. "Who?"

"The queen of Galea. Your bride to be. I envy her."

He turned away from her as she sat lightly at the edge of her chair. Richard pulled a deep breath, trying to clear his swimming head, and went around the table to sink into his own chair.

"Duchess, I was so sorry to hear of your husband's death."

She averted her eyes. "Thank you, Lord Rahl, but don't be troubled for me; I have little grief for the man. Don't misunderstand me, I didn't wish him harm, but . . ."

Richard's blood heated. "Did he hurt you?"

When she glanced away with a self-conscious shrug, Richard had to forcibly resist the urge to take her in his arms and comfort her. "The duke had a vile temper." Her graceful fingers stroked the sleek fur at the edge of her ermine robe. "But it wasn't as bad as it must sound. I rarely had to face him; he was away most of the time, in one bed or another."

Richard's mouth dropped opened. "He would forsake you to be with other women?" Her reluctant nod confirmed it was so.

"It was an arranged marriage," she explained. "Though he was of noble blood, for him it was a move up in station. He gained his title by marriage to mine."

"What did you gain?"

The ringlets of curls at the sides of her face swayed across her cheekbones as she glanced up. "My father gained a ruthless son-in-law to run the family holdings, and at the same time he rid himself of a useless daughter."

Richard came halfway out of his chair. "Don't say such a thing about yourself. If I had known, I would have seen that the duke had a lesson . . ." He sank back down. "Forgive my presumption, Duchess."

Her tongue leisurely wet the corners of her mouth. "Had I known you, when he struck me, perhaps I would have been bold enough to have sought your protection."

Struck her? Richard ached to have been there, to have been able to do something about it.

"Why didn't you leave him? Why would you endure it?"

Her gaze sought the low fire in the hearth. "I couldn't. I'm the daughter of the queen's brother. Divorce in such high ranks is not permitted." She suddenly blushed with a self-conscious smile. "But listen to me ramble on about my petty problems. Forgive me, Lord Rahl. Others have a great deal more trouble in their lives than an unfaithful husband with a ready hand. I'm not an unhappy woman. I have responsibilities to my people that keep me occupied."

She lifted a slender finger, pointing. "Could I have just a sip of tea? My throat is dry from worry thinking you . . ." The blush revisited her cheeks. "Thinking you would chop off my head for coming to you against your orders."

Richard shot to his feet. "I'll get you some tea that's hot."

"No, please, I don't want to inconvenience you. And just a sip is all I need, really."

Richard snatched up the mug and offered it to her.

He watched her lips mold themselves to the rim. He glanced at the tray, striving to put his mind back to business. "What is it you wished to see me about, Duchess?"

After she had taken a sip, she set the mug down, turning the handle back around before him the way it had been. There was a hint of a red print from her lips left on the rim. "Those responsibilities I spoke of. You see, the queen was on her deathbed when Prince Fyren was killed, and died herself soon after. The prince, though he had uncounted bastard offspring, was not married and so had no issue of standing."

Richard had never seen eyes of such a soft brown. "I'm not an expert on matters of royalty, Duchess. I'm afraid I don't follow."

"Well, what I'm trying to say is that with the queen and her only descendant dead, Kelton is without a monarch. Being the next in the line of succession—the daughter of the queen's deceased brother—I will succeed to queen of Kelton. There is no one I need turn to, to seek direction in the matter of our surrender."

Richard struggled to keep his mind on her words and not her lips. "You mean that you have the power to surrender Kelton?"

She nodded. "Yes, Your Eminence."

He felt his ears redden at the title she had given him. He picked up the mug, seeking to hide as much of his coloring face as possible. Richard realized he had put his lips where hers had been when he tasted the piquant print left on the rim. He let the mug linger as he felt the smooth honey-sweet warmth slide across his tongue. With a shaking hand, he set the mug on the silver tray.

Richard rubbed his sweaty palms on his knees. "Duchess, you heard what I had to say. We fight for freedom. If you surrender to us, you will not be losing something, but gaining. Under our rule, for example, it will be a crime for a man to harm his wife, the same as it would be were he to harm a stranger on the street."

Her smile had a hint of merry scolding to it. "Lord Rahl, I'm not sure even you will ever have enough power to proclaim such to be law. In some places in the Midlands it is only a token fine for a man to kill his wife should she provoke him with any of a list of misdeeds. Freedom would only give men everywhere the same license."

Richard ran a finger around the rim of his mug. "Harming an innocent, whoever they be, is wrong. Freedom is not a sanction for wrongdoing. People in some lands shouldn't have to suffer acts that in a neighboring land are a crime. When we are united, there will be no such injustices. All people will have the same freedoms, and the same responsibilities, to live by a just law."

"But surely you cannot expect that by proclaiming such tolerated customs outlawed, they will stop."

"Morality comes from the top, such as parent to child. The first step, then, is to set down just laws and show that all of us must live by their maxims. You can never stop all wrongdoing, but if you don't punish it, then it proliferates until anarchy wears the robes of tolerance and understanding."

She brushed her fingers through the delicate hollow at the base of her neck. "Lord Rahl, the things you say fill me with a rush of hope for the future. I pray to the good spirits that you succeed."

"Then will you join with us? Will you surrender Kelton?"

Her soft brown eyes came up in supplication. "There is a condition."

Richard swallowed. "I have sworn no conditions. Everyone will be treated the same, as I have told you. How could I vow equity if I didn't live by my word and rule?"

She wet her lips again as fear visited her eyes. "I understand," she said in a whisper almost lost in the quiet. "Forgive me for thinking to selfishly gain something for myself. A man of honor such as yourself could not understand how a mere woman such as I could sink to such a level."

Richard wanted to thrust his knife into his chest for allowing fear to haunt her.

"What is your condition?"

Her gaze settled in her lap along with her nested hands. "After your speech, my husband and I were almost home, and . . ." She grimaced as she swallowed. "We were almost safely home when we were attacked by that monster. I never even saw it coming. I was holding my husband's arm. There was a flash of steel." A moan escaped her throat. Richard had to force himself to stay in his seat. "My husband's insides spilled down the front of me." She gasped back a cry. "The knife that killed him put three slices in my sleeve as it passed."

"Duchess, I understand, there's no need to . . ."

She held up a trembling hand, imploring silence so she could finish. She pulled up the silken sleeve of her dress to reveal three slices across the flesh of her forearm. Richard recognized the three cuts of a mriswith blade. He had never wished that he knew how to use his gift to heal as much as at that moment. He would have done anything to take the angry red cuts from her arm.

She drew the sleeve down, seeming to read the concern on his face. "It's nothing. A few days and it will be healed." She tapped her chest, between her breasts. "It's what they did to me in here that will not heal. My husband was an expert swordsman, but he had no more chance than would I against those creatures. I will never forget the feel of his warm blood down the front of me. I'm embarrassed to admit that I screamed inconsolably until I could tear that dress off my body and wash the blood from my naked flesh. For fear I'll wake and think I'm still in that dress, I've since had to sleep without any bedclothes."

Richard wished she had used words that hadn't put such an explicit picture in his head. He watched the rise and fall of her silken dress. He forced himself to take a drink of tea, only to be confronted unexpectedly with her lip print. He wiped a bead of sweat from behind his ear.

"You were speaking of a condition?"

"Forgive me, Lord Rahl. I wanted you to understand my fear, so you might consider my condition. I was so frightened." She hugged her arms to herself, causing the dress to fold between her breasts as they pressed together.

Richard looked down at his tray of dinner as he rubbed his fingertips on his forehead. "I understand. The condition?"

She stiffened with courage. "I will surrender Kelton if you will offer me your personal protection."

Richard looked up. "What?"

"You killed those creatures out front. It's said that none but you can kill them. I'm terrified of those monsters. If I side with you, then the Order may send them after me. If you will allow me to stay here under your protection until the danger is over, then Kelton is yours."

Richard leaned forward. "You just want to feel safe?"

She nodded with a slight wince, as if she feared he would lop off her head for what she was to say next. "I must be given a room near yours, so that if I scream, you will be close enough to come to my aid."

"And . . ."

She finally gathered the courage to meet his eyes.

"And . . . nothing. That's the condition."

Richard laughed. The anxiety released its constriction of his chest. "You just want to be protected, much as my guards protect me? Duchess, that's not a condition, that's merely a simple favor—a perfectly reasonable and proper desire for shelter from our merciless enemies. Granted." He pointed. "I'm staying in the guest rooms, off that way. They're all empty. As one who sides with us, you're an honored guest, and may have your choice. You can have one right beside mine, if you would feel safer."

She had not even smiled before, in comparison with the radiance that came to her face now. Her hands crossed over her breasts. She let out a huge sigh as if liberated from the greatest of dreads. "Oh, Lord Rahl, thank you."

Richard brushed his hair back from his forehead. "First thing tomorrow, a delegation, escorted by our troops, will leave for Kelton. Your forces must be brought under our command."

"Brought under . . . yes, of course. Tomorrow. They will have a personal letter from me, and the names of all our officials to be informed. Kelton is hereby a part of D'Hara." She bowed her head, her dark curls slipping across her rosy cheeks. "We are honored to be the first to join. All Kelton will fight for freedom."

Richard let out a huge sigh of his own. "Thank you, Duchess . . . or should I call you Queen Lumholtz?"

She sat back, her wrists draped on the arms of the chair, her hands pendent. "Neither." One leg slid upward as she crossed it over the other. "You should call me Cathryn, Lord Rahl."

"Cathryn, then, and please, call me Richard. Quite frankly, I'm getting tired of everyone calling me . . ." As he stared into her eyes, he forgot what he was going to say.

With a coy smile, she leaned forward, one breast slipping past the table's brink. Richard realized he was sitting on the edge of his chair again as he watched her twist a ringlet of black hair around a finger. He focused on the tray of food before himself in an attempt to control his roving eyes.

"Richard, then." She giggled, a sound not in the least bit girlish, but both husky and womanly at the same time, and not at all ladylike. He held his breath, lest he sigh out loud. "I don't know if I can get used to addressing such a great man as the Master of all D'Hara so intimately."

Richard smiled. "Perhaps it will simply take practice, Cathryn."

"Yes, practice," she said in a breathy voice. She suddenly blushed. "Look at me, going on again. Those painfully handsome gray eyes of yours do make a woman forget herself. I had better leave you to your dinner before it gets cold." Her gaze lingered on the tray between them. "It looks delicious."

Richard jumped up. "Let me have some brought for you."

She withdrew from the brink of the table, putting her shoulders back against the chair. "No, I couldn't. You're a busy man, and you've already been too kind."

"I'm not busy. I was just having a bite before I went to bed. At least you could sit with me while I ate, and perhaps share a little of it with me? There's more here than I can eat—it would just go to waste."

She drew closer to him again, pressing against the table. "Well, it does look sumptuous . . . and if you aren't going to eat it all . . . maybe just a nibble, then."

Richard grinned. "What would you like? Stew, spiced eggs, rice, lamb?"

At the mention of lamb she let out a throaty murmur of pleasure. Richard threaded the gold-rimmed white plate across the tray. He hadn't had any intention of eating the lamb himself; since the gift had awakened in him he wasn't able to eat meat. Something to do with the magic at the time the gift manifested itself, or perhaps it was as the Sisters had told him: all magic must be in balance. Since he was a war wizard, maybe he couldn't eat meat in order to balance the killing he sometimes had to do.

Richard offered her the knife and fork. Smiling again, she shook her head and with her fingers picked up the lamb chop. "Keltans have a saying that if it's good, nothing should come between you and the experience."

"Then I hope it's good," Richard heard himself say. For the first time in days he didn't feel lonely.

With her brown eyes fixed on his, she leaned forward on her elbows and took a dainty bite. Transfixed, Richard waited.

"So . . . is it good?"

In answer, her eyes rolled back in her head and her lids slid closed while she hunched her shoulders and moaned in perfect rapture. Her gaze came down, restoring the torrid connection. Her mouth enveloped the meat, and her flawless white teeth tore off a succulent chunk. Her lips were slick with it. He didn't think he had ever seen anyone chew so slowly.

Richard pulled the doughy center of the bread in two, giving her the one with the most butter. With the crust, he scooped rice out of the brown cream. His hand paused before his mouth as she took the butter off in one long lick.

She let out a throaty purr of approval. "I love how soft and slippery it feels against my tongue," she explained in little more than a whisper. From her glistening, dangling fingers, she let the chunk of bread drop to the tray.

She watched his eyes as she dragged her teeth across the bone, gnawing along its ridge. With sucking nibbles, she scoured the length clean. The piece of bread waited before Richard's mouth.

Her tongue stroked across her lips. "Best I've ever had."

Richard realized that his fingers were empty. He thought that he must have eaten the scoop of rice until he saw the white splat on the tray under him.

She plucked an egg from the bowl, pressed her red lips around it, and bit it in half. "Umm. Luscious." She placed the round end of the other half to his lips. "Here, try it."

Its silken surface had a mildly spicy tang against his tongue and a flexible, resilient feel. She pushed it all the way in with one finger. It was chew or choke. He chewed.

Her gaze left his to roam the tray. "What have we here? Oh, Richard, don't tell me it's . . ." She swirled her first and second fingers around the bowl with the pears. She sucked the thick white sauce off her first finger. Some of the coating on the other dribbled down her hand to her wrist. "Oh, yes. Oh, Richard, this is fabulous. Here."

She put her second finger up to his lips. Before he realized it, she had the whole length in his mouth. "Suck it clean," she insisted. "Isn't that the best you've ever had?" Richard nodded, trying to catch his breath after she drew her finger out. She tilted her wrist. "Oh, please, lick it off before it gets on my dress." He took her hand up in his and put it to his mouth. The taste of her galvanized him. His lips on her flesh made his heart pound painfully.

She let out a throaty laugh. "That tickles. Your tongue is rough."

He let her hand go, rousing from the intimate connection. "Sorry," he whispered.

"Don't be silly. I didn't say I didn't like it." Her eyes found his. Lamplight glowed softly on one side of her face, firelight on the other. He envisioned raking his fingers through her hair. Her breaths were the mate of his. "I did like it, Richard."

So did he. The room seemed to be spinning. The sound of his name on her lips sent waves of euphoria coursing through him. With the greatest of effort, he forced himself to stand.

"Cathryn, it's late, and I'm really tired."

She rose willingly, eagerly, a graceful movement that betrayed her shape through the silken dress. His control threatened to unravel completely as she slipped her arm around his, pressing close. "Show me which room is yours?"

He could feel her firm breast crushed against his arm as he led her out into the hall. Ulic and Egan stood not far away with their arms folded. Farther off, at each end of the hall, Cara and Raina came to their feet. None of the four showed any reaction to his having Cathryn on his arm. Richard said nothing to them as he headed for the guest rooms.

With urgent insistence, Cathryn's free hand stroked his shoulder. The heat of her flesh against him warmed him to his bones. He didn't know if his legs would make the journey.

When he found the wing with the guest rooms, he gestured Ulic and Egan close. "Take shifts. I want one of you on watch at all times. I don't want anyone, or anything, coming into this hall tonight." He glanced to the two Mord-Sith waiting at the far end. "That includes them." They asked no questions and vowed it would be so before they planted themselves.

Richard took Cathryn halfway down the hall. She was still caressing his arm. Her breast was still pressed against it.

"I trust this room will do."

Her lips parted as her chest heaved. Her delicate fingers clutched at his shirt. "Yes," she whispered in a pant, "this room."

Richard summoned every ounce of strength. "I'll take the one right next to it. You'll be safe here."

"What?" The blood drained from her face. "Oh, please, Richard . . ."

"Sleep well, Cathryn."

She tightened her grip on his arm. "But . . . but, you have to come in. Oh, please, Richard. I'll be afraid."

He squeezed her hand as he took it from his arm. "Your room is safe, Cathryn, don't be concerned."

"There could be something inside, waiting. Please, Richard, come in with me?"

Richard smiled reassuringly. "There's nothing inside. I could sense it if there were danger anywhere near. I'm a wizard, remember? You're perfectly safe, and I'll be only a few steps away. Nothing will disturb your rest, I swear it."

He opened the door, handed her a lamp off a bracket beside the door, and put a hand to the small of her back, urging her in.

She turned and ran a finger down the center of his chest. "I'll see you tomorrow?"

He took her hand from his chest and kissed it in as courtly a fashion as he could muster. "Count on it. We have a lot of work to do first thing tomorrow."

He pulled her door closed and then went to the next. The two Mord-Sith's eyes never left him. He watched as they slid their backs down the wall to sit on the floor. Each folded her legs, as if to say they intended to be there all night, and each gripped her Agiel in both hands.

Richard glanced at the door to Cathryn's room, his gaze lingering a long moment. The little voice in the back of his head was screaming frantically. He wrested open the door to his room. Inside, he laid his face against the closed door as he caught his breath. He compelled himself to throw the bolt.

He sank down on the edge of the bed, putting his face in his hands. What was the matter with him? His shirt was soaked with sweat. Why should he be having such thoughts about this woman? But he was. Dear spirits, he was. He remembered that the Sisters of the Light thought men suffered from uncontrollable urges.

With dazed effort, he drew the Sword of Truth from its scabbard, sending its soft, clear ring around the dark room. Richard planted the point on the floor and with both hands held the hilt to his forehead, letting the wrath inundate him. He felt its fury storm through his soul, and hoped it would be enough.

From a dim corner of his mind, Richard knew he was in a dance with death, and this time his sword couldn't save him. He also knew he had no choice.

CHAPTER 21

SISTER PHILIPPA MADE THE most of her already ample height as she stiffened her back while managing to look down her thin, straight nose without making it seem as if she were really looking down her nose. But she was.

"Surely, Prelate, you have not considered this matter thoroughly enough. Perhaps if you were to reflect on it a bit more you would realize that three thousand years of results attests to the need."

With her elbow on the table, Verna rested her chin in the heel of her loose fist while scanning through a report, making it impossible to look at her without seeing the gold sunburst-patterned ring of office. She glanced up just to make sure Sister Philippa was, in fact, looking at her.

"Thank you, Sister, for your wise advice, but I have already considered the matter at length. There is no need to put any more digging into a dry well; it just makes you thirstier, which raises your hopes, but not any water."

Sister Philippa's dark eyes and exotic features rarely showed emotion, but Verna detected a tightening in the muscles in her narrow jaw.

"But, Prelate . . . we won't be able to ascertain if a young man is progressing properly, or has learned enough to be released from his Rada'Han. It's the only way."

Verna grimaced at the report she was reading. She set it aside for later action and gave her full attention to her advisor. "How old are you, Sister?"

Sister Philippa's dark gaze didn't waver. "Four hundred seventy-nine, Prelate."

Verna had to admit to herself that she felt a bit of envy. The woman looked hardly older than she, yet she was in fact on the order of three hundred years older. The twenty-odd years away from the palace's spell had cost Verna time she could never recover. She would never have the life span to learn what this woman would.

"How many of those years at the Palace of the Prophets?"

"Four hundred seventy, Prelate." The inflection on the title was hard to detect, unless one had been listening for it. Verna had been listening.

"So, you are saying, then, that the Creator has granted you a span of four hundred and seventy years to learn his work, to work with and teach young men to control their gift and become wizards, and in all that time, you have failed to be able to come to a determination of the nature of your students?"

"Well, no, Prelate, that's not exactly what—"

"Are you trying to tell me, Sister, that a whole palace full of Sisters of the Light are not smart enough to determine if a young man, who has been under our charge and tutelage for near to two hundred years, is ready for advancement, without subjecting him to a brutal test of pain? Do you have so little faith in the Sisters? In the Creator's wisdom in choosing us to do this work? Are you trying to tell me that the Creator chose us, gave us, collectively, thousands of years of experience, and we are still too stupid to do the work?"

"I think that perhaps the Prelate is—"

"Permission denied. It's an obscene use of the Rada'Han, giving that kind of pain. It can tear the fabric of a person's mind. Why, young men have even died in the test.

"You go tell those Sisters that I expect them to come up with a strategy for accomplishing the task without blood, vomit, or screaming. You might even suggest they try something revolutionary, like . . . oh, I don't know, maybe talking to the young men? Unless the Sisters think they would be outwitted, in which case I would like them to admit as much to me in a report, for the record."

Sister Philippa stood silent a moment, probably considering the worth of further arguing. Reluctantly, she at last bowed. "Very wise, Prelate. Thank you for enlightening me."

She turned to leave, but Verna called her back. "Sister, I know how you feel. I was taught the same as you, and believed as you. A young man of a mere twenty-odd years taught me how wrong I had been. Sometimes the Creator chooses to bring His light to us in ways we don't expect, but He does expect us to be ready to receive His wisdom when it's presented to us."

"You speak of young Richard?"

Verna picked with a thumbnail at the disorderly edges in the stack of reports awaiting her attention. "Yes." She abandoned her official tone. "What I learned, Philippa, is that these young men, these wizards, are going to be sent out into a world that will test them. The Creator wants us to determine if we have taught them to endure with integrity the pain they will see, and feel." She tapped her chest. "In here. We must determine if they can make the painful choices the Creator's light sometimes requires. That is the meaning of the test of pain. Their ability to endure torture tells us nothing of their heart, their courage, or their compassion.

"You yourself, Philippa, have passed a test of pain. You would have fought to be Prelate. You've worked for hundreds of years toward the goal of being at least in serious contention. Events cheated you out of that chance, yet you have never said one bitter word to me, though you must feel the pain every time you look at me. Instead, you have done your best to advise me in the post, and have worked in the interest of the palace, despite that pain.

"Would I be better served had I insisted you be tested by torture to become my advisor? Would that have proven anything?"

Sister Philippa's cheeks had mantled. "I won't lie by pretending to agree with you, but at least I now understand that you have indeed been shoveling dirt out of the hole, and are not simply abandoning it as dry because you didn't want to sweat. I will carry out your directive at once, Verna."

Verna smiled. "Thank you, Philippa."

Philippa betrayed the slightest hint of a smile. "Richard created quite an upheaval around here. I thought he was going to try to kill us all, and he turns out to have been a greater friend to the palace than any wizard in three thousand years."

Verna barked a laugh. "If you only knew how many times I had to pray for the strength not to strangle him."

As Philippa left, Verna could see through the door into the outer office that Millie was awaiting permission to enter and do the cleaning. Verna stretched with a yawn, picked up the report she had set aside, and went to the door. She waved Millie into her office as she turned her attention to her two administrators, Sisters Dulcinia and Phoebe.

Before Verna could speak, Sister Dulcinia stood with a stack of reports. "If you're ready, Prelate, we have these in order for you."

Verna took the stack, about the weight of an infant, and rested it on a hip. "Yes, all right, thank you. It's late. Why don't you two be off."

Sister Phoebe shook her head. "I don't mind, Prelate. I enjoy the work, and—"

"And tomorrow is another long day of it. I won't have you nodding off because you don't get enough sleep. Now, be off, the both of you."

Phoebe scooped up a sheaf of papers, probably to take to her own office so she could continue working. Phoebe seemed to think that they were in a paper race; whenever she suspected there was even a remote chance Verna might actually catch up, she worked frantically, producing more of the stuff, almost as if by magic. Dulcinia plucked her cup of tea from the desk, leaving the papers. She worked at a measured pace, never lowering herself to scrambling to stay ahead of Verna, but she still managed to produce stacks of reports, sorted and annotated, almost at will. Neither needed to fear that Verna would catch up with them; every day set her further behind.

Both Sisters bade their farewells, offering their hope that the Creator would grant the Prelate a restful sleep.

Verna waited until they had reached the outer door. "Oh, Sister Dulcinia, I have a little matter I'd like you to take care of tomorrow."

"Of course, Prelate. What is it?"

Verna placed the report she had brought on Dulcinia's desk where it would be the first thing she would see when she sat down in the morning. "A request for support from a young woman and her family. One of our young wizards is to be a father."

Phoebe squealed. "Oh, that's wonderful! We pray that, with the

Creator's blessing, it will be a boy, and have the gift. There hasn't been one born with the gift in the city since . . . well, I can't even remember the last time. Maybe this time . . ."

Verna's scowl finally brought her to silence. Verna turned her attention to Sister Dulcinia. "I want to see this young woman, and the young man responsible for her condition. Tomorrow, you will arrange an appointment. Perhaps her parents should be there as well, since they are requesting assistance."

Sister Dulcinia, a blank expression on her face, leaned in a little. "Is there a problem, Prelate?"

Verna hiked the load of reports up higher on her hip. "I should say there is. One of our young men got the woman pregnant."

Sister Dulcinia set her tea down on the corner of the desk as she took a step closer. "But Prelate, we allow our charges to go into the city for this very reason. It not only lets them dissipate their impulses so they may devote themselves to their studies, but it also, on occasion, nets us one with the gift."

"I will not sanction the palace meddling in creation and the lives of innocent people."

Sister Dulcinia's blue eyes glanced the length of Verna's simple, dark blue dress. "Prelate, men have uncontrollable urges."

"So do I, but with the Creator's help I've so far managed not to strangle anyone."

Phoebe's laugh was cut short by a scalding glance from Sister Dulcinia. "Prelate, men are different. They can't control themselves. Allowing this simple diversion keeps their minds focused on their lessons. The palace can well afford the recompense. It's a small price to pay in view of the fact that it on occasion results in gaining us a young wizard."

"The charge of the palace is to teach our young men to use their gift in a responsible fashion, with restraint, and knowing full well the consequences of wielding their ability. When we encourage them to act in the exact opposite fashion with regard to other aspects of their lives, it undermines our teachings.

"As to the occasional result of one with the gift being born from these indiscriminate couplings, there is no evidence that it's of benefit. Who is to say that were they to act with more responsibility and control, the results of meaningful couplings in their future wouldn't produce more than a dismal percentage of offspring with the gift. For all we know, their lascivious indiscretion could be diluting their ability to pass on the gift."

"Or developing it to its highest chances, poor though they are."

Verna shrugged. "Perhaps. But I do know that those fishermen out on the river don't spend their entire lives fishing the exact same spot because they once caught a fish there. Since we are netting few fish, I think it's time for us to move on."

Sister Dulcinia clasped her hands in an effort to be patient. "Prelate, the Creator blessed people with their nature, such as it is, and there is no way we can alter it. Men and women are going to go on doing what gives them pleasure."

"Of course they are, but as long as we pay the cost of the results, we encourage more of it. If there are no consequences, then there will be no self-control. How many children have grown up without the benefit of a father because we give pregnant young women gold? Does that gold replace nurturing? How many lives have we altered, to their detriment, with our gold?"

Dulcinia spread her hands in dismay. "Our gold helps them."

"Our gold encourages the women in the city to act irresponsibly, and to bed our young men because it means a life of support without qualifications." Verna swept her free hand around, indicating the city. "We are demeaning these people with our gold. We have rendered them little more than breeding stock."

"But we have used this method for thousands of years to help augment those with the gift we can find. Hardly any with the gift are born anymore."

"I realize that, but we're in the business of teaching people, not breeding them. Our gold reduces them to creatures acting out of want of gold, instead of people having a child out of love."

Sister Dulcinia was stricken mute for only a moment. "How can we be seen as so heartless as to deny the help of a little of our gold? Lives are more important than gold."

"I've seen the reports; it's hardly a 'little' amount of gold. But that's beside the point; the point is that we are breeding our Creator's fellow children like livestock, and in so doing, we are breeding contempt for values."

"But we teach our young men values! As the Creator's highest creation, people respond to the teaching of values because they have the intellect to understand its importance."

Verna sighed. "Sister, suppose we preached truthfulness, and at the same time gladly handed out a penny for each lie told. What do you venture would be the result?"

Sister Phoebe covered her mouth as she laughed. "I'd venture we'd soon be penniless."

Sister Dulcinia's blue eyes were ice. "I didn't realize you were so heartless, Prelate, as to let the Creator's newborn children go hungry."

"The Creator gave their mothers breasts so they might suckle their children, not so they could wile gold from the palace."

Sister Dulcinia's face went crimson. "But, men have uncontrollable urges!"

Verna's voice lowered with heat. "The only time a man's urges are truly uncontrollable is when a sorceress casts a glamour. No Sister has cast a glamour spell over any of the women in the city. Need I remind you that were a Sister to do so, she would be lucky to be put out of the palace, if not hanged? As you well know, a glamour is the moral equivalent to rape."

Dulcinia's face had gone white. "I'm not saying—"

Verna glanced to the ceiling in thought. "As I recall, the last time a Sister was caught casting a glamour, was . . . what? Fifty years ago?"

Sister Dulcinia's gaze sought refuge but found none. "It was a novice, Prelate, not a Sister."

Verna kept her glare on Dulcinia. "You were on the tribunal, as I also recall." Dulcinia nodded. "And you voted to hang her. A poor young woman who had only been here for a few brief years, and you voted to put her to death."

"It's the law, Prelate," she said without looking up.

"It is the maximum of the law."

"Others voted the same as I."

Verna nodded. "Yes they did. A tie, six-six. Prelate Annalina broke the deadlock by voting to have the young woman banished."

Sister Dulcinia's penetrating blue eyes finally came up. "I still say she was wrong. Valdora vowed undying vengeance. She swore to destroy the Palace of the Prophets. She spat in the Prelate's face and promised someday to kill her."

Verna wrinkled her brow. "I always wondered, Dulcinia, why you were selected to be on the tribunal."

Sister Dulcinia swallowed. "Because I was her instructor."

"Really. Her teacher." Verna clicked her tongue. "Where do you suppose the young woman ever learned to cast a glamour?"

The color returned to Sister Dulcinia's face in a rush. "We were never able to establish that with certitude. Probably her mother. A mother often teaches a young sorceress such things."

"Yes, I've heard that, but I wouldn't know. My mother wasn't gifted; she was a skip. Your mother was gifted, if I recall. . . ."

"Yes, she was." Sister Dulcinia kissed her ring finger while whispering a prayer to the Creator, a private act of supplication and devotion done frequently, but rarely in front of others. "It's getting late, Prelate. We don't wish to keep you any longer."

Verna smiled. "Yes, good night, then."

Sister Dulcinia bent in a formal bow. "As you command, Prelate, tomorrow I will see to the matter of the pregnant woman and young wizard, after I clear it with Sister Leoma."

Verna lifted an eyebrow. "Oh? And now Sister Leoma outranks the Prelate, yes?"

"Well, no, Prelate," Sister Dulcinia stammered. "It's just that Sister Leoma likes me to . . . I just thought you would want me to inform your advisor of your action . . . so that she would not be caught . . . unawares."

"Sister Leoma is my advisor, Sister, I will inform her of my actions, if I deem it necessary."

Phoebe's round face tilted from one woman to the other as she silently watched the exchange.

"As you wish, Prelate, it will be done," Sister Dulcinia said. "Please forgive my . . . enthusiasm, in assisting my Prelate."

Verna shrugged, as best she could with the load of reports. "Of course, Sister. Good night."

Thankfully, they both departed without further argument. Grumbling to herself, Verna lugged the stack of reports into her office and dumped them on her desk beside the ones she had yet to get to. She eyed Millie, off in a corner scrubbing with a rag at a spot no one would ever see were it to be left there for the next hundred years.

The dimly lit office was silent but for the swishing of Millie's rag and her mumbling to herself under her breath. Verna ambled over to the bookcase near where the woman was on her knees working and ran a finger along the volumes without really seeing the gold-leafed titles on the worn spines of the ancient leather covers.

"How are your old bones, tonight, Millie?"

"Oh, don't get me started, Prelate, or I'll soon have your hands all over me trying to heal what can't be healed. Age, you know." Her knee nudged the bucket closer as her hand moved on to scrub at another place on the carpet. "We all get old. The Creator Himself must have intended it, as no mortal can heal it. Though I've had more time than most are granted, working here at the palace, I mean." Her tongue poked out of the corner of her mouth as she applied more force to the rag. "Yes, the Creator has blessed me with more years than I know what to do with."

Verna had never seen the sinewy little woman in anything other than a resolute state of movement. Even when she spoke, her rag constantly wiped at dust, or a thumb rubbed at a spot, or a nail picked at a crust of dirt no one else could see.

Verna pulled out a volume and opened it. "Well, I know that Prelate Annalina appreciated having you around all those years."

"Oh, yes, many years, it was. My, my, many years."

"A Prelate, I'm coming to discover, has precious little opportunity for friendship. It was good that she had yours. I'm sure I'll find no less comfort in having you around."

Millie mumbled a curse at a reluctant bit of dirt. "Oh yes, we had many a talk late into the night. My, my, but she was a wonderful woman. Wise, and kind. Why, she would listen to anyone, even old Millie."

Verna smiled as she absently turned a page in the book, a volume on the arcane laws of a long dead kingdom. "It was so good of you to help her, with her ring and the letter, I mean."

Millie looked up, a grin coming to her thin lips. Her hand had actually stopped wiping. "Ah, so you'll be wanting to know about that, like all the others."

Verna snapped the book closed. "Others? What others?"

Millie dunked her rag in the soapy water. "The Sisters—Leoma, Dulcinia, Maren, Philippa, those others. You know them, I'm sure." She licked the end of a finger and rubbed it on the bottom of the dark woodwork, squeaking off a spot. "There might have been a few more, I don't recall. Age, you know. They all came to me after the funeral. Not together, mind you," she said with a chuckle.

"You know, each alone, their eyes watching the shadows as they asked the same as you."

Verna had forgotten her pretense at the bookcase. "And what did you tell them?"

Millie rung her rag. "The truth, of course, same as I'll tell you, if you've a mind to hear it."

"Yes," Verna said, reminding herself to keep the edge out of her voice. "Since I'm the Prelate now and all, I think I should hear about it. Why don't you rest a bit, and tell me the story."

With a grunt of ache, Millie struggled to her feet and turned her sharp eyes on Verna. "Why, thank you, Prelate. But I've got work to do, you know. I wouldn't want you thinking I'm a slacker, seeking to work my tongue instead of my rag."

Verna patted the wiry woman's shoulder. "No fear of that, Millie. Tell me about Prelate Annalina."

"Well now, she was on her deathbed when I saw her. I cleaned Nathan's rooms, too, you know, so that's when I saw her, when I went to Nathan's. The Prelate trusted no one but me to go in there with that man. Can't say as I blame her, though the Prophet was always kind to me. Except when he would go off about something or another, yelling, you know. Not at me, understand, but at his condition and all, being locked in his apartments for all those years. Takes a toll on a man, I suppose."

Verna cleared her throat. "I imagine it was difficult for you to see the Prelate in such a condition."

Millie put a hand to Verna's arm. "Don't you just know it. Broke my heart, it did. But she was in her usual kind humor, despite the pain."

Verna was biting the inside of her lip. "You were telling me about the ring, and the letter."

"Oh, yes." Millie squinted, then reached out and picked a bit of lint from the shoulder of Verna's dress. "You should let me brush this out for you. It doesn't do to have people think . . ."

Verna took the woman's callused hand. "Millie, this is a bit important to me. Could you please tell me about how you came to have the ring?"

Millie smiled apologetically. "Ann told me she was dying. Said it right out, she did. 'Millie, I'm dying.' Well, I was in tears. She had been my friend for a good long time. She smiled and took my hand, just like you have it now, and told me that she had one last task she wished me to do. She pulled her ring off her finger and handed it to me. In my other hand, she put that letter sealed with wax and imprinted with the sunburst off the ring.

"She told me how when her funeral was going on, I should put the ring on top of the letter, on the pedestal I was to take in there. She told me to be careful not to touch the ring to the letter until just at the end, or the magic she had put around it could kill me. She warned me several times to remember to be careful not to touch them together until I did it all proper. She told me just what to do, in what order. So that's what I done. I never saw her again, after she gave me the ring."

Verna stared off out the open doors to the garden she had never had time to visit. "When was this?"

"That's a question none of the others asked," Millie mumbled to herself. She stroked a thin finger back and forth across her lower lip. "Let's see now. Quite a while back, it was. It was way back before the winter solstice. Yes, it was right after the attack, the day you left with young Richard. Now, there was a nice boy. Kind as a sunny day, he was. Always smiled at me with a how-do-you-do. Most of the other boys don't even see me, right there before their eyes, but young Richard always saw me, he did, and had a pleasant word for me, too."

Verna only half listened. She remembered the day Millie spoke of. She and Warren had gone with Richard to get him through the shield that kept him bound to the palace. After they passed through the shield, they went to the Baka Ban Mana people, and took them all to the Valley of the Lost, their ancestral homeland, a homeland they had been driven from three thousand years before in order that the towers that separated the Old from the New World be put up. Richard needed their spirit woman to help him.

Richard had used unimaginable power, not only Additive Magic, but Subtractive, too, to destroy the towers, and cleanse the valley, returning it to the Baka Ban Mana before he went on his desperate mission to stop the Keeper of the dead from escaping through the gateway and into the world of the living. Winter solstice had come and gone, so she knew he had succeeded.

Suddenly, Verna turned to Millie. "That was almost a month ago. Well before she died."

Millie nodded. "That seems about right to me."

"You mean to say that she gave you the ring almost three weeks before she died?" Millie nodded. "Why so long?"

"She said she wanted to give it to me before she slipped any further, and wouldn't be able to say good-bye to me, or be able to give proper instructions."

"I see. And when you went back after that, before she died, did she slip as she thought?"

Millie shrugged as she let out a sigh. "That was the only time I saw her. When I went back to see her, and to clean, the guards said that Nathan and the Prelate had left strict orders that no one was to be allowed in. Something about Nathan not being disturbed as he tried his best to heal her. I didn't want him to fail, so I tiptoed away, quiet as I could."

Verna sighed. "Well, thank you for telling me, Millie." Verna glanced at her desk, and the waiting stacks of reports. "I'd best be back at my work, too, or everyone will think me lazy."

"Oh, that's a shame, Prelate. Such a warm, beautiful night, you should enjoy your private garden."

Verna grunted. "I've so much work to do I've never even poked my nose out to look at the Prelate's private garden."

Millie started toward her bucket, but suddenly spun back. "Prelate! I just remembered something else that Ann told me."

Verna straightened her dress at her shoulders. "She told you something else? Something you told the others that you forgot to tell me?"

"No, Prelate," Millie whispered as she scurried closer. "No, she told me, and told me to tell none but the new Prelate. For some reason, it's been completely out of my memory until this moment."

"With all the rest, she may have spelled the message, to make you forget it for all but the new Prelate."

"That could be," Millie said as she rubbed her lip. She looked into Verna's eyes. "Ann would do things like that, sometimes. Sometimes, she could be devious."

Verna smiled without humor. "Yes, I know. I, too, have been on the receiving end of her manipulations. What is the message?"

"She said to tell you to be sure not to work too hard."

Verna rested a hand on a hip. "That's the message?"

Millie nodded as she leaned close and lowered her voice. "And she said that you should use the garden to relax. But she took my arm and pulled me close then, looking right into my eyes, and told me to tell you also to be sure to visit the Prelate's sanctuary."

"Sanctuary? What sanctuary?"

Millie turned and pointed through the open doors. "Out in the garden there's a little building nestled in the trees and shrubs. She called it her sanctuary. I've never been in it. She never allowed me to go in there to clean. She cleaned it herself, she said, because a sanctuary was a sacrosanct place where a body could be alone, and where no one else ever set foot. She would go there, from time to time, I think to pray for guidance from the Creator, or perhaps just to be alone. She said to be sure to tell you to go there and visit it."

Verna let out an exasperated breath. "Sounds like her way of telling me I would need the Creator's help to get through all the paperwork. She did have a twisted sense of humor, sometimes."

Millie chuckled. "Yes, Prelate, that she did. Twisted." Millie put her hands to her blushing cheeks. "May the Creator forgive me. She was a kind woman. Her humor was never meant to be hurtful."

"No, I suppose not."

Verna rubbed her temples as she started for her desk. She was tired, and dreaded the prospect of reading more mind numbing reports. She halted and turned back to Millie. The doors to the garden were opened wide, letting in the fresh night air.

"Millie, it's late, why don't you go have some dinner, and get some rest. Rest is good for tired bones."

Millie grinned. "Really, Prelate? You don't mind your office being layered in dirt?"

Verna laughed under her breath. "Millie, I've been out-of-doors for so many years that I've grown fond of dirt. It's fine, really. Have a good rest."

As Verna stood in the doorway to her garden, looking out into the night, at moonlight dappled ground beneath trees and vines, Millie gathered up her rags and bucket. "A good night to you, then, Prelate. Enjoy your visit to your garden."

She heard the door close and the room fall silent. She stood feeling the warm, moist breeze and inhaled the fragrant aroma of leaf and flower and earth.

Verna took a last look back at her office, and then stepped out into the waiting night.

CHAPTER 22

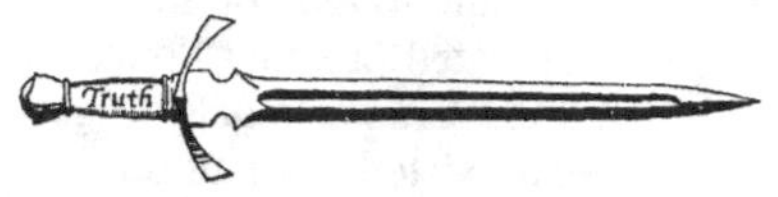

VERNA TOOK A DEEP, refreshing breath of the humid night air. It was like a tonic. She could feel her muscles relaxing as she strolled down a winding, narrow path, among beds of peeping lilies, flowering dogwood, and lush huckleberry bushes, as she waited for her eyes to adjust to the moonlight. Spreading trees reached over the dense shrubs, seeming to offer their branches for her to touch, or the sweet fragrance of their foliage and blossoms for her to inhale.

Though it was too early for most trees to be in bloom, in the Prelate's garden there were a few rare everblossoms—squat, gnarled, outspreading trees that bloomed throughout the year, though they fruited only in season. In the New World she had come across a small forest of everblossoms, and discovered them to be a favorite haunt of the elusive night wisps—frail creatures appearing to be nothing more than sparks of light, and only visible at night.

After the night wisps had been convinced of their benign intentions, she and the two Sisters she had been with at the time had spent several nights there, talking with the wisps of simple things and learning about the benevolent nature of the wizards and Confessors who guided the alliance of the Midlands. Verna had been pleased to learn that the people of the Midlands protected places of magic, and left the creatures inhabiting them to live their lives in unmolested solitude.

While there were wild places in the Old World where magic creatures dwelled, they were nowhere near as numerous or as varied as those wondrous places in the New World. Verna had learned a bit of tolerance from some of those creatures—that the Creator had sprinkled the world with many fragile wonders, and sometimes mankind's highest calling was to simply let them be.

In the Old World that view was not widely held, and there were many places where wild magic had been brought under control lest people be injured or killed by things not amenable to reason. Magic could often be "inconvenient." In many ways, the New World was still a wild place, as the Old World had been thousands of years ago, before man made it a safe, if somewhat sterile, place through its notions of stewardship.

Verna missed the New World. She had never felt so at home as she did there.

Ducks sleeping with their heads tucked back under their wings bobbed at the edge of a pond beside the path, while unseen frogs croaked from the reeds. Verna saw an occasional fluttermouse swoop down across the surface of the water to snatch a bug from the air. Moon shadows played across the grassy bank as the gentle breeze caressed the trees overhead.

Just beyond the pond, a small side trail turned off toward a stand of trees among a thicket of underbrush hardly touched by the moonlight. Verna somehow felt this was the place she sought, and strolled off the main path, toward the waiting shadows. The grounds here seemed to be ruled by the wildness of nature, as opposed to the cultured look of much of the garden.

Through a narrow opening in the wall of thorn glove, Verna found an enchanting little stuccoed building with four gables, the rake of each tiled roof swooping down in a gentle curve to eaves no higher than her head. A towering maidenhair tree stood off the face of each gable, its branches lacing together overhead. Sweetbriar hugged the ground close to the walls, suffusing the cozy enclosure with a fragrant scent. A round window, too high to see through, was set in the peak of each gable.

At one gabled wall, where the path ended, Verna found a rough-hewn, round-topped door with a sunburst pattern carved in its center. There was a pull handle, but no lock. A tug produced no movement, not even a wiggle. The door was shielded.

Verna ran her fingers along the edge, feeling for the nature of the shield, or its keyway. She felt only an icy chill that made her recoil at its touch.

She opened herself to her Han, letting the sweet light inundate her with its warm, familiar comfort. She nearly gasped with the glory of being just that much closer to the Creator. The air suddenly smelled of a thousand scents; against her flesh it felt of moisture, dust, pollen, and salt from the ocean; in her ears it carried the sounds of a world of insects, small animals, and fragments of words carried for miles in its airy, volatile fingers. She listened carefully for any sounds that might betray anyone near, at least anyone with no more than Additive Magic. She heard none.

Verna focused her Han on the door before her. Her probe told her that the entire building was encased in a web, but not one she had ever felt before: it had elements of ice woven through with spirit. She didn't even know ice could be woven with spirit. The two fought each other like cats in a sack, but there it was, the two of them purring contentedly, as if they belonged together. She had absolutely no idea how such a shield could be breached, much less undone.

Still joined with her Han, an impulse came to her, and she reached up, touching the sunburst pattern on her ring to that on the door. The door swung silently open.

Verna stepped inside and placed the ring on the sunburst pattern carved on the inside of the door. It obediently swung closed. With her Han she could feel the shield seal tight around her. Verna had never felt so isolated, so alone, so safe.

Candles sprang to flame. She surmised that they must be tied to the shield. The light from the ten candles, five each in two candlesticks with branching arms, was more than sufficient to light the inside of the small sanctuary. The candlesticks stood to each side of a small altar draped with a white cloth trimmed in gold thread. Atop the white cloth rested a perforated bowl, probably for burning aromatic gums. A red brocade kneeling pad edged with gold tassels sat on the floor before the altar.

Each of the four alcoves formed by the gables was only large enough for the comfortable-looking chair occupying one of them.

One of the others held the altar, another a tiny table with a three-legged stool, and the last, along with the door, a box bench with a neatly folded quilted comforter, probably for the lap, as lying down looked to be out of the question; the area in the center wasn't much larger than the alcoves.

Verna turned about, wondering what it was she was supposed to do here. Prelate Annalina had left a message to make sure she visited the place, but why? What was she to accomplish here?

She flopped down in the chair, her eyes searching the faceted walls that followed the in-and-out of the gable ends. Maybe she was supposed to come here to relax. Annalina knew the work of being Prelate; maybe she simply wanted her successor to know of a place where she could be alone, a place to get away from people always bringing her reports. Verna drummed her fingers on the arm of the chair. Not likely.

She didn't feel like sitting. There were more important things to do. There were reports waiting, and they were hardly likely to begin reading themselves. Hands clasped behind her back, Verna paced, as best she could, around the tiny room. This was certainly a waste of time. She finally let out an exasperated breath and lifted her fist toward the door, but stopped before she touched the ring to the sunburst pattern.

Verna turned back, staring for a moment, then lifted her skirts and knelt on the pad. Perhaps Annalina wanted her to pray for guidance. A Prelate was expected to be a pious person, although it was absurd to think one needed a special place to pray to the Creator. The Creator had created everything, everywhere was His special place, so why would one need a special place to seek guidance? A special place could never approach the meaningfulness of one's own heart. No place could compare to joining with her Han.

With an irritated sigh, Verna folded her hands. She waited, but wasn't in the mood to pray to the Creator in a place in which she was under obligation to do so. It vexed her to think that Annalina was dead yet still manipulated her. Verna's eyes roved the bare walls as her toe tapped against the floor. That woman was reaching out from the world beyond to enjoy a final morsel of control. Hadn't she had enough of that in all the years she was Prelate? One would think that would be enough, but no, she had to have it all planned out so that even after she was dead, she could still . . .

Verna's eyes settled on the bowl. There was something in the bottom, and it wasn't ashes.

She reached in and lifted out a small package wrapped in paper and tied with a bit of string. She turned it over in her fingers, inspecting it. This had to be it. This had to be what she was sent here for. But why leave it in here? The shield—no one but the Prelate could enter. This was the only place to put something if you didn't want anyone but the Prelate to have it.

Verna pulled the ends of the bow and dropped the string back in the bowl. Laying it in a palm, she lifted back the paper and stared at what was inside.

It was a journey book.

Finally, movement returned to her fingers and she extracted the book from the paper to thumb through the pages. Blank.

Journey books were objects of magic, like the dacra, that had been created by the same wizards who had invested the Palace of the Prophets with both Additive and Subtractive Magic. None since, for three thousand years, except Richard, had been born with Subtractive. Some had learned it through the calling, but none but Richard had been born with it.

Journey books had the ability to transmit messages; what was written in one with the stylus stored in the spine would appear by magic in its twin. As near as they could determine, the message written in one appeared in the twin simultaneously. Since the stylus could also be used to wipe old messages away, the books were never used up, and could be used over and over.

They had been carried by Sisters who went on journeys to recover boys born with the gift. More often than not, the Sisters had had to travel through the barrier, through the Valley of the Lost, going into the New World to recover the boy and put a Rada'Han around his neck so that the gift would not harm him while he learned to control his magic. Once beyond the barrier there was no turning back for instructions or guidance; one journey through and back was all that was possible for each Sister. Until now—Richard had destroyed the towers and their storms of spells.

A young boy with no understanding of the gift could not control it, and his magic sent out telltale signs that could be detected by Sisters at the palace who were sensitive to such disturbances in the flows of power. Not enough Sisters had this talent to risk sending them on journeys, so others were sent, and they carried a journey book to be able to communicate with the palace. If Sisters were to go after the boy, and something happened—he moved, for example—they would need guidance to find him in his new location.

Of course, a wizard could teach the boy to control the gift in order to avoid its many dangers, and in fact that was the preferred method, but wizards were not always available, or willing. The Sisters had long ago established an accord with the wizards in the New World. In the absence of a wizard, the Sisters of the Light were allowed to save a boy's life by taking him to the Palace of the Prophets for training in the use of his gift. For their part, the Sisters had vowed never to take a boy who had a wizard willing to teach him.

It was a truce backed by a death sentence to any Sister who ever again entered the New World if the agreement were ever violated. Prelate Annalina had violated that agreement in order to bring Richard to the palace. Verna had been the unwitting instrument of the violation.

At any one time there could be several Sisters gone on a journey to recover a boy. Verna had found a whole box of journey books back in her office, tied together in matching pairs. The journey books were twinned, each working only with its correct twin. Precautions were always taken before a journey was undertaken; the two books were taken to separate locations and tested, just to be sure a Sister wasn't sent off with the wrong book. Journeys were dangerous, that was why the Sisters also carried a dacra up their sleeve.

Usually, a journey lasted a few months, and on rare occasions they had lasted as long as a year. Verna's journey had lasted over twenty years. Nothing like that had ever happened before, but then, it had been three thousand years since one like Richard had been born. Verna had lost twenty years she could never recover. She had aged in the outside world. The twenty-odd years of aging her body had undergone would have taken near to three hundred years at the Place of the Prophets. She had not simply given up twenty years to go on Prelate Annalina's mission; she had in reality given up close to three hundred years.

Worse, Annalina had known all along where Richard was. Even though she had done as she had in order to allow the proper prophecies to come to pass so they could stop the Keeper, it hurt that she had never told Verna that she was being sent out to throw away that much of her life as a decoy.

Verna reprimanded herself. She had not thrown anything away. She had been doing the Creator's work. Just because she hadn't known all the facts at the time made it no less important. Many people toiled their whole lives at meaningless things. Verna had toiled at something that had saved the world of the living.

Besides that, those twenty years were perhaps the best years of her life. She had been out in the world on her own, with two other Sisters of the Light, learning about strange places and strange peoples. She had slept under the stars, seen distant mountains, plains, rivers, rolling hills, villages, towns, and cities that few others had seen. She had made her own decisions and accepted the consequences. She had never had to read reports; she had lived the stuff of reports. No, she had not lost anything. She had gained more than any of the Sisters sitting back here for three hundred years would ever gain.

Verna felt a tear drop onto her hand. She reached up and wiped her cheek. She missed her journey. All that time she had thought she hated it, and only now did she realize how much it meant to her. She turned the journey book over in her trembling fingers, feeling the familiar size and weight—the familiar grain of the leather, the familiar three little bumps at the top of the front cover.

She jerked the book up to her eyes, looking in the candlelight. The three bumps, the deep scratch at the bottom of the spine—it was the same book. She couldn't mistake her journey book, not after carrying it for twenty years. It was the very same book. She had looked at all the books in the box in her office, absently searching for this one, and she had not found it. It had been here.

But why? She held up the paper it had been wrapped in and saw there was writing on the paper. She held it near the candle in order to read it.

Guard this with your life.

She turned the paper over, but that was all it said. *Guard this with your life.*

Verna knew the Prelate's hand. When she had been on her journey to recover Richard, and after she had found him but was forbidden to interfere with him in any way, or to use his collar to help control him, yet was expected to bring him back, a grown man, unlike any other they had ever recovered, she had sent an angry message to the palace: *I am the Sister in charge of this boy. These directives are beyond reason if not absurd. I demand to know the meaning of these instructions. I demand to know upon whose authority they are given.*

She had received back a message: *You will do as you are instructed, or suffer the consequences. Do not presume to question the orders of the palace again. —In my own hand, The Prelate.*

The message of reprimand the Prelate had sent her was burned in her memory. The handwriting was engraved in her memory. The hand on the piece of paper was the same.

That message had been a thorn in her side, forbidding her to do the very things she had been trained to do. It was only back at the palace that she discovered that Richard had Subtractive Magic, and had she used the collar he would have very likely killed her. The Prelate had been saving her life, but it nettled her that once again she had not been informed. Verna guessed that was what annoyed her the most: the Prelate not telling her why.

She understood, of course. There had been Sisters of the Dark at the palace, and the Prelate could not take any risk or the whole world would be consumed; but emotionally it still vexed her. Reason and passion were not always in agreement. As Prelate, she was coming to see that sometimes you couldn't convince people of the need of something, and the only option was simply to give an order. Sometimes you had to use people to do what must be done.

Verna dropped the paper in the bowl and ignited it with a flow of Han. She watched it burn, just to be sure it was entirely reduced to ash.

Verna squeezed the journey book, her journey book, tightly in her hand. It was good to have it back. Of course, it wasn't really hers, it belonged to the palace, but she had carried it so many years that it felt like hers, like an old, familiar friend.

The thought struck her abruptly—where was the other one? This book had a twin. Where was its twin? Who had it?

She regarded the book with sudden trepidation. She was holding something potentially dangerous, and once again Annalina was not telling her all of it. It was entirely possible that its twin was held by a Sister of the Dark. This could be Annalina's way of telling her to find its twin, and she would find a Sister of the Dark. But how? She couldn't simply write, "Who are you, and where are you?" in the book.

Verna kissed her ring finger, her ring, and then stood.

Guard this with your life.

Journeys were dangerous. Sisters had been captured, and on occasion killed, by hostile peoples who were protected by magic of their own. In those instances, only her dacra, a knifelike weapon with the ability to instantly extinguish life, could protect her, if she were quick enough. Verna still had hers up her sleeve. On the back of her belt Verna had long ago sewn a pouch to secret the journey book and keep it safe.

She slipped the little book into its glovelike pouch. Verna patted her belt. It felt good to have the journey book back there.

Guard this with your life.

Dear Creator, who had the other?

When Verna burst through the door to her outer office, Sister Phoebe jumped up as if someone had stuck her in the rump with a sharp stick.

Her round face went red. "Prelate . . . you startled me. You weren't in your office. . . . I thought you had gone to bed."

Verna's gaze swept the desk scattered with reports. "I thought I told you that you had done enough work for one day, and to go get some rest."

Phoebe twisted her fingers together as she winced. "You did, but I remembered some tallies I had forgotten to verify, and I was afraid you would see them and call me to account, so I ran back to check the numbers."

Verna had somewhere to go, but rethought how she had planned to go about it. She clasped her hands.

"Phoebe, how would you like to do a task that Prelate Annalina always trusted to her administrators?"

Sister Phoebe's fingers stilled. "Really? What is it?"

Verna gestured back toward her office. "I've been out in my garden, praying for guidance, and it has come to me that in these trying times I should consult the prophecies. Whenever Prelate Annalina did the same, she always had her administrators clear the vaults so that she wouldn't feel encumbered by prying eyes watching what she read. How would you like to order the vaults cleared for me, like her administrators did for her?"

The young woman bounced on the balls of her feet. "Really, Verna? That would be splendid."

Young woman indeed, Verna thought in annoyance, they were the same age, even if they didn't look it. "Let's be off then. I have palace business to attend to."

Sister Phoebe snatched up her white shawl, throwing it over her shoulders as she bolted through the door.

"Phoebe." The round face peeked back around the doorframe. "If Warren is in the vaults, have him stay. I have a few questions, and he would be better able to direct me to the proper volumes than any of the others would. It will save me time."

"All right Verna," Phoebe said in a breathless voice. She liked doing paperwork, probably because it made her feel useful in a way she never would have until she had another hundred years of experience, but Verna had cut that time short by appointing her the Prelate's administrator. The prospect of wielding orders, though, seemed to be of even more interest than paperwork. "I'll run ahead and have them cleared by the time you get there." She grinned. "I'm glad it was me here, instead of Dulcinia."

Verna remembered how she and Phoebe used to be of such like personalities. Verna wondered if she really had such an immature temperament when Annalina had sent her on her journey. It seemed to her that in the years she had been gone she had grown older than Phoebe in more than just appearance. Perhaps she had simply learned more out in the world, rather than in the cloistered life of the Palace of the Prophets.

Verna smiled. "Almost seems like one of our old pranks, doesn't it?"

Phoebe giggled. "Sure does, Verna. Except it won't end in us stringing a thousand prayer beads." She dashed off down the hall, her skirts and shawl flapping behind.

By the time Verna had made it down into the heart of the palace, to the huge, round, six-foot-thick stone door leading into vaults carved from the bedrock atop which sat the palace, Phoebe was just leading six Sisters, two novices, and three young men out.

Novices and young men were given lessons at all hours of the day and night. Sometimes they were even awakened in the dead of night for lessons, such as ones down in the vaults. The Creator didn't keep hours; they were expected to learn that in His work they didn't, either. They all bowed as one.

"The Creator's blessing on you," Verna said to them as a group. She was about to apologize for chasing them from the vaults when they were busy, but she cut herself off, reminding herself that she was the Prelate and didn't need to make excuses to anyone. The Prelate's word was law, and was followed without question. Still, it was hard not to explain herself.

"All clear, Prelate," Sister Phoebe said in an august tone. Phoebe inclined her head toward the room beyond. "Except the one you asked to see. He's in one of the small rooms."

Verna nodded to her assistant and then turned her attention to the novices, who were in a state of wide-eyed awe. "And how are your studies coming?"

Trembling like leaves on a quaking aspen, both girls curtsied. One swallowed. "Very well, Prelate," she squeaked, her face going red.

Verna remembered the first time the Prelate had addressed her directly. It had seemed as if the Creator Himself had spoken. She remembered how much the Prelate's smile had meant to her, how it had sustained and inspired her.

Verna squatted down and in each arm hugged a girl to herself. She kissed each forehead.

"If you ever have a need, don't be afraid to come to me, that's what I'm here for, and I love you like all the Creator's children."

Both girls beamed, and performed curtsies more steady the second time. Their round eyes stared at the gold ring on her finger. As if it had reminded them, they each kissed their own ring finger, whispering a prayer to the Creator. Verna did the same. Their eyes widened at the sight.

She held her hand out. "Would you like to kiss the ring that symbolizes the Light we all follow?" They nodded earnestly, going to a knee in turns to kiss the sunburst-patterned ring.

Verna squeezed each small shoulder. "What are your names?"

"Helen, Prelate," one said.

"Valery, Prelate," the other said.

"Helen and Valery." Verna didn't need to remind herself to

smile. "Remember, novices Helen and Valery, that while there are others, such as the Sisters, who know more than you, and will teach you many things, there is no one closer to the Creator than you, not even me. We are all His children."

Verna felt more than a little uncomfortable being the object of veneration, but she smiled and waved as the group headed off down the stone hall.

After they had rounded a corner, Verna pressed her hand to the cold metal plate set in the wall, the plate that was the keyway to the shield guarding the vaults. The ground shook beneath her feet as the huge, round door began to move. It was rare for the main vault door to be closed; except under special circumstances, only the Prelate ever sealed the entrance. She stepped into the vault as the door grated closed behind her, leaving her in tomblike silence.

Verna passed the old, worn tables with papers scattered all over them, along with some of the simpler books of prophecy. The Sisters had been giving lessons. The lamps set about the carved stone walls did little to diminish a feeling of perpetual night. Long rows of bookcases stretched off to either side among massive pillars supporting the vaulted ceiling.

Warren was in one of the back rooms. The small, hollowed-out alcoves were restricted, and so had separate doors and shields. The room he was in was one with the oldest prophecies written in High D'Haran. Few people knew High D'Haran, among them Warren, and Verna's predecessor.

When she stepped into the lamplight, Warren, slouched against the table with his arms folded atop it, only glanced up. "Phoebe told me you wanted to use the vaults," he said in a distracted voice.

"Warren, I need to talk to you. Something has happened."

He flipped a page in the book before him. He didn't look up. "Yes, all right."

She frowned and then drew a chair to the table beside him, but didn't sit. With a flick of her wrist, Verna brought a dacra to her left hand. The dacra, with a silver rod in place of a blade, was used the same as a knife, but it wasn't the wound it caused that killed; the dacra was a weapon possessing ancient magic. Used in conjunction with the wielder's Han, it drained the life force from the victim, regardless of the nature of the wound. There was no defense against its magic.

Warren looked up with tired, red eyes as she leaned closer. "Warren, I want you to have this."

"That's a weapon of the Sisters."

"You have the gift, it will work for you as well as me."

"What do you want me to do with it?"

"Protect yourself."

He frowned. "What do you mean?"

"The Sisters of the . . ." She glanced back into the main room. Even if it was empty, there was no telling how far one with Subtractive Magic could hear. They had heard Prelate Annalina name them. "You know." She lowered her voice. "Warren, though you have the gift, it will not protect you against them. This will. There is no protection against this. None." She spun the weapon in her hand with practiced grace, walking it over the backs of her fingers as it twirled. The dull silver color was a blur in the lamplight. She caught the rodlike blade and held the handle out to him. "I found extras in my office. I want you to have one."

He flipped his hand dismissively. "I don't know how to handle that thing. I only know how to read the old books."

Verna snatched his violet robes at his neck and drew his face close. "You just stick it in them. Belly, chest, back, neck, arm, hand, foot—it doesn't matter. Just stick them while you're shrouded in your Han, and they will be dead before you can blink."

"My sleeves aren't tight like yours. It will just fall out."

"Warren, the dacra doesn't know where you keep it, or care. Sisters practice for hours on end, and carry them in our sleeve so they will be readily at hand. We do that for protection when we go on journeys. It doesn't matter where you carry it, only that you do. Keep it in a pocket, if you wish. Just don't sit on it."

With a sigh, he took the dacra. "If it will make you happy. But I don't think I could stab anyone."

She released his robes as she looked away. "You would be surprised what you can do, when you have to."

"Is this what you came for? You found an extra dacra?"

"No." She drew the little book from its pouch behind her belt and tossed it on the table before him. "I came because of this."

He glanced at her out of the corner of his eye. "Going somewhere, Verna?"

Scowling, she smacked his shoulder. "What's the matter with you?"

He pushed the book away. "I'm just tired. What's so important about a journey book?"

She lowered her voice. "Prelate Annalina left a message that I should go to her private sanctuary, in her garden. It was shielded with a web of ice and spirit." Warren lifted an eyebrow. She showed him her ring. "This opens it. Inside I found this journey book. It was wrapped in a piece of paper that said only 'Guard this with your life.'"

Warren picked up the journey book and thumbed through the blank pages. "She probably just wants to send you instructions."

"She's dead!"

Warren cocked an eyebrow. "Do you think that would stop her?"

Verna smiled in spite of herself. "Maybe you're right. Maybe we burned the other with her, and she intended to run my life from the world of the dead."

Warren's expression slipped back to sullen. "So, who has the other one?"

Verna smoothed her dress behind her knees and sat, scooting the chair closer. "I don't know. I'm worried that it could be a tell-tale of sorts. She might have meant it to mean that if I discovered the other, it would identify our enemy."

Warren's smooth brow wrinkled up. "That doesn't make any sense. Why would you think that?"

"I don't know, Warren." Verna wiped a hand across her face. "It was the only thing I could think of. Can you think of anything that would make more sense? Why else would she not tell me who had the other? If it was someone meant to help us, someone on our side, then it would only make sense for her to have told me the name, or at least that it was a friend who had the other."

Warren returned his stare to the table. "I suppose."

Verna checked her tone before she spoke. "Warren, what's wrong? I've never seen you like this before."

She shared a long look with his troubled blue eyes. "I've read some prophecies I don't like."

Verna searched his face. "What do they say?"

After a long pause, he reached down, and with two fingers

turned a piece of paper around and pushed it toward her. Finally, she picked it up and read it aloud.

"When the Prelate and the Prophet are given to the Light in the sacred rite, the flames will bring to boil a cauldron of guile and give ascension to a false Prelate, who will reign over the death of the Palace of the Prophets. To the north, the one bonded to the blade will abandon it for the silver sliph, for he will breathe her back to life, and she will deliver him into the arms of the wicked."

Verna swallowed, afraid to meet Warren's eyes. She set the paper on the table and folded her hands in her lap to stop their trembling. She sat silently staring down, not knowing what to say.

"This is a prophecy on a true fork," Warren said, at last.

"That's an audacious statement, Warren, even for one as talented with prophecies as you. How old is this prophecy?"

"Not yet a day."

Her wide eyes came up. "What?" she whispered. "Warren, are you saying that . . . that it came to you? That you have at last given a prophecy?"

Warren's red eyes stared back. "Yes. I went into a kind of trance, and in this state of rapture, I had a vision of fragments of this prophecy, along with the words. That was the way it happened for Nathan, too, I believe. Remember that I told you I was beginning to understand prophecy in a way I never had before? It's through the visions that the prophecies are truly meant to be revealed."

Verna swept her hand around. "But the books hold prophecies, not visions. The words prophesy."

"The words are only a way to pass them down, and only meant to be clues that trip the vision in one who has the gift for prophecy. All the studying the Sisters have done for the last three thousand years is only a partial understanding of them. The written words were meant to pass knowledge to wizards through the visions. That's what I learned when this one came to me. It was like a door opening in my mind. All this time, and the key was right inside my own head."

"You mean you can read any of these, and have a vision that will reveal its true meaning?"

He shook his head. "I'm a child, who has taken his first step. I've a long way to go before I'll be vaulting over fences."

She looked at the page on the table and then glanced away as she twisted the ring around and around on her finger. "And does this one, the one that came to you, mean what it sounds like?"

Warren licked his lips. "Like an infant's first step, which is not very steady, this is not the most stable of prophecies. You might say it's sort of a practice prophecy. I've found others that I think are the same sort of first attempts, like this one here—"

"Warren, is it true or not!"

He tugged his sleeves down his arms. "It's all true, but the words, as in all prophecies, while true, are not necessarily what they would seem."

Verna leaned close as she gritted her teeth. "Answer the question, Warren. We're in this together. I have to know."

He flipped his hand, as he often did when trying to diminish the importance of something. To Verna, though, that flip of a hand was like a flag of warning. "Look, Verna, I'll tell you what I know, what I saw in the vision, but I'm new at this, and I don't understand it all, even though it's my prophecy."

She kept a steady glare on him. "Tell me, Warren."

"The Prelate in the prophecy is not you. I don't know who it is, but it isn't you."

Verna closed her eyes as she sighed. "Warren, that's not as bad as I thought. At least it's not to be me who does this terrible thing. We can work to turn this prophecy to a false fork."

Warren looked away. He stuffed the paper with his prophecy into an open book and flopped it closed. "Verna, for someone else to be Prelate, that has to mean you will be dead."

CHAPTER 23

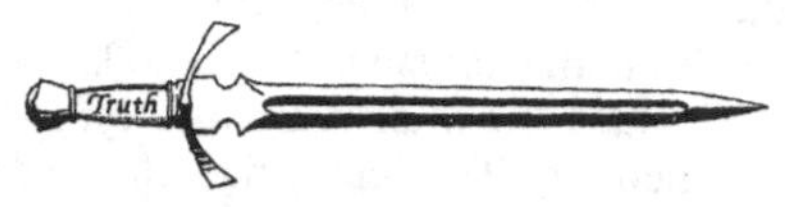

WHEN HIS WHOLE BODY suddenly flushed with the sweet agony of desire, he knew, even though he couldn't see her, that she had entered the room. His nostrils filled with her unmistakable scent, and already he ached to surrender. Like a furtive movement in the mist, he couldn't discern the essence of the threat, but somehow in the dim recesses of his awareness he knew without doubt that there was one, and the exquisite peril, too, excited him.

With the desperation of a man being stormed by an overpowering foe, he clawed for the hilt of his sword, hoping to rally his resolve and stay the hand of submission. It wasn't bared steel he sought, though, but the bared teeth of anger, a rage that would sustain him and give him the will to resist. He could do it. He had to; everything turned on this.

His hand anchored on the hilt at his belt, and he felt the flood of perfect fury coursing through his body and mind.

When Richard glanced up, he could see the approach of Ulic and Egan's heads above the knot of people before him. Even if he hadn't seen them, to see the space between them where she would be, he knew she was there. Soldiers and dignitaries began parting to make way for the two big men and their charge. Heads tilted in waves, reminding him of the rings of ripples in a pond, as they passed whispers to others. Richard recalled that the prophecies had also named him "the pebble in the pond"—the generator of ripples in the world of life.

And then he saw her.

His chest constricted with longing. She was wearing the same rose-colored silk dress that she had worn the night before, having no change of clothes with her. Richard recalled vividly how she had said she slept naked. He could feel his heart hammering.

With great effort, he struggled to put his mind to the task at hand. She looked with wide eyes at the soldiers she knew; they were her Keltish palace guard. Now, they wore D'Haran uniforms.

Richard had been up early, preparing everything. He hadn't been able to get much sleep anyway, and the sleep he had gotten had been wracked with dreams of longing.

Kahlan, my love, can you ever forgive me my dreams?

With this many D'Haran troops in Aydindril, he had known there would be supplies of all sorts available, so he had ordered spare uniforms brought out. The Keltans, being disarmed as they were, were in no position to argue, but after they had put on the dark leather and mail, and had had a chance to see how fierce they looked in the new outfits, they began to grin with approval. They were told that Kelton was now a part of D'Hara, and were given back their weapons. They stood in rank, now, proud and straight as they kept an eye on the representatives of the other lands who had yet to surrender.

As it had turned out, the bad luck of the storm that had allowed Brogan to escape had also carried good fortune as a balance; the dignitaries had wanted to wait out the foul weather before departing, so Richard had taken what the fates had offered him and had brought them back to the palace before they were to leave later that morning. Only the highest, the most important, of those officials were present. He wanted them to witness the surrender of Kelton: one of the most powerful lands of the Midlands. He wanted them to have one final lesson.

Richard stood as Cathryn started up the steps at the side of the dais, her gaze sweeping the faces watching her. Berdine stepped back to give her room. Richard had positioned the three Mord-Sith at the far ends of the platform, where they wouldn't be too close to him. He wasn't interested in anything they might have to say.

When Cathryn's brown-eyed gaze finally settled on him, he had to lock his knees to keep his legs from buckling. His left hand, gripping the hilt of his sword, was beginning to throb. He reminded himself that he didn't need to be holding the sword to command its magic and chanced removing his hand to wiggle some feeling back into his fingers while he contemplated the tasks before him.

When the Sisters of the Light had tried to teach him to touch his Han, they had had him use a mental picture to concentrate his inner will. Richard had selected an image of the Sword of Truth to be his focus, and he had it firmly fixed in his mind, now.

But for the battle with the people gathered before him today, his sword would be of no use. Today he would need the deft maneuvers devised with the aid of General Reibisch, his officers, and knowledgeable members of the palace staff, who had also helped with the arrangements. He hoped he had it all right.

"Richard, what—"

"Welcome, Duchess. Everything has been prepared." Richard scooped up her hand and kissed it in a manner he judged befitting a queen being greeted before an audience, but touching her only fired his heat. "I knew you would want these representatives to witness your bravery at being the first to join with us against the Imperial Order, the first to break the path for the Midlands."

"But I . . . well, yes . . . of course."

He turned to the watching faces. They were a considerably more quiet and compliant group than they had been the last time, as they waited in tense anticipation.

"Duchess Lumholtz—whom you all know is soon to be named queen of Kelton—has committed her people to the cause of freedom, and wished you to be here to witness as she signs the documents of surrender."

"Richard," she whispered as she leaned a little closer, "I must . . . have them looked over by our barristers first . . . just to be sure everything is clear, and there will be no misunderstandings."

Richard smiled reassuringly. "Though I'm sure you will find them quite clear, I've already anticipated your concern and took the liberty of inviting them to the signing." Richard held a hand out to the other end of the dais. Raina seized a man's arm and urged him up the steps. "Master Sifold, would you give your future queen your professional opinion?"

He bowed. "As Lord Rahl says, Duchess, the papers are quite clear. There is no room for misinterpretation."

Richard lifted the ornately decorated document from the desk. "With your permission, Duchess, I would like to read it to the gathered representatives, so they may see that Kelton wishes this joining of our forces to be unequivocal. So they may see your bravery."

Her head rose with pride before the eyes of the representatives of the other lands. "Yes. Please do, Lord Rahl."

Richard glanced to the waiting faces. "Please bear with me; this isn't long." He held the paper up before himself and read it aloud. "Know all peoples, that Kelton hereby surrenders unconditionally to D'Hara. Signed, in my hand, as the duly appointed leader of the Keltish people, the Duchess Lumholtz."

Richard set the document back on the desk and dunked the quill pen in a bottle of ink before offering it to Cathryn. She stood stiff and unmoving. Her face had gone ashen.

Fearing she would balk, he had no choice. Summoning strength he knew he was stealing from what he would need later, he put his lips close to her ear, enduring silently the torturous wave of longing at the warm fragrance of her flesh.

"Cathryn, after we finish here, would you go for a walk with me, just the two of us, alone? I dreamed of nothing but you."

Radiant color bloomed in her cheeks. He thought she might put an arm around his neck and thanked the spirits when she didn't.

"Of course, Richard," she whispered back. "I, too, dreamed of nothing but you. Let's get this formality over with."

"Make me proud of you, of your strength."

Richard thought that, surely, her smile would make others in the room blush. He could feel his ears burn at the meaning her smile conveyed.

She took the quill pen, brushing his hand as she did so, and held it up. "I sign this surrender with a quill from a dove, to signify that what I do is done willingly, in peace, and not as one defeated. I do it out of love for my people, and a hope for the future. That hope is this man here—Lord Rahl. I swear the undying vengeance of my people on any of you who would think to harm him."

She bent and scrawled her sweeping signature across the bottom of the surrender document.

Before she could straighten, Richard produced more papers and slid them under her.

"What . . ."

"The letters you spoke of, Duchess. I didn't want to weigh you down with the tedium of having to do the work yourself when we could put the time to a better purpose. Your aides helped me draw them up. Please check them, just to be sure all is as you intended when you made the offer last night.

"Lieutenant Harrington, of your palace guard, helped with the names of General Baldwin, commander of all Keltish forces, Division Generals Cutter, Leiden, Nesbit, Bradford, and Emerson, and a few of the guard commanders. There's a letter to each for you to sign, ordering them to turn over all command to my D'Haran officers. Some of your palace guard officers will accompany a detachment of my men along with the new officers.

"Your adjutant aide, Master Montleon, has been of invaluable assistance with the instructions to Finance Minister Pelletier; Master Carlisle, the deputy administrator of strategic planning; the governors in charge of the trade commission, Cameron, Tuck, Spooner, Ashmore; as well as Levardson, Doudiet, and Faulkingham of the office of commerce.

"Coadjutant Schaffer, of course, drew up the list of your mayors. We didn't want to offend anyone by leaving them out, of course, so he had several aides help him work up a complete list. There are letters here for them all, but of course the letters of instruction are the same, with just the proper name to each, so you only have to check over one, and then just sign the rest. We'll handle it from there. I have men ready to ride with the official document pouches. A man from your guard will accompany each, just to make sure there's no confusion. We have all the men from your guard here to witness your signature."

Richard drew a breath and straightened as Cathryn, still holding the pen in midair, blinked at all the papers Richard had pushed before her. Her aides had all come up to surround her, proud of the job they had accomplished in such short order.

Richard leaned close to her again. "I hope I got it all as you wished, Cathryn. You said you'd take care of it, but I didn't want to be away from you while you toiled at the work, so I rose early and took care of it for you. I hope you're pleased."

She glanced over letters, pushing them aside to look at others underneath. "Yes . . . of course."

Richard slid a chair closer. "Why don't you have a seat?"

When she had sat, and started signing her name, Richard pushed his sword out of the way and sat beside her, in the Mother Confessor's chair. He settled his gaze on the people watching, and kept it there as he listened to the pen scratching. He kept the rage on a slow boil in order to concentrate.

Richard turned back to the smiling Keltish officials behind and to each side of her chair. "You've all performed a valuable service this morning, and I would be honored if you would be willing to continue in an official capacity. I'm sure I could use your talents in administering the growing D'Hara."

After they had all bowed and thanked him for his generosity, he once again turned his attention to the silent group watching the proceedings. The D'Haran soldiers, especially the officers, having spent months stationed in Aydindril, had learned a great deal about trade in the Midlands. In the four days he had been with them searching for Brogan, Richard had learned all he could, and had added to that knowledge earlier that morning. When he knew the questions to ask, Mistress Sanderholt had proven to be a woman of vast knowledge gathered over years of having prepared the dishes of many lands. Food, as it turned out, was a reservoir of knowledge about a people. Her keen ear didn't hurt, either.

"Some of the papers the duchess is signing are trade instructions," Richard told the officials as Cathryn bent over her work. His eyes lingered on her shoulders. He willed them away. "Since Kelton is now part of D'Hara, you must understand that there can be no trade between Kelton and those of you who have not joined with us."

He turned his gaze on a short, round man with a curly black and gray beard. "I realize, Representative Garthram, that this will put Lifany in an uncomfortable position. With Galea and Kelton's borders now ordered sealed to anyone not part of D'Hara, you will have a very difficult time with trade.

"With Galea and Kelton to your north, D'Hara to your east, and the Rang'Shada Mountains to the west, you will be hard-pressed to find a source of iron. Most of what you purchased came from Kelton, and they bought grain from you, but Kelton will just have to buy their grain from the Galean warehouses now. Since they're now both D'Haran there is no longer any reason for past animosity to hinder trade, and their armies are under my command so they won't be wasting effort worrying about one another and instead will devote their attention to sealing the borders.

"D'Hara, of course, has a use for Keltish iron and steel. I suggest you find another source, and quickly, as the Imperial Order will probably attack from the south. Possibly right through Lifany, I would suspect. I will have no man spilling blood to protect lands not yet joined with us, nor will I reward hesitation with trade privileges."

Richard turned his gaze to a tall, gaunt man with a ring of wispy white hair around the base of his knobby skull. "Ambassador Bezancort, I regret to inform you that the letter, here, to Kelton's Commissioner Cameron, instructs him that all agreements with your homeland of Sanderia are hereby canceled until and unless you, too, are part of D'Hara. When spring comes, Sanderia will not be allowed to drive their herds up from your plains to spring and summer on the highlands of Kelton."

The tall man lost what little color he had to begin with. "But, Lord Rahl, we have no place to spring and summer them; while those plains are a lush grassland in the winter, they are a brown and barren wasteland in the summer. What would you have us do?"

Richard shrugged. "I would suppose you'll have to slaughter your herds in order to salvage what you can before they starve."

The ambassador gasped. "Lord Rahl, these agreements have been in place for centuries. Our whole economy is based on the husbandry of our sheep."

Richard lifted an eyebrow. "It's not my concern; my concern is with those who stand with us."

Ambassador Bezancort raised his hands in an imploring gesture. "Lord Rahl, my people would be ruined. Our whole country would be devastated if we were forced to slaughter our herds."

Representative Theriault took an urgent step forward. "You can't allow those herds to be slaughtered. Herjborgue depends on that wool. Why, why . . . it would ruin our industry."

Another spoke up. "And then they couldn't trade with us, and we would have no way to buy crops that won't grow in our land."

Richard leaned forward. "Then I suggest you impress these arguments on your leaders, and do your best to convince them that surrender is the only way. The sooner the better." He looked out at the other dignitaries. "As interdependent as you all are I'm sure you will soon come to realize the value of unity. Kelton is part of D'Hara, now. The trade routes will be closed to any who fail to stand with us. I told you before, there are no bystanders."

A riot of protests, appeals, and supplications filled the council chambers. Richard stood, and the voices fell to silence.

The Sanderian ambassador lifted a bony finger in accusation. "You are a ruthless man."

Richard nodded, the magic heating his glare. "Be sure to tell that to the Imperial Order, if you choose to join with them." He looked down on the other faces. "You all had peace and unity through the Council and the Mother Confessor. While she was away, fighting for you and your people, you threw that unity aside for ambition, for naked greed. You acted like children fighting over a cake. You had a chance to share it, but instead chose to try to steal it all from your smaller siblings. If you come to my table, you will have to mind your manners, but you each will have bread."

No one offered an argument this time. Richard straightened his mriswith cape on his shoulders when he realized Cathryn had finished signing and was watching him with those big brown eyes. He couldn't maintain the grip on the sword's anger in the glow of her sweet gaze.

He turned back to the representatives, the rage gone from his tone. "The weather is clear. You had best be off. The sooner you convince your leaders to agree to my terms, the less inconvenience your people will suffer. I don't want anyone to suffer. . . ." His voice trailed off.

Cathryn stood next to him and looked down at the people she knew so well. "Do as Lord Rahl asks. He has given you enough of his time." She turned and addressed one of her aides. "Have my clothes brought over at once. I'll be staying here, at the Confessors' Palace."

"Why is she staying here?" one of the ambassadors asked as his brow wrinkled in suspicion.

"Her husband, as you know, was killed by a mriswith," Richard said. "She is staying here for protection."

"You mean there is danger for us?"

"Very possibly," Richard said. "Her husband was an expert swordsman, yet he . . . well, I hope you will be careful. If you join with us then you are entitled to be guests of the palace, and the protection of my magic. There are plenty of empty guest rooms, but they will remain empty until you surrender."

Accompanied by worried chatter, they headed for the doors.

"Shall we go?" Cathryn asked in a breathy voice.

His task done, Richard felt the sudden emptiness being filled with her presence. As she took his arm and they started away, he summoned the last shred of his will to stop at the end of the dais, where Ulic and Cara were standing.

"Keep us in sight at all times. Understand?"

"Yes, Lord Rahl," Ulic and Cara said as one.

Cathryn tugged on his arm, urging his ear close. "Richard." Her warm breath carrying his name sent a shudder of longing through him. "You said we would be alone. I want to be alone with you. Very alone. Please?"

It was from this moment that Richard had borrowed strength. He could no longer hold the image of the sword in his mind. In desperation, he put Kahlan's face there in its stead.

"There is danger about, Cathryn. I can sense it. I won't risk your life carelessly. When I don't feel the danger, then we can be alone. Please try to understand, for now."

She looked distraught, but nodded. "For now."

As they stepped off the platform, Richard's gaze snagged on Cara's. "Don't let us out of your sight for anything."

CHAPTER 24

PHOEBE PLOPPED DOWN THE reports in a narrow vacant spot on the polished walnut table. "Verna, may I ask you a personal question?"

Verna scrawled her initials across the bottom of a report from the kitchens requesting replacements for the large cauldrons that had burned through. "We've been friends for a good long time, Phoebe; you may ask me anything you wish." She again scrutinized the request, and then above her initials she wrote a note denying permission and telling them to instead have the cauldrons repaired. Verna reminded herself to show a smile. "Ask."

Phoebe's round cheeks flushed as she twisted her fingers together. "Well, I mean no offense, but you're in a unique position, and I could never ask anyone else but a friend like you." She cleared her throat. "What's it like to get old?"

Verna snorted a laugh. "We're the same age, Phoebe."

She wiped her palms at the hips of her green dress as Verna waited. "Yes . . . but you've been away for more than twenty years. You've aged that much, just like those outside the palace. It will take me near to three hundred years to age to where you are right now. Why, you look like a woman of almost . . . forty."

Verna sighed. "Yes, well, a journey will do that to you. At least mine did."

"I don't want to ever go on a journey and get old. Does it hurt, or something, to so suddenly be old? Do you feel . . . I don't know, like you're not attractive and life is no longer sweet? I like it when men view me as desirable. I don't want to get old like . . . . It worries me."

Verna pushed away from the table and leaned back in her chair. Her strongest urge was to strangle the woman, but she took a breath and reminded herself that it was a friend's sincere question asked out of ignorance.

"I would guess that everyone views it in their own unique way, but I can tell you what it means for me. Yes, it hurts a bit, Phoebe, to know that something is gone and can never be recovered, as if I was somehow not paying attention and my youth was stolen from me while I was waiting for my life to start, but the Creator balances it with good, too."

"Good? What good could come of it?"

"Well, inside I'm still myself, but wiser. I find that I have a clearer understanding of myself and what I want. I appreciate things I never did before. I see better what's really important in doing the Creator's work. I suppose you could say I feel more content, and worry less about what others think of me.

"Even though I've aged, that doesn't diminish my longing for others. I find comfort in friends, and yes, to answer what you're thinking, I still long for men much the same as I always did, but now I have a wider appreciation for them. I find callow youth less interesting. Men need not simply be young to stir my feelings, and the simple hold less appeal."

Phoebe's eyes were wide as she leaned forward attentively. "Reeeally. Older men stir longings in you?"

Verna checked her tongue. "What I meant by older, Phoebe, was men older like me. The men that catch your interest, now? Fifty years ago you wouldn't have considered walking with a man the age you are now, but now it seems natural to you because you're that age, and men now the age you were back then seem immature to you. See what I mean?"

"Well . . . I guess."

Verna could read it in her eyes that she didn't. "When we first came here as young girls, like the two down in the vaults last night, novices Helen and Valery, what did you think of women who were the age you are now?"

Phoebe covered a giggle with her hand. "I thought them impossibly old. I never thought I'd be this age."

"And, now, how do you feel about your age?"

"Oh, it isn't old at all. I guess I was just foolish at that young age. I like being this age. I'm still young."

Verna shrugged. "It's much the same for me. I view myself in much the way you view yourself. I no longer see older people as simply old, because I now know that they're the same as you or I; they view themselves the same as you or I view ourselves."

The young woman wrinkled her nose. "I guess I see what you mean, but I still don't want to get old."

"Phoebe, in the outside world you would have lived nearly three lives by now. You, we, have been given a great gift by the Creator to be able to have as many years as we do, living here at the palace, in order to have the time necessary to train young wizards in their gift. Appreciate what you were given; it's a rare benevolence that touches only a handful."

Phoebe nodded slowly and behind the slight squint Verna could almost see the labor of contemplative reasoning. "That's very wise, Verna. I never knew you were so wise. I always knew you were smart, but you never seemed wise to me before."

Verna smiled. "That's one of the other advantages. Those younger than you think you wise. In a land of the blind, a one-eyed woman could be queen."

"But it seems so frightening, to have your flesh go limp and wrinkly."

"It happens gradually; you become somewhat accustomed to yourself growing older. To me, the thought of being your age again seems frightening."

"Why's that?"

Verna wanted to say that it was because she feared walking around with such an underdeveloped intellect, but she reminded herself once again that she and Phoebe had shared a good part of their lives as friends. "Oh, I guess because I've been through some of the thorn hedges you have yet to face, and I know their sting."

"What sort of thorns?"

"I think they're different for each person. Everyone has to walk her own path."

Phoebe wrung her hands as she leaned over even more. "What were the thorns on your path, Verna?"

Verna stood and pushed the stopper back into the ink bottle. She stared down at her desk, not seeing it. "I guess," she said in a distant tone, "the worst was returning to have Jedidiah look at me with eyes like yours, eyes that saw a wrinkled, dried-up, old, unattractive hag."

"Oh please, Verna, I never meant to suggest that—"

"Do you even understand the thorn in that, Phoebe?"

"Why, to be thought old and ugly, of course, even though you are not that. . . ."

Verna shook her head. "No." She looked up into the other's eyes. "No, the thorn was to discover that appearance was all that ever mattered, and that what was inside"—she tapped the side of her head—"didn't hold any meaning for him, only its wrapping."

Even worse than returning to see that look in Jedidiah's eyes, though, was to discover that he had given himself over to the Keeper. In order to save Richard's life as Jedidiah was about to kill him, Verna had buried her dacra in his back. Jedidiah had betrayed not only her, but the Creator, too. A part of her had died with him.

Phoebe straightened, looking a bit puzzled. "Yes, I guess I know what you mean, when men . . ."

Verna waved her hand in a dismissive gesture. "I hope I've been of help, Phoebe. It's always good to talk to a friend." Her voice took on the clear ring of authority. "Are there any petitioners to see me?"

Phoebe blinked. "Petitioners? No, not today."

"Good. I wish to go pray and seek the Creator's guidance. Would you and Dulcinia please shield the door; I wish not to be disturbed."

Phoebe curtsied. "Of course, Prelate." She smiled warmly. "Thank you for the talk, Verna. It was like old times in our room after we were ordered to be sleeping." Her gaze darted to the stacks of papers. "But what about the reports? They're falling further behind."

"As Prelate, I cannot ignore the Light that directs the palace and the Sisters. I must also pray for us, and ask for His guidance. We are, after all, the Sisters of the Light."

The look of awe returned to Phoebe's eyes. Phoebe seemed to believe that in assuming the post, Verna had somehow become more than human, and could somehow touch the hand of the Creator in a miraculous way. "Of course, Prelate. I will see to the placement of the shield. No one will disturb the Prelate's meditation."

Before Phoebe went through the door, Verna called her name in a quiet tone. "Have you learned anything yet about Christabel?"

Phoebe's eyes turned away in sudden disquiet. "No. No one knows where she went. We've had no word on where Amelia or Janet have disappeared to, either."

The five of them, Christabel, Amelia, Janet, Phoebe, and Verna had been friends, had grown up together at the palace, but Verna had been closest to Christabel, though they were all a bit jealous of her. The Creator had blessed her with gorgeous blond hair and comely features, but also with a kind and warm nature.

It was disturbing that her three friends seemed to have vanished. Sisters sometimes left the palace for visits home, while their families were still living, but they requested permission first, and besides, the families of those three would all have passed away of old age long ago. Sisters, too, sometimes went away for a time, not only to refresh their minds in the outside world, but also to simply have a break from decade upon decade at the palace. Even then, they almost always would tell the others that they had to leave for a time, and where they were going.

None of her three friends had done that; they had simply shown up missing after the Prelate died. Verna's heart ached with the worry that they simply couldn't accept her as Prelate, and had chosen instead to leave the palace, but as much as it hurt, she prayed it was that, and not something darker that had taken them.

"If you hear anything, Phoebe," Verna said, trying to hide her concern, "please come tell me."

After the woman had gone, Verna placed her own shield inside the doors, a telltale shield she had devised herself; the delicate filaments spun from the spirit of her own unique Han, magic she would recognize as her own. Should anyone try to enter, they probably wouldn't detect the diaphanous shield, and would tear the fragile threads. Even if they did manage to detect it, their mere presence and the act of probing for a shield would still unavoidably tear it, and if they then repaired the weave with Han of their own, Verna would know that, too.

Hazy sunlight filtered through the trees near the garden wall, infusing the quiet wooded area of the retreat with a muted, dreamy light. The small woodlot ended at a clump of sweetbay, their branches heavy with hairy white buds. The trail beyond meandered into a well-tended patch of blue and yellow flowering groundcover surrounding islands of taller lace-lady ferns and monarch roses. Verna broke a twig off one of the sweetbays and idly savored its spicy aroma as she surveyed the wall while striding along the path.

At the rear of the plantings stood a thicket of shining sumac, the ribbon of small trees placed deliberately to screen the high wall protecting the Prelate's garden and give the illusion of more expansive grounds. She eyed the squat trunks and spreading branches critically; they might do, if nothing better could be found. She moved on; she was already late.

On a small side trail around the back side of the wild place where the Prelate's sanctuary stood hidden, she found a promising spot. Once she had lifted her dress and stepped through the shrubs to reach the wall, she could see that it was perfect. Sheltered all around by pine was a sunlit area where pear trees had been espaliered against the wall. While they were all trained and pruned, one seemed to be particularly suitable; its limbs to each side alternated like the steps of a single-pole ladder.

Just before Verna hiked her skirts up and started to climb, the texture of the bark caught her eye. She rubbed a finger along the top edge of stout limbs, seeing that they were callused and rough. It would appear she was not the first Prelate to want to surreptitiously depart the Prelate's compound.

Once she had climbed atop the wall and had checked that no guards were in sight, she found there was a convenient abutment to a reinforcing pilaster to step down on, and then a drain tile, and then a decorative stone sticking out, and then a low spreading limb of a smoky oak, and then a round rock not two feet from the wall and an easy hop to the ground. She brushed off the bark and leaves and then straightened her gray dress at the hips and ordered the simple collar. She slipped the Prelate's ring into a pocket. As she draped her heavy black shawl over her head and tied it under her chin, Verna grinned with the thrill of having found a secret way to escape her prison of paper.

She was surprised to find the palace grounds uncommonly deserted. Guards patrolled their posts, and Sisters, novices, and young men in collars dotted the paths and stoned walkways as they went about their business, but there were few city people to be seen, most of them old women.

Every day, during the daylight hours, people from the city of Tanimura poured across the bridges to Halsband Island to seek advice from the Sisters, to petition for intervention in disputes, to request charity, to seek guidance in the Creator's wisdom, and to worship in the courtyards all over the island. Why they would think they needed to come here to worship had always seemed odd to Verna, but she knew these people viewed the home of the Sisters of the Light as hallowed ground. Perhaps they simply enjoyed the beauty of the palace grounds.

They weren't enjoying it now; there were virtually no city people to be seen. Novices assigned to guide visitors paced in boredom. Guards at the gates to restricted areas chatted among themselves, and those who glanced her way saw only another Sister going about her business. The lawns were empty of reposing guests, the formal gardens displayed their beauty to no one, and the fountains sprayed and splashed without the accompaniment of astonished gasps from adults or delighted squeals from children. Even the gossip benches sat vacant.

In the distance, the drums beat on.

Verna found Warren sitting on the dark, flat rock at their meeting place in the rushes on the city side of the river. He was skipping stones out onto the swirling waters prowled by one lone fishing boat. Warren jumped up when he heard her approach.

"Verna! I didn't know if you were ever going to come."

Verna watched the old man bait his hooks as his skiff rolled gently beneath his steady legs. "Phoebe wanted to know what it was like to get old and wrinkled."

Warren brushed dirt from the seat of his violet robes. "Why would she ask you?"

Verna only sighed at his blank expression. "Let's get going."

The journey through the city toward the outskirts proved as strange as the palace grounds. While some of the shops in the wealthy sections were open and doing a bit of trade with a scattering of people, the market in the indigent section was vacant, its tables empty, cook fires cold, and shopwindows shuttered. The lean-to shelters were deserted, the looms in the workshops abandoned, and the streets silent but for the constant, grating presence of the drums.

Warren acted as if there were nothing unusual about the ghostly streets. As the two of them turned down a narrow, deeply shadowed, dusty street lined with dilapidated buildings, Verna had had enough and finally erupted in fury.

"Where is everyone! What's going on!"

Warren stopped and turned to give her a puzzled look as she stood, fists on hips, in the center of the empty street. "It's Ja'La day."

She fixed him with a scowl. "Ja'La day."

He nodded, the puzzled frown deepening. "Yes. Ja'La day. What did you think happened to all the . . ." Warren slapped his forehead. "I'm sorry, Verna; I thought you knew. We've become so accustomed to it I just forgot you wouldn't know."

Verna folded her arms. "Know what?"

Warren returned to take her arm and start her walking again. "Ja'La is a game, a contest." He pointed over his shoulder. "They built a big playing field in the bowl between two hills on the outskirts of the city, over that way, about . . . oh, I guess it must have been fifteen or twenty years ago, when the emperor came to rule. Everyone loves it."

"A game? The entire city empties out to go watch a game?"

Warren nodded. "I'm afraid so. Except a few—mostly older people; they don't understand it and aren't too interested, but most everyone else is. It's become the people's passion. Children start playing it in the streets almost as soon as they can walk."

Verna eyed a side street and checked behind, the way they had come. "What kind of game is this?"

Warren shrugged. "I've never been to an official game, yet; I spend most of my time down in the vaults, but I've delved into the subject a bit. I've always been interested in games and how they fit into the structure of different cultures. I've studied ancient peoples and their games, but this gives me the chance to observe a living game for myself, so I've read up on it and made inquiries.

"Ja'La is played by two teams on a square Ja'La field marked out with grids. In each corner is a goal, two for each team. The teams try to put the 'broc'—a heavy, leather-covered ball a little smaller than a man's head—in one of their opponents' goals. If they do, then they get a point, and the other team gets to pick a grid square from which they begin their turn at attack.

"I don't understand the strategy, it gets complex, but five-year-olds seem to be able to grasp it in no time."

"Probably because they want to play, and you don't." Verna untied her shawl and flapped the ends, trying to cool her neck. "What's so interesting about it that everyone would want to go crowd together in the sun to see it."

"I guess it takes them away from their toil for a day of festivity. It gives them an excuse to cheer and scream, and to drink and celebrate if their team wins, or to drink and console one another if their team loses. Everyone gets quite worked up over it. More worked up than they should."

Verna thought it over a moment as she felt a refreshing breeze cool her neck. "Well, I guess that sounds harmless."

Warren glanced over out of the corner of his eye. "It's a bloody game."

"Bloody?"

Warren sidestepped a pile of dung. "The ball is heavy and the rules loose. The men who play Ja'La are savage. While they must of course be adept at handling the broc, they're selected mostly because of their brawn and their brutal aggressiveness. Not many a game goes by without at least some teeth getting knocked out, or a bone broken. It isn't rare for a neck to get broken, either."

Verna stared incredulously. "And people like to watch that?"

Warren grunted a humorless confirmation. "From what the guards tell me, the crowd gets ugly if there isn't blood, because they think it means their team isn't trying hard enough."

Verna shook her head. "Well, it doesn't sound like anything I would enjoy watching."

"That isn't the worst of it." Warren kept his eyes ahead as he strode along the shadowed street. To the sides, shutters so faded it was hard to tell they had ever been painted stood closed over narrow windows. "The losing team is brought out onto the field when the game is over, and each is flogged. One lash with a big leather whip for each point scored against them, administered by the winning team. And the rivalry between teams is bitter; it isn't unheard of for men to die from the flogging."

Verna walked in stunned silence as they turned a corner. "The people stay for this flogging?"

"I think that's what they go for. The entire crowd supporting the winning team counts out the number of lashes as they're laid on. Emotions run pretty high. People get really worked up over Ja'La. Sometimes there are riots. Even with ten thousand troops trying to keep order, things can get out of hand. The players sometimes start the brawl. The men who play Ja'La are brutes."

"People really like rooting for a team of brutes?"

"The players are heroes. Ja'La players virtually have the run of the city, and can do no wrong. Rules and laws rarely apply to Ja'La players. Crowds of women follow the players around, and after a game there's usually a team orgy. Women fight over who will be with a Ja'La player. The spree goes on for days. To have been with a player is an honor of the highest order, and is so highly contested that bragging rights require witnesses."

"Why?" was all she could think to say.

Warren threw up his hands. "You're a woman; you tell me! When I've been the first in three thousand years to solve a prophecy, I've never had a woman throw her arms around my neck, or want to lick the blood off my back."

"They do that?"

"Fight over it. If he's pleased with her tongue, he might pick her. I hear the players are pretty arrogant, and like to make the eager women earn the honor of being under him."

Verna looked over and saw that Warren's face was glowing red. "They even want to be with the losing players?"

"It's irrelevant. He's a Ja'La player: a hero. The more brutal, the better. The ones who have killed an opponent with a Ja'La ball are renowned, and are most sought after by the women. People name babies after them. I just don't understand it."

"You're just seeing a small sampling of people, Warren. If you were to go into the city instead of spending all of your time down in the vaults, women would want to be with you, too."

He tapped his bare neck. "They would if I still had a collar, because they would see the palace's gold around my neck, that's all; they wouldn't want to be with me because of who I am."

Verna pursed her lips. "Some people are attracted by power. When you have no power yourself, it can be very seductive. That's just the way life is."

"Life," he repeated with a sour grunt. "Ja'La is what everyone calls it, but its full name is Ja'La dh Jin—the Game of Life, in the old tongue of the emperor's homeland of Altur'Rang, but everyone simply calls it Ja'La: the Game."

"What does 'Altur'Rang' mean?"

" 'Altur'Rang' is from their old tongue, too. It doesn't translate well, but it means, approximately, 'the Creator's chosen,' or 'destiny's people,' something like that. Why?"

"The New World is split by a mountain range called the Rang'Shada. It sounds like the same language."

Warren nodded. "A *shada* is an armored war gauntlet with spikes. Rang'Shada would roughly mean 'war fist of the chosen.'"

"A name from the old war, I guess. Spikes would certainly apply to those mountains." Verna's head was still spinning with Warren's story. "I can't believe this game is allowed."

"Allowed? It's encouraged. The emperor has his own personal Ja'La team. It was announced this morning that when he comes for his visit, he's going to bring his team to play Tanimura's top team. Quite an honor, from what I gather, as everyone is beside themselves with excitement at the prospect." Warren glanced around, and then turned back to her again. "The emperor's team doesn't get flogged if they lose."

She lifted an eyebrow. "The privilege of the mighty?"

"Not exactly," Warren said. "If they lose, they get beheaded."

Verna's hands dropped away from the points of her shawl. "Why would such a game be encouraged by the emperor?"

Warren smiled a private smile. "I don't know, Verna, but I have my theories."

"Such as?"

"Well, if you have conquered a land, what problems do you suppose might present themselves?"

"You mean insurrection?"

Warren brushed back a lock of his curly blond hair. "Turmoil, protests, civil unrest, riots, and yes, insurrection. Do you remember when King Gregory ruled?"

Verna nodded as she watched an old woman far up a side street draping wet clothes over a balcony railing. It was the only person she had seen in the last hour. "What happened to him?"

"Not long after you left, the Imperial Order took over and that was the last we heard of him. The king was well thought of, and Tanimura prospered, along with the other cities under his rule in the north. Since then, times have become hard for the people. The emperor allowed corruption to flourish and at the same time ignored important matters of commerce and justice. All those people you've seen living in squalor are refugees come to Tanimura from smaller towns, villages, and cities that were sacked."

"They seem a quiet and content lot for refugees."

An eyebrow lifted over a blue eye. "Ja'La."

"What do you mean?"

"They have little hope of a better life under the Imperial Order. The one thing they can have hope for, dream about, is to become a Ja'La player.

"The players are selected because of their talent at the game, not because they have rank or power. The family of a player need never want for anything again; he can provide for them—in abundance. Parents encourage their children to play Ja'La, hoping they will become paid players. Amateur teams, classed by age group, start with five-year-olds. Anyone, no matter their background, can become a paid Ja'La player. Players have even come from the ranks of the emperor's slaves.

"But that still doesn't explain the passion for it."

"Everyone is part of the Imperial Order now. No devotion to one's former land is allowed. Ja'La lets people be devoted to something, to their neighbors, to their city, through their team. The emperor paid to have the Ja'La field built—a gift to the people. The people are distracted from the conditions of their lives, over which they have no control, and into an outlet that doesn't threaten the emperor."

Verna flapped the ends of her shawl again. "I don't think your theory casts a shadow, Warren. From a young age, children like to play games. They do it all day. People have always played games. When they get older, they have contests with the bow, with horses, with dice. It's part of human nature to play at games."

"This way." Warren caught her sleeve and pointed with a thumb, turning her down a narrow alley. "And the emperor is channeling that tendency into something more than natural. He need not worry about their minds wandering to thoughts of their freedom, or even simple matters of justice. Their passion, now, is Ja'La. Their minds are dulled to everything else.

"Instead of wondering why the emperor is coming, and what it will mean for their lives, everyone is aflutter because of Ja'La."

Verna felt her stomach lurch. She had been wondering just why the emperor was coming. There had to be a reason for him to come all this way, and she didn't think it was just to watch his team play Ja'La. He wanted something.

"Aren't the people worried about defeating such a powerful man, or his team, anyway?"

"The emperor's team is very good, I'm told, but they don't have any special privilege or advantage. The emperor takes no affront at his team losing, except, of course with his players. If an opponent bests them, the emperor will acknowledge their skill and heartily congratulate them and their city. People long for that honor—to best the emperor's renowned team."

"I've been back for a couple months, and I've never seen the city empty out for this game before."

"The season just started. Official games are only allowed to be played in the the Ja'La season."

"That doesn't fit with your theory, then. If the game is a distraction from more important matters of life, why not let them play it all the time?"

Warren gave her a smug smile. "Anticipation makes the fervor stronger. The prospects for the upcoming season are talked about endlessly. By the time the season finally arrives the people are worked up into a fever pitch, like young lovers returned to the embrace after an absence—their minds are dull to anything else. If the game went on all the time, the ardor might cool."

Warren had obviously thought long and hard on his theory. She didn't think she believed in it, but he seemed to have an answer for everything, so she changed the subject.

"Where did you hear this, about him bringing his team?"

"Master Finch."

"Warren, I sent you to the stables to find out about those horses, not to gab about Ja'La."

"Master Finch is a big Ja'La enthusiast and was all excited about today's opening game, so I let him ramble on about it so I could find out what you wanted to know."

"And did you?"

They came to an abrupt halt, looking up at a carved sign displaying a headstone, shovel, and the names BENSTENT and SPROUL.

"Yes. Between telling me how many lashes the other team was going to get, and telling me how to make money betting on the outcome, he told me that the missing horses have been gone for quite a time."

"Since right after winter solstice, I'd bet."

Warren shielded his eyes with a hand as he peered into the window. "You'd win the bet. Four of his strongest horses, but full tack for only two, are gone. He's still searching for the horses, and swears he'll find them, but he thinks the tack was stolen."

From behind the door in the back of the dark room, she could hear the sound of a file on steel.

Warren took his hand from his face and checked the street. "Sounds like there's someone here who isn't a Ja'La enthusiast."

"Good." Verna tied the shawl under her chin and then pulled open the door. "Let's go hear what this gravedigger has to say."

CHAPTER 25

ONLY THE SMALL, STREET-SIDE window coated with ancient layers of dirt, and an open door in the back, lit the dim, dusty room, but it was enough to see a path through the cluttered mounds of sloppy rolls of winding sheets, rickety workbenches, and simple coffins. A few rusty saws and planes hung on one wall, and a disorderly stack of pine planks leaned against another.

While people of means frequented undertakers who provided guidance in the selection of ornate, expensive coffins for their loved ones, people with precious little money could afford no more than the services of simple gravediggers who supplied a plain box and a hole to put it in. While the departed loved ones of those who came to gravediggers were no less precious to them, they had to worry about feeding the living. Their memories of the deceased, however, were no less gilded.

Verna and Warren paused at the doorway out into a tiny pit of a work yard, its borders steep and high with lumber stacked upright against a fence to the back and stuccoed buildings at each side. In the center, with his back to them, a gangly, barefoot man in tattered clothes stood facing away from them as he filed the blades of his shovels.

“My condolences on the loss of your loved one,” he said in a gravelly but surprisingly sincere voice. He resumed drawing the file against the steel. “Child, or adult?”

“Neither,” Verna said.

The hollow-cheeked man glanced back over his shoulder. He wore no beard, but looked as if his efforts at shaving were rare enough that he was close to crossing the line. “In between, then? If you’ll tell me the size of the departed, I can work a box to fit.”

Verna clasped her hands. “We’ve no one to bury. We’re here to ask you some questions.”

He quieted his hands and turned around fully to look them up and down. “Well, I can see that you can afford more than me.”

“You aren’t interested in Ja’La?” Warren asked.

The man’s droopy eyes came a little more alert as he took another look at Warren’s violet robes. “Folks don’t fancy the likes of me around at festive occasions. Spoils their good time to look on my face, like it were the face of death itself walking among ’em. Aren’t shy about telling me I’m not welcome, either. But they come by when they’ve need of me. They come, then, and act like they never turned their eyes away before. I could let ’em go pay for a fancy box what the dead won’t see, but they can’t afford it, and their coin don’t do me no good if I grudge ‘em their fears.”

“Which are you,” Verna asked, “Master Benstent, or Sproul?”

His flaccid eyelids bunched into creases as his eyes turned up to her. “I’m Milton Sproul.”

“And Master Benstent? Is he about, too?”

“Ham’s not here. What’s this about?”

Verna bowed her mouth in a nonchalant expression. “We’re from the palace, and wanted to ask about a tally we were sent. We just need to be sure it’s correct, and everything is in order.”

The bony man turned back to his shovel and stroked the file across the edge. “Tally’s correct. We’d not cheat the Sisters.”

“Of course we aren’t suggesting any such thing, it’s just that we can’t find any record of who it was you buried. We just need to verify the deceased, and then we can authorize payment.”

“Don’t know. Ham done the work and made out the tally. He’s an honest man. He wouldn’t cheat a thief to get back what was stole from him. He made out the tally and told me to send it over, that’s all I know.”

"I see." Verna shrugged. "Then I guess we'll need to see Master Benstent in order to clear this up. Where can we find him?"

Sproul took another stroke with his file. "Don't know. Ham was getting on in years. Said he wanted to spend what little time was left to him being with his daughter and grandchildren. He left to be with them. They live downcountry somewheres." He circled his file in the air. "Left his half of the place, such as it is, to me. Left me his half of the work, too. Guess I'll have to take on a younger man to do the digging; I'm getting old myself."

"But you must know where he went, and about this tally."

"Said I don't. He packed up all his things, not that that was much, and bought himself a donkey for the journey, so I reckon it must be a goodly distance." He pointed his file over his shoulder toward the south. "Like I said, downcountry.

"The last thing he told me was to be sure I sent the tally to the palace, because he done the work and it was only fair that they pay for what was done. I asked him where to send the payment, as he done the work, but he said to use it to hire a new man. Said it was only fair what with him leaving me on such short notice."

Verna considered her options. "I see." She watched him take a dozen strokes on his shovel, and then turned to Warren. "Go outside and wait for me."

"What!" he whispered heatedly. "Why do you—"

Verna held up a finger to silence him. "Do as I say. Take a little walk around the area to be sure . . . our friends aren't looking for us." She leaned a little closer with a meaningful look. "They might be wondering if we need any assistance."

Warren straightened and glanced to the man filing his shovel. "Oh. Yes, all right. I'll go look and see where our friends have gotten to." He fumbled with the silver brocade on his sleeve. "You won't be long, will you?"

"No. I'll be out shortly. Go on now, and see if you see them anywhere."

After Verna heard the front door shut, Sproul glanced over his shoulder. "Answer's still the same. I told you what . . ."

Verna produced a gold coin in her fingers. "Now, Master Sproul, you and I are going to have a candid conversation. What's more, you are going answer my questions truthfully."

He frowned suspiciously. "Why'd you send him out?"

She no longer made an effort to show him a pleasant smile. "The boy has a weak stomach."

He took an unconcerned stroke with his file. "I told you the truth. If you want a lie, then just tell me and I'll build you one to fit."

Verna shot him a menacing scowl. "Don't you even think of lying to me. You may have told the truth, but not all the truth there is to tell. Now, you are going to tell me the rest of it, either in exchange for this token of my appreciation—" Verna used her Han to snatch the file from his hand and send it sailing up into the air until it vanished from sight. "—or in appreciation for my sparing you any unpleasantness."

Whistling with speed, the file streaked out of the sky to slam into the ground, burying itself a scant inch from the gravedigger's toes. Only the tang stuck above the dirt, and that glowed red. With angry mental effort, she drew the hot steel up in a long, thin line of molten metal. Its white-hot glow illuminated his shocked expression, and she, too, could feel the sizzling heat on her face. His eyes had gone wide.

She waggled a finger, and the ductile line of glowing steel wavered before his eyes, dancing in time with her finger's movement. She swirled her finger and the hot steel coiled around the man, holding mere inches from his flesh.

"One twitch of my finger, Master Sproul, and I bind you up in your file." She opened her hand, holding her palm up. A howl of flame ignited, hovering obediently in the air. "After I have you bound up, then I will start at your feet, and I'll cook you an inch at a time, until you give me the whole truth."

His crooked teeth chattered. "Please . . ."

She brought the coin up in her other hand, and showed him a humorless smile. "Or, as I say, you can choose to tell me the truth in exchange for this token of my appreciation."

He swallowed, eyeing the hot metal around him, and the hissing flame in her hand. "It seems I do recall some more of it. I'd be most pleased if you'd let me set the story straight with the rest I'm now remembering."

Verna extinguished the flame above her hand, and with an abrupt effort, flipped the Han's heat to its opposite, to bitter cold. The glow left the metal like a candle's flame being snuffed. The steel went from red hot to icy black, and shattered, the fragments dropping around the stiff gravedigger like hail.

Verna lifted his hand and pressed the gold into it, closing his fingers around the coin. "I'm so sorry. I seem to have broken your file. This will more than cover it, I'm sure."

He nodded. It was likely more gold than the man could earn in a year. "I've got more files. It's nothing."

She laid a hand on his shoulder. "All right, Master Sproul, why don't you tell me what else you remember about that tally." She tightened her grip. "Every last bit of it, no matter how unimportant you consider it. Understand?"

He licked his lips. "Yes. I'll tell you every bit. Just like I said, Ham did the work. I didn't know nothing about it. Said he had some digging to do for the palace, but nothing more. Ham's the closemouthed sort, and I never paid it no mind.

"Right after, he broke it on me, real sudden like, that he was quitting, and going off to live with his daughter, just like I told you. He was always talking about going to live with his daughter, before he had to dig his own hole, but he didn't have no money and she's no better off, so I never paid him no mind. Then he bought that donkey, a good one, too, so I knew he weren't mooning this time. He said he didn't want the money from the work for the palace. Said to hire a new man to help me.

"Well, the next night, before he left, he brought over a bottle of liquor. Good stuff what cost more than the bottles we always bought. Ham never could keep a secret from me when he gets to drinking, everyone knows the truth of that. He don't tell what he shouldn't to others, understand, he's a man to be trusted, but he'll tell me everything, if he's been drinking."

Verna took her hand back. "I understand. Ham is a good man, and your friend. I don't want you to worry about betraying a confidence, Milton. I'm a Sister. You aren't doing wrong to confide in me, and you need not fear I will bring trouble to you for it."

He nodded, clearly relieved, and managed a weak smile. "Well, like I said, we had that bottle, and we was talking old times. He was leaving, and I knew I'd be missing him. You know. We was together for a long time, not that we didn't . . ."

"You were friends. I understand. What did he say?"

He loosened his collar. "Well, we was drinking, and feeling all misty-eyed about breaking up. That bottle was stronger than what we was used to. I asked him where his daughter lived, so I could send him the pay from the tally to help out with things. I got this place, after all, and I can get by. I got work. But Ham says no, he don't need it. Don't need it! Well, I was powerful curious after he said that. I asked him where he got money, and he said he saved it. Ham never saved nothing. If he had it, it was because he just got it, that's all, and hadn't spent it yet.

"Well, that's when he told me to be sure to send the tally to the palace. He was real insistent, I guess because he felt bad about leaving me with no help. So, I asks him, 'Ham, who'd you put in the ground for the palace?'"

Milton leaned toward her, lowering his voice to a gravely whisper. "'Didn't put no one in the ground,' Ham says, 'I took 'em out.'"

Verna snatched the man's dirty collar. "What! He dug someone up? Is that what he meant? He dug someone up?"

Milton nodded. "That's it. Have you ever heard of such a thing? Digging up the dead? Putting 'em in the ground don't bother me, it's what I do, but the idea of digging 'em up gives me the shivers. Seems a desecration. Course, at the time, we was drinking to old times and all, and we was in stitches over it."

Verna's mind was racing in every direction at once. "Who did he exhume? And on whose orders?"

"All's he said was 'for the palace.'"

"How long ago?"

"A good long time. I don't remember . . . wait, it was after the winter solstice, not long after, maybe just a couple of days."

She shook him by the collar. "Who was it? Who did he dig up!"

"I asked him. I asked him who it were they wanted back. He told me, he says, 'They didn't care who, I'm just to bring 'em, wrapped up all pretty in clean winding sheets.'"

Verna worked her fingers on his collar. "Are you sure? You were drinking—he might have just been making up drunken stories."

He shook his head as if he feared she were going to bite it off. "No. I swear. Ham don't make up stories, or lie, when he drinks. When he drinks he would tell me anything true. No matter what sin he done, when he drinks he confesses it to me true. And I remember what he told me; it was the last night I saw my friend. I remember what he said.

"He said to be sure to get the tally to the palace, but to wait a few weeks as they was busy, they'd told him."

"What did he do with the body? Where did he take it? Who did he give it to?"

Milton tried to back away a bit, but her grip on his collar didn't allow it. "I don't know. He said he took 'em to the palace in a cart covered over real good, and he said they give him a special pass so as the guards wouldn't check his load. He had to dress in his best clothes so people wouldn't recognize him for what he was, so as not to frighten the fine people at the palace, and especially so as not to upset the delicate sensibilities of the Sisters, who were communing with the Creator. He said he done as he was told, and he was proud that he done it right, 'cause no one got disturbed by his going there with the bodies. That's all he said about it. I don't know no more, I swear it on my hope to go to the Creator's light after this life be done."

"Bodies? You said bodies. More than one?" She fixed him with a dangerous glare as she tightened her grip. "How many? How many bodies did he dig up and deliver to the palace?

"Two."

"Two . . ." she repeated in a whisper, wide-eyed. He nodded.

Verna's hand fell away from his collar.

Two.

Two bodies, wrapped in clean winding sheets.

Her fists tightened as she growled in a rage.

Milton swallowed, holding up a hand. "One other thing. I don't know if it matters."

"What?" She asked through gritted teeth.

"He said that they wanted 'em fresh, and one was small, and weren't too bad, but the other gave him a time, because he were a big one. I didn't think to ask him more about it. I'm sorry."

With great effort, she managed a smile. "Thank you, Milton, you've been a great help to the Creator."

He scrunched his shirt closed at the neck. "Thank you, Sister. Sister, I've never had the nerve to go to the palace, being what I am, and all. I know folks don't like to see me around. Well, I've never gone. Sister, could you give me the Creator's blessing?"

"Of course, Milton. You have done his work."

He closed his eyes with a murmured prayer.

Verna gently touched his forehead. "The Creator's blessing on His child," she whispered as she let the warmth of her Han flow into his mind. He gasped in rapture. Verna let her Han seep through his mind. "You will remember nothing of what Ham told you about the tally while you were drinking. You will recall only that he said he did the work, but you know nothing of its nature. After I've left, you will not recall my visit."

His eyes rolled beneath his eyelids for a time before coming open at last. "Thank you, Sister."

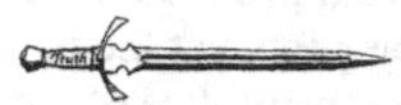

Warren was pacing on the street outside. She stormed past him without stoping to say anything. He ran to catch up.

Verna was a thunderhead. "I'll strangle her," she growled under her breath. "I'll strangle her with my bare hands. I don't care if the Keeper takes me, I'll have her throat in my hands."

"What are you talking about? What did you find out? Verna, slow down!"

"Don't talk to me right now, Warren. Don't say a word!"

She swept through the streets, her fists whipping in time to her furious strides, a storm rampaging across the land. The churning knot of fury in her stomach threatened to ignite in lightning. She didn't see the streets or buildings, or hear the drums thundering in the background. She forgot Warren trotting behind her. She could see nothing but a vision of vengeance.

She was blind to where she was, lost in a world of rage. Without knowing how she had gotten there, she found herself crossing one of the back bridges onto Halsband Island. In the center crest above the river she stamped to a halt so abruptly that Warren almost collided with her.

She snatched the silver braiding at his collar. "You get yourself down into the vaults and link up that prophecy."

"What are you talking about?"

She shook him by his robes. "The one that says that when the Prelate and the Prophet are given to the Light in the sacred rite, the flames will bring to boil a cauldron of guile and give ascension to a false Prelate who will reign over the death of the Palace of the

Prophets. Find the branches. Link it up. Find out everything you can. Do you understand!"

Warren snatched his robes free and tugged them straight. "What's this about? What did the gravedigger tell you?"

She held up a cautionary finger. "Not now, Warren."

"We're supposed to be friends, Verna. We're in this together, remember? I want to know—"

Her voice was thunder on the horizon. "Do as I tell you. If you press me right now, Warren, you are going to go for a swim. Now go link up that prophecy, and as soon as you find anything, you come tell me."

Verna knew about the prophecies in the vaults. She knew that it could easily take years to link branches. It could take centuries. What choice was there?

He brushed dust from his robes, giving his eyes an excuse to look elsewhere. "As you wish, *Prelate*."

As he turned to go, she could see that his eyes were red and puffy. She wanted to catch his arm and stop him, but he was already too far away. She wanted to call out to him and tell him that she wasn't angry at him, that it wasn't his fault that she was the false Prelate, but her voice failed her.

She found the round rock beneath the limb and sprang up the wall. Bothering with only two branches on the pear tree, she dropped to the ground inside the Prelate's compound and, when she regained her feet, started running. Panting in hurt, she slapped her hand repeatedly against the door to the Prelate's sanctuary, but it wouldn't open. Remembering why, she dug in her pocket and found the ring. Inside, she pressed it against the sunburst on the door to close it, and then with all her anger and anguish, heaved the ring across the room, hearing it clatter against the walls and skitter across the floor.

Verna pried the journey book from the secret pouch sewn on the back of her belt and plopped down on the three-legged stool. Gasping for her breath, she fumbled the stylus from the spine of the little black book. She opened it, spreading it flat on the small table, and stared at the blank page.

She tried to think through the rage and resentment. She had to consider the possibility that she could be wrong. No. She wasn't wrong. Still, she was a Sister of the Light, for what that was worth, and knew better than to risk everything on presumption. She had to think of a way to verify who had the other book, and she also had to do it in a way that wouldn't betray her identity if she was wrong. But she wasn't wrong. She knew who had it.

Verna kissed her ring finger as she whispered a prayer beseeching the Creator's guidance, and asking, too, for strength.

She wanted to vent her wrath, but before all else, she had to make sure. With trembling fingers, she picked up the stylus and began to write.

You must first tell me the reason you chose me the last time. I remember every word. One mistake, and this journey book feeds the fire.

Verna closed the book and tucked it back into its secret pouch in her belt. Shaking, she pulled the comforter from its resting place atop the box bench and dragged it to the overstuffed chair. Feeling more lonely than she had ever felt in her entire life, she curled up in the chair.

Verna remembered her last meeting with Prelate Annalina, when Verna had returned with Richard after all those years. Annalina hadn't wanted to see her, and it had taken weeks to finally be granted an audience. As long as she lived, no matter how many hundreds of years that might be, she would never forget that meeting, or the things the Prelate had told her.

Verna had been furious to discover the Prelate had withheld valuable information. The Prelate had used her and never told her the reasons. The Prelate had asked if Verna knew why she had been selected to go after Richard. Verna said she had thought it was a vote of confidence. The Prelate said it was because she suspected that Sisters Grace and Elizabeth, who had been on the journey with her and had been the first two to be selected, were Sisters of the Dark, and she had privileged information from prophecy that said the first two Sisters would die. The Prelate said she had used her prerogative to pick Verna as the third Sister to go.

Verna asked, "You chose me, because you had faith that I was not one of them?"

"I chose you, Verna," the Prelate said, "because you were far down on the list, and because, all in all, you are quite unremarkable. I doubted you were one of them. You are a person of little note. I'm sure Grace and Elizabeth made their way to the top of the list because whoever directs the Sisters of the Dark considered them expendable. I direct the Sisters of the Light. I chose you for the same reason.

"There are Sisters who are valuable to our cause; I could not risk one of them on such a task. The boy may prove a value to us, but he is not as important as other matters at the palace. It was simply an opportunity I thought to take.

"If there had been trouble, and none of you made it back, well, I'm sure you can understand that a general would not want to lose his best troops on a low-priority mission."

The woman who had smiled at her when she was little, filling her with inspiration, had broken her heart.

Verna drew the comforter up as she blinked at the watery walls of the sanctuary. All she had ever wanted was to be a Sister of the Light. She had wanted to be one of those wondrous women who used her gift to do the Creator's work here in this world. She had given her life and her heart to the Palace of the Prophets.

Verna remembered the day they came and told her that her mother had died. Old age, they said.

Her mother didn't have the gift, and so was of no use to the palace. Her mother didn't live close, and Verna only rarely saw her. When her mother did travel to the palace for a visit, she was frightened because Verna didn't age to her eyes, the way a normal person aged. She could never understand it, no matter how many times Verna tried to explain the spell. Verna knew it was because her mother feared to really listen. She feared magic.

Though the Sisters made no attempt to conceal the existence of the spell about the palace that slowed their aging, people without the gift had difficulty fathoming it. It was magic that had no meaning to their lives. The people were proud to live near the palace, near its splendor and might, and although they viewed the palace with reverence, that reverence was edged with fearful caution. They didn't dare to focus their minds on things of such power, much the same way as they enjoyed the warmth of the sun, but didn't dare to stare at it.

When her mother died, Verna had been at the palace for forty-seven years, yet appeared to have aged only to adolescence.

Verna remembered the day they came and told her that Leitis, her daughter, had died. Old age, they said.

Verna's daughter, Jedidiah's daughter, didn't have the gift, and so was of no use to the palace. It would be better, they said, if she were raised by a family who would love her and give her a normal life; a life at the palace was no life for one without the gift. Verna had the Creator's work to do, and so acquiesced.

Joining the gift of the male and the female created a better, though still remote, chance of the offspring being born with the gift. Thus, Sisters and wizards could look forward to approval, if not official encouragement, should they conceive a child.

As per the arrangement the palace always made in such circumstances, Leitis didn't know that the people who raised her weren't her real parents. Verna guessed it was for the best. What kind of mother could a Sister of the Light be? The palace had provided for the family, to insure Verna wouldn't worry for her daughter's well-being.

Several times Verna had visited, as a Sister merely bringing the Creator's blessing to a family of honest, hardworking people, and Leitis had seemed happy. The last time Verna had visited, Leitis had been gray and stooped, and was able to walk only with the aid of a cane. Leitis didn't remember Verna as the same Sister who had visited when she was playing catch-the-fox with her young friends, sixty years before.

Leitis had smiled at Verna, at the blessing, and said, "Thank you, Sister. So talented, for one so young."

"How are you, Leitis? Have you a good life?"

Verna's daughter smiled distantly. "Oh, Sister, I've had a long and happy life. My husband died five years ago, but other than that, the Creator has blessed me." She had chuckled. "I only wish I still had my curly brown hair. It was once as lovely as yours, yes it was—I swear it."

Dear Creator, how long had it been since Leitis had passed on? It had to be fifty years. Leitis had had children, but Verna had scrupulously avoided learning so much as their names.

The lump in her throat as she wept was nearly choking her.

She had given so much to be a Sister. She had just wanted to help people. She had never asked for anything.

And she had been played a fool.

She hadn't wanted to be Prelate, but she was just beginning to think she could use the post to better the lives of people, to do the work for which she had sacrificed everything. Instead, she was again being played for a fool.

Verna clutched the comforter to herself as she cried in racking sobs until the light was long gone from the little windows in the peaks and her throat was raw.

In the heart of the night, she finally decided to go to her bed. She didn't want to stay in the Prelate's sanctuary; it only seemed to be mocking her. She was not the Prelate. She had finally exhausted all her tears, and felt only numb humiliation.

She couldn't get the door to open, and had to crawl around on the floor until she found the Prelate's ring. After she had closed the door, she put the ring back on her finger, a reminder, a beacon, of the dupe she was.

She shuffled woodenly into the Prelate's office, on her way to the Prelate's bed. The candle had guttered and gone out, so she lit another on the desk still stacked with waiting reports. Phoebe worked hard at seeing to it that it stayed that way. What was Phoebe going to think when she found out that she wasn't really the Prelate's administrator? That she had been appointed by a quite unremarkable Sister of little note?

Tomorrow, she would have to apologize to Warren. This wasn't his fault. She shouldn't take it out on him.

Just before she went through the door to the outer office, she stopped in her tracks.

Her diaphanous shield was shredded. She looked back at the desk. No new reports had been added to the piles.

Someone had been snooping around.

CHAPTER 26

SHEETS OF RAIN RAKED the deck of the ship. The barefoot men crouched, tense and ready, their bulging muscles glistening in the faint yellow lamplight as they watched the distance close, and then, with a sudden burst of effort, they leapt into the darkness. After they landed, they sprang up to catch the lead-weighted fists at the ends of light heaving lines lofted across the murky chasm after them. Hand over hand, the men hauled across the heavy docking lines attached to the heaving lines.

Moving with swift efficiency, they looped the wrist-thick dock lines around the massive pilings, planted their feet, and bent their backs against the drag, using the pilings for purchase. Wet wood creaked and groaned as the lines took up the tension. The rows of men straining against the burden gave ground until they brought the slow but seemingly inexorable headway of the *Lady Sefa* to a halt. Grunting in unison, they began taking back the ground they had yielded, and the ship slowly drew toward the rain-slicked pier as men aboard dropped bundled rope fenders over the side to protect the hull.

Sister Ulicia, bunched together with Sisters Tovi, Cecilia, Armina, Nicci, and Merissa under a tarp drumming in the pelting rain, watched as Captain Blake paced the deck, angrily shouting orders at men running to see them carried out. He hadn't wanted to bring the *Lady Sefa* into the narrow wharf in such weather, to say nothing of the dark, but instead to anchor in the harbor and bring the women ashore in the longboat. Ulicia was in no mood to be drenched as they were rowed a half mile to shore, and had summarily dismissed his pleas about having to launch all the boats to tow the ship in with the sweeps. One glare had cut off his reiteration of the dangers, and sent him tight-lipped to the task.

The captain snatched his sodden hat from his head as he stopped before them. "We'll have you ashore shortly, ladies."

"It didn't appear as difficult as you made it out to be, Captain," Ulicia said.

He wrung his hat. "We got her in. Though why you'd want to come way down the coast to Grafan Harbor is beyond me. Getting back to Tanimura over land from this forsaken army outpost is not going to be the ease it would have been had you let us take you straight there by sea."

He left unsaid that it would have had them off his ship days sooner, which was undoubtedly the reason he had offered, with effusive graciousness, to take them straight back to Tanimura as they had originally wanted. Ulicia would have liked nothing better, but she had had no choice in the matter. She had done as she was ordered.

She peered up, beyond the wharf, to where she knew he waited. Her companions' eyes, too, stared into the same darkness.

The hills overlooking the harbor were visible only in the crackling flashes of lightning, appearing suddenly out of the void, and except when the lightning sporadically revealed the lay of the high ground, the feeble glow of lights coming from the massive stone fortress hunkered high on a distant hill appeared to be floating in the inky sky. Only in the brief illumination could she see the bleak, rain-slicked stone walls.

Jagang was there.

Being before him in the dream was one thing—she could eventually wake—but being before him in the flesh was quite another. There would be no waking, now. She clutched the link tighter to herself. For Jagang, there was going to be no waking, either. Her true Master would have him, and make him pay.

"Looks like you're expected."

Ulicia snatched herself from her thoughts and redirected her attention to the captain. "What?"

He pointed with his hat. "That coach must be for you ladies; there sure enough isn't anyone else about but all those soldiers."

Staring off into the gloom, she finally saw the black coach, with its team of six huge geldings, waiting on the road at the top of the wall above the wharf. Its door stood open. Ulicia had to remind herself to let the breath go from her lungs.

It would be over soon. Jagang would pay. They had only to see it through.

Once her eyes had recognized the still, dark shapes, she was able to begin picking out soldiers. They were everywhere. Fires dotted the closer hills all about the harbor, and she knew that for every fire that managed to burn in the pouring rain, there were twenty or thirty that wouldn't catch flame. Without counting the fires she could see, she could easily tell there were hundreds.

The gangway rumbled across the deck as the sailors slid it out through the opening in the bulwark. With a dull thud, one end dropped on the dock. As soon as it touched down, sailors trotted down the plank with the Sisters' baggage and headed up the pier toward the coach.

"It's been a pleasure doing business with you, Sister," Captain Blake lied. He fumbled with his hat as he waited for them to be on their way. He turned to the men on the lines. "Stand ready to slip the lines, lads! We don't want to lose the tide!"

No cheer went up, but only because they feared the result were they to show their happiness to be rid of their passengers. On their sea voyage back to the Old World it had been necessary to measure out a few more lessons in discipline—lessons not one of them would ever forget.

As they waited silently for the order to cast off, none of the sailors so much as glanced at the six women. At the end of the gangway four men stood in readiness, eyes fixed on the ground, each gripping a pole supporting the corner of a canvas tarp to hold over the Sisters' heads to keep them from being drenched.

With as much power as was crackling around Ulicia and her five companions, she could easily have used the Han to shield herself and her five Sisters from the rain, but she didn't want to use the link until it was time; she didn't want to take a chance by giving Jagang any warning. Besides, it pleased her to make these insignificant worms carry the tarp over their heads. They were all lucky she didn't want to reveal the link, or she would have slaughtered the lot of them. Slowly.

As Ulicia started moving, she could feel each of her Sisters move, too. Each of them had not only the gift they were born with, the female Han, but each had been through the ritual, and each also possessed its opposite; the male Han they had appropriated from young wizards. Besides the Additive gift they were born with, each also possessed its opposite: Subtractive Magic.

And now it was all linked.

Ulicia had not been sure it would work; Sisters of the Dark, and beyond that Sisters of the Dark who had also succeeded in absorbing the male Han, had never before attempted to link their power. It had been a dangerous risk, but the alternative was unacceptable. That it worked had given them all a heady flush of relief. That it had worked beyond their wildest hopes left Ulicia intoxicated with the swift and violent flux of magic coursing through her.

She had never suspected such awesome power could be gathered. Short of the Creator or the Keeper, there was no power on the face of the earth that could approach what they now controlled.

Ulicia was the link's dominant node, and the one who would command and direct the force. It was all she could do to contain the inner blaze of Han. Wherever her gaze settled, it howled to be released. Soon enough, it would be.

Linked as they were, the female and male Han, the Additive and Subtractive Magic, they had enough destructive force to make wizard's fire seem a candle by comparison. With a mere thought, she could level the hill atop which sat the fortress. With a mere thought, she could instantly level everything in the range of her sight, and possibly beyond.

If she could be sure Jagang was in the fortress, she would have already unleashed the cataclysmic fury, but if he wasn't, and they failed to find and kill him before they fell asleep again, then he would have them. First they must face him, to be sure he was there, and then she would release such power as had never been seen in this world, and turn Jagang to dust before he could blink. Her Master would have his soul, then, and see to it that Jagang's punishment went on without end.

At the end of the gangway the four sailors moved around them, sheltering them from the rain. Ulicia could feel the muscles in each of her Sisters flex as they moved up the pier. Through the link, she could feel each little ache, or pain, or pleasure they felt. In her mind, they were one. In her mind, they were of one thought, one need: to rid themselves of this leech of a man.

Soon enough, Sisters, soon enough.

And then we go after the Seeker?

Yes, Sisters, and then we go after the Seeker.

As they marched up the pier, a squad of grisly-looking soldiers trotted past in the opposite direction, their weapons clanging as they went. They ran up the slippery gangway without pause. The squad's corporal came to a halt before the blustering ship's captain. She couldn't hear the soldier's words, but she saw Captain Blake throw his arms up and she could hear him scream, "What!" The captain angrily threw down his hat and started a flurry of objections she couldn't make out. Had she extended the link, she would be able to, but she didn't dare risk it, yet. The soldiers drew steel. Captain Blake planted his fists on his hips and after a short pause turned to the men on the dock.

"Make the lines fast, boys," he yelled down at them. "We're not leaving tonight."

When Ulicia reached the coach, a soldier held his hand out, commanding them to enter. Ulicia let the others climb in first. She could feel the comfort of the weight coming off the legs of the two older women as they sat on the thinly padded leather seat. The soldier ordered the four sailors that had accompanied them to stand to the side and wait. As she stepped in and pulled the door closed, Ulicia saw the soldiers on the ship herding all the sailors from the *Lady Sefa* down the gangway.

Emperor Jagang probably intended to kill them to eliminate any witnesses to connect him with Sisters of the Dark. Jagang was doing her a favor. He would not get the chance to kill the ship's crew, of course, but since the sailors were not being allowed to leave, she would. She smiled at her Sisters. Through the link, they each knew her thoughts. Each of the other five returned a satisfied smile. Their sea voyage had been miserable; the sailors would pay.

On the slow ride to the fortress, as they gained a rise, Ulicia was surprised to see, when the lightning flashed, the extent of the army Jagang had gathered. Every time the lightning thundered through the hills, she could see tents as far as there was land. They covered the rolling hills like blades of grass in spring. Their numbers made the city of Tanimura seem a village. She had not known there were this many men at arms in the whole of the Old World. Well, perhaps they, too, would be useful.

When the forks of lightning ripped under the boiling clouds and shook the ground, she could see, too, the grim fortress where Jagang waited. Through the link, she could see the fortress through their eyes, too, and could feel their fear. They all wanted to blast that hilltop into oblivion, but every one of them knew that they couldn't, not yet.

There would be no mistaking Jagang when they saw him—none of them could fail to recognize that smirking face—but they had to see him first, to be certain.

When we see him, Sisters, and know he is there, then he will die.

Ulicia wanted to see fear in that man's eyes, the kind of fear he had put in their hearts, but she dared not risk giving him any indication of what they were about to do. Ulicia didn't know what he was capable of; they had, after all, never before been visited in the dream that was not a dream by any but their Master, the Keeper, and she was not about to take the slightest chance by giving him any warning, just for the satisfaction of seeing him quake.

She had deliberately waited until they were sailing into Grafan Harbor before she revealed her plan to her Sisters, just to be safe. Their Master would see to Jagang's punishment. It was their job to simply deliver his soul to the underworld and into the Keeper's grasp.

The Keeper would be more than pleased when they restored his power in this world, and would reward them with a view of Jagang's torment, should they wish it. And they would wish it.

The coach lurched to a halt before the imposing maw of the fortress. The women were ordered out of the coach by a burly soldier wearing a hide mantle and enough weapons to single-handedly slaughter a good-sized army. The six of them marched silently through the rain and mud and in under the barreled roof beyond the iron portcullis. They were led into a dark entryway where they were told to stand and wait, as if any of them had any intention of sitting on the filthy, cold, stone floor.

They were, after all, wearing their finest dresses: Tovi in a dark dress slimming to her size; Cecilia, her brushed and neat gray hair complementing her deep green dress banded with lace at the collar; Nicci in a simple dress, black, as her dresses always were, laced at the bodice in a way that accented the shape of her bosom; Merissa in a red dress, a color she favored, and with good reason, the way it set off her thick mane of dark hair, to say nothing of exhibiting her exquisite form; Armina in a dark blue dress that revealed her reasonably shapely figure and went well with her sky blue eyes; and Ulicia in her own becoming attire, a shade of blue much lighter than Armina's and trimmed with tasteful ruffles at her cleavage and wrists, and unadorned at the waist so as not to hide her well-formed hips.

They all wanted to look their best when they killed Jagang.

The block stone walls of the room were bare of everything but two hissing torches in brackets. As they waited, Ulicia could feel the anger of each of the others rising, along with hers and, too, their collective apprehension.

When the sailors, surrounded by soldiers, came through the portcullis, one of the two guards in the stone room opened the inner door into the fortress and with a rude tilt of his head ordered the Sisters through. The corridors were as austere as the entry room had been; this was an armed fortress, not a palace, after all, and it made no pretension of comfort. As they followed their guards, Ulicia saw no more than crude wooden benches and torches set in rusty iron brackets. Doors were rough planks with iron strap hinges, and there was not so much as a single oil lamp to be seen as they worked their way into the heart of the stronghold. It appeared little more than barracks for troops.

The guards came to a large double door and turned their backs to the stone at each side after opening the doors. One of them pompously lifted a thumb, ordering them into the greatroom beyond. Ulicia vowed to her Sisters that she would remember his face, and he would pay the price for his arrogance. Ulicia led the other five women in as the sailors came up the hall behind, accompanied by the echo of boots on stone and the clatter of the weapons of the men guarding them.

The room was huge. Windows without glass high up on the walls revealed the lightning outside, and let the rain run down the dark stone in glistening rivulets. A pit to each side of the floor held roaring fires. Their sparks and churning smoke ascended to billow out the open windows, but still left a reeking haze to hang in the air. In a ring of rusted brackets around the room, torches spit and hissed, adding the smell of pitch to the stink of sweat. Everything in the dim room flickered in the firelight.

Between the twin crackling fires they could see, in the gloom beyond, a massive plank table set with a wealth of food. Only one man sat at the table, on the opposite side, casually watching them as he sawed off a chunk of roasted suckling pig.

In the murky, flickering light, it was hard to be sure. They had to be sure.

Behind the table, against the wall, stood a row of people who were obviously not soldiers. The men wore white trousers and nothing else. The women wore baggy-legged garments running from ankle to neck to wrist and cinched at the waist with a white cord. Except for the cord, the outfits were so sheer that the barefoot women might as well have been naked.

The man raised his hand and waggled his first two fingers, ordering them forward. The six women advanced across the cavernous room, that because of its dark stone that swallowed the firelight, seemed to close in about them. On an enormous bearskin before the table sat two more of the absurdly clad slaves. The women behind the table, against the wall, stood hands at their sides, bodies stiff and unmoving. Each of the young women had a gold ring pierced through the center of her lower lip.

The fires behind them popped and snapped as the six Sisters advanced into the gloom. One of the men in white trousers poured wine into a mug for the man when he held it out to his side. None of the slaves looked at the six women. Their attention was on the man sitting alone at the table.

Ulicia and her Sisters all recognized him, now.

Jagang.

He was of average height, but stout, with massive arms and chest. His bare shoulders bulged from a fur vest opened in the middle, displaying a few dozen gold and jeweled chains lying against the hair in the deep cleft between his prodigious chest muscles. The chains and jewels looked to have once belonged to kings and queens. Silver bands encircled his arms above bulky biceps. Each of his thick fingers bore a gold or silver ring.

Each of the Sisters knew well the pain those powerful fingers could inflict.

His shaved head gleamed in the fluttering firelight. It matched his brawn. Ulicia couldn't imagine him with hair atop his head; it could only diminish his menace. His neck looked like it belonged to a bull. A gold ring in the flare of his left nostril held a thin gold chain running to another ring at midheight in his left ear. He was clean-shaven except for a two-inch braid of mustache growing only above the corners of his smirk, and another braid in the center under his lower lip.

His eyes, though, were what riveted anyone upon whom they settled. There were no whites to them at all. They were a murky gray, clouded over with sullen, dusky shapes that shifted in a field of inky obscurity, yet there was no doubt whatsoever as to when he was looking at you.

They were twin windows into nightmare.

The smirk departed, leaving in its place a treacherous glare. "You're late," he said in a deep, grating voice that they each recognized as readily as his nightmare eyes.

Ulicia wasted no time with a reply, nor did she betray any indication of what she was about to do. Twisting the flow of Han, she even controlled their hatred, allowing only one facet of their feelings—fear—to touch their faces, lest they give him any warning of their confidence, and betray a reason for it.

Ulicia committed to obliterating everything from her toes outward—for the next twenty miles.

With violent and unceremonious abruptness, she yanked the restraining blocks from the furious force bottled behind it. As quick as thought, with thundering fury, the Additive and Subtractive Magic exploded outward in a murderous blast. The very air howled as it burned. The room ignited with a blinding flash of twin magics—opposites that twisted in a deafening discharge of wrath.

Even Ulicia was stunned at what she had unleashed.

The fabric of reality seemed to rip.

Her last thought was that surely, she had destroyed the entire world.

CHAPTER 27

LIKE SNOWFLAKE PATCHES OF a dark dream drifting down, everything came slowly back into her vision—the twin fires first, then the torches, then the dark stone walls, and finally the people.

Her whole body was numb for a stunned moment before the feeling returned to her flesh in a million painful pinpricks. She hurt everywhere.

Jagang tore off a big bite of roast pheasant. He chewed a moment, and then wagged the leg bone at her.

"You know your problem, Ulicia?" he asked, still chewing. "You use magic that you can unleash as quick as a thought."

The smirk returned to his greasy lips. "I, on the other hand, am a dream walker. I use the time between fragments of thought, in that stillness when there is nothing, to do what I do. I slip in where no other can go."

He gestured with the bone again as he swallowed. "You see, for me, in that space between thought, time is infinite, and I can do as I wish. You might as well be stone statues trying to chase me."

Ulicia felt her Sisters through the link. It was still there.

"Crude. Very crude," he said. "I've seen others do it much better, but then they'd been practiced at it. I left the link—for now.

For now, I want you all to feel each other. I'll break it later. Just as I can break the link, I can break your minds, too." He took a gulp of wine. "But I think that's so unproductive. How can you teach people a lesson, really teach them a lesson, if their minds don't understand it?"

Through the link, Ulicia felt Cecilia lose control of her bladder, and the warm urine running down her legs.

"How?" Ulicia heard herself ask in a hollow voice. "How can you use the time between thoughts?"

Jagang picked up his knife and sliced off a slab of meat on an ornate silver platter to his side. He stabbed the bloody center of the slice with the knifepoint and then rested his elbows on the table. "What are we all?" He waved around the skewered hunk of meat as it dripped red down his knife. "What is reality—the reality of our existence?"

He drew the meat off the knife with his teeth and chewed as he went on. "Are we our bodies? Is a small person less than a big person, then? If we were our bodies, then when we lost an arm, or a leg, would we be less, would we begin to fade from existence? No. We are the same person.

"We are not our bodies; we are our thoughts. As they form, they define who we are, and create the reality of our existence. Between those thoughts, there is nothing, simply the body, waiting for our thoughts to make us who we are.

"Between your thoughts, I come. In that space between your thoughts time has no meaning to you, but it has meaning to me." He took a swig of wine. "I am a shadow, slipping between the cracks of your existence."

Through the link, Ulicia could feel the others trembling. "That isn't possible," she whispered. "Your Han can't spread time, break it apart."

His condescending smile caught her breath short. "A small, simple wedge, inserted into a crack in the largest, most massive boulder, can split it apart. Destroy it.

"I am that wedge. That wedge is now hammered into the cracks in your minds."

She stood silently as his thumb gouged off a long strip of pork from a roasted suckling pig. "When you sleep, your thoughts float and drift and you are vulnerable. When you sleep, you are a beacon I can find. Then, my thoughts slip into the cracks. The spaces where you fade in and out of existence are chasms to me."

"And what do you want with us?" Armina asked.

He tore off a bite of the pork dangling from his meaty fingers. "Well, among my uses for you, we have a mutual enemy: Richard Rahl. You know him as Richard Cypher." He arched an eyebrow over one of his dark, seething eyes. "The Seeker.

"Up until now he's been invaluable. He did me a huge favor by destroying the barrier, which kept me on this side. My body, anyway. You, the Sisters of the Dark, the Keeper, and Richard Rahl made it possible for me to bring the race of man to ascendancy."

"We have done no such thing," Tovi protested in a meek voice.

"Ah, but you have. You see, the Creator and the Keeper vied for dominance in this world, the Creator simply to prevent the Keeper from swallowing it into the world of the dead, and the Keeper simply because he has an insatiable appetite for the living."

His inky-eyed gaze rose to meet theirs. "In your struggle to free the Keeper, to give him this world, you gave the Keeper power here, and that, in turn, baited Richard Rahl to come to the defense of the living. He restored the balance.

"In that balance, just as in the space between your thoughts, I come.

"Magic is the conduit to those other worlds, giving them power here. By reducing the amount of magic in the world I will lessen the Creator and the Keeper's influence here. The Creator will still send his spark of life, and the Keeper will still take it away when its end has come, but beyond that, the world will belong to man. The old religion of magic will be consigned to the midden heap of history, and eventually, to myth.

"I am a dream walker; I have seen the dreams of men, I know their potential. Magic suppresses these boundless visions. Without magic, man's mind, his imagination, will be unleashed, and he will be all-powerful.

"That's why I have the army I do. When magic is dead, I will still have them. I keep them well practiced for that day."

"And how is Richard Rahl your enemy?" Ulicia asked, hoping to keep him talking while she tried to think of what they could do.

"He had to do as he did, of course, or you darlins would have given the world to the Keeper. That aided me, but now he interferes with my plans. He's young, and ignorant of his talents. I, on the other hand, have spent the last twenty years perfecting my ability."

He waved the knifepoint in front of his eyes. "Only in the last year have my eyes turned—the mark of a dream walker. Only now am I entitled to the most feared appellation in the ancient world. In the ancient tongue, 'dream walker' is synonymous with 'weapon.' The wizards who created this weapon came to regret it."

He licked the grease off his knife as he watched them. "It's a mistake to forge weapons with minds of their own. You are my weapons now. I don't make the same mistake.

"My power allows me to enter the minds of anyone when they sleep. In those who don't have the gift I can only exert a limited amount of influence, and they are of small use to me anyway, but in those who are gifted, like you six, I can do anything I wish. Once my wedge is in your mind, it is no longer yours. It's mine.

"The magic of the dream walkers was powerful, but unstable. None has been born with the ability in the last three thousand years, since the barrier went up and trapped us here. But now, a dream walker treads this world again."

He shook with a menacing chuckle. The tiny braids at the corners of his mouth danced. "That would be me."

Ulicia almost told him to get to the point, but stopped herself just in time. She had no desire to see what he would do when he was done talking. She needed the time to try to think of something. "How do you know all this?"

Jagang tore a strip of charred fat from the roast and nibbled on it as he went on. "In a buried city in my homeland of Altur'Rang, I found an archive from the ancient times. Ironic, the value of books, to a warrior like me. The Palace of the Prophets has books of immense value, too, if you know how to use them. Too bad the Prophet died, but I have other wizards.

"A fragment of magic from the ancient war, a shield of sorts, was passed down from its originator to all those descendants with the gift born to the House of Rahl. This bond shields people's minds so I can't enter. Richard Rahl has that ability, and has begun to use it. Before he learns too much, he must be brought to task.

"Along with his betrothed." He paused with a distant, brooding look. "The Mother Confessor dealt me a small setback, but she's being brought to task by my unwitting puppets up north. The fools, in their zeal, have created some complications, but I've yet to truly jerk their strings. When I do, they'll jump to my tune; I have that wedge planted deep. I've spent great effort to bend events to my advantage so as to put Richard Rahl and the Mother Confessor in the palm of my hand."

He squeezed a fist of meat from the roasted suckling pig. "You see, he's been born a war wizard, the first in three thousand years, but then, you knew that. A wizard like that will prove an invaluable weapon to me. He can do things none of you can, so I don't want to kill him; I want to control him. When he's outlived his usefulness, then he'll need killing."

Jagang sucked the pig fat from his rings. "You see, control is more important than killing. I could have killed you six, but then what good would you be? As long as you're under my dominion, you're no threat to me, and of use in oh, so many ways."

Jagang turned his wrist up, pointing his knife at Merissa. "You've all vowed vengeance against him, but you, my darlin, have vowed to bathe in his blood. I may yet give you the chance."

Merissa's face paled. "How . . . could you know that? I said that when I was awake."

He chuckled at the look of panic on her face. "If you don't want me to know something, darlin, then you shouldn't dream about what you've said while you were awake."

Through the link, Ulicia felt Armina come near to fainting.

"Of course, you six must first be brought to task. You must learn who it is that's in control of your lives." With his knife he indicated the silent slaves behind him. "You'll become as obedient as these, here."

For the first time, Ulicia took a good look at the partially clad people around the room. She nearly gasped aloud. The women were all Sisters. Worse, most were her Sisters of the Dark. She took a quick survey; not all of them were here. The men, mostly young wizards who had been released after their training at the palace, were also ones who had given a soul oath to the Keeper.

"Some are Sisters of the Light, and serve well, for fear of what I'll visit upon them should they displease me." With a finger and thumb, Jagang stroked the thin gold chain between the rings in his nose and ear, "but I like your Sisters of the Dark the best; I've brought them all to task, even those at the palace." Ulicia felt as if another pin had been knocked from under her. "I have business at the Palace of the Prophets. Important business."

The gold chains at his chest glinted in the firelight as he spread his arms. "They're all quite obedient." His inky gaze turned to those behind. "Aren't you, my darlins?"

Janet, a Sister of the Light, kissed her ring finger as tears crept down her cheeks. Jagang laughed. His ring sparkled in the firelight as he pointed a thick finger at her.

"See that? I permit her to do that. It keeps her filled with false hope. Would I prevent it, then she might kill herself, because she doesn't have the fear of death like those sworn to the Keeper. Isn't that right, my darlin Janet?"

"Yes, Excellency," she answered in a cowed voice. "You own my body in this life, but my soul belongs to the Creator when I die."

Jagang laughed, a morbid, grating sound. Ulicia had heard it before, and she knew she was going to be its cause again.

"You see? That's what I tolerate in order to maintain my control. Of course she will now have to serve a week in the tents as punishment." His inky glare caused Janet to shrink back. "But then you knew that before you said it, didn't you my darlin?"

Sister Janet's voice trembled. "Yes, Excellency."

Jagang's murky, clouded eyes returned to the six before him. "I like the Sisters of the Dark best because they have sound reason to fear death." He twisted the pheasant in half. Bones snapped and popped. "They've failed the Keeper, to whom they've sworn their souls. If they die, it's no escape. If they die, the Keeper will have his revenge for their failure." He laughed, a deep, resonant, mocking sound. "As he'll have you six, for eternity, if you displease me enough to earn death."

Ulicia swallowed. "We understand . . . Excellency."

Jagang's nightmare gaze made her forget to breathe. "Oh no, Ulicia, I don't think you truly do. When your lessons are finished, though, you will."

With his nightmare gaze on Ulicia, he reached under the table and dragged a shapely woman out by her blond hair. She winced in pain as his powerful fist lifted her. She was dressed the same as the others. Through the sheer fabric, Ulicia could see older, yellow bruises, and newer, purple ones. There was a bruise on her right cheek, and a fresh, huge, blue-black one on her left jaw, with a line of four cuts left by his rings.

It was Christabel, one of the Sisters of the Dark Ulicia had left at the palace. The Sisters of the Dark at the palace were to have laid the groundwork for their return. Apparently, they now laid the groundwork for Jagang's arrival. What he could want with the Palace of the Prophets, she couldn't fathom.

Jagang turned his hand over, pointing. "Stand before me."

Sister Christabel scurried around the table to stand before Jagang. She quickly smoothed her disheveled hair, and wiped her mouth with the back of her hand before bowing. "How may I serve you, Excellency?"

"Well, Christabel, I need to teach these six their first lesson." He tore the other leg off the pheasant. "In order to do that, you must die."

She bowed. "Yes, Excell—" She froze, realizing what he had just said. Ulicia could see her legs trembling as she straightened, but still, the woman dared say nothing.

He gestured with the pheasant leg to the two women sitting before him on the bearskin, and they scrambled away. Jagang smiled that terrifying smirk of his. "Good-bye, Christabel."

Her arms flung into the air as she collapsed to the ground with a shriek. Christabel thrashed madly on the floor, screamed so loudly it hurt Ulicia's ears. The six women standing above her at the edge of the bearskin watched with wide eyes, holding their breath. Jagang gnawed on his pheasant leg. The bloodcurdling screams went on and on as Christabel's head whipped from side to side and her whole body flopped and bounced as she twitched violently.

Jagang occupied himself with his pheasant leg and having his wine mug refilled. No one spoke as he finished the leg and turned to take a few grapes.

Ulicia could stand it no longer. "How long until she dies?" she asked in a hoarse voice.

Jagang lifted an eyebrow. "Until she dies?" He threw his head back as he roared in laughter. His fists, bristling with huge rings, pounded the table. No one else in the room so much as smiled. His burly body shook. The thin chain between his nose and ear danced as his laughter died out in fits.

"She was dead before she hit the floor."

"What? But she . . . she's still screaming."

Christabel suddenly was silent, her chest as still as stone.

"She's been dead from the first instant," Jagang said. A slow smile spread on his lips as he fixed the black void of his gaze on Ulicia. "That wedge I told you about. Just like the one I have in your minds. What you see is her soul screaming. You are seeing her torment in the world of the dead. The Keeper looks to be displeased with his Sister of the Dark."

Jagang lifted a finger and Christabel resumed her wild thrashing and screaming.

Ulicia swallowed. "How long . . . how long until she . . . stops?"

He licked his lips. "Until she rots."

Ulicia felt her knees trembling, and through the link she could feel the other five on the verge of screaming in mad panic, just as Christabel was. This was the displeasure the Keeper would visit upon them if they didn't restore his influence in this world.

Jagang snapped his fingers. "Slith! Eeris!"

Light shimmered against the wall. Ulicia gasped as two caped forms seemed to appear out of the dark stone.

The two scaled creatures glided silently around the table and bowed. "Yesss, dreamssss walker?"

Jagang waggled his thick finger, indicating the screaming woman on the floor. "Throw her down the privy pit."

The mriswith flipped their capes back over their shoulders and bent, lifting the thrashing, shrieking body of a woman Ulicia had known for well over a hundred years, a woman who had helped her, and been an obedient servant to the Keeper's wishes. She was to have had a reward for her service. They all were.

Ulicia looked to Jagang as the two mriswith left the room with their load for the privy pit. "What do you want us to do?"

Jagang lifted a hand and with two grease-slicked fingers motioned a soldier at the side of the room to come forward. "These six belong to me. Ring them."

The husky man, draped in furs and hung with weapons, bowed. He went to the closest, Nicci, and with filthy fingers unceremoniously pulled on her lower lip, distending it grotesquely. Her wide blue eyes filled with panic. Ulicia gasped with Nicci. Through the link, she could feel the young woman's stunned pain and terror as the blunt, rusty iron pick stabbed with a twisting motion through the margin of the lip. The soldier stuck the wooden-handled pick back in his belt and pulled a gold ring from his pocket as he held out her lower lip. With the help of his teeth, he spread the split in the ring and then shoved it through the bleeding wound. He twisted the ring around and used his teeth to close the gap.

The unshaven, filthy, stinking soldier came to Ulicia last. By then she was shuddering uncontrollably, having felt it done to each of the others. As he yanked on her lower lip, she desperately tried to think of an escape. It was like drawing a bucket from an empty well. Tears of pain flooded from her eyes as the ring was poked through.

Jagang wiped grease from his mouth with the back of his hand while he watched with amusement as blood trickled down all their chins. "You six are my slaves, now. If you don't give me cause to kill you, I have use for you at the Palace of the Prophets. When I'm finished with Richard Rahl, I may even let you kill him."

His eyes came up again, the sullen shapes in them shifting in a way that caught her breath. All traces of mirth vanished, leaving unbridled menace in its place. "But first, I'm not finished with your lessons."

"We understand quite well our alternatives," Ulicia said hurriedly. "Please—you have no need to fear our loyalty."

"Oh I know that," Jagang whispered. "But I still haven't finished with your lessons. Your first one was only the beginning. The rest won't be nearly so quick."

Ulicia's legs were in danger of giving way. Since Jagang had begun coming into her dreams, her waking life had turned into a nightmare. There must be a way to stop this, but she could think of none. She had a vision of herself, returning to the Palace of the Prophets as one of Jagang's slaves, in one of those outfits.

Jagang glanced past her. "Have you boys been listening?"

Ulicia heard Captain Blake answer that they had. She started. She had forgotten all about the thirty sailors standing behind her at the back of the room.

Jagang gestured with two fingers for them to come closer. "In the morning you may leave. I thought, though, that for tonight you would like to have these ladies."

Each of the six went rigid.

"But—"

Her words were cut short by the way the floating shapes shifted suddenly in his mirky eyes. "From now on, if you use your magic against my wishes, even if it's to stop yourself from sneezing, you'll share Christabel's fate. In your dreams I've shown you a small taste of what I can do to you while you're alive, and you've now seen a small taste of what the Keeper will do to you if you die. You have but one path to tread. If I were you, I'd not put one foot wrong."

Jagang returned his gaze to the sailors behind them. "They're yours for the night. Knowing these six from their dreams, I know you have scores to settle. Do to them as you wish."

The sailors' voices rose in gleeful oaths.

Through the link, Ulicia could feel a hand grip Armina's breast, another pull Nicci's head back by her hair as the lace at her bodice was pulled loose, and another hand slide up the inside of her own thigh. She choked back a scream.

"There's some minor rules," Jagang said, stopping the hands on them. "If you violate them, I'll gut you all like a sack of fish."

"And what would the rules be, Emperor?" a sailor asked.

"You can't kill them. They're my slaves—they belong to me. I want them returned in the morning in good enough condition so that they can serve me. That means no broken bones and such. You'll draw lots as to which one you get. I know what'll happen if I let you choose for yourselves. I don't want any of them neglected."

The sailors all chuckled in agreement, and all spoke up that it was more than fair. They vowed the rules would be followed.

Jagang returned his attention to the six women. "I have a gigantic army of big burly soldiers, and nowhere near enough whores to go around. Puts my men in an ugly mood. Until I have other duties for you, you'll serve in that capacity for all but four hours a day. Be thankful you have my ring in your lip; it'll keep them from killing you while they're having their fun."

Sister Cecilia spread her hands. She glowed with a kindly, innocent smile. "Emperor Jagang, your men are young and strong. I'm afraid they would find no enjoyment being with an old woman such as myself. I'm sorry."

"I'm sure they'll grin with delight to have you. You'll see."

"Emperor, Sister Cecilia is right. I'm afraid I, too, am too old and fat," Tovi said in her best elderly voice. "We would bring your men no satisfaction."

"Satisfaction?" He took a bite of the roast on the point of his knife. "Satisfaction? Are you daft? This has nothing to do with satisfaction. I assure you, my men will enjoy your warm charms—but you misunderstand."

He waggled a finger at them, the greasy rings on his fingers glinting in the firelight. "You six were Sisters of the Light, and then Sisters of the Dark. You're probably the most powerful sorceresses in the world. This is to teach you that you're little more than dung beneath my boots. I'll do with you as I please. Those with the gift are my weapons, now.

"This is to teach you a lesson. You have no say in it. Until I decide otherwise, I give you to my men to use. If they want to twist your fingers and take bets on who can make you scream the loudest, then they will. If they want any other sort of pleasure from you, then they'll have it. They have quite varied tastes, and as long as they don't kill you, they're free to indulge them."

He shoved the rest of the piece of meat in his mouth. "After these fellows are done with you, anyway. Enjoy my gift, boys. Do as I ask, follow my rules, and I may have use of you in the future. Emperor Jagang treats his friends well."

A cheer for the emperor went up from the sailors.

Ulicia would have fallen when her legs buckled had not an arm circled her waist to pull her back tight against an eager sailor. She could smell his foul breath.

"Well, well, well, lass. Looks like you ladies are going to come out to play after all, and after you were so nasty to us."

Ulicia could hear herself whimper. Her lip throbbed in pain, but she knew it was only the beginning. She was so stunned by what was happening that she couldn't form a clear thought.

"Oh," Jagang said, stopping everyone. He gestured with his knife to Merissa. "Except that one. You can't have her," he said to the sailors. He waggled two fingers. "Step forward, darlin."

Merissa took two strides to the fur. Through the link, Ulicia could feel her legs trembling.

"Christabel was mine, exclusively. She was my favorite. But she's dead now, just to serve as a lesson for you." He glanced to where the sailors had already pulled her dress open. "You will take her place."

He returned his inky gaze to her eyes. "You did say, if I recall correctly, that you would lick my feet, if you must. You must." At Merissa's look of surprise, Jagang smiled that deadly smile of his, framed by the little braids at the ends. "I told you, darlin, you dream things you've said when you're awake."

Merissa nodded weakly. "Yes, Excellency."

"Take off that dress. You might need something nice for later, if I choose to let you kill Richard Rahl for me." He looked to the other women as Merissa did as she was ordered. "I'm going to leave the link on you for now so you can each feel the lessons the others get. I wouldn't want you to miss out on any of it."

When Merissa had finished, Jagang turned the knife between a finger and thumb, and pointed it down. "Under the table, darlin."

Ulicia could feel the coarse fur rug against Merissa's knees, and then the rough stone floor under the table. The sailors leered at the sight.

Through sheer force of will, from her reservoir of hatred for this man, Ulicia tapped strength and drew resolve. She was the leader of the Sisters of the Dark. Through the link, she spoke to the others. *"We have all been through the ritual. Worse than this has been done to us. We are Sisters of the Dark; remember who is our true Master. For now we are slaves to this leech, but he has made a huge mistake if he thinks we don't have minds. He has no power of his own except to use ours. We will think of something, and then Jagang will pay. Oh, sweet Master, will he ever pay."*

"But what are we going to do until then!" Armina screamed.

"Silence!" Nicci commanded. Ulicia could feel the probing fingers on Nicci, and she could feel the white heat of her rage, and she could feel her heart of black ice. *"Remember each face. They will each pay. Listen to Ulicia. We'll think of something, and then we will teach them all lessons only we could envision."*

"And don't any of you dare dream any of this," Ulicia warned. *"The one thing we cannot afford is to let Jagang kill us, or all hope is lost. As long as we live, we have a chance to earn our way back into our Master's favor. We've been promised a reward for our souls, and I intend to have it. Have strength, my Sisters."*

"But Richard Rahl is mine," Merissa hissed. *"Any who takes him in my stead will answer to me—and the Keeper."* Even Jagang, had he been able to hear her, would have blanched at the venom in her warning. Through the link, Ulicia felt Merissa push her thick hair back out of the way. She could taste what Merissa tasted.

"I'm done with you. . . ." Jagang paused a moment as he drew a breath. He waved the knife. "Be gone."

Captain Blake snatched Ulicia by the hair. "Time for payback, lass."

CHAPTER 28

SHE BLINKED AS SHE looked down the length of the rusty sword held at her face. The point was no more than an inch away.

"Really, is this necessary? I told you that you could steal what you wanted and we wouldn't do anything to stop you, but I have to tell you that you're the third band of dangerous outlaws who have robbed us in the last couple of weeks, and we've nothing of value left."

By the way the lad's hand was shaking, he didn't look to be very practiced at his craft. By the way his skin clung to his bones, he didn't look to be very successful at it, either.

"Be quiet!" He snuck a look in the direction of his companion. "Have you found anything?"

The second young outlaw, squatting among the packs in the snow, and as thin as the first, darted glances around at the darkening woods to each side of the little-traveled road. He checked behind, to the bend in the road not far away where it vanished behind a screen of snow-crusted fir trees. In the center of the bend, just before the road vanished, was a bridge over a stream still rushing despite the fact it was winter. "No. Just old clothes and junk. No bacon, not even any bread."

The first danced back and forth on the balls of his feet, ready to bolt at the first sign of trouble. He brought his other hand up to the hilt to help hold the weight of the poorly made sword. "You look well fed. What do you two eat, old woman! Snow?"

She folded her hands against her belt as she sighed. She was tiring of this. "We work for our food as we go. You should try it. Work, I mean."

"Yeah? It's winter, old woman, in case you hadn't noticed. There's no work. Last autumn the army took our stores. My parents don't have anything to get them through the winter."

"I'm sorry, son. Perhaps . . ."

"Hey! What's this, old man?" He had his finger through the dull silver collar. He gave it a yank. "How do you get this off? Answer me!"

"I told you," she said, avoiding the silent fury of the wizard's blue eyes, "my brother is deaf and dumb. He doesn't understand your words, and he can't answer them."

"Deaf and dumb? Then you tell me, how do you get this thing off?"

"It's just an iron memento that was welded on long ago. It's worthless."

A hand came off the sword as her assailant leaned warily toward her and with a finger lifted her cape aside. "What's this? A purse! I found her purse!" He yanked the heavy bag of gold coins from her belt. "It must be full of gold!"

She chuckled. "I'm afraid its just a bag of hard biscuits. You're free to have one, if you'd like, but don't try to bite down on them or you'll break your teeth. Suck on it awhile."

He fished out a gold coin and put it between his teeth. He winced with a sour expression. "How can you eat these things? I've eaten bad biscuits, but these aren't even good enough to be called bad."

So easy with a young mind, she thought. Too bad it wasn't that easy on an adult.

He spat to the side and tossed the bag of gold to the snow before patting her cape, searching for anything else she might have concealed.

She sighed impatiently. "Would you boys get on with this robbery. We'd like to make the next town before dark."

"Nothin'," the second said. "They don't have nothin' worth the trouble of carrying off."

"They got horses," the first said as he squeezed fistfuls of her heavy cape, feeling for anything it might be holding. "At least we can take the horses. They'll bring something."

"Please do," she said. "I'm tired of being slowed by leading those old nags around. You would be doing me a favor. All four are lame and I don't have the heart to put them out of their misery."

"The old woman's right," the second said as he pulled one of the limping horses along, testing it. "All four. We can walk faster. We try to take these bags of bones with us and we'll get caught sure."

The first was still running his hand down her cape. It halted on her pocket. "What's this?"

Her voice took on an edge. "Nothing of interest to you."

"Yeah?" He fingered the journey book from her pocket.

As he thumbed through the blank pages, she caught sight of a message. At last.

"What's this?"

"Just a notebook. Can you read, son?"

"No. There don't appear to be hardly nothin' worth reading anyway."

"Take it anyway," the second said. "It might be worth something if nothin's written in it."

She looked back to the young man holding the sword on her. "I've had just about enough of this. Consider the robbery over."

"It's over when I say it's over."

"Give it back," Ann said in a level voice as she held her hand out. "And then be on your way before I drag you to town by your ear and have your parents come to collect you."

He brandished the sword as he leapt back defensively. "Look, don't you go getting feisty or you'll taste steel! I know how to use this thing!"

The still evening air suddenly thundered with horses' hooves. She had been watching as the soldiers had slipped up, around the bend and over the little bridge, unnoticed by the two young men because of the rushing water, until at the last moment when they charged in. As her assailant turned in shock, Ann snatched the sword from his hands. Nathan snatched the knife from the other.

Mounted D'Haran soldiers suddenly towered above them. "What's going on here?" the sergeant asked in a calm, deep voice.

The two young men stood frozen in panic. "Well," Ann said, "we ran into these two, here, and they were telling us how we should be careful of outlaws. They live in the neighborhood. They were showing us how to protect ourselves and giving us a demonstration of their blade work."

The sergeant folded his hands over the pommel. "Is that right, boy?"

"I . . . we . . ." His pleading eyes turned to her. "That's right. We live nearby, and we was just telling these two travelers to be careful as we heard tell that there are outlaws about."

"And quite a show of swordsmanship it was. As I promised, young man, you get a biscuit for the show. Hand me my sack of biscuits, there."

He bent and snatched up the heavy purse of gold, holding it out to her. Ann pulled two coins out and pressed one into the hand of each young man.

"As promised, a biscuit for each. Now you boys best be getting home before dark, or your parents will worry. Give them my biscuit as thanks for sending you out to warn us to be careful."

He nodded dumbly. "All right. Good night, then. Take care of yourselves."

Ann held her hand out. She fixed the young man with a dangerous squint. "If you're done looking at my notebook, I'll have it back."

His eyes widened at the look in hers, and then he thrust the journey book into her hand as if it were burning his fingers, which it was.

Ann smiled. "Thank you, son."

He wiped the hand on his tattered coat. "Good-bye, then. And be careful."

He turned to leave. "Don't forget this." He turned back cautiously. She held the hilt out to him. "You father would be awfully angry if you forgot to bring back his sword."

He lifted it carefully. Nathan, not about to let this go without a bit of theatrics, walked the spinning knife across the backs of his fingers. He tossed the knife in the air, catching it behind his back, and then whirled it under his armpit and into his other hand. Ann rolled her eyes as he slapped the blade, reversing the spin. He caught the knife by its blade and handed it, handle first, to the other wide-eyed young man.

"Where'd you learn to do that, old man?" the sergeant asked.

Nathan scowled. If there was one thing Nathan didn't like, it was being called "old man." He was a wizard, a prophet, of unparalleled ability, and thought he should be viewed with wonder, if not open awe. She was restraining his gift by choking it off with his Rada'Han, or no doubt the sergeant's saddle would be aflame by now. She was also preventing him from speaking. Nathan's tongue was at least as dangerous as his power.

"I'm afraid my brother is deaf and dumb." She gestured to the two outlaws with a shooing motion of her hand. They waved and scrambled for the woods, kicking up snow as they went. "My brother has always amused himself by practicing hand tricks."

"Ma'am, are you sure those two aren't causing you any trouble?"

"Oh, no," she scoffed.

The sergeant lifted his reins, the twenty men behind him doing the same in response, ready to take out after him. "Well, I think we'll have a little talk with them, anyway. A little talk about thieving."

"If you do, be sure to ask them to tell you about how the D'Haran soldiers stole their families' stores of food, and how they're starving because of it."

The square-jawed soldier lowered the reins. "I don't know anything about what was done before, but the new Lord Rahl has given explicit orders that there will be no stealing of anything by the army."

"The new Lord Rahl?"

He nodded. "Richard Rahl, the Master of D'Hara."

From the corner of her eye, she saw a smile twitch across Nathan's lips. It was a smile for a properly taken fork in a prophecy. Though it had to be, were they to succeed, it brought her no smile, but an inner pang of agony for the path ahead now confirmed. Only the alternative was worse. "Yes, I do believe I've heard the name, now that you mention it."

The sergeant stood in the stirrups and turned back to his men. "Ogden, Spaulding!" Their horses kicked up snow when they leaped ahead. "Go after those boys and take them to their families. Find out if what they say is true about their stores being stolen by troops. If it is, find out the number in their families and if there are any others in the neighborhood under the same circumstances. Take a report back to Aydindril at once and see to it that they get what they need to eat, to see them through the winter."

The two men saluted with a fist to the dark leather and mail over their hearts and then galloped their horses down the tracks leading into the woods. The sergeant turned back to her. "Lord Rahl's orders," he explained. "Are you headed to Aydindril?"

"Yes, we're hoping to find safety there, like the others traveling north."

"You'll find it, then, but it comes at a cost. I'll tell you the same as all the others. Whatever your former homeland, you will now be subjects of D'Hara. Your allegiance is required, along with a small portion of what you earn in your labor, if you wish to come to territory held by D'Hara."

She lifted an eyebrow. "It would seem the army is still thieving from the people?"

"It might seem so to you, but not to Lord Rahl, and his word is law. All pay the same in order to support the troops who have been charged with protecting our freedom. If you don't wish to pay, you are free not to seek that protection and freedom."

"Seems like Lord Rahl has things well in hand."

The sergeant nodded. "He is a powerful wizard."

Nathan's shoulders shook with a silent laugh.

The sergeant's eyes narrowed. "What's he laughing about, if he's supposed to be deaf and dumb?"

"Oh he is, but he's also a half-wit." Ann strolled toward the horses. As she crossed in front of the broad-shouldered wizard, she landed a sharp elbow in his gut. "Laughs like that at the oddest times." She scowled up as Nathan coughed. "He's liable to start drooling in a moment, if he keeps at it."

Ann stroked a gentle hand along Bella's sleek, powerful, golden flanks. Bella danced with delight at her touch. The big mare hopefully stuck her tongue out; she liked nothing better than having someone tug on it. Ann obliged her and then scratched behind an ear. Bella whinnied with a horse giggle and stuck the tongue out again, hoping for the game to continue.

"You were saying, Sergeant, about how Lord Rahl is a powerful wizard?"

"That's right. He slew the creatures you'll see on pikes before the palace."

"Creatures?"

"He calls them mriswith. Ugly, scaled, lizardlike things. They've killed a number of people, but Lord Rahl himself cut them to pieces."

Mriswith. That was certainly not good news.

"Is there a town near, where we could find food and lodging for the night?"

"Ten Oaks is just over the next rise, maybe two miles. There's a small inn there."

"And how far to Aydindril?"

He appraised their four horses as she stroked Bella's ear. "With animals as fine as those, I doubt it will take you more than seven or eight days."

"Thank you, Sergeant. It's good to know there are soldiers about in case there are outlaws in the neighborhood."

He glanced over at Nathan, taking in his towering form, his long white hair that brushed his shoulders, his strong, clean-shaven jaw, and his hooded, penetrating, dark azure eyes. Nathan was a ruggedly handsome man filled with vigor, despite the fact that he was close to a thousand years old.

The sergeant looked back to her, clearly preferring to exchange glances with a squat old woman rather than with Nathan. Even with his power choked off, Nathan presented an intimidating presence. "We're looking for someone: the Blood of the Fold."

"Blood of the Fold? You mean those pompous fools from Nicobarese in the red capes?"

The sergeant snugged the reins as his horse tried to step sideways. Others of the twenty horses pawed the snow, looking for grass, or nibbled hopefully at dry branches to the side of the road, tails lazily swishing the cool evening air. "That's them. Two men, one the lord general of the Blood, another officer, and a woman. They escaped from Aydindril, and Lord Rahl has ordered them brought back. We have men out everywhere scouring the countryside."

"Sorry, but I haven't seen a sign of them. Is Lord Rahl staying at the Wizard's Keep?"

"No, at the Confessors' Palace."

Ann signed. "That's good, at least."

His brow drew together. "Why is that good?"

She hadn't realized she had spoken her relief aloud. "Oh, well, it's just that I'm hoping to see this great man, and if he stays at the Keep, then I wouldn't be able to. It's protected by magic, I hear. If he comes out on a balcony at the palace to greet the people, I might get to see him.

"Well, thank you for your help, Sergeant. I think we best get to Ten Oaks before it gets pitch black. Don't want one of my horses to step in a hole and break a leg."

The sergeant bid her a good night and led his column of men up the road, away from Aydindril. Only after they were more than out of earshot did she withdraw the block from Nathan's voice. It was difficult to maintain such control for long periods of time. Ann mentally braced for the inevitable tirade as she started gathering up their packs from the snow.

"We best be on our way," she told him.

Nathan drew himself up with an imperious scowl. "You would give gold to robbers? You should have—"

"They were only boys, Nathan. They were hungry."

"They tried to rob us!"

Ann smiled as she tossed a pack over Bella. "You know as well as I that that would not have happened, but I gave them a little more than gold. I don't think they will be trying that again."

He grunted. "I hope the spell you put on it burns their fingers to the bone."

"Help me with our things. I want to get to the inn. There was a message in the journey book."

Nathan was struck speechless for only an instant. "Took her long enough. We left her enough hints for a child of ten to figure it out long before now. We did everything but leave a note pinned to her dress that said, 'By the way, the Prelate and the Prophet aren't really dead, you dolt.'"

Ann cinched Bella's girth strap tight. "I'm sure it wasn't as easy for her as you make it out to be. It seems obvious to us only because we knew. She had no reason to suspect. Verna figured it out; that's all that is important."

Nathan replied with a lofty snort before he finally started helping by gathering up the rest of the packs. "Well, what did she say?"

"I don't know yet. When we get settled for the night we'll find out."

Nathan lifted a finger in her direction. "You pull the deaf-and-dumb trick on me again and you will live to regret it."

She turned an angry scowl on him. "And if we again come across people and you start yelling that you've been abducted by a mad witch and held prisoner in a magic collar, I'll make you deaf and dumb for real!"

Nathan huffed sourly as he went back to work. As he turned to his horse, she saw him smile to himself in satisfaction.

By the time they found the inn, and after they had left their horses with a boy at the stable out back, the stars were out and the small winter moon was visible over a distant mountain slope. The woodsmoke hugging the ground also carried the aroma of stew. She gave the stableboy a penny to carry in their things.

Ten Oaks was a small community, and the inn had only a dozen locals at the few tables, most drinking and smoking pipes over stories of soldiers they had seen, and rumored alliances forged by the new Lord Rahl, who not all were sure was really in command of Aydindril, as was claimed. Others asked them to then explain why the D'Haran troops had suddenly become so disciplined, if it wasn't because someone had finally brought them to task.

Nathan, wearing high boots, brown trousers, a ruffled white shirt buttoned up over his Rada'Han, an open dark green vest, and a heavy dark brown cape hanging almost to the floor, strolled up to the short counter set before a few bottles and kegs. With a noble air, he flipped his cape back over a shoulder as he settled a boot to the footrail. Nathan relished wearing clothes other than the black robes he always wore at the palace. He called it "playing down."

The humorless innkeeper smiled only after Nathan had slid silver his way and advised that for the high price of lodging, it had better include a meal. The innkeeper shrugged and agreed.

Before she knew it, Nathan was already spinning a tale that he was a merchant traveling with his mistress while his wife was home raising his twelve strapping sons. The man wanted to know what sort of merchandise Nathan dealt in. Nathan leaned close, lowered his commanding voice, and winked at the man as he told him that it would be safer if he didn't know.

The impressed innkeeper straightened and handed Nathan a mug on the house. Nathan toasted the Ten Oaks Inn, the innkeeper, and the patrons before he started for the stairs, telling the innkeeper to bring a mug for his "woman" when he brought their stew. Every eye in the inn followed him, marveling at the impressive stranger among them.

Pressing her lips tight, Ann vowed not to let herself be distracted again, giving Nathan enough time to make up their pretense at being there. It was the journey book that had distracted her. She wanted to know what it said, but she was apprehensive about it, too. Something could easily have gone wrong, and one of the Sisters of the Dark could have the book and have discovered the two of them were still alive. They couldn't afford that. She pressed her fingers against a pang in her stomach. For all she knew, the Palace of the Prophets was already in the hands of the enemy.

The room was small, but clean, with two narrow pallets, a whitewashed stand holding a tin washbasin and chipped ewer, and a square table atop which Nathan set an oil lamp he had carried in from the bracket beside the door. The innkeeper was not far behind with bowls of lamb stew and brown bread, followed by the stableboy with their bags. After both had gone and closed the door, Ann sat and scooted her chair up to the table.

"Well," Nathan said, "aren't you going to give me a lecture?"

"No, Nathan, I'm tired."

He flourished a hand. "I thought it only fair, in view of the deaf-mute business." His expression turned dark. "I've been held in this collar all but the first four years of my life. How would you feel, being a captive your whole life?"

Ann mused to herself that, being his keeper, she was nearly as much a captive as he. She met his glare. "Though you never believe me when I say it, Nathan, I will tell you again that I wish it weren't so. It brings me no pleasure to keep one of the Creator's children a prisoner for no crime but his birth."

After a long silence, he withdrew the glare. His hands clasped behind his back, Nathan strolled the room, giving it a critical appraisal. His boots thumped across the plank floor. "Not what I'm accustomed to," he announced to no one in particular.

Ann pushed away the bowl of stew and set the journey book on the table, staring at the black leather cover for a time before finally opening it and turning to the writing.

You must first tell me the reason you chose me the last time. I remember every word. One mistake, and this journey book feeds the fire.

"My, my, my," she murmured. "She's being very cautious. Good." Nathan peered over Ann's shoulder as she pointed. "Look at the strokes, at how hard she pressed. Verna looks to be angry."

Ann stared at the words. She knew what Verna meant.

"She must really hate me," Ann whispered as the words on the page wavered in her watery gaze.

Nathan straightened. "So what? I hate you, and it never seems to bother you."

"Do you, Nathan? Do you really hate me?"

His only answer was a dismissive grunt. "Have I told you that this plan of yours is madness?"

"Not since breakfast."

"Well it is, you know."

Ann stared at the words in the journey book. "You've worked before to influence which fork is taken in prophecy, Nathan, because you know what can happen down the wrong path, and you also know how vulnerable the prophecies are to corruption."

"What good will it do everyone if you get yourself killed with this foolhardy plan? And me with you! I'd like to live to see a thousand, you know. You're going to get us both killed."

Ann rose from her chair. She laid a gentle hand on his muscular arm. "Tell me then, Nathan, what you would do. You know the prophecies; you know the threat. You yourself are the one who warned me. Tell me what you would do, if it were up to you."

He shared a gaze with her for a long moment. The fire left his eyes as he put a big hand over hers. "The same as you, Ann. It's our only chance. But it doesn't make me feel any better knowing the danger to you."

"I know, Nathan. Are they there? Are they in Aydindril?"

"One is," he said quietly as he squeezed her hand, "and the other will be there around the time we arrive; I have seen it in the prophecy.

"Ann, this age that is upon us is tangled with a warren of prophecies. War draws prophecies like dung draws flies. Branches go in every direction. Every one of them must be negotiated properly. If we take the wrong path on any of them, we walk into oblivion. Worse, there are gaps where I don't know what must be done. Worse yet, there are others involved who must also take the correct fork, and we have no control over them."

Ann could find no words, and so nodded instead. She sat back at the table and inched her chair close. Nathan straddled the other chair and broke off a chunk of brown bread, chewing while he watched her draw the stylus from the spine of the journey book.

Ann wrote, *Tomorrow night, when the moon is up, go to the place you found this.* She closed the book and returned it to a pocket in her gray dress.

Nathan spoke around his mouthful of bread. "I hope she is smart enough to justify your faith."

"We trained her as best we could, Nathan; we sent her away from the palace for twenty years so she might learn to use her wits. We have done all we can. Now we must have faith in her." Ann kissed the finger where the Prelate's ring had been all those years. "Dear Creator, give her strength, too."

Nathan blew on a spoonful of hot stew. "I want a sword," he announced.

Her brow wrinkled. "You're a wizard with full command of his gift. Why in the name of Creation would you want a sword?"

He regarded her as if she were witless. "Because I would look dashing with a sword at my hip."

CHAPTER 29

"PLEASE?" CATHRYN WHISPERED.

Richard stared into her soft brown eyes as he gently touched the side of her radiant face, brushing a black ringlet back from her cheek. When they looked into each other's eyes, it was near to impossible for him to look away unless she did so first. He was having that difficulty now. Her hand on his waist sent warm sensations of longing coursing through him. He struggled desperately to put an image of Kahlan in his mind in order to resist the compulsion to take Cathryn in his arms and say yes. His body burned to do so.

"I'm tired," he lied. Sleep was the last thing he wanted. "It's been a long day. Tomorrow we'll be together again."

"But I want—"

He touched her lips to silence her. He knew that if he heard those words from her again, it would be one time too many. The implied offer of her lips as they sucked the end of his finger with a wet kiss was nearly as impossible to resist as the overt invitation of her words. In the fog of his mind, he could hardly form coherent thoughts.

He managed to form one: *Dear spirits, help me. Give me strength. My heart belongs to Kahlan.*

"Tomorrow," he managed.

"You said that yesterday, and it took me hours to find you," she whispered as she kissed his ear.

Richard had been using the mriswith cape to make himself invisible. It was just a little easier to resist when she couldn't appeal to him directly, but it only delayed the inevitable. When he saw her frantic to find him, he couldn't bear to see her in distress as she searched for him, and would end up going to her.

As her hand came up to his neck, he took it and administered it a quick kiss. "Sleep well, Cathryn. I'll see you in the morning."

Richard glanced to Egan standing ten feet away, with his back to the wall and his arms folded as he stared ahead, as if he saw nothing. Beyond, in the shadows at the end of the gloomy hall, Berdine stood guard, too. She made no pretense at not seeing him standing at the door with Cathryn pressed up against him. She observed without expression. His other guards, Ulic, Cara, and Raina were getting some sleep.

Richard slipped a hand behind his back and turned the doorknob. His weight against the door caused it to spring open, and as it did he stepped aside and Cathryn stumbled into her room. She caught herself by his hand. Looking into his eyes, she kissed his hand. His knees nearly buckled.

Knowing he could resist her no longer if he didn't remove himself from the sight of her, he took back his hand. He was mentally making excuses to himself as to why it would be all right to give in. What could it hurt? Why was it so bad? Why did he think it would be so wrong?

It felt like there was a thick blanket over his thoughts, suffocating them before they could get to the surface.

Voices in his head tried to rationalize why he should stop this foolish resistance and simply enjoy the charms of this gorgeous creature who was making it more than stone cold obvious that she wanted him, who in fact was begging him. He felt a lump in his throat at his desire for her. He was near tears from struggling to find reasons to stop himself.

His thinking churned in a mental stupor. Part of him, the largest part, desperately struggled to make him abandon his resistance, but a small, dim part of his mind fought fiercely, trying to hold him back, trying to warn him that something was wrong. It made no sense. What could be wrong? Why was it wrong? What was it in him that was trying to stop him?

Dear spirits, help me.

An image of Kahlan came to him, and he saw her smile that smile she gave no other but him. He saw her lips moving. She said she loved him.

"I need to be alone with you, Richard," Cathryn said. "I can't wait any longer."

"Good night, Cathryn. Sleep well. I'll see you in the morning." He pulled the door closed.

Panting with exhaustion at the effort, he closed the door to his room after he entered. His shirt was soaked with sweat. With a weak arm, he reached up and shoved the bolt to the door into place. It broke as he drove it home. He stared at the bracket as it swung, hanging by one screw. In the dim light coming from the fire in the hearth, he couldn't see the other screws on the ornate carpets.

He was so hot he could hardly breathe. Richard pulled the baldric over his head and dropped his sword to the floor on his way to the window. With the effort of a drowning man, he twisted the latch and threw the window open, gasping as if he couldn't get his breath. Cold air filled his lungs, but did little to cool him.

His room was on the ground floor, and he briefly contemplated stepping over the sill and rolling in the snow. He decided against it, and settled on letting the cold air waft over him as he stared out into the night, at the moonlit, secluded garden.

Something was wrong, but he couldn't make himself grasp it. He wanted to be with Cathryn, but something inside was fighting it. Why? He couldn't understand why he would want to fight his desire for her.

He thought again about Kahlan. That was why.

But if he loved Kahlan, why would he be having such an intense desire for Cathryn? He could think of little but her. He was having trouble keeping the memory of Kahlan in his head.

Richard shuffled to the bed. He instinctively knew that he had reached the end of his ability to resist his lust for Cathryn. He sat on the edge of the bed, in a daze as his head spun.

The door opened. Richard looked up. It was her. She was

wearing something so sheer that the dim light in the hall silhouetted her body underneath. She crossed the room toward him.

"Richard, please," she said in that soft voice that paralyzed him, "don't send me away this time. Please. I will die if I can't be with you right now."

Die? Dear spirits, he didn't want her to die. Richard nearly burst into tears at the very thought.

She glided closer, into the firelight. The softly pleated nightdress reached the floor, but did nothing to hide what was beneath it, merely softening her body into a vision of beauty beyond anything he could have imagined. The sight ignited him. He could think of nothing but what he was seeing, and how much he wanted her. If he didn't have her, he would die of unrealized desire.

As she stood over him, with one hand behind her back, she smiled as she stroked his face with the other. He could feel the heat of her flesh. She bent and brushed her lips against his. He thought he would die of pleasure. Her hand went to his chest.

"Lie down, my love," Cathryn whispered as she pushed him back.

He flopped back on the bed, staring up at her through the numb agony of desire.

Richard thought of Kahlan. He was powerless. Richard dimly remembered some of the things Nathan had told him about using his gift: it was within him, and anger could bring it out. But he felt no anger. Instinct was how a war wizard used his gift, Nathan had told him. He remembered abandoning himself to that instinct when he was about to die at the hands of Liliana, a Sister of the Dark. He had given sanction to the inner power. He had let his instinctive use of need bring the power to life.

Cathryn put a knee on the bed. "At long last, my love."

In helpless abandon, Richard gave himself over to that calm center, the instinct beyond the veil within his mind. He let himself fall into that dark void. He relinquished control of his actions to what would be. He was lost either way.

Clarity ignited, scorching the fog away in seething ripples.

He looked up to see a woman for whom he had no feelings. With cold lucidity, he understood. Richard had been touched by magic before; he knew its feel. The shroud had been shattered. There was magic about this woman. With the fog gone, he could feel its cold fingers in his mind. But why?

Then he saw the knife.

The blade glinted in the firelight as she lifted it over her head. With a wild rush of strength, he flung himself to the floor as Cathryn buried the knife in the bedding. She drew it back again as she dove toward him.

It was too late for her now. He cocked his legs to kick her back, but in a confusion of sensations and realizations, Richard felt the presence of a mriswith, and at nearly the same time, he saw it materialize as it dove through the air above him.

And then the world went red. He felt warm blood splatter his face as he saw the filmy nightdress slashed open; severed edges of diaphanous material fluttered as if in a blast of wind. The three blades ripped Cathryn nearly in two. The mriswith crashed to the floor beyond.

Richard spun out from underneath her and sprang to his feet as she toppled back, the shocking gore of her insides sloshing across the carpet. Her terrible gasps died out in heaving pants.

Richard crouched, his feet and his hands spread, facing the mriswith on the other side of her. The mriswith had a three-bladed knife in each claw. Between them, Cathryn writhed in the agony of death.

The mriswith took a step back toward the window, its beady eyes staying on Richard. It took another step, drawing its black cape over one scaled arm as its gaze swept the room.

Richard dove for his sword. He slid to a stop as the mriswith planted a clawed foot atop the scabbard, holding it to the floor.

"No," it hissed. "She was going to killssss you."

"The same as you!"

"No. I protectssss you, skin brother."

Dumbfounded, Richard stared up at the dark shape. The mriswith flung the cape around itself and dove through the window into the night, vanishing as it leapt. Richard lunged toward the window to grab it. His arms caught only air as he landed across the windowsill, hanging halfway out into the night. The mriswith was gone. He could no longer feel its presence in his mind.

In the emptiness left by the departure of the mriswith, Richard's mind filled with the mental image of Cathryn squirming in a mass of her guts. He vomited out the window.

When his racking heaves finished, and his head stopped spinning, he staggered back to where she lay to kneel beside her. He thanked the spirits that she was dead, and no longer suffered. Even if she had tried to kill him, he couldn't stand to watch her suffering in the throes of death.

He stared at her face. He couldn't imagine the feelings he had had for her that he now only dimly remembered. She was just an ordinary woman. But she had been shrouded in magic. It was some sort of spell that had overpowered his reason. He had come to his senses with no time to spare. His gift had broken the spell.

The top half of her slashed nightdress was thrown up around her neck. A cold feeling that gave him goose bumps turned his attention to her breasts. Richard's eyes narrowed, and he leaned closer, staring. He reached out and touched her right nipple. He touched the left. It wasn't the same.

He carried a lamp to the fire and lit it with a long splinter of kindling. He returned to the body and held the lamp near her left breast. Richard wet his thumb on his tongue and rubbed the smooth nipple. It came off. With her nightdress, he cleaned the paint from her breast, to leave a smooth, unbroken mound of skin. Cathryn had no left nipple.

The calm center within radiated an aura of comprehension. This was connected to the spell she had over him. He didn't know how, but it was.

Richard suddenly sat back on his heels. He sat a moment, wide-eyed, and then sprang up, running to the door. He stopped. Why should he be thinking this? He had to be wrong.

What if he wasn't?

He opened the door just enough to slip through and then shut it behind himself. Egan glanced his way, his arms still folded, and resumed his stance. Richard peered down the hall, to Berdine, in her red leather, leaning against the wall. She was watching him.

Richard crooked his finger, gesturing her to come to him. She straightened and then strolled up the hall. Berdine glanced to the door as she stopped before him. She frowned up to his eyes.

"The duchess wishes to be with you. Go back to her."

"Go get Cara and Raina, and the three of you get back here." His voice took on the heat of his glower. "Right now."

"Is something—"

"Right now!"

She looked to the door again and then strode off without further word. When she had disappeared around the hall at the end of the corridor, Richard turned to Egan, who was again watching him.

"Why did you let her come into my room?"

Egan's brow wrinkled in puzzlement. He lifted a hand toward the door. "Well . . . the way she is . . . dressed. She said you wanted her tonight, and that you told her to put that on and come to you." Egan cleared his throat. "It was obvious why you wanted her. I thought you would be angry if I kept her from you after you had told her to come to you in the night."

Richard turned the knob and flung open the door. He held his arm out in invitation. Egan hesitated and then entered.

He stiffened as he stood over her remains. "Lord Rahl, I'm sorry. I saw no mriswith. I would have stopped it if I had, or at least have tried to warn you—I swear." He groaned. "Dear spirits, what a way to die. Lord Rahl—I've failed you."

"Look in her hand, Egan."

He glanced along the length of her arm, to see the knife still clutched in her fist. "What the . . . ?"

"I didn't ask her to come to me. She came to my room to kill me."

Egan's eyes turned away. He clearly knew the implications. Any past Lord Rahl would execute a guard for such a failure.

"She fooled me too, Egan. It's not your fault. But don't you ever let a woman, other than my future wife, into my room again. Understand? If a woman comes to my room, you get my permission to let her in, no matter what."

He clapped a fist to his heart. "Yes, Lord Rahl."

"Egan, please roll her up in that carpet and get her out of here. Put her in her room for now. Take up your post in the hall, and when the three Mord-Sith return, send them in."

Without questioning the instructions, Egan bent to the task. With his strength and size, it was only a minor effort.

After he had inspected the broken door bolt, Richard pulled out a chair from the table and turned it around, next to the fireplace, and sat facing the door. He hoped he was wrong. What was he going to do if he wasn't? He sat in the quiet, listening to the fire crackle, and waited for the three women.

"Come," he called out in response to the knock.

Cara entered, followed by Raina, both in their brown leather, with Berdine bringing up the rear. The first two glanced about casually as they crossed the room. Berdine swept the room with a more focused search. The three came to a halt before him.

"Yes, Lord Rahl?" Cara asked without emotion. "You wish something?"

Richard folded his arms. "Show me your breasts. All three of you."

Cara's mouth opened to say something, but she closed it and, setting her jaw, started undoing the buttons running up the side of her ribs. Raina glanced to Cara and saw that she was doing as ordered. Reluctantly at first, she started undoing the buttons, too. Berdine watched the other two. Slowly, she started slipping the buttons at the side of her red leather outfit.

When finished, Cara gripped the top of the leather at the side, but didn't open it. Smoldering resentment settled in her expression. Richard rearranged the unsheathed sword in his lap and crossed his legs.

"I'm waiting," he said.

Cara took a final breath of resignation and pulled the front of her outfit open. In the flickering light coming from the recently stoked fire in the hearth, Richard studied each nipple and the wavering shadow cast by each raised knob in the center. Both had the proper contour of flesh, and not the flat profile of paint put there to mimic.

He shifted his gaze to Raina in silent command. He said nothing as he waited. He could see her fighting to keep silent, and at the same time fighting to decide what to do. She pressed her lips tight in indignation, but finally reached up and yanked the leather aside. Richard gave her breasts the same careful appraisal. Her nipples, too, were both real.

His gaze slid to Berdine. She was the one who had threatened him. She was the one who had lifted her Agiel to him.

It wasn't humiliation, but rage that had her face as red as her outfit. "You said we didn't have to do this! You promised us! You said you would not—"

"Show me."

Cara and Raina shifted their weight uncomfortably, not liking this one bit, as if they expected he was choosing one of them for the night, but at the same time neither was willing to do anything to go against the wishes of the Lord Rahl. Still, Berdine didn't move.

He hardened his glare. "That's an order. You are sworn to obey me. Do as I say."

Tears of anger leaked from her eyes. She reached up and tore the leather aside.

She had only one nipple. Her left breast was smooth and unbroken. Her chest heaved with ire.

The other two stared at her smooth left breast in open astonishment. By the looks on their faces, Richard knew they had seen her breasts before. When their Agiel suddenly spun into their fists, he knew that this wasn't what they had expected to see this time.

Richard came to his feet, addressing Cara and Raina. "Forgive me for doing that to you." He gestured for all of them to cover themselves. Berdine stood shaking in rage, not moving, as the other two began to button their leather up the side.

"What's going on?" Cara asked him, her dangerous eyes on Berdine the whole time she worked at the tight buttons.

"I'll tell you later. You two may leave."

"We're not going anywhere," Raina said in a grave tone as her eyes, too, stayed on Berdine.

"Yes you are." Richard pointed toward the door. He lifted a finger to Berdine. "You stay right there."

Cara stepped protectively closer to him. "We're not—"

"Don't argue with me, I'm not in the mood! Out!"

Cara and Raina flinched back in surprise. With a final furious sigh, Cara motioned to Raina and left the room, closing the door behind them.

Berdine's Agiel spun up into her fist. "What did you do with her?"

"Who did this to you, Berdine?" he said in a gentle voice.

She stepped closer. "What did you do with her!"

Richard, his mind now clear, could feel the spell around her as she put herself close to him. He could feel the distinctive tingle of magic, its uncomfortable, prickling sensation in his gut. This was not benevolent magic.

In her eyes, he could see more than magic; he could see the fury of a Mord-Sith unleashed.

"She died trying to kill me."

"I knew I should have done it myself." She shook her head in disgust. "Kneel," she commanded through gritted teeth.

"Berdine, I'm not—"

She lashed out with her Agiel, striking him across the shoulder, knocking him back. "Don't you dare address me by my name!"

She had been faster than he had expected. He gasped with the pain as he clutched his shoulder. Every memory of an Agiel being used against him came stunningly fresh to his mind.

He was abruptly flushed with doubt. He didn't know if he could do this. But his only alternative was to kill her, and he had sworn he wouldn't do that. The bone-burning torture searing through his shoulder made his resolve falter.

Berdine stalked closer. "Pick up your sword."

He stiffened his will as he regained his feet. Berdine laid the Agiel on his shoulder, forcing him to his knees. He struggled to maintain his focus. Denna had taught him to endure this. He must now. He picked up the sword and staggered to his feet again.

"Try to use it on me," she commanded.

Richard looked to her cold blue eyes, fighting the tug of panic within his soul. "No." He tossed the sword on the bed. "I am the Lord Rahl. You are bonded to me."

She screamed in fury as she drove the Agiel into his gut. The room spun as he realized he was on his back. Breathless, he again struggled to his feet when she commanded it.

"Use your knife! Fight me!"

With shaking fingers, Richard pulled his knife from the sheath at his belt and held it hilt first to her. "No. Kill me, if that's what you really want."

She snatched the knife from his hand. "You make this easy for me. I intended to make you suffer, but your death is all that is required."

Richard, his insides in an agony of lingering, burning pain, used all his strength to puff his chest out. He pointed. "Here is my heart, Berdine. The Lord Rahl's heart. The Lord Rahl you are bonded to." He tapped his chest again. "Stab me here, if you wish to kill me."

She gave him a gruesome smile. "Fine. You shall have your wish."

"No, not my wish—yours. I don't want you to kill me."

She faltered. Her brow twitched. "Protect yourself."

"No, Berdine. If this is what you wish, then you must choose it for yourself."

"Fight me!" She struck him across the face with the Agiel.

It felt like his jaw shattered and all his teeth were knocked out. The pain stabbed into his ear, nearly blinding him with hurt. Panting, in a cold sweat, he straightened.

"Berdine, you have two magics in you. One is your bond to me, the other is what was put there when they took your nipple. You cannot continue to carry both. One has to be broken. I'm your Lord Rahl. You are bonded to me. The only way you can kill me is to break that bond. My life is in your hands."

She lunged at him. He felt the back of his head smack against the floor. Berdine was atop him, screaming in fury.

"Fight me, you bastard!" She pounded his chest with one fist as she held the knife up in the other. Tears streamed from her eyes. "Fight me! Fight me! Fight me!"

"No. If you want to kill me, then you have to do it on your own."

"Fight me!" She struck his face. "I can't kill you if you don't fight me! Defend yourself!"

Richard enfolded her in his arms and pulled her to his chest. He pushed his heels against the carpet and slid himself back, taking her with him as he sat up against the bed.

"Berdine, just as you are bonded to me, I protect you. I won't let you die like this. I want you alive. I want you as my protector."

"No!" she screamed. "I must kill you! You must fight me so I can! I can't do it unless you try to kill me! You must!"

Weeping in angry exasperation, she pressed the knife against his throat. Richard did nothing to stop her.

He drew his hand down her wavy brown hair. "Berdine, I've sworn to fight to protect those who want to live free. That's my bond to you. I won't do anything to harm you. I know you don't want to kill me; you've sworn on your life to protect me."

"I'll kill you! I will! I'll kill you!"

"I believe in you, Berdine, in your oath to me. I put my life in your word and your bond."

She gasped in racking sobs as she looked into his eyes. She shook as she wept uncontrollably. Richard didn't move against the sharp blade at his throat.

"Then you must kill me," she cried. "Please . . . I can stand it no longer. Please . . . kill me."

"I will never do anything to harm you, Berdine. I've given you your freedom. You are answerable to yourself."

Berdine let out a long wail of misery and then threw the knife across the floor. She collapsed against him, throwing her arms around his neck.

"Oh, Lord Rahl," she sobbed, "forgive me. Forgive me. Oh, dear spirits, what have I done."

"You have proven your bond," he whispered as he held her.

"They hurt me," she wept, "they hurt me so much. Nothing ever hurt like that before. It hurts so to fight it now."

He held her tight. "I know, but you must fight it."

She put a hand to his chest and pushed back. "I can't." Richard didn't think he had ever seen anyone in such misery. "Please, Lord Rahl—kill me. I can't stand the pain. I beg you, please, kill me."

Richard, in an agony of empathy for her suffering, drew her back to his chest and hugged her, stroking her head, trying to comfort her. It did no good; she only cried harder.

He set her back against the bed as she shook and wept. Without thinking about what he was doing, or even understanding the reason, he cupped his hand over her left breast.

Richard sought the calm center, the place without thought, the fount of peace within, and cloaked himself in instinct. He felt the searing pain seep through him. Her pain. He felt what had been done to her, and what the lingering magic was doing to her now. As he had done with the pain of the Agiel, he endured it.

In his empathy, he felt the torment of her life, the torture of what it meant to become a Mord-Sith, and the anguish of her former self lost. His eyes closed, he took it unto himself. Though he didn't see the events involved, he understood the trail of scars they left through her soul. He hardened his will in order to endure the suffering of it. He stood, a rock, in a torrent of hurt rushing into his own soul.

He was that rock for her. He let his loving regard for this innocent, this fellow victim of suffering, flow into her. Without fully understanding the feelings he was having, he let his instinct guide him. He felt himself soaking up her suffering so that she wouldn't have to endure it, so he could help her, and at the same time he felt an inner warmth flowing outward through his hand on her flesh.

Through that hand it seemed he was connected to her spark of life, to her soul.

Berdine's crying slowed, her breathing evened out, and her muscles went slack as she sank back against the bed.

Richard felt the pain that had come into him from her begin to dissipate. Only then did he realize he was holding his breath with the agony of it, and let the breath go.

The warmth flowing from within him began to fade, too, and at last was gone. Richard removed his hand, and brushed her wavy hair back from her face. Her eyes came open, her dazed, blue-eyed gaze meeting his.

They both looked down. She was whole again.

"I'm myself again," she whispered. "I feel as if I have just awakened from a nightmare."

Richard pulled the red leather up across her breasts, covering her. "Me too."

"There has never been a Lord Rahl such as you before," she said in wonder. "The spirits be praised, there never has."

"Greater truth has never been spoken," a voice behind said.

Richard turned to see the tearstained faces of the other two women kneeling behind him.

"Are you all right, Berdine?" Cara asked.

Berdine, still looking a bit stunned, nodded. "I am myself again."

None of them was as stunned as Richard.

"You could have killed her," Cara said. "If you had tried to use your sword, she would have had your magic, but you could have used your knife. For you, it would have been easy. You didn't have to suffer her Agiel. You could have just killed her."

Richard nodded. "I know. But that pain would have been worse."

Berdine tossed her Agiel to the floor before him. "I give this over to you, Lord Rahl."

The other two pulled the gold chains down over their hands and dropped their Agiel to the floor along with Berdine's.

"I, too, give mine over to you, Lord Rahl," Cara said.

"And I, Lord Rahl."

Richard stared at the red rods on the floor before him. He thought about his sword, and how much he hated the things he did with it, how he hated the killing he had done with it, and the killing he knew he would do again. But he could not yet give up the sword.

"This means more to me than you can know," he said, unable to meet their eyes. "That you would do this is what matters. It proves your hearts and your bond. Forgive me, all of you, but I must ask you to keep them for now." He handed back their Agiel. "When this is over, when we are free of the threat, then we can all give up the phantoms that haunt us, but for now we must fight for those who count on us. Our weapons, terrible as they are, allow us to continue the struggle."

Cara laid a gentle hand to his shoulder. "We understand, Lord Rahl. It shall be as you say. When this is over, we can be free of not only those enemies from without, but within, too."

Richard nodded. "Until then, we must be strong. We must be the wind of death."

In the silence, Richard wondered what mriswith were doing in Aydindril. He thought about the one that had killed Cathryn. It was protecting him, it had said. Protecting him? Impossible.

As he thought about it, though, he couldn't recall a mriswith actually attacking him, personally. He remembered the first attack, outside the Confessors' Palace, with Gratch. Gratch had attacked them, and Richard had come to the aid of his friend. They had been intent on killing "green eyes," as they had call the gar, but they never specifically attacked him.

The one tonight had had the best chance of all—Richard had been without his sword—yet it didn't attack him, and instead escaped without a fight. It had addressed him as "skin brother." Just to wonder what that could mean gave him goose bumps.

Richard idly scratched his neck.

Cara rubbed a finger on the back side of his neck where he had just scratched. "What's this?"

"I don't know. Just a spot that's always itching."

CHAPTER 30

VERNA PACED INDIGNANTLY BACK and forth in the little sanctuary. How dare Prelate Annalina do this? Verna had told her that she had to tell her the words so as to prove it was really her, to say once again that she regarded Verna as an unremarkable Sister of little note. Verna wanted the Prelate to say those cruel words again so she would know that Verna knew she was being used, and of little value to the palace, in the Prelate's eyes.

If she was going to be used, and follow the Prelate's orders like an earnest Sister was duty bound to do, it would be knowingly, this time.

Verna was done weeping. She was not going to jump whenever that woman cavalierly crooked a finger. Verna had not devoted her entire life to being a Sister of the Light, worked so hard, for so many years, to be treated with such disrespect.

The thing that made her the most angry was that she had done it again. Verna had told the Prelate that she first had to say the words to prove it was really her, or Verna would feed the journey book to the fire. Verna had set the rules: prove yourself first. Instead, the Prelate had crooked her finger, and Verna had jumped.

She should just throw the journey book in a fire—destroy it. Let the Prelate try to use her then. Let her see that Verna was finished with being played for a fool. See how she liked having her wishes disregarded. It would serve her right.

That was what she should have done, but she hadn't. She still had the book tucked in her belt. Despite her hurt, she was still a Sister. She had to be sure. The Prelate still hadn't proved to her that she was really alive, and had the other book. When she was sure, then Verna would throw the book in the fire.

Verna stopped pacing and looked out through one of the windows in the gable ends. The moon was up. This time, there would be no grace if her instructions weren't followed. She vowed that either the Prelate did as requested, and prove her identity, or Verna was going to burn the book. This was the Prelate's last chance.

Verna pulled the branched candlestick away from the small altar draped with a white cloth trimmed in gold thread and set it beside the little table. The perforated bowl, in which Verna had found the journey book in the first place, set atop the white cloth on the altar. Instead of the journey book, it now held a small flame. If the Prelate failed again to do as instructed, the journey book was going back into that bowl, into the flames.

She pulled the small black book from its pouch in her belt and set it on the little table as she pulled the three-legged stool close. Verna kissed the Prelate's ring on her ring finger, took a deep breath, said a prayer beseeching the Creator's guidance, and opened the book.

There was a message. Pages of it, in fact.

My dearest Verna, it began. Verna pursed her lips. Dearest Verna indeed.

My dearest Verna, First, the easy part. I asked you to go to the sanctuary because of the danger involved. We cannot take any chance that others will read my messages, much less discover that Nathan and I are alive. The sanctuary is the only place I could be sure no one else would read this, and that is the only reason I failed to follow your reasonable precaution before now. You, of course, should expect me to prove myself, and now that I can be sure that you are alone and safe from discovery, I will provide the proof.

In accordance with this caution of only using the sanctuary to communicate, you must be sure to erase all messages before you leave the protection of the sanctuary.

Before I go on—the proof. As you requested, this is what I told you in my office the first time I saw you after you returned from your journey to recover Richard:

"I chose you, Verna, because you were far down on the list, and because, all in all, you are quite unremarkable. I doubted you were one of them. You are a person of little note. I'm sure Grace and Elizabeth made their way to the top of the list because whoever directs the Sisters of the Dark considered them expendable. I direct the Sisters of the Light. I chose you for the same reason.

"There are Sisters who are valuable to our cause; I could not risk one of them on such a task. The boy may prove a value to us, but he is not as important as other matters at the palace. It was simply an opportunity I thought to take.

"If there had been trouble, and none of you made it back, well, I'm sure you can understand that a general would not want to lose his best troops on a low-priority mission."

Verna turned the book over on the table and put her face in her hands. There was no doubt—it was Prelate Annalina who had the other journey book. She was alive, as probably was Nathan.

She glanced to the little fire burning in the bowl. The hurt of those words burned in her chest. Reluctantly, with trembling fingers, she turned the book back over, and read on.

Verna, I know that those words must have broken your heart to hear. I do know that it broke my heart to say them, because they were not true. It must seem to you that you are being used in a nefarious way. It is wrong to lie, but it is worse to let the wicked triumph because you adhere to the truth at the expense of good sense. If the Sisters of the Dark were to ask me what my plans were, I would lie. To do otherwise is to allow wickedness to triumph.

I will now tell you the truth, realizing that you have no reason to believe that this time, my words are true, but I believe in your intelligence and know that if you weigh my words, you will be able to see the truth in them.

The true reason I chose you to go after Richard is because of all the Sisters, you were the one I trusted with the fate of the world. You know, now, the battle Richard won against the Keeper. Without him, we would have all been lost to the world of the dead. A low-priority mission it was not. It was the most important journey any Sister had ever been sent on. I trusted only you.

Over three hundred years before you were born, Nathan warned me of the danger to the world of life. Five hundred years before Richard was born, Nathan and I knew that a war wizard would come into this world. The prophecies told us some of what must be accomplished. The challenge was unlike any we have faced before.

When Richard was born, Nathan and I traveled by ship, around the great barrier, to the New World. We recovered a book of magic from the Wizard's Keep in Aydindril to keep it out of Darken Rahl's hands and gave the book to Richard's stepfather, securing his promise that he would make Richard learn it. Only through such trials, and events in his life at his home, could this young man be forged into the kind of person with the wits to stop the first threat, Darken Rahl, his real father, and later restore the balance to the world of life. He is perhaps the most important person born in the last three thousand years.

Richard is the war wizard who will lead us in the final battle. The prophecies tell us this, but not whether we will prevail. This is now a battle for mankind. Our only chance was to make sure, above all else, that he was not tainted in his training as a man. In this battle, magic is needed, but heart must rule it.

I sent you to bring him to the palace because you were the only one I could trust to accomplish the task. I knew your heart and soul, and I knew you were no Sister of the Dark.

I'm sure you are now wondering how I could let you search for him for more than twenty years when I knew where he was all the time. I also could have waited, and sent you after him when he was grown, and at last revealed his whereabouts when he triggered his gift. I am shamed to admit that I was using you, too, much as I used Richard.

For the challenges that lie ahead, I needed to teach you things you could not learn at the Palace of the Prophets, while Richard grew and learned some of the essential things he required. I needed you to be able to use your wits, and not the reams of rules that the Sisters at the palace thrive on. I had to let you develop your innate skills in the real world. The battle ahead lies in the real world; the cloistered world of the palace is no place to learn about life.

I don't expect you to ever forgive me. That, too, is one of the burdens a Prelate must bear: the hatred of one she loves like her own daughter.

When I told you those awful words, that, too, was to a purpose. I had to finally break you of the palace's teaching that you must always do as you were trained, and blindly follow orders. I had to make you angry enough to do what you judged was right. Since you were little, I could always count on your temper.

I couldn't trust that if I told you the reasons, you would understand, or do as was necessary. Sometimes, a person can only properly affect events by using their own moral propriety, and not by carrying out orders. It is so stated in prophecy. I trusted that you would choose right over training, if you came to the conclusion yourself.

The other reason I told you those things in my office was because I suspected that one of my administrators was a Sister of the Dark. I knew my shield would not keep my words from her ears. I let my words betray me so she would attack me, and force their hand. I knew I could very possibly be killed, but I chose that fate over the possibility of the world being plunged into the grip of the Keeper. Sometimes, a Prelate must even use herself.

So far, Verna, you have lived up to my every expectation of you. You have played a vital role in saving the world from the Keeper. With your help, we have thus far succeeded.

The very first time I laid eyes on you, I smiled, because you had an angry scowl on your face. Do you remember why? I will tell you, if you don't. Every novice brought to the palace was given a test. Sooner or later, we wrongly blamed her for a small offense of which she was innocent. Most cried. Some pouted. Some bore the shame of guilt with stoic resignation. Only you became angry at the injustice. In that, you proved yourself.

Nathan had found a prophecy that said the one we needed would be delivered to us not with a smile, or a pout, or a brave face, but with an angry scowl. When I saw that look on your face, and your little arms folded in a fit, I nearly laughed aloud. At last, you had been delivered into our hands. From that day I have been using you in the Creator's most important work.

I chose you to be the Prelate in the illusion of my death because you are still the one Sister I trust above all others. There is more than a good chance that I will be killed on my present journey with

Nathan, and if I do die, you will be the Prelate for real. That is the way I wish it.

Your justifiable hatred weighs on my heart, but it is the Creator's forgiveness that is important, and I know I will have that much, at least. I will suffer your scorn as my burden in this life, as I suffer other burdens for which there is no relief. It is the price of being Prelate of the Palace of the Prophets.

Verna pushed the book away, unable to read more of the words. Her head fell to her folded arms as she sobbed. Though she didn't recall the nature of the injustice of which the Prelate spoke, she remembered the sting of it, and her anger. Mostly, she remembered the Prelate's smile, and how it made the world right again.

"Oh, dear Creator," Verna wept aloud, "you truly have a fool for a servant."

If she had felt heartache before, for thinking the Prelate had used her, she now felt agony over the anguish the Prelate had had to endure. When she was finally able to bring her tears to a halt, she pulled the little book back before her and read on.

But the past is past, and we must now go on with what must be done. The prophecies say that the greatest danger now lies before us. The tests that have come before would have ended the world of life in a final, terrible flash. In an instant, all would be irrecoverably lost. Richard passed those tests, and kept us from that fate.

Now a greater trial is upon us. It is not from other worlds, but from our own. This is a battle for the future of our world, the future of mankind, and the future of magic. In this, in the struggle for the minds and hearts of men, there is no final flash, no instant end, but the inexorable, grinding struggle of war, as the shadow of enslavement slowly creeps across the world, and darkens the spark of magic, through which comes the Creator's light.

The ancient war, started thousands of years ago, is again aflame. We, in protecting this world from others, have unavoidably brought it to pass. This time, there will be no cessation of war because of the efforts of hundreds of wizards. This time, we have only one war wizard to lead us. Richard.

I cannot tell you all of it now. Some, I simply do not know, and as much as it pains me to have to leave you in the dark about some things I do know, understand that because of forks in prophecies that must be correctly taken, it is necessary that some of the people involved act instinctively, and not by instruction. To do otherwise would make the correct forks impassable. Part of our job is to hope to teach people to act in the right way, so that when the test comes, they will do what must be done. Forgive me, Verna, but I must once again trust some things to the fates.

I hope that you are learning, as Prelate, that you cannot always explain everything to others, but that you must sometimes simply give them a task, and expect them to do it.

Verna sighed. She knew the truth of that. She, herself, had given up on trying to explain everything all the time, and had started to simply ask that instructions be carried out as spoken.

Some things, though, I can and must tell you so you can help us. Nathan and I have gone on a mission of vital importance. For now, only he and I can know its nature.

Should I live, I intend to return to the palace. Before then, you must find out who are loyal Sisters of the Light, novices, and young men. You must also identify all who have given their souls to the Keeper.

"What!" Verna heard herself say aloud. "How can I do that!"

I leave it up to you to find a way. You don't have a lot of time. This is important, Verna; it must be before Emperor Jagang arrives.

Nathan and I believe Jagang is what was called in the ancient war a "dream walker."

Verna felt the sweat between her shoulder blades trickle down her spine. She recalled her talk with Sister Simona, and how the woman had screamed uncontrollably at the mere mention of Jagang's name. Sister Simona said that Jagang came to her in her dreams. Everyone thought Sister Simona was crazy.

Warren, too, had spoken of the dream walker, and that in the old war they were a form of weapon. Their visit to Sister Simona had confirmed what he believed.

Above all else, remember this: No matter what happens, your only salvation is to remain loyal to Richard. A dream walker can take just about anyone's mind and enslave them to his will—those with the gift more so than others. There is only one protection—Richard. An ancestor of his created a magic that protects them and any loyal to them, bonded in cause to them, from the power of the dream walkers. This magic is passed down to any Rahl born with the gift. Nathan, of course, has this same protective element to his gift, but he is not the one who can lead us. He is a prophet, and not a war wizard.

Verna could read between the lines that being a loyal follower of Nathan would be madness. The man was lightning itself in a collar.

By going against palace law of your own free will and helping Richard escape, you became bonded to him. This bond protects you from the power of the dream walker, but not from his waking force of arms and minions. This is part of the reason I had to deceive you that day in my office. It made you, of your own free will, choose to help Richard over your training and orders.

Goose bumps ran up Verna's arms. Had she convinced the Prelate to reveal her plans, telling Verna to help Richard escape, then she would have been as vulnerable as Sister Simona to the dream walker.

Nathan is protected, of course, and I have been bonded to Richard for a good long time. I pledged myself to him when I first saw him. In my own way, I have been letting him set his own rules as to how he fights for our side. At times, I must tell you, it is difficult. Though he does as is needed to protect the innocent, free people who need his help, he has a mind of his own, and does things that, if I had my way, he would not do. At times, he can be as much of a trial as Nathan. Such is life.

I am finished telling you what I had to reveal. I am sitting here in a room in a cozy inn, waiting for you to read this. When you have read this message over as many times as you wish, I'll be waiting here should you wish to ask me anything. You must understand that I have had hundreds of years working at events and prophecies, and there is no way I can impart all that knowledge to you in one night, much less in a journey book, but I will tell you what I can of what you wish to know.

Also, you must understand that there are certain things I cannot tell you for fear of tainting prophecy and events. Every word I tell you carries a danger of that, though some more than others, but it is necessary that you know some of it.

With these things in mind, I await your questions. Ask.

Verna sat up straight at the end of the writing. Ask? It would take a hundred years to ask all she wanted to know. Where was she to start? Dear Creator, what were the important questions?

She read the entire message again, to be sure she hadn't missed anything, and then sat, staring at the blank page beyond. Finally, she picked up the stylus.

My dearest Mother, I beg you forgive me the things I thought of you. I am humbled by your strength, and shamed by my foolish pride. Please don't get yourself killed. I am not worthy to be Prelate. I am an ox that you are asking to soar like a bird.

Verna sat, watching the book for the return message to appear if the Prelate really was waiting.

Thank you, child. You have lightened my heart. Ask what you need to know, and if I can, I will answer your questions. I will sit here all night, if I can help you with your burden.

Verna smiled for the first time in days. This time, the tears were sweet, and not bitter.

Prelate, are you truly safe? Is everything well with you and Nathan?

Verna, perhaps you enjoy having your friends calling you Prelate, but I do not. Please call me by my name, as all my true friends do.

Verna laughed out loud. She, too, was frustrated that people insisted on calling her "Prelate." Words continued to appear as Ann's message went on.

And yes, I am fine, as is Nathan, who is presently occupied. Today he bought himself a sword, and is now having a sword fight with invisible enemies in our room. He thinks a sword will make him look "dashing." He is a thousand-year-old child, and, at this moment, is grinning like a child as he lops the heads off his invisible foes.

Verna read the message again, just to be sure she was reading it right. Nathan with a sword? The man was even more deranged than she had thought. The Prelate must have her hands full.

Ann, you said I must find out who is sworn to the Keeper. I have no idea how to do this. Can you help?

If I knew how to do it, Verna, I would tell you. A few made me suspect them, but most did not. I was never able to find a way to divine who were the Keeper's. I have other matters I must deal with, so I must leave this one to you to solve. Keep in mind that they can be as clever as the Keeper himself. Some, who I was certain were against us, because of their disagreeable nature, were loyal to us. Some who revealed themselves and escaped on the ship, I would have trusted with my life. I would be dead now, had I.

Ann, I don't know how to do this! What if I fail?

You must not fail.

Verna wiped her sweaty palms on her dress.

But even if I can find a way to identify them, then what am I to do with this information? I cannot fight Sisters with the power they have.

Once you accomplish the first part, Verna, I will tell you. Know that the prophecies are vulnerable to tampering, and in danger. Just as Nathan and I use them to help us influence events so as to take the proper fork, so, too, can our enemies use them.

Verna sighed in frustration.

How can I work to identify our enemies, when there is so much work to do as Prelate? All I do is read reports, and yet I fall farther and farther behind. Everyone is depending on me, and waiting on me. How did you find the time to accomplish anything, with all the reports?

You read the reports? My goodness, Verna, but you are ambitious. You certainly are more conscientious as Prelate than I.

Verna's mouth dropped open.

You mean that I don't have to read the reports?

Well, Verna, look at the value in reading them. Because you read the reports, you discovered that the horses were missing from the stables. We could have easily bought horses after we left the palace, but took those instead so as to leave a sign. We could have paid for the bodies instead of going through the complicated arrangements we did, but then you wouldn't have been able to talk to the gravedigger. We took care to leave signs you could follow so as to discover the truth. Some of the signs we left were quite troublesome, such as the one with the discovery of our "bodies," but were necessary, and you did a good job in figuring it out.

Verna felt her face flush. She had never thought to look into the matter of the bodies being discovered already prepared and in winding sheets. She had completely missed that clue.

But I must confess, Ann went on, *that I hardly ever bothered to read reports. That is what assistants are for. I simply told them that they were to use their judgment and wisdom and, in keeping with the best interest of the palace, handle the matters involved in the reports. Then, every once in a while, I would stop before them and pull out some reports that they had dealt with and read their disposition. It always kept them diligent in their task, for fear I would read their instructions given in my name, and find them unsatisfactory.*

Verna was astonished. *You mean to say that I can simply tell my assistants, or advisors, how I wish matters managed, and then have them handle the reports? I don't have to read them all? I don't have to initial them all?*

Verna, you are Prelate. You can do as you wish. You run the palace, it does not run you.

But, Sisters Leoma and Philippa, my advisors, and Dulcinia, one of my administrators, all told me how it must be done. They are so much more experienced than I. They made it seem I would be failing the palace were I not to handle the reports myself.

Did they now, Ann wrote almost instantly. *My, my. I think that if I were you, Verna, I would do a bit less listening, and a little more talking. You have a fine scowl. Use it.*

Verna grinned at that. Already she was picturing the scene. There were going to be some changes in the Prelate's office come morning.

Ann, what is your mission? What are you trying to accomplish?

I have a small task in Aydindril, and then I hope to return.

It was plain that Ann wasn't going to tell her, so Verna thought about what else she wanted to know, and what she needed to tell the Prelate. One thing of importance came to mind.

Warren gave a prophecy. His first, he said.

There was a long pause. Verna waited. When the message finally came, its hand was a bit more carefully drawn.

Do you remember it, word for word?

Verna could not forget a word of that prophecy. *Yes.*

Before Verna could begin to write the prophecy, a message suddenly began to splash across the page. The scrawl was huge and angry, the letters drawn in big blocks.

Get that boy out of the palace! Get him out!

A line snaked across the page. Verna sat up straighter. It was obvious that Nathan had taken the stylus away from Ann and had written the message, and Ann was in the process of getting it back. There was another long pause, and at last Ann's handwriting appeared again.

Sorry. Verna, if you are certain that you remember the prophecy, word for word, then write it down so we may see it. If you are unsure of any of it, tell me. This is important.

I remember it word for word, as it pertains to me, Verna wrote. *It says:*

"When the Prelate and the Prophet are given to the Light in the sacred rite, the flames will bring to boil a cauldron of guile and give ascension to a false Prelate, who will reign over the death of the Palace of the Prophets. To the north, the one bonded to the blade will abandon it for the silver sliph, for he will breathe her back to life, and she will deliver him into the arms of the wicked."

There was another pause. *Hold, please, while Nathan and I study this.*

Verna sat and waited. The bugs outside chirped, and the frogs peeped. Verna stood, keeping an eye to the book, and stretched her back as she yawned. Still, there was no message. She sat and rested her chin in her fist, and her eyes drooped as she waited.

At last, a message began to appear.

Nathan and I have been going over this, and Nathan says that it is an immature prophecy, and because of that, he cannot fully decipher it.

Ann, I am the false Prelate. It troubles me greatly that this prophecy says I will reign over the death of the palace.

An immediate message came back. *You are not the false Prelate in this prophecy.*

Then what does it mean?

There was a shorter pause this time. *We do not know its full meaning, but we do know that you are not the false Prelate named in it.*

Verna, listen carefully. Warren must leave the palace. It is too dangerous for him to remain any longer. He must go into hiding. He could be seen leaving in the night. Tomorrow morning, have him go into the city on the pretense of an errand. In the confusion of people it will be hard for anyone to follow him. Have him get away through that confusion. Give him gold so he will not have any trouble doing what he needs.

Verna put a hand to her heart as she gulped a breath. She bent back over the book. *But Prelate, Warren is the only one I can trust. I need him. I don't know the prophecies like he does, and will be lost without him.* She left unsaid that he was her only friend, the only friend she could trust.

Verna, the prophecies are in danger. If they get their hands on a prophet The hastily scribbled message halted abruptly. After a moment it resumed, more carefully written. *He must get away. Do you understand?*

Yes, Prelate. I will see to it first thing in the morning. Warren will do as I ask. I will trust in your instructions, that it is more important for him to leave than to aid me.

Thank you, Verna.

Ann, what is the danger to the prophecies?

She waited a moment in the quiet of the sanctuary, until the writing began again. *Just as we try to help our effort by knowing the danger down various forks in prophecy, so, too, can those who wish to rule mankind use this information to guide events down forks they want to come to pass. Used in this fashion, the prophecies can defeat us. If they have a prophet, they can have a better understanding of the prophecies, and how to direct events to their advantage.*

Tampering with forks can invoke chaos that even they don't expect and can't control. This is dangerous in the extreme. They could inadvertently walk us all off a cliff.

Ann, are you saying that Jagang is going to try to take the Palace of the Prophets, and the prophecies in the vaults?

Pause. *Yes.*

Verna paused herself. The realization of the nature of the struggle ahead came over her in icy goose bumps.

How can we stop him?

The Palace of the Prophets cannot fall so easily as Jagang thinks. Though he is a dream walker, we have control of our Han. That power is also a weapon. Though we have always used our gift to preserve life and help bring the Creator's light to the world, a time may come when we have to use our gift to fight. For this, we must know who is loyal to us. You must find out who is untainted.

Verna thought carefully before she began to write. *Ann, do you intend to call upon us to become warriors, to use our gift to strike down the Creator's children?*

I am telling you, Verna, that you will have to use what you know to help prevent the world from being taken forever into the darkness of tyranny. Though we struggle to help the Creator's children, we also carry a dacra, don't we? We can't help people if we are dead.

Verna rubbed her thighs when she realized they were trembling. She had killed people, and the Prelate knew it. She had killed Jedidiah. She wished she had brought something to drink; her throat felt as if it were turning dry as dust.

I understand, she wrote at last. *I will do what I must.*

I wish I could give you better guidance, Verna, but right now I don't know enough. Events are already rushing ahead in a torrent. Without direction, and probably on sheer instinct, Richard has already taken precipitous action. We are not sure what he is up to, but from what I gather he already has the Midlands in an uproar. The boy doesn't rest for a minute. He seems to make up his own rules as he goes.

What has he done? Verna asked, fearing the answer.

He has somehow taken command of D'Hara, and has captured Aydindril. He has declared the Midlands alliance dissolved, and demanded the surrender of all lands.

Verna gasped. *It is the Midlands that must fight the Imperial Order! Has he lost his mind? We can't afford to have him bring D'Hara and the Midlands to war!*

He has already done it.

The Midlands isn't going to surrender to him.

From what I gather, Galea and Kelton are already in his fist.

He must be stopped! The Imperial Order is the threat. It is they who must be fought. We can't allow him to start a war in the New World—the diversion could be fatal.

Verna, magic is marbled through the Midlands like a juicy roast. The Imperial Order will steal that roast one slice at a time, as they did the Old World. Timid alliances will balk at starting a conflagration over one slice, and let it go instead, then the next slice will be taken in the name of appeasement and peace, and then the next, all the while weakening the Midlands and strengthening the Order. While you were gone on your journey, they took all of the Old World, in less than twenty years.

Richard is a war wizard. It is his instincts that guide him, and everything he has learned and holds dear forge his actions. We have no choice but to trust in him.

In the past, the threat was a single individual, like Darken Rahl. In this, it is a monolithic threat. Even if we could somehow eliminate Jagang, another would take his place. This is a battle of beliefs, fears, and ambitions of all people, not a single leader.

It is much the same as the way people fear the palace. If a leader came to the fore, we could not eliminate the threat by eliminating the leader; the fear would still be in people's heads, and taking their leader would only intensify their belief that they are justified in their fear.

Dear Creator, Verna wrote back, *then what are we to do?*

There was a pause for a time. *As I said, child, I don't have all the answers. But I can tell you this: In this, the final trial, we all play a part, but it is Richard who is the key. Richard is our leader. I don't agree with all the things he does, but he is the only one who can lead us to victory. If we are to prevail, we must follow him. I am not saying we cannot try to advise and guide him in what we know, but he is a war wizard, and this is the war he was born to fight.*

Nathan has warned that there is a place in the prophecies called the Great Void. If we end on this fork, he believes that there is nothing beyond for magic, and thus no prophecy illuminating it. Mankind will go off forever into that unknown without magic. Jagang wishes to take the world into that void.

Remember this above all else: No matter what, you must remain loyal to Richard. You can talk to him, advise him, reason with him, but you must not fight him. Loyalty to Richard is the only thing keeping Jagang from your mind. Once a dream walker has your mind, you are lost to our side.

Verna swallowed. The stylus shook in her hand. *I understand. Is there anything I can do to help?*

For now, the things I have already told you. You must act quickly. The war has already charged ahead of us. I hear there are mriswith in Aydindril."

Verna's eyes opened wide at the last of the message. "Dear Creator," she said aloud, "give Richard strength."

CHAPTER 31

VERNA SQUINTED IN THE light. The sun was just up. She groaned as she rose from the overstuffed chair and stretched her cramped muscles. She had corresponded with the Prelate late into the night, and then, too tired to go to her bed, had curled up in the chair and fallen asleep. After Verna had heard about Richard and the mriswith in Aydindril, the two had written back and forth about palace business.

The Prelate answered countless questions Verna asked about the running of the palace, the way things worked, and how to handle her advisors, administrators, and other Sisters. The lessons Ann imparted were eye-opening.

Verna had never realized the extent of palace politics and how nearly every facet of palace life and law revolved around it. A Prelate's power was derived in part from making the correct alliances, and using duties and power carefully assigned to control opposition. Divided into factions, responsible for their own niche and given wide leeway in narrowly defined areas, the more influential Sisters were diverted from joining in opposition to the Prelate. Information was granted or withheld in a carefully controlled process, keeping opposing groups balanced in influence and power. This balance kept the Prelate the pivot point, and in control of palace objectives.

Though the Sisters couldn't remove a Prelate from office, except for treason against the palace and Creator, they could mire the workings of the palace in petty bickering and power struggles. The Prelate had to control that energy and focus it to worthwhile goals.

It seemed that running the palace, doing the Creator's work, was really handling personalities and their attendant feelings and sensibilities, rather than simply assigning tasks that needed to be done. Verna had never viewed the running of the palace in this way. She had always seen them as one happy family, all intent on the Creator's work, running smoothly on direction from the Prelate. That, she had learned, had been because of the deft handling of the Sisters by the Prelate. Because of her, they all worked to a purpose, seeming to Verna to be satisfied with their part in the scheme of things.

After the talk with Annalina, Verna felt even more inadequate at her post, but at the same time more prepared to rise to the task. She had never known the vast extent of the Prelate's knowledge about the most trivial of palace matters. It was no wonder that Prelate Annalina had made the job look so easy; she was a master at it—a juggler who could keep a dozen balls in the air at once while smiling and patting a novice on the head.

Verna rubbed her eyes as she yawned. She had gotten only a few hours' sleep, but she had work to do, and couldn't lie about any longer. She tucked the journey book, all its pages wiped clean, back into her belt and headed back to her office, stopping along the way to splash water from the pond on her face.

A pair of green ducks swam closer, interested in what she was doing mucking about in their world. They circled about a bit before deciding to preen themselves, apparently content that she had no interest other than to share their water. The sky was a glorious pink and violet in the new day, the air clean and fresh. Though deeply worried about what she had learned, she also felt optimistic. Like everything around her in the light of the new day, she felt as if her mind had been enlightened, too.

Verna shook the water from her hands as she fretted about how she was going to discover which Sisters were sworn to the Keeper. Just because the Prelate had faith in her, and had ordered it, that didn't mean she would succeed. She sighed, and then kissed the Prelate's ring, asking the Creator to please help her figure out a way.

Verna couldn't wait to tell Warren about the Prelate, and all the things she had learned in talking with her, but she was heavy-hearted, too, because she was going to have to ask him to go into hiding. She didn't know how she was going to manage without him. Maybe if he was able to find a safe place not too far, she could still visit him occasionally, and not feel so alone.

In her office, Verna smiled when she saw the teetering stacks of waiting reports. She left the doors to the garden open to let in the cool morning air, and let out the stale air of her office. She began straightening the reports, shuffling the papers into order and making the stacks straight, lining them up along the edge. For the first time, she was able to see some of the wood of the tabletop.

Verna looked up when the door opened. Phoebe and Dulcinia, each carrying more reports in the crook of an arm, both started when they saw her.

"Good morning," Verna said in a bright voice.

"Forgive us, Prelate," Dulcinia said. Her penetrating blue eyes caught when she saw the neat stacks of reports. "We didn't realize the Prelate would be at work so early. We didn't mean to interrupt. We can see that you've a lot of work to do. We'll just put these down with the others, if we may."

"Oh yes, please do," Verna said, holding an inviting hand out toward her desk. "Leoma and Philippa will be pleased you brought them to me."

"Prelate?" Phoebe said, her round face set in puzzlement.

"Oh, you know what I mean. My advisors of course like to make sure the palace runs as smooth as a new greased wheel. Leoma and Philippa fret over the task."

"Task?" Dulcinia asked, her frown growing.

"The reports," Verna said, as if it should be obvious. "They wouldn't want ones so new at the job as you two to be undertaking such responsibility. Maybe if you continue to work hard, and prove yourselves, I will someday trust you with them. If they think it wise, of course."

Dulcinia's frown darkened. "What did Philippa say, Prelate? What aspect of my experience does she find inadequate?"

Verna shrugged. "Don't misunderstand me, Sister. My advisors haven't derided you in any way; they are most scrupulous about praising you, in fact. It's just that they've made it clear that the reports are important, and have urged me to see to them myself. I'm sure they will come around, in a few years, and have the confidence to advise me when you are ready."

"Ready for what?" Phoebe asked in bewilderment.

Verna waggled her hand toward the stacks of reports. "Well, it's the duty of the Prelate's administrators to read the reports and dispose of them. The Prelate only needs to occasionally oversee the disposition, to confirm that her administrators are doing a proper job. Since my advisors urged me to handle the reports myself, I assumed it was obvious that they . . . well, I'm sure they meant no offense, seeing as how they always compliment the both of you." Verna clicked her tongue. "Though they do then go on to remind me that I should handle the reports myself, in the best interest of the palace."

Dulcinia stiffened with indignation. "We already read those reports—every one—to make sure they're in order. We know more about them than anyone. The Creator knows I see those reports in my sleep! We know when something is amiss, and note it for you, don't we? We bring tallies to your attention when they don't reconcile, don't we? Those two have no business telling you that you must do it yourself."

Verna strolled to a bookshelf, busying herself with a fictitious search for a particular volume. "I'm sure they only have the best interest of the palace in mind, Sister. You being so new at the post, and all. I think you read too much into their advice."

"I'm as old as Philippa! I have as much experience as she!"

"Sister, she made no accusation," Verna said in her most humble tone as she glanced over her shoulder.

"She advised you to handle the reports, didn't she?"

"Well, yes, but . . ."

"She's wrong. The both of them are wrong."

"They are?" Verna asked, turning away from the bookcase.

"Of course." Dulcinia looked to Phoebe. "We could have those reports, the whole lot of them, worked, ordered, assessed, and ruled on in a matter of a week or two, couldn't we, Sister Phoebe."

Phoebe lifted her nose. "I should think we could have it done in under a week. We know more about how to handle those reports than anyone." Her face flushed as she glanced to Verna. "Except you, of course, Prelate."

"Really? It's a huge responsibility. I wouldn't want to put you in over your heads. You have only been at the jobs a short time. Do you think you are already seasoned enough?"

Dulcinia huffed. "I should say we are." She marched to the desk and scooped up a huge stack. "We'll see about this. You just come and check any we've done, and you'll find you would have handled matters in the exact same manner we do. We know what we're doing. You'll see." She scowled. "And those two will see, too."

"Well, if you really think you can handle it, I'm willing to give you a chance. You are my administrators, after all."

"I should say we are." Dulcinia tilted her head toward the desk. "Phoebe, grab a stack."

Phoebe lifted a large column of reports, staggering back a step to keep them balanced. "I'm sure the Prelate has more important matters to attend to than doing work her administrators can just as easily handle."

Verna folded her hands at her belt. "Well, I did appoint you because I believed in your abilities. I guess it only fair that I allow you to prove them. After all, a Prelate's administrators are of vital importance to the running of the palace."

Dulcinia's lips spread in a cunning smile. "You'll see just how vital we are to helping you, Prelate. And so will your advisors."

Verna lifted her eyebrows. "I'm already impressed, Sisters. Well, I do have some matters to look into. What with being so busy with reports, I've not had a chance to check up on my advisors, and make sure that they're handling their duties properly. I guess it's about time I did that."

"Yes," Dulcinia said as she followed Phoebe out the door, "I think that would be wise."

Verna let out a huge sigh when the door closed. She had thought she would never see the end of those reports. She gave a mental thank-you to Prelate Annalina. She realized she was grinning, and straightened her face.

Warren didn't answer her knock, and when she peeked into his room she saw his bed didn't look slept in. Verna winced when she remembered that she had ordered him to the vaults to link up those prophecies. Poor Warren had probably been sleeping with his books, doing as she had commanded. She recalled with shame how she had spoken to him when she had been so angry after her talk with the gravedigger. Now, she was relieved and overjoyed to know that the Prelate and Nathan were alive, but at the time she had been livid and had taken it out on Warren.

Instead of causing a stir, she descended the stairs and corridors without an escort to empty the vaults for her. She thought it would be safer if she were to simply pay a short visit to the vaults on a minor inspection and tell Warren to come to her at their meeting spot by the river. This information was far too dangerous to convey even in the safety of the empty vaults.

Maybe Warren could come up with an idea of how they could unmask the Sisters of the Dark. Warren's cleverness was surprising at times. She kissed her ring in an attempt to banish the anguish when she remembered her duty to send him away. She had to get him away at once.

With a sad smile, she thought that maybe he could get some wrinkles on his annoyingly smooth face, and catch up with her while she remained under the palace's spell.

Sister Becky, her pregnancy becoming obvious to all, was lecturing a group of older novices on the intricacies of prophecy. She was pointing out the danger of false prophecy because of forks that had been taken in the past. Once an event in a prophecy had taken place, and if it carried an "either/or" fork, then the prophecy had been resolved by events; one branch of the fork had proven true, and the other branch then became a false prophecy.

The difficulty was that yet other prophecies were linked to each branch, but when they were given it wasn't yet decided which fork would come to pass. Once resolved, any prophecy linked to the dead branch became false, too, but because it was often impossible to determine which fork many prophecies were linked to, the vaults were clogged with this dead wood.

Verna moved to the back wall and listened for a time as the novices asked questions. It was frustrating for them to learn the scope of the problems facing one trying to work with prophecy, and how many of the things they asked had no answer. Verna now knew from what Warren had told her that the Sisters had even less understanding of the prophecies than they thought.

Prophecy was really meant to be interpreted by a wizard whose gift possessed that aptitude. In the last thousand years, Nathan was the only wizard they had come across who had the ability to give prophecy. She now knew that he understood them in a way no Sister had ever known, except perhaps Prelate Annalina. She now knew that Warren, too, had that latent talent for prophecy.

As Sister Becky went on with an explanation of linkage through key events and chronology, Verna quietly moved off toward the back rooms where Warren usually worked, but found them all empty, and their books returned to the shelves. Verna puzzled over where to look next. It had never been difficult to find Warren, but that was because he was almost always in the vaults.

Sister Leoma met her as she was returning up the aisles between the long rows of shelves. Her advisor smiled in greeting and bowed her head of long, straight white hair, tied behind with a golden ribbon. Verna detected worry in the creases of her face.

"Good morning, Prelate. The Creator's blessing on this new day."

Verna returned the warm smile. "Thank you, Sister. A fine day it is, too. How are the novices doing?"

Leoma glanced off toward the tables with the young women sitting around it in concentration. "They will make fine Sisters. I've been observing the lessons, and there's not an inattentive one in the lot." Without returning her gaze to Verna, she asked, "Have you come to find Warren?"

Verna twisted the ring on her finger. "Yes. There were a few matters I thought to ask him to check for me. Have you seen him about?"

When Leoma turned back at last, her creases had deepened into true concern. "Verna, I'm afraid Warren is not here."

"I see. Well, do you know where I could find him?"

She let out a deep breath. "What I mean, Verna, is that Warren is gone."

"Gone? What do you mean gone?"

Sister Leoma's gaze drifted away to the shadows among the shelves. "I mean he has left the palace. For good."

Verna's mouth dropped opened. "Are you sure? You must be mistaken. Perhaps you . . ."

Leoma smoothed back a wisp of white hair. "Verna, he came to me, night before last, and told me he was leaving."

Verna wet her lips. "Why didn't he come to me? Why wouldn't he tell the Prelate that he was leaving?"

Leoma drew her shawl tighter. "Verna, I'm sorry to have to be the one to tell you, but he said you and he had words, and he thought that it would be for the best if he were to leave the palace. For now, at least. He made me promise that I wouldn't tell you for a couple of days so he could be away. He didn't want you coming after him."

"Coming after him!" Verna's fists tightened. "What makes him think . . ." Verna's head was spinning, trying to understand, and suddenly trying to call back words that were days ago uttered. "But . . . did he say when he would be back? The palace needs his talent. He knows about the books down here. He can't just up and leave!"

Leoma glanced away again. "I'm sorry, Verna, but he's gone. He said that he didn't know when, or if, he would return. He said that he thought it would be for the best, and that you would come to see that, too."

"Did he say anything else," she whispered hopefully.

She shook her head.

"And you just let him go? Didn't you try to stop him?"

"Verna," Leoma said in a gentle tone, "Warren had his collar off. You yourself released him from his Rada'Han. We can't force a wizard to remain at the palace against his will when you've released him. He is a free man. It is his choice, not ours."

It all came over her in an icy wave of tingling dread. She had released him. How could she expect him to remain to help her when she treated him in such a humiliating fashion? He was her friend, and she had dressed him down as if he were a first-year boy. He was not a boy. He was a man. His own man.

And now he was gone.

Verna forced herself to speak. "Thank you, Leoma, for telling me."

Leoma nodded and after giving Verna's shoulder a squeeze of reassurance, walked back toward the lessons in the distance.

Warren was gone.

Reason told her that the Sisters of the Dark might have taken him, but in her heart she could only blame herself.

Verna's faltering steps bore her to one of the little rooms, and after the stone door had closed, she sank weakly into a chair. Her head fell into her arms, and she began to weep, realizing only now how much Warren had meant to her.

CHAPTER 32

KAHLAN LEAPED OUT OF the wagon bed, rolling through the snow when she landed. She sprang to her feet and scrambled toward the shrieks as rocks still crashed down around her, rebounding into the trees on the low side of the narrow trail, snapping branches and thudding into the huge trunks of the old pines.

She jammed her back against the side of the wagon. "Help me!" she screamed to men already in a dead run toward her.

Arriving only seconds after her, they threw themselves up against the wagon, taking up the weight. The man cried out louder.

"Wait, wait, wait!" It sounded like they were killing him. "Just hold it there. Don't lift anymore."

The half dozen young soldiers strained to hold the wagon where it was. The rock that had piled down on top had added considerably to the burden.

"Orsk!" she called out.

"Yes, Mistress?"

Kahlan started. In the darkness, she hadn't seen the big, one-eyed D'Haran soldier standing right behind her.

"Orsk, help them hold the wagon up. Don't lift it—just hold it still." She turned to the dark trail behind as Orsk muscled his way in beside the others and clamped his massive hands onto the lower edge of the wagon. "Zedd! Somebody get Zedd! Hurry!"

Pushing her long hair back over her wolf-hide mantle, Kahlan knelt beside the young man under the axle hub. It was too dark to see how badly he was injured, but by his panting grunts, she feared it was serious. She couldn't figure out why he cried out louder when they started to lift the weight off him.

Kahlan found his hand and took it in both of hers. "Hold on, Stephens. Help's coming."

She grimaced when he crushed her hand in his grip as he let out a wail. He clutched her hand as if he were hanging from a cliff and her hand was the only thing keeping him from falling into death's dark grasp. She vowed that she would not take her hand back even if he broke it.

"Forgive me . . . my queen . . . for slowing us."

"It was an accident. It wasn't your doing." His legs squirmed in the snow. "Try to stay still." With her free hand, she brushed hair back from his brow. He quieted a bit at her touch, so she held the hand to the side of his icy face. "Please, Stephens, try to be still. I won't let them put the weight down on you. I promise. We'll get you out from under there in a just a moment, and the wizard will set you back to right."

She could feel him nod under her hand. No one near had a torch, and in the feeble moonlight ghosting through the thick branches she couldn't see what the problem was. It seemed that lifting the wagon caused him more pain than he felt when it was on him.

Kahlan heard a horse galloping up and saw a dark figure leap off as the horse skidded to a halt, twisting its head against the pull of the reins. When the man hit the ground, a flame ignited in his upturned sticklike hand, lighting his thin face and mass of wavy white hair sticking out in disarray.

"Zedd! Hurry!"

When Kahlan looked down in the sudden, harsh illumination,

she saw the extent of the problem, and felt a wave of nausea surge up like a hot hammer.

Zedd's calm, hazel eyes glided over the scene in quick appraisal as he knelt on the other side of Stephens.

"The wagon grazed a piling timber holding back the scree," she explained.

The trail was narrow and treacherous, and in the darkness, on the curve, they hadn't seen the piling in the snow. The timber must have been old and rotted. When the hub bumped it, the timber snapped, and the beam it had supported tumbled down, allowing a sluice of rock to come down on them.

As the rock drove the back of the wagon sideways, the iron rim of the rear wheel caught in a frozen rut beneath the snow and the spokes of the rear wheel snapped. The hub knocked Stephens from his feet and came down atop him.

Kahlan could now see in the light that one of the splintered spokes jutting from the hub canted at the end of the broken axle had impaled the young man. When they tried to hoist the wagon, it lifted him by that spoke driven at an angle up under his ribs.

"I'm sorry, Kahlan," Zedd said.

"What do you mean you're sorry? You must . . ."

Kahlan realized that although her hand still throbbed, the grip on it had gone slack. She looked down and saw the mask of death. He was now in the spirits' hands.

The pall of death sent a shudder through her. She knew what it was to feel the touch of death. She felt it now. She felt it every waking moment. In sleep it saturated her dreams with its numb touch. Her icy fingers reflexively brushed at her face, trying to wipe away the ever-present tingle, almost like a hair tickling her flesh, but there was never anything there to brush away. It was the teasing touch of magic, of the death spell, that she felt.

Zedd stood, letting the flame float to a torch that a man nearby was holding out, igniting it into wavering flame. While Zedd held one hand out as if in command to the wagon, he motioned the men away with his other. They cautiously took their shoulders away, but remained poised to catch the wagon if it suddenly fell again. Zedd turned his palm up and, in harmony with his arm's movement, the wagon obediently rose into the air another couple of feet.

"Pull him out," Zedd ordered in a somber tone.

The men seized Stephens by his shoulders and hauled him off the spoke. When he was out from under the axle, Zedd turned his hand over and allowed the wagon to settle to the ground.

A man fell to his knees beside Kahlan. "It's my fault," he cried in anguish. "I'm sorry. Oh, dear spirits, it's my fault."

Kahlan gripped the driver's coat and urged him to his feet. "If it's anyone's fault, then I'm to blame. I shouldn't have been trying to make distance in the dark. I should have . . . It's not your fault. It was an accident, that's all."

She turned away, closing her eyes, still hearing the phantoms of his screams. As was their routine, they hadn't used torches so as not to reveal their presence. There was no telling what eyes might see a force of men moving through the passes. While there was no evidence of pursuit, it was foolhardy to be overconfident. Stealth was life.

"Bury him as best you can," Kahlan told the men. There would be no digging in the frozen ground, but at least they could use the rock from the scree to cover him. His soul was with the spirits, and safe, now. His suffering was over.

Zedd asked the officers to get the trail cleared and then went with the men to find a place to lay Stephens to rest.

Amid the mounting noise and activity, Kahlan suddenly remembered Cyrilla, and climbed back into the wagon bed. Her half sister was wrapped in a heavy layer of blankets and nestled among piles of gear. Most of the rock had fallen in the back of the wagon, missing her, and the blanket had protected her from the smaller stones the pile of gear didn't stop. It was a wonder that no one had been crushed by one of the larger boulders that had crashed down in the darkness.

They had put Cyrilla in the wagon instead of the coach because she was still unconscious, and they thought that in the wagon they could lay her down so she would be more comfortable. The wagon was probably beyond repair. They would have to put her in the coach, now, but it wasn't far.

In the bottleneck in the trail, men started gathering, some squeezing past at officers' instructions and moving on into the night, while others brought out axes to cut trees and repair the support wall, while still others were told to throw the small stones and roll the larger rocks from the trail so they could get the coach through.

Kahlan was relieved to see that Cyrilla was unhurt by any of the rocks, and relieved, too, that she was still in her near constant stupor. They didn't need Cyrilla's screams and cries of terror at the moment; there was work to be done.

Kahlan had been riding in the wagon with her in case she happened to wake. After what had been done to her back in Aydindril, Cyrilla panicked at the sight of men, becoming terrified and inconsolable if Kahlan, Adie, or Jebra wasn't there to calm her.

In her rare spells of lucidity, Cyrilla made Kahlan promise, over and over, that she would be queen. Cyrilla worried for her people, and knew that she was in no state to help them. She loved Galea enough to refuse to burden her land with a queen in no condition to lead them. Kahlan had reluctantly assumed the responsibility.

Kahlan's half brother, Prince Harold, wanted nothing to do with a monarchial burden. He was a soldier, as was his and Cyrilla's father, King Wyborn. After Cyrilla and Harold had been born, Kahlan's mother had taken King Wyborn as her mate, and Kahlan was born. She was born a Confessor; the magic of the Confessors took precedence over petty matters of royalty.

"How is she?" Zedd asked as he tugged his robes off a snag while climbing into the wagon.

"The same. She was unhurt by the rockfall."

Zedd put fingers to her temples for a moment. "There is nothing wrong with her body, but the sickness still holds reign over her mind." He shook his head with a sigh as he rested an arm on his knee. "I wish the gift could cure maladies of the mind."

Kahlan saw the frustration in his eyes. She smiled. "Be thankful. If you could, you would never have time to eat."

As Zedd chuckled, she glanced to the men around the wagon, and saw Captain Ryan. She gestured him closer.

"Yes, my queen?"

"How far to Ebinissia?"

"Four, maybe six hours."

Zedd leaned toward her. "Not a place we want to reach in the dead of the night."

Kahlan caught his meaning and nodded. For them to reclaim the Crown city of Galea, they had a lot of work to do; the first of it was taking care of the thousands of corpses littering the city. It was not a scene they wanted to encounter in the middle of the night after a hard day's march. She didn't look forward to returning to the sight of that slaughter, but it was a place no one would expect to find them, and they could be safe there for a time. From that base, they could begin pulling the Midlands back together.

She turned back to Captain Ryan. "Is there anywhere near we can set up camp for the night?"

The captain gestured up the road. "The scouts said there's a small, upland valley not far ahead. There's an abandoned farm there where Cyrilla will be comfortable for the night."

She drew a strand of hair back from her face and hooked it behind an ear, noting that Cyrilla was no longer referred to as "queen." Kahlan was queen now, and Prince Harold had made sure all knew it. "All right, send word ahead, then. Get the valley secured and set up camp. Post sentries and scout the area. If the surrounding slopes are deserted, and the valley is cut off from view, then let the men have fires, but keep them small."

Captain Ryan smiled and tapped a fist to his heart in salute. Fires would be a luxury, and hot food would do the men good. They deserved it, after the hard march. They were almost home; tomorrow they would be there. Then the worst of the work would begin: taking care of the dead, and putting Ebinissia back to order. Kahlan would not let the Imperial Order's victory over Ebinissia stand. The Midlands would have the city back, and it would live again to strike back.

"Did you take care of Stephens?" she asked the captain.

"Zedd helped us find a place, and the men are taking care of it. Poor Stephens. He fought all through the battles against the Order, when we started with five thousand, saw four of every five of his companions killed, and he ends up dying in an accident after it's over. I know he would have wanted to die defending the Midlands."

"He did," Kahlan said. "It's not over; we won only a battle, though an important one. We are still at war with the Imperial Order, and he was a soldier in that war. He was helping with our effort, and died in the line of duty, just as much as those men killed in combat. There is no difference. He died a hero of the Midlands."

Captain Ryan stuffed his hands in the pockets of his heavy,

brown wool coat. "I think the men would appreciate hearing those words, and would find courage in them. Before we move on, could you say something over his grave? It would mean a lot for the men to know their queen will miss him."

Kahlan smiled. "Of course, Captain. It would be my honor."

Kahlan stared after the captain as he moved off to see to things. "I shouldn't have been pushing on after dark."

Zedd stroked a reassuring hand along the back of her head. "Accidents can happen in broad daylight. This very likely would have happened in the morning, had we stopped sooner, and then it would be blamed on being still half asleep."

"I still feel to blame. It just doesn't seem fair."

His smile marked no humor. "Fate does not seek our consent."

CHAPTER 33

IF THERE WERE ANY bodies at the farm, the men had removed them by the time Kahlan reached it. They had started a fire in the roughly built hearth, but it hadn't had time to thaw the iron chill from the deserted home.

Cyrilla was carefully carried to the remains of a straw mattress in a back bedroom. There was another cramped room with two pallets, probably for children, and the main room with a table and little else. By the broken bits of a cupboard and chest, and the remains of personal items, Kahlan knew the Order had been through here on their way to Ebinissia. She wondered again what the men had done with the bodies; she didn't want to find them in the night if she had to go outside to relieve herself.

Zedd peered around at the room as he rubbed his hands on his stomach.

"How long until dinner is ready?" he asked in a cheery tone.

He wore heavy maroon robes with black sleeves and cowled shoulders. Three rows of silver brocade circled the cuffs of his sleeves. Thicker, gold brocade ran around the neck and down the front, the outfit gathered at the waist with a red satin belt set with a gold buckle. Zedd hated the flashy accoutrements that Adie had insisted he purchase as a disguise. He preferred his simple robes, but they were long gone, as was his fancy hat with the long feather that he had "lost" somewhere along the way.

Kahlan grinned in spite of herself. "I don't know. What are you cooking?"

"Me? Cook? Well, I suppose . . ."

"Dear spirits, spare us that man's cooking," Adie said from the doorway. "We would be better served to eat bark and bugs."

Adie limped into the room, followed by Jebra, the seer, and Ahern, the coach driver who had carried Zedd and Adie on their recent journeys. Chandalen, who had accompanied Kahlan from the Mud People's village months ago, had departed after Kahlan had been with Richard one wondrous night in a place between worlds. He wanted to return to his home and people. She couldn't blame him; she knew what it was to miss friends and loved ones.

With Zedd and Adie, she felt as if they were almost all together. When Richard caught up with them, then truly they would all be together again. Though it would probably be weeks yet, Kahlan still couldn't help being excited by each breath, because each breath brought her one moment closer to having her arms around him.

"My bones do be too old for this weather," Adie said as she crossed the room.

Kahlan retrieved a simple wooden chair and dragged it along as she took Adie's arm and walked her to the fire. She put the chair close to the flames and urged the sorceress to sit and warm herself. Unlike Zedd's original clothes, Adie's simple, flaxen robes, with yellow and red beads sewn at the neck in ancient symbols of her profession, had survived their journey. Zedd scowled every time he saw them, thinking it more than a little odd that her simple robes had managed to make the journey and his had been lost.

Adie always smiled and said it was a wonder and insisted that he looked grand in his fine clothes. Kahlan suspected she really did like him better in his new outfit. Kahlan, too, thought Zedd looked grand, though not so wizardlike as his traditional fashion made him look. Wizards of his high rank wore the simplest robes. There was no rank above Zedd: First Wizard.

"Thank you, child," Adie said as she warmed her hands near the flames.

"Orsk," Kahlan called.

The big man scurried forward. The scar over his missing eye was white in the firelight. "Yes, mistress?" He stood ready to carry out her instructions. What they might be was of no importance to him, his only concern being that he had a chance to please her.

"There's no pot in here. Could you get us one, so we can make some dinner?"

His dark leather uniform creaked as he bowed and turned to hurry from the room. Orsk had been a D'Haran soldier from the Imperial Order's camp. He had tried to kill her, and in the struggle she touched him with her power, the magic of the Confessors destroying forever who he had been and filling him with blind loyalty to her. That blind loyalty and devotion was a wearing presence to Kahlan, a constant reminder of what and who she was.

She tried not to see the man he had been: a D'Haran soldier who had joined with the Imperial Order, one of the killers who had participated in the slaughter of the helpless women and children of Ebinissia. As the Mother Confessor, she had sworn no mercy on any of the men of the Order, and there had been none. Only Orsk still lived. Though he lived, the man who had fought for the Order was dead.

Because of the death spell Zedd had cast over her to aid in their escape from Aydindril, few knew Kahlan as the Mother Confessor. Orsk only knew her as his mistress. Zedd, of course; Adie; Jebra; Ahern; Chandalen; her half brother, Prince Harold; and Captain Ryan knew her true identity, but everyone else thought the Mother Confessor was dead. The men she had fought with knew her only as their queen. Their memory of her being the Mother Confessor had been confused and muddled into remembering her as Queen Kahlan, no less their leader, but not the Mother Confessor.

After snow had been melted, Jebra and Kahlan added beans and bacon, cut up a few sweet roots to toss into the pot, and spooned in some molasses. Zedd stood rubbing his hands as he watched the ingredients being added. Kahlan grinned at his childlike eagerness and, from a pack, retrieved some hard bread for him. He was pleased, and ate the bread while the beans boiled.

While dinner cooked, Kahlan thawed leftover soup they had brought in a small pot and took it in to Cyrilla. She set a candle on a slat she stuck in a crack in the wall and sat on the edge of the bed in the quiet room. She wiped a warm cloth on her half sister's forehead for a while, and was happy to see Cyrilla's eyes open. A panicked gaze darted around the dim room. Kahlan grabbed Cyrilla's jaw and forced her to look up into her eyes.

"It's me, Kahlan, my sister. You are safe, alone with me. You are safe. Be at ease. Everything is all right."

"Kahlan?" Cyrilla clutched at Kahlan's white fur mantle. "You promised. You won't go back on your word. You mustn't."

Kahlan smiled. "I promised, and I will keep the promise. I am the queen of Galea, and will be the queen until the day you wish the crown back."

Cyrilla sagged back in relief, still clutching the fur mantle. "Thank you, my queen."

Kahlan urged her to sit up. "Come on, now. I've brought you some warm soup."

Cyrilla turned her face from the spoon. "I'm not hungry."

"If you want me to be the queen, then you must treat me as queen." A questioning frown came to Cyrilla's face. Kahlan smiled. "This is an order from your queen. You will eat the soup."

Only then would Cyrilla eat. When she had finished it all, and had started shaking and crying again, Kahlan hugged her tight until she slipped into a trancelike state, staring blindly up at nothing. Kahlan tucked the heavy blankets tight around her and kissed her forehead.

Zedd had scrounged up a couple of barrels, a bench, a stool from the barn, and somewhere found another chair. He had asked Prince Harold and Captain Ryan to join Adie, Jebra, Ahern, Orsk, Kahlan, and himself for dinner. They were close to Ebinissia, and had to talk about their plans. Everyone crowded around the small table as Kahlan broke up hard bread and Jebra dished out steaming bowls of beans from the pot sitting in the fire. When the seer was finished, she sat down on the short bench beside Kahlan, all the while giving Zedd puzzled looks.

Prince Harold, a barrel-chested man with a head of long, thick, dark hair, reminded Kahlan of her father. Harold had only that day returned with his scouts from Ebinissia.

"What news have you from your home?" she asked him.

He broke his bread with his thick fingers. "Well," he sighed, "it was the same as you described it. It doesn't look as if anyone else has been there. I think it'll be safe enough for us there. With the Order's army destroyed—"

"The one in this area," Kahlan corrected.

He conceded the point with a wave of his bread. "I don't think we'll have any trouble for now. We don't have many men yet, but they're good men, and we have enough to protect the city from up in the passes in the mountains all around, as long as they don't come in numbers like before. Until the Order brings more men, I think we can hold the city." He gestured toward Zedd. "And we have a wizard."

Zedd, busy spooning beans into his mouth, only slowed enough to grunt in agreement.

Captain Ryan swallowed a big mouthful of beans. "Prince Harold is right. We know these mountains. We can defend the city until they bring a large force. By then, maybe we'll have more men joining with us, and we can start to move."

Harold dunked his bread in his bowl, scooping up a chunk of bacon. "Adie, what do you judge our chances of getting help from Nicobarese?"

"My homeland be in turmoil. When Zedd and I were there, we learned that the king be dead. The Blood of the Fold has moved to seize power, but not all the people be pleased about it. The sorceresses be most displeased. If the Blood takes power, those women will be hunted down and killed. I expect them to back the forces in the army who resist the Blood."

"With civil war," Zedd said, interrupting his speedy spoon work, "it doesn't bode well for sending troops to aid the Midlands."

Adie sighed. "Zedd be right."

"Maybe some of the sorceresses could help?" Kahlan asked.

Adie stirred her spoon in her beans. "Maybe."

Kahlan looked to her half brother. "But you have troops from other areas you can call in."

Harold nodded. "We sure do. At least sixty or seventy thousand, perhaps as many as a hundred thousand could be marshaled, though not all of those will be well trained or well armed. It'll take time to get them organized, but when we do, then Ebinissia will be a force to be reckoned with."

"We had nearly that many here before," Captain Ryan reminded them without looking up from his bowl, "and it wasn't enough."

"True," Harold said flourishing his bread. "But that's just for a beginning." He looked to Kahlan. "You can bring more of the lands together, can't you?"

"That's our hope," she said. "We must rally the Midlands around us, if we're to have a chance."

"What about Sanderia?" Captain Ryan asked. "Their lances are the best in the Midlands."

"And Lifany," Harold said. "They make a lot of weapons, and know how to use them."

Kahlan picked a soft pinch out of the center of her bread. "Sanderia relies on Kelton for summer grazing for their sheep herds. Lifany buys iron from Kelton, and sells them grain. Herjborgue relies on Sanderia's wool. I think they all might go where Kelton goes."

Harold stabbed his spoon into his beans. "There were Keltish dead among the ones who attacked Ebinissia."

"And Galeans." Kahlan put the bread in her mouth and chewed for a moment as she watched him clench his spoon as if it were a knife. He glared into his bowl.

"There were insurgents and murderers from many lands who joined them," she said after she had swallowed. "That does not mean their homelands will. Prince Fyren of Kelton had committed his land to the Imperial Order, but he's dead, now. We are not at war with Kelton; they are part of the Midlands. We are at war with the Imperial Order. We need to stand together. If Kelton joins with us, the others will almost have to, but if they go with the Order, then we will have trouble convincing the others to join us. We need to win over Kelton and bond them to us."

"I'd bet on Kelton joining with the Order," Ahern said.

Everyone turned his way. He shrugged. "I'm Keltish. I can tell you that they'll go where the Crown goes; its the way of our people. With Fyren dead, then that would make Duchess Lumholtz next in line. She and her husband, the duke, will go to the side they think will win, no matter who that may be. At least that's my opinion from what I've heard about her."

"That's foolish!" Harold threw his spoon down. "As much as I don't trust Keltans—no offense intended, Ahern—and know their scheming ways, at the heart of it, they're Midlanders. They may want to grab whatever scrap of a farm lies on a disputed border and call it Keltish, but the people are still Midlanders.

"The spirits know that Cyrilla and I had our fights, but when it came to trouble, we stood together. Same with our lands; when D'Hara attacked last summer, we fought to protect Kelton, despite some of our disagreements. If it means the future of the Midlands, they'll go with us. The Midlands means more than what anyone come new to the crown has to say about it." Harold snatched up his spoon and waved it at Ahern. "What have you to say about that?"

Ahern shrugged. "Nothing, I guess."

Zedd's eyes moved between the two men. "We are not here to argue. We are here to fight a war. Speak what you believe, Ahern. You are Keltish, and would know more of it than we."

Ahern scratched his windburned face as he thought on Zedd's words. "General Baldwin, the commander of all Keltish forces, and his generals, Bradford, Cutter, and Emerson, will go where the Crown goes. I don't know the men, I'm just a driver, but I go a lot of places and I hear a lot of talk, and that's what's always said of them. People have a joke that if the queen tossed her crown out the window and it caught on a buck's antlers, the whole of the army would be grazin' on grass within a month."

"And from the talk you hear, do you really believe this duchess become queen will go with the Order just for a chance at power, if it means breaking with the Midlands?" Zedd asked.

Ahern shrugged. "It's just my opinion, understand, but I think it would be so."

As Kahlan spooned out a sweet root without looking up, she spoke. "Ahern's right. I know Cathryn Lumholtz, and her husband, the duke. She will be queen, and even though she takes counsel from her husband, she is of like mind anyway. Prince

Fyren would have been king, and I thought he would have stuck with us no matter what, but someone from the Order won him to their side, and he betrayed us. I'm sure the Order will make Cathryn Lumholtz similar offers. She will see power in those offers."

Harold reached across the table and snatched up some more bread. "If she does, and Ahern's right, then we've lost Kelton. If we've lost Kelton, then we've got the first crack of ruin."

"This not be good," Adie observed. "Nicobarese be in trouble, Galea be weakened when so many of her army be killed in Ebinissia, and Kelton be leaning toward the Order, and with her will go a number of lands that be trade partners."

"And then there are some of the others who when—"

"Enough." The quiet, clear ring of authority in Kahlan's voice lowered a pall of silence over the table. She remembered what Richard always said when they were in more trouble than they knew how to wiggle out of: think of the solution, not the problem. If your mind was filled only with thoughts of why you were going to lose, then you couldn't think of how to win.

"Stop telling me why we can't bring the Midlands back together, and why we can't win. We already know there are problems. We need to discuss the solutions."

Zedd smiled over his spoon. "Well put, Mother Confessor. I think we must have some ideas. For one, there are a number of smaller lands that will remain loyal to the Midlands no matter what. We must gather their representatives in Ebinissia, and begin rebuilding the council."

"That's right," Kahlan said. "They might not be as powerful as Kelton, but there is a quality to numbers that has influence."

Kahlan opened her fur mantle. The crackling fire was warming the room a bit and the food was warming her belly, but it was worry that was beginning to make her sweat. She couldn't wait for Richard to join them; he would have ideas. Richard never sat around letting events dictate as they would. She watched the others as they bent over their bowls, each with a frown as they pondered their options.

"Well," Adie said as she set her spoon down, "I be sure we could get some sorceresses from Nicobarese to join with us. They would be a powerful aid. While some would refuse to fight, as it be against their convictions, they would not be averse to helping in other ways. None want to see the Blood, or their allies, the Imperial Order, take the Midlands. Most know the terror of times past, and would not want them to come anew."

"Good," Kahlan said. "That's good. Do you think you could go there and convince them to join with us, maybe get some of the regular army to help, too? After all, the civil war is a part of the larger war, and it would not be going on if at least some didn't want to aid the Midlands."

Adie's completely white eyes regarded Kahlan for a moment. "For something this important, of course I will try."

Kahlan nodded. "Thank you, Adie." She looked to the others. "What else? Any ideas?"

Harold rested an elbow on the table as he frowned in thought. He waggled his spoon. "I think if I sent some officers, as an official delegation, to some of the smaller lands, they could be convinced to send representatives to Ebinissia. Most hold Galea in high regard, and know how the Midlands has protected their freedom. They will come to our aid."

"And perhaps," Zedd said with a sly smile, "if I went to visit this Queen Lumholtz, as First Wizard, mind you, I could convince her that the Midlands is not without power of its own."

Kahlan knew Cathryn Lumholtz, but she didn't want to douse the warm hope of Zedd's idea. She was the one, after all, who had said they needed to think of solutions instead of the problems.

What held her in the grip of terror, was the thought of being the Mother Confessor who lost the Midlands.

When dinner was finished, Prince Harold and Captain Ryan went to see to the men. Ahern threw his longcoat around his broad shoulders and said he had to check on his team.

After they were gone, Zedd caught Jebra's arm as she went about helping Kahlan collect the bowls.

"Do you want to tell me, now, what it is you're seeing every time you look my way?"

Jebra turned her blue eyes from his gaze and gathered another spoon into her hand with the others. "It's nothing."

"I would like to be the judge of that, if you don't mind."

She halted, and at last looked up at him. "Wings."

Zedd lifted an eyebrow. "Wings?"

She nodded. "I see you with wings. You see? It makes no sense.

It has to be a vision that means nothing. I told you, I get those kind sometimes."

"That's it? Just wings?"

Jebra fussed with her short, sandy hair. "Well, you are up in the air, with these wings, and you are dropped into a huge ball of flame." The fine wrinkles at the corners of her eyes deepened. "Wizard Zorander, I don't know what it means. It's not an event—you know how my visions work sometimes—but a sense of events. I don't know what they mean, all jumbled together like that."

Zedd released her arm. "Thank you, Jebra. If you learn anything else, you will tell me?" She nodded. "And at once. We need all the help we can get."

Her eyes sought the floor as she nodded again. Her head tilted toward Kahlan. "Circles. I see the Mother Confessor running around in circles."

"Circles?" Kahlan asked as she stepped closer. "Why am I running in circles?"

"I can't tell."

"Well, I feel as if I'm running in circles right now, trying to find a way to pull the Midlands back together."

Jebra looked up hopefully. "That may be it."

Kahlan offered her a smile. "Maybe it is. Your visions aren't always of calamity."

As they all started to go back to cleaning up, Jebra spoke again. "Mother Confessor, we mustn't leave your sister alone with any ropes."

"What do you mean?"

Jebra let out a breath. "She is dreaming of hanging herself."

"You mean that you have seen a vision of her hanging herself?"

Jebra laid a concerned hand to Kahlan's arm. "Oh no, Mother Confessor, I've not seen that. It's just that I can see the aura, see that she is dreaming of doing it. It does not mean she will, only that we must watch her, so she won't have the chance before she can recover."

"That sounds like sound advice," Zedd offered.

Jebra tied the leftover bread in a cloth. "I will sleep with her tonight."

"Thank you," Kahlan said. "Why don't you let me finish cleaning up, and you go to bed now, in case she wakes."

Zedd, Adie, and Kahlan shared the chores after Jebra took her bedroll into the room with Cyrilla. When they were finished, Zedd placed a chair before the fire for Adie. Kahlan loosely twined her fingers together and stood looking into the flames.

"Zedd, when we send the delegations to the smaller lands to ask them to come to a council in Ebinissia, it would be easier to convince them if it were an official delegation from the Mother Confessor."

Zedd finally broke the quiet. "They all think the Mother Confessor is dead. If we let them know you're alive, then you become a target, and it would bring the Order down on us before we could gather a strong enough force."

Kahlan turned and gripped his robes. "Zedd, I'm tired of being dead."

He patted her hand on his arm. "You're the queen of Galea, and you can use your influence in that way, for now. If the Imperial Order finds out you're alive, then we'll have more trouble than we're prepared to handle."

"If we're going to unite the Midlands, then they need a Mother Confessor."

"Kahlan, I know you don't want to do anything to jeopardize the lives of those men out there. They've just won a costly battle; they aren't strong enough yet. We need more gathered to our side. If anyone knows you are the Mother Confessor, then you become a target and they will have to fight to protect you. If you must fight, it must be for the right reasons. We don't need more problems than we can handle right now."

Kahlan pressed the tips of her fingers together as she stared into the fire. "Zedd, I am the Mother Confessor. I'm terrified I will be the Mother Confessor who presides over the destruction of the Midlands. I was born a Confessor. It's more than my job. It is who I am."

Zedd hugged her shoulders. "Dear one, you are still the Mother Confessor. That's why we must hide your identity for now. We need the Mother Confessor. When the time comes, you will rule over the Midlands again, a Midlands stronger than it has ever been. Have patience."

"Patience," she muttered.

"Ah, well," he said with a grin, "there is magic in patience, too, you know."

"Zedd be right," Adie said from her chair. "The wolf does not survive if he announces to the herd he be a wolf. He makes his plans of attack, and only at the last moment, lets the prey know that it be he, the wolf, who be after them."

Kahlan rubbed her arms. There was more to it—another reason.

"Zedd," she whispered with the pain of it, "I can't stand this spell any longer. It's driving me mad. I can feel it all the time, like death walking in my flesh with me."

Zedd pulled her head to his shoulder. "My daughter used to say the same thing. Those very words, in fact, 'like death walking in my flesh with me.'"

"How did she stand it all those years?"

Zedd sighed. "Well, when Darken Rahl raped her, I knew that if he thought she was alive, he would come after her. There was no choice. I wanted to protect her more than I wanted to go after him. I took her to the Midlands, where Richard was born, and then she had another reason to hide. If Darken Rahl ever knew, he might have come after Richard, too, so she had to endure it."

Kahlan shuddered. "All those years. I wouldn't have the strength. How could she stand it?"

"Well, there was no alternative, for one thing, and for another, she said that after a time she became used to it a bit, and it wasn't so bad as it was in the beginning. The feeling will ease a bit over time. You will get used to it, and hopefully, you will not have to go on long like this."

"I hope so," Kahlan said.

The firelight flickering on Zedd's thin face. "She also said that having Richard lessened the burden."

Kahlan's heart leapt at the mere mention aloud of his name. She grinned. "That will surely help." She clutched Zedd's arm. "He'll be here soon. He won't let anything hold him back. He'll be here in a couple of weeks at the most. Dear spirits, how will I ever wait that long?"

Zedd chuckled. "You have as little patience as that boy. You two were made for each other." He brushed back her hair. "Your eyes look better already, dear one."

"Then when Richard is with us, and we start pulling the Midlands back together, you can take this death spell off me. Then the Midlands will have a Mother Confessor again."

"It can't be soon enough for me, either."

Kahlan frowned. "Zedd, if you go away to see Queen Cathryn, and I need to get this spell off, how can I do it?"

Zedd looked back at the flames. "You can't. If you were to announce that you were the Mother Confessor, people would believe you no more than if Jebra were to announce that she was the Mother Confessor. The spell won't leave because you simply declare who you are."

"Then how do I get it off?"

Zedd sighed. "Only I can do that."

Kahlan felt a sudden flush of fear. She didn't want to voice it, but she would be trapped with the spell if anything happened to Zedd.

"But surely there must be another way to remove the spell. Perhaps Richard?"

Zedd shook his head. "Even if Richard knew how to be a wizard, he could not remove the web. Only I can do it."

"And that's the only way?"

"Yes." He looked back to her eyes. "Unless, of course, another with the gift were to deduce your true identity. If such a man were to see you, understand who you were, and name you aloud, then it would break the spell, and all would once again know your identity."

There was no hope of that. She felt her hopes sink. Kahlan squatted and shoved another stick of wood in the fire. The only way she was going to get the death spell off was for Zedd to do it, and he wasn't going to do it until he was good and ready.

As Mother Confessor, she would not order a wizard to do something both knew was wrong.

Kahlan watched the sparks swirling up. She brightened. Richard would be with her soon, and it wouldn't be so bad, then. When Richard was with her she wouldn't think about the spell; she would be too busy kissing him.

"What's funny?" Zedd asked.

"What? Oh, nothing." She stood and brushed her hands off on her pants. "I think I'll go check on the men. Maybe some cold air will get this spell off my mind."

The cold air did feel good. She stood in the clearing outside the small farmhouse and took a deep breath. The woodsmoke smelled good. She recalled the previous days when they were on the march, and her feet and fingers felt frozen, when her ears burned with the bite of cold, and her nose ran, how she daydreamed about woodsmoke because it meant the warmth of a fire.

Kahlan strolled across the field outside the house. She stared up at the stars, her breath drifting slowly in the still air. She could see small fires dotting the valley beyond, and she could hear the murmurs of conversation of the men sitting around the fires. She was glad they, too, could have fires this night. Soon they would be at Ebinissia and they could be warm again.

Kahlan took a deep breath of the cold air, trying to forget the spell. The whole sky was aglitter with stars, like sparks from a huge fire. She wondered what Richard was doing right now, and if we was riding hard, or getting sleep. She longed to see him, but she also wanted him to get enough sleep. When he finally reached her, she could sleep in his arms. She grinned at the thought.

Kahlan frowned as a swath of stars went dark. Almost as soon as they darkened, they winked back to points of light. Had she really seen them go dark for an instant? Must be her imagination, she thought.

She heard a thud as something hit the ground. No alarm went up. Only one thing could get through the ring of defenders and not raise an alarm. She tingled in sudden gooseflesh, and it wasn't the spell.

Kahlan yanked her knife free.

CHAPTER 34

SHE SAW GLOWING GREEN eyes. In the faint light coming from the small winter moon and the stars, she saw a great hulk step toward her. Kahlan wanted to cry out, but her voice wasn't there.

When the huge beast's lips drew back, she saw the entire length of its prodigious fangs. She staggered back a step. She was squeezing the knife handle so hard that her fingers ached. If she was quick, and if she didn't panic, she might have a chance. If she called out, would Zedd hear her? Would anyone hear her? Even if they did, they were too far away. They wouldn't be able to get to her in time.

In the dim light she could see by its size that it was a short-tailed gar. It would have to be a short-tailed gar; they were the smartest, the biggest, the most deadly. Dear spirits, why couldn't it be a long-tailed gar?

Kahlan stared as it lifted something from its chest. Why was it just standing there? Where were its blood flies? It looked down, looked up at her, and looked down again. The eyes glowed a menacing green. Its lips drew back farther, vapor clouding the air when it let out a gurgling sound.

Kahlan's eyes went wide. Could it be? "Gratch?"

The gar suddenly started jumping up and down, howling with excitement and flapping its wings.

Kahlan sagged with heady relief. She sheathed her knife and stepped closer to the towering beast, but she was still cautious.

"Gratch? Is that you, Gratch?"

The gar vigorously nodded his huge, grotesque head. "Grrratch!" He called out in a deep growl that resonated in her breastbone. He thumped his chest with both claws. "Grrratch!"

"Gratch, did Richard send you?"

The gar's wings flapped more energetically at the mention of Richard's name.

She came closer. "Did Richard send you?"

"Grrratch luuug Raaaach aaarg."

Kahlan blinked. Richard had told her that Gratch tried to talk. She suddenly giggled. "Kahlan loves Richard, too." She tapped her chest. "I'm Kahlan, Gratch. I'm so happy to meet you."

She gasped as the gar lunged forward and scooped her up in his furry arms, lifting her feet clear of the ground. Her first thought was that he was surely going to crush her, but he was surprisingly gentle as he held her to his smooth chest. Kahlan reached around the great body and hugged the gar's sides. She couldn't get her arms even halfway around him,

Kahlan could never have imagined doing such a thing, but now she was brought nearly to tears, because Gratch was Richard's friend, and Richard had sent the gar to her. It was almost as if it were a hug sent from Richard himself.

The gar carefully set her on the ground. He studied her with his glowing green eyes. She stroked a hand along the fur at the side of his chest as the hulking creature reached down and tenderly stroked her hair with a huge, deadly claw.

Kahlan grinned up at the wrinkled face full of fangs. Gratch let out a purling gurgle. His wings moved in slow, contented sweeps as she stroked his fur, and he stroked her hair.

"You're safe here with us, Gratch. Richard told me all about you. I don't know how much you can understand, but you're among friends."

When his lips drew back, again exposing the full length of his fangs, she suddenly realized it was a smile. It was the ugliest smile she had ever seen, but it had an innocent quality to it that made her grin, too. She had never in her life thought that gars could smile. It truly was a marvel.

"Gratch, did Richard send you?"

"Raaaach aaarg." Gratch thumped his chest. He flapped his wings hard enough that it briefly lifted his feet from the ground. Then he reached out and tapped Kahlan's shoulder.

Kahlan's mouth fell opened. The gar was telling her something, and she understood. "Richard sent you to find me?"

Gratch went wild with glee that she understood. He scooped her up in his arms again. She laughed at the whole marvelous nature of it all.

When he set her down again, she asked, "Was it hard to find me?"

He let out a whine and shrugged.

"It was a little bit hard?"

Gratch nodded. Kahlan knew a wide variety of languages, but she couldn't help laughing again at the very idea of communicating with a gar. She shook her head in wonder. Who but Richard would think to befriend a gar?

Kahlan took a claw up in her hand. "Come on in the house. There is someone I want you to meet."

Gratch gurgled his assent.

Kahlan paused in the doorway. Zedd and Adie looked up from their chairs beside the fire.

"I'd like to introduce a friend," she said as she pulled Gratch in behind her by a claw. He ducked under the doorframe, folding his wings to fit through, and then once inside, straightened to nearly his full height behind her, still stooping a bit to fit under the ceiling.

Zedd toppled backward in his chair, his skinny arms and legs flailing at the air.

"Zedd, stop it. You're going to frighten him," she scolded.

"Frighten him!" Zedd croaked. "You told me that Richard said it was a baby gar! That thing is nearly full-grown!"

Gratch's massive eyebrows drew together in a frown as he watched the wizard scramble to his feet and tug at his tangled robes.

Kahlan held a hand out. "Gratch, this is Richard's grandfather, Zedd."

The leathery lips drew back, showing the fangs again. Gratch held his claws out and started across the room. Zedd flinched and stumbled back.

"Why's he doing that? Has he had dinner?"

Kahlan laughed so hard she could hardly get the words out. "He's smiling. He likes you. He wants a hug."

"A hug! Most certainly not!"

It was too late. With only three strides, the gar had closed the distance in the small room and was already scooping up the bony wizard in his huge, furry arms. Zedd let out a muffled cry. Gratch gurgled a giggle as he lifted Zedd from his feet.

"Bags!" Zedd tried unsuccessfully to back away from the gar's breath. "This flying rug has eaten! And you don't want to know what!"

Gratch finally set Zedd down. The wizard scrambled back a few steps and shook his finger at the beast. "Now, look here, we'll have no more of that! You just keep your arms to yourself."

Gratch wilted, again letting out a purling whine.

"Zedd!" Kahlan admonished. "You've hurt his feelings. He's Richard's friend, and ours, too, and he's had a difficult time finding us. The least you can do is be nice to him."

Zedd harrumphed. "Well . . . perhaps you're right." He peered up at the hopeful beast. "I'm sorry, Gratch. On occasion, I suppose it would be all right for you to hug me."

Before the wizard could lift his arms to try to hold the gar back, Gratch had again scooped him up and was hugging him like a rag doll, Zedd's feet swinging to and fro. Gratch at last set the gasping wizard to the floor.

Adie held out a hand, to shake. "I be Adie, Gratch. I be pleased to meet you."

Gratch ignored the hand and threw his furry arms around her, too. Kahlan had often seen Adie smile, but she rarely let out her raspy laugh. She was laughing now. Gratch laughed with her, in his own, rumbling way.

When order was restored to the room, and everyone had caught their breath, Kahlan saw Jebra's wide eyes peeking out from a slit in the bedroom door. "It's all right, Jebra. It's Gratch, a friend of ours." Kahlan clamped a restraining grip to the fur of Gratch's arm. "You can hug her later."

Gratch shrugged with a nod. Kahlan turned him toward her and took up one of his claws in both of her hands. She looked up into his glowing green eyes.

"Gratch, did Richard send you on ahead to tell us he will be here soon?" Gratch shook his head. Kahlan swallowed. "But he's on his way? He's left Aydindril, and he's on his way to catch up with us?"

Gratch studied her face. His claw came up and stroked her hair. Kahlan saw that he had a lock of her hair on a leather thong at his throat, along with the dragon's tooth. He slowly shook his head again.

Kahlan's heart sank like a rock in a well. "He's not on his way? But he sent you to me?"

Gratch nodded, adding a small flap of his wings.

"Why? Do you know why?"

Gratch nodded. He reached over his shoulder and caught hold of something hanging on his back by another thong. He pulled a long red object over his shoulder and held it out to her at the end of the thong.

"What is it?" Zedd asked.

Kahlan started working the knot free. "It's a document case. Maybe it's a letter from Richard."

Gratch nodded at the guess. When she had freed the knot, she asked Gratch to sit down. He squatted contentedly to the side as Kahlan drew the rolled and flattened letter from the pouch.

Zedd sat beside Adie next to the fire. "Let's hear the boy's excuses, and they had better be good ones, or he is in a lot of trouble."

"I agree with you about that," she said under her breath. "There's enough wax on this thing for two dozen letters. We need to teach Richard how to seal a document." She turned it in the light. "It's the sword. He's pressed the hilt of the Sword of Truth into the wax."

"So we will know it's truly from him," Zedd observed as he fed a piece of wood into the fire.

When she had finished breaking all the wax, Kahlan unfurled the letter and turned her back to the fire so she could read it.

" 'My Dearest Queen,' " she read aloud, " 'I pray to the good spirits that this letter reaches your hands . . .' "

Zedd shot to his feet. "That's a message."

Kahlan frowned at him. "Well of course it is. It's his letter."

He waved his thin hand. "No, no. I mean he's telling us something. I know Richard—I know the way he thinks. He's telling us he fears that if someone were to get their hands on this letter, it might betray us . . . or him, so he's warning us that he can't say everything he might like to."

Kahlan pulled her lower lip through her teeth. "Yes, that would make sense. Richard usually thinks things through."

Zedd gestured as he turned to make sure his bony bottom would hit the chair as he sat. "Go on."

" 'My Dearest Queen, I pray to the good spirits that this letter reaches your hands, and it finds you and your friends well and safe. Much has happened, and I must beg your understanding.

" 'The alliance of the Midlands is ended. Overhead, Magda Searus, the first Mother Confessor, and her wizard, Merritt, glare down upon me, because they have witnessed its end, and because it is I who have ended it.

" 'Realize that I know full well the weight of thousands of years of history staring down upon me from overhead, but please try to understand that if I had not acted, then our only future would be as slaves to the Imperial Order, and then that history would be forgotten.' "

Kahlan put a hand to her chest over her thumping heart, and paused to gulp air before she went on.

" 'Months ago, the Imperial Order began the undoing of the alliance, winning converts to their side, and unraveling the unity that was the Midlands. As we fought the Keeper, they fought to steal the security of our home. Perhaps there would have been a chance to bring unity once more, had we the luxury of time, but the Order presses their plans, and denies us that luxury. With the Mother Confessor dead, I was forced to do what must be done to forge unity.' "

"What? What has he done?" Zedd croaked.

Kahlan shot him a silencing glare over the top of the trembling letter, and then went on.

" 'Delay is weakness, and weakness is death at the hands of the Order. Our beloved Mother Confessor knew the cost of failure, and has charged us with carrying this war to victory; she has declared this a war without mercy on the Imperial Order. Her wisdom in this was infallible. The alliance, however, was fragmented with self-interest. This was a prelude to ruin. I was forced to act.

" 'My troops have captured Aydindril.' "

Zedd exploded. "Bags and double bags! What's he talking about! He has no troops! He just has his sword and this flying rug with fangs!"

Gratch rose with a growl. Zedd flinched.

Kahlan blinked away the tears. "Be quiet, both of you."

Zedd glanced from her to the gar. "Sorry, Gratch, no offense intended."

They both sank back down as she went on.

" 'Today I gathered the representatives of the lands here in Aydindril and informed them that the alliance of the Midlands is dissolved. My troops have surrounded their palaces and will shortly have disarmed their soldiers. I told them, as I will tell you, that there are only two sides in this war: our side, and the Imperial Order. There will be no bystanders. We will have unity, one way, or another. All lands of the Midlands must surrender to D'Hara.' "

"D'Hara! Bags!"

Kahlan didn't look up as tears dripped from her face. "If I have to tell you again to be quiet, you will wait outside while I read this letter."

Adie took a fistful of Zedd's robes and pulled him down into his chair. "Read on."

Kahlan cleared her throat. " 'I explained to the representatives that you, the queen of Galea, were to marry me, and through your surrender and our union, it shows that this is a union forged in peace, with common goals and mutual respect, and not a matter of conquest. Lands will be allowed to retain their heritage and lawful traditions, but not their sovereignty. Magic in all forms will be protected. We will be one people, with one army, under one command, and under one law. All lands that join us through their surrender will have a say in formulating those laws.' "

Kahlan's voice broke. " 'I must ask you to return at once to Aydindril and surrender Galea. I must deal with matters of various lands, and your knowledge and assistance would be invaluable.

" 'I informed the representatives that surrender is mandatory. There will be no favoritism. Any who fail to surrender will be put under siege. They will not be allowed to trade with us until they surrender. If they do not surrender willingly, with all the benefits that that entails, and we are compelled to gain their surrender by force of arms, then they will not only forfeit those benefits, but incur sanctions as well. As I said, there will be no bystanders. We will be one.

" 'My queen, I would give my life for you, and want nothing more than to be your husband, but if my actions turn your heart against me, I would not force your hand in marriage. Understand, though, that the surrender of your land is necessary and vital. We must live by one law. I cannot afford to show special favors to any land, or we are lost before we begin.' "

Kahlan had to pause to gasp back a sob. She could hardly read the watery words wavering before her eyes.

" 'Mriswith have attacked the city.' " A low whistle came from between Zedd's teeth. She ignored it and read on. " 'With Gratch's help, I have put their remains on pikes to decorate the front lawn of the Confessors' Palace so all may see the fate of our enemies. Mriswith can be invisible at will. Besides myself, only Gratch can detect them when they are shrouded by their cloaks. I fear they will come for you, so I have sent Gratch for protection.

" 'We must remember one thing above all others: the Order wishes to destroy magic. They are not shy about using it, though. It is our magic they wish to destroy.

" 'Please tell my grandfather that he, too, must return at once. His ancestral home is in danger. This is why I had to take Aydindril, and cannot leave; I fear to let the enemy have my grandfather's ancestral home, and the dire consequences that would ensue.' "

Zedd couldn't keep silent. "Bags," he whispered to himself as he came to his feet again. "Richard's talking about the Wizard's Keep. He didn't want to write it, but that's what he's referring to. How could I be so stupid? The boy is right; we can't let them have the Keep. There are things of powerful magic in there that the Order would dearly pay to put their hands on. Richard doesn't know about the magic in there, but he's smart enough to understand the danger. I've been a blind fool."

With a cold fright Kahlan realized the truth of it, too. If the Order were to take the Keep, they would have access to enormously powerful magic.

"Zedd, Richard is there all alone. He knows almost nothing about magic. He doesn't know anything about the kind of people in Aydindril who can use magic. He's a fawn in a bear's den. Dear spirits, he has no idea of the danger he's in."

Zedd nodded grimly. "The boy's in over his head."

Adie let out a mocking laugh. "In over his head? He has stolen Aydindril and access to the Keep right from under the nose of the Order. They have sent mriswith against him, and he puts them on pikes outside the palace. He probably has the lands on the verge of surrender into a union that can fight the Order, the very thing we were trying to think how to accomplish. He be using the very thing that be our problem—trade, and uses even that as a weapon to force their hand. He not be waiting to try to reason with them. He has simply put a knife to their throats. If they start falling to him, he could very well soon have the whole of the Midlands in his fist. The important lands, anyway."

"And with them all joined with D'Hara, as one force, one command," Zedd said, "it could be a force that could stand against the Order." He turned to Kahlan. "Is there any more?"

She nodded. "A bit. 'Though I fear greatly for my heart, I fear, too, the results should I fail to act, for the shadow of tyranny that will forever darken the world. If we don't do this, then Ebinissia's fate will have been only the beginning.

" 'I will put my faith in your love, though I can't help fearing this test of it.

" 'Though I am surrounded by bodyguards, and one has already laid down her life for me, their presence is not what I need to feel secure. You all must return to Aydindril at once. Do not delay. Gratch will keep you safe from the mriswith until you are with me. Signed, yours in this world, and those beyond, Richard Rahl, Master of D'Hara.' "

Zedd whistled through his teeth again. "Master of D'Hara. What has that boy done?"

Kahlan lowered the letter in her trembling hands. "He has destroyed me, that is what he has done."

Adie lifted a thin finger in her direction. "Now, you listen to me, Mother Confessor. Richard knows very well what he be doing to you, and has laid his heart open to you for it. He told you that he writes that letter under the image of Magda Searus because he be pained by what he must do, and understands what it means to you. He would rather lose your heart than let you be killed by what will come if he bows to the past instead of minding the future. He has done what we could not do. We would be begging for unity, he has demanded it, and put teeth to the demand. If you wish to truly be the Mother Confessor, and put the safety of your people above all else, then you will help Richard."

Zedd lifted an eyebrow, but remained silent.

At the name, Gratch spoke up. "Grrratch luuug Raaaach aaarg."

Kahlan wiped a tear from her cheek and sniffled. "I love Richard, too."

"Kahlan," Zedd said, reassuringly, "just as the spell will be removed from you in time, I'm sure that you will once again be the Mother Confessor."

"You don't understand," she said, holding back the tears. "For thousands of years a Mother Confessor has always protected the Midlands through the alliance. I will be the Mother Confessor who failed the Midlands."

Zedd shook his head. "No. You will be the Mother Confessor who had the strength to save the people of the Midlands."

She put a hand to her heart. "I'm not so sure."

Zedd stepped closer. "Kahlan, Richard is the Seeker of Truth. He carries the Sword of Truth. I am the one who named him. As First Wizard, I recognized him as the one with the instincts of the Seeker.

"He is acting on those instincts. Richard is a rare person. He reacts as the Seeker, and with the use of the gift. He is doing what he thinks he must. We must put our faith in him, even if we don't fully understand why he is doing what he is doing. Bags, he may not even fully understand why he's doing what he is doing."

"Read the letter again to yourself," Adie said. "Listen to his words with your heart and you will feel his heart in them. And remember, too, that there may be things he didn't dare to put on the paper in case it be captured."

Kahlan wiped the back of her hand across her nose. "I know it sounds selfish, but that's not it. I am the Mother Confessor; a trust has been passed down to me from all those who have gone before me. When I was chosen, that trust was put into my hands. It became my responsibility. When I ascended to Mother Confessor, I swore oaths."

With a bony finger, Zedd lifted her chin. "An oath to protect your people. There is no sacrifice too great for that."

"Maybe so. I will think on it." Besides her tears, Kahlan fought to keep down the hackles of anger. "I love Richard, but I would never do something like this to him. I just don't think he understands what he is doing to me—to the Mother Confessors before me who have given their lives."

"I think he does," Adie said in a soft rasp.

Zedd's face suddenly went nearly as white as his hair. "Bags," he whispered. "You don't think Richard would be foolish enough to go into the Keep, do you?"

Kahlan's head came up. "There are spells to protect the Keep. Richard doesn't know how to use his magic. He won't know how to get past them."

Zedd leaned closer to her. "You said he has Subtractive Magic, in addition to his Additive. The spells are Additive. If Richard has any use of his Subtractive, he will be able to walk right through even the most powerful of the spells I put on the Keep."

Kahlan gasped. "He told me that at the Palace of the Prophets he was able to simply walk through all the shields because they were Additive. The only one that stopped him was the perimeter shield and that was because it had Subtractive, too."

"If that boy goes into the Keep, there are things in there that could kill him in a heartbeat. That's why we put shields there—so no one can get near them. Bags, there are shields that even I have not dared pass through. For someone that doesn't know what he's doing, that place is a death trap."

Zedd grabbed her by the shoulders. "Kahlan, do you think he would go into the Keep?"

"I don't know, Zedd. You practically raised him. You would know better than I."

"He wouldn't go in there. He knows how dangerous magic can be. He's a smart boy."

"Unless he wants something."

He peered at her with one eye. "Wants something? What do you mean?"

Kahlan wiped the last of the tears from her cheek. "Well, when we were with the Mud People, he wanted a gathering. The Bird Man warned him that it would be dangerous. An owl brought a spirit message. It hit him right in the head, cut his scalp, and then dropped to the ground dead. The Bird Man said it was a dire warning from the spirits of the danger to Richard. Richard called the gathering anyway. That was when Darken Rahl came back from the underworld. If Richard wants something, nothing will stop him."

Zedd winced. "But he doesn't want anything right now. He has no need to go in there."

"Zedd, you know Richard. He likes to learn things. He may decide to just go have a peek, out of curiosity."

"A peek can be just as deadly."

"He said in the letter that one of his guards was killed." Kahlan frowned. "In fact, he said 'she.' Why would his guard be a woman?"

Zedd flailed his arms impatiently. "I don't know. What were you going to say about the guard being killed?"

"For all we know, it could be that someone from the Order is already in the Keep, and killed her by using magic from the Keep. Or, it could be that he fears the mriswith want to take the Keep, and he will go there to try to protect it."

Zedd ran a thumb down his smooth jaw. "He has no idea of the dangers in Aydindril, but worse, he has no inkling of the deadly nature of the things in the Keep. I remember telling him one time that objects of magic, like the Sword of Truth, and books, were kept there. I never thought to say many were dangerous."

Kahlan clutched his arm. "Books? You told him that there were books there?"

Zedd grunted. "Big mistake."

Kahlan let out a sigh. "I should say so."

Zedd threw his arms up. "We have to get to Aydindril at once!" He gripped Kahlan by her shoulders. "Richard doesn't have control of his gift. If the Order uses magic to take the Keep, Richard won't be able to stop them. We could lose this war before we have a chance to fight back."

Kahlan's fists tightened. "I can't believe it. We've spent weeks running from Aydindril, and now we have to run back there. It will take weeks more."

"The sun has already set on the days we made those choices. We must concentrate on what we can do tomorrow; we can't relive yesterday."

Kahlan eyed Gratch. "Richard sent us a letter. We can send him one back, and warn him."

"That won't help him hold the Keep should they use magic."

Kahlan's head was spinning with fragments of thoughts and

hurried solutions. "Gratch, could you carry one of us back to Richard?"

Gratch eyed each of them, his gaze lingering on the wizard. At last, he shook his head.

Kahlan chewed her lower lip in frustration. Zedd paced back and forth before the fire, muttering to himself. Adie stared off in thought. Kahlan suddenly gasped.

"Zedd! Could you use magic?"

Zedd halted his pacing and looked up. "What sort of magic?"

"Like you did with the wagon today. Lifting it with magic."

"I can't fly, dear one. Just lift things."

"But could you make us lighter, like the wagon, so that Gratch could then carry us?"

Zedd twisted up his wrinkled face. "No. It would be too hard to maintain the effort. It works on spiritless things, like rocks or wagons, but it's altogether another matter to do it to living things. I could lift us all up a bit, but only for a few minutes."

"Could you do it for just yourself? Could you make yourself light enough so that Gratch could carry you?"

Zedd brightened. "Yes, perhaps. It would take a great effort to maintain it for that much time, but I think I might be able to do it."

"Could you do it, too, Adie?"

Adie sagged in her chair. "No. I do not have the power he does. I could not do it."

Kahlan swallowed back her apprehension. "Then you have to go, Zedd. You can get to Aydindril weeks before we could travel there. Richard needs you right now. We can't wait. Every minute's delay is a danger to our side."

Zedd threw his skinny arms up. "I can't leave you defenseless!"

"I have Adie."

"What if the mriswith come, as Richard is worried about? Then you wouldn't have Gratch. Adie can't help with a mriswith."

Kahlan clutched his black sleeve. "If Richard goes in the Keep, he could be killed. If the Order gets the Wizard's Keep, and the magic in it, then we are all dead. This is more important than my life. This is about what happened to everyone in Ebinissia. If we let them win, then a great many will die, and the living will be condemned to slavery. Magic will be extinguished. This is a battle decision.

"Besides, no mriswith has come yet. Just because they've

attacked Aydindril, that doesn't mean they will attack anywhere else. Anyway, the spell hides my identity. No one knows the Mother Confessor is alive, or that I am she. They have no reason to come after me."

"Flawless logic. I can see why you were chosen as the Mother Confessor. But I still think it's foolhardy." Zedd appealed to the sorceress. "What do you think?"

"I think the Mother Confessor be right. We must consider what be the most important action we can take. We must not risk everyone for a danger to a few."

Kahlan stood before Gratch. With the way he was squatting down, she was eye to eye with him. "Gratch, Richard is in great danger." Gratch's tufted ears twitched. "He needs Zedd to help him. And you too. I'll be safe enough; no mriswith have been here. Can you get Zedd to Aydindril? He's a wizard and can make himself easy for you to carry. Will you do it for me? For Richard?"

Gratch's glowing eyes moved among the three of them, considering. At last he rose. His leathery wings spread as he nodded. Kahlan hugged the gar, and he returned the tender embrace.

"Are you tired, Gratch? Do you want to rest, or can you leave right now?"

Gratch flapped his wings in answer.

In growing alarm, Zedd looked from one to the other. "Bags. This is the most foolish thing I've ever done. If I was meant to fly, I'd have been born a bird."

Kahlan offered a weak smile. "Jebra said she had a vision of you with wings."

Zedd planted his fists on his bony hips. "She also said she saw me being dropped into a ball of fire." He tapped his foot. "All right. Let's get going, then."

Adie stood to seize him in a hug. "You be a brave old fool."

Zedd grumbled in disgust. "Fool, indeed." He finally returned the embrace. He let out a sudden yelp when she pinched his bottom.

"You look handsome in your fine robes, old man."

Zedd was overcome with a helpless grin. "Well, I guess I do." A frown returned. "A little anyway. Take care of the Mother Confessor. When Richard finds out I left her to make her own way back, he may do more than pinch me."

Kahlan threw her arms around the skinny wizard, feeling suddenly forsaken. Zedd was Richard's grandfather, and it had made her feel at least a little better having that much of Richard with her.

When they parted, Zedd cast a wincing glance to the gar. "Well, Gratch, I guess we had best be on our way."

In the cold night air, Kahlan caught the wizard's sleeve. "Zedd, you have to talk some sense into Richard." Her voice heated. "He can't do this to me. He's being unreasonable."

Zedd studied her face in the dim light. He spoke softly, at last. "History is rarely made by reasonable men."

CHAPTER 35

"DON'T TOUCH ANYTHING," RICHARD reminded them again as he scowled over his shoulder. "I mean it."

The three Mord-Sith didn't answer. They turned to look up at the high ceiling of the arched entry and then at the huge, intricately joined blocks of dark granite just inside the raised, massive portcullis marking the entrance to the Wizard's Keep.

Richard glanced back past Ulic and Egan, to the wide road that had led them up the mountainside and at last over a stone bridge two hundred and fifty paces long that spanned a chasm with near vertical sides that dropped away for what seemed thousands of feet. He wasn't sure of the full depth of the yawning abyss because in the far distance below, clouds hugging the ice-slicked walls obscured the bottom. Walking over the bridge and looking down into that dark, jagged maw made him dizzy and light-headed. He couldn't imagine how the stone bridge could have been erected over such an obstacle.

Unless one had wings, there was but this single way into the Keep.

Lord Rahl's official escort of five hundred men waited back on the other side of the bridge. They had intended to come with him into the Keep until they had reached that spot, having just rounded a switchback, and every eye, including his, had looked up at the vastness of the Keep, its soaring walls of dark stone, its ramparts, bastions, towers, connecting passageways, and bridges, all of which presented an unmistakable sensation of sinister menace jutting from the stone of the mountain, somehow looking alive, as if it were watching them. Richard's knees had gone weak at the sight, and when he ordered them to wait there, none had raised so much as a single word of protest.

It had taken considerable will for Richard to force himself to go on, but the idea of all those men seeing their Lord Rahl, their wizard, balk at going into the Wizard's Keep kept his feet moving when he would have wished otherwise. Besides, he needed to do this. Richard summoned courage by remembering Kahlan telling him that the Keep was protected by spells, and that there were places even she couldn't go because those spells so sapped one of courage that they couldn't proceed. That's all it was, he assured himself, just a spell to keep the curious away, only a feeling, and not a real threat.

"It's warm here," Raina said, her dark eyes looking about in astonishment.

Richard realized she was right. Once they were beyond the iron portcullis, the air had lost its chill with each step, until it was like a fine spring day inside. The somber, steel gray sky into which the sheer mountainside ascended above the Keep, and bitter wind on the road up, held no hint of spring, though.

The snow on his boots was beginning to melt. They all took off their heavy mantles and tossed them in a pile to the side, against the stone wall. Richard checked that his sword was clear in its scabbard.

The towering, arched opening they passed beneath was a good fifty feet long. Richard saw that it was merely a breach in the outer wall. Beyond, the road continued through an open area before tunneling into the base of a high stone wall and disappearing into the gloom beyond. Probably just went to the stables, he told himself. No reason to go in there.

Richard had to resist the urge to shroud himself in his black mriswith cape and become invisible. He had been doing that more and more of late, finding comfort not only in the solitude it provided, but in an odd, indefinably pleasurable sensation it invoked, almost like the reassurance of the magic of the sword at his hip, always there, always at his beck and call, always his ally and champion.

All around, intricate junctures of masonry walls created of the bleak courtyard a craggy canyon, its walls dotted by a number of doors. Richard chose to follow a stepping-stone path through the gravel of granite fragments, to the largest of the doors.

Berdine suddenly clutched his arm so hard he winced in pain, turning away from the door to pry off her fingers.

"Berdine," he said, "what are you doing? What's the matter?"

He extricated his arm from her grasp, but she grabbed it again. "Look," she finally said in a tone of voice that made the hair at the back of his neck stand on end. "What do you suppose that is?"

Everyone turned to see where she pointed with her Agiel.

Rock fragments and stones rolled in waves, as if some huge stone fish swam beneath their surface. As the unseen thing underneath came closer, they all inched toward the center of their stepping-stone. The gravel crunched and gnashed as it undulated in waves, like water in a lake.

Berdine's grasp on his arm tightened painfully as the crest of the waves approached. Even Ulic and Egan gasped with the rest of them as it seemed to pass beneath the stepping-stones under their feet, the waves lapping stone chips up onto the rocks upon which they stood. Once beyond, the rolling movement of the gravel abated until all was still.

"All right, just what was that?" Berdine blurted out. "And what would have happened to us if we had gone a different way, to one of the other doors, instead of along the only path to this one?"

"How should I know?"

She blinked up at him. "You're a wizard. You're supposed to know these things."

Berdine would have fought Ulic and Egan by herself, without a second thought, if he were to command it, but unseen magic was something altogether different. All five of them were fearless against steel, but none of them were the least bit shy about letting him see their anxiety toward magic. They had explained it to him any number of times: they were the steel against steel, so that he could be the magic against magic.

"Look, all of you, I've told you before that I don't know very much about being a wizard. I've never been to this place before. I don't know anything about it. I don't know how to protect you. Now, will you do as I asked, and wait with the soldiers on the other side of the bridge? Please?"

Ulic and Egan folded their arms in mute reply.

"We're going with you," Cara insisted.

"That's right," Raina added.

"You can't stop us," Berdine said as she finally released his arm.

"But it could be dangerous!"

"And we must protect you," Berdine said.

Richard scowled down at her. "How? By squeezing the blood out of my arm?"

Berdine turned red. "Sorry."

"Look, I don't know about the magic here. I don't know the dangers, much less how to stop them."

"That is why we must go," Cara explained with exaggerated patience. "You don't know how to protect yourself. We might be of help. Who's to say that an Agiel—" She lifted a thumb to Ulic and Egan. "—or muscles, aren't what will be needed? What if you fall down a simple hole with no ladder, and there is no one to hear you call for help? You could be hurt by something not magic, you know."

Richard sighed. "Well, all right. I guess you have a point." He shook a finger at her. "But if you get your foot bitten off by some stone fish or something, don't you complain to me about it."

The three women grinned in satisfaction. Even Ulic and Egan smiled. Richard let out a weary sigh.

"Come on, then."

He turned toward the twelve-foot-tall door set back in an alcove. The wood was gray and weathered, and spanned with simple but massive iron straps spiked on with cut nails as big as his fingers. Above the door, words were carved in the stone lintel, but they were in a language none of them could understand. As

Richard reached for the lever, the door began to move inward on silent hinges.

"And he says he doesn't know how to use his magic," Berdine mocked.

Richard checked the resolve in their eyes one last time. "Remember, don't touch anything." They nodded. He heaved a resigned sigh and turned toward the doorway, scratching the back of his neck.

"Didn't the unguent I brought rid you of your rash?" Cara asked as they stepped through the doorway into the cheerless room beyond. It smelled of damp stone.

"No. Not yet, anyway."

Inside the vast entry chamber their voices echoed off the beamed ceiling, which was some thirty feet high. Richard slowed as he peered around the near empty room and came to a halt.

"The woman I bought it from promised me it would cure your rash. She said it was made with the usual, common ingredients, like white rhubarb, juice of laurel, butter, and soft-boiled egg, but when I told her that it was most important, she added some special, costly elements. She said she put in betony, pig's ulcer, a swallow's heart, and because I am your protector, she had me bring her my moon blood. She stirred it in with a red hot nail. I stayed and watched, just to make sure."

"I wish you had told me this before I'd used it," Richard muttered as he started ahead into the gloomy chamber.

"What?" He waved off her question. "Well, I warned her that it had better work, for the amount I paid, and told her that if it didn't, I would be back and she would rue the day she failed. She promised it would work. You did remember to put some on your left heel, like I told you, didn't you?"

"No, I just put in on the rash." Now he wished he hadn't.

Cara threw her hands up. "Well, no wonder. I told you that you had to put it on your left heel, too. The woman said the rash was probably a disruption in the basing of your aura, and you had to put it on your heel, too, to complete the connection to the earth."

Richard only half listened to her; he knew she was merely trying to find courage in the sound of her own voice, by keeping the subject mundane.

High overhead to their right, a row of small windows poured long slanting shafts of daylight across the room. Ornately carved wooden chairs stood watch to each side of an arched opening at the far end. Beneath the row of windows hung a tapestry, its image too faded to be discerned. The opposite wall held a row of candles in simple iron sconces. A heavy trestle table sat near the center of the room, bathed in a brilliant shaft of light. The room was otherwise bare.

They crossed the floor, accompanied by the echoes of the sounds of their boots on the tiles. Richard saw that there were books on the table. His hopes elevated; books were why he had come. It could be weeks yet before Kahlan and Zedd made it back, and he feared that he might need to take action to protect the Keep before then. He was becoming restive and worried while he waited.

With the D'Haran army holding Aydindril, his biggest threat right now was an assault to seize the Keep. He hoped to find books that might impart some knowledge, maybe even tell him how to use some of his magic, so that if someone with magic attacked, he might gain a key to warding them off. He feared the Order would try to snatch some of the magic preserved in the Keep. Mriswith, too, were in his thoughts.

There were nearly a dozen books on the table, all the same size. The words on the covers were not in a language he could understand. Ulic and Egan stood with their backs to the table while Richard slid some of the books aside with a finger to better see ones underneath. Something looked familiar about them.

"They look like the same book, but in different languages," he remarked, half to himself.

He turned around one that caught his eye so he could look at the title, and suddenly realized that though he couldn't read it, he had seen the language before, and he recognized two of the words. The first, *fuer*, and the third, *ost*, were words he knew only too well. The title was in High D'Haran.

A prophecy that Warren had shown him in the vaults at the Palace of the Prophets had referred to Richard, calling him *fuer grissa ost drauka*: the bringer of death. The first word in this title, *fuer*, meant "the," and the third, *ost*, meant "of."

"Fuer Ulbrecken ost Brennika Dieser." Richard let out a frustrated sigh. "I wish I knew what it meant."

"*The Adventures of Bonnie Day.* I think."

Richard turned to see Berdine looking past his shoulder at the table. She stepped back, her blue eyes glancing away as if she thought she had done something wrong.

"What did you say," he whispered.

Berdine pointed at the book on the table. "*Fuer Ulbrecken ost Brennika Dieser.* You said you wished to know what it meant. I think it means *The Adventures of Bonnie Day.* It's an old dialect."

The Adventures of Bonnie Day was a book Richard had owned since his early youth. It had been his favorite book, and he had read it so often he practically knew it by heart.

Only after going to the Palace of the Prophets in the Old World had he discovered that the book had been written by Nathan Rahl, a prophet and Richard's ancestor. Nathan had written the book as a primer on prophecy, he said, and had given it to boys who had potential. Nathan had told Richard that with the exception of Richard, all who had possessed the book had met with fatal accidents.

When Richard was born, the Prelate and Nathan had come to the New World and stolen the Book of Counted Shadows from the Keep in order to prevent it from falling into Darken Rahl's hands. They gave it to Richard's stepfather, George Cypher, and extracted his promise to make Richard memorize the entire book, word for word, and then destroy it. The Book of Counted Shadows was needed in order to open the Boxes of Orden, back in D'Hara. Richard still knew that book by heart—every word.

Richard remembered fondly the happy times of his youth, living at home with his father and brother. He had loved his older brother, and looked up to him. Who knew then the treacherous turns life would take? There was no going back to those innocent times.

Nathan had also left behind a copy of *The Adventures of Bonnie Day* for him. He must have also left these copies, in other languages, here at the Keep when he had been here right after Richard had been born.

"How do you know what it says?" Richard asked.

Berdine swallowed. "It's in High D'Haran, but an old dialect of the tongue."

Richard realized, by the way her eyes had gone wide, that he must have a frightening look on his face. He put in an effort to smooth his features.

"You mean to say that you understand High D'Haran?" She

nodded. "I was told that it's a dead language. A scholar I know who could understand High D'Haran told me that almost no one anymore knows it. How do you?"

"From my father," she said. The emotion left her voice. "It was one of the reasons Darken Rahl chose me to be Mord-Sith." Her face had gone emotionless, too. "Few people still understood High D'Haran. My father was one of them. Darken Rahl used High D'Haran to work some of his magic, and he didn't like that there were others who knew the old tongue."

Richard didn't have to ask what had happened to her father.

"I'm sorry, Berdine."

He knew that in their training, those forced into the bondage of becoming Mord-Sith were compelled to torture their fathers to death. It was called the third breaking, their final test.

She showed no reaction. She had retreated behind the iron mask of her training. "Darken Rahl knew that my father had taught me some of the old tongue, but being Mord-Sith, I was no threat to him. He consulted with me, on occasion, to hear my interpretation of various words. High D'Haran is a difficult language to translate. Many words, especially in the older dialects, have shades of meaning that can only be understood by their context. I am no expert, by any means, but I understand some. Darken Rahl was a master at High D'Haran."

"And do you know the meaning of *fuer grissa ost drauka*?"

"A very ancient dialect. I'm not terribly well versed in versions that old." She thought a moment. "I think the literal translation is 'the bringer of death.' Where did you hear this?"

He didn't want to think of the complications of the other meanings at the moment. "An old prophecy. It gives me this name."

Berdine clasped her hands behind her back. "Unfairly, Lord Rahl. Unless it is in reference to your skill at handling your enemies, not your friends."

Richard smiled. "Thank you, Berdine."

Her smile returned, like the sun from behind fading storm clouds.

"Let's go see what else we can find of interest in here," he said, heading for the arched opening at the far end of the chamber.

As he went through the doorway, Richard felt a tingling, tickling sensation pass across his flesh in a razor's-edge line. Once beyond the opening, it was gone. He turned when he heard Raina call his name.

The rest of them, on the other side, pressed their hands up against the air as if it were a sheet of impenetrable glass. Ulic beat his fist against it, but to no avail.

"Lord Rahl!" Cara called out. "How do we pass through?"

Richard returned to the doorway. "I'm not sure. I have magic that allows me to pass shields. Here, Berdine, give me your hand. See if that will work."

He stuck his hand back through the invisible barrier, and she gripped his wrist without hesitation. Slowly, he pulled her hand toward him until it penetrated the shield.

"Oh, that's cold," she complained.

"You all right? You want to try the rest of the way?"

When she nodded, he pulled her on. Once through, she shuddered and shook herself as if she were crawling with bugs.

Cara put her hand out toward the doorway. "Now me."

Richard began to reach for her, but stopped. "No. The rest of you wait here until we come back."

"What!" Cara shrieked. "You have to take us with you!"

"There are dangers I know nothing about. I can't be watching out for all of you and at the same time pay attention to what I'm doing. Berdine is enough in case I need protection. The rest of you wait here. If anything happens, you know how to get out."

"But you have to take us," Cara pleaded. "We can't leave you without protection." She turned. "Tell him, Ulic."

"She's right, Lord Rahl. We should be with you."

Richard shook his head. "One is enough. If something happened to me, then you wouldn't be able to get back out through the shield. If anything happens, and we don't return, I'm depending on you to carry on. If anything happens, you are in charge, Cara. If anything happens, get help for us, if you can. If you can't, well, take care of things until my grandfather Zedd and Kahlan get here."

"Don't do this!" Cara looked more distraught than he had ever seen her. "Lord Rahl, we can't afford to lose you."

"Cara, it will be all right. We'll be back, I promise. Wizards always keep their promises."

Cara huffed in anger. "Why her?"

Berdine flipped her brown braid back over her shoulder as she flashed Cara a self-satisfied smile. "Because Lord Rahl likes me best."

"Cara," Richard said as he scowled at Berdine, "it's because you're the leader. If anything happens to me, I want you to be in charge."

Cara stood a moment, considering. A self-satisfied smile of her own finally spread on her lips. "All right. But you better never pull a trick like this again."

Richard winked at her. "If you say so." He looked up the gloomy corridor. "Come on, Berdine. Let's go have a look around so we can finish and get out of this place."

CHAPTER 36

PASSAGEWAYS RAN IN EVERY direction. Richard tried to keep to what he thought was the main one so that he could find his way out. As they passed rooms, he stuck his head in to see if there were any books or anything else that might be helpful. Most were simple, empty stone rooms. A few had tables and chairs, with chests or other plain furniture, but nothing of particular interest. One whole hall had rooms with beds. The wizards who stayed at the Keep must have lived unassuming lives, at least some of them. There were thousands of rooms and he had seen only a few.

Berdine peeked past him whenever he looked into a room, to see what he was seeing. "Do you know where we are going?"

"Not exactly." He glanced off down another side hall. The place was a labyrinth. "But I think we should find some stairs. Start at the bottom and work our way up."

She pointed back over her shoulder. "I saw some down a hall to our left, just back there."

The stairs were where she said they would be. He hadn't noticed them because it was just a hole in the floor with spiral stone steps descending down into darkness, and he had been looking for a stairwell. Richard reprimanded himself for not thinking to bring a lamp, or candle. He had a flint and steel in his pocket, and guessed that if he could find some straw or old cloth, he could get a small flame going and light one of the candles he had seen in iron sconces.

As they descended into the darkness, Richard felt, as well as heard, a low hum coming from below. The stone, which had been disappearing in darkness, began to reveal itself in a bluish green light, as if someone were turning up the wick on a lamp. By the time they reached the bottom of the steps, he could see clearly in the eerie light.

Just around the corner at the bottom of the steps, he found the source of the light. In a ringed iron bracket sat a globe, about as wide as his hand, and looking to be glass. It was the origin of the light.

Berdine looked up at him, her face outlined in the strange illumination. "What makes it glow?"

"Well, there's no flame, so I would guess it has to be magic."

Richard cautiously reached toward the light. It brightened. He touched a finger to it, and the bluish green cast changed to a warmer yellow color.

Since touching it seemed to cause no harm, Richard carefully lifted it from the bracket. It was heavier than he expected. Rather than being a hollow sphere of blown glass, it seemed to be solid. In his hand, it threw off a warm, useful light.

Richard could see that far off down the tunnel-like hall there were other such spheres in brackets. In the distance, the closest barely glowed with bluish green light. As they passed them, each brightened at his approach, and dimmed as he moved on with the one he had taken.

At an intersection, the hall joined a wider, more welcoming corridor. Light pink stone ran in a band down both sides, and at places the passageway opened into cavernous rooms with padded benches.

Opening the wide, double doorways in one of the corridor's big rooms, he discovered a library. The library looked cozy and inviting with its polished wood floor, paneled walls, and white-washed ceiling. There were tables beside the rows of shelves, and comfortable-looking chairs. Glassed windows at the far side overlooked the city of Aydindril and made the room bright and airy.

He moved on to the next cavernous chamber in the hall, and discovered that it, too, had a library off of it. It appeared that the corridor ran parallel to the face of the Keep, and along a whole row of libraries. They found another two dozen of the huge library rooms by the time they reached the end of the corridor.

Richard had never imagined that this many books existed. Even the vaults at the Palace of the Prophets, with all the books it held, seemed sparse to him after seeing this many volumes. It would take a year just to read all the titles. He felt suddenly overwhelmed. Where was he to start?

"This must be what you were looking for," she said.

Richard frowned. "No, it's not. I don't know why, but this isn't it. This is too ordinary."

Berdine walked beside him as they moved on through passageways and down several stories when they came to a stairwell, her Agiel swinging on the chain at her wrist, and ever at the ready. At the bottom of the stairs stood an ornate, gold-leafed doorframe before a chamber beyond that, rather than stonework, had been excavated from inky rock, perhaps once a cave that had been enlarged. In places where the rock had been broken away, it left behind glossy, sharp facets. Fat columns looked to have been left in places as the rock had been carved out in order to support a low, craggy ceiling.

At the gold doorway Richard encountered a shield for the fourth time since he had entered the Keep, but this was different than the first three. The first three all had the same feel; this was nothing like the others. As he put his hand through, the vertical plane between the doorframe glowed red from no visible source, and the sensation, instead of the tingling, was hot where the red light touched him. It was the most uncomfortable shield he had ever felt. He feared it might singe the hair off his arm, but it didn't.

Richard pulled his arm back. "This one is different. If it's more than you want to do, you stop me." He put his arms around Berdine to better protect her. She tensed. "Don't worry, I'll stop if you want me to."

She nodded, and he shuffled into the doorway. When the red light touched the red leather on her arm, she flinched. "It's all right," she said. "Keep going." He pulled her through, and released her. Only after he took his arms from around her did she seem to relax.

The glow of the sphere Richard held out cast sharp shadows among the columns, and he could see that there were small recesses carved in the stone all around the room. At the wall around the edge of the room, there were perhaps sixty or seventy such niches. Though he couldn't make out what was in them, he could tell that each held objects of different sizes and shapes.

Richard felt the hairs on the back of his neck stiffen as his gaze swept over the nooks from a distance. He didn't know what the things were, but he instinctively knew that they were more than dangerous.

"Stay close to me," he told her. "We want to stay away from the walls." He pointed with his chin across the vast room. "Over there. That passageway is where we want to go."

"How do you know?"

"Look at the floor." The rough, natural stone was worn smooth in a winding track cutting across the center of the chamber. "We'd better stay on this path."

Her blue eyes glanced up in unease. "You be careful. If anything happens to you I'll never get out of this place to get help from the others. I'll be trapped down here."

Richard smiled and then started out across the dead silent cavern. "Well, that's the risk you take for being my favorite."

Her unease didn't diminish at his attempt to lighten the mood. "Lord Rahl, do you really think that I believe I am your favorite."

Richard checked that they were still on the path. "Berdine, I only said that because it's what you always say."

She thought in silence as they moved cautiously across the room. "Lord Rahl, may I ask you a question? A serious question? A personal question?"

"Sure."

She pulled her wavy brown braid over her shoulder and held on to it. "When you marry your queen, you will still have other women, won't you?"

Richard frowned down at her. "I don't have other women now. I love Kahlan. I'm loyal in my love to her."

"But you are the Lord Rahl. You can have any you wish. Even me. That is what the Lord Rahl does; he has many women. You have but to snap your fingers."

Richard got the distinct impression that she was definitely not making an offer. "Is this about when I put my hand on you, on your breast?" She glanced away and nodded. "Berdine, I did that to help you, not because . . . well, not because of anything else. I hoped you would know that."

She quickly laid a concerned hand on his arm. "I do know. That's not what I mean. You've never touched me in the other way. What I mean is that you never make those requirements of me." She chewed her lower lip. "The way you put your hand on me has me feeling very ashamed."

"Why?"

"Because you risked your life to help me. You are my Lord Rahl, and I have not been honest with you."

Richard gestured, guiding them on the path around a column twenty men couldn't have held hands around. "You're getting me confused, Berdine."

"Well, I say that I am your favorite so that you will not think I don't like you."

"You are trying to say you don't like me?"

She clutched his arm again. "Oh no. I love you."

"Berdine, I told you I have—"

"Not like that. I mean I love you as my Lord Rahl. You have freed me. You have seen that I am more than simply Mord-Sith, and you have trusted me. You saved my life and returned me to whole. I love you for the kind of Lord Rahl you are."

Richard shook his head as if to clear it. "You're not making any sense. What does this have to do with you always saying that you're my favorite."

"I say that so you won't think I wouldn't willingly go to your bed if asked. I feared that if you knew that I didn't want to, then you would force me, to be perverse."

Richard held the light out as they reached the passageway leading from the room. It looked a simple block hall. "Stop fretting about it." He motioned her onward. "I've told you I wouldn't."

"I know. And after what you did—" She touched her left breast.

"—I believe you. But I didn't before. I'm beginning to see that you really are different in more ways than a few."

"Different from who?"

"Darken Rahl."

"Well, you're right about that." As they walked on down the long hall, again he suddenly looked at her. "Are you trying to tell me that you're in love with someone, and you have only been saying those things to me so that I wouldn't think you were trying to avoid my affections, and therefore wouldn't be provoked to force you?"

Her fist tightened on her braid as her blue eyes closed for a moment. "Yes."

"Really? I think that's wonderful, Berdine." At the end of the hall, they came to a broad room, the walls lined with bundled tufts of fur and hair hanging from framed panels. Richard studied the displays from a distance. He recognized one tuft as gar fur.

Richard looked over as he started out again and grinned. "Who is it?" He waved his hand, feeling a sudden flush of embarrassment that, considering her odd mood at the moment, he might be overstepping his bounds. "Unless you don't want to tell me. You don't have to tell me. I don't want you to feel you have to. It's your business, if you choose."

Berdine swallowed. "Because of the things you have done for us, for me, I wish to confess."

Richard made a face. "Confess? Telling me who you're in love with isn't a confession, it's—"

"Raina."

Richard's mouth snapped shut. He looked back to the way they were going. "Green tiles, left foot only. Right foot only on the white ones, until we cross this space. Don't skip a green or white tile. Touch the pedestal before you step from the last tile."

She followed him as he stepped carefully from the green to the white tiles until they had reached the stone floor on the other side, touched the pedestal, and moved into a tall, narrow corridor of sparkling silver stone, like a cleft in a huge jewel.

"How did you know that—the green-tile-white-tile business?"

"What?" He glanced back with a frown. "I don't know. It must have been a shield or something." He looked back to her as she walked with her eyes on the floor. "Berdine, I love Raina, too. And Cara, and you, and Ulic and Egan. Kind of like family. Is that what you mean?" She shook her head without looking up. "But . . . Raina is a woman."

Berdine shot him a cool scowl.

"Berdine," he said after a long silence, "you had better not tell Raina this or—"

"Raina loves me, too."

Richard straightened, not knowing quite what to say. "But how can . . . you can't . . . I don't see . . . Berdine, why are you telling me this?"

"Because you have always been honest with us. At first, when you told us things, we thought you would not do as you said. Well, not all of us. Cara has always believed you, but I did not."

Her expression slipped back to the distant countenance of a Mord-Sith. "When Darken Rahl was our Lord Rahl, he found out, and he ordered me to his bed. He laughed at me. He . . . liked to take me to his bed because he knew. It was his way of humiliating me. I thought that if you knew, too, you would do the same, so I tried to hide it from you by making you think I fancied you."

Richard shook his head. "Berdine, I wouldn't do that to you."

"I know that, now. That is why I had to confess to you, because you've always been honest with me, but I was not honest with you."

Richard shrugged. "Well, then I'm glad you feel better." He thought as he turned her down a winding hall of plastered walls. "Did Darken Rahl make you this way, by choosing you to become a Mord-Sith? Is that what made you hate men?"

She frowned up at him. "I do not hate men. I just, I don't know, I just always looked at girls from the time I was young. Boys didn't interest me in that way." She drew her hand down her braid. "Now you hate me?"

"No. No, I don't hate you, Berdine. You are my protector, the same as always. But can't you try to not think about her or something? It just isn't right."

She smiled distantly. "When Raina smiles at me in her special way, and the day is suddenly wonderful, it seems right. When she touches my face, and my heart races, it seems right. I know my heart is safe in her care." Her smile withered. "But now you think I am despicable."

Richard looked away, shame coming over him in a cold wave.

"That's the way I feel about Kahlan. One time, my grandfather said I should forget about her, but there was no way I could."

"Why would he say that?"

Richard couldn't tell her that it was because Kahlan was a Confessor, and Zedd was doing it for Richard's best interest; no one was supposed to be able to love a Confessor. He felt bad that he couldn't be honest with Berdine now. He shrugged. "He didn't think she was the one for me."

Richard pulled her through another of the tingly kind of shields when they reached the end of the hall. The triangular room had a bench. He sat her down beside him and set the glowing ball between them.

"Berdine, I think I can see how you feel. I know how I felt when my grandfather said I should forget Kahlan. No one else can tell you what to feel. You either do, or you don't. Though I don't understand or approve of this, all of you are becoming my friends. Being a friend means you don't have to be exactly alike, and you are still friends."

"Lord Rahl, I know that you can never accept me, but I had to tell you. Tomorrow, I will return to D'Hara. You should not have to have one you do not approve of as your guard."

Richard thought a minute. "Do you like boiled peas?"

Berdine frowned. "Yes."

"Well, I hate boiled peas. Does that make you like me any less, because I dislike something you like? Or make you want to abandon being my protector?"

She made a face. "Lord Rahl, this is different from boiled peas. How can you have faith in someone you do not approve of?"

"It's not that I don't approve of you, Berdine. It's just that to me it doesn't seem right. But it doesn't have to. Look, I had a friend when I was younger, another woods guide. Giles and I spent a lot of time together, because we had a lot in common.

"He fell in love with Lucy Fleckner. I hated Lucy Fleckner; she was cruel to Giles. I couldn't understand how he could care for her. I didn't like her, and I thought he should feel the same. I lost my friend because he couldn't be the way I thought he should be. I didn't lose him because of Lucy, I lost him because of me. I lost all the good things we had because I wasn't willing to let him be who he was. I've always regretted what I lost.

"I guess this is something like that. As you learn to be other than Mord-Sith, like I learned as I grew up, you'll find that being a friend is to like a person for who they are, even the parts you don't understand. The reasons you like them makes the things you don't understand unimportant. You don't have to understand, or do the same, or live their lives for them. If you truly care for them, then you want them to be who they are; that was why you liked them in the first place.

"I like you, Berdine, and that's all that matters."

"True?"

"True."

She put her arms around his neck and hugged him. "Thank you, Lord Rahl. After you saved me, I feared you would wish you hadn't. I'm glad I told you, now. Raina will be relieved to know you will not do to us as Darken Rahl did."

As they stood, a part of the stone wall slid to the side. Richard took her hand and led her from the odd room, through the new doorway, down a stairway and through a dank, wet room with a stone floor that mounded into a huge hump in the center.

"If we are becoming your friends, then I can tell you what you did that I don't like, what I don't approve of, and how you did a wrong?" Richard nodded. "I don't like what you did to Cara. She is angry at what you did to her."

Richard glanced back in the strange room that seemed to swallow the light. "Cara? Angry with me? What did I do to her?"

"You have treated her badly because of me." When Richard wrinkled his face in puzzlement, she went on. "When I was under that spell, and I threatened you with my Agiel after you came back from looking for Brogan, you became angry with all of us. You treated them like they had done it too, though it was only I."

"I didn't know what was going on. I felt threatened by Mord-Sith because of what you did. She should realize that."

"She does, but when you found out at last, and made me whole again, you never told Cara and Raina that you were wrong to treat them as if they had threatened you the same as I. They did not."

Richard felt his face flush in the darkness. "You're right. Now I feel terrible. Why didn't she say something?"

Berdine lifted an eyebrow. "You are Lord Rahl. If you decided to beat her because you did not like the way she said good morning, she would not say anything."

"Then why are you saying something?"

Berdine followed him into a strange corridor with a cobblestone floor only two feet wide and smooth, round, tubelike, walls covered completely in gold. "Because you are a friend."

As he looked over his shoulder and smiled his thanks, she reached out to touch the gold. Richard snatched her wrist before she could touch it. "Do that and you're dead."

She frowned at him. "Why do you tell us that you do not know anything about this place, and then you walk through it like you have lived here your whole life?"

Richard blinked at the question. His eyes suddenly went wide with the realization. "Because of you."

"Me!"

"Yes," Richard said in astonishment. "By talking to me, you distracted my conscious mind. You had me so intent on the things you were saying, and on thinking about them, that it let my gift guide me. I never even realized it as it was happening. Now that I've been through this way, I know the dangers and the way back. I can get back, now." He squeezed her shoulder. "Thank you, Berdine."

She grinned. "What are friends for?"

"I think we're through the worst. This way."

At the end of the gold tunnel was a round tower room at least a hundred feet across, with stairs spiraling up around the inside of the outer wall. At irregular intervals, small landings interrupted the steps at doors. In the gloomy expanse above, shafts of light pierced the darkness. Most of the windows above were small, but one looked huge. Richard couldn't tell for sure how far the tower rose, but it had to be close to two hundred feet. Below, the circular shaft descended into dank obscurity.

"I don't like the looks of it," Berdine said as she peered over the edge of the iron rail at the landing. "This looks like the worst of it to me."

Richard thought he saw something move in the murk below. "Stay close and keep your eyes open." He fixed his gaze on the spot where he thought he had seen movement, trying to see it again. "If anything happens, you have to try to get out."

Berdine glanced with disapproval over the railing. "Lord Rahl, it has taken us hours to get down here. We have been through more shields than I can remember. If anything happens to you, I am dead, too."

Richard considered his options. It might be better if he were cloaked in his mriswith cape. "You wait here. I'll go have a look."

Berdine snatched his shirt at his shoulder and yanked him around to face her fiery blue eyes. "No, you will not go alone."

"Berdine—"

"I am your protector. You will not go alone. Is that understood?"

She had that penetrating, iron look in her eyes that made his tongue fear a mistake. He finally let out a breath.

"All right. But you stay close and do as I say."

She cocked her head. "I always do as you say."

CHAPTER 37

AS HIS HORSE SWAYED under him, Tobias Brogan idly watched the Creator's five messengers walking not far ahead and off to one side. It was unusual to see them. Since they had unexpectedly appeared four days earlier, they were always around, but rarely seen, and even when they were visible they were still hard to see, being all white like the snow, or when it was dark, all black like the night. He marveled at the way they were able to simply vanish before his eyes. The Creator's power was indeed miraculous.

His choice of messengers, though, left Tobias uneasy. The Creator had told Tobias, in his dreams, not to question His plans and, thankfully, had finally accepted Tobias's supplications of forgiveness for the effrontery of an inquiry. All right-minded children feared the Creator, and Tobias Brogan was nothing if not right-minded. Still, the scaled creatures hardly seemed the appropriate choice to carry divine guidance.

He suddenly straightened in his saddle. Of course. The Creator wouldn't want to reveal His intentions to the profane by letting them see disciples who looked the part. Evil would expect the beauty and glory of the Creator to hound them, but would not be spooked to go to ground at the sight of disciples in this guise.

Tobias let out a relieved sigh as he watched the mriswith leaning in, conferring with one another, and with the sorceress, in whispers. She called herself a Sister of the Light, but she was still a sorceress, a *streganicha*, a witch. He could understand the Creator using the mriswith as messengers, but he couldn't understand why He would give *streganicha* such authority.

Tobias wished he knew what they had to talk about all the time. Ever since the *streganicha* had joined them the day before, she had kept company almost exclusively with the five scaled creatures, having precious few words for the lord general of the Blood of the Fold. The six of them kept to themselves, as if they only happened to be traveling the same direction as Tobias and his company of a thousand.

Tobias had seen but a handful of the mriswith dispatch hundreds of D'Haran soldiers, and so felt less uneasy about only having two fists of his men with him. The rest of his force of over a hundred thousand of the Fold waited a little more than a week out of Aydindril. Tobias had been told by the Creator, when He had come in a dream that first night with his army, that they were to remain behind, to participate in the conquest of Aydindril.

"Lunetta," he said in a quiet tone as he watched the Sister gesticulating in her conversation with the mriswith.

She stepped her horse closer to his right side. She took his cue and kept her voice low. "Yes, my lord general?"

"Lunetta, have you seen the Sister use her power?"

"Yes, Lord General, when she moved the windfall from our way."

"Could you tell her power from that?" Lunetta gave him a slight nod. "Does she have the power you do, my sister?"

"No, Tobias."

He smiled over at her. "That be good to know." He glanced around to make sure no one was near, and the six were still visible. "I am becoming puzzled by some of the things the Creator has been telling me in the last few nights."

"Do you wish to tell Lunetta?"

"Yes, but not now. We'll talk about it later."

She idly stroked her pretties. "Perhaps when we can be alone. It be time to stop soon."

Tobias didn't miss the demure smile, or the offer. "We'll not be stopping early tonight." He lifted his nose as he took a deep whiff of the cold air. "She's so close I can almost smell her."

Richard counted the landings on his way down so he would be able to find their way back. He thought he could remember the rest of it because of the sights along the way, but the inside of the tower was disorienting. It smelled of rot, like a deep bog, probably because water that came in the open windows collected in the bottom.

At the next landing platform, Richard saw a shimmering to the air as he approached. In the light coming from the globe he was holding, he could see something standing to the side. Its edges glowed in the humming light. Though the thing wasn't solid, he recognized it as a mriswith standing with its cape drawn around itself.

"Welcome, skin brother," it hissed.

Berdine flinched. "What was that?" she whispered urgently.

Richard caught hold of her wrist as she tried to put herself in front of him—she had her Agiel in her fist—and pulled her to the other side of him as he continued on. "It's just a mriswith."

"Mriswith!" she whispered in a hoarse tone. "Where?"

"Right here on the landing, by the rail. Don't be afraid, it won't hurt you."

She clutched his black cape after he forced down her arm with the Agiel. They stepped onto the landing.

"Have you come to wake the sliph?" the mriswith asked.

Richard frowned. "Sliph?"

The mriswith opened its cape to point with the three-bladed knife in its claw down the stairs. When it did so, it became solid and fully visible, a figure of dusky scales and cape. "The sliph is down there, skin brother." Its beady eyes came back up. "She is accessible, at last. Soon, it will be time for the *yabree* to sing."

"Yabree?"

The mriswith lifted its three-bladed knife and gave it a little wiggle. Its slit of a mouth widened into sort of a smile. "*Yabree.* When the *yabree* sing, it will be the time of the queen."

"The queen?"

"The queen needs you, skin brother. You must help her."

Richard could feel Berdine trembling as she pressed against him. He decided that he should be going before she became too frightened, and started down the steps.

Two landings down, she was still hanging on to him. "It's gone," she whispered in his ear.

Richard looked back up and saw that she was right.

Berdine muscled him into the recess of a doorway, flattening his back up against a wood door. Her penetrating blue eyes were intense with agitation. "Lord Rahl, that was a mriswith."

Richard nodded, a little puzzled by her ragged panting.

"Lord Rahl, mriswith kill people. You always kill them."

Richard lifted a hand toward the landing above. "It wasn't going to hurt us. I told you that. It didn't attack us, did it? There was no need to harm it."

Her brow furrowed with concern. "Lord Rahl, are you all right?"

"I'm fine. Now, come on. Maybe the mriswith gave us a good hint of what we might be looking for."

She shoved him back against the door when he tried to move. "Why did it call you 'skin brother'?"

"I don't know. I guess because it has scales, and I have skin. I think it called me that to let me know it meant no harm. It wanted to help."

"Help?" she repeated incredulously.

"It didn't try to stop us, did it?"

She finally let go of his shirt, but it took longer for her blue eyes to release their hold on him.

At the bottom of the tower, a walkway with an iron railing ringed the outside wall of the tower. In the center lurked black water with rocks breaking the surface in several places. Salamanders clung to the stone below the walkway, and rested partially submerged at the rocks. Insects swam through the thick, inky water, skittering around bubbles that occasionally ascended to release rings as they burst.

Halfway around the walkway, Richard knew he had found what

he was looking for: something not ordinary, like the libraries, or even the strange rooms and corridors.

A wide platform in the walkway before where a door had been was littered with sooty stone fragments, chips, and dust. Chunks of wood from the door now floated in the dark water beyond the iron railing. The doorway itself had been blown away, and was now perhaps twice its previous size. The jagged edges were blackened, and in some places the stone itself was melted like candle wax. Twisting streaks on the stone wall ran off in every direction away from the blasted hole, as if lightning had flailed against the wall and burned it.

"This is not old," Richard said, running his finger through the black soot.

"How can you tell?" Berdine asked as she peered about.

"Look. See here? The mold and slime have been burned away, scoured right off the rock, and haven't had time to grow back. This happened recently—sometime within the last few months."

The room inside was round, perhaps sixty feet across, its walls scorched in ragged lines as if lightning had gone wild in the place. A circular stone wall took up the center, like a huge well, nearly half the width of the room. Richard leaned over the waist-high wall, holding out the glowing globe. The smooth stone walls of the hole fell away forever. He could see the stone for hundreds of feet before the light failed to penetrate farther. It looked bottomless.

Above was a domed ceiling nearly as high as the room was wide. There were no windows or other doors. To the far side, Richard could see a table and a few shelves.

When they rounded the well, he saw the body, lying on the floor beside a chair. All that was left were bones inside a few scraps of cloth robes. Most of the robes had long ago rotted away, leaving the skeleton encircled by just a leather belt. Sandals remained, too. When he touched the bones, they crumbled like baked dirt.

"He has been here a very long time," Berdine said.

"You're right about that."

"Lord Rahl, look."

Richard stood and looked to the table where she pointed. There was an inkwell, dry for perhaps centuries, a pen to the side, and an open book. Richard leaned over and blew a cloud of dust and stone chips from the book.

"It's in High D'Haran," he said as he held it up next to the glowing sphere.

"Let me see." Her eyes moved from side to side as she studied the strange characters. "You're right."

"What does it say?"

She carefully took the book in both hands. "This is very old. The dialect is older than any I have ever seen. Darken Rahl showed me an old dialect that he said was over two thousand years old." She looked up. "This is older."

"Can you read it?"

"I could only understand a bit of the book we found when we came in the Keep." She considered the last page with writing on it. "I understand much less of this," she said as she turned some of the pages back.

Richard gestured impatiently. "Well, can you understand any of it?"

She stopped turning and scrutinized the writing. "I think it says something about finally having success, but that success means he would die here." She pointed. "See? *Drauka.* That word is the same I think—'death.' " Berdine looked at the blank leather cover, then turned back through the book, scanning the pages.

Her blue eyes came up at last. "I think it's a journal. I think this is the journal of the man who died in here."

Richard felt goose bumps dance up his arms. "Berdine, this is what I was looking for. This is something not ordinary, not a book others have seen, like in the library. Can you translate it?"

"A bit, perhaps, but not much." Her features sagged with disappointment. "I'm sorry, Lord Rahl. I just don't know dialects this old. It's the same problem I would have with the book we saw at first. I don't know enough of the words to be able to fill in the blanks correctly. I would only be guessing."

Richard pinched his lower lip as he thought. He looked down at the bones, wondering what this wizard had been doing in this room, and what had kept it sealed, and worse yet, what had unsealed it.

Richard twisted back to her. "Berdine! That book upstairs—I know that book. I know the story. If I helped you, telling you what I remember of what it says, could that help you decipher the words, and then use those translated words to help translate this journal?"

As she considered, her face brightened. "If we worked together, it might. If you could tell me what a sentence says, then I would be able to know the meaning of words I don't recognize. We might be able to do it."

Richard carefully closed the journal. "You hold on to this with your life. I'll hold the light. Let's get out of here. We have what we came for."

When he and Berdine came through the doorway, Cara and Raina practically leapt out of their skin with relief. Richard even saw Ulic and Egan close their eyes with a sigh and a silent thank-you to the good spirits for a prayer answered.

"There are mriswith in the Keep," Berdine told the other two women at their tumbling questions.

Cara gasped. "How many did you have to kill, Lord Rahl?"

"None. They didn't attack us. We weren't in danger from them. But there were enough other dangers." He waved off her furious questions. "We'll talk about it later. With Berdine's help, I found what I was looking for." He tapped the journal in Berdine's hands. "We need to get back and start translating it." He picked up the book from the table and gave it to Berdine.

As he started for the doorway out, he stopped and turned back to Cara and Raina. "Uh, while I was down there, and I was thinking that I could be killed if I did something wrong, it came to me that I didn't want to die without telling you two something."

Richard put his hands in his pockets as he stepped closer. "I realized when I was down there that I never told you that I was sorry for the way I treated you both."

"You did not know Berdine was under a spell, Lord Rahl," Cara said. "We don't blame you for wanting to keep us all at arm's length."

"I didn't know Berdine was under a spell, but I do now, and I want you to know that I wrongly thought ill of you. You never gave me cause. I'm sorry. I hope you can forgive me."

Smiles warmed Cara and Raina's faces. He didn't think they had ever looked less like Mord-Sith than at that moment.

"We forgive you, Lord Rahl," Cara said. Raina nodded her agreement. "Thank you."

"What happened down there, Lord Rahl?" Raina asked.

"We had a talk about friendship," Berdine answered.

At the base of the Keep road, where the city of Aydindril started and other roads joined to come into the city, stood a small market, nothing like the one on Stentor Street, but it looked to serve those arriving with a variety of goods.

As Richard was moving past, with his five bodyguards around him and his escort of troops marching behind, something caught his eye in the fading light and he came to a halt before a small, rickety table.

"Would you like one of your honey cakes, Lord Rahl?" a small, familiar voice asked.

Richard smiled down at the little girl. "How many do you still owe me?"

The girl turned. "Grandmamma?"

The old woman rose to her feet, clutching the tattered blanket to herself as her faded blue eyes fixed on Richard.

"My, my," she said with a grin, showing the gaps from missing teeth. "Lord Rahl can have as many as he wants, dear." She bowed her head. "So good to see you well, my Lord Rahl."

"You, too . . ." He waited for her name.

"Valdora," she said. She stroked a hand down the little girl's light brown hair. "And this is Holly."

"Pleased to see you again, Valdora and Holly. What are you doing here instead of Stentor Street?"

Valdora shrugged under her blanket. "With the new Lord Rahl making the city safe, more people are coming all the time, and perhaps there will even be activity at the Wizard's Keep once again. We hope to catch some of these new people."

"Well, I don't think I'd put my hopes in the Keep thriving again any time soon, but you will certainly have first chance at those come new to Aydindril." Richard surveyed the cakes on her table. "How many do I still have coming?"

Valdora chuckled. "I would have a lot of baking to do to catch up with what we owe you, Lord Rahl."

Richard winked at her. "Tell you what. If I could have one each for these five friends of mine, and one for myself, we will bargain it as even."

Valdora's gaze passed over his five guards. She bowed her head again. "Done, Lord Rahl. You have brought me more satisfaction than you could know."

CHAPTER 38

AS VERNA HURRIED TOWARD the gate to the Prelate's compound, she noticed Kevin Andellmere standing guard in the darkness. She was impatient to get to the sanctuary, to tell Ann that she had at last figured it out, and she now knew almost every one of the Sisters loyal to the Light, but she hadn't seen Kevin in weeks. Despite her heart-pounding rush, she stopped.

"Kevin, is that you?"

The young soldier bowed. "Yes, Prelate."

"I haven't seen you around for quite a time, have I?"

"No, Prelate. Bollesdun, Walsh, and I were called back to our command."

"Why?"

Kevin shifted his weight. "I'm not sure, exactly. My commander was curious about the spell over the palace, I think. I've known him for near to fifteen years, and he's aged. He wanted to see with his own eyes if it were true that we hadn't. He said Bollesdun, Walsh, and I look the same as we did when he first saw us, fifteen years ago. He said he had doubted it when he heard it said, but he believed it, now. He had his commanders who knew us come look for themselves."

Verna felt her forehead break out with beads of perspiration. With a cold wash of understanding, she knew why the emperor was coming to the Palace of the Prophets. She had to tell the Prelate. There was no time to lose.

"Kevin, are you a loyal soldier of the Empire, of the Imperial Order?"

Kevin slid his hand up on his pike. His voice hesitated. "Yes, Prelate. I mean, when the Order conquered my homeland, I had little choice; I was made a soldier in the Order. I fought for a time up north, near the wilds. Then, when the Order took over our kingdom, I was told I was a soldier for the Order, and assigned to the palace.

"Can't get a better guard job than this. I'm glad to be back guarding your compound. Bollesdun and Walsh are glad to be back, too, to their posts at the Prophet's compound.

"My officers have always treated me decent, at least, and I always get paid. It's not much, but it always comes, and I see plenty of people who have no work, and have a hard time eating."

Verna put a gentle hand to his arm. "Kevin, what do you think of Richard?"

"Richard?" A grin came over his face. "I liked Richard. He bought me expensive chocolates for me to give my lady."

"Is that all he means to you? Chocolates?"

He scratched his eyebrow. "No . . . I didn't mean it that way. Richard was . . . a good man."

"Do you know why he bought you those chocolates?"

"Because he was nice. He cared about people."

Verna nodded. "Yes, he did. He hoped that by giving you chocolates, when the time came for him to escape, it would make you see him as a friend and keep you from fighting him so he wouldn't have to kill you. He didn't want you as an enemy trying to kill him."

"Kill him? Prelate, I would never have—"

"If he hadn't been kind to you, you might have been loyal to the palace first, and tried to stop him."

He glanced to the ground. "I've seen him use his sword. I guess the gift was more than chocolates."

"That it was. Kevin, if a times comes, and you have to choose—Richard, or the Order—which would you choose?"

His face twisted in discomfort. "Prelate, I'm a soldier." He let out a groan. "But Richard is a friend. I guess that if I had to, I'd be hard-pressed to raise a weapon against a friend. Any of the palace guard would be. They all like him."

She squeezed his arm. "Be loyal to your friends, Kevin, and you will be all right. Be loyal to Richard, and it will save you."

He nodded. "Thank you, Prelate. But I don't fear I will have to choose."

"Kevin, listen to me. The emperor is an evil man." Kevin didn't say anything. "You just remember that. And keep my words to yourself, will you?"

"Yes, Prelate."

As Verna marched into her outer office, Phoebe came halfway out of her chair when she saw her. "Good evening, Prelate."

"I have to pray for guidance, Phoebe. No visitors."

Something Kevin had said abruptly snagged in her mind. It didn't make sense. "Guards Bollesdun and Walsh have been assigned to the Prophet's compound. We don't have a prophet. Find out why they're there and who ordered it, and give me a report first thing in the morning." Verna shook a finger. "First thing."

"Verna—" Phoebe sank back into her chair and looked down to her desk. Sister Dulcinia turned her white face away, putting her attention to her reports. "Verna, there are some Sisters here to see you. They wait inside."

"I gave no one permission to wait in my office!"

Phoebe didn't look up. "I know, Prelate, but—"

"I'll see to this. Thank you, Phoebe."

Verna was masked in a furious scowl as she stormed into her office. No one was allowed in her office without her explicit permission. She didn't have time to waste with nonsense. She had figured out how to tell the Sisters of the Light from the Sisters of the Dark, and she knew why Emperor Jagang was coming to Tanimura, to the Palace of the Prophets. She had to send a message to Ann. She had to know what she was to do.

She saw the figures of four women in the dark room as she closed the distance. "What is the meaning of this!"

Verna recognized Sister Leoma as she stepped forward into the candlelight.

And then, in a blinding flash of pain, the world went black.

"Do as I say, Nathan."

He leaned down toward her, quite a distance, considering their difference in height, and gnashed his teeth. "You could at least give me access to my Han! How can I protect you?"

Ann watched in the darkness as the column of five hundred men followed the Lord Rahl up the street. "I don't want you to protect me. We can't take the chance. You know what to do. You must not interfere until he has rescued me, or we won't have a chance of capturing one so dangerous."

"What if he doesn't 'rescue' you?"

Ann tried not to think of that possibility. She tried not to think of what was going to happen even if events took the correct fork. "Must I now lecture a prophet on prophecy? You must let it happen. Afterward, I will remove the block. Now, take the horses to a stable for the night. Make sure they are well fed."

Nathan snatched the reins from her. "Have it your way, woman." He turned back. "You had better hope that I never get this collar off, or we are going to have a very long talk. You won't be able to do a proper job of holding up your end of the conversation, though, because you will be bound and gagged at the time."

Ann chuckled. "Nathan, you're a good man. I trust in you. You must trust in me."

He shook a finger at her. "If you get yourself killed . . ."

"I know, Nathan."

He growled. "And they say I'm the one who is mad." He turned back to her. "At least you could get yourself something to eat. You haven't eaten all day. There's a market just over there. Promise me you will at least have something to eat."

"I'm not—"

"Promise me!"

Ann sighed. "All right, Nathan. If it will make you happy, I will have something to eat. But I'm not very hungry." He lifted a finger in admonition. "I said I promise. Now go on."

After he had finally stormed off with the horses, she proceeded on toward the Keep. Her stomach churned with the fear of walking into a prophecy blind. She didn't like the idea of going to the Keep again, but she liked it even less considering the prophecy involved. Still, she had to do this. It was the only way.

"Honey cake, ma'am? They're only a penny, and quite good."

Ann looked down at a little girl in a big coat standing behind a rickety table. Honey cake. Well, she hadn't promised what she would eat. A honey cake would do.

Ann smiled at the pretty face. "All alone out here at night?"

The girl turned and pointed. "No, m'lady, my grandmamma is here with me."

A squat woman was curled up, all covered over in a tattered blanket, apparently asleep. Ann fished around in a pocket and pulled out a coin.

"A silver for you, my dear. You look to need it more than I."

"Oh, thank you, m'lady." She pulled a honey cake from under the table. "Please take this one. It's one of the special ones, with the most honey. I save them for the nicest people who stop at my stand."

Ann smiled as she took the honey cake. "Well, thank you, my dear."

As Ann started up the road to the Keep, the little girl began packing up her things.

Ann savored the sweet honey cake as she eyed the people milling about the small market, looking for one who would be trouble. She didn't see any who looked dangerous, but she knew one was. She put her attention back to the road. What would be, would be. She wondered if it would really ease the anxiety if she knew how it would come. Probably not.

In the darkness, no one saw her take the road to the Keep, and at last she was alone. She wished Nathan were with her, but in a way, it was nice to be alone at last, if only for a brief time. It did give her time, without Nathan's presence, to think about her life, and what changes this would mean. So many years.

In a way, what she was doing was like condemning to death those she loved. What choice had she?

She licked her fingers clean when she finished the honey cake. It hadn't settled her stomach, as she had hoped it would. By the time she crossed under the iron portcullis, her stomach was in churning turmoil. What was wrong with her? She had faced dangers before. Maybe, as she got older, she found life more precious, and held on more tenaciously, fearing to let it slip.

By the time she lit a candle inside the Keep, she knew something was wrong. She felt on fire. Her eyes burned. Her joints ached. Was she sick? Dear Creator, not now. She needed strength.

When she felt the stabbing pain under her breastbone, she crossed an arm across her middle and slumped into a chair. She groaned as the room spun. What was . . . ?

The honey cake.

It had never occurred to her that it could come this way. She had been wondering how one could overpower her; she was not without her Han, after all, and it was strong in her, stronger than nearly any other sorceress. How could she be so stupid? She doubled over in the chair with a searing lash of pain.

In her wavering vision, she saw two figures enter the room, one short, one taller. Two? She hadn't expected two. Dear Creator, two could ruin everything.

"Well, well. Look what the night netted me."

Struggling with the effort, Ann tilted her head up. "Who . . . is . . . it?"

They stepped closer. "Don't you remember me?" The old woman in the blanket cackled. "Don't recognize me, all old and wasted? Well, you're to blame for that. I must say, you look hardly a day older. I could still have my youth, were it not for you, my dear, dear, Prelate. Then you would recognize me."

Ann gasped as the twisting pain bore down on her.

"Honey cake not setting well?"

"Who . . ."

The old woman put her hands to her knees and leaned down. "Why, Prelate, surely, you must remember? I promised you that you would pay for what you did to me. And you don't even remember the cruel thing you did? Did it mean that little to you?"

Ann's eyes widened in sudden recognition. She would never have recognized her after all these years, but the voice, the voice was the same.

"Valdora."

The old woman cackled again. "Well, dear Prelate, I'm honored you would remember one so lowly as I." She bowed with exaggerated courtesy. "I hope you also remember what I promised you. You do remember, don't you? I promised to see you dead."

Ann felt herself hit the floor as she writhed in agony. "I thought that . . . after you . . . reflected on your actions . . . you would see the wrong in your ways. I can see, now, that . . . I was right to put you . . . from the palace. You . . . have no right to serve as a Sister."

"Oh, don't you concern yourself, Prelate. I've started my own palace. My granddaughter here is my student, my novice. I teach her better than your Sisters could ever teach. I teach her everything."

"You teach her . . . to poison people?"

Valdora laughed. "Oh, the poison won't kill you. Just a little something to incapacitate you until I could bind you up all helpless in a web. You'll not die so easily." She leaned down closer, her voice coming like venom. "You are going to be a long time dying, Prelate. You may even last all the way to morning. A person can die a thousand times over in a single night."

"How could you have . . . known . . . I would come?"

The woman straightened. "Oh, I didn't. When I saw the Lord Rahl, and he gave me one of your coins, I thought he might end up bringing me a Sister, too. I had no idea, not in my wildest hopes, that he would bring me the Prelate herself. Delivered right into my hands. My, my, what a marvel. No, I never even dared hope. I would have been more than happy just to skin one of your Sisters, or even your student, Lord Rahl, to do you a pain. But now I can fulfill my deepest, darkest desires."

Ann tried to call her Han. Through the layer of pain, she realized the honey cake had contained more than simple poison. It had been bound up with a spell.

Dear Creator, this was not going the way it should.

The room was getting dim. She felt a jerk of pain in her scalp. She felt the stone scrape along her back. She saw the pretty, smiling face of the girl walking along at her side.

"I forgive you, child," Ann whispered.

And then, the blackness smothered her.

CHAPTER 39

KAHLAN CLUTCHED ADIE'S ARM in one hand and a sword in the other as they ran. In the darkness, they both stumbled over Orsk, falling hard. Kahlan yanked her hand back from the warm mass of his guts in the snow.

"How . . . how could he be here!"

Adie panted, trying to catch her breath. "It be impossible."

"There's enough moon to see. I know we're not going in circles." She took a quick swipe against the snow, smearing the gore from her hands. She scrambled to her feet, pulling Adie up with her. There were bodies, clad in red capes, scattered all about. They had had only one fight. There couldn't be other bodies. And Orsk . . .

Kahlan swept her gaze along the tree line, looking for the men on horseback. "Adie, remember the vision Jebra had? She saw me going in circles."

Adie brushed the snow from her face. "But how?"

Kahlan knew Adie couldn't run much more. She had used her power to fight, and she was near dead with exhaustion. The force of her magic unleashed had been a terror to the attackers, but there were too many. Orsk must have killed twenty or thirty by himself. Kahlan hadn't seen Orsk killed, but she had come across his body three times now. He had been cut nearly in two.

"Which way do you think we must go to get away?" she asked the sorceress.

"They be back there." Adie pointed. "We must go this way."

"That's what I think, too." She pulled Adie the other way. "We've been doing what we think we should, and it's not working. We have to try something else. Come on. We must do what we think is wrong."

"It could be a spell," Adie offered. "If it is, you be right. I be too tired to feel it if there be one."

They charged through the bramble and down a steep slope, half running, half sliding down the snow. Before she bounded over the edge she saw the horsemen spring from the cover of trees. The snow at the bottom was drifted into deep banks. They both struggled through them toward trees. It was like trying to run in a quagmire.

A man suddenly came out of the night and drove down the slope after them. Kahlan didn't wait for Adie to try to use her magic. There was no time if she failed.

Kahlan spun, bringing the sword around. The man in the red cape swept his sword up defensively as he plunged onward. He wore an armored breastplate. Her strike would be wasted on his armor. He was protecting his face—an instinctive reaction, but a fatal move against someone trained by her father, King Wyborn. Men in armor fought with false confidence.

With all her strength, Kahlan took her sword low instead. It jolted to a halt when it hit his femur. The man, the muscle of his thigh cleaved, tumbled with a helpless cry to the trampled ground.

Another man leapt over top of him toward her. His red cape sailed open in the night air. Kahlan brought her sword up, slashing the inside of his thigh, severing the artery. As he fell past her, she hacked his hamstring.

The first cried out in panic. The second man cursed at the top of his lungs, calling her every vile name she had ever heard as he crawled ahead, brandishing his sword, provoking her to dare to fight him.

Kahlan remembered her father's counsel: *Words can't cut you. Ward only for steel. Fight only steel.*

She didn't waste the time to finish them; they would probably bleed to death in the snow, and even if they didn't, maimed as they were, they couldn't come after her. Clutching each other's arms, she and Adie fled onward into the trees.

Panting in the darkness, they wove their way through the snow-crusted fir trees. Kahlan realized Adie was shivering. She had lost her heavy cloak at the very beginning. Kahlan pulled off her wolf-hide mantle and threw it around Adie's shoulders.

"No, child," Adie began to protest.

"Wear it," Kahlan commanded. "I'm sweating, and anyway, it only slows my sword." In truth, her sword arm was so weary she could hardly lift the thing, much less swing it. Only fright powered her muscles. For now, that was enough.

Kahlan no longer knew which way she was running. The two of them simply ran for their lives. When she wanted to go right, she went left instead. The trees they ran through were too thick to see the stars, or the moon.

She had to get away. Richard was in danger. Richard needed her. She had to get to him. Zedd should be there by now, but anything could go wrong. Zedd might not make it. She had to.

Kahlan slapped a balsam branch aside, struggling into a small open area of ledge wind-blown nearly clean of snow. She started to a halt. Before her stood two horses.

Tobias Brogan, the lord general of the Blood of the Fold, smiled down at her. A woman in tattered scraps of colored cloth sat on a horse beside him.

Brogan knuckled his mustache. "And what have we here?"

"Two travelers," Kahlan said in voice as cold as the winter air. "Since when has the Blood taken to robbing and butchering helpless travelers?"

"Helpless travelers? Hardly. The two of you must have killed over a hundred of my men."

"We have been defending our lives from the Blood of the Fold, which if it thinks it can get away with it, attacks people it doesn't even know."

"Oh, I know you, Kahlan Amnell, Queen of Galea. I know more than you think. I know who you be."

Kahlan's fist tightened on the hilt of the sword.

Brogan stepped his big dappled gray closer, a gruesome grin overcoming his face. He rested an arm on the pommel as he leaned forward, his dark eyes holding her in their malevolent grip.

"You, Kahlan Amnell, be the Mother Confessor. I see you for who you be, and you be the Mother Confessor."

Kahlan's muscles locked tight, her breath held prisoner in her lungs. How could he know that? Had Zedd removed the spell? Had something happened to Zedd? Dear spirits, if anything happened to Zedd . . .

With a cry of rage, she brought the sword around in a mighty swing. At the same time, the woman in the tattered rages flung a hand out. With a grunt of effort, Adie cast out a shield. The blow of air from the woman atop the horse brushed past Kahlan's face, flicking her hair out. Adie's shield had saved her.

Kahlan's sword flashed in the moonlight. The night air cracked as her blade sundered the horse's leg under Brogan.

The horse screamed as it thudded to the ground, pitching Brogan into the trees. At the same time, a gout of flame from Adie enveloped the other horse's head. It reared wildly, throwing the woman whom Kahlan now knew to be a sorceress, too.

Kahlan snatched Adie's hand and yanked her away. They scrambled desperately into the brush. All around, she could hear men and horses crashing through the trees. Kahlan didn't try to think where she was going; she simply ran.

There was one thing she hadn't resorted to, yet; she was saving her power as her last recourse. It could only be used once, and then would take hours to recover. Most Confessors took a day or two to recover their magic. The fact that Kahlan could recover her power within a couple of hours marked her as one of the most powerful Confessors to have ever been born. That power didn't seem like much, now. One chance.

"Adie." Kahlan gasped, trying to catch her breath. "If you can, if they catch us, try to slow one of the two women."

Adie didn't need further explanation. She understood; both the women chasing them were sorceresses. If Kahlan had to use her power, that would be the best use of it.

Kahlan ducked at a flash of light. A tree beside them crashed down with a deafening roar. As the snow cleared in rolling clouds, the other woman, the one who had been afoot, marched forward.

Beside the woman was a dark, scaled creature, looking half man, half lizard. Kahlan heard a cry come from her throat. It felt as if her bones wanted to jump out of her unmoving flesh.

"I've had quite enough of this nonsense," the woman said as she strode forward, the scaled thing at her side.

Mriswith. It had to be mriswith. Richard had described them to her. This nightmare creature could only be a mriswith.

Adie darted closer, casting sparkling light toward the woman. The woman flicked her hand, almost indifferently, and Adie went down, the sparkles settling harmlessly to the snow.

The woman bent, took Adie's wrist, and cast her away like a chicken for later plucking. Kahlan burst into action, diving forward with her sword.

The thing, the mriswith, swept before her like a gust of wind. She saw its dark cape billow open as it spun past. She heard the ring of steel.

She realized she was on her knees. Her empty sword hand tingled and stung. How could it move that fast? When she looked up, the woman was closer. Her hand came up, and the air shimmered. Kahlan felt a blow to her face.

She blinked the blood from her eyes, seeing the woman lift her hand again, her fingers curling.

The woman's arms suddenly splayed in the air as she was hit from behind by a mighty wallop. Adie must have used everything she had left. The invisible blast of magic from Adie, hard as a hammer, threw the woman forward. Kahlan caught her hand as she tried desperately to snatch it back.

It was too late. Everything slowed in Kahlan's mind. The sorceress seemed to be suspended in midair, Kahlan gripping her hand. Time was Kahlan's, now. She had all the time in the world.

The sorceress began to gasp. She began to look up. She began to flinch. In the calm center of her power, her magic, Kahlan was in control. The woman had no chance.

As Kahlan watched, she could feel the magic within, the Confessor's magic, rip through every fiber of her being, screaming onward.

In that timeless place of her mind, Kahlan released her power.

Lightning without sound jolted the night.

As the concussion slammed through the air, even the stars above seemed to stagger, as if a celestial fist had struck the great, silent bell of the night sky.

The shock shuddered the trees. A cloud of snow lifted, billowing outward in a ring.

The impact of magic had knocked the mriswith from its feet.

The woman looked up, her eyes wide, her muscles slack.

"Mistress," she whispered, "command me."

Men were crashing through the trees. The mriswith was staggering to its feet.

"Protect me!"

The sorceress sprang up, spinning with a hand out. The night ignited.

Lightning ripped through the trees in an arc. Tree trunks exploded as the twisting line of light sliced across them. Splintered wood spun through the air, trailing smoke. Men were no less naked before the rending violence than were the trees. Not so much as a scream escaped their lungs, nor would it have been heard above the pandemonium.

The mriswith vaulted toward her. Scales, like the feathers of a bird hit by a rock from a sling, filled the air.

The night roared with fire. The air was rife with flame, flesh, and bone.

Kahlan wiped blood from her eyes, trying to see, as she scooted backward across the snow. She had to get away. She had to find Adie.

She bumped into something. She thought it must be a tree. A fist snatched her by the hair. She reached for her power, realizing too late that it was gone.

Kahlan spit blood from her mouth. Her ears rang. And then there was pain. She couldn't push herself up. Her head felt as if a tree had fallen on it. She heard a voice above her.

"Lunetta, put a stop to this at once."

Kahlan turned her head in the snow and saw the sorceress she had touched with her power seem to grow bigger, to come apart. Her arms went in two different directions. That was all Kahlan could recognize as a cloud of red misted the air where the woman had been.

Kahlan slumped into the numbing snow. No. She couldn't give up. She twisted up onto her knees, pulling her knife. Brogan's boot caught her in the middle.

Looking up at the stars, she tried to draw a breath. She couldn't. Cold panic swept through her as she tried to get air. It wouldn't come. Her stomach muscles clenched in spasms, but she couldn't get a breath.

Brogan knelt beside her, pulling her up by her shirt. Breath finally came in convulsing coughing, choking pulls.

"At last," he whispered. "At last, I have the prize of prizes—the Keeper's most precious pet, the Mother Confessor herself. Oh, you have no idea how I've dreamed of this day." He backhanded her across the jaw. "No idea at all."

Kahlan labored for air as Brogan twisted the knife from her grip. She fought to keep her mind from going black. She had to remain conscious if she was to think, if she was to fight.

"Lunetta!"

"Yes, my lord general, I be here."

Kahlan felt the buttons on her shirt pop off as he ripped it open. She weakly lifted an arm to check his hands. He batted the arm away. Her arms felt too heavy to lift.

"First, Lunetta, we must take her before her power returns. Then we will have all the time we want to question her before she pays for her crimes."

He leaned closer in the moonlight, leaning a knee into her gut, holding her down. She fought to get air back into her lungs, but then it rushed out with a scream as his brutal fingers wrenched her left nipple.

She saw the knife come up in his other hand.

With wide eyes, she saw a white glimmer before Brogan's grin. In the moonlight, three blades poised before his bloodless face. Kahlan's eyes, along with Brogan's, turned to see two mriswith above them.

"Releassse her," the mriswith hissed, "or die."

Kahlan covered the piercing pain in her breast when he had done as he was told. Her eyes watered with the intensity of hurt. At least it helped clear them of the blood.

"What be the meaning of this," Brogan growled. "She be mine. The Creator wishes her punished!"

"You will do as the dreamssss walker commandsss, or you will die."

Brogan cocked his head. "He wishes this?" The mriswith hissed confirmation. "I don't understand. . . ."

"You question?"

"No. No, of course not. It will be as you advise, sacred one."

Kahlan was afraid to sit up, hoping they would tell Brogan to let her go, next. Brogan stood, backing away.

Another mriswith appeared with Adie, shoving her to the ground beside Kahlan. The sorceress's touch on Kahlan's arm said without words that she was all right, if bruised and cut. Adie put an arm around Kahlan's shoulders and helped her sit up.

Kahlan hurt everywhere. Her jaw throbbed where Brogan had hit her, her stomach ached, and her forehead stung. Blood was still running into her eyes.

One of the mriswith selected two rings from a number looped over its wrist, and shoved them at the sorceress in tattered rags—Lunetta, Brogan had called her. "The other is dead. You must do it instead."

Lunetta, looking puzzled, took the rings. "Do what?"

"Use your gift to put these around their neck, so they can be controlled."

Lunetta pulled and one of the collars snapped, coming open. She seemed surprised, even pleased. Holding it out, she bent over Adie.

"Please, sister," Adie whispered in her native tongue, *"I be from your homeland. Help us."*

Lunetta paused, looking into Adie's eyes.

"Lunetta!" Brogan kicked her rump. "Hurry up. Do as the Creator wishes."

Lunetta snapped the metal collar around Adie's neck, then shuffled over to Kahlan and did the same. Kahlan blinked at the childlike smile Lunetta gave her.

Kahlan reached up after Lunetta straightened, and felt the collar. In the moonlight, she thought she recognized it, but when she felt the smooth metal and could no longer find the seam, she was sure. It was a Rada'Han, like the Sisters of the Light had put around Richard's neck. She knew that those sorceresses used the collar to control him. The purpose must be the same for them: to control their power. Kahlan suddenly feared that her power would not be returning in a few hours.

When they reached the coach, Ahern was there, at the point of a mriswith blade. He had told Kahlan, Adie, and Orsk to dive out of the coach on a curve and he would lead their pursuers away from her. A bold, and brave, move that, in the end, had failed.

Kahlan was suddenly relieved she had made everyone else go to Ebinissia, as planned. Kahlan had told Jebra to care for Cyrilla, and the rest of the men to carry out their plans to bring Ebinissia back from the ashes. Kahlan's sister was home. If Kahlan died, Galea still had a queen.

Had she brought any of those gallant young men, these mriswith, these nightmare creatures of the wind, would have gutted them all, as they had done to Orsk.

She felt a pang of sorrow for Orsk, and then a claw shoved her into the coach. Adie was pushed in right behind her. Kahlan heard a brief conversation, and then Lunetta climbed in the coach, sitting across from Kahlan and Adie. A mriswith entered and sat beside Lunetta, its beady eyes taking account of them. Kahlan pulled her shirt closed and tried to wipe the blood from her eyes.

She heard more talking outside, something about replacing the runners on the coach with wheels. Through the window, she saw Ahern, at swordpoint, climb up to the driver's seat. The man in the red cape followed him up, and then another of the mriswith.

Kahlan felt her legs trembling. Where were they taking them? She was so close to Richard. She clenched her teeth, holding back a wail. It wasn't fair. She felt a tear roll down her cheek.

Adie's hand slid between their legs, and by its little movement against her thigh, she read the comfort in that touch.

The mriswith leaned toward them as its slit of a mouth seemed to widen in a grim smile. It lifted the three-bladed knife in its claw, giving it a little wiggle before their eyes.

"Try to esssscape, and I will ssslice the bottoms of your feet." It cocked its smooth head. "Understand?"

Kahlan and Adie both nodded.

"Speak," it added, "And I ssslice out your tonguesss."

They nodded again.

It turned to Lunetta. "With your gift, through the collar, seal their power. Like I show you." It put a claw to Lunetta's forehead. "Understand?"

Lunetta smiled with comprehension. "Yes. I see."

Kahlan heard Adie grunt, and at the same time she felt something tighten in her own chest. It was the place where she always felt her power. In dismay, she wondered if she would ever feel it return. She remembered the forlorn emptiness when the Keltish wizard had used magic to make her lose the connection with her power. She knew what to expect.

"She bleeds," the mriswith said to Lunetta. "You must heal her. Skin brother would not be pleased if she were scarred."

She heard the whip snap, and Ahern's whistle. The coach lurched ahead. Lunetta leaned forward to heal her wound.

Dear spirits, where were they taking her?

CHAPTER 40

ANN'S EYES STUNG WITH tears as a shuddering cry escaped her throat. She had long ago forsaken her determination to keep from crying out. Who but the Creator would hear, or care?

Valdora lifted the knife, greasy with blood. "Hurt?" A gap-toothed grin came to her as a chuckle fought its way out. "How do you like it when someone else chooses what will happen to you? That's what you did. You chose how I would die. You denied me life. Life I could have had at the palace. I would still be young. You chose to let me die."

Ann flinched as the knife point pricked her side. "I asked a question, Prelate. How do you like it?"

"No more than you, I would expect."

The grin returned. "Gooood. I want you to know the pain I've lived with all these years."

"I left you with a life the same as everyone else has. A life to live as you would. You were left with what the Creator gave you, the same as everyone else come into this world. I could have had you executed."

"For casting a spell! I'm a sorceress! That's what the Creator gave me, and I used it!"

Though Ann knew the arguments were pointless, she favored them over Valdora going back to her silent knifework.

"You used what the Creator gave you to take from others what they would not have given willingly. You thieved their affections, their hearts, their lives. You had no right. You sampled devotion like candies at a fair. You bound them to you with glamours and then cast them away to snare another."

The knife pricked her again. "And you banished me!"

"How many lives did you bring to ruin? You were counseled, you were warned, you were punished. Still, you continued. Only after all this were you put out of the Palace of the Prophets."

Ann's shoulders throbbed with a dull ache. She was stretched out naked on a wooden table, her wrists bound with magic over her head at one end, and her ankles at the other. The spell chafed worse than coarse hemp rope. She was as helpless as a hog hung up to be bled.

Valdora had used a spell, something else she had learned who knew where, to block Ann's Han. She could feel it there, like a warm fire on a winter's night, just beyond a window, inviting, promising warmth, but out of reach.

Ann stared up at the window near the top of the wall in the little stone room. It was nearing daylight. Why hadn't he come? He should have come to rescue her by now, and then she was to somehow capture him. But he hadn't come.

It still wasn't daylight. He still might come. Dear Creator, let him come soon.

Unless it was the wrong day. Panic raced through her mind. What if they had miscalculated? No. She and Nathan had gone over the charts. This was the right day, and besides, it was the events, more than the day itself, that fueled the prophecy. The fact that she had been captured said that it was the right day. If she had been captured a week before, then that would have been the right day. This day was within the window of opportunity. The prophecy was being fulfilled. But where was he?

Ann realized that Valdora's face was gone. She wasn't beside her. She should have kept talking. She should . . .

She felt a sudden, sharp, searing pain as the knife cut down the sole of her left foot. Her whole body jerked against the restraints. Sweat once again beaded on her brow and trickled through her scalp. Again the pain came, another cut, accompanied by another impotent cry.

Her screams reverberated from the stone as Valdora ripped a strip of flesh from the sole of her foot.

She was shaking uncontrollably; her head lolled to the side. The little girl, Holly, was looking into her eyes. Ann felt tears run over the bridge of her nose, and into her other eye, to finally fall away.

Trembling, she stared into Holly's eyes, wondering what vile things Valdora was teaching such an innocent child. She would turn this small creature's heart to stone.

Valdora held up the little white curl of flesh. "Look, Holly, how cleanly it comes off, if you do as I say. Would you like to try your hand, my dear?"

"Grandmamma," Holly said, "must we do this? She has done nothing to harm us. She is not like the others; she never tried to hurt us."

Valdora gestured with the knife for emphasis. "Oh, but she has, dear one. She hurt me. She stole my youth."

Holly glanced at Ann as she shivered with the lingering pain. The little girl had an odd mask of calm, for one so young. She would have made an outstanding novice, and one day a fine Sister. "She gave me a silver. She didn't try to hurt us. This is not fun. I don't want to do it."

Valdora chuckled. "Well, do it we will." She wiggled the knife. "You listen to your grandmamma. She deserves it."

Holly coolly considered the old woman. "Just because you're older than me, that doesn't make you right. I'll watch no longer. I'm going outside."

Valdora shrugged. "If you wish. This is between the Prelate and me. If you do not wish to learn anything, then go outside and play."

Holly strode from the room. Ann could have kissed her for her courage.

Valdora's face glided closer. "Just you and me, now, Prelate." Her jaw muscles flexed. "Shall, we, get—" She jabbed the knife-point into Ann's side to punctuate each word. "—down, to, business?" She tilted her head to better look into Ann's eyes. "Near time to die, Prelate. I think I'd like to see you scream to death. Shall we try?"

"Over there!" Zedd tried to point, as best he could, confined as he was. "There's a light in the Keep."

Though dawn was beginning to lighten the sky, it was still dark enough to pick out the yellow glow coming from several windows. Gratch saw what Zedd was seeing, and banked toward the Keep.

"Bags," he muttered, "if that boy is already in the Keep, I'll . . ."

Gratch growled at Zedd's obvious reference to Richard. He could feel the growl against his back pressed to the gar's chest more than he could hear it. Zedd glanced to the ground, far below.

"I'll have to save him. That's all I meant, Gratch. If Richard is in trouble, I'll have to get down there to save him."

Gratch gurgled with satisfaction.

Zedd hoped Richard wasn't in trouble. The effort of maintaining the spell to make himself light enough for Gratch to carry him for the last week had sapped nearly all his strength. He didn't think he would be able to stand, much less use his power to save anyone. He would need days of rest after this.

Zedd stroked the huge, furry arms around him. "I love Richard, too, Gratch. We'll help him. Both of us will protect him." Zedd's eyes widened. "Gratch! Watch where you're going! Slow down!"

Zedd held his arms up before his face as the gar swooped down toward the rampart. Peeking between his arms, he could see the stone approach at alarming speed. He gasped as Gratch tightened his grip and flapped his wings, trying to halt their plummeting descent.

Zedd realized he was losing his grip on his spell. He was too exhausted to hold on any longer, and he was becoming too heavy for Gratch to carry. In desperation, he drew the spell back, like catching an egg rolling from the edge of a table.

Just in time, he snatched the spell before it winked out, and yanked it back.

Gratch's flapping finally netted enough air to slow them, and he pulled up before they hit. With a graceful flutter of his huge, leathery wings, the gar set them on the rampart. Zedd felt the furry arms come off his sweat soaked robes.

"Sorry Gratch. I almost lost my grip on the magic. I almost got us both hurt."

Gratch absently grunted acknowledgment. His glowing green eyes were searching the darkness. There were walls going everywhere up here, and a hundred places to hide. Gratch seemed to be searching them all.

A low growl rumbled in the gar's throat. The green glow intensified. Zedd searched the dark recesses, but saw nothing. Gratch did.

Zedd flinched when, with a sudden roar, the gar bounded into the darkness.

Massive claws ripped at the night air. Fangs tore at nothing.

Zedd began to see shapes seeming to come out of the air. Capes billowed open, and knives flashed as the things danced and spun around the gar.

Mriswith.

The creatures let out clicking hisses as they lunged at the great fur beast. Gratch caught them on claws, ripping their scaled hides open, spilling their blood and insides. Their howls as they died drew a shiver up Zedd's spine.

Zedd felt the air move as one swept past, intent on the gar. The wizard threw his hand out, casting a ball of liquid fire that caught the mriswith, igniting its cape, and then spilled flame over the rest of it.

The rampart was suddenly alive with the creatures. Zedd, digging deep to bring up the power, snapped back a line of dense air, throwing several over the edge. Gratch threw one at the wall with such violence that it burst open when it hit.

Zedd wasn't prepared for the pitched battle that was suddenly all around him. Through his numb exhaustion, Zedd's frenetic quest for ideas couldn't engender anything more ingenious than simple magic of fire and air.

A mriswith turned suddenly, bringing around its bladed claw. Zedd threw a line of air as sharp as an axe. It cleaved the mriswith's head. He used a web to snare several away from Gratch and cast them over the side of the wall. At this outer rampart, it was a drop of several thousand feet—straight down.

The mriswith, for the most part, ignored Zedd, so resolute were they with taking down the gar. Why did they want so badly to kill the gar? By the way Gratch was dispatching them, it seemed they held a primal hatred for the winged beast.

A wedge of light suddenly stabbed through the predawn darkness as a door opened. A small figure stood silhouetted in the light. In the illumination, Zedd could see the mriswith all lunging for the gar. He rushed forward, throwing a fist of fire that engulfed three of the scaled creatures spinning forward with their knives flashing.

A mriswith hurtled past, slamming Zedd's shoulder, knocking him from his feet. He saw the mriswith pile into the gar, knocking him back against the crenellated wall.

Zedd saw them all, in one seething mass, tumble over the edge, and fall into the night, just as his head hit the stone.

The door squeaked open. As Valdora rose from her work, Ann gasped to catch her breath, and at the same time fought the darkness trying to shroud her mind. She couldn't do it any longer. She was at the end. She had no more screams left. Dear Creator, she could not hold out any longer. Why hadn't he come to rescue her?

"Grandmamma." Holly grunted with effort as she labored to drag something, inch by inch, into the room. "Grandmamma. Something has happened."

Valdora turned to the girl. "Where did you find him?"

Ann struggled to lift her head. Holly huffed and strained to lift a skinny old man up by his maroon robes and lean him against the wall. Blood trickled down the side of his head and matted his wavy white hair sticking out in disarray.

"He's a wizard, Grandmamma. He's near to dead. I saw him having a fight with a gar, and some other creatures all covered with scales."

"What makes you think he's a wizard?"

Holly straightened, panting as she stood over the old man on the floor. "He was using his gift. He was casting balls of fire."

Valdora frowned. "Reeeally. A wizard. How interesting." She scratched her nose. "What happened to the creatures, and the gar?"

Holly wheeled her arms about as she described the battle. "And then they all jumped on the gar, and all of them fell over the side. I went to the edge and looked, but I couldn't see them anymore. They all fell down the mountain."

Ann's head thumped back to the table. Dear Creator, it was a wizard who was supposed to rescue her.

It was all for naught. She was going to die. How could she have been so vain as to believe she could do something this risky and get away with it. Nathan was right.

Nathan. She wondered if he would ever find her body to know what had happened, or would even care if his warden was dead. She was a foolish, foolish, old woman, who thought herself more clever than she was. She had tampered with prophecy one time too many, and it had bitten her. Nathan was right. She should have listened.

Ann flinched when she saw Valdora leaning over her with a wicked grin. She pushed the knifepoint up under Ann's chin.

"Well, dear Prelate, it seems I have a wizard to dispatch." She drew the knifepoint across Ann's throat. She could feel it tugging at the skin, cutting and scratching as it dragged along.

"Please, Valdora, ask Holly to leave the room. You shouldn't let your granddaughter see you kill someone."

Valdora turned. "You'd like to watch, wouldn't you, dear?"

Holly swallowed. "No, Grandmamma. She never tried to hurt us."

"I've told you, she hurt me."

Holly pointed. "I brought him in here so you could help him."

"Oh, no. Can't have that. He must die, too."

"And what did he do to hurt you?"

Valdora shrugged. "If you don't want to watch, then go. It won't hurt my feelings."

Holly turned, pausing a moment to glance down at the old man. She reached out and touched his shoulder in a comforting way, and then hurried away.

Valdora turned back. She laid the knife against Ann's cheek, under her eye. "Should I gouge out your eyes, first?"

Ann closed her eyes, unable to witness the terror any longer.

"No!" Valdora jabbed the point under her chin. "Don't close your eyes! You will watch! If you don't open them, I will gouge them out then."

Ann opened her eyes. She held her lower lip between her teeth as she watched Valdora put the point to her chest and lift the handle straight up.

"At last," Valdora whispered. "Vengeance."

She lifted the knife. It paused in midair as she pulled a deep breath.

Valdora's body twitched as a sword blade erupted from the center of her chest.

Her eyes widened, and she let out a gurgling squeal as the knife dropped to the floor.

Nathan put a foot to Valdora's back and drew the sword out of the woman. She went down hard to the stone floor.

Ann let out a wail of relief. Tears streamed from her eyes as the bonds holding her wrists and ankles broke.

Nathan, tall and grim, gazed down at her lying on the table. "You foolish woman," he whispered, "what have you let be done to you?"

He bent and took her up in his arms as she wept like a child. His arms felt as sweet as the Creator's as he held her to his breast.

As her crying slowed, he parted from her, and she saw that the front of him was soaked with blood. Her blood.

"Remove the block, and then lie back and let me see if I can possibly heal this mess."

Ann pushed his hand away. "No. First I must do what I came to do." She pointed. "It is he. The wizard we've come for."

"Can't it wait?"

She wiped blood and tears from her eyes. "Nathan, I have gone through this dreadful prophecy this far. Let me finish. Please?"

With a disgusted sigh, he reached in a pouch beside his scabbard at his belt and pulled out a Rada'Han. He handed it over as she slid off the table. When her feet touched the floor, the pain crumpled her. Nathan caught her with a big arm and helped her to kneel before the unconscious wizard.

"Help me, Nathan. Open it for me. She broke most of my fingers."

With trembling hands, she placed the collar around the wizard's neck. Pushing with her palms, she at last managed to snap it shut, locking on not only the collar, but its magic. The prophecy was fulfilled.

Holly stood in the doorway. "Is Grandmamma dead?"

Ann sagged back on her heels. "Yes, my dear child. I'm sorry." She held out a hand. "How would you like to watch a healing, instead of a hurting?"

Holly gently took the hand. She glanced to the wizard on the floor. "And him? Will you heal him, too?"

"Yes, Holly, him too."

"That was why I brought him in: to be helped. Not to be killed. Grandmamma helped people sometimes. She wasn't always mean."

"I know," Ann said.

A tear rolled down the girl's cheek. "What is to become of me, now?" she whispered.

Ann smiled through the tears. "I am Annalina Aldurren, Prelate of the Sisters of the Light, and have been for a good long time. I've taken in many young women with the gift, like you, and have taught them to be wonderful women who heal and help people. I would be most happy if you would come with us."

Holly nodded, a smile coming to her tearstained face. "Grandmamma took care of me, but she was mean to other people, sometimes. Mostly those who would try to hurt us, or cheat us, but you never did. It was wrong for her to hurt you. I'm sorry she wasn't nicer. I'm sorry she had to be mean, and die."

Ann kissed the girl's hand. "Me, too. Me, too."

"I have the gift." She looked up with big, doleful eyes. "Can you teach me to heal with it?"

"It would be my honor."

Nathan picked up his sword and, with a dramatic flourish, slid it back into its scabbard. "You want to be healed, now? Or would you prefer to bleed to death so I can try my hand at resurrection?"

Ann winced as she came to her feet. "Heal me, my savior."

He squinted. "Then allow me access to my power, woman. I can't heal with my sword."

Ann closed her eyes as she lifted a hand, focusing her inner sense on his Rada'Han, removing the block in the flow of his Han. "It is done."

Nathan grunted. "I know it's done; I can feel it back, you know."

"Help me onto the table, Nathan." Holly held her hand as she was lifted up.

Nathan peered down at the wizard on the floor. "Well, you've finally got him. Far as I know, one such as he has never been collared before." His penetrating blue eyes turned to her. "Now that you've got a wizard of the First Order, the true madness of this whole plan of yours begins."

Ann sighed as his healing hands at last caressed her. "I know. Hopefully, Verna has her end of matters well in hand by now."

CHAPTER 41

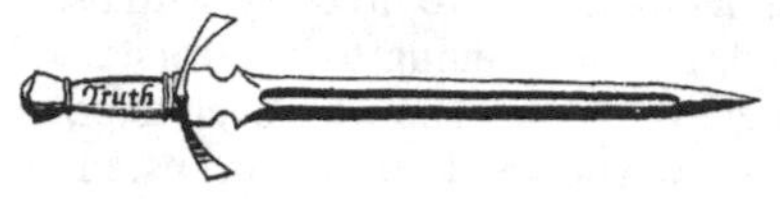

ZEDD GASPED AS HIS eyes popped opened. He sat bolt upright. A big hand on his chest pushed him back down.

"Take it easy, old man," a deep voice said.

Zedd goggled up at the square-jawed face. His shoulder-length white hair fell forward as he leaned over, putting both hands to the sides of Zedd's head.

"Who are you calling 'old,' old man?"

The penetrating blue eyes, beneath an intimidating raptor's brow, smiled along with the rest of his face. It was a mixed visage Zedd found unsettling. "Now that you mention it, I guess I am a bit older than you."

There was something familiar about that face. It came to him in a rush. Zedd shoved the hands away and sat up, pointing a bony finger at the tall man beside the table.

"You look like Richard. Why do you look like Richard?"

His cheeks drew back with a wide smile. The brow was still looking very hawklike. "He's a relative of mine."

"Relative! Bags!" Zedd peered closer. "Tall. Muscular. Blue eyes. Hair looks of similar texture. That jaw. Worse, the eyes." Zedd folded his arms. "You're a Rahl," he pronounced.

"Very good. You know Richard, then."

"Know him! I'm his grandfather."

His brow elevated. "Grandfather . . ." He wiped his face with one of his big hands. "Dear Creator," he muttered, "what has that woman gotten us into."

"Woman? What woman?"

With a sigh, he took the hand away from his face. The smile returned and he bowed. A rather good bow, Zedd thought. "Allow me to introduce myself. I'm Nathan Rahl." He straightened. "And may I have your name, friend?"

"Friend!"

Nathan rapped his knuckles on Zedd's forehead. "I just healed your cracked skull. That should count for something."

"Well," Zedd grumbled, "perhaps you're right. Thank you, Nathan. I'm Zedd. A talented bit of healing, if my skull really was cracked."

"Oh, it was. I seem to get quite a bit of practice. How do you feel?"

Zedd took stock of himself. "Well, fine. I feel fine. My strength is back. . . ." He groaned, remembering what had happened. "Gratch. Dear spirits, I have to get out of here."

Nathan planted a restraining hand on Zedd's chest. "We have to have a little talk, friend. At least I hope we can become friends. We unfortunately have a lot in common, besides being related to Richard."

Zedd blinked up at the tall man. "Like what?"

Nathan unbuttoned his ruffled shirt at the top. The whole front of him was covered with dried blood. Nathan hooked a finger through a dull silver collar around his neck and lifted it a bit.

Zedd's voice lowered to a somber timber. "Is that what I think it is?"

"You're a pretty smart fellow, I've no doubt, or you wouldn't be of such value."

Zedd returned his gaze to the blue eyes. "And what unfortunate thing do we have in common?"

Nathan reached out and tugged something at Zedd's neck. Zedd's hands shot up to feel the smooth metal collar. He could find no seam.

"What is the meaning of this? Why would you do this?"

Nathan heaved a sigh. "Not me, Zedd." He pointed. "Her."

A squat old woman with gray hair tied in a loose knot at the back of her head was walking through the doorway. She held the hand of a little girl.

"Ah," she said, as her fingers touched the top of the dark brown dress buttoned to her throat. "I see Nathan has you back to right. I'm so pleased. We were worried."

"Is that so," Zedd said noncommittally.

The old woman smiled. "Yes." She looked at the little girl, stroking her straight, light brown hair. "This is Holly. She dragged you in here. She saved your life."

"I seem to remember seeing her. Thank you for your help, Holly. You have my gratitude."

"I'm so glad you're healed," the girl said. "I was afraid that gar might have killed you."

"Gar? Did you see him? Is he all right?"

She shook her head. "He went over the wall with all those monsters."

"Bags," Zedd whispered through his teeth. "That gar was a friend."

The woman lifted an eyebrow. "A gar? Well, I'm sorry, then."

Zedd turned his glare on the woman. "What is this collar doing around my neck?"

She spread her hands. "I'm sorry, but it's necessary for now."

"You will remove it."

Her smile stayed where it was. "I understand your concern, but it must remain in place, for now." She folded her hands at her waist. "I'm afraid I haven't been introduced. What is your name?"

Zedd's voice came low and dangerous. "I am First Wizard Zeddicus Zu'l Zorander."

"I'm Annalina Aldurren, Prelate, of the Sisters of the Light." Her smile warmed. "You may call me Ann. All my friends do, Zedd."

With his eyes locked on the woman, Zedd hopped off the table. "You are not my friend." She took a step back. "You will address me as Wizard Zorander."

"Easy, friend," Nathan cautioned.

Zedd turned a glare on him that closed his mouth and straightened his spine.

She shrugged. "As you wish, Wizard Zorander."

Zedd tapped the collar at his neck. "Remove this at once."

Her smile clung tenaciously to her face. "It must remain."

Zedd began closing the distance between them. Nathan strode forward, apparently to restrain him. Without turning his eyes from the Prelate, Zedd lifted an arm, pointing a thin finger toward Nathan. The big man, his arms flailing, slid backward, as if he were standing on ice in a gale, until he was flattened against the far wall.

Zedd lifted his other hand, and the ceiling lit, glowing with bluish light. As his hand lowered, a razor-thin plane of light, like the surface of a still lake, lowered, passing over them. Ann's eyes widened. The plane of light descended until it settled on the floor, turning it to a churning layer of boiling light. The light coalesced into points of brilliant intensity.

From the points, lightning erupted. Crackling cords of white fire climbed the walls all around, filling the room with a pungent smell. Zedd circled a finger and the lightning leapt from the wall to his collar. Flashes struck out at the metal. The room shook in sympathy with the dancing thunder. Stone dust filled the air.

The table lifted and then exploded in a cloud of dust that was sucked into the streams of twisting light. The room quaked and groaned as huge blocks of stone loosened and began chattering out of their place in the wall.

Through the fury of power, Zedd realized it wasn't working. The collar absorbed the violence without breaking. He whipped an arm out, cutting the cacophony and light. The room rang in sudden silence. Enormous stone blocks hung halfway from the wall. The entire floor was charred and black, yet none of them were burned.

Through his analysis of the Prelate, the girl, and Nathan via the light bond, he now knew the exact extent of the power of each, their strengths, and weaknesses. She could not have made the collar, it had been made by wizards, but she could use it.

"Are you quite through?" Ann asked. Her smile was finally gone.

"I have not yet begun."

Zedd lifted his arms. He would channel enough power to level a mountain, if he had to. Nothing happened.

"That will be enough," she said. Some of her smile returned. "I can see where Richard gets some of his fury."

Zedd thrust out a finger. "You! You're the one who collared him."

"I could have taken him when he was a child, instead of letting him grow up with your love and guidance."

Zedd could count on the fingers of one hand the times in his life he had truly lost control of his temper, and worse, his reason. He was rapidly approaching the need to start counting on his other hand. "Don't try to placate me with your self-righteous justifications; there can be none for slavery."

Ann sighed. "A Prelate, like a wizard, must sometimes use people. I'm sure you understand that. I regret having had to use Richard, and that I must use you, but I have no choice." A wistful smile passed across her face. "Richard was a handful in a collar."

"If you think Richard was trouble, you have seen nothing yet. Wait until you find out the trouble his grandfather will bring down on you." Zedd ground his teeth. "You put one of your collars around his neck. You abducted boys from the Midlands. You have broken the truce that has stood for thousands of years. You know the consequences of such a transgression. The Sisters of the Light will pay the price."

Zedd was standing at the brink of the abyss, at the brink of violating the Wizard's Third Rule, yet he couldn't bring his reason under control. That, in fact, was the only way to violate the Third Rule.

"I know the consequences of the Imperial Order taking the world. I know you don't understand right now, Wizard Zorander, but I hope you will come to see that we fight on the same side."

"I understand a lot more than you think I do. You are aiding the Order through this. I've never had to make my allies prisoners to fight for what's right!"

"Really. What would you call the Sword of Truth?"

Seething, he refused to argue with the woman. "You will remove this collar. Richard needs my help."

"Richard will have to take care of himself. He's a smart boy. You are partly responsible for that. That's why I let him grow up with you."

"The boy needs my help! He needs to know how to use his power. If I don't get to him, he could come up into the Keep. He doesn't know the dangers here. He doesn't know how to use his gift. He could be killed. I can't let that happen. We need him."

"Richard has already been up to the Keep. He spent most of yesterday there, and he left unharmed."

" 'Once lucky,' " Zedd quoted, " 'twice confident, and thrice dead.' "

"Have faith in your grandson. We must help him in other ways. There is no time to waste. We must be going."

"I'm not going anywhere with you."

"Wizard Zorander, I'm asking you to help. I'm asking you to cooperate and come with us. Much is at stake. Please do as I ask, or I will be forced to use the collar. You would not like that."

"Listen to her, Zedd," Nathan said. "I can testify that you won't like it. You don't have a choice. I understand how you feel, but it will be easier if you just do as she asks."

"What manner of wizard are you?"

Nathan stood a bit taller. "I'm a prophet."

At least the man was honest. He hadn't recognized the light bond for what it was, and didn't know what Zedd could read from it. "And are you happy about being held in slavery?"

Ann laughed aloud. Nathan didn't; his eyes betrayed the composed, simmering, deadly fury of a Rahl. "I assure you, sir, it is not by my choice. I've been railing against it most of my life."

"She may know how to subjugate a wizard who is a prophet, but she is going to find out just why I hold the rank of First Wizard. I earned the rank in the last war. Both sides in that war called me 'the wind of death.' "

It had been one of the fingers he counted.

Turning away from Nathan, Zedd fixed the Prelate with a look of such cold menace that she swallowed as she retreated a step. "By breaking the truce, you have condemned any Sister caught in the Midlands to death. By the terms of the truce, they have just been sentenced. Each of you has lost the right to trial or mercy. Any of you caught will be executed on sight without prejudice."

Zedd thrust his fists into the air. Lightning laced from the clear sky, hammering the Keep above them. A deafening howl rose, and a ring of light expanded outward, racing through the sky, leaving a trail of clouds like smoke from flame.

"The truce is ended! You now stand in enemy territory, and upwind of death.

"If you take me away by this collar, I promise you that I will go to your homeland and lay waste to the Palace of the Prophets."

Stone faced, Prelate Annalina Aldurren regarded him silently for a moment. "Don't make promises that you can't keep."

"Try me."

A distant smile touched her lips. "We really must be going."

With a grim glare, Zedd nodded. "So be it."

Verna only incrementally became aware that she was awake. It was as dark with her eyes open as with them closed. She blinked, trying to ascertain if she really was conscious.

Deciding that she really was awake, she called her Han in order to light a flame. It wouldn't come. She sank deeper into herself, and pulled more power.

Straining with all her might, she at last managed to light a small flame in her palm. There was a candle on the floor beside the pallet where she sat. She sent the flame into the candle wick, sagging with relief that she could see at last without the monumental effort required to hold forth a flame with her Han.

The room was bare except for the pallet, the candle, a small tray with bread and a tin cup of water, and what looked to be a chamber pot against the far, plastered wall. Not too far—the room was not very big. There were no windows, only a heavy wooden door.

Verna recognized the room; it was one of the rooms in the infirmary. What was she doing in the infirmary?

Looking down, she realized she was naked. She turned to the side, and saw her clothes in a pile. When she turned, she felt something at her throat. Reaching up tentatively, she groped at her neck.

A Rada'Han.

Her flesh went atingle. Dear Creator, she had a Rada'Han around her neck. Panic washed through her in a dizzying rush. She clawed at her neck, trying to get it off. She heard a cry coming from her own throat as she was whimpered in terror while yanking frantically at the unyielding ring of metal.

In horror, she realized what the boys felt to have this instrument of domination bound to them. How many times had she, herself, used a collar to make someone do as she wished?

But only to help them, only in their best interest—only to help them. Did they feel this same helpless dread?

She remembered with shame using the collar on Warren.

"Dear Creator, forgive me," she cried. "I only wanted to do your work."

Sniffling back the tears, she brought herself back under control. She had to figure out what was happening. She knew that this collar wasn't around her neck to help her; it was to control her.

Verna fumbled at her hand. The Prelate's ring was gone. Her heart sank; she had failed in her guardianship. She kissed the naked finger, beseeching strength.

She pounded her fist against the door when the handle produced no movement. She summoned all her power, focusing it on the handle, trying to make the lever lift. It wouldn't budge. She lashed out at the hinges she knew to be on the other side. Furiously, she concentrated, applying her Han to the task. Tongues of light, green with mental bile, lashed at the door, licked through the cracks and flickered under the gap at the bottom.

Verna cut the impotent flow of Han, remembering seeing Sister Simona trying the very same thing hour after hour, with the same ineffectual results. The shield on the door couldn't be broken by one in a Rada'Han. She knew better than to waste her strength on useless effort. Simona might be crazy, but she was not.

Verna slumped back down on the pallet. Her fists pounding against the door would not get her out. Her gift would not get her out. She was trapped.

Why was she here? She looked down at her finger, where the Prelate's ring belonged. That was why.

With a gasp, she remembered the real Prelate. Ann had given her a mission, and was depending on her to get the Sisters of the Light away before Jagang arrived.

She dove for her clothes, searching frantically through them. Her dacra was gone. That was probably why they had stripped her: to make sure she had no weapon. That was what had been done to Sister Simona, for her own protection, to be sure she wouldn't hurt herself. They couldn't let a crazy woman have a deadly weapon.

Her fingers found her belt. She yanked it from the pile of clothes and, fumbling along its length, found the bulge in the thickness of leather.

Trembling with hope, Verna held the belt near the candle. She pulled open the false seam. There, nestled inside the secret pocket, was the journey book. She clutched the belt to her breast, thanking the Creator as she rocked on the pallet, holding her belt tight to her. She had at least this much.

When she had finally calmed, she pulled her clothes close to the weak light and dressed, feeling better, at least, not to be naked and helpless. She was no less helpless, but at least she didn't have to suffer the indignation of being a naked prisoner. She was beginning to feel the least little bit better.

Verna didn't know how long she had been unconscious, but she realized she was ravenous. She devoured the crust of bread, and gulped down the water.

After her belly was at least partially satisfied, she turned her thoughts to how she had come to be in this room. Sister Leoma. She remembered Sister Leoma and three others waiting for her in her office.

Sister Leoma was high up on her list of suspected Sisters of the Dark. Though she hadn't been put to a test, she had been a part of putting Verna in here. That was proof enough. It had been dark and she hadn't seen the other three, but she had a list of suspects in her head. Phoebe and Dulcinia had let them in—against her orders. However reluctantly, they had to be placed on the list, too.

Verna started pacing the small room. She was beginning to get angry. How dare they think they could get away with this?

They had gotten away with it.

A scowl settled in. No, they hadn't. Ann had given her this responsibility and she would live up to that faith. She would get the Sisters of the Light away from the palace.

Verna touched her fingers to her belt. She should send a message. Dare she, in here? What if she were caught? It could ruin everything. But she had to let Ann know what had happened.

Her pacing halted abruptly. How was she going to tell Ann that she had failed, and that because of her, all the Sisters of the Light were in mortal danger and she had no way to do anything about it? Jagang was coming. She had to escape. With her in this prison, none of the Sisters would know to escape.

And Jagang was going to have them all.

Richard leaped from the horse as it skidded to a halt. He glanced down the road and saw the others far below galloping to catch him. He rubbed the horse's nose and then started to tie the reins to an iron lever on the dropgate mechanism.

He glanced over the gears and levers, and then tied the reins to the end of a gear shaft instead. The place he had at first started tying the reins was the release lever to the huge gate. A good yank, and the portcullis could come crashing down on the horse.

Without waiting for the others, Richard started into the Wizard's Keep. He was furious that no one had awakened him. A light is burning in the windows of the Keep for half the night, he thought, and no one has the nerve to wake the Lord Rahl and tell him.

And then, not an hour before, he had seen the lightning, and the bloom of light racing outward in an expanding ring through a clear sky, leaving in its wake a smoky layer of clouds.

A thought coming to him, Richard paused before he went into the Keep and turned to look down on the city. At the bottom of the Keep road other roads branched off, leading away from Aydindril.

What if someone had been in the Keep? What if they had taken something? He had better tell the soldiers to hold anyone trying to leave. As soon as the others reached the Keep, he would send one back down to tell the soldiers to bring back anyone leaving and to seal the roads.

Richard watched the people on the road. Most were coming into the city, not leaving. There were a few leaving, though: what looked to be a few families with handcarts; some soldiers going out on patrol; a couple of wagons with trade goods; and four horses, close together, trotting past the people on foot. He would have them all stopped and checked.

But checked for what? He could take a look at the people

himself, after the soldiers brought them back, and maybe tell if they carried anything magic.

Richard turned back toward the Keep. He didn't have the time. He needed to find out what had been going on up here, and besides, how would he know if it were a thing of magic? It would be a waste of time better spent. He needed to get to work with Berdine and translate the journal, not paw through families' belongings. People were still leaving, not wanting to live under D'Haran rule. Let them.

He marched through the shields inside, knowing that the others would be blocked when they arrived. The five of them would be upset he hadn't waited for them. Well, maybe the next time they would wake him if they saw lights in the Keep.

Shrouded in his mriswith cape, he made his way upward, toward where he had seen the lightning hit the Keep. He avoided passageways that he could sense were dangerous, and found other routes that at least didn't raise the hair at the back of his neck. Several times he sensed mriswith, but they didn't come near.

In a wide room with four corridors leading from it, Richard stopped. Several doors stood closed. One had a trail of blood leading to it. He squatted and inspected the smeared trail of blood and determined that it was actually two trails: one leading into the room, and one leading out.

Richard flung open the mriswith cape and drew his sword. The clear ring of steel echoed down the corridors. With the point of the blade, he pushed the door open.

The room was empty, but it was far from ordinary. The wood floor was scorched. Sooty, jagged lines were seared into the stone as if an enraged lightning storm had been trapped in the room. Most puzzling, though, was the stone block of the walls; here and there huge blocks of stone hung halfway from the wall, as if they had come near to toppling out of their place. The room looked like it had nearly come apart in an earthquake.

There were blood splatters all over the floor, and to the side a big pool of it, but because of the fire that had blackened the floor, it was all dry as dust, and told him little.

Richard followed the trail of blood from the room until it led to a door to the outer rampart. He stepped out into the cold air and immediately saw the splashes of blood spilled across the stone. It was recent—within the last day.

Mriswith, and parts of mriswith, littered the windswept rampart. Even though they were frozen, now, they still stank. Against one wall, a good five feet up, was a huge splat of blood, and below it, on the ground, a dead mriswith, its scaled hide burst open. If the spray of blood had been on the ground, instead of the wall, Richard would have thought it had fallen from the sky and been killed from the impact.

His eyes gliding over the mess, Richard thought it looked like what was left when Gratch fought mriswith. He shook his head in dismay, wondering what had happened.

He followed a trail of blood to a notch in the crenellated wall and found blood staining the stone to each side. He stepped into the notch and peered over the edge. It was a dizzying sight.

The stone blocks of the Keep plunged nearly vertically, flaring slightly toward their foundation far below, and beneath that the stone of the mountain itself fell away for what looked to be several thousand feet. From the notch in the wall, a trail of blood ran down the face, disappearing in the distance below. There were several big splotches in the bloody trail; something had gone over the edge, smacking the wall on the way down. He would have to send soldiers out to see what, or who, had gone over the edge.

He ran a finger through different trails of blood at the edge; most of it reeked of mriswith. Some did not.

Dear spirits, what had happened up here? Richard pressed his lips together as he shook his head. He drew the black mriswith cape around himself and vanished as he pondered, thinking, too, for some reason, about Zedd. He wished Zedd were here with him.

CHAPTER 42

THIS TIME, WHEN VERNA saw the little flap open at the bottom of the door, she was ready. She dove toward it, shoving the tray aside and putting her face against the floor, trying to see out.

"Who's out there! Who is it! What's going on? Why am I being held here? Answer my questions!" She could see a woman's boots and the hem of a dress. Probably a Sister who cared for those in the infirmary. The woman straightened. "Please! I need another candle! This one's almost gone!"

She could hear the disinterested footfalls vanish back up the hall, and then the sound of the door and the big bolt being dropped into place as she ground her teeth and pounded her fist on the door. Verna finally slumped down on the pallet, comforting her hand. She had been pounding the door too often, of late. Her frustration was overcoming her sense, she knew.

In the windowless room, she had no idea anymore if it was day or night. She assumed that they brought her food in the day, and so tried to keep track of time in that way, but sometimes it seemed they brought food only hours apart, and at other times she was nearly starved to death before they brought it. She sorely wished they would do something about the chamber pot.

They didn't bring her enough food, either. Her dress was getting quite loose at the hips and bust. She had wished, for the last several years, that she could be a bit smaller, as she had been before she went on her journey twenty years before. She had been thought attractive, in her youth. Her extra weight always seemed a reminder of that lost youth and beauty.

She laughed maniacally. Maybe they thought so, too, and had decided to put the Prelate on a fast. Her laughter died. She had wished Jedidiah would see what was on the inside, instead of just the outside, and here she was longing for the outside, just as he did. A tear rolled down her cheek. Warren had never ignored what was inside. She was a fool.

"I pray you are safe, Warren," she whispered to the walls.

Verna slid the tray across the floor toward the candle. She flopped down and snatched up the tin cup of water. Before she gulped it down, she stopped, cautioning herself to make it last. They never brought her enough water. Too often she gulped it down and then spent the next day lying in her bed daydreaming about diving into a lake with her mouth open, guzzling down as much as she wanted.

She put the cup to her lips and took a dainty sip. When she set it back on the tray, she saw something new, something other than the half loaf of bread. There sat a bowl of soup.

Verna reverently lifted it, inhaling the aroma. It was a thin onion broth, but it seemed a queen's feast. Nearly in tears with joy, she took a swallow, savoring the rich flavor. She tore off a chunk of bread and dunked it in the soup. It tasted better than chocolate, better than anything she had ever eaten. She broke the rest of the bread into small pieces and dumped them all in the bowl. Swelling in the soup, it made the bread seem more than she could eat. But she did.

As she ate, she worked the journey book from its pouch in her belt. Her hopes sagged again, as there was no new message. She had told Ann what had happened, and she had received back a hastily scrawled message that said only "You must escape and get the Sisters away." She had received no message since.

After she had tipped up the bowl and drained the last of the soup, she blew out the candle, saving it for later. She put the half cup of water behind the candle so as to help insure she wouldn't spill it in the dark, and then lay back on the pallet, rubbing her full stomach.

She woke from a dead sleep when she heard the door lever clang as it was lifted. Verna put the back of a hand to her eyes, protecting them from the dazzling illumination that stabbed into the room. She scooted back against the wall as the door closed. A woman stood holding a lamp. Verna squinted in its blinding brightness.

The woman set the lamp on the floor and straightened to fold her hands at her waist. She stood watching, saying nothing.

"Who is it? Who's there?"

"Sister Leoma Marsick," came the terse reply.

Verna blinked as her eyes finally acclimated to the lamplight. Yes, it was Leoma. Verna could make out her wrinkled face and long white hair hanging back over her shoulders.

Leoma was the one in the Prelate's office. The one who had put her in here.

Verna sprang for the woman's throat.

Confused for a moment, she realized she was sitting back on her pallet, and her behind smarted from the rough landing. She felt the disturbing sensation of the Rada'Han preventing her from rising. She tried to move her legs, but they wouldn't respond. It was a singularly terrifying sensation. She gasped for air, fighting back a cry of panic. She stopped trying to fight it, to stand, and the alarm eased, but the disquieting, extrinsic feeling didn't.

"That will be quite enough, Verna."

Verna made sure her voice was under control before she spoke. "What am I doing in here?"

"You were being held until your trial had concluded."

Trial? What trial? No. She would not give Leoma the satisfaction. "That would seem appropriate." Verna wished she could stand; it was shaming to have Leoma looking down upon her like this. "And has it, then?"

"That is why I'm here. I've come to inform you of the decision of the tribunal."

Verna bit off her caustic reply. Of course these traitors found her guilty of some fraudulent charge. "And their decision, then?"

"You have been found guilty of being a Sister of the Dark."

Verna was struck speechless. She stared up at Leoma, but couldn't bring forth a word at the pain of having Sisters convict her of that. She had worked nearly her whole life to see the Creator honored in this world. Rage boiled up, but she held it in check, remembering Warren's admonition about her temper.

"Sister of the Dark? I see. And how could I have been convicted of such an accusation without evidence?"

Leoma chuckled. "Come now, Verna, surely you would not believe you could get away with such a high crime and leave no evidence."

"No, I suppose you managed to find something. Do you intend to tell me, then, or did you simply come here to gloat over having at last managed to make yourself Prelate?"

Leoma lifted an eyebrow. "Oh, I have not been named Prelate. Sister Ulicia was chosen."

Verna flinched. "Ulicia! Ulicia is a Sister of the Dark! She fled with five of her collaborators!"

"Quite the contrary. Sisters Tovi, Cecilia, Armina, Nicci, and Merissa have all returned and have been reinstated to their positions of authority as Sisters of the Light."

Verna struggled mightily, but unsuccessfully, to rise to her feet. "They were caught attacking Prelate Annalina! Ulicia killed her! They all fled!"

Leoma sighed, as if having to explain the most simple of things to an ignorant novice. "And who caught them attacking Prelate Annalina?" She paused. "You. You and Richard.

"The six Sisters have testified how they were attacked by a Sister of the Dark, after Richard had killed Sister Liliana, and they fled for their lives until they could arrange their return in order to save the palace from your grip. The misunderstanding has been set straight.

"It was you, a Sister of the Dark, who masterminded that accusation. You and Richard were the only witnesses. It was you who killed Prelate Annalina, you and Richard Rahl, whom you then aided in escaping. We heard testimony by Sisters who overheard you telling one of the guards, Kevin Andellmere, that he must be loyal to Richard, your accomplice, instead of the emperor."

Verna shook her head in disbelief. "So you took the word of six of the Keeper's minions, and on that basis, because there are more of them than one of me, convicted me?"

"Hardly. There were days and days of testimony and evidence presented. So much, in fact, that your trial has taken nearly two weeks; we wanted to make sure, in the interest of justice, and considering the seriousness of the charges, that we were completely fair and thorough. A great number of witnesses came forth to reveal the extent of your nefarious work."

Verna threw her hands up. "What are you talking about?"

"You have been methodically destroying the work of the pal ace. Thousands of years of tradition and effort have been overturned in your effort to bring the work of the Sisters of the Light to ruin. The problems you caused were extensive.

"The people in the city rioted because you had ordered the palace to halt payments to women who become pregnant by our young wizards. Those children are one of our main sources of boys with the gift. You wished to strangle that source. You stopped our young men from going to the city to see to their needs, and produce those offspring with the gift.

"It came to a head last week when we had a riot that had to be put down by the guards. The people were about to storm the palace, because of our cruelty in letting those young women and their children starve. Many of our young men joined in the uprising because you cut off their right to palace gold."

Verna wondered just what the true nature of the "uprising" had been, considering that young wizards were involved. But she didn't think Leoma would be forthcoming with the truth of it. Verna knew that there were good men among those young wizards, and feared their fate.

"Our gold corrupts the morals of everyone it touches," Verna said. She knew it was a waste to try to defend herself; this woman was not amenable to reason, or the truth.

"It has worked for thousands of years. But of course you would not want the benefits of this design to come to fruit in order to aid the Creator. These orders have been reversed, as have others of your ruinous directives.

"You would not want us to be able to determine if young men were prepared to face the world—you want them to fail—and so you disallowed the test of pain. That order, too, has been reversed.

"You have been defiling palace doctrine since the day you became Prelate. You yourself are the one responsible for the Prelate's death, and then you use your underworld tricks to install yourself as Prelate so you may destroy us.

"You never listened to the advice of your advisors, because you never had any intent of preserving the palace. You no longer even bother to look at reports, but instead burden inexperienced administrators with your work while you lock yourself in your sanctuary to confer with the Keeper."

Verna sighed. "That's it, then? My administrators don't like having to work? Some avaricious people are unhappy because I refuse to hand out gold from the palace treasury simply because they choose to get pregnant rather than establish their own families to bring children into the world? Some Sisters are disgruntled because I won't allow our young men to indulge in unrestrained self-gratification? The words of six Sisters who flee rather than stay to be questioned are suddenly taken seriously? And you even name one of them Prelate! All without so much as a single piece of hard evidence?"

A smile finally came to Leoma's lips. "Oh, we have hard evidence, Verna. We do indeed."

With a smug expression, she reached into a pocket and pulled out a piece of paper. "We had some very hard, very condemning evidence, Verna." She solemnly unfurled the paper as her austere gaze again settled on Verna. "And one other witness. Warren."

Verna flinched as if she had been struck across the face. She recalled the messages she had received from the Prelate and Nathan. Nathan had been in a panic that Warren must get away from the palace. Ann had been emphatic that Verna make sure Warren left at once.

"Do you know what this is, Verna?" Verna dared not speak, or even blink. "I think you do. It's a prophecy. Only a Sister of the Dark would be so arrogant as to leave such an incriminating document lying about. We found it down in the vaults, stuffed in a book. Perhaps you've forgotten all about it? Let me read it, then.

"When the Prelate and the Prophet are given to the Light in the sacred rite, the flames will bring to boil a cauldron of guile and give ascension to a false Prelate, who will reign over the death of the Palace of the Prophets."

Leoma folded the paper and slipped it back into her pocket. "You knew Warren was a prophet, and you took off his collar. You let a prophet roam free—a grievous offense in itself."

"And what makes you think Warren gave this prophecy," Verna asked cautiously.

"Warren testified that he did. It took a while for him to decide to speak his guilt in giving prophecy."

Verna's voice heated. "What did you do to him?"

"We used his Rada'Han, as is our duty, to elicit the truth. In the end, he confessed that the prophecy was his."

"His Rada'Han? You put a collar back on him!"

"Of course. A prophet must be collared. As Prelate, it was your duty to see it done. Warren is back in a collar, and under shields and guard at the prophet's quarters, where he belongs.

"The Palace of the Prophets has once again been set back to the way it is meant to be. This prophecy was the final, condemning piece of evidence. It proved the duplicity in your actions, and revealed your true intent. Fortunately, we were able to act before you could bring the prophecy to fruition. You have failed."

"You know none of that is true."

"Warren's prophecy proves your guilt. It names you a false Prelate, and reveals your plans to destroy the Palace of the Prophets." Her smile returned. "It created quite a stir when it was read before the tribunal. Quite a condemning piece of 'hard evidence,' I would say."

"You vile beast. I will see you dead."

"I would expect no less from one such as you. Fortunately, you are in no position to make good on your threats."

Looking up into Leoma's eyes, Verna kissed her ring finger. "Why don't you kiss your finger, Sister Leoma, and beseech the Creator's help in this time of trouble for the Palace of the Prophets?"

Wearing a mocking smile, Leoma spread her hands. "The palace has no trouble, now, Verna."

"Kiss your finger, Leoma, and show the beloved Creator your solicitude for the well-being of the Sisters of the Light."

Leoma didn't bring her hand to her lips. She couldn't, and Verna knew it. "I have not come here to pray to the Creator."

"Of course not, Leoma. You and I both know that you're a Sister of the Dark, as is the new Prelate. Ulicia is the false Prelate in the prophecy."

Leoma shrugged. "You, Verna, are the first Sister ever to be convicted of such a high crime. There is no longer any doubt. The conviction cannot be overturned."

"We're alone, Leoma. No one can hear us behind all those shields, except, of course, one with Subtractive Magic, and you've no need to fear those ears. None of the true Sisters of the Light can hear anything we say. If I tried to tell anyone anything you might have to say, no one would believe me.

"So let's drop the pretense, Leoma; we both know the truth."

A small smile spread onto Leoma's lips. "Go on."

Verna took a calming breath and folded her hands in her lap. "You haven't killed me, as Ulicia killed Prelate Annalina. You wouldn't have bothered to go through this whole sham if you intended to kill me; you could have killed me in my office. You obviously want something. What is it?"

Leoma chuckled. "Ah, Verna, you always were one to cut right to the heart of the matter. You're not very old, but I must admit, you are a smart one."

"Yes, I'm just brilliant; that's why I'm sitting here. What is it your master, the Keeper, wants you to get from me?"

Leoma pursed her lips. "At the moment, we serve another master. It is what he wants that is important."

Verna frowned. "Jagang? You've given an oath to him, too?"

Leoma's gaze darted away for an instant. "Not exactly, but that's beside the point. Jagang wants things, and he shall have them. It's my duty to see to it that he gets what he wants."

"And what is it you want from me?"

"You must forsake your loyalty to Richard Rahl."

"You're dreaming, if you think I'll do that."

An ironic smile came to Leoma's face. "Yes, I have been dreaming, but that, too, is beside the point. You must give up your bond to Richard."

"Why?"

"Richard has a way of interfering with the emperor's control of events. You see, loyalty to Richard blocks Jagang's power. He wishes to see if this loyalty can be broken so that he can enter your mind. It's an experiment, of sorts. It's my task to convince you to forsake that loyalty."

"I'll do no such thing. You can't make me abandon my fidelity to Richard."

Leoma's smile turned grim as she nodded. "Oh, yes, I can, and I will. I have a great deal of motivation. Before Jagang finally arrives to establish his headquarters here, I will break the bond to his enemy."

"How? By cutting off my Han? You think that will break my will?"

"You forget so easily, Verna? You forget the other uses the Rada'Han has? You forget the test of pain? Sooner or later, you will be on your knees begging to swear fidelity to the emperor.

"You make a grave mistake if you think I will balk at such a gruesome task. You make a grave mistake if you forget what I am, or think I have an ounce of sympathy. We have weeks yet, before Jagang arrives. We have all the time we need. Those weeks under the test will seem like years to you, until you submit, but submit you will."

Verna stiffened. She had forgotten the test of pain. She felt the constriction of terror rising in her throat again. She had seen it done to young men in a Rada'Han, of course, but it was never done for more than an hour, with years between tests.

Leoma stepped closer and kicked the cup of water aside.

"Shall we begin, Sister Verna?"

CHAPTER 43

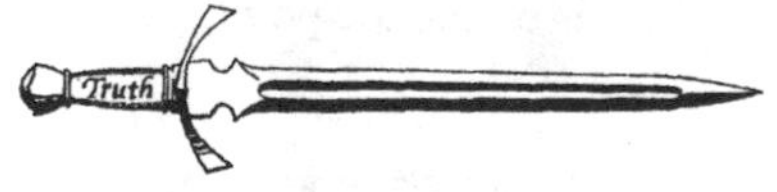

RICHARD WINCED WHEN HE saw the boy knocked senseless. Some of the bystanders pulled him aside, and another boy took his place. Even from behind the high window in the Confessors' Palace, he could hear the cheers from the crowd of children watching the boys play the game he had seen children in Tanimura playing: Ja'La.

In his homeland of Westland, he had never heard of Ja'La, but children in the Midlands played it just as did those in the Old World. The spirited game was fast-paced and looked exciting, but he didn't think children should have to pay the price of having their teeth knocked out for the fun of a game.

"Lord Rahl?" Ulic called. "Lord Rahl, are you here?"

Richard turned from the window and let the comforting shroud go as he flung the black mriswith cape back over his shoulders.

"Yes, Ulic. What is it?"

The big guard strode into the room when he saw Richard seem to appear out of the air. He was used to the sight. "There's a Keltish general here asking to see you. General Baldwin."

Richard touched his fingertips to his forehead as his mind searched. "Baldwin, Baldwin." He looked up. "General Baldwin. Yes, I remember. He's the commander of all Keltish forces. We sent him a letter about Kelton's surrender. What does he want?"

Ulic shrugged. "He would say only that he wants to speak with Lord Rahl."

Richard turned to the window, pushing the heavy gold drape back with a hand as he idly leaned against the painted window casing. He watched a boy doubled over, recovering from a hit with the broc. The boy straightened and went back to the play.

"How many men accompanied the general to Aydindril?"

"A small guard of five, maybe six hundred."

"He was told that Kelton had surrendered. If he meant trouble, he wouldn't march into Aydindril with so few men. I guess I had better see him." He turned back to the attentive Ulic. "Berdine is busy. Have Cara and Raina escort the general in."

Ulic clapped a fist to his heart and started to turn away, but turned back when Richard called his name. "Have the men found anything more at the bottom of the mountain below the Keep?"

"No, Lord Rahl, nothing more than all those parts of mriswith. The snow at the base of that cliff is drifted so deep that it will be spring, when it melts, before we can discover what else fell from the Keep. The wind could have carried whatever fell anywhere, and the soldiers have no idea where in that vast tract to dig. The mriswith arms and claws they found were light enough so that they didn't drive under the snow. Anything heavier could have gone down ten, maybe twenty feet in that light, windblown fluff."

Richard nodded in disappointment. "One other thing. The palace must have seamstresses. Find the head seamstress and ask her to please come see me."

Richard pulled his black mriswith cape around himself without really thinking about what he was doing, and went back to watching the Ja'La game. He was impatient for Kahlan and Zedd to arrive. It shouldn't be long, now. They must be close. Surely Gratch had found them and they would all be together soon.

He heard Cara's voice behind him, at the door. "Lord Rahl?"

Richard turned, letting the cape fall open as he relaxed. Standing tall between the two Mord-Sith was a sturdily built older man with a white-flecked dark mustache, the ends of which grew down to the bottom of his jaw, and graying black hair growing down over his ears. His pate shone through where his hair was thinning.

He wore a heavy, semicircular serge cape, richly lined with green silk and fastened on one shoulder with two buttons. A tall, embroidered collar was turned down over a tan surcoat decorated with a heraldic emblem slashed through with a diagonal black line dividing a yellow and blue shield. The man's high boots covered his knees. Long black gauntlets, their flared cuffs lying over the front, were tucked through a wide belt set with an ornate buckle.

As Richard became visible before his eyes, the general's face paled and he lurched to a halt.

Richard bowed. "General Baldwin, I'm pleased to meet you. I am Richard Rahl."

The general at last regained his composure and returned the bow. "Lord Rahl, I am honored that you would see me on such short notice."

Richard gestured. "Cara, please bring a chair for the general. He must be weary from his travel."

After Cara had placed a simple tufted leather chair before the table, and the general had seated himself, Richard sat in his own chair behind the table. "What can I do for you, General Baldwin?"

The general glanced up at Raina standing behind his left shoulder, and Cara behind his right. Both women stood relaxed and silent with their hands clasped behind their backs, sending the unequivocal message that they had no intention of going anywhere.

"You may speak freely, General. I trust these two to watch over me when I sleep."

He took a breath and seemed to relax a bit, accepting the assurance. "Lord Rahl, I've come about the queen."

Richard had thought that might be it. He folded his hands on the table. "I'm very sorry about what happened, General."

The general rested an arm on the table as he leaned in. "Yes, I've heard about the mriswith. I saw some of the loathsome beasts on the pikes outside."

Richard had to stop himself when he almost said that they might be beasts, but they weren't loathsome. A mriswith, after all, had killed Cathryn Lumholtz as she was trying to murder him, but the general wasn't likely to understand, so Richard kept it to himself, and said instead, "I deeply regret that your queen was killed while under my roof."

The general flipped his hand dismissively. "I meant no imputation, Lord Rahl. What I mean is that I've come about Kelton being without a king or queen, now that Cathryn Lumholtz is dead. She was the last successor to the throne, and with her sudden death, it presents a problem."

Richard kept his voice friendly, but official. "What sort of problem? You are part of us, now."

The man distorted his features in an offhanded expression. "Yes, we received the surrender documents. But the queen who led us is now dead. While she was in power, she acted within her authority, but we find ourselves at a loss as to how to proceed."

Richard frowned. "You mean you need a new queen, or king?"

He shrugged apologetically. "It is our way to have a monarch lead our people. Even if it's only symbolic, now that we've surrendered to the union with D'Hara, it gives the Keltish people esteem to have a king or queen. Without one the people feel that they are no more than nomads, without roots—without anything in common to tie them together.

"Since there is no Lumholtz in line of succession, one of the other Houses could come to the fore. None has the right to claim the throne, but one could eventually win the right. A contested throne could cause a civil war, though."

"I see," Richard said. "You realize, of course, that whoever you choose for your king or queen doesn't make any difference as far as your surrender is concerned. The surrender is irrevocable."

"It's not so simple. That's why I've come to seek your help."

"How can I help?"

The general kneaded his chin. "You see, Lord Rahl, Queen Cathryn surrendered Kelton to you, but now she's dead. Until we have a new monarch, we are your subjects. You are the equivalent of our king until a true monarch is named. However, if one of these Houses ascends to the throne, it could be that they see it differently."

Richard kept his tone from sounding as threatening as he felt. "I don't care how they see it. That river has been crossed."

The general waggled his hand as if to implore patience. "I think the future lies with you, Lord Rahl. The problem is that if the wrong House finally comes to the throne, they might have different ideas. Quite frankly, I would never have thought that the House of Lumholtz would have chosen to go with you and D'Hara. You must have been very persuasive to make the queen see reason.

"Some of these dukes and duchesses are talented at playing games of power, but not at what is in the best interest of all. These duchies are almost sovereign, and their subjects bow only to a monarch. There are those who would speak persuasively for Kelton to heed the word of the Crown, and not D'Hara, should one of the wrong Houses come to the throne and declare the surrender invalid. Civil war would be the result.

"I'm a soldier, and view events with a soldier's eyes. A soldier likes least of all fighting in a civil war. I have men from every duchy. Civil war would tear the unity of the army apart, destroy us, and leave us vulnerable to true enemies."

Richard filled the silence. "I'm listening, go on."

"As I said, as a man who understands the value of unity, of unified authority, I think the future lies with you. Right now, until there is a new ruler on the throne, you are the law."

General Baldwin leaned sideways against the table and lowered his voice meaningfully. "Since you are the law at the moment, if you were to name a king or queen, then that would settle the matter. See what I mean? The Houses would be obligated to honor the new ruler, and go with you, if the new ruler says it is to be as has already been done."

Richard squinted. "You make it sound like a game, General. Moving this piece on the board to block an opposing piece before the opponent has his turn to take your marker."

He smoothed down his mustache. "It's your move, Lord Rahl."

Richard leaned back in his chair. "I see." He thought a moment, not knowing how he was going to get out of this. Maybe he could ask the general's advice as to which House would be loyal. He didn't think that would be wise, though, trusting a man who just walked in and announced his intent to help. It could be a ruse.

He glanced at Cara, who stood to the side behind the general. Her shoulders were hunched and her face wore a silent, confounded expression. When he moved his gaze to Raina, she signaled that she, too, didn't have any suggestions.

Richard rose and went to the window, staring out at the people in the city. He wished Kahlan were here. She knew all about this kind of thing: the ways of royalty and rulers. This taking-over-the-Midlands business was constantly proving more complicated than he had expected.

He could simply order this nonsense stopped, and send in D'Haran troops to enforce his orders, but that would waste valuable men taking care of what should already be settled. He could leave the matter until later, but he needed Kelton to remain loyal—other lands' surrender hinged on Kelton. He already had Kelton, but if he made a mistake, all his plans could end in ashes.

Richard wished Kahlan would hurry up and get to Aydindril. She could tell him what he needed to do. Perhaps he could stall until she and Zedd arrived, and with her advice, do the right thing. She should be here soon. But would it be soon enough?

Kahlan, what should I do?

Kahlan.

Richard turned back to the waiting general. "Since Kelton needs a monarch to stand as a symbol of hope and leadership for all Keltish people, I shall name one for you."

The general waited expectantly.

"By my authority as Master of D'Hara, to whom Kelton owes its allegiance, I name your queen.

"From this day forward, Kahlan Amnell is the Queen of Kelton."

General Baldwin's eyes widened as he came out of his chair. "You name Kahlan Amnell as our queen?"

Richard hardened his gaze as his hand settled on the hilt of his sword. "I do. All Kelton will bow to her. Like your surrender, this order is irrevocable."

General Baldwin dropped to his knees, his head hanging low. "Lord Rahl, I can hardly believe you would do this for my people. We are grateful."

Richard, his hand on the verge of drawing his sword, paused at the general's words. He hadn't expected such a reaction.

The general finally came to his feet before the table. "Lord Rahl, I must leave at once to bring this glorious news to our troops. They will be as honored as I to be the subjects of Kahlan Amnell."

Richard, unsure how to react, remained noncommittal. "I'm pleased that you would accept my choice, General Baldwin."

The general spread his arms. "Accept? This is beyond my hopes, Lord Rahl. Kahlan Amnell is the queen of Galea. It has been a cause of strife in our land that the Mother Confessor herself would serve as queen to our rival, Galea, but to now have her as our queen, too, well, it will prove that the Lord Rahl holds us in the same high esteem as Galea. When you are wedded to her, you will be wedded to our people, too, the same as the Galeans."

Richard was stiff and speechless. How did the man know that Kahlan was the Mother Confessor? Dear spirits, what had happened?

General Baldwin reached out and pulled Richard's hand from his sword, clasping it in a warm embrace. "Lord Rahl, this is the greatest honor our people have ever received: to have the Mother Confessor herself as our queen. Thank you, Lord Rahl, thank you."

General Baldwin was grinning joyously, but Richard was on the verge of panic. "It is my hope, General, that this will seal our unity."

Waving a hand, the general laughed with glee. "For all time, Lord Rahl. Now, if you will excuse me, I must return at once to let our people know of this great day."

"Of course," Richard managed to get out.

General Baldwin clasped hands with Cara and Raina before rushing from the room. Richard stood stunned.

Cara frowned. "Lord Rahl, is something wrong? Your face is as pale as ashes."

Richard finally took his gaze from the door the general had gone through, and looked to her. "He knew that Kahlan is the Mother Confessor."

Cara's brow twitched as if she were mystified. "Everyone knows that your bride-to-be, Kahlan Amnell, is the Mother Confessor."

"What?" he whispered. "You know, too?"

She and Raina nodded, Raina speaking. "Naturally. Lord Rahl, you do not look well. Are you ill? Perhaps you should sit down."

Richard looked from Raina's questioning face back to Cara. "She had a spell on her to protect her. No one knew she was the Mother Confessor. No one. A great wizard used magic to hide her identity. You never knew before."

Cara frowned, truly puzzled, now. "We didn't? That's most odd, Lord Rahl. It seems to me that I've always known she was the Mother Confessor." Raina nodded her agreement.

"Impossible," Richard said. He turned to the door. "Ulic! Egan!"

They burst through the door almost instantly, poised and ready for combat. "What is it, Lord Rahl?"

"Who am I to marry?"

Both men straightened in surprise. "The Queen of Galea, Lord Rahl," Ulic said.

"Who is she!"

The two men shared a confused glimpse at one another. "Well," Egan said, "she is the queen of Galea—Kahlan Amnell, the Mother Confessor."

"The Mother Confessor is supposed to be dead! Don't any of you remember the speech I gave to all the representatives, down in the council chambers? Don't you remember how I talked about how they should honor the memory of the dead Mother Confessor by joining with D'Hara?"

Ulic scratched his head. Egan stared at the floor while he sucked the tip of a finger in concentration. Raina looked to the others, hoping they would have an answer. Cara's face finally brightened.

"I think I remember, Lord Rahl," she said. "But I think you were speaking of past Mother Confessors in general, not your bride-to-be."

Richard looked from one face to another as each nodded.

"Look, I know you don't understand, but this involves magic."

"You're right, then, Lord Rahl," Raina said, turning more serious. "If there's a magic spell involved, then the spell would deceive us. You have magic, so you would be able to discern the difficulty. We must trust in what you tell us about magic."

Richard rubbed his hands together as he looked off, his eyes unable to find a place to settle. Something was wrong. Something was terribly wrong. But what? Maybe Zedd lifted the spell. Maybe he had a reason. It could be that there was nothing wrong. Zedd was with her. Zedd would protect her. Richard spun around.

"The letter. I sent them a letter. Maybe Zedd removed the spell because he knows that I've taken Aydindril from the Imperial Order, so he didn't think there was any need to keep her spelled."

"That sounds reasonable," Cara offered.

Richard felt a wave of worry rise into his throat. What if Kahlan was furious that he had ended the alliance of the Midlands and had demanded the surrender of the lands to D'Hara, and so she had insisted that Zedd take off the spell to let people know the Midlands still had a Mother Confessor? If so, that would mean she wasn't in trouble, but that she was angry with him. Anger he could accept. Trouble, he could not. If she was in trouble, he had to help her.

"Ulic, please go find General Reibisch and bring him to me at once." Ulic tapped a fist to his chest and rushed from the room. "Egan, you go visit some of the officers and men. Don't act as if it's anything out of the ordinary. Just engage them in conversation about me, maybe my marriage or something like that. See if others also know that Kahlan is the Mother Confessor."

Richard paced and thought as he waited for General Reibisch to arrive. What should he do? Kahlan and Zedd should be here at any time, but what if something was wrong? Even if Kahlan was angry about what he had done, that wouldn't stop her from coming to Aydindril, it would only make her want to talk him out of it, or lecture him on the history of the Midlands and what he was destroying.

Maybe she would want to tell him that their marriage was off, and she never wanted see him again. No. He could not believe that. Kahlan loved him, and even if she was angry, he refused to believe that she would willingly put anything before her love for him. He had to believe in her love, just as she had to believe in his.

The door opened and Berdine struggled into the room with her arms full of books and papers. She had a pen between her teeth. She smiled as best she could with the pen in her mouth, and dumped the things on the table.

"We need to talk," she whispered, "if you're not busy."

"Ulic went out to look for General Reibisch. It's urgent that I talk to him."

Berdine glanced to Cara, Raina, and the door. "Do you want me to leave, Lord Rahl? Is something wrong?"

Already, Richard had learned enough to know he was right about the journal they had found being important. He could do nothing until Reibisch returned.

"Who am I to marry?"

Berdine opened a book on the table as she sat in his chair and shuffled through the papers she had brought. "Queen Kahlan Amnell, the Mother Confessor." She looked up hopefully. "Do you have a bit of time? I could use your help."

Richard sighed and went around the desk to stand beside her. "Until General Reibisch gets here I've got time. What do you need?"

With the back end of her pen, she tapped the open journal. "I've almost got this bit here translated, and it seems he was emphatic about it when he wrote it, but I'm missing two words that I think are important." She pulled the High D'Haran version of *The Adventures of Bonnie Day* around before them. "I've found a place with the same two words in this. If you can remember what it says, I'll have it."

Richard had read *The Adventures of Bonnie Day* countless times, it was his favorite book, and he thought he could recite it by heart. He had discovered that he could not. He knew the book well, but remembering the exact words proved harder than he had thought it would be. He could remember the story, but not the exact story, word for word. Unless he could tell her the exact words of a sentence, the gist of the story wasn't often of much help.

He had gone to the Keep several times and searched for a version of the book he could read so they could cross-reference the D'Haran version, but he hadn't been able to find one. It was frustrating that he couldn't be of more help.

Berdine pointed to a place in *The Adventures of Bonnie Day.* "I need these two words. Can you tell me what this sentence says?"

Richard's hopes rose. It was the beginning of a chapter. He had had the most success with the beginnings of chapters because the starting places were memorable.

"Yes! This is the chapter where they leave. I remember. It starts, 'For the third time that week, Bonnie violated her father's rule about not going into the woods alone.' "

Berdine leaned over, looking at the line. "Yes, this is 'violated,' I've already got that one. This word here is 'rule,' and this one 'third'?"

Richard nodded when she glanced up. Grinning with the thrill of discovery, she dipped her pen in the bottle of ink and started writing on one of the sheets of paper she had brought, filling in a few of the blank places. When she finished, she proudly slid the paper over in front of him.

"This is what it says in this bit of the journal."

Richard picked up the paper and held it up in the light coming over his shoulder from the window.

The arguments rage on among us. Wizard's Third Rule: Passion rules reason. I fear this most insidious of rules may be our ruin. Though we know better, I fear some of us are violating it anyway. Each faction presses that their course of action is reason, but in the desperation, I fear all are passion. Even Alric Rahl sends frantic word of a solution. Meanwhile, the dream walkers scythe through our men. I pray the towers can be completed, or we are all lost. Today I said good-bye to friends leaving for the towers. I wept to know I will never see those good men again in this world. How many will die in the towers for the cause of reason? But alas, I know the worse cost should we violate the Third Rule.

When Richard finished the translation, he turned away, toward the window. He had been in those towers. He knew that wizards had given their life force into them to ignite the tower's spells, but they had never seemed real people to him before. It was chilling to read the anguish in the words of the man whose bones had lain in that room in the Keep for thousands of years. Through the words in the journal, his bones seemed to be coming to life.

Richard thought about the Third Rule, trying to reason it out for himself. Before, for the first and second, he had had Zedd, and then Nathan to explain it for him, to help him see how the rules worked in life. He would have to work this one out himself.

He recalled going down to the roads leading out of Aydindril, to talk to some of the people fleeing the city. He had wanted to know why they would leave, and had been told by fearful people that they knew the truth: that he was a monster who would slaughter them for his twisted pleasure.

When pressed, they quoted rumor as if it were fact seen with their own eyes, rumor of how the Lord Rahl had children as slaves in the palace, how he took countless young women to his bed, leaving them senseless from the experience to wander the streets naked. They claimed to know young women and girls whom he had gotten pregnant, and furthermore knew people who had actually seen the miscarriages of some of these poor victims of his rape, and they had been hideous, misshapen freaks, the spawn of his evil seed. They spat at him for the crimes he committed against helpless people.

He asked them how they could be so frank with him if he were such a monster. They said that they knew he wouldn't do them harm in the open, that they had heard how he pretended to be compassionate in public so as to fool people, so they knew he would do nothing to them in front of the crowds, and they would soon have their womenfolk away from his evil clutches.

The more Richard tried to put to rest the baffling beliefs, the more tenaciously the people clung to them. They said they had heard these things from too many others for it to be anything but true. Such common knowledge could not be false, they said, as it would be impossible to fool so many people. They were passionate in their belief and their fear, and would hear no arguments of logic. They simply wanted to be left alone to run to the protection they had heard was offered by the Imperial Order.

Their passion was going to bring them to true ruin. He wondered if this could be how violation of the Third Rule hurt people. He didn't know if it was a solid enough example. It seemed tangled with the First Rule: People would believe any lie, either because they wanted it to be true, or because they feared it was. It seemed it could be several rules mixed together, violated in tandem, and he couldn't tell where one ended and the other began.

And then Richard recalled the day back home in Westland when Mrs. Rencliff, who could not swim, had wrenched her arms from the men trying to hold her back, refusing to wait for the rowboat, and had leapt into a flood swollen river after her boy who had fallen in. The men rushed up a few minutes later with the rowboat and saved the boy's life. Chad Rencliff grew up without a mother; they never found her body.

Richard's skin prickled as if ice had touched it. He understood. Wizard's Third Rule: Passion rules reason.

It was a distressing hour of detailing the way people's passion instead of reason brought them to harm, and worse, wondering how magic could add ruin to the equation, as he knew it would, before Ulic finally returned with the general.

General Reibisch clapped a fist to his heart as he entered the room. "Lord Rahl, Ulic said you were in a hurry to see me."

Richard gripped the bearded man's dark uniform. "How long will it take you to get men ready to leave on a search?"

"Lord Rahl, they're D'Harans. D'Haran soldiers are always ready to leave on a moment's notice."

"Good. You know my bride-to-be, Queen Kahlan Amnell?"

General Reibisch nodded. "Yes. The Mother Confessor."

Richard winced. "Yes, the Mother Confessor. She's on her way here from the southwest. She's past due, and there may be trouble. She had a spell over her to protect her identity as the Mother Confessor, so that her enemies couldn't hunt her. Somehow, the spell has been removed. It might be nothing, but it could be that it means trouble. For sure, her enemies will now know of her."

The man scratched his rust-colored beard. His grayish green eyes came up at last. "I see. What would you like me to do?"

"We have close to two hundred thousand men in Aydindril, with another hundred thousand scattered all around the perimeter of the city. I don't know exactly where she is, except that she's supposed to be to the southwest and on her way here. We have to protect her.

"I want you to get a force together, half the troops in the city, a hundred thousand at least, to go out after her."

The general stroked his scar as he heaved a sigh. "That's a lot of men, Lord Rahl. Do you think we need to take that many from the city?"

Richard paced between the desk and the general. "I don't know exactly where she is. If we take too few we could miss her by fifty miles and wander off without ever making contact. With that many men we can fan out as we go, cast a wide net, covering all the roads and trails so we don't miss her."

"You will be going with us, then?"

Richard desperately wanted to go find Kahlan and Zedd. He glanced to Berdine sitting behind the desk as she worked, and thought about the words of warning from a three-thousand-year-old wizard. Wizard's Third Rule: Passion rules reason.

Berdine needed his help to translate the journal. He was already learning important things about the last war, and the towers, and the dream walkers. A dream walker again walked the world.

If he did go, and Kahlan slipped past him where he searched, it might take longer for him to join with her than if he simply waited in Aydindril. And then there was the Keep. Something had happened at the Keep, and it was his duty to guard the magic there.

Richard's passion told him to go—he desperately wanted to go search for Kahlan—but in his mind's eye, he saw Mrs. Rencliff diving into the dark, rushing water, refusing to wait for the boat. These men were his boat.

The troops could find Kahlan and protect her. He could do nothing to add to that protection. Reason told him to wait here, as much anxiety as that would cause him. Like it or not, he was a leader now. A leader had to act with reason, or everyone would pay the price of his passion.

"No, General. I'll remain in Aydindril. Get the troops together. Take the best trackers." He looked to the man's eyes. "I know I don't have to tell you how important this is to me."

"No, Lord Rahl," the general said in a compassionate tone. "Don't worry, we'll find her. I'll go with the men to make certain that everything is done with the same care as you would do it if you were there." He put his fist to his heart. "Every one of our lives before harm touches your queen."

Richard laid a hand to the man's shoulder. "Thank you, General Reibisch. I know I could do no more than you will. May the good spirits be with you."

CHAPTER 44

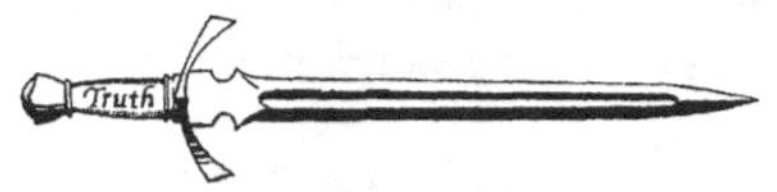

"PLEASE, WIZARD ZORANDER."

The skinny wizard didn't glance up from spooning beans and bacon into his mouth. She didn't know how the man could eat as much as he did.

"Are you listening?"

It wasn't like her to yell, but she was near the end of her patience. This was proving to be even more trouble than she had envisioned. She knew she had to do this, to cultivate his hostility, but this was too much.

With a pleased sigh, Wizard Zorander tossed his tin bowl down with their packs. "Good night, Nathan."

Nathan lifted an eyebrow as Wizard Zorander crawled into his bedroll. "Good night, Zedd."

Nathan, too, was becoming dangerously difficult to deal with since she had captured the old wizard. He had never had such a talented cohort before. Ann sprang to her feet and stood with her fists on her hips as she glared down at the white hair sticking from the blanket.

"Wizard Zorander, I'm begging you."

It infuriated her to implore his aid in such a humble fashion, but she had learned the hard way what the results could be when she used the power of his collar to bring him to task through unpleasant means. How the man could manage to get those tricks through the block she had locked on his collar mystified her, but get them through he did, to the great amusement of Nathan. She was not amused.

Ann was near tears. "Please, Wizard Zorander."

His head turned up, the firelight casting the lines of his bony face in harsh shadows. His hazel eyes fixed on her.

"If you open that book again, you will die."

With ghostlike stealth, he slipped spells around her shields when she least expected it. She was at a loss to understand how he had put a light spell on the journey book. She had opened it that night and had seen the message from Verna that she had been captured and put in a collar, and then everything had gone terribly wrong.

Opening the book had triggered the light spell. She had seen it swell and flare. A bright, burning cinder had shot up into the air, and the old wizard had calmly told her that if she didn't close the book by the time the glowing spark of light hit the ground, she would be incinerated.

With one eye on the hissing spark as it descended, she had managed only to scrawl a hurried message to Verna that she must escape and get the Sisters away. She had closed the book just in time. She knew he was not jesting about the deadly nature of the spell around the book.

She could see the softly glowing spell around it now. She had never seen one quite like it, and how he had managed to set it when she thought she had his power blocked, she couldn't fathom. Nathan didn't understand it either, but he seemed quite interested. She knew of no way to open the book without being killed.

Ann squatted down beside the bedroll. "Wizard Zorander, I know you have good reason to rail against me, but this is a matter of life and death. I must get a message through. The lives of Sisters are at stake. Wizard Zorander, please. Sisters could die. I know you are a good man, and wouldn't want that."

He brought a finger out from under the blanket and pointed it at her. "You bonded me into slavery. You have brought this upon yourself and your Sisters. I told you, you broke the truce, and have sentenced your Sisters to death. You are endangering the lives of ones I love. They could die because you wouldn't let me help them. You took me from protecting the things of magic in the

Keep. You are endangering the lives of my people in the Midlands. They could all die because of what you have done to me."

"Can't you understand that all our lives are tied together? This is a war against the Imperial Order, not between us. I have no wish to harm you, only to have you help me."

He grunted. "Don't forget what I told you: either you or Nathan had better remain awake at all times. If I catch you asleep, and Nathan isn't awake to protect you, you will never wake again. Fair warning, though you don't deserve it."

He rolled over and pulled the blanket up.

Dear Creator, was this happening the way the prophecy intended, or had everything gone terribly wrong? Ann moved around the fire to Nathan.

"Nathan, do you think you could talk some sense into him?"

Nathan glanced down at her. "I told you that this part of the plan is the true madness. Collaring a young man is one thing, collaring a wizard of the First Order is quite another. This is your plan, not mine."

She clenched her teeth as she snatched his shirt. "Verna could be killed in that collar. If she is killed, our Sisters could die, too."

He took a spoonful of beans. "I've been warning you against this plan from the beginning. You were nearly killed at the Keep, but this part of the prophecy is even more dangerous. I've talked to him; he's telling you the truth. As far as he is concerned, you are placing his friends in mortal danger. If he can, he will kill you in order to escape and go help them. No doubt in my mind."

"Nathan, after all the years we've been together, how could you be so callous about this?"

"You mean, after all these years of captivity, how can I still rebel against it?"

Ann turned her face away as a tear ran down her cheek. She swallowed back the lump in her throat.

"Nathan," she whispered, "in all the time you've known me, have you ever once seen me do anything cruel to someone other than because I had to, to protect lives? Have you ever once known me to struggle other than to preserve life and freedom?"

"I presume you mean other than my freedom."

She cleared her throat. "And I know I will have to answer to the Creator for that, but I do it because I must, and because I care for you, Nathan. I know what would happen to you out in the world.

You would be hunted down and killed by people who don't understand you."

Nathan tossed his bowl atop the others. "You want first watch or second?"

She turned back to him. "If you want your freedom so badly, what's keeping you from falling asleep on your watch, so I will be killed?"

His piercing blue eyes took on an acrimonious set. "I want this collar off. The one thing I will not do is kill you to accomplish the task. If I were willing to pay that price, you would be dead a thousand times over, and you know it."

"I'm sorry, Nathan. I know you're a good man, and I'm fully aware of the vital part you've played in helping me preserve life. Forcing you to help me makes my heart ache."

"Force me?" He laughed. "Ann, you're more fun than any woman I've ever met. Most of it I wouldn't have missed for anything. What other woman would buy me a sword? Or give me need to use it?

"That foolhardy prophecy says you have to bring him angry, and you're doing a splendid job of it. I fear it might even work. I'll take first watch. Don't forget to check your bedroll. No telling what he might have enticed in there this time. I still haven't figured out the snow fleas."

"Me neither. I'm still itching." She absently scratched her neck. "We're almost home. At the rate we're running, it won't be long."

"Home," he mocked. "And then you kill us."

"Dear Creator," she whispered to herself, "what choice have I?"

Richard leaned back in his chair and yawned. He was so tired he could hardly keep his eyes open. When he stretched and yawned, it caused Berdine, sitting next to him, to do the same. Across the room at the door, Raina was infected by their yawns.

A knock came and Richard shot to his feet. "Come!"

Egan stuck his head in. "A messenger is here."

Richard motioned, and Egan's head disappeared. A D'Haran soldier in a heavy cape and smelling of a horse hurried in and saluted with a fist to his heart.

"Sit down. You look like you've had a hard ride," Richard said.

The soldier straightened his battle axe at his hip as he glanced to the chair. "I'm fine, Lord Rahl. But I'm afraid I've nothing to report."

Richard sank down in his chair. "I see. No sign? Nothing?"

"No, Lord Rahl. General Reibisch said to tell you they're making good time, and are scouring every inch, and wanted me to assure you that our men have missed nothing, but so far they've found no sign."

Richard sighed in disappointment. "All right. Thank you. You'd best go get something to eat."

The man saluted and took his leave. Every day for two weeks, starting a week after the force had departed in search of Kahlan, messengers had been returning to give Richard a report. Since the force had started splitting up to cover different routes, each group was sending its own messenger. This was the fifth of the day.

Hearing the reports of what had happened weeks ago, when the messengers had left their troops, was like watching history happen. Everything he heard unfolding had happened in the past. For all Richard knew, they could have found Kahlan a week ago and were on their way back while he was still hearing reports of failure. He kept that constant hope foremost in his mind.

He had filled the time and kept his mind from wandering into worried thoughts by working on translating the journal. It gave him much the same feeling as getting the reports every day, like watching history happen. Richard was rapidly coming to understand more of the argot form of High D'Haran than Berdine.

Because he knew the story of *The Adventures of Bonnie Day*, they had been working on that the most, making long lists of words as they discovered their meanings, giving them something to refer to when they worked on the journal. As he learned words, Richard was able to read more of the book, piecing together the exact wording, enabling him to fill in more of the blanks in his memory, and thus learn yet more words.

It was often easier for him, now, to simply use what he had learned to translate from the journal than to show Berdine and have her do it. He was beginning to see High D'Haran in his sleep, and speak it when awake.

The wizard who wrote the journal never named himself; it was not an official record, but a private journal, so he had no need to call himself by name. Berdine and Richard had taken to calling him Kolo, short for *koloblicin*, a High D'Haran word meaning "strong advisor."

As Richard was able to understand more and more of the journal, a frightening picture was beginning to emerge. Kolo had written his journal during the ancient war that had spawned the creation of the Towers of Perdition in the Valley of the Lost. Sister Verna had once told him that the towers had stood guard over that valley for three thousand years, and had been placed to halt a great war. After learning how desperate these wizards had been to activate the towers, Richard was beginning to feel more and more troubled about having destroyed them.

Kolo had mentioned in one place that his journals had been with him since he was a boy, and he filled about one a year, so this one, number forty-seven, must have been written when he was somewhere in his early to mid-fifties. Richard intended to go to the Keep and search for Kolo's other journals, but this one still had many secrets to reveal.

Apparently Kolo was a trusted advisor to the others in the Keep. Most of the other wizards had both sides of the gift, Additive and Subtractive, but a few had only Additive. Kolo felt great sorrow for, and was protective of, those born with only that one side of the gift. These "unfortunate wizards" were said to be viewed by many as next to helpless, but Kolo thought that they could contribute in their own unique way and petitioned on their behalf for full status in the Keep.

In Kolo's time hundreds of wizards lived at the Keep, and it was alive with families, friends, and children. The now empty halls had at one time rung with laughter, conversation, and lighthearted rapport. Several times Kolo mentioned Fryda, probably his wife, and his son and younger daughter. Children were restricted to certain levels in the Keep, and went to lessons where they studied typical subjects like reading, writing, and mathematics, but also prophecy and the use of the gift.

But over this great Keep, teeming with life, work, and the joy of families, hung a pall of dread. The world was at war.

Among Kolo's other duties was his turn at standing guard over the sliph. Richard remembered the mriswith in the Keep asking him if he had come to wake the sliph. It had pointed down at the room where they had found Kolo's journal and said she was accessible at last. Kolo, too, referred to the sliph as "she," sometimes mentioning that "she" was watching him as he wrote in the journal.

Because it was such a struggle to decipher the journal from High D'Haran, they had abandoned skipping around since it only tended to confuse them. It was easier to start at the beginning and translate every word as they went, thus learning Kolo's idiosyncrasies in the way he used language, making it easier to recognize patterns in his expressions. They were only about a fourth of the way into the journal, but the process was speeding up considerably as Richard was learning High D'Haran.

While Richard leaned back and yawned again, Berdine bent toward him. "What is this word?"

" 'Sword,' " he responded without hesitation. He remembered the word from *The Adventures of Bonnie Day.*

"Huh. Look here. I think Kolo is speaking about your sword."

The front legs of Richard's chair thumped down as he came forward. He took the book and the piece of paper she had been using to write out the translation. Richard scanned the translation, and then went back to the journal, forcing himself to read it in Kolo's words.

The third attempt at forging a Sword of Truth failed today. The wives and children of the five men who died roam the halls, wailing in inconsolable anguish. How many men will die before we succeed, or until we abandon the attempt as impossible? The goal may be worthy, but the price is becoming terrible to bear.

"You're right. It seems he's talking about when they were trying to make the Sword of Truth."

Richard felt a chill at learning that men had died in the making of his sword. In fact, it made him feel a little sick. He had always thought of the sword as an object of magic, thinking that maybe it had simply been a plain sword at one time that some powerful wizard had cast a spell over. Learning that people died in the effort to make it made him feel ashamed that he took it for granted most of the time.

Richard went on to the next part of the journal. After an hour of consulting the lists and Berdine, he had it translated.

Last night, our enemies sent assassins through the sliph. Had the man on duty not been so alert, they would have succeeded. When the towers are ignited, the Old World will truly be sealed away, and the sliph will sleep. Then we can all rest easier, except the unlucky man on guard. We have concluded that we will have no way of knowing when the spells will be ignited, if they ever are, or if anyone is in the sliph, so the guard cannot be called away in time. When the towers are brought to life, the man on guard will be sealed in with her.

"The towers," Richard said. "When they completed the towers, sealing the Old World from the New World, that room was also sealed. That's why Kolo was down there. He couldn't get out."

"Then why is the room open now?" Berdine asked.

"Because I destroyed the towers. Remember I told you that it looked like Kolo's room had been blasted open within the last few months? How the mold on the walls had been burned away and hadn't had time to regrow? It must have happened because I destroyed the towers. It also unsealed Kolo's room for the first time in three thousand years."

"Why would they seal the room with the well?"

Richard had to force himself to blink. "I think this sliph thing Kolo keeps talking about lives in that well."

"What is this sliph? The mriswith mentioned it, too."

"I don't know, but somehow they used the sliph, whatever it is, to travel to other places. Kolo talks about the enemy sending assassins through the sliph. They were fighting the people in the Old World."

Berdine lowered her voice in worry as she leaned toward him. "You mean to say that you think these wizards could travel from here all the way to this Old World, and back?"

Richard scratched the itch at the back of his neck. "I don't know, Berdine. It sounds that way."

Berdine was still staring at him as if she thought he might be about to show further evidence that he was going mad. "Lord Rahl, how could that be possible?"

"How should I know?" Richard glanced out the window. "It's late. We'd better get some sleep."

Berdine yawned again. "Sounds like a good idea."

Richard shut Kolo's journal and tucked it under an arm. "I'm going to read a bit in bed until I fall asleep."

Tobias Brogan peered at the mriswith on the coach, and the one inside, and to the others among his columns of men, the sunrise glinting off their armor. He could see all the mriswith; none were invisible to sneak up on him and listen. His anger boiled at the sight of the side of the Mother Confessor's head in the coach. It enraged him that she was still alive, and that the Creator had forbade him from laying a blade to her.

He glanced sideways briefly, to make sure Lunetta was close enough to hear him if he spoke softly.

"Lunetta, I'm beginning to become very disturbed about this."

She stepped her horse closer as they rode so she could speak with him, but she didn't look over in case any of the mriswith were watching. The Creator's messengers or not, she didn't like the scaled creatures.

"But Lord General, you said that when the Creator has come to speak with you he told you that you must do this. You are most honored to be visited by the Creator, and to do his work."

"I think the Creator . . ."

The mriswith on the coach stood and pointed with a claw as they crested the hill. "Seeee!" it cried out in a sharp hiss, adding a guttural clicking after the word.

Brogan lifted his head to see a great city spread out below them, with the glittering sea beyond. In the center of the vast sprawl of buildings, with a golden, sunlit river splitting to go around the island atop which it sat, was a huge palace, its towers and roofs sparkling in the sunrise. He had seen cities before, he had seen palaces before, but he had never seen such as this. Despite not wanting to be here, he was awed.

"It be beautiful," Lunetta breathed.

"Lunetta," he whispered. "The Creator visited me again last night."

"Really, my lord general? That be wonderful. You be honored to be visited so often of late. The Creator must have great plans for you, my brother."

"The things he tells me are becoming more and more unsound."

"The Creator? Unsound?"

Brogan's gaze slid over to meet his sister's. "Lunetta, I believe there is trouble. I believe the Creator is going insane."

CHAPTER 45

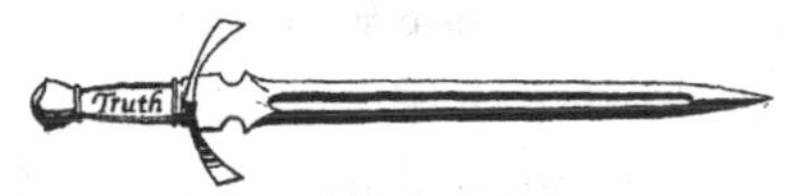

WHEN THE COACH STOPPED, the mriswith climbed out, leaving the door open. Kahlan glanced out the window to one side and the door to the other, seeing that the mriswith were moving off to talk. The two of them were at last alone.

"What do you think is going on?" she whispered. "Where are we?"

Adie leaned to the side, looking out the window. "Dear spirits," she whispered in dismay, "we be in the heart of enemy territory."

"Enemy territory? What are you talking about? Where are we?"

"Tanimura," Adie whispered. "That be the Palace of the Prophets."

"The Palace of the Prophets! Are you sure?"

Adie straightened in the seat. "I be sure. I spent time here when I be younger, fifty years ago."

Kahlan stared incredulously. "You went to the Old World? You have been to the Palace of the Prophets?"

"It be a long time ago, child, and a long story. We not have time for the story just now, but it be after the Blood killed my Pell."

They rode until well after dark, and were on their way long before the sun came up each day, but Kahlan and Adie were at least able to get some sleep in the coach. The men riding horseback got little sleep. A mriswith, and sometimes Lunetta, always guarded them, and they hadn't been able to speak more than a few words in weeks. The mriswith didn't care if they slept, but had warned them what would happen if they spoke. Kahlan didn't doubt their word.

Over the weeks as they traveled south, the weather had become warmer, and she no longer shivered in the coach, she and Adie pressed together for a little warmth.

"I wonder why they brought us here?" Kahlan said.

Adie leaned closer. "What I wonder is why they haven't killed us."

Kahlan peeked out the window to see a mriswith speaking with Brogan and his sister. "Because we are of more value to them alive, obviously."

"Value for what?"

"What do you think? Who would they want? When I tried to rally the Midlands, they sent that wizard to kill me, and I had to flee as Aydindril slipped into the hands of the Imperial Order. Who is forging the Midlands in opposition to them now?"

Adie's eyebrows went up above her white eyes. "Richard."

Kahlan nodded. "That's all I can think of. They had started to take the Midlands, and were having success by getting lands to join with them. Richard changed the rules, and disrupted those plans by forcing the lands to surrender to him."

Kahlan stared off out the window. "As much as it hurts to admit it, Richard may have done the only thing that has a chance to save the people of the Midlands."

"How can we be used to get to Richard?" Adie patted Kahlan's knee. "I know he loves you, Kahlan, but he not be stupid."

"Neither is the Imperial Order."

"What else could it possibly be, then?"

Kahlan looked into Adie's white eyes. "Have you ever seen the Sanderians hunt a mountain lion? They tie one of their lambs to a tree, letting it bleat for its mother. Then they sit and wait."

"You think we be lambs tied to a tree?"

Kahlan shook her head. "The Imperial Order may be vicious and cruel, but they are not stupid. By now they will not believe Richard is, either. Richard would not trade one life in exchange for the freedom of all, but he has also shown them that he is not afraid to act. They could be tempting him to think he could effect a rescue without having to surrender anything."

"Do you think they be right?"

Kahlan sighed. "What do you think?"

Adie's cheeks pushed back in a humorless smirk. "As long as you be alive, he would draw his sword on a lightning storm."

Kahlan watched Lunetta climb down from her horse. The mriswith were walking away, toward the rear of the columns of crimson-caped men.

"Adie, we have to escape, or Richard will come after us. The Order must be counting on his coming, or we would be dead."

"Kahlan, I cannot even light a lamp with this cursed collar around my neck."

Kahlan sighed in frustration as she looked back out the window and saw the mriswith moving off into the dark woods. As they walked, they drew their capes around themselves and vanished.

"I know. I can't touch my power either."

"Then how can we escape?"

Kahlan watched the sorceress dressed in scraps of different-colored cloth as she approached the coach. "If we could turn Lunetta to our side, she could help us."

Adie let out a disagreeable grunt. "She will not turn against her brother." Adie's brow wrinkled in puzzled thought. "She be an odd one. There be something strange about her."

"Strange? Like what?"

Adie shook her head. "She touches her power all the time."

"All the time?"

"Yes. A sorceress, or a wizard for that matter, only calls upon their power when they need it. She be different. For some reason, she be touching her power all the time. I have never seen her not clutching it around herself, like her colored cloth patches. It be very odd."

Both of them fell to silence as Lunetta huffed with the effort of climbing into the coach. She dropped into the seat opposite and gave them a pleasant smile; she looked to be in a good mood. Kahlan and Adie returned the smile. As the coach lurched ahead, Kahlan rearranged herself in the seat, taking the opportunity to check out the window. She didn't see any mriswith, but that didn't always mean anything.

"They be gone," Lunetta said.

"What?" Kahlan cautiously asked.

"The mriswith be gone." They all grabbed the handles in the coach as it bounced over ruts. "They told us to go on alone."

"To where?" Kahlan asked, hoping to engage the woman in conversation.

Lunetta's eyes brightened beneath her fleshy brow. "The Palace of the Prophets." She leaned forward excitedly. "It be a place full of *streganicha.*"

Adie scowled. "We not be witches."

Lunetta blinked. "Tobias says we be *streganicha*. Tobias be the Lord General. Tobias be a great man."

"We not be witches," Adie repeated. "We be women with the gift, given us by the Creator of all things. The Creator would not give us something vile, would he?"

Lunetta didn't hesitate for an instant. "Tobias says the Keeper gave us our vile magic. Tobias never be wrong."

Adie smiled at the growing scowl on Lunetta's face. "Of course not, Lunetta. Your brother seems a great and powerful man, just as you say." Adie rearranged her robes as she crossed a leg. "Do you feel as if you be evil, Lunetta?"

Lunetta frowned in thought a moment. "Tobias says I be evil. He tries to help me do good, to make up for the Keeper's taint. I help him root out evil so he can do the Creator's work."

Kahlan could tell that Adie was getting nowhere, except perhaps to anger Lunetta, and so changed the subject before things went too far. Lunetta, after all, had control of their collars.

"Have you been to the Palace of the Prophets often?"

"Oh, no," Lunetta said. "This be the first time. Tobias says it be a house of evil."

"Why would he take us there, then?" Kahlan asked in an offhanded manner.

Lunetta shrugged. "The messengers said we are to go there."

"Messengers?"

Lunetta nodded. "The mriswith. They be the Creator's messengers. They tell us what to do."

Kahlan and Adie sat in stunned silence. At last Kahlan found her voice. "If it's a house of evil, it seems odd that the Creator would want us to go there. Your brother doesn't seem to trust the Creator's messengers." Kahlan had seen Brogan casting scowls in their direction as they walked off into the woods.

Lunetta's beady eyes moved between them. "Tobias said I should not talk about them."

Kahlan twined her fingers together over a knee. "You don't think the messengers would hurt your brother, do you? I mean, if the palace is a place of evil, as your brother says . . ."

The squat woman leaned forward. "I would not let them. Mamma said I was always to protect Tobias, because he be more important than me. Tobias be the one."

"Why did your mamma—"

"I think we should be quiet now," Lunetta said in a dangerous tone.

Kahlan relaxed back in the seat and looked out the window. It didn't seem to take much to raise Lunetta's ire. Kahlan decided that it would be best if Lunetta were not pressed for now. Lunetta had already experimented with the control the collar afforded her, at Brogan's urging.

Kahlan watched as the buildings of Tanimura went past the window and tried to imagine Richard being here, seeing the same sights. It made her feel closer to him, seeing things his eyes had seen, and eased the terrible longing in her heart.

Dear Richard, please don't come into this trap to save me. Let me die. Save the Midlands, instead.

Kahlan had seen a great many cities, every one in the Midlands, and this was the equal to most. On the outskirts, there were ramshackle huts, many no more than lean-tos erected against some of the older, shabby buildings and warehouses. As they moved on into the city, the buildings became more grand, and there were shops of every sort. They passed several large markets with jumbles of people in every bright color of dress.

Everywhere in the city was the constant beat of drums. It was a slow rhythm, and grating on the nerves. As Lunetta glanced around, her eyes searching out the men at drums when they became louder as they rode along, Kahlan could see that she didn't like them either. Out the window, Kahlan could see Brogan riding close to the coach, and the drums were making him jumpy, too.

The three of them grabbed at the handles again as the coach bounced up onto a stone bridge. The iron wheels let out a grating racket as they rolled over the stone. Through the window, Kahlan could see the palace looming overhead as they crossed the river.

In an expansive courtyard of green lawns fringed with trees near soaring sections of the palace, the coach rocked to a halt. The crimson-caped men all about sat tall in their saddles, making no move to dismount.

Brogan's sour face suddenly appeared in the window. "Get out," he growled. Kahlan started to rise. "Not you. I'm talking to Lunetta. You stay where you are until you're told to move." He knuckled his mustache. "Sooner or later, you're mine. Then you pay for your filthy crimes."

"The mriswith aren't going to let their little lapdog have me," Kahlan said. "The Creator won't allow one such as you to put your filthy hands on me. You are nothing more than dirt under the Keeper's fingernails, and the Creator knows it. He hates you."

Kahlan felt the collar send a searing pain into her legs, preventing her from moving, and another shard into her throat, squelching her voice. Lunetta's eyes were ablaze. But Kahlan had said what she had wanted to say.

If Brogan killed her, Richard wouldn't come into this trap to rescue her.

Brogan's eyes bulged and his face went as crimson as his cape. He ground his teeth. Suddenly, he reached into the coach for her. Lunetta seized his hand, pretending she thought it was meant for her.

"Help me down, my lord general? My hip do be aching from the bumpy ride. The Creator do be kind to give you such strength, my brother. Heed his words."

Kahlan tried to call out, to taunt him, but her voice wouldn't come. Lunetta was preventing her from talking.

Brogan seemed to come to his senses, and grudgingly helped Lunetta climb down. He was about to turn back to the coach when he saw someone approaching. She waved him away with an arrogant flip of her hand. Kahlan couldn't hear what the woman said, but Brogan snatched up the reins to his horse and motioned his men to follow him.

Ahern was told to get down from the driver's seat and to go with the men of the Blood. He cast her a quick, sympathetic glance over his shoulder. Kahlan prayed to the good spirits that they wouldn't kill him, now that his coach had delivered its cargo. In a racket of sudden movement, the men on horseback all followed after Brogan and Lunetta.

The early-morning air quieted as the men moved off, and

Kahlan felt the grip of the collar at her neck slacken. Again she remembered with anguish making Richard put one of these collars around his neck, and every day she thanked the good spirits that he had finally come to understand that she had done it to save his life, to keep his gift from killing him. But the collars she and Adie wore were not to help them, as Richard's had been. These collars were no more than manacles in another form.

A young woman strode up to the door and peered in. She wore a clinging red dress that left little doubt as to the perfection of her figure. The long mass of hair that framed her face was as dark as her eyes. Kahlan suddenly felt like a clod of dirt in this stunningly sensuous woman's presence.

The woman's eyes took in Adie. "A sorceress. Well, perhaps we can find a use for you." Her knowing gaze turned to Kahlan. "Come along."

She turned without further word and started away. Kahlan felt a hot stab of pain in her back that propelled her out of the coach, stumbling to catch her balance when she landed on the ground. She turned just in time to put a hand out for Adie before she fell. The two of them rushed to catch up with the woman before she gave them another jab of pain.

Kahlan and Adie hurried along at the woman's heels, Kahlan feeling like a bumbling fool the way the collar's control made her legs twitch, shepherding her along, urging her to keep up, while the woman in the red dress strode along with the bearing of a queen. Adie was not prodded along as was Kahlan. Kahlan ground her teeth, wishing she could strangle the haughty woman.

There were other women, and a few men in robes, strolling along in the fine morning air. Seeing all the clean people was a keen reminder of the layers of road dust covering her. She hoped, though, that they wouldn't let her have a bath; maybe Richard wouldn't recognize her under all the dirt. Maybe he wouldn't come for her.

Please, Richard, protect the Midlands. Stay there.

They walked on down roofed walkways that had vine-covered lattices to the sides holding fragrant white blossoms and then were led through a gate in a high wall. Guards' eyes took in the sight, but they didn't make any move to challenge the woman leading them. After crossing a shady path under spreading trees, they entered a large building that looked nothing like the rat-infested dungeon Kahlan had expected. It looked more a proper guest wing for visiting dignitaries to the palace.

The woman in the red dress slowed to a halt before a carved door set back in a massive stone casing. She flicked the lever on the door and threw it open, entering ahead of them. The room was elegant, with heavy drapes overlooking a drop of perhaps thirty feet. There were several chairs richly upholstered in gold brocade fabric, a mahogany table and desk, and a canopied bed.

The woman turned to Kahlan. "This is to be your room." She displayed a brief smile. "We want you to be comfortable. You will be our guests until we are done with you.

"Try to go through the shield I leave on the door and window, and you will be on your hands and knees vomiting until your ribs feel as if they are breaking. That's just for the first infraction. After the first, you will find you have no desire to attempt such a thing again. You don't want to know about the second infraction."

She lifted a finger to Adie, but kept her dark eyes on Kahlan. "Cause me any trouble, and I will punish your friend here. Even if you think you have a strong stomach, I assure you, you will find otherwise. Do you understand?"

Kahlan nodded, afraid she wasn't supposed to speak.

"I asked a question," she said in a wickedly quiet tone. Adie crumpled to the floor with a cry. "You will answer me."

"Yes! Yes, I understand! Don't hurt her, please!"

When Kahlan turned to help Adie as she gasped for breath, the woman told her to leave the "old woman" to recover on her own.

Kahlan reluctantly straightened, letting Adie come to her feet. The woman's critical gaze glided down the length of her and back up. The smirk on her face heated Kahlan's blood.

"Do you know who I am?" the woman asked.

"No."

An eyebrow arched. "Well, well, that naughty boy. I guess I shouldn't be surprised that Richard didn't mention me to his future wife, considering."

"Considering what?"

"I am Merissa. Now do you know who I am?"

"No."

She let out a soft laugh, as annoyingly elegant as the rest of her. "Oh, he's so naughty, keeping such lascivious secrets from his future wife."

Kahlan wished she could keep her mouth shut, but she couldn't. "What secrets?"

Merissa shrugged indifferently. "When Richard was a student here, I was one of his teachers. I spent a great deal of time with him." The smirk returned. "Many a night, we spent in each other's arms. I taught him many things. Such a strong and attentive lover. If you've ever lain with him, then you would be the beneficiary of my more . . . tender instruction."

Merissa's soft lilting laugh returned as she strode from the room, giving Kahlan one last smiling look before she shut the door.

Kahlan stood clenching her fists so hard her nails were cutting her palms. She wanted to scream. When Richard had been taken away to the Palace of the Prophets, it was in a collar she had made him put on. He thought it was because she didn't love him. He thought she had sent him away and never wanted to see him again.

How could he resist a woman as beautiful as Merissa? He would have had no reason to.

Adie gripped her shirt at the shoulder and pulled her around. "Don't you listen to her."

Kahlan felt her eyes filling with tears. "But . . ."

"Richard loves you. She only be tormenting you. She be a cruel woman, and be enjoying to make you suffer." Adie lifted a finger as she quoted an old proverb. " 'Never let a beautiful woman pick your path for you when there be a man in her line of sight.' Merissa has Richard in her line of sight. I have seen that look of lust before. It not be a lust to have your man. It be a lust for his blood."

"But . . ."

Adie shook the finger. "Don't you lose your faith in Richard because of her. That be what she wants. Richard loves you."

"And I will be the death of him."

With a sob of agony, Kahlan fell into Adie's arms.

CHAPTER 46

RICHARD RUBBED HIS EYES. He wished he could read faster, because the journal was becoming so engrossing, but it still took time. He had to think about many of the words, and he still had to search for the meaning for a few, but as the days passed he was getting to the point where at times it didn't seem as if he was translating, but simply reading. Whenever he realized he was reading High D'Haran without conscious effort, he would begin stumbling over the meaning of words again.

Richard was intrigued by the intermittent references to Alric Rahl. It seemed that this ancestor of his had devised a solution to the problem of the dream walkers. He was only one of many working on a way to prevent the dream walkers from taking people's minds, but he had been particularly insistent that he had the solution.

Spellbound, Richard read how Alric Rahl had sent word from D'Hara that he had already woven this protective web over his people, and in order for the others to be protected by the same web, they had to pledge undying fidelity to him, and they, too, would be safe under this bond. Richard realized that this was the origin of the D'Harans' bond to him. Alric Rahl had created this spell to protect his people from the dream walkers, not to enslave them. Richard felt pride in his ancestor's benevolent act.

He was hardly able to breathe as he read the journal, hoping against hope that they would believe Alric Rahl, even though he knew that they hadn't. Koto had been cautiously interested in proof, but remained dubious. He reported that most of the other wizards thought Alric was up to some kind of trick, insisting that the only thing a Rahl was interested in was ruling the world. Richard groaned with disappointment when he read how they had sent a message refusing to swear fidelity and bind themselves to Alric.

Annoyed by a persistent sound, Richard turned to look out the window and saw that it was black as pitch outside. He hadn't even realized the sun had set. The candle he seemingly had just lit was half gone. The annoying noise was water dripping from icicles. Spring was taking the bite out of the weather.

Taking his mind off the journal brought back the pang of frantic worry about Kahlan. Every day messengers returned to give reports of nothing found. How could she have vanished?

"Any messengers waiting to see me?"

With a chafed expression, Cara shifted her weight. "Yes," she mocked, "there are several out there, but I told them that you were too busy sweet-talking me to be bothered right now."

Richard sighed. "I'm sorry, Cara. I know you'll tell me if a messenger arrives." He shook a finger at her. "Even if I'm asleep."

She smiled. "Even if you're asleep."

Richard looked around the room and frowned. "What happened to Berdine?"

Cara rolled her eyes. "She told you hours ago that she was going to go get some sleep before her watch. You said 'Yes, good night' to her."

Richard looked back to the journal. "Yes, I guess I did."

He read again a section about how the wizards were becoming fearful that the sliph would bring something through that they wouldn't be able to stop. The war was a frightening mystery to Richard. Each side created things of magic, mostly creatures designed for one purpose, such as the dream walkers, and the other side had to react with a counter to it, if they could. It was appalling to discover that some of these creatures were created out of people—out of wizards themselves. They were that desperate.

Day by day, they became more and more concerned that before the towers could be completed, the sliph—which in itself was created of their magic to allow them to move great distances to attack the enemy and turned out to be a great danger as well as a benefit—would bring something unexpected that they couldn't handle. They said that when the towers were competed, the sliph could go to sleep. Richard wondered constantly what the sliph was and how it could go to "sleep," and how they would wake it later, after the war, as they said they hoped to do.

The wizards decided that because of the danger of attack through the sliph, some of the more important, valuable, or more dangerous things, had to be moved from the Keep for protection. The last of the items deemed most in need of safekeeping had long ago been taken to this haven, and then Kolo said:

Today, one of our most coveted desires, possible only through the brilliant, tireless work of a team of near to one hundred, has been accomplished. The items most feared lost, should we be overrun, have been protected. A cheer went up from all in the Keep when we received word today that we were successful. Some thought it would not be possible, but to the astonishment of all, it is done: the Temple of the Winds is gone.

Gone? What was the Temple of the Winds, and where did it go? Kolo's journal didn't provide an explanation.

Richard scratched the back of his neck as he yawned. He could hardly keep his eyes open any longer. There was so much more to read, but he needed sleep. He wanted Kahlan back so he could protect her from the dream walker. He wanted to see Zedd so he could tell him about the things he had learned.

Richard rose and shuffled toward the door.

"Going off to bed to dream about me?" Cara asked.

Richard smiled. "Always do. Wake me if—"

"If a messenger comes. Yes, yes, I think you've mentioned it."

Richard nodded and started for the door. Cara caught his arm.

"Lord Rahl, they will find her. She will be safe. Rest well; D'Harans are looking, and they will not fail."

Richard patted her shoulder as he left. "I'll leave the journal here, so when Berdine wakes she can work on it."

He yawned and rubbed his eyes as he went to his room, not far down the hall. He only bothered to pull off his boots and slip the baldric over his head, placing the Sword of Truth on a chair before he fell into the bed. Despite his worries about Kahlan, he was asleep in seconds.

He was having a troubling dream about her when a loud knock woke him. He rolled over onto his back. The door burst open and there was sudden light. He could see Cara carrying a lamp. She moved to the side of his bed, lighting another lamp.

"Lord Rahl, wake up. Wake up."

"I'm awake." He sat up. "What is it? How long have I been asleep?"

"Maybe four hours. Berdine has been working on the book for a couple of hours, and got all excited about something and wanted to wake you to help her, but I wouldn't let her."

"Then why did you wake me now? Is it a messenger?"

"Yes. A messenger is here."

Richard almost flopped back into bed. Messengers never brought any news.

"Lord Rahl, get up. The messenger has news."

Richard came awake as if a bell had rung in his head. He swung his feet over the side of the bed and pulled his boots on in one big rush. "Where is he?"

"They're bringing him."

Just then, Ulic rushed in, helping a man he had with him. The soldier looked as if he had been riding hard for weeks. He could hardly stand on his own.

"Lord Rahl, I bring a message." Richard gestured for the young soldier to sit on the edge of the bed, but he waved off the offer, wanting to talk instead. "We found something. General Reibisch told me to tell you first not to be frightened. We didn't find her body, so she must still be alive."

"What did you find!" Richard realized he was shaking.

The man reached under the leather of his uniform and pulled something out. Richard snatched it up and let it unfold so he could see it. It was a crimson cape.

"We found the site of a battle. There were dead men wearing these capes. Lots of dead men. Maybe a hundred." He pulled out something else and handed it over.

Richard unfolded it. It was a roughly cut piece of faded blue cloth with four gold tassels along one edge.

"Lunetta," he breathed. "This is Lunetta's."

"General Reibisch said to tell you that there was a battle. There were many dead Blood of the Fold. There were trees that were blown down by blasts of fire, as if magic had been used in the battle. There were burned bodies, too.

"They found only one body that was not Blood of the Fold. He was a D'Haran. A big man with only one eye, with a scar over where the other was sewn shut."

"Orsk! That's Orsk! He was Kahlan's guard!"

"General Reibisch said to tell you that there was no sign that she or anyone else with her was killed. It appears that they put up a furious fight, but then they were captured."

Richard grabbed the soldier's arm. "Do the trackers have any idea which direction they went?" Richard was furious with himself because he hadn't gone. If he had gone, he would already be on the trail. Now it would take him weeks to catch up.

"General Reibisch said to tell you that the trackers are pretty sure they went south."

"South? South?" Richard had been sure that Brogan would flee with his prize to Nicobarese. With that many bodies, Gratch must have fought furiously. They must have captured him, too.

"They said they couldn't be sure because it happened so long ago. It snowed more, and now the snow is melting, so it's hard to track, but he believes they went to the south, and his whole force is going after your queen."

"South," Richard murmured. "South."

He raked his fingers back through his hair, trying to think. Brogan had fled rather than join with Richard and his cause against the Order. The Blood of the Fold had joined with the Imperial Order. The Imperial Order ruled the Old World. The Old World was to the south.

General Reibisch was tracking her south—going after his queen. South.

What was it the mriswith in the Keep had said?

The queen needs you, skin brother. You must help her.

They were trying to help him. His mriswith friends were trying to help him.

Richard snatched up his sword and shoved his head through the loop of leather baldric. "I have to go."

"We go with you," Cara said. Ulic nodded his agreement.

"You can't go where I go. Take care of things for me." He turned to the soldier. "Where's your horse?"

He pointed. "Out that way and over in the next courtyard. But she's pretty footsore."

"She only has to get me to the Keep."

"The Keep!" Cara clutched his arm. "Why are you going to the Keep?"

Richard pulled his arm away. "That's the only way to get to the Old World in time."

She started objecting, but he was already running down the hall. Others were joining in the rush to catch up with him. He could hear the jangle of armor and weapons behind, but he didn't slow. He didn't listen to Cara's pleas as he tried to think.

How was he going to do it? Was it possible? It had to be. He would do it.

Richard burst out the door, pausing for only an instant, and then tore off toward the courtyard where the soldier said he had left his horse. He stumbled to a stop when he came upon the horse in the darkness. He gave the sweaty animal a quick pat of introduction as she danced sideways, and then he vaulted up into the saddle.

As he pulled the horse around by the reins, he could just hear Berdine's voice in the distance as she ran toward him.

"Lord Rahl! Stop! Take off the cape!" Richard gave the horse his heels as he saw Berdine waving Kolo's journal. He didn't have time for her. "Lord Rahl! You must take off the mriswith cape!"

Not likely, he thought. The mriswith were his friends.

"Stop! Lord Rahl, listen to me!" The horse leapt into a gallop, the black mriswith cape billowing out behind. "Richard! Take it off!"

The weeks of tedious, patient waiting seemed to be exploding into the sudden need for desperate action. His passion to get to Kahlan overwhelmed all other thought.

The sound of thundering hooves drowned out Berdine's voice. The wind tore at his cape, the palace rushed by in a blur, and the night swallowed him.

"What are you doing here?"

Brogan turned to the voice. He hadn't heard the Sister coming up behind them.

He scowled at the older woman with long white hair tied loosely behind her back. "What business is that of yours?"

She clasped her hands. "Well, since this is our palace, and you are a guest, that makes it our business when one of our guests goes places in our home where he has been specifically forbidden to go."

Brogan squinted with indignation. "Do you have any idea just who you be speaking to?"

She shrugged. "Some petty, self-important officer, I would say. One too pompous to know when he is treading on dangerous ground." She cocked her head. "Have I gotten it right?"

Brogan closed the distance. "I be Tobias Brogan, Lord General of the Blood of the Fold."

"My, my," she mocked. "How impressive. Now, it seems I don't recall saying, 'You may not visit the Mother Confessor unless you are the lord general of the Blood of the Fold.' You hold no value for us except that which we assign you. You do no task but what we assign you."

"Which *you* assign *me*! The Creator Himself assigns me task!"

She snorted with a laugh. "The Creator! My but don't you think a lot of yourself. You are a part of the Imperial Order, and you do what we tell you."

Brogan was an inch away from slicing this disrespectful woman into a thousand pieces. "What be your name?" he growled.

"Sister Leoma. Do you think you can remember that much in your tiny brain? You were told to remain with your fancy troops in the barracks. Now, get yourself back there, and don't let me catch you in this building again, or you will cease to be of value to the Imperial Order."

Before Brogan could explode in anger, Sister Leoma turned to Lunetta. "Good evening, my dear."

"Good evening," Lunetta said in a cautious voice.

"I've been meaning to have a talk with you, Lunetta. As you can see, this is a house of sorceresses. Women with the gift are greatly respected here. Your lord general here is of little value to us, but one of your ability would be most welcome. I would like to offer you a place with us. You would be held in high esteem. You would have responsibility and respect." She glanced down at Lunetta's outfit. "We would certainly see to it that you were better clothed. You wouldn't have to wear those ugly rags."

Lunetta clutched her colored patches tighter and inched closer to Brogan's side. "I be loyal to my lord general. He be a great man."

Sister Leoma smirked. "Yes, I'm sure he is."

"And you be wicked women," Lunetta said in a suddenly steady, suddenly dangerous tone. "My mamma told me so."

"Sister Leoma," Brogan said. "I will remember the name." He tapped the trophy case at his belt. "You can tell the Keeper that I will remember your name. I never forget the name of a baneling."

A malicious smile spread across Leoma's face. "The next time I speak with my Master in the underworld, I will tell him your words."

Brogan pulled Lunetta around and headed for the door. He would be back, and the next time, he would have what he wanted.

"We need to go talk to Galtero," Brogan said. "I've had about enough of this nonsense. We've wiped out nests of banelings bigger than this one."

Lunetta touched a worried finger to her lower lip. "But, Lord General, the Creator has told you to do as these women say. He told you that you must give the Mother Confessor to them."

Brogan took long strides through the darkness once outside. "What did mamma tell you about these women?"

"Well . . . she said . . . that they be bad."

"They be banelings."

"But Lord General, the Mother Confessor be a baneling. Why would the Creator tell you to give her to these women if they be banelings?"

Brogan turned his eyes down to her. In the faint light, he could see her looking up in confusion. His poor sister didn't have the intellect to figure it out.

"Isn't it obvious, Lunetta? The Creator has revealed himself through his treacherous ways. He be the one to create the gift. He tried to trick me. It be up to me, now, to purge the world of evil. Everyone with the gift must die. The Creator be a baneling."

Lunetta gasped in awe. "Mamma always said you be the one headed for greatness."

After setting the glowing sphere on the table, Richard stood before the great, silent well in the center of the room. What was he to do? What was the sliph, and how did he call her?

He paced around the waist-high round wall, looking down into the darkness, but saw nothing.

"Sliph!" he called down into the bottomless hole. His own voice echoed back up.

Richard paced back and forth, pulling on his hair, frantically trying to think of what to do. The tingle of a presence flushed across his flesh. He halted his pacing and looked up to see a mriswith standing near the door.

"The queen needs you, skin brother. You must help her. Call the sliph."

He rushed over to the dark, scaled creature. "I know she needs me! How do I call the sliph!"

The slit of a mouth spread in what looked to be a smile. "You are the first in three thousand years to be born with the power to wake her. You have already broken the shield keeping us from her. You must use your power. Call the sliph with your gift."

"My gift?"

The mriswith nodded, its beady eyes staying on Richard. "Call her with your gift."

Richard finally turned away from the mriswith and went back to the stone wall around the great pit. He tried to remember how he had used his gift in the past. It always came on instinct. Nathan had said that that was the way it worked with him, with a war wizard: need—through instinct.

He had to let his need bring forth the gift.

Richard let the need burn through him, through the calm center. He didn't try to summon the power, but he screamed with the need of it.

He thrust his fists into the air, tilting his head back. He let the need fill him. He wanted nothing else. He let the unconscious restraints go. He didn't try to think of what to do, he simply demanded it be done.

He needed the sliph.

He let out a silent cry of fury.

Come to me!

He loosed the power, like letting out a deep breath, demanding the task be done.

Light ignited between his fists. That was it—the call—he knew it, he felt it, he understood it. He knew, too, what to do. The softly glowing mass rotated between his wrists as lacy veins of light twisted up his arms, flowing into the pulsing force between.

When he felt the power reach its peak, he cast his hands downward. With a howl, the orb of light shot away, down into the blackness.

As it descended, it became a ring of light around the stone. The ring of light and the glowing mass became smaller and smaller, the howl diminishing in the far distance, until he could neither hear nor see what he had unleashed.

Richard hung over the stone wall, looking into the bottomless abyss, but all was silent and dark. He could hear only his own panting. He stood and glanced over his shoulder. The mriswith watched, but made no move to help; what was needed was up to Richard. He hoped it would be enough.

In the stillness of the Keep, in the quiet of the mountain of dead stone towering around him, there came a distant rumbling.

A rumbling of life.

Richard leaned back over the wall, looking down, but saw nothing. Yet, he could feel something. The stone beneath his feet quaked. Stone dust floated in the jittering air.

Richard looked down in the well again and saw a reflection. The well was filling—not filling as water fills, but something was racing up the shaft with impossible speed, roaring with a howling shriek of velocity as it came. The howl grew as the thing rushed upward.

Richard flung himself back from the stone wall, scarcely fast enough. He was sure it would shoot out of the well and blast through the ceiling. Nothing moving that fast could stop in time. Yet it did.

All was abruptly still. Richard sat up, propping himself up with his arms behind on the floor.

A lustrous metallic hump slowly mounded above the edge of the stone wall surrounding the well. It drew up into a bulk, rising impossibly of its own accord, like water standing in the air, only it wasn't water. Its glossy surface reflected everything about it, like polished armor, distorting the images reflected off its surface as it grew and moved.

It looked like living quicksilver.

The lump, joined to the body of it in the well as if by a neck, continued to contort, bending into edges and planes, folds and curves. It warped into a woman's face. Richard had to remind himself to take a breath. He now understood why Kolo called the sliph "she."

The face finally saw him on the floor. It looked like a smooth statue made of silver—except it moved.

"Master," she said in an eerie voice that echoed around the room. Her lips hadn't moved as she spoke, but she smiled as if well pleased. The silver face warped into curiosity. "You have called me? You wish to travel?"

Richard sprang to his feet. "Yes. Travel. I wish to travel."

The pleasant smile returned. "Come, then. We will travel."

Richard brushed the stone dust from his hands onto his shirt. "How? How do we . . . travel?"

The silver brow drew together. "You have not traveled before?"

Richard shook his head. "No. But I need to now. I need to get to the Old World."

"Ah. I have been there often. Come, and we will travel."

Richard hesitated. "What do I do? What do you want me to do?"

A hand formed up and touched the top of the wall. "Come to me," the voice said, echoing around the room. "I will take you."

"How long does it take?"

The frown returned. "Long? From here to there. That long. I am long enough. I have been there."

"I mean . . . hours? Days? Weeks?"

She didn't seem to understand. "The other travelers never spoke of this."

"Then it must not take very long. Kolo never mentioned it, either." The journal could be frustrating at times because Kolo never explained what was, to his people, common knowledge. He hadn't been trying to teach, or pass on information.

"Kolo?"

Richard pointed at the bones. "I don't know his name. I call him Kolo."

The face stretched out of the well to look over the wall. "I do not remember seeing this."

"Well, he's dead. He didn't look like that before." Richard decided he better not explain who Kolo was or she might remember and be upset. He didn't need any emotion, he needed to get to Kahlan. "I'm in a hurry. I'd appreciate it if we could hurry."

"Step closer so I may determine if you can travel."

Richard moved up to the wall and stood still while the quicksilver hand came out to touch his forehead. He flinched back. It was warm. He had expected cold. He returned to the hand and let the palm glide over his forehead.

"You can travel," the sliph said, "You have both sides required. But you will die if you are like this."

"What do you mean, 'like this'?"

The quicksilver hand lowered beside him, pointing at the sword, but being careful not to get too close. "That object of magic is incompatible with life in the sliph. With that magic in me, any life also in me will be ended."

"You mean I must leave it here?"

"If you wish to travel, you must, or you will die."

Richard was decidedly uneasy about leaving the Sword of Truth unguarded, especially after learning of the men with families who had died to make it. He pulled the baldric off over his head and stared at the scabbard in his hands. He looked over his shoulder at the mriswith watching him. He could ask his mriswith friend to guard the sword.

No. He could ask no one to take the responsibility of guarding something so dangerous and coveted. The Sword of Truth was his responsibility, not anyone else's.

Richard drew the sword from the scabbard, letting the clear ring of its steel reverberate around the room, die out slowly. The rage of the magic didn't die out, though; it thundered through him.

He held up the blade, looking down its length. He could feel the raised gold wire of the word TRUTH biting into his palm. What was he to do? He needed to go to Kahlan. He needed to have the sword be safe in his absence.

It came to him through the call of need.

He turned the sword down, gripping the hilt in both hands. With a grunt of effort powered by the magic, by the storms of fury it engendered, he thrust the sword downward.

Sparks and stone chips flew as Richard drove the sword up to its hilt into a huge stone block of the floor. When he took his hands away, he could still feel the magic within him. He had to leave the sword, but he still had the magic; he was the true Seeker.

"I'm still linked to the sword's magic. I retain the magic within me. Will that kill me?"

"No. Only that which generates the magic is deadly, not that which receives it."

Richard climbed up on the stone wall, suddenly beginning to worry about this. No, he had to do it. He needed to.

"Skin brother." Richard turned to the mriswith when it called to him. "You are without a weapon. Take this." It tossed one of its three-bladed knives up to Richard. As it arced gently through the air, Richard caught it by the handle. The side guards lay against each side of his wrist as he grasped the weapon's crossways handgrip in his fist. It felt surprisingly good in his hand, like an extension of his arm.

"The *yabree* will sing to you, soon."

Richard nodded. "Thank you."

The mriswith returned a slow smile.

Richard turned to the sliph. "I don't know if I can hold my breath long enough."

"I told you, I am long enough to reach where we travel."

"No, I mean I need air." He made a display of inhaling and exhaling. "I need to breathe."

"You breathe me."

He listened to her voice echo around the room. "What?"

"To live when you travel, you must breathe me. The first time you travel, you will be afraid, but you must do this. Those who do not, die in me. Do not be afraid; I will keep you alive when you breathe me. When we reach the other place, you must then breathe me out, and breathe in the air. You will be just as afraid to do that as you will be to breathe me, but you must do it or you will die."

Richard stared incredulously. Breathe this quicksilver? Could he bring himself to do such a thing?

He had to get to Kahlan. She was in danger. He had to do this. He needed to do this.

Richard swallowed, and then took a deep, sweet breath. "All right, I'm ready to go. What do I do?"

"You do not do. I do."

A liquid silver arm came up and slipped around him, its warm, undulating grip compressing to grasp him. The arm lifted him off the wall and plunged him down into the silver froth.

Richard had sudden a vision: he remembered Mrs. Rencliff being pulled under the raging floodwater.

CHAPTER 47

VERNA BLINKED IN THE bright light of a lamp when the door opened. It felt as if her heart rose into her throat. It seemed too soon for Leoma to return. Already, she was quivering with dread, tears welling up in her eyes, and Leoma hadn't even begun the test of pain.

"Get in here," Leoma snapped to someone.

Verna sat up and saw a small, thin woman move into the doorway. "Why do I have to do this?" complained a familiar voice. "I don't want to clean her room. This isn't part of my job!"

"I have to work in here with her, and the smell is near to making me blind. Now get yourself in here and clean up some of this stink, or I'll lock you in here with her just to teach you proper respect for a Sister."

Grumbling, the woman waddled into the room, lugging her heavy bucket of soapy water. "Stinks it does," she announced. "Stinks with the likes of her." The bucket thumped down on the floor. "Filthy Sister of the Dark."

"Just get some soap and water around this place, and be quick about it. I have work to do."

Verna looked up to see Millie staring at her. "Millie . . ."

Verna turned her face away but not in time as Millie spat at her. She wiped the spittle off her cheek with the back of her hand.

"Filthy scum. To think I trusted you. To think I respected you as the Prelate. And all the time you served the Nameless One. You can rot in here for all I care. The place stinks with your filthy walking corpse. I hope they flail the hide off—"

"Enough," Leoma said. "Just clean up and then you can remove yourself from her loathsome presence."

Millie grunted in disgust. "Won't be soon enough for me."

"None of us enjoys being in the same room with an evil one such as her, but it's my duty to question her, and at least you could make it smell a little better for me."

"Yes, Sister, I'll do it for you, then, for a true Sister of the Light, so you won't have to bear her stink at least." Millie spat in Verna's direction again.

Verna was near to tears, humiliated to know that Millie thought those terrible things of her. Everyone else did, too. She was no longer positive that they were untrue. Her mind was so dizzied by the tests of pain that she could no longer trust that she was thinking straight to believe in her own innocence. Perhaps it was wrong to be loyal to Richard; he was, after all, a mere man.

When Millie finished, then Leoma would start again. She heard herself sob at the helplessness of her situation. When Leoma heard the sob, she smiled.

"Empty that reeking chamber pot," Leoma said.

Millie huffed in disgust. "All right, all right, just hold your skirts on and I'll empty it."

Millie pushed the bucket of soapy water closer to Verna's pallet and collected the brimming chamber pot. Holding her nose, she carried it out of the room at arm's length.

After she had shuffled off down the hall, Leoma spoke. "Notice anything different?"

Verna shook her head. "No, Sister."

Leoma lifted her eyebrows. "The drums. They've stopped."

Verna started with the realization. They must have stopped while she was asleep.

"Do you know what that means?"

"No, Sister."

"It means that the emperor is close, and will be arriving soon. Maybe tomorrow. He wants results from our little experiment. Tonight, you either forsake your fidelity to Richard, or you will answer to Jagang. Your time has run out. You think on that, while Millie finishes cleaning up a bit of your stink."

Muttering curses, Millie returned with the empty chamber pot. After she put it in the far corner, she went back to scrubbing the floor. She dunked her rag in the water and slopped it on the floor, working her way toward Verna.

Verna licked her cracked lips as she stared at the water. Even if the water was soapy, she wouldn't care. She wondered if she would be able to get a gulp of it down before Leoma stopped her. Probably not.

"I shouldn't have to do this," Millie grouched to herself, but loud enough for the other two to hear. "It's bad enough that I now have to clean the Prophet's room, now that we have another. I thought I was done with going in there to clean the room of a madman. I think it's about time a younger woman had to do the work. Strange man, he is. Prophets are all loony, they are. I don't like that Warren any more than the last one."

Verna nearly burst into tears at the mention of Warren's name. She missed him so. She wondered if they were treating him well. Leoma answered her unspoken question.

"Yes, he is a bit odd. But the tests with the collar are bringing him back into line. I'm seeing to that."

Verna turned her eyes away from Leoma. She was doing it to him, too. Oh, dear Warren.

With a knee, Millie pushed her bucket closer as she scrubbed the floor. "Don't you be watching me. I don't like your filthy eyes on me. Gives me the shivers it does, like having the Nameless One himself watching me."

Verna turned her eyes down. Millie tossed the rag into the bucket and dunked her hands in deep to wash it out. She looked back over her shoulder as she worked the rag in the water.

"I'll be finished soon. Not soon enough for me, but soon. Then you can have this vile traitor to yourself. I hope you won't be kind to her."

Leoma smiled. "She will get what she deserves."

Millie brought her hands out of the soapy water. "Good." She jammed one wet, callused hand against Verna's thigh. "Move your feet! How can I wash the floor when you sit there like a lump?"

Verna felt something rigid against her thigh after Millie took her hand away.

"That Warren is a pig, too. Keeps his room a mess. I was just there earlier today, and it stunk nearly as bad as this sty."

Verna moved her hands to each side of her legs and put them under her thighs as if to balance herself while she lifted her feet for Millie. Her fingers found something hard, and thin. At first, her dull mind couldn't decipher the feel. It came to her with a jolt of recognition.

It was a dacra.

Her chest constricted. Her muscles stiffened. She could hardly make herself breathe.

Millie suddenly spat in her face again, causing her to flinch and turn away. "Don't you be looking at an honest woman like that! Keep your eyes off me."

Verna realized Millie must have seen her eyes open wide.

"I'm done," she said as she straightened her sinewy frame, "unless you want me to give her a bath, and if you do, you'd better think again. I'm not touching that evil woman."

"Just get your bucket and go," Leoma said, her impatience growing.

Verna had the dacra gripped so tightly in her fist that it was making her fingers tingle. Her heart hammered so hard she thought it might crack a rib.

Millie shuffled out of the room without looking back. Leoma pushed the door closed.

"This is your last chance, Verna. If you still refuse, you will be turned over to the emperor. You will soon wish you had cooperated with me, I can promise you that much."

Come closer, Verna thought. Come closer.

She felt the first wave of pain coursing up through her. She flopped back on the pallet, turning away from Leoma. Come closer.

"Sit up and look at me when I speak to you."

Verna could only let out a small cry, but she stayed where she was, hoping to lure Leoma closer. She would have no chance if she lunged from this far; the woman would hobble her before she made the distance. She had to be closer.

"I said sit up!" Leoma's footsteps approached.

Dear Creator, please bring her close enough.

"You will look at me and tell me you renounce Richard. You must renounce him so the emperor can enter your mind. He will know when you have quit your loyalty, so don't think to lie."

Another step. "Look at me when I speak to you!"

Another step. A fist snatched her hair and jerked her head upward. She was close enough, but her arms seared with pain, and she couldn't lift her hand. *Oh, dear Creator, don't let her start the test with my arms. Let her start with my legs. I need my arms.*

Instead of beginning in her legs, the nerve-burning pain shot down her arms. With all her strength, Verna tried to lift the hand with the dacra. It would not move. Her fingers twitched with stabs of pain.

Despite her straining, her fingers tugged opened in spasms and the dacra fell out.

"Please," she wept, "don't do my legs this time. I'm begging you, don't do my legs."

Leoma's fist in her hair tilted her head back, and the woman struck her across the face. "Legs, arms, it doesn't matter. You will submit."

"You can't make me. You're going to fail and . . ." Verna got no more out before the hand struck her face again.

The searing pain jumped to her legs, and they flopped uncontrollably with the jolts. Verna's arms tingled, but she could at last move them. Her hand groped blindly along the pallet, frantically searching for the dacra.

Her thumb touched it. She curled her fingers around the cool metal handle, pulling it up in her fist.

Summoning all her strength and resolve, Verna plunged the dacra into Leoma's thigh.

Leoma cried out, releasing Verna's hair.

"Still!" Verna panted. "I have a dacra in you. Stay still."

One hand slowly lowered to comfort her leg above the dacra in her thigh muscle. "You can't possibly think this will work."

Verna swallowed, catching her breath. "Well now, I guess we are going to find out, aren't we? Seems I have nothing to lose. You do—your life."

"Be careful, Verna, or you will find out just how sorry you can be for doing something like this. Take it out, and I will pretend this didn't happen. Just take it out."

"Oh, I don't think that's such wise advice, advisor."

"I have control of your collar. All I have to do is block your Han. If you make me do that, it will go worse on you."

"Really, Leoma? Well, I think I should tell you that on my journey of twenty years, I learned a great deal about using a dacra.

While it's true that you can block my Han through the Rada'Han, there are two things you had better think on.

"First, while you can block my Han, you can't block it fast enough for me not to touch just the tiniest flow first. From my experience, I judge that that would be enough. If I touch my Han, you will be dead instantly.

"Secondly, for you to block my Han, you must link with it through the collar. That gives you the ability to manipulate it; that's how it works. Do you suppose that the act of blocking my Han by touching it would in itself power the dacra and kill you? I'm not sure myself, but I must tell you that from my end, the handle end, I'm willing to put it to the test. What do you think? Do you want to put it to the test, Leoma?"

There was a long silence in the dimly lit room. Verna could feel warm blood oozing over her hand. At last Leoma's small voice filled the quiet. "No. What do you want me to do?"

"Well, first of all, you are going to take this Rada'Han off me, and then, since I appointed you as my advisor, we are going to have a little talk—you are going to advise me."

"After I take the collar off, then you will remove the dacra, and I will tell you what you want to know."

Verna looked up at the panicked eyes watching her. "You are hardly in a position to make demands. I ended up in this room because I was too trusting. I've learned my lesson. The dacra remains where it is until I'm finished with you. Unless you do as I say, you have no value to me alive. Do you understand that, Leoma?"

"Yes," came the resigned reply.

"Then let's begin."

Like an arrow he shot ahead with blistering speed, yet at the same time he glided with the slow grace of a turtle beneath still waters on a moonlit night. There was no heat, no cold. His eyes beheld light and dark together in a single, spectral vision, while his lungs swelled with the sweet presence of the sliph as he breathed her into his soul.

It was rapture.

Abruptly, it ended.

Sights exploded about him. Trees, rocks, stars, moon. The panorama gripped him in terror.

Breathe, she told him.

The thought horrified him. *No.*

Breathe, she told him.

He remembered Kahlan, his need to help her, and let out the sweet breath, emptying his lungs of the rapture.

With a reluctant yet needful gasp, he sucked in the alien air.

Sounds rushed in around him—insects, birds, bats, frogs, leaves in the wind, all chattering, whooping, clicking, whistling, rustling—painful in their omnipresence.

A comforting arm set him up on the stone wall as the night world around him settled into a familiar presence in his mind. He saw his mriswith friends scattered about in the dark woods beyond the stone ruins around the well. A few sat on scattered blocks, and a few stood among the remains of columns. They seemed to be at the edge of an ancient, crumbling structure.

"Thank you, sliph."

"We are where you wished to travel," she said, her voice echoing out through the night air.

"Will you . . . be here, when I want to travel again?"

"If I am awake, I am always ready to travel."

"When do you sleep."

"When you tell me, Master."

Richard nodded, not sure at all what he was nodding to. He looked out on the night as he stepped away from the sliph's well. He knew the woods, not by sight, but by their manifest feel. It was the Hagen Woods, though it had to be a place much deeper in their vast tract than he had ever ventured, because he had never seen this place of stone. By the stars he knew the direction of Tanimura.

Mriswith were coming in numbers from the somber, surrounding woods to the ruins. Many passed him with a "Welcome, skin brother." As they passed, the mriswith tapped their three-bladed knives to his, causing both to ring.

"May your *yabree* sing soon, skin brother," each said as they tapped.

Richard didn't know the proper response, and so said only, "Thank you."

As the mriswith slunk past him to the sliph, tapping his *yabree,* the humming ring lasted longer each time, its pleasant purr warming his whole arm. As other mriswith approached, he altered his course so that he might tap his *yabree* to theirs.

Richard looked to the rising moon, and the position of the stars. It was early evening, with a faint glow still in the western sky. He had left Aydindril in the dead of night. This couldn't be the same night. It had to be the next night. He had spent almost a full day in the sliph.

Unless it was two days. Or three. Or a month, or even a year. He had no way to tell; he knew only that it was at least one day. The moon was the same size; maybe it was only a day.

He paused to let another mriswith tap his *yabree*. Behind, mriswith were entering the sliph. A whole line of them stood waiting their turn. Only seconds passed before the next stepped off the wall to drop into the shimmering quicksilver.

Richard stopped to feel his *yabree* sending a warming purr all though him. He smiled with the singing hum, the soft song pleasant in his ears, and in his bones.

He felt a disturbing need that interrupted the joyful song.

He stopped a mriswith. "Where am I needed?"

The mriswith pointed with its *yabree*. "She will take you. She knows the way."

Richard wandered off in the direction the mriswith had indicated. In the darkness near a ruined wall, a figure waited. The singing of his *yabree* urged him onward with need.

The figure wasn't a mriswith, but a woman. In the moonlight, he thought he recognized her.

"Good evening, Richard."

He took a step back. "Merissa!"

She smiled congenially. "How is my student? It's been a while. I hope you are well, and your *yabree* sings for you."

"Yes," he stammered. "It sings of a need."

"The queen."

"Yes! The queen. She needs me."

"Are you ready, then, to help her? To free her?"

After he nodded, she turned and led him on into the ruins. Several mriswith joined them as they entered the broken doorways. Through vine-rimmed gaps in the walls, moonlight streamed in, but when the walls became more solid, blocking the moonlight, she lit a flame in her palm as she glided along. Richard followed her up stairs coiling into the gloomy ruins and down halls that looked to have been undisturbed for thousands of years.

The illumination from the light in her palm suddenly became inadequate as they entered a huge chamber. Merissa sent the small flame into torches to either side, bringing flickering light to the vast room. Long-dead balconies covered with dust and spiderwebs ringed the room, looking down on a tiled pool making up the main floor. The tiles, once white, were now dark with stains and dirt, and the murky water in the pool was laced with strings of muck. Overhead the partly domed ceiling was open in the center, with structures rising up beyond the opening.

The mriswith slipped up beside him, standing close. Both tapped their *yabree* to his. The pleasant singing resonated with the calm center within him.

"This is the place of the queen," one said. "We can come to her, and when the young are born they may leave, but the queen cannot leave here."

"Why?" Richard asked.

The other mriswith stepped forward and reached out with a claw. As it came in contact with something unseen, a whole domed shield lit with a soft glow. The sparkling dome fit neatly within the one of stone, except it had no hole in the top. The mriswith pulled its claw back, and the shield became invisible again.

"The old queen's time is passing, and she is at last dying. We have all eaten of her flesh, and a new queen emerged from the last of her young. The new queen sings to us through the *yabree*, and tells us that she is rich with young. It is time for the new queen to move on, and establish our new colony.

"The great barrier is gone and the sliph is awakened. Now you must help the queen so we may establish new territories."

Richard nodded. "Yes. She needs to be free. I can feel her need. It fills me with the singing. Why haven't you freed her?"

"We cannot. Just as you were needed to still the towers, and to wake the sliph, only you can free the queen. It must be done before you hold two *yabree*, and they both sing to you."

Guided by his instinct, Richard moved to the stairs at the side. He could sense that the shield was stronger at the base; it had to be breached at the top. He held the *yabree* to his chest as he climbed the stone steps. He tried to imagine how wondrous two would be.

Its comforting song soothed him, but the queen's need drove him on. The mriswith remained behind, but Merissa followed him.

Richard moved as if he had made the journey before. The stairs led outside, and then up spiraling steps beside the ruins of columns. The moonlight cast jagged shadows among the craggy stone still standing among the devastation.

They at last reached the top of a small circular observation tower, pillars rising to the side of it, connected overhead by the remains of an entablature decorated with gargoyles. It looked as if at one time it had circled the entire dome, connecting towers like the one atop which they stood. From the high tower, Richard could look down through the opening of the dome. The curved roof bristled with huge columns, like spikes, radiated out and down in rows.

Merissa, in a red dress, the only color he had ever seen her wear when she had come to give him instruction, pressed up close behind him, looking silently down into the dark dome.

Richard could feel the queen in the mirky pool below, calling to him, urging him to free her. His *yabree* sang through his bones.

Casting his hand down, he let his need flow outward. He cast the other arm out, pointing the *yabree* down along with the fingers of his other hand. The steel knives knelled, vibrating from the power coursing out of him.

The blades of the *yabree* rang, rising in pitch, until the night screamed. The sound was painful, but Richard didn't allow it to abate. He called it onward. Merissa turned away, covering her ears as the air reverberated with the howl of the *yabree*.

The domed shield below quaked, glowing as its vibrations intensified. Sparkling cracks appeared and raced along its surface. With a deafening knell, the shield shattered; pieces of it, like glowing glass, rained down toward the pool, sparking out as they fell.

The *yabree* went silent, and the night was once again still.

A bulk below stirred, shaking itself free of the strands of weed and muck. Wings spread, testing their strength, and then, with frenetic strokes, the queen lifted into the air. With needful beats of her wings, she lifted to the edge of the dome, her claws snatching and catching at the stone for support. Partially folding her newly tested wings, she began climbing the stone of the tower upon which Richard and Merissa stood. With sure, slow, powerful pulls, she hauled her glistening bulk up the column, her claws finding purchase in the cracks, crags, and crannies in the stone.

At last she stopped, clinging to the pillar beside Richard like a clawed salamander clinging to a slimy log. In the bright light of the moon, Richard could see that she was as red as Merissa's dress. At first Richard thought he was seeing a red dragon, but upon closer scrutiny he could see the differences.

Her legs and arms were more heavily muscled than a dragon's, and covered over with smaller scales more like the mriswith's. A raised row of interlocking plates ran the length of her spine from the end of her tail to a nest of spikes at the back of her head. Atop the head, at the base of several long, supple spines, was a raised protrusion crowned with rows of scaleless flesh that occasionally fluttered as she exhaled.

The queen's head snaked about, looking, searching. Her wings unfurled, slowly sweeping the night air. She wanted something.

"What do you seek?" Richard asked.

Twisting her head down toward him, she huffed a breath that engulfed him with an odd aroma. It somehow made him feel her need more acutely; the aroma had meaning he could understand, saying, *"I wish to go to this place."*

She then turned her head out to the night beyond the pillars. She blew out, emitting a long, low, vibrating rumble that seemed to shudder through the air. Richard could see her expelling air through the fleshy ribbons atop her head. They fluttered as she trumpeted, creating the sound. With the heady aroma still filling his nostrils, he looked to the sweep of night before the tower.

The air shimmered, brightening as an image began to emerge before him. The queen trumpeted again, and the image brightened further. It was a scene Richard recognized—it was Aydindril, as if he were seeing it through an eerie, ocher fog. Richard could see the buildings of the city, the Confessors' Palace, and, as she trumpeted again, brightening the image floating before him in the night sky, the Wizard's Keep towering above on the mountainside.

Her head swung around to him, again huffing an aroma, but it was different from the first. It carried a different meaning: *"How do I get to this place?"*

Richard grinned with the wonder of being able to understand her meaning through an aroma. He grinned, too, with the knowledge that he could help her.

He extended his arm, and a glow shot out from it, illuminating the sliph. "There. She will take you."

The queen flapped her wings as she sprang from the column and once clear of the stone spread them wide to glide down to the sliph. The queen couldn't fly very well, Richard understood; she could use her wings to aid her somewhat but she couldn't fly to Aydindril. She needed help to get there. Already, the sliph was embracing the queen as she folded her wings. The quicksilver took her in, and the red queen was gone.

Richard stood smiling with the pleasure of the *yabree* singing in his hand, humming through his bones.

"I'll meet you at the bottom, Richard," Merissa said. He felt her suddenly seize him by the shirt at the back of his neck, and with the power of her Han, fling him over the side of the tower.

By instinct, Richard reached out, just managing to snatch the lip of the dome's opening as he fell past. He swung by his fingers, his feet dangling over a drop of at least a hundred feet. His *yabree* clattered as it hit the stone far below. Flushed with rushing panic, he felt as if he were waking in a nightmare.

The song was gone. Without the *yabree*, his mind suddenly felt startlingly wide awake. He shuddered with terror at realizing the insidious seduction, and what it had been doing to him.

Leaning over to see him hanging there, Merissa threw a bolt of fire down at him. He swung his feet in, and the flames just missed him. She wouldn't make the same mistake twice, he knew.

Richard frantically felt under the rim of the dome for something to grab. His fingers found a fluted support rib. With desperate need to get away from Merissa, he gripped it and swung down under the dome as another bolt of fire shot past to erupt in the murky pool below, throwing strings of scum up into the air.

Hand over hand, propelled by fear, not only of Merissa, but also of the height, he started down the rib. Merissa headed for the stairs. As he descended, the rib steepened, becoming nearly vertical as it approached the edge of the dome.

Grunting with effort as he hurried, his fingers aching, Richard was overwhelmed by shame. How could he be so stupid? What was he thinking? It came to him with sickening comprehension.

The mriswith cape.

He remembered Berdine running out, holding Kolo's journal, screaming at him to take off the cape. He remembered reading in the journal how not only they, but their enemies, too, created things of magic that brought about the changes needed to give people certain properties, such as strength and stamina, or the power to focus a line of light into a destructive point, or the ability to see great distances, even at night.

The mriswith cape must be one of those things, used to give wizards the ability to become invisible. Koto had mentioned how many of the weapons they developed had gone terribly awry. It could be, too, that the mriswith were developed by the enemy.

Dear spirits, what trouble had he caused? What had he done? He had to get the cape off his back. Berdine had been trying to warn him.

Wizard's Third Rule: Passion rules reason. He had been so passionate to get to Kahlan that he had not used his reason and listened to Berdine's warning. How was he going to stop the Order now? His folly had aided them.

Richard strained to hold the rib as it became nearly vertical. Ten more feet.

Merissa appeared in a doorway. He saw a bolt of lightning arc across the room. He let go, and dropped to the ground, wishing that he could fall faster. The loud crack of the lightning hurt his ears as it came perilously close to taking off his head. He had to get away from her. He had to run.

"I've met your bride-to-be, Richard."

Richard froze in his tracks. "Where is she?"

"Come out of there, and we'll talk about it. I'll tell you all about how I'm going to enjoy hearing her scream."

"Where is she!"

Merissa's laughter echoed around the dome. "Right here, my student. Right here in Tanimura."

In a fury, Richard unleashed a bolt of lightning. It lit the chamber, thundering across the room to where he had seen her last. Stone chips trailing smoke sailed through the air. He only dimly wondered how he had done such a thing. Need.

"Why! Why would you want to hurt her?"

"Oh, Richard, it's not her I care about hurting. It is you. Her pain will give you pain; it's that simple. She is merely a means to your blood."

Richard eyed the passageways. "Why do you want my blood?"

As soon as he had finished asking, he ducked down and headed for a passageway.

"Because you have ruined everything. You locked my master back in the underworld. I was to have my reward. I was to have immortality. I did my part, but you ruined it."

A twisting bolt of black lightning sliced a clean void through a wall right beside him. She was using Subtractive Magic. She was a sorceress with unimaginable power, and she could tell where he was; she could sense him. Then why was she missing?

"But worse," she said as a slender finger tapped the gold ring through her lower lip, "because of you, I must serve that pig Jagang. You have no idea of the things he did to me. You have no idea of the things he makes me do. All because of you! All because of you, Richard Rahl! But I will make you pay. I have sworn to bathe in your blood, and I shall."

"What about Jagang? You're going to make him angry if you kill me."

Fire erupted behind him, racing him to the next column.

"Quite the contrary. Now that you have done what was required of you, you are no longer of use to the dream walker. As a reward, I am being allowed to do away with you as I wish, and I have some grand wishes."

Richard realized he was not going to be able to get away from her like this. He could be behind a wall, and she would be able to sense him with her Han.

He thought again about Berdine, and just as he reached up and clutched a fistful of the mriswith cape to rip it off his back, he paused. Merissa wouldn't be able to see him with her Han if he was shrouded with the cape's magic. But the cape's magic was the force that created the mriswith.

Kahlan was a captive. Merissa said her pain would give him pain. He couldn't allow them to hurt Kahlan. He had no choice.

He flung the cape around himself, and vanished.

CHAPTER 48

"THAT IS THE LAST of them, as I promised."

Verna stared into the eyes of a woman she had known for a hundred and fifty years. Her heart was sick. Known not well enough. There were many she had not known well enough.

"What does Jagang want with the Palace of the Prophets?"

"He has no power, beyond that of an ordinary man, except his ability as a dream walker." Leoma's voice trembled, but she went on. "He uses others, especially those with the gift, to accomplish what he wishes. He is going to use our knowledge to reveal the forks on the prophecies that will bring him victory, and then see to it that the correct action is taken in order to carry the world down that fork.

"He is a very patient man. It took him nearly twenty years to conquer the Old World, all the time perfecting his ability, probing the minds of others, and gathering the information he needed.

"He not only intends to use the prophecies in the vaults, but he intends to make the Palace of the Prophets his home. He knows about the spell; he has stationed men here as a test to make sure that it works for those without the gift, and that there is no harmful effect. He is going to live here and direct the conquest of the rest of the world, with the help of the prophecies, from this place.

"Once all lands fall to him, he will hold dominion over the world for hundreds upon hundreds of years, enjoying the spoils of his tyranny. To his mind, nothing so great has ever been dreamed, much less accomplished. It will be as near as a ruler can come to immortality."

"What else can you tell me?"

Leoma rung her hands. "Nothing. I've told you all. Let me go, Verna?"

"Kiss your ring finger, and beg the Creator's forgiveness."

"What?"

"Forsake the Keeper. It's your only hope, Leoma."

Leoma shook her head. "I can't do that, Verna. I won't."

Verna had no time to waste. Without further word or argument, she seized her Han. Light seemed to come from within Leoma's eyes and she crashed to the floor, dead.

Verna slipped silently down to the end of the empty hall, to Sister Simona's room. Feeling the joy of being able to manipulate her Han at will, she brought down the shield. Carefully, so as not to startle her, she knocked and then opened the door, hearing Simona scurry for the far corner.

"Simona, it's Verna. Don't be afraid, dear."

Simona let out a shuddering cry. "He comes! He comes!"

Verna lit a gentle glow of Han in her palm. "I know. You're not crazy, Sister Simona. He does come."

"We must escape! We must get away," she cried. "Oh, please, we must get away before he gets here. He comes in my dreams and taunts me. I'm so afraid." She fell to kissing her ring finger.

Verna gathered the trembling woman in her arms. "Simona, listen carefully to me. I have a way to save you from the dream walker. I can make you safe. We can get away."

The woman stilled, blinking up at Verna. "You believe me?"

"Yes. I know you're telling the truth. But you must believe me, too, when I tell you the truth that I know a magic that will protect you from the dream walker."

Simona wiped the tears from her filthy cheek. "Is it truly possible? How can it be done?"

"You remember Richard? The young man I brought back?"

Simona nodded with a smile as she cuddled in Verna's arms. "Who could forget Richard? Trouble and wonder in one package."

"Listen, now. Besides the gift, Richard has a magic which was passed down from his ancestors who fought the original dream walkers. It's a magic that protects him, too, from the dream walkers. It also protects anyone who swears fidelity to him, who is loyal to him in every way. That was the reason the spell was originally cast—to fight the dream walkers."

Her eyes widened. "That can't be possible—mere loyalty conferring magic."

"Leoma has had me locked in a room down the hall. She put a collar around my neck and used the test of pain to try to break my will and make me renounce Richard. She told me that the dream walker wanted to come to me in my dreams, like he does you, but my fidelity to Richard prevented it. It works, Simona. I don't know how, but it does. I'm protected from the dream walker. You can be, too."

Sister Simona wiped wisps of gray hair back from her face. "Verna, I'm not crazy. I want this collar off my neck. I want to escape the dream walker. We must escape. What would you have me do?"

Verna gripped the small woman tighter. "Will you help us? Will you help the rest of the Sisters of the Light escape, too?"

Simona put her cracked lips to her ring finger. "On my oath to the Creator."

"Then swear an oath to Richard, too. You must be bonded to him."

Simona pushed away and knelt with her forehead to the floor. "I swear fidelity to Richard. I swear my life to him on my hope to be sheltered by the Creator in the next world."

Verna urged Simona to sit up. She put her hands to the side of the Rada'Han, letting her Han flow into it, join with it, the room droning with the effort. The collar snapped and fell away.

Simona let out a joyful cry as she hugged Verna. Verna embraced her tightly; she knew the joy of having the Rada'Han off her neck.

"Simona, we must be going. We have much work to do, and not much time. I need your help."

Simona wiped away her tears. "I'm ready. Thank you, Prelate."

At the door with the bolt held on with the intricate web, Verna and Simona worked their Han together. The web had been set by three Sisters, and though Verna had that much power, it would still be a challenge to undo it. With Simona's added help, the web slipped away easily.

The two guards outside the door started in surprise when they saw the filthy prisoners. Pikes came down.

Verna recognized one of the guards. "Walsh, you know me, now raise that pike."

"I know you've been convicted of being a Sister of the Dark."

"I know you don't believe that."

The point was menacingly close to her face. "What makes you think so?"

"Because if it were true, I would have simply killed you in order to escape."

He was silent for a moment as he considered. "Keep talking."

"We are at war. The emperor wishes to put the world under his fist. He uses the true Sisters of the Dark, like Leoma, and the new Prelate, Ulicia. You know them, and you know me. Who do you believe?"

"Well . . . I'm not so sure."

"Then let me put it in terms that make it clear. You remember Richard?"

"Of course. He's a friend."

"Richard is at war with the Imperial Order. The time is upon you to choose sides. You must decide your loyalty, right now, right here. Richard, or the Order."

His lips pressed together as he fought a mental battle. Finally, the butt of his pike thumped to the floor. "Richard."

The other guard's eyes shifted between Walsh and Verna. His pike suddenly thrust forward with the cry, "The Order!"

Verna already had a firm grip on her Han. Before the blade touched her, the man was blown back with such force that when he hit the wall, his head split open. He toppled to the floor, dead.

"I guess I chose right," Walsh said.

"You did indeed. We must get the true Sisters of the Light, and the loyal young wizards, and we must be away from here at once. There isn't a moment to waste."

"Let's go," Walsh said, holding his pike out, pointing the way.

Outside, in the warm night air, a thin figure sat on a bench nearby. When she recognized them, she sprang up.

"Prelate!" she whispered with tearful joy.

Verna hugged Millie so tight the old woman squeaked for release. "Oh, Prelate, forgive the hateful things I said. I didn't mean a word of it, I swear."

Verna, nearly in tears, squeezed the woman again, and then kissed her forehead a dozen times. "Oh, Millie, thank you. You are the Creator's best work. I will never forget what you've done for me, for the Sisters of the Light. Millie, we must escape. The emperor is going to take the palace. Will you come with us, please, so you will be safe?"

Millie shrugged. "Me? An old woman? On the run from cut-throat Sisters of the Dark and magic monsters?"

"Yes. Please?"

Millie grinned in the moonlight. "Sounds more fun than scrubbing floors and emptying chamber pots."

"All right, all of you listen then, we . . ."

A tall shadow stepped out from behind the corner of the building. Everyone fell still and silent as the figure approached.

"Well, Verna, it looks as if you found your way out. I thought you might." She stepped close, where they could see her. It was Sister Philippa, Verna's other advisor. She kissed her ring finger. Philippa's narrow mouth spread in a smile. "Thank the Creator. Welcome back, Prelate."

"Philippa, we must get the Sisters away tonight, before Jagang gets here, or we will be captured and used."

"What are we to do, Prelate?" Sister Philippa asked.

"All of you, listen carefully, now. We must hurry, and we must be more than careful. If we are caught, we will all be in collars."

Richard was winded from his run from the Hagen Woods, so he slowed to a trot to catch his breath. He saw Sisters prowling the grounds of the palace, but they didn't see him. Though he was shrouded in the mriswith cape, he couldn't search the entire palace; it would take days. He had to find out where Kahlan, Zedd, and Gratch were being held so he could get back to Aydindril. Zedd would know what to do.

Zedd would probably furiously upbraid him for his stupidity, but Richard deserved it. His stomach was in a knot thinking about the trouble he had caused. He could not even credit his wits for his foolhardy actions not ending in his being killed. How many lives had he put in jeopardy by his reckless actions?

Kahlan was probably going to be more than furious with him. And why not?

Richard shuddered to think why the mriswith went to Aydindril. He felt a pang of dread for his friends there. Maybe the mriswith only wanted to establish a new home, like the Hagen Woods here, and would stay there and keep to themselves. An inner voice laughed at his wishful thinking. He had to get back there.

Stop thinking about the problem, he reprimanded himself. Think about the solution.

He would get his friends out of here first, and then he would worry about the rest.

It was puzzling that Kahlan, Zedd, and Gratch would be held at the palace, but he didn't doubt what Merissa had told him; she had thought she had him, and so would have had no reason to lie. He couldn't understand why the Sisters of the Dark would hide their catch in a place that could be a danger to them.

Richard halted. A small group of people was crossing the lawn in the moonlight. He couldn't see who they were, and was about to go find out, but decided that his first thought was the correct one: go see Ann. The Prelate would be able to help him. Other than Prelate Annalina and Sister Verna he didn't know which of the Sisters he could trust. He waited until the people moved off down a covered corridor before he started out again.

When he had left the palace months ago, he knew there could still be Sisters of the Dark among the sorceresses here, and they must be the ones who had hidden Kahlan away, but he didn't know who they were. He could look for Verna, but he didn't know where she would be. He did know where to find the Prelate, though, so that was where he would start.

If he had to, he would tear the Palace of the Prophets down, stone by stone, to find Kahlan and his friends, but he was wary of violating the Wizard's Third Rule again, and decided that this time he would start out, at least, with reason instead of passion.

Dear spirits, where did one end and the other begin?

At the outer gate to the Prelate's compound, Kevin Andellmere was standing guard. Richard knew Kevin, and was reasonably sure that he could be trusted. "Reasonably sure" wasn't good enough, so Richard kept the mriswith cape closed around himself and slipped past Kevin into the inner compound. In the distance,

Richard could hear the raucous laughter of several men coming up a walkway, but they were a goodly distance away.

Richard knew the Prelate's former administrators. One had been killed when the other, Sister Ulicia, had attacked the Prelate. After the attack, Sister Ulicia and five other Sisters of the Dark had fled aboard the ship, the *Lady Sefa*. The desks outside the Prelate's office were empty, now.

No one was around out in the hall, or the outer office, and the door to the Prelate's office was open, so Richard let the mriswith cape fall open as he relaxed his concentration. He wanted Ann to recognize him.

The moonlight coming through the double doors in the rear of the dark room silhouetted her enough for Richard to tell that she was sitting in her chair at the table. He could see in the faint light that her head was tilted down. She must be napping.

"Prelate," he said gently, so as not to startle her awake. She stirred, her head coming up a bit, and her hand lifting. "I need to talk with you, Prelate. It's Richard. Richard Rahl."

A glow lit in her upturned palm.

Sister Ulicia smiled up at him. "Come to talk, have you? How very interesting. Well, a talk would be nice."

As her wicked grin widened, Richard took a step back, his hand going for thc hilt of his sword.

He had no sword.

He heard the door slam shut behind him.

He spun and saw four of his teachers: Sisters Tovi, Cecilia, Armina, and Merissa. He saw as they closed the distance that each wore a ring in her lower lip. Only Nicci was missing. They all grinned like hungry children staring at a candy reward at the end of a three-day fast.

Richard felt his need ignite within.

"Before you do anything foolish, Richard, you had better listen first, or you will die where you stand."

He paused and looked to Merissa. "How did you beat me back here?"

She arched an eyebrow over a dark, malevolent eye. "I returned on my horse."

Richard turned back to Ulicia. "This was all planned, wasn't it? You did this to trap me."

"Oh, yes, my boy, and you have done your part splendidly."

He pointed back at Merissa while he spoke to Ulicia. "How did you know I wouldn't be killed when she threw me off that tower?"

Ulicia's smile vanished as she glared up at Merissa. Richard realized by seeing that look that Merissa had been acting outside of instructions.

Ulicia brought her gaze back to Richard. "The point is, you are here. Now, I want you to calm down, or someone could get hurt; you may have been born with both sides of the gift, but we have use of both magics, too. Even if you managed to kill one or two of us, there is no way you will get us all, and then Kahlan will die."

"Kahlan . . ." Richard glared down at her. "I'm listening."

Ulicia folded her hands. "You see, Richard, you have a problem. Fortunately for you, we also have a problem."

"What sort of problem?"

Her eyes hardened with distant menace. "Jagang."

The others moved around the table to stand beside Ulicia. None of them were smiling anymore. The loathing in their eyes at the name Jagang, even the kindly seeming Tovi and Cecilia, looked as if it could burn stone.

"You see, Richard, it's almost time for bed."

Richard frowned. "What?"

"You don't have any visits from Emperor Jagang in your dreams. We do. He is becoming a problem to us."

Richard could feel the control around her voice. This woman wanted something more than life itself.

"Problems with the dream walker, Ulicia? Well, I wouldn't know. I sleep like a baby."

Richard usually knew when a person with the gift was touching their Han; he could sense it, or see it in their eyes. The air about these women fairly sizzled. There seemed enough power bottled up behind all those eyes to melt a mountain. Apparently, it wasn't enough. A dream walker must be a formidable opponent.

"All right, Ulicia, let's get to the point. I want Kahlan, and you want something. What is it?"

Ulicia fingered the ring through her lip as she looked away from his eyes. "This has to be decided before we sleep. I have only just told my Sisters of the plan I devised. We couldn't find Nicci to include her. If we go to sleep before this is resolved, and any of us dreams of it . . ."

"Resolved? I want Kahlan. Just tell me what you want."

Ulicia cleared her throat. "We want to swear loyalty to you."

Richard stared, unable to blink. He wasn't sure he had just heard what he thought he had heard. "You're all Sisters of the Dark. You know me, and you all want to kill me. How can you break your oath to the Keeper?"

Ulicia's iron gaze came up. "I did not say that we wished to do that. I said we would like to swear loyalty to you, in this, the world of life. I don't think, in view of the overall picture, that the two are incompatible."

"Not incompatible! Are you crazy, too!"

Her eyes took on an ominous set. "Do you want to die? Do you want Kahlan to die?"

Richard made an effort to calm his racing mind. "No."

"Then be quiet and listen. We have something you want. You have something we want. Each of us has conditions. For instance, you want Kahlan, but you want her alive and well. Am I correct?"

Richard returned the ominous glare in kind. "You know it is. But what makes you think I would make a pact with you? You tried to kill Prelate Annalina."

"Not only tried, but succeeded."

Richard closed his eyes with an anguished groan. "You admit to murdering her, and then you expect I would trust . . ."

"I'm running out of patience, young man, and your bride-to-be is running out of time. If you don't get her away before Jagang gets here, I can assure you, there is no hope you will ever see her again. You have no time to search."

Richard swallowed. "All right. I'm listening."

"You put the lock back on the Keeper's gateway to this world. You thwarted the plans we laid. In so doing, you diminished the Keeper's power in this world, restoring the balance between him and the Creator. In the balance you created, Jagang makes his move to take the world for himself.

"He has also taken us. He can come to us any time he wishes. We are his prisoners, no matter where we are. He has demonstrated to us just how unpleasant a captor he can be. There is no way for us to escape him, but one."

"You mean the bond to me."

"Yes. Now, if we do as Jagang has instructed, then we continue on in his good graces, as it were. While it is . . . unpleasant, at least we live. We want to live.

"If we swear fidelity to you, we can break the hold Jagang has on us, and escape."

"You mean you want to kill him," Richard observed.

Ulicia shook her head. "We want never to see his face again. We don't care what he does, we just want out of his clutches.

"I will tell you the truth of it. We will return to our work of bringing our Master, the Keeper, to dominance. If we succeed, we will be rewarded. I don't know if it's possible for us to succeed, but that is the risk you will have to bear."

"What do you mean, that's the risk I'll have to bear? If you're bonded to me, then you have to work toward my ends: fighting against the Keeper and the Imperial Order."

Ulicia's lips spread with a cunning smile. "No, my boy. I've thought this out very carefully. Here is my offer: We swear fidelity to you, you ask us where Kahlan is, and we tell you. In return, you can ask nothing else of us, and must allow us to leave immediately. You won't see us, we won't see you."

"But if you work to free the Keeper, that's against me, and violates the bond. It won't work!"

"You are looking at it through your eyes. The protection your bond provides is invoked through the conviction of the person bonded—their doing what they think is called for by their fidelity.

"You want to take the world. You think this is for the good of the people of the world. Have all the people you've tried to win to your side believed you, and stayed to stand with you? Or have some seen your benevolent offers as something else, as abuse, and fled in fear of you?"

Richard remembered the people leaving Aydindril. "I guess I can understand, in a way, but . . ."

"We don't view loyalty through your moral filter; we view our loyalty by our own standards. To our sensibilities, as Sisters of the Dark, as long as we are doing nothing that is directly harming you, we will not be breaking our loyalty because not harming you is definitely to your benefit."

Richard put his fists on the table and leaned toward her. "You want to free the Keeper. That will harm me."

"It's a matter of perception, Richard. It's power we want, the same as you, no matter the morals in which you wish to couch your ambition.

"Our efforts are not directed against you. If we should happen to succeed on behalf of the Keeper, everyone would be vanquished, including Jagang, so it won't matter if we incidentally lose the protection of the bond. It may not fit your mores, but it fits ours, and so the bond will work.

"And who knows, it could even be that by some miracle, you might win your war against the Order, and kill Jagang. Then we won't need a bond. We can have patience to see what will happen. Just don't be foolish enough to return to Aydindril. Jagang is taking it back, and there is nothing you can do to stop him."

Richard straightened and blinked down at her, trying to reason it out. "But . . . I would be setting you free to go out and work for evil."

"Evil by your morals. The truth is you would be giving us the chance to try, but that does not mean we will succeed. However, it also gives you Kahlan, and the chance to try to stop the Imperial Order, and to try to frustrate our attempts to win our struggle. You have thwarted us in the past.

"It buys each of us something very important. It buys us our freedom, and it buys Kahlan hers. A fair trade, I think."

Richard stood silently considering this mad offer; he was that desperate.

"So, if you bow down and offer me your fidelity, your bond, then you tell me where Kahlan is, and then you run off as you propose, what assurance have I that you have told me the truth of where Kahlan is?"

Ulicia cocked her head with a clever smile. "Simple. We swear, you ask. If we lie to your direct question, the bond would be broken, and we would be back in Jagang's clutches."

"What if I break my end, and after you tell me where Kahlan is, I make another demand of you? You would have to uphold it to remain bonded and be protected from Jagang."

"That's why our offer carries the condition of only one question: where is Kahlan? If you do more, then we will kill you, the same as if you turn us down. We will be no worse off than we are right now. You die, and Jagang gets Kahlan to do with as he will, and he will, I assure you. He has very perverse tastes." Her gaze turned to the young woman beside her. "Just ask Merissa."

Richard looked at Merissa and saw the blood drain from her face. She tugged down her red dress enough to show him the top half of her breast. Richard felt the blood drain from his own face. He turned his eyes away.

"He will only allow my face to be healed. The rest he orders left, for his . . . amusement. This is the least of what he did to me. The very least of what he did to me," Merissa said in a bone cold voice. "All because of you, Richard Rahl."

Richard had a flash of a vision of Kahlan with Jagang's ring through her lip and those lurid marks on her. His knees went weak.

He pulled his lower lip through his teeth as he looked back to Ulicia. "You aren't the Prelate. Give me her ring." Without hesitation, she pulled it off and handed it to him. "You want to swear loyalty, I get to ask where Kahlan is, you must tell me true, and then you leave?"

"That is our offer."

Richard heaved a sigh. "Bargain struck."

Ulicia closed her eyes with a sigh of freedom after Richard shut the door on his way out. He was in a hurry. She didn't care; she had what she wanted. She was going to sleep without the fear of Jagang coming in the dream that was not a dream.

Their five lives for one. Quite a bargain.

And she hadn't even had to tell him everything. But she had had to tell him more than she wished. Still, quite a bargain.

"Sister Ulicia," Cecilia said with a tone of surety in her voice that had been missing for months, "you have done the impossible. You have broken Jagang's hold on us. The Sisters of the Dark are free, and it has cost us nothing."

Ulicia took a deep breath. "I wouldn't be so sure of that. We have just struck an uncharted course across untrodden ground in an unknown land. But for now, we are free. We must not waste our chance. We must leave at once."

She glanced up as the door banged opened.

A grinning Captain Blake swaggered into the office. Two smirking sailors trailed in behind, one slowing to grope Armina on his way past. She made no attempt to ward off his hands.

Captain Blake teetered before her. He placed his hands on the table and leaned over. She could smell liquor on his breath as he leered at her.

"Well, well, lass. We meet again."

Ulicia betrayed no emotion. "So we do."

His hungry gaze was too low to meet her eyes. "The *Lady Sefa* just made port, and we lonely sailors thought we should have some company for the night. The boys enjoyed the last time with you ladies so much that they thought to do it all over again."

She affected a timorous tone. "I hope you plan to be more gentle than the last time."

"Matter of fact, lass, the boys was saying how they didn't think we did all we could to enjoy ourselves." He leaned over even more, reached out with his right hand, grabbed her nipple, and pulled her forward in her chair. He smiled at her cry. "Now, before I get in an ugly mood, you whores get your behinds down to the *Lady Sefa* with us, where we can put 'em to a good use."

Ulicia brought her fist around and slammed a knife through the back of the captain's left hand, pinning it to the table. She touched a finger of her other hand to the ring in her lip, and with a flow of Subtractive Magic, it winked out of existence.

"Yes, Captain Blake, let's all of us go down to the *Lady Sefa* and have another very intimate visit with you and your crew."

With a fist of Han, she clouted him back, the knife embedded in the table slicing his hand in two as it was yanked away. A gag of air filled his mouth when he opened it to scream.

CHAPTER 49

"SOMETHING BE GOING ON out there," Adie whispered. "It must be them." She fixed her white eyes on Kahlan. "You be sure you wish to do this? I be willing, but . . ."

"We have to," Kahlan said as she glanced at the fire to make sure it was still going strong. "We must escape. If we can't escape, and we're killed, well then, Richard won't be lured to come here to fall into their trap, and he can stay where he is and, with Zedd's help, protect the people of the Midlands."

Adie nodded. "We try, then." She sighed. "I know I be right that she be doing it, but I do not know the reason."

Adie had told her that Lunetta did something very peculiar: she was shrouded in her power all the time. Such a task was so extraordinary, Adie had said, that it required the use of a talisman invested with magic. With Lunetta, that talisman could only be one thing.

"Like you said, Adie, even if you don't know the reason, she wouldn't do something like that if it weren't important."

Kahlan crossed her lips with a finger when she heard the squeak of the floor in the hall. Adie's gray and black jaw-length hair swayed as she quickly blew out the lamp and moved back behind the door. The fire still provided light, but the flickering flames made the shadows dance, and would only add to the confusion.

The door opened. Kahlan, standing to the opposite side of the door from Adie, took a deep breath, mustering her courage. She hoped they had removed the shield, or they were going to be in a lot of trouble for nothing.

The two figures stepped into the room. It was them.

"What are you doing in here, you greasy little nick!" Kahlan yelled.

Brogan, with Lunetta behind him, rounded on Kahlan. She spat in his eyes.

His face gone red, he grabbed for her. Kahlan brought her boot up between his legs. When he cried out, Lunetta reached for him. From behind, Adie cracked a log across the squat sorceress's head.

Brogan threw himself on Kahlan, grappling with her, punching her in the ribs. Adie snatched Lunetta's outfit of colored patches as she fell. The whole thing ripped as Adie, her mighty effort powered by desperation, rolled the nearly senseless woman out of her patchwork clothes.

Lunetta, dazed and slow, cried out as Adie spun around with her prize and heaved it into the roaring fire.

Kahlan saw the patches of colored cloth flame up in the hearth as she and Brogan toppled to the floor. She heaved him over the top of her as she crashed to the ground and then rolled to her feet. As Brogan turned to get his footing, she kicked him in the face.

Lunetta squealed in distress. Kahlan kept her eyes on Brogan as he sprang up with blood running from his nose. Before he could charge at her again, he saw his sister behind Kahlan and froze.

Kahlan darted a quick glance behind. A woman was pawing frantically at the fire, futilely trying to recover the flaming patches of colored cloth.

The woman was not Lunetta.

It was an attractive, older woman, in a white shift.

Kahlan's eyes went wide at the sight. What happened to Lunetta?

Brogan screamed out in fury. "Lunetta! How dare you do a glamour in front of others! How dare you use magic to make them think you be pretty! Stop it at once! Your taint be ugly!"

"Lord General," she cried, "my pretties. My pretties be burning. Please, my brother, help me."

"You filthy *streganicha*! Stop it, I say!"

"I can't," she wept, "I can't without my pretties."

With a growl of rage, Brogan slammed Kahlan aside and dashed to the fire. He lifted Lunetta by her hair and struck her with his fist. She fell back, knocking Adie to the floor with her.

He kicked his sister as she tried to stand. "I've had enough of your disobedience and your profane taint!"

Kahlan snatched up a log and swung at him, but he ducked and it caught only his shoulders. His fist in her gut drove her back.

Kahlan gasped to get her breath. "You ugly pig! Leave your beautiful sister alone!"

"She be loony! Loony Lunetta!"

"Don't listen to him, Lunetta! Your name means 'little moon'! Don't listen to him!"

Brogan screamed in fury and threw his hands out toward Kahlan. With a loud crack, lightning lit the room. It missed her only because he was raging out of control and striking wildly. Plaster and other debris blasted through the air.

Kahlan was stunned near to paralysis. Tobias Brogan, the Lord General of the Blood of the Fold, the man committed to exterminating magic, had the gift.

Screaming again, Brogan threw a fist of air that caught Kahlan square in the chest and slammed her against the wall. She crumpled to the floor, dazed and senseless.

Lunetta shrieked louder when she saw what Brogan had done. "No, Tobias! You must not use the taint!"

He fell on his sister, strangling her, pounding her head against the floor. "You be the one who did it! You be using the taint! You be using a glamour! You made the lightning!"

"No, Tobias, you be the one doing it. You must not use the gift. Mamma told me you must not use it."

He lifted her by a fistful of her white shift. "What are you talking about? What did Mamma tell you, you vile *streganicha*?"

The comely woman panted and gulped. "That you be the one, my brother. The one for greatness. She said I must not make people to notice me—so they would look only to you. She said you be the one who be important. But she said I must not let you use your gift."

"Liar! Mamma never said any such thing! Mamma didn't know anything!"

"Yes, Tobias, she knew. She be touched with a little of the gift. The Sisters came to take you away. We loved you, and didn't want them to take our little Tobias."

"I don't have the taint!"

"It be true, my brother. They said you had the gift, and they wanted to take you to the Palace of the Prophets. Mamma told me that if they went back without you they would bring others. We killed them. Mamma and me. That be how you got the scar by your mouth—in our fight with them. She said we had to kill them so they wouldn't send others. She said I must never let you use the gift or they would come to take you."

Brogan's chest heaved with rage. "All lies! You did the lightning, and you be using a glamour for others!"

"No," she wept. "They burned my pretties. Mamma said you be destined to be great, but it could all be ruined. She taught me how to use the pretties to hide my looks and to keep you from using the gift. We wanted you to be great.

"My pretties be gone. You made the lightning."

Brogan stared off with wild eyes, as if seeing things none of the rest of them saw. "It not be the taint," he whispered. "It just be me. The taint be evil. This not be evil. It just be me."

Brogan's eyes focused again as he saw Kahlan struggle to rise. The room flashed with blinding light as he threw another lightning bolt across the room. It raked the wall over her head as she dived for the floor. Brogan sprang to his feet to come for her.

"Tobias! Stop! You must not use your gift!"

Tobias Brogan gazed back at his sister with an eerie calm. "This be a sign. The time has come. I always knew it would." Blue flashes flickered between his fingertips as he held a hand up before his face. "This not be the taint, Lunetta, but divine power. The taint would be ugly. This be beautiful.

"The Creator has relinquished his right to dictate to me. The Creator be a baneling. I have the power, now. The time has come to use it. I must sit in judgment of man, now." He turned to Kahlan. "I be the Creator, now."

Lunetta lifted an imploring arm. "Tobias, please—"

He wheeled back toward her, deadly snakes of light writhing at his hands. "What I have be glorious. I will hear no more of your filth and lies. You and Mamma be banelings." He drew his sword, the light coiling up the blade, and waved it in the air.

She frowned with mental effort. "You must not use your power, Tobias. You must not." The flickering light at his hands cut off.

"I will use what be mine!" The light at his fingers ignited once more and danced up the blade. "I be the Creator, now. I have the power, and I say you must die!"

His eyes gleamed with madness as he stared, transfixed, at the light crackling at his fingertips.

"Then you," Lunetta whispered, "be the true baneling, and I must stop you, as you have taught me."

A glowing line of rose-colored light flared from Lunetta's hand and pierced Tobias Brogan through the heart.

In the smoky stillness, he drew a last gasp, and collapsed.

Not knowing what Lunetta would do, Kahlan didn't move, remaining as still as a fawn in the grass. Adie reached out with a tender hand, offering comforting words in their native tongue.

Lunetta didn't seem to hear. She crawled woodenly to her brother's body and cradled his head in her lap. Kahlan thought she might be sick.

Suddenly, Galtero stepped into the room.

He snatched Lunetta by the hair and pulled her head back. He didn't see Kahlan in the rubble against the wall behind him.

"*Streganicha,*" he whispered viciously.

Lunetta made no effort to resist. She seemed in a numb daze. Brogan's sword lay nearby. Kahlan dove for it. Frantic, she snatched up the sword. She wasn't fast enough.

Galtero sliced his knife across Lunetta's throat.

Before Lunetta had hit the floor, Kahlan ran him through.

As he toppled she yanked the sword free. "Adie, are you hurt?"

"Not on the outside, child."

"I understand, but we don't have time for sorrow right now."

Kahlan grasped Adie's hand, and after carefully checking to insure that Lunetta had indeed removed the shield before they had entered, the two of them stepped out into the hall.

At either end lay the remains of a Sister: their guards. Lunetta had killed them both.

Kahlan heard boots clambering up the steps. She and Adie leapt over the bloody mess at the other end of the hall and dashed down the service stairs and out the back way. They looked about in the darkness, seeing no one, but hearing a commotion in the distance—the clash of steel. Together, hand in hand, they ran for their lives.

Kahlan could feel tears coursing down her face.

With her head down, so the Sister wouldn't recognize her, Ann crossed the distance in the dim light of the vaults. Zedd trailed in her footsteps. The woman behind the table stood with a suspicious frown and marched forward.

"Who is it?" Sister Becky's voice was terse. "No one is allowed down here anymore. All have been warned."

Ann felt a thrust of Han smack her shoulder to bring her to a halt as Sister Becky rushed up before her. When Ann raised her head, Becky's eyes went wide.

Ann drove the dacra into her, and the eyes seemed to light from within before the woman went down.

Zedd leapt out to the side. "You killed her! You just killed a pregnant woman!"

"You," Ann whispered, "condemned her to death. I pray you have ordered the execution of a Sister of the Dark, and not the Light."

Zedd wrench her around by the arm. "Have you lost your mind, woman!"

"I ordered the Sisters of the Light to get out of the palace. I told them they had to escape. I have begged you countless times to let me use the book. I needed to confirm that they have done as ordered. Since you refused to allow me to use the journey book, I am forced to assume my instructions were carried out."

"That's no excuse to kill her! You could have simply incapacitated her!"

"If my orders were followed, then she is a Sister of the Dark. I have no chance in a fair fight with one of them. Neither do you. We couldn't take the risk."

"And what if she's not one of the Keeper's Sisters!"

"I can't risk everyone else on a mere chance."

Zedd's eyes flashed with cold fury. "You are mad."

Ann lifted an eyebrow. "Oh? And you would risk the lives of thousands to fret over one who you are reasonably sure was an enemy bent on stopping you? Did you get to be a Wizard of the First Order by such choices?"

He released her arm. "All right, you've gotten me here. What is it you want?"

"Check the vault first, to make sure there are no others."

They each stole down one side, Ann checking between the rows of bookshelves to watch the old wizard and make sure he was doing as instructed. If he tried to run, she could bring him back by the Rada'Han, and he knew it.

She liked Richard's grandfather, but need demanded she cultivate his hatred. For this, he had to be in a fury, and willingly take the chance she would give him.

When they reached the rear of the gloomy vaults, they had found no others. Ann kissed her naked ring finger and thanked the Creator. She blocked the emotion of having killed Sister Becky, telling herself that she would not be guarding the vaults unless she were sworn to the Keeper, and a pawn of the emperor. She tried not to think of the innocent unborn child she had also killed.

"Now what?" Zedd snapped when they met in the rear, near one of the small, restricted rooms.

"Nathan will do his part. I brought you here to do your part, the other half of what is needed.

"The palace is charged with a spell cast three thousand years ago. I have been able to determine that it's a bifurcated web."

Zedd's eyebrows went up. His curiosity overcame his indignation. "That's quite a claim. I've never heard of anyone able to spin a bifurcated web. Are you sure?"

"No one now can spin such a web, but the wizards of old had such power."

Zedd drew a thumb down his smooth jaw as he stared off. "Yes, they would have had the power, I imagine." His gaze returned to her eyes. "To what purpose?"

"The spell alters the grounds of the palace. The outer shield, where we left Nathan, is the shell encasing it all. It creates the environment in which this half can exist in this world. The spell here, on this island, is linked to other worlds. Among other things, it alters time. That's why we age more slowly than people living outside the spell."

The old wizard pondered. "Yes, that would explain it."

Ann glanced away from his eyes. "Nathan and I are both almost one thousand years old. I have been Prelate of the Sisters of the Light for nearly eight centuries."

Zedd straightened his robes at his bony hips. "I've known of the spell, how it extends life spans in order to give you the time to do your foul work."

"Zedd, when the wizards of old began jealously guarding their power and refused to train young men with the gift so as to prevent a threat to their domination, the Sisters of the Light were formed to help these young men lest they die. Not everyone likes the idea, but there it is.

"Without a wizard to help them, the task falls to us. We don't have the same Han as the male, and so it takes us a great deal of time to accomplish the task. The collar keeps them alive, keeps their gift from harming them, from driving them mad, until we can teach them what they need.

"The spell around the palace gives us the time we need. It was laid down for us three thousand years ago, when a few wizards helped with our cause. They had the power to cast a bifurcated web."

Zedd was, for the moment, becoming intrigued. "Yes. Yes, I can see what you mean. Bifurcation would invert the force, kind of like twisting a length of gut, and create an area where the center could be bent to do extraordinary things. The ancient wizards could accomplish deeds I can only dream of doing."

Ann was keeping a constant watch, to make sure they were alone. "Bifurcating a web bends it back on itself, creating an outer and inner region. There are two nodes, like with the twisted gut you mentioned, where this bending would have to take place: one at the outer shield, and one at the inner."

Zedd peered at her with one eye. "But the node on the inner half, where the true event takes place, would be vulnerable to breach. Though created by necessity, it would be a dangerous flaw. Do you know where the inner node is located?"

"We stand in it."

Zedd straightened. He glanced around. "Yes, I can see the thought that went into it—placing it in the bedrock under everything else where it would be best protected."

"That's why, on the off chance it could bring havoc, we unequivocally forbid wizard's fire anywhere on Halsband Island."

Zedd absently waved a hand. "No, no. Wizard's fire wouldn't

harm such a node." He turned to her with a suspicious glare. "What are we doing here?"

"I brought you here to give you the opportunity to do what you wish to do—to destroy the spell."

He stared, he blinked, and he stared some more. At last, he spoke. "No. It wouldn't be right."

"Wizard Zorander, this is a highly inconvenient time for you to be overcome with morals."

He folded his skinny arms. "This spell was placed by wizards greater than I will ever be, greater than I can even imagine. This is a wonder, a thing of profound mastery. I won't destroy such a piece of work."

"I broke the truce!"

Zedd lifted his chin. "Breaking the truce condemns any Sister who comes to the New World to death. We are not in the New World. Breaking the truce says nothing about me going to the Old World and doing harm. By the terms of the truce, I have no right to do such a thing."

She leaned closer with a dark look. "You promised me that if I took you away by that collar, endangering your friends, you would come to my homeland and lay waste to the Palace of the Prophets. I am giving you your chance."

"It was a temporary, passionate outburst. Reason has returned to my head." He fixed her with a scolding scowl. "You've been using devious tricks and sly deception to try to convince me you're a vile, contemptible, immoral malefactor, but you have failed to fool me. You are not the evil sort."

"I've shackled you! I abducted you!"

"I won't destroy your home and your life. Doing so, destroying the spell, would alter the pattern of the lives of the Sisters of the Light and, in essence, be ending their lives prematurely. The Sisters and their charges live by standards of time that to me seem strange, but to them are normal.

"Life is perception. If a mouse with a life span of only a few years were to have the magic to make my life as short as its life, that, to my perception, would be killing me, though to the mouse it would seem he were granting no less than a normal life span. That's what Nathan meant when he said you were killing him.

"I would be shortening their lives to the same as the rest of us, but by their expectations and the oath they have taken, that would be the same as killing them before they have a chance to live. I won't do it."

"If I have to, Wizard Zorander, I'll use the collar to give you pain until you agree."

He smirked. "You have no conception of the tests of pain I have passed to become a wizard of the First Order. Go ahead, do your best."

Ann pressed her lips together in exasperation. "But you have to! I've put a collar around your neck! I've done terrible things to you to make you angry enough to do this! The prophecy says the anger of a wizard is necessary to destroy our home!"

"You've been playing me for a dancing frog." His hazel eyes hovered closer. "I don't dance unless I know the tune."

Ann sagged in frustration. "The truth is that Emperor Jagang is going to take the Palace of the Prophets for his own use. He's a dream walker, and controls the minds of the Sisters of the Dark. He intends to use the prophecies to find the forks he needs to win the war, and then he's going to live under the spell for hundreds of years, ruling the world and everyone in it as his own."

Zedd considered her with a scowl. "Now, that gets my blood to boiling. That's a worthy reason to level the palace. Bags, woman, why didn't you just tell me the truth in the beginning?"

"Nathan and I have been working on this fork in the prophecies for hundreds of years. The prophecy says a wizard will level the palace in fury. Failure is too dark a vision for the world to take any risk, so I did the thing I thought would work. I've been trying to make you furious enough to want to destroy the Palace of the Prophets." Ann rubbed her tired eyes. "It was a desperate act, because of a desperate need."

Zedd grinned. "Desperate act. I like that. I like a woman who can appreciate the occasional need for acts of desperation. Shows spirit."

Ann clutched his sleeve. "Will you do it, then? We don't have any time to spare; the drums have stopped. Jagang could be here at any moment."

"I'll do it. We'd better get back near the entrance, though."

When they were back near the huge round door to the vaults, Zedd reached into a pocket and pulled out what appeared to be a stone. He tossed it on the floor.

"What's that?"

Zedd glanced back over his shoulder. "Well, I conjecture you told Nathan to cast a light web."

"Yes. Other than Nathan, a few sisters, and myself, no one knows how to spin a light web. I think Nathan has enough power to breach the outer node once a cascade is begun on this inner one, but I know neither of us has the power to start the one needed in here. That's why I needed to bring you here. I fear only a wizard of the First Order will have the power necessary."

"Well, I'll do my best," Zedd grumbled, "but I've got to tell you, Ann, as vulnerable as a node would be, it's still a spell cast by wizards the vastness of whose power I can only imagine."

He spun his finger around, and the stone on the floor before him popped and snapped as it rapidly grew to a broad, flat rock. He stepped up onto it.

"You get out of here. Go wait outside. Make sure Holly is safe while I do this. If anything goes wrong, and I can't control the cascade of light, you won't have time to get out of here."

"Act of desperation, Zedd?"

He answered with a grunt as he turned back to the room and lifted his arms. Already, sparkling colors were rising from the rock, engulfing him with spiraling shafts of humming light.

Ann had heard of wizard's rocks, but she had never seen one, and didn't know how they worked. She could feel the power that began emanating from the old wizard when he had stepped up on the thing.

She hurried from the vault as he wished. She wasn't sure if he really wanted her out of the room for her own safety, or if he didn't want her to see how he was going to do such a thing. Wizards did tend to guard their secrets. Besides that, Zedd was proving to be even more devious than Nathan—an achievement she would have thought impossible.

Holly wrapped her thin little arms around Ann's neck when she squatted down by the dark niche.

"Has anyone come past?"

"No, Ann," Holly whispered.

"Good. Let me squeeze in here with you, while we wait until Wizard Zorander is finished with his task."

"He yells a lot, and says a lot of bad words, and waves his arms around like he's going to call a storm around us, but I think he's nice."

"You aren't still itching from snow fleas." Ann smiled in the dark of the small hiding place among the rock. "But I think you may be right."

"My grandmamma would get angry, sometimes, like when people meant to hurt us, but you could tell she really meant it. Wizard Zorander doesn't really mean it. He's just pretending."

"You are more perceptive than I have been, child. You're going make a splendid Sister of the Light."

Ann held Holly's head to her shoulder as she waited in the silence. She hoped the wizard would hurry. If they were caught in the vaults, there was no way out, and a fight with Sisters of the Dark, despite his power, would prove more than dangerous.

Time dragged on with agonizing stubbornness. Ann could tell by her slow, steady breathing that Holly had fallen asleep against her shoulder. The poor child hadn't been getting enough sleep—none of them had, rushing day and most of the nights, too, to get to Tanimura in time, to beat Jagang to the palace. They were all exhausted.

Ann started when there was a tug on her dress at her shoulder. "Let's get out of here," Zedd whispered.

Pulling Holly with her, she squeezed back out of their hiding place. "Did you do it?"

Zedd, looking worse than merely vexed, glanced back through the huge round door to the vaults.

"I can't get the confounded thing to work. It's like trying to start a fire under water."

She clutched his robes in a fist. "Zedd, we have to do this."

He turned his worried eyes to her. "I know. But the ones who wove this web had Subtractive Magic. I have only Additive. I've tried everything I know. The web around this place is stable beyond my ability to breach. It can't be done. I'm sorry."

"I've woven a light web in the palace. It can be done."

"I didn't say I didn't weave one, I said I can't get it to ignite. Not down here in the node, anyway."

"You tried to ignite it! Are you crazy?"

He shrugged. "Act of desperation, remember? I had my suspicions about it working, so I had to test it. Good thing I did, or we would have thought it would work. It won't. It will ignite only for life. It won't expand and consume the spell."

Ann sagged. "At least if anyone goes in there, hopefully Jagang, it will kill them. Until they discover it, anyway, and then they will drain the shield and have the vaults to do with as they will."

"It will cost them dearly. I've left a few 'tricks' of my own in there. The place is a death trap."

"Is there nothing else we can do?"

"It's big enough to take down the entire palace, but I can't set it off. If these Sisters of the Dark really can wield Subtractive Magic, as you say, we could ask one of them if they would try to ignite the light web for us."

Ann nodded. "That's all we can do, then. We have to hope the things you left in there will kill them. Even if we can't destroy the palace, maybe that will be enough." She took Holly's hand. "We had better get out of here. Nathan will be waiting. We must escape before Jagang arrives, or the Sisters discover us."

CHAPTER 50

WHEN SHE SAW THE flash of steel in the moonlight, Verna ducked behind a stone bench. The sounds of battle rolled up the lawns toward her from lower down on the palace grounds. Some of the others had told her that the crimson-caped soldiers had arrived not long ago to join with the Imperial Order, but they now seemed bent on killing everyone in sight.

Two men in the crimson capes raced up out of the darkness. From the other direction, where she had seen the flash of steel, someone sprang out and in an instant had cut them down.

"It's two of the Blood," a woman's voice whispered. The voice sounded familiar. "Come on, Adie."

Another thin form emerged from the shadows. The woman had used a sword, and Verna had her Han to defend herself. She took a chance, and stood.

"Who is it? Show yourself."

Moonlight glinted off the sword as it rose. "Who wants to know?"

She hoped she wasn't taking a foolish chance, but there were friends among the women here. Still, she kept a firm grip on her dacra.

"It's Verna."

The shadowed figure paused. "Verna? Sister Verna?"

"Yes. Who is it," she whispered back.

"Kahlan Amnell."

"Kahlan! It can't be." Verna rushed out into the moonlight and lurched to a halt before the woman. "Dear Creator, it is." Verna threw her arms around her. "Oh, Kahlan. I was so worried you were killed."

"Verna, you can't know how glad I am to see a friendly face."

"Who is it with you?"

An old woman stepped closer. "A long time, it has been, but I still remember you well, Sister Verna."

Verna stared, trying to place the face of the old woman. "I'm sorry, but I don't recognize you."

"I be Adie. I was here for a time, fifty years ago, in my youth."

Verna's eyebrows went up. "Adie! I remember Adie."

Verna left unsaid that she remembered Adie as a rather young woman. She had learned long ago not to say such things aloud; those from the outside world lived by a different pace of time.

"I think you may remember my name, but not my face. It be a long time ago." Adie embraced Verna in a warm hug. "You be one I remember. You be kind to me when I be here."

Kahlan interrupted the brief reminiscing. "Verna, what's going on here? We were brought here by the Blood of the Fold, and have just managed to escape. We have to get out of here, but it seems the place is erupting in battle."

"It's a long story, and I have no time right now to tell it all. I'm not sure I even know it all. But you're right, we must escape at once. The Sisters of the Dark have taken the palace, and Emperor Jagang of the Imperial Order is due to arrive at any time. I have to get the Sisters of the Light away from here at once. Come with us?"

Kahlan scanned the lawns for trouble. "All right, but I have to go get Ahern. He's been steadfast; I can't leave him behind. He'll be wanting to get his team and coach, if I know Ahern."

"I still have Sisters out collecting all those loyal," Verna said. "We're to meet just over there, on the other side of that wall. The guard hiding on the other side, beside the gate, is loyal to Richard, as are all the rest guarding the gates in that wall. His name is Kevin. He can be trusted. When you get back, just tell him you're a friend of Richard. It's a code he knows. He'll let you into the compound."

"Loyal to Richard?"

"Yes. Hurry. I have to go inside to get a friend out. You can't let your man bring his team through this way, though; the palace grounds are becoming a battlefield. He'll never make it.

"The stables are at the north end. That's the way we're leaving. I have Sisters guarding the small bridge there. Have him head north to the first farm on the right with a stone wall around the garden. That's our secondary meeting place, and it's secure. For the moment, anyway."

"I'll hurry," Kahlan said.

Verna caught her arm. "We can't wait for you if you don't get back here in time. I must get a friend and then we must escape."

"I don't expect you to wait. Don't worry, I have to get away, too. I think I'm the bait to draw Richard here."

"Richard!"

"Another long story, but I have to get away before they can use me to lure him here."

The night suddenly lit, as if by silent lightning, except it didn't go out like lightning. They all turned to the southeast and saw massive balls of flame boiling up into the night sky. Thick black smoke billowed into the air. It seemed the entire harbor was aflame. Huge ships were thrown into the air atop colossal columns of water.

The ground suddenly shook, and at the same time the air boomed with the rumbling sound of distant explosions.

"Dear spirits," Kahlan said. "What's going on?" She glanced about. We're running out of time. Adie, stay with the Sisters. I hope to be back soon."

"I can get the Rada'Han off," Verna called out, but too late. Kahlan had already dashed away into the shadows.

Verna took Adie's arm. "Come on. I'll take you to some of the other Sisters behind the wall. One of them will get that thing off you while I go inside."

Verna's heart pounded as she slipped through the halls inside the prophet's compound after leaving Adie with the others. As she moved deeper into the dark halls, she braced herself for the possibility that Warren was dead. She didn't know what they had done to him, or if they had decided to simply eliminate him. She didn't think she could endure it if she were to find his body.

No. Jagang wanted a prophet to help him with the books. Ann had warned her, what seemed ages ago, to get him away at once.

The thought entered her mind that maybe Ann wanted her to get Warren away to keep the Sisters of the Dark from killing him because he knew too much. She put the troubling thoughts from her mind as she scanned the halls for any sign that a Sister of the Dark might have slipped into the building to hide from the battle.

Before the door to the prophet's apartments, Verna took a deep breath, and then moved into the inner hall, through the layers of shields that had kept Nathan a prisoner in the place for near to a thousand years, and now kept Warren.

She breached the inner door into the gloom. The far double doors to the prophet's small garden stood open, letting in the warm night air and a shaft of moonlight. A candle on a side table was lit, but provided little illumination.

Verna's heart pounded as she saw someone rise from a chair.

"Warren?"

"Verna!" He rushed forward. "Thank the Creator you escaped!"

Verna felt a clutch of dismay as her hopes and longings sparked her old fears. She retreated from the brink. She shook a finger at him. "What kind of foolishness was that, sending me your dacra! Why didn't you use it and save yourself—to escape! That was reckless sending it to me. What if something had happened? You already had it, and you let it out of your hands! What were you thinking?"

He smiled. "I'm glad to see you, too, Verna."

Verna dammed up her feelings behind a gruff reply. "Answer my question."

"Well, first of all, I've never used a dacra, and worried I might do something wrong, and then we would lose our only chance. Secondly, I have this collar around my neck, and unless I get it off, I can't get through the shields. I feared that if I couldn't get Leoma to take it off, if she would rather die than do it, then it would all be for naught.

"Third," he said, taking a tentative step toward her, "if only one of us was to have a chance to get away, I wanted it to be you."

Verna stared at him a long moment, a lump rising in her throat. She could help herself no longer and threw her arms around his neck.

"Warren, I love you. I mean I really truly love you."

He embraced her tenderly. "You have no idea how long I dreamed of hearing you say those words, Verna. I love you, too."

"What about my wrinkles?"

He smiled a sweet, warm, glowing Warren smile. "Someday, when you get wrinkles, I'll love them, too."

For that, and everything else, she let herself go and kissed him.

A small knot of crimson-caped men burst around the corner, intent on killing him. He spun into them, kicking one in the knee as he brought his knife up into the gut of a second. Before their swords could block him, he had cut another's throat and broken a nose with an elbow.

Richard was livid—lost in the thundering rage of the magic storming through him.

Even though the sword wasn't with him, the magic was still his; he was the true Seeker of Truth, and was bonded irrevocably to its magic. It coursed through him with lethal vengeance. The prophecies had named him *fuer grissa ost drauka*, High D'Haran for the bringer of death, and he moved now like its shadow. He understood the words, now, as they had been written.

He whirled through the men of the Blood of the Fold as if they were mere statues, toppling before a ruinous wind.

In a moment, all was silent again.

Richard panted in rage as he stood over the bodies, wishing they were Sisters of the Dark instead of their minions. He wanted those five.

They had told him where Kahlan had been held, but when he arrived, she was gone. Smoke still hung in the air from the battle. The room had been raked by what looked to be the furor of magic unleashed. He had found the bodies of Brogan, Galtero, and a woman he didn't recognize.

Kahlan, if she had been there, might have escaped, but he was frantic with apprehension that she had been spirited away by the Sisters, that she was still a captive, and that they would hurt her, or worse yet, that they would give her to Jagang. He had to find her.

He needed to get his hands on a Sister of the Dark so he could make her talk.

Around the palace grounds, a confusing battle raged. It appeared to Richard that the Blood of the Fold had turned on everyone in the palace. He had seen dead guards, dead cleaning staff, and dead Sisters.

He had also seen a great many dead of the Blood. The Sisters of the Dark scythed them down mercilessly. Richard had seen one charge of near to a hundred men cut down in an instant by one Sister. He had also seen a relentless charge of men from all directions overrun another Sister. They tore her apart like a pack of dogs at a fox.

When he reached the Sister who had cut down the attack, she had vanished, and so he was looking for another. One of them was going to tell him where Kahlan was. If he had to kill every Sister of the Dark at the palace, one of them was going to talk.

Two Blood of the Fold caught sight of him and came up the path at a dead run. Richard waited. Their swords caught only air. He took them down with his knife almost without thinking about it, and was moving again before the second man had finished pitching face-first to the ground.

He had lost track of the number of the Blood of the Fold he had killed since the battle had begun. He ripped through them only if they attacked him; he wasn't able to avoid all the soldiers he saw. If they came at him, it was by their choice, not his. It wasn't them he wanted—it was a Sister.

Near a wall, Richard hugged the moon shadows beneath a clump of aromatic, spreading witch hazels as he moved toward one of the covered walkways. He flattened against a pilaster in the wall as he saw a shape dart from the walkway. As it approached he could tell by the flow of hair and the shape that it was a woman.

At last, he had a Sister.

When he stepped out in front of her, he saw the flash of a blade slashing toward him. He knew that every Sister carried a dacra; it was probably that, rather than a knife. He also knew how deadly a dacra was, and how skilled they were with the weapon. He dared not take the hazard lightly.

Richard whipped his leg around, kicking the weapon from her hand. He would have broken her jaw so she couldn't cry out for help, but he needed her to be able to talk. If he was fast enough, she would raise no alarm.

He caught her wrist, sprang up behind her back, snatched her other fist as she brought it up to hit him, and clamped her wrists together with one hand. He swept his knife arm around her throat and with a yank, toppled back. As he landed on his back, with her atop his chest, he hooked his legs over hers to keep her from kicking him. She was pinned and helpless in a heartbeat.

He pressed the blade to her throat. "I'm in a *very* bad mood," he said through gritted teeth. "If you don't tell me where the Mother Confessor is, you are going to die."

She panted, catching her breath. "You are about to slit her throat, Richard."

For what seemed an eternity, his mind, filtering her words through his fury, tried to make sense of what she had said. It seemed a riddle to him.

"Are you going to kiss me, or are you going to cut my throat?" she asked, still panting.

It was Kahlan's voice. He released her wrists. She turned around, her face inches from his. It was her. It was really her.

"Dear spirits, thank you," he whispered before he kissed her.

His fury stilled like a lake becalmed on a moonlit summer night. With aching bliss, he held her to him.

His fingers gently touched her face, touching his dream come to life. Her fingers trailed along his cheek as she gazed at him, needing words no more than he. For a moment, the world stopped.

"Kahlan," he said at last, "I know you're angry with me, but . . ."

"Well, if I hadn't broken my sword, and had to pick up a knife, you wouldn't have had such an easy time. But I'm not angry."

"That's not what I meant. I can explain—"

"I know what you meant, Richard. I'm not angry. I trust you. You have some explaining to do, but I'm not angry. The only thing you could do to make me angry would be if you ever get more than ten feet from me for the rest of your life."

Richard smiled. "You aren't going to ever be angry with me, then." His smile withered as his head thumped back to the ground. "Oh, yes you are. You don't know the trouble I've caused. Dear spirits, I've . . ."

She kissed him again—tender, soft, warm. He ran his hand down the back of her long, thick hair.

He held her away by her shoulders. "Kahlan, we have to get out of here. Right now. We're in a lot of trouble. I'm in a lot of trouble."

Kahlan rolled off him and sat up. "I know. The Order is coming. We need to hurry."

"Where's Zedd, and Gratch? Let's get them and be gone."

Her head tilted toward him. "Zedd and Gratch? They aren't with you?"

"Me? No. I thought they were with you. I sent Gratch with a letter. Dear spirits, don't tell me you didn't get the letter. No wonder you aren't angry with me. I sent—"

"I got the letter. Zedd used a spell to make himself light enough for Gratch to carry him. Gratch took Zedd back to Aydindril weeks ago."

Richard felt a hot wave of nausea. He remembered the dead mriswith all over the rampart at the Keep.

"I never saw them," he said in a whisper.

"Maybe you left before they arrived. It must have taken you weeks to get here."

"I only left Aydindril yesterday."

"What?" she whispered, wide-eyed. "How could . . ."

"The sliph brought me. She got me here in less than a day. At least, I think it was less than a day. It may have been two. I had no way of telling, but the moon looked the same. . . ."

Richard realized he was rambling, and made himself stop.

Kahlan's face was becoming watery in his vision. His voice sounded hollow to him, as if it were someone else speaking. "I found a place on the Keep where there had been a fight. There were dead mriswith all over. I remember thinking it looked like Gratch had killed them. It was at the edge of a high wall.

"There was blood at a notch in the wall, and all down the side of the Keep. I ran my finger through the blood. Mriswith blood stinks. Some of the blood wasn't from a mriswith."

Kahlan took him in her comforting arms.

"Zedd, and Gratch," he whispered. "That must have been them."

Her arms tightened. "I'm sorry, Richard."

He lifted her arms away and stood, giving her a hand up. "We have to get out of here. I've done something terrible, and Aydindril is in trouble. I've got to get back there."

Richard's gaze caught on the Rada'Han. "What's this doing around your neck?"

"I was captured by Tobias Brogan. It's a long story."

Even before she had finished speaking, he curled his fingers around the collar. Without cognitive reasoning, but through the need and fury, he felt the power swell from the calm center and surge through his arm.

The collar shattered in his hand like sunbaked dirt.

Kahlan's fingers groped at her neck. She let out a sigh of relief verging on a wail.

"It's back," she whispered as she leaned against him, putting a hand to her breastbone. "I can feel my Confessor's power. I can touch it again."

He squeezed her with one arm. "We'd better get out of here."

"I've just gone and freed Ahern. That's where I broke my sword—on one of the Blood. He took a bad fall," she explained to his frown. "I told Ahern to head north with the Sisters."

"Sisters? What Sisters?"

"I found Sister Verna. She's gathering the Sisters of the Light, the young men, novices, and guards, and escaping with them. I'm on my way to meet her. I left Adie with them. Hurry, and we may be able to catch them before they leave. They're not far."

Kevin's mouth dropped when he stepped out from behind the wall to challenge the two of them. "Richard!" he whispered. "Is it really you?"

Richard smiled. "Sorry, I don't have any chocolates, Kevin."

Kevin pumped Richard's hand. "I'm loyal, Richard. Nearly all the guards are loyal."

Richard frowned in the dark. "I'm . . . honored, Kevin."

He turned and called out in a loud whisper. "It's Richard!"

A crowd gathered around after he and Kahlan had slipped through the gate and behind the wall. In the flickering light of distant fires down at the docks, Richard saw Verna and threw his arms around her.

"Verna, I'm so glad to see you!" He held her out at arm's length. "But I have to tell you, you need a bath."

Verna laughed. It was a rare, good sound to hear. Warren squeezed past her and with a gleeful laugh embraced Richard.

Richard held Verna's hand out and pressed the Prelate's ring into it, closing her fingers around it. "I heard about Ann dying. I'm so sorry. This is her ring. I think you would know better than I what to do with it."

Verna brought the hand closer to her face, staring at the ring. "Richard . . . where did you get this?"

"I made Sister Ulicia give it to me. She had no business wearing it."

"You made . . ."

"Verna was named Prelate, Richard," Warren said as he put a reassuring hand to her shoulder.

Richard grinned. "I'm proud of you, Verna. Put it back on, then."

"Richard, Ann isn't . . . The ring was taken from me. . . . I was convicted by a tribunal . . . and removed as Prelate."

Sister Dulcinia stepped forward. "Verna, you are the Prelate. At the trial, every Sister here with us voted with you."

Verna searched all the faces watching her. "You did?"

"Yes," Sister Dulcinia said. "We were overruled by the others, but we all believed in you. You were named by Prelate Annalina. We need a Prelate. Put the ring back on."

Verna nodded her tearful gratitude to the Sisters as they voiced their agreement. She slipped the ring back on her finger and kissed it. "We have to get everyone away at once. The Imperial Order is coming to take the palace."

Richard gripped her arm and pulled her back around. "What do you mean 'the Imperial Order is coming to take the palace'? What do they want with the Palace of the Prophets?"

"The prophecies. Emperor Jagang intends to use them to know the forks in the books so he can alter events to his advantage."

The other Sisters behind Verna gasped. Warren slapped a hand over his face as he groaned.

"And," Verna added, "he plans to live here, under the palace's spell, so he can rule the world after the prophecies help him crush all opposition."

Richard released her arm. "We can't let him do that. We would be frustrated at every fork. We wouldn't have a chance. The world would suffer under his tyranny for centuries."

"There's nothing we can do about it," Verna said. "We have to get away or we'll all be killed here, and then there's no chance for us to help—to think of a way to fight back."

Richard swept his gaze across the gathered Sisters, many of whom he knew, and then looked back to Verna. "Prelate, what if I were to destroy the palace?"

"What! How can you do that?"

"I don't know. But I destroyed the towers, and they were made by the wizards of old, too. What if there were a way?"

Verna licked her lips as she stared off. The crowd of Sisters stood silent. Sister Phoebe pushed her way through the others.

"Verna, you can't allow it!"

"It may be the only way to stop Jagang."

"But you can't," Phoebe said, on the verge of tears. "It's the Palace of the Prophets. It's our home."

"It's going to be the dream walker's home, now, if we leave it for him."

"But Verna," Phoebe said, gripping Verna's arms, "without the spell, we will grow old. We'll die, Verna. Our youth will be gone in a twinkling. We'll get old and die before we have a chance to live."

With a thumb Verna wiped a tear from the other's face. "Everything dies, Phoebe, even the palace. It can't live forever. It has served its purpose, and now, if we don't do something, its purpose will turn to harm."

"Verna, you can't do this! I don't want to get old."

Verna hugged the young woman. "Phoebe, we're Sisters of the Light. We serve the Creator in his work to make the lives of the people in this world better. The only chance we have to better their lives, now, is to become like the rest of the Creator's children; to live among them.

"I understand your fear, Phoebe, but trust in me that it won't be as you fear. Time feels different to us under the spell of the palace. We don't feel the slow passing of centuries, the way those outside imagine, but the rapid pace of life. It really doesn't feel much different when you live outside.

"Our oath is to serve, not simply to live long. If you wish to live a long and empty life, Phoebe, you can remain with the Sisters of the Dark. If you wish to live a meaningful, helpful, fulfilled life, then come with us, with the Sisters of the Light, to our new life beyond what has been."

Phoebe stood silent, tears running down her cheeks. Off in the distance, fire roared, and occasional explosions punctuated the night. The cries of men at battle were coming closer.

At last, Phoebe spoke. "I am a Sister of the Light. I wish to go with my Sisters . . . wherever that takes us. The Creator will still watch over us."

Verna smiled, running a tender hand down Phoebe's cheek. "Anyone else?" she asked, looking among the others gathered. "Does anyone else have any objection? If you do, it must be heard now. Don't come to me later and say you didn't have the chance. I give it now."

All the Sisters shook their heads. Soon they were all voicing their wish to go.

Verna twisted the ring on her finger as she looked up at Richard. "Do you think you can destroy the palace? The spell?"

"I don't know. Do you remember when you first came for me, and Kahlan used that blue lightning? Confessors have an element of Subtractive Magic from the wizards who created their power. Maybe that will do some harm to the vaults, if I can't."

Kahlan's fingers touched his back as she whispered. "Richard, I don't think I can do that. That magic was invoked for you—to defend you. I can't call it for anything else."

"We have to try. If nothing else, we can set the prophecies afire. If we start a fire among all those books, they'll all be consumed, and then at least Jagang can't use them against us."

A small group of women and half a dozen young men came rushing up to the gate. "Friends of Richard," came the urgent whisper. Kevin opened the gate, letting the breathless group in.

Verna clutched a woman's arm. "Philippa, did you find them all?"

"Yes." The tall woman paused to catch her breath. "We have to get out of here. The emperor's advance guard are in the city. Some are already coming across the south bridges. The Blood of the Fold are engaging them in pitched battle."

"Did you see what's going on at the docks?" Verna asked.

"Ulicia and some of her Sisters are down there. Those women are ripping the entire harbor apart. It looks like the underworld unleashed." Philippa put trembling fingers to her lips as she closed her eyes for a moment. "They have the men from the *Lady Sefa*." Her voice faltered. "You can't imagine what they're doing to those poor men."

Philippa turned, dropped to her knees, and vomited. Two of the other sisters who had returned with her did the same. "Dear Creator," Philippa managed between retches, "you cannot conceive of it. I will have nightmares the rest of my life."

Richard turned to the shouts and cries of battle. "Verna, you have to get out of here right now. There's no time to waste."

She nodded. "You and Kahlan can catch up with us."

"No. Kahlan and I have to get to Aydindril at once. I don't have time to explain right now, but she and I have the magic required that will allow it. I wish I could take the rest of you, but I can't. Hurry. Head north. There's an army of a hundred thousand D'Haran soldiers heading south looking for Kahlan. You'll have more protection with them, and they with you. Tell General Reibisch that she is safe with me."

Adie stepped through the others and took Richard's hands. "How be Zedd?"

Richard's voice caught in his throat. He closed his eyes against the pain. "Adie, I'm sorry, but I haven't seen my grandfather. I fear he may have been killed at the Keep."

Adie wiped her cheek as she cleared her throat. "I be sorry, Richard," she whispered in her raspy voice. "Your grandfather be a good man. But he takes too many desperate chances. I have warned him."

Richard hugged the old sorceress as she wept softly against his chest.

Kevin came in a rush from the gate, sword in hand. "We either have to go now, or we have to fight."

"Go," Richard said. "We won't win this war if you die in this battle. We must fight by our rules, not Jagang's. He'll have those with the gift with him, not just soldiers."

Verna turned to the gathered Sisters, novices, and young wizards. She took the hands of two young girls who looked to be in need of reassurance. "All of you, listen. Jagang is a dream walker. The only protection is our bond to Richard. Richard has been born with the gift, and with a magic passed down from his ancestors that protects against dream walkers. Leoma tried to break that bond to allow Jagang to enter my mind and take me. Before we go, all of you, bow down and swear fidelity to Richard to be certain we will be protected from our enemy."

"If it is your wish to do this," Richard said, "then do it as was set down by Alric Rahl, the one who created the bond and its protection. If you wish to do this, then I ask you to give the devotion as it was passed down, as it was meant to be."

Richard told them the words, as he had said them himself, and then stood silent, feeling the weight of responsibility, not only to those gathered, but to the thousands in Aydindril who were depending on him, as the Sisters of the Light and their charges went to their knees and with one voice rising into the night above the sound of battle, proclaimed their bond.

"Master Rahl guide us. Master Rahl teach us. Master Rahl protect us. In your light we thrive. In your mercy we are sheltered. In your wisdom we are humbled. We live only to serve. Our lives are yours."

CHAPTER 51

RICHARD PRESSED KAHLAN UP against the wall in the dank, dark stone corridor as he waited for the knot of crimson-caped soldiers to pass the intersection. As the echo of their boots faded in the distance, Kahlan stretched up on her toes and whispered, "I don't like it down here. Are we going to be able to get out of this place alive?"

He pressed a quick kiss to the worry lines on her brow. "Of course we're going to get out of here alive. I promise." He took her hand and ducked under a low beam. "Come on, the vaults are just ahead."

The stone of the bleak passageway was streaked with pale yellow stains where water leaked between joints and over the blocks. In places on the ceiling, drops of water hung from stone icicles the color of egg yolk, to drip occasionally onto ripply stone mounds on the floor. Beyond two torches, the passageway widened and the ceiling rose up to accommodate the huge round door to the vaults.

As they came in sight of the six-foot-thick stone door, Richard knew something was wrong. Not only could he see an eerie light beyond, but the hairs at the back of his neck were standing on end, and he could feel the whisper of magic against his arms, like spiderwebs brushing the hairs.

He rubbed at the tickling sensation on his arms as he leaned close, "Do you feel anything odd?"

She shook her head. "But there's something funny about the light."

Kahlan's step faltered. Richard saw the body at the same time as they approached the round opening into the vaults. Ahead, a woman lay curled up on the floor, as if she were asleep, but Richard knew she wasn't sleeping. She was as still as the stone.

As they stepped closer, they could see beyond the wall to the right that there near to a dozen dead Blood of the Fold scattered about the floor. Richard winced at the sight, and a queasy feeling settled in his stomach. Each man was sliced cleanly in half, armor, cape, and all, at midchest. The floor was a lake of blood.

His apprehension burgeoned with every slow step toward the round opening in the rock.

"Look, I have to go get something first," he said. "You wait here until I get back. It should only take a few minutes."

Kahlan tugged him back by his shirtsleeve. "You know the rules."

"What rules?"

"You're not allowed to get more than ten feet from me for the rest of your life, or I get angry."

Richard stared into her green eyes. "I'd rather have you angry than dead."

Her brow drew down into a scowl. "You only think that now. I've been waiting too long to be with you to let you go off by yourself now. What's so important that would make you want to go in there? We can try to do something from out here—throw in torches, set the place ablaze, or something. All that paper should burn like tinder grass. We don't need to go in there."

Richard smiled. "Did I ever tell you how much I love you?"

She cuffed his arm. "Talk. What are we risking our lives for?"

Richard yielded with a sigh. "There's a book of prophecy in the back that's over three thousand years old. It has prophecies in it about me. It helped me before. If we're successful at destroying all these books, I'd like to at least take that one with us. It may be a help again."

"What's it say about you?"

"It calls me *'fuer grissa ost drauka.'* "

"What does that mean?"

Richard turned back to the vault. "The bringer of death."

She was silent a moment. "So how do we get back there?"

Richard surveyed the dead soldiers. "Well, for sure we don't walk." He held his hand up to his chest. "Something cut them down at about this high. Whatever we do, we don't stand up."

At about that height, a wafer-thin haze, like a stratified layer of smoke, hung in the air in the vault room. It seemed to be glowing, as if lit from something, but Richard couldn't tell what.

On their hands and knees, they crawled into the vault and under the strange blush of light. They stayed near the wall until they reached the bookshelves so they wouldn't have to crawl through the pools of blood. Once beneath the glowing haze, it seemed even more peculiar. It didn't seem to be like any fog or smoke Richard had ever seen before; it seemed to be made of light.

A grating sound caused them to pause, motionless. Richard looked back over his shoulder and saw the six-foot-thick stone door swinging closed. He judged that no matter how fast they moved, they wouldn't be able to make it back before the door closed shut.

Kahlan turned from the door. "Are we locked in here? How are we going to get out? Is there another way out?"

"It's the only way out, but I can open it," Richard said. "The door works in conjunction with a shield. If I put my hand to the metal plate on the wall, it'll open."

Her green eyes studied his face. "Richard, are you sure?"

"Pretty sure. It always worked in the past."

"Richard, after all we've been through, now that we're together, I want both of us to get out of here alive."

"We will. We have to; there are people who need our help."

"In Aydindril?"

He nodded, trying to find the words for what he had been wanting to say to her, words to fill the space he feared was between them, the space he feared he had put there.

"Kahlan, I didn't do what I did there because I wanted something for myself—I swear. I want you to know that. I know how much I've hurt you, but it was the only thing I could think to do before it was too late. I only did it because I truly believe that it's our only chance to keep the Midlands from falling to the Imperial Order.

"I know that the goal of the Confessors is to protect people, not to simply hold dominion. I trusted that you would see that I was acting on those goals, if not your wishes. I wanted to protect people, not rule them, but I've been heartsick over what I've done to you."

Dead silence stretched in the stone room for a long moment. "Richard, when I first read your letter, I was crushed. A sacred trust was placed in my hands, and I didn't want to be known as the Mother Confessor who lost the Midlands. On the way here, with that collar around my neck, I've had a lot of time to think.

"The Sisters did something noble tonight. They've sacrificed a three-thousand-year legacy for a higher purpose: to help people. I may not be happy about what you did, and you still have some explaining to do, but I'll listen with love in my heart, not just for you, but for the people of the Midlands who need us.

"Over the weeks as we traveled here, I thought about how we must live in the future and not the past. I want the future to be a place where we can live in peace and safety. That's more important than anything else. I know you, and I know that you wouldn't do as you did for selfish reasons."

Richard brushed the backs of his fingers down her cheek. "I'm proud of you, Mother Confessor."

She kissed his fingers. "Later, when people aren't trying to kill us and we have the time, I'll fold my arms and frown and tap my foot like the Mother Confessor is supposed to, while you stutter and stammer and try to explain the sense of what you did, but for now, could we just get out of this place?"

His worry eased, Richard smiled and started off again, crawling past the rows of bookcases. The thin layer of glowing haze over their heads seemed to stretch across the entire room. Richard wished he knew what it was.

Kahlan hurried closer to his side. Richard checked for trouble down each row they passed, guiding them around the inexplicable feel of danger whenever he encountered it. He didn't know if the sense of danger was a true perception or not, but he dared not ignore the feelings. He was learning to trust in his instincts and be less concerned with proof.

When they entered the small alcove in the back, he scanned the books on the shelf, and saw the one he wanted. The problem was that it was above the level of the haze. He knew better than to try to reach through it; he didn't know exactly what the glow of light was, but he knew it was magic of some sort, and he had seen what it had done to the soldiers.

With Kahlan's help, they rocked the bookcase until it fell over. When it toppled against the table, the books pitched out, but the one he wanted landed on the table. The layer of glowing haze hovered mere inches above the book. Richard carefully eased his hand along the tabletop, feeling the tingling sensation of the magic floating just above his arm. At last, he caught the book with his fingers and drew it off the edge.

"Richard, something's wrong."

He picked up the book and thumbed through it quickly to confirm that it was the right one. Though he could read the High D'Haran words, now, and he recognized some of them, he didn't have time to address what the book said.

"What? What's wrong?"

"Look at the fog over us. When we came in, it was chest high. It must have been what cut down those men. Look at it now."

Without his noticing, it had descended to just above the table. He tucked the book under his belt. "Follow me, and hurry."

Richard scrambled out of the room with Kahlan right at his heels. He didn't know what would happen if the glowing magic reached them, but he didn't have much trouble imagining.

Kahlan cried out. Richard turned and saw her sprawled flat on the floor.

"What is it?"

She tried to drag herself ahead by her elbows, but went nowhere. "Something has me by my ankle."

Richard clambered back to her and grabbed her wrist.

"It let go. As soon as you touched me, it let go."

"Grab hold of my ankle and let's get out of here."

She gasped. "Richard! Look."

The glow over their heads had lowered when he touched her, as if the magic had felt the touch, felt its prey, and was lowering in pursuit. It barely gave them room to crawl. Richard, with Kahlan holding his ankle, raced for the door.

Before they reached the door, the line of light overhead lowered until Richard could feel its heat against his back.

"Get down!"

She flattened to her stomach when he ordered it, and they squirmed forward on their bellies. When they at last reached the door, Richard flopped over on his back. The haze hovered inches above them.

Kahlan grabbed ahold of his shirt and pulled herself close. "Richard, what are we going to do?"

Richard stared up at the metal plate. It was above the glowing layer that extended from wall to wall. He could no longer get to the plate without reaching through the menacing light over them.

"We have to get out of here, or that thing is going to kill us, just like it killed those men. I have to stand."

"Are you crazy? You can't do that!"

"I have the mriswith cape. Maybe if I use that, the light won't find me."

Kahlan threw an arm over his chest. "No!"

"I'm dead anyway if I don't try."

"Richard, no!"

"Do you have a better idea? We're running out of time."

She growled in anger and extended her arm toward the door. Blue lightning exploded from her fist. The door sizzled with streaks of blue light racing around the perimeter of the door.

The thin layer of hazy light recoiled back, as if alive, and the touch of her magic was painful. The door, however, didn't move.

As the light retreated, bunching in the center of the room, Richard sprang up and slapped a hand to the plate. The door groaned and began to move. The crackling blue flashes from Kahlan died out as the door inched opened. The glow began to flatten and spread once more.

Richard snatched Kahlan's hand. He stood and squeezed through the opening, pulling her with him. They fell to the ground once outside, panting and holding on to one another.

"It worked," she said, catching her breath from the fright. "I knew you were in danger, so my magic worked."

As the door opened the rest of the way, the slick of light seeped into the corridor toward them.

"We have to get out of here," he said as they came to their feet.

They trotted backward, keeping an eye on the creeping fog that pursued them. They both grunted when they smacked into an invisible barrier. Richard groped along its surface, but could find no opening. He turned back to see the light almost upon them.

With a rage of need, without thought, Richard threw his hands out.

Ropes of black lightning, undulating voids in the existence of light and life, like eternal death itself, blasted outward, twisting and curling away from his outstretched hands. The crack of lightning as the Subtractive Magic ripped into the world was deafening. Kahlan winced. She covered her ears and shrank from the sight.

In the center of the vaults, the hazy glow seemed to ignite. He felt a powerful, low-pitched thump in his chest and the stone beneath his feet.

The bookshelves were blown back, flinging a blizzard of papers into the air to flame briefly like thousands of sparks from a bonfire. The light howled as if alive. He could feel the black lightning exploding from within himself, power and fury beyond his comprehension, burning through him and twisting into the vault.

Kahlan tugged on his arms. "Richard! Richard! We have to run! Richard! Listen to me! Run!"

Kahlan's voice sounded as if it came to him from a great distance. The black ropes of Subtractive Magic abruptly ceased. The world returned, rushing into the void of his awareness, and he felt alive again. Alive, and aghast.

The invisible barrier blocking their escape was gone. Richard snatched Kahlan's hand and ran. Behind, the core of light tumbled and wailed, brightening all the time as the sound rose in pitch.

Dear spirits, he thought, what have I done?

They ran through the stone corridors, up stairs, and through halls that became more elaborate at each level, paneled and carpeted, with lamps lighting their way instead of torches. Ahead of them their shadows stretched out, but it wasn't from the lamps—it was from the living light behind.

They burst through a door, out into a night alive with battle. Men wearing crimson capes fought bare-armed men Richard had never seen before. Some wore beards, and many a head was shaved smooth, but each had a ring through his left nostril. In their strange leather belts and straps, some studded with spikes, and layers of hides and fur, they looked to be wild, savage men, an impression aided by the way they fought: gruesome smiles bared gritted teeth as they swung swords, axes, and flails, slogging into their opponents, sweeping aside strikes and pushing ahead with round bucklers set with long center spikes.

Though he had never seen the men before, Richard knew they had to be the Imperial Order.

Richard didn't slow, but wove his way through openings in the battle, pulling Kahlan behind as he raced for a bridge. When one of the Imperial Order soldiers lunged at him, driving a boot toward him to stop him, Richard sidestepped, hooked his arm under the man's leg, and flipped him aside, hardly slackening his headlong rush. When one of the Order's soldiers came at him, Richard drove an elbow into the man's face, knocking him aside.

In the center of the east bridge, which led into the countryside where lay the Hagen Woods, a half-dozen men of the Blood grappled with a like number of the Order. When a sword swung at him, Richard ducked under it, shouldering the man over the edge into the river before dashing on through the opening it created.

Behind, over the sounds of battle, the clash of steel and the cries of men, he could hear the wail of the light. He ran, his legs pumping seemingly of their own volition to escape; what they fled from was something worse than swords or knives. Kahlan needed no help in keeping up; she was right beside him.

Once they were on the other side of the river and not far into the city, the night vanished in a harsh glare that cast sudden inky shadows pointing away from the palace. The two of them ducked behind the plastered wall of a closed-up shop and, squatting down, gasped to catch their breath. Richard peeked around the side of the building and saw dazzling light blazing from all the windows in the palace, even those in the high towers. Light seemed to be oozing through the joints in the stone.

"Can you run some more?" he asked as he panted.

"I didn't want to stop," she said.

Richard knew the city well between the palace and the countryside. He led Kahlan though the confused, frightened, ululating mass of people, up streets tight with buildings and those wide with trees, until they reached the outskirts of Tanimura.

Halfway up the hill out of the valley where the city lay, he felt a hard thud in the ground that nearly took his feet out from under him. Without looking back, Richard swept an arm around Kahlan and dove with her into a low cut in the granite. Sweaty and exhausted, they clung together as the ground shook.

They stuck their heads up just in time to see the light ripping apart the massive towers and stone walls of the Palace of the

Prophets as if they were paper before a hurricane. The whole of Halsband Island seemed to rend. Parts of trees and huge chunks of lawns lifted into the air along with stone of every size. A blinding flash drove a dome of dark debris before it. The river was stripped of water and bridges.

The curtain of light expanded outward with a clacking roar. The city beyond the island somehow stood up against the fury.

Overhead, the sky lit as if a celestial vault were flaring in sympathy with the bedazzling core below. The skirts of the shimmering bell of light overhead cascaded to the ground miles away from the city. Richard remembered that boundary; it was the outer shield that kept him here when he wore a Rada'Han.

"Bringer of death, indeed," Kahlan whispered as she watched, awestruck. "I didn't know you could do such a thing."

"Neither did I," Richard said under his breath.

A blast of air tore at the grass as it roared headlong up the hill. They ducked down as a roiling wall of sand and dirt raced past.

They cautiously sat up when all went still. Night had returned, and in the sudden darkness, Richard couldn't see much below, but he knew—the Palace of the Prophets was gone.

"You did it, Richard," Kahlan said at last.

"We did it," he answered as he stared down at the dead, dark hole in the center of the city lights.

"I'm glad you brought that book. I want to know what else it says about you." A smile began to spread on her lips. "I guess Jagang won't be living there."

"I guess not. Are you all right?"

"Fine," she said. "But I'm glad it's over."

"I'm afraid it's only just begun. Come on, the sliph will get us back to Aydindril."

"You still haven't told me what this sliph is."

"I don't think you would believe me. You'll just have to see it for yourself."

"Quite impressive, Wizard Zorander," Ann said, turning away.

Zedd gave a dismissive grunt. "Not my doing."

Ann wiped the tears from her cheeks, glad for the darkness so he couldn't see them, but she had to work to keep her voice from betraying her emotion. "You may not have thrown on the torch, but you did the work of stacking the pyre. Quite impressive. I've seen a light web tear apart a room, but this . . ."

He laid a gentle hand on her shoulder. "I'm sorry, Ann."

"Yes, well, what must be, must be."

Zedd squeezed her shoulder as if to say he understood. "I wonder who threw the torch?"

"The Sisters of the Dark can use Subtractive Magic. One of them must have accidentally ignited the light web."

Zedd peered over at her in the dark. "Accidentally?" He took his hand back as he voiced only a dubious snort.

"That had to have been it," she said as she sighed.

"A little bit more than an accident, I would say." She detected a hint of pride in his wistful whisper.

"Like what?"

He ignored her question. "We'd better find Nathan."

"Yes," Ann said, suddenly remembering the prophet. She squeezed Holly's hand. "This is where we left him. He has to be around here somewhere."

Ann stared off toward the moonlit hills in the distance. She could see a group of people moving up the north road: a coach and a band of people, mostly on horseback. There were too many not to be able to sense them. It was her Sisters of the Light. Thank the Creator; they had gotten away after all.

"I thought you could find him by that infernal collar."

Ann began casting about in the brush. "I can, and it tells me he should be right here somewhere. Perhaps the blast injured him. Since the spell was destroyed, he had to have been here doing his part with the outer shield, so maybe he was hurt. Help me look."

Holly searched, too, but stayed close. Zedd wandered off toward an open, flat place. Guided by the way the branches and brush were bent and broken, he was looking near the center of the node, where the power would have been concentrated. As she stooped to look among the low places in the rocks, Zedd called out to her.

Ann took Holly's hand and hurried to the old wizard. "What is it?"

He pointed. Standing up, so they couldn't miss it, stuck in

a crack in a round hump of granite, was something round. Ann wiggled it free.

She stared incredulously. "It's Nathan's Rada'Han."

Holly gasped. "Oh, Ann, maybe he was killed. Maybe Nathan was killed by the magic."

Ann turned it around. It was locked closed. "No, Holly." She stroked a comforting hand down the child's hair. "He wasn't killed, or there would be some trace of him. But dear Creator, what does this mean?"

"What does it mean?" Zedd chuckled. "It means he got free. He stuck it in that rock so you would be sure to see it, as if to thumb his nose at you. Nathan wanted us to know he got the collar off on his own. He must have linked the power of the node to it, or something." Zedd sighed. "Well, he's gone. Now, get mine off."

Ann's hand holding the Rada'Han lowered as she looked out into the night. "We have to find him."

"Take my collar off, as you promised, and then you can gad off after him. Without me, I might add."

Ann felt her anger heating. "You're coming with me."

"With you? Bags, I'm doing no such thing!"

"You're coming."

"You intend to break your word!"

"No, I intend to keep it, just as soon as we find that troublesome prophet. You have no idea of the complications that man can cause."

"What do you need me for!"

She shook her finger at him. "You're coming with me whether you like it or not, and that's all there is to it. When we find him, then I take that collar off. Not before."

He shook his fists in a sputtering fit while Ann strode off to collect the horses. Her gaze wandered to the moonlit hill in the distance, to the band of Sisters heading north. When Ann reached the horses, she squatted down before Holly.

"Holly, as your first assignment as a novice to be a Sister of the Light, I have a very important, urgent duty for you."

Holly nodded seriously. "What is it, Ann?"

"It's critical that Zedd and I go find Nathan. I hope it won't be long, but we must hurry before he gets away."

"Before he gets away!" Zedd howled behind her. "He's had

hours. He's got a huge lead. There's no telling where that man went. He's already 'gotten away.' "

Ann glanced back over her shoulder. "We have to find him." She turned back to Holly. "We need to hurry, and I don't have time to go catch up with the Sisters of the Light over on that hill there. I need you to go to them and tell Sister Verna everything you know about what's happened."

"What should I tell her?"

"Whatever you know about what you've seen and heard while you've been with us. Tell her the truth, and don't make anything up. It's important that she know what's going on. Tell her that Zedd and I are going after Nathan, and that when we can we will join up with them, but our first priority is finding the Prophet. Tell her to head north, as they're doing, to escape the Order."

"I can do that."

"It's not far, and the road right over here will take you to the road they will be riding up, so you won't miss them. Your horse knows and likes you, so she'll take good care of you. You'll be there in just an hour or two, and then you'll have all the Sisters to keep you safe, and love you. Sister Verna will know what to do."

"I'll miss you until you catch up with us," Holly said, her voice choked with tears.

Ann hugged the little girl. "Oh, child, I'll miss you so much, too. I wish I could take you with us, you've been such a help, but we must hurry if we're to catch Nathan. The Sisters, especially Prelate Verna, need to know what's happened. It's important; that's why I must send you."

Holly bravely snuffled back the tears. "I understand. You can count on me, Prelate."

Ann helped the girl up into the saddle and kissed her hand as she put the reins in them. Ann watched and waved farewell as Holly trotted off toward the Sisters of the Light.

She turned to the fuming wizard. "We'd best be going if we're to catch Nathan." She patted his bony shoulder. "It won't be long. Just as soon as we catch him, I'll have that collar off your neck, I promise."

Chapter 52

The Hagen Woods were as dark and uninviting as ever, but Richard was sure that the mriswith were gone. In their journey through the gloomy wood he hadn't sensed even one of them. The place, though forbidding, was deserted; the mriswith had all left for Aydindril. He shuddered to think what that meant.

Kahlan sighed nervously, twining her fingers together, as she stared at the sliph's pleasant, smiling, quicksilver face. "Richard, before we do this, just in case something goes wrong, I want to tell you that I know about what happened when you were a captive here, and I don't hold it against you. You thought I didn't love you, and you were alone. I understand."

Richard leaned closer as he frowned. "What are you talking about? What things I did?"

She cleared her throat. "Merissa. She told me all about it."

"Merissa!"

"Yes. I understand, and I don't blame you. You thought you would never see me again."

Richard blinked in astonishment. "Merissa is a Sister of the Dark. She wants to kill me."

"But she told me how when you were here before, she was your teacher. She said that . . . Well, I met her, and she's beautiful. You were lonely, and I don't blame you."

Richard took her by the shoulders and forced her to turn away from staring at the sliph. "Kahlan, I don't know what Merissa told you, but I'm telling you the truth: since the day I met you, I've loved no one but you. No one. Yes, when you made me put on the collar and I thought I would never see you again, I was lonely, but I never betrayed your love, even when I thought I had lost it. Even though I thought you didn't want me, I never . . . with Merissa, or anyone else."

"Really?"

"Really."

She smiled her special smile, the one she gave no one but him. "Adie tried to tell me the same thing. I was afraid I would die before I could see you again, and wanted you to know that I love you, no matter what. Part of me is afraid of doing this. I'm afraid I'll drown in there."

"The sliph felt you, and she says you can travel. You have an element of Subtractive Magic, too. Only those with both magics can travel. It'll work. You'll see." He smiled encouragement. "It's nothing to be afraid of, I promise. It's unlike anything you've ever felt before. It's wondrous. All right, now?"

She nodded. "All right." She threw her arms around him and hugged him so hard she pressed the wind out of him. "But if I drown, I just want you to know how much I love you."

Richard helped her up onto the stone wall around the sliph and then glanced around at the dark woods beyond the ruins. He didn't know if there really were eyes watching or it was simply his apprehension. He didn't sense a mriswith, though, and if one were watching him, he would. He decided that it must just be his past experiences in Hagen Woods that made him apprehensive.

"We're ready, sliph. Do you know how long it will take?"

"I am long enough," came the echoing reply.

Richard sighed and tightened his grip on Kahlan's hand. "Do as we've told you." She nodded, gasping her last breaths. "I'll be with you. Don't be afraid."

The liquid silver arm lifted them, and the night went truly black. Richard gripped Kahlan's hand tightly as they plunged downward, knowing how hard it had been for him to breathe in the sliph the first time. When she returned the squeeze, they were already in the weightless void.

The familiar sensation of rushing and drifting at the same time returned, and Richard knew they were on their way to Aydindril. As before, there was no heat, no cold, no sense of being soaked in the quicksilver wet of the sliph. His eyes beheld light and dark together in a single, spectral vision, while his lungs swelled with the sweet presence of the sliph as he inhaled her silken essence.

Richard was joyous, knowing that Kahlan could feel the same rapture he felt; he could sense it through the slow pressure on his hand. They let go, to take strokes through the still rush.

Richard swam on through the darkness and light. He felt Kahlan grip his ankle to be towed along after him.

Time meant nothing. It could have been a glimmer of a moment or the slow passing of a year as he soared ahead with Kahlan holding on to his ankle. As before, abruptly, it ended.

Sights of the room in the Keep exploded about him, but he knew what to expect, and this time there was no terror.

Breathe, the sliph said.

He let out the sweet breath, emptying his lungs of the rapture, and pulled in a breath of the alien air.

He felt Kahlan come up behind him, and in the silence of Kolo's room, he heard her expel the sliph and inhale the air. Richard bobbed up, the sliph sloughing off him as he boosted himself up onto the wall and over. Once his feet hit the floor, he turned and bent to help Kahlan out.

Merissa smiled at him.

Richard went rigid. At last his mind worked. "Where's Kahlan! You're bonded to me! You gave an oath!"

"Kahlan?" came the melodious voice. "She's right here." Merissa reached down into the quicksilver. "But you won't be needing her anymore. And I'm keeping my oath—an oath to myself."

She lifted Kahlan's limp form by the back of her collar. With the aid of her power, Merissa heaved Kahlan out of the sliph's well. Kahlan hit the wall and slumped, unbreathing, to the floor.

Before Richard could rush to her, Merissa rapped the blades of a *yabree* against the stone. The sweet song gripped him, making his legs go weak and impotent as he stared, spellbound, at Merissa's smiling face.

"The *yabree* sings for you, Richard. Its song calls you."

She drifted closer, bringing the humming *yabree* closer. She held it up, turning the resplendent object of his hunger, displaying it, tantalizing him with it. Richard wet his lips as his bones resonated with the purring hum of the *yabree.* The vibrant sound transfixed him.

She floated closer, finally offering it to him. His fingers at last touched it, and the song coursed through every fiber of his body, charmed every corner of his soul. Merissa smiled as his fingers curled around the crossbar. He shuddered with the enchantment of having it in his grasp. His fingers tightened in painful pleasure.

She brought another *yabree* out from under the silvery pool. "That's only the half of it, Richard. You need both."

She laughed, a pleasant, lilting sound, as she tapped the second *yabree* against the stone. The song nearly blinded him with its longing for his touch. He struggled to keep his knees from buckling. He had to get to the second *yabree.* He leaned over the wall, stretching for it.

Merissa's grin mocked him, but he didn't care, he only wanted, needed, to have the twin to his *yabree* in his other hand.

"Breathe," the sliph said.

Distracted, Richard glanced over. The sliph was looking at the woman slumped on the floor against the wall. He was about to speak, when Merissa tapped the second *yabree* against the stone again.

His legs went boneless. He held his left arm, with the *yabree* in his fist, over the wall to hold himself up.

"Breathe," the sliph said again.

Through the enchanting, purring song singing through his bones, Richard struggled to make sense of who it was against the wall that the sliph was speaking to. It seemed important, but he couldn't reason why. Who was it?

Merissa's laugh echoed around the room as she tapped the *yabree* again.

Richard let out a helpless cry both of ecstasy and longing.

"Breathe," the sliph said again, more insistent.

Through the numbing song of the *yabree*, it came to him. His inner need surged up, sluicing through the benumbing melody that encased him.

Kahlan.

He looked at her. She wasn't breathing. An inner voice cried out for help.

When the *yabree* sang again, his neck muscles went flaccid. His swirling gaze focused on something in the stone under him.

Exigency stirred his muscles. His hand extended. His fingers touched it. His grip enveloped it, and a new need coursed through his bones. A need he knew well.

With an explosion of fury, Richard yanked the Sword of Truth from the stone floor, and the room rang with a new song.

Merissa fixed him with a murderous glare as she again rapped the *yabree* against the stone. "You will die, Richard Rahl. I have sworn to bathe in your blood, and I will."

With the last of his strength, powered by the sword's wrath, Richard heaved himself against the top of the stone wall and stretched down, plunging the blade into the quicksilver of the sliph.

Merissa shrieked.

Silver veins fluxed through her flesh. Her screams echoed around the stone room as her arms reached up in a frantic effort to escape the sliph, but it was too late. The metamorphosis coursed through her, and she waxed as glossy as the sliph, like a silver statue in a silver reflecting pool. The hard edges of her face softened, and what had been Merissa dissolved into the lapping waves of quicksilver.

"Breathe," the sliph said to Kahlan.

Richard threw the *yabree* aside as he dashed across the room. He scooped Kahlan up in his arms and carried her to the well. He draped her over the wall, wrapped his arms around her abdomen, and squeezed.

"Breathe! Kahlan, breathe!" He compressed again. "Do it for me! Breathe! Please, Kahlan, breathe."

Her lungs expelled the quicksilver, and she gasped a sudden, desperate breath, and then another.

At last, she turned in his arms and fell against him. "Oh, Richard, you were right. It was so wonderful I forgot to breathe. You saved me."

"But he killed the other," the sliph observed. "I warned him about the object of magic he carries. It is not my fault."

Kahlan blinked at the silver face. "What are you talking about?"

"The one that is part of me, now."

"Merissa," Richard explained. "It's not your fault, sliph. I had to do it, or she would have killed both of us."

"Then I am discharged of responsibility. Thank you, Master."

Kahlan spun back to him, glancing down at the sword. "What happened? What do you mean, Merissa?"

Richard untied the thong at his throat, reached over his shoulder, and pulled the mriswith cape off his back.

"She followed us through the sliph. She tried to kill you, and to . . . well, she wanted to take a bath with me."

"What!"

"No," the sliph corrected, "she said she wanted to bathe in your blood."

Kahlan's mouth dropped open. "But . . . what happened?"

"She is with me, now," the sliph said. "For all time."

"That means she's dead," Richard said. "I'll explain when we have more time." He turned to the sliph. "Thank you for your help, sliph, but I need you to sleep, now."

"Of course, Master. I will sleep until I am needed again."

The shiny silver face softened and melted back into the pool of quicksilver. Richard, without conscious direction, crossed his wrists. The lustrous pool took on a glow. The sliph stilled, and began sinking into the well, slowly at first, and then with gathering speed, until she was gone.

Kahlan stared up at him when he straightened. "I think there are a lot of things you are going to need to explain to me."

"When we have time, I promise."

"Where are we, anyway?"

"In the lower parts of the Keep, at the base of one of the towers."

"Lower parts of the Keep?"

Richard nodded. "Down under the library."

"Under the library! No one can go below the library level. There are shields that have kept every wizard from the lower Keep for as long as anyone knows."

"Well, that's where we are and that, too, we'll have to talk about later. We have to get down to the city."

They stepped out of Kolo's room, and immediately they both flattened themselves against the wall. The red mriswith queen was in the pool beyond the railing. She spread her wings protectively over a clutch of hundreds of eggs the size of large melons as she trumpeted a warning that echoed around the inside of the huge tower.

From what little light that came in from the openings overhead, Richard could see that it was late afternoon. It had taken less than a day, at least he hoped just one day, to reach Aydindril. In thc light, he could also see the vast extent of the clutch of splotchy gray and green eggs atop the rock.

"It's the mriswith queen," Richard hastily explained as he climbed the railing. "I have to destroy those eggs."

Kahlan shouted his name, trying to call him back, as he vaulted the railing, into the dark, slimy water. Richard held out his sword as he waded through the waist-deep water toward the slick rocks in the center. The queen rose up on her claws, venting a clacking bellow.

Her head snaked close to him, her jaws snapping. In that moment, Richard swung the sword. The grotesque head recoiled. She huffed a cloud of acrid aroma at him that carried a clear message of warning. Relentlessly, Richard slogged ahead. Her jaws gaped, revealing long, sharp teeth.

Richard couldn't let the mriswith have Aydindril. And if he didn't destroy these eggs, then there would be even more mriswith to deal with.

"Richard! I tried to use the blue lightning, but it won't work down here! Come back!"

The hissing queen snapped at him. Richard stabbed at the head when it came close, but she kept just out of reach and roared in anger. Richard was able to keep the head at bay while he groped for a handhold.

He found a crag to grasp, and scrambled up onto the dark, slimy rocks. He swung the sword, and when the menacing jaws pulled back, he hacked at the eggs. Stinking yolk oozed across the dark stone as he broke the thick, leathery shells.

The queen went wild. Her wings flapped, lifting her clear of the rock and out of the reach of Richard's sword. Her tail lashed around, snapping like a huge whip. When the tail came close, Richard swung the sword to keep her at bay. He was more interested in destroying the eggs at the moment.

Her teeth snapped as she lunged at him. Richard thrust the sword, piercing her neck with a glancing strike, enough that the queen reeled back in pain and fury. Her frantically flapping wings knocked him sprawling across the rock. Richard rolled to the side to avoid the slashing claws. Her tail thrashed at him again, and her jaws snapped. Richard was forced to forget the eggs for the moment and defend himself. If he could kill her, it would simplify the task.

The queen squealed in anger. A moment later, Richard heard a crunching sound. He turned toward the noise and saw Kahlan smashing eggs with a board that had been part of the door to Kolo's room. He scrambled across the slippery rock to put himself between Kahlan and the enraged queen. He slashed at the head when it tried to bite them, at the tail when it tried to sweep him from the rock, and at the claws when they tried to rip him apart.

"You just keep it away," Kahlan said as she swung the board, smashing eggs and wading into the gooey, yellow muck, "and I'll take care of these."

Richard didn't want Kahlan in danger, but he knew she was defending her city, too, and he couldn't ask her to go hide. Besides, he needed her help. He had to get down to the city.

"Just hurry," he said between dodging and attacking.

The huge red bulk flung itself at him, trying to crush him against the rock. Richard dove to the side, but the queen still came down on his leg. He cried out in pain and slashed with the sword as the beast gnashed at him.

The board suddenly whacked down on top of the fleshy slits atop the queen's head. She staggered back in howling pain, her wings flapping wildly, and her claws raking the air. Kahlan hooked an arm through his and helped pull him away as the red body lifted. They both tumbled back into the stagnant water.

"I got them all," Kahlan said. "Let's get out of here."

"I have to get her, or she'll just lay more."

But the mriswith queen, seeing all her eggs destroyed, switched from attack, to escape. Her wings beat madly, lifting her into the air. She lunged at the wall, fastened her claws to the stone, and began to climb toward a large opening high up on the tower.

Richard and Kahlan pulled themselves out of the reeking pool and onto the walkway. Richard started for the stairs that wound their way up around the inside of the tower, but when he put weight on his leg, he crashed to the floor.

Kahlan helped him stand. "You can't get to her now. We

destroyed all the eggs, we'll just have to worry about her later. Is your leg broken?"

Richard leaned against the railing, rubbing the painful bruise as he watched the queen climb out the opening high up in the tower. "No, she just mashed it against the rock. We have to get down to the city."

"But you can't walk."

"I'll be all right. The pain is easing up. Let's go."

Richard took one of the glowing spheres to light the way and, with Kahlan giving him support, they started out of the belly of the Keep. She had never been in the rooms and halls he took her through. He had to hold her in his arms to help her get through the shields, and constantly caution her what she mustn't touch, and where she must not step. She repeatedly questioned his warnings, but followed his insistent orders, muttering to herself that she had never known these peculiar places existed in the Keep.

By the time they had wound their way up through the rooms and halls to the top, his leg, though it still hurt, was working better. He could walk, if with a limp.

"At last, I know where we are," Kahlan said when they came up to the long hall before the libraries. "I was worried we would never get out from down there."

Richard headed toward the corridors he knew to be the way out. Kahlan protested that he couldn't go that way, but he insisted that that was the way he always went, and she reluctantly followed. He held her to get her through the shield into the great hall at the entrance, and they were both glad for the excuse.

"How much farther?" she asked as she looked around the near barren room.

"Right here. This is the door out."

When they went through the door to the outside, Kahlan turned around twice in astonishment. She snatched his shirt and gestured to the door. "There? You went in there! That's the way you went into the Keep?"

Richard nodded. "That's where the stone path led."

She pointed angrily above the door. "Look what it says! And you went in there?"

Richard glanced up at the words carved in the stone lintel above the huge door. "I don't know what those words mean."

"Tavol de ator Mortado," she said, reading the words aloud. "It means 'Path of the Dead.' "

Richard glanced briefly at the other doors beyond the expanse of stone chips and gravel. He remembered the thing that had come for them under the gravel.

"Well, it seemed the biggest door, and the path led right to it, so I thought that was the way to go in. Kind of makes sense, when you think about it. I am named 'the bringer of death.' "

Kahlan rubbed her arms in dismay. "We were frightened you would come up into the Keep. We were scared to death you would go in there and be killed. Dear spirits, I can't believe you weren't. Not even the wizards would go in this entrance. That shield just inside wouldn't allow me to pass without your help; that alone means it's perilous beyond. I can pass all the shields except those protecting the most dangerous places."

Richard heard a crunching of rock, and saw movement in the gravel. He pulled Kahlan back onto the center of a stepping-stone as the thing took a snaking course toward them.

"What's the matter?" she asked.

Richard pointed. "Something's coming."

Kahlan cast him a frown over her shoulder and walked out onto the gravel. "You're not afraid of this, are you?" She squatted and burrowed her hand into the gravel as the thing beneath came to her. She wiggled her hand around as if scratching a pet.

"What are you doing!"

Kahlan grappled playfully with the thing under the gravel. "It's just a stone hound. Wizard Giller conjured him up to frighten away a woman who was pestering him all the time. She was afraid to cross the gravel, and of course no one in their right mind would dare to go into the Path of the Dead." Kahlan stood. "You mean . . . don't tell me you were afraid of the stone hound."

"Well . . . no, not exactly . . . but . . ."

Kahlan put her fists on her hips. "You went into the Path of the Dead, and through those shields, because you were afraid of a stone hound? That's why you didn't go to the other doors?"

"Kahlan, I didn't know what the thing under the gravel was. I'd never seen anything like it before." He scratched his elbow. "All right, so, I was afraid of it. I was trying to be cautious. And I couldn't read the words, so I didn't know that this door was dangerous."

She shot a stymied look skyward. "Richard, you could have—"

"I didn't get killed in the Keep, I found the sliph, and I got to you. Now, come on. We need to get down to the city."

She put her arm around his waist. "You're right. I guess I'm just edgy from . . ." She lifted a hand toward the door. "From all that happened in there. That mriswith queen frightened me. I'm just thankful that you made it."

Arm in arm, they hurried through the towering, arched opening through the outer wall.

As they rushed under the huge portcullis, a powerful red tail whipped around from beyond the corner, felling them both. Before Richard could get his wind back, wings were beating overhead. Claws ripped at him. He felt searing pain in his left shoulder as a claw hooked him. Kahlan was sent tumbling across the ground by the thrashing tail.

While he was being hauled closer to the gaping jaws by the claw embedded in his shoulder, he yanked his sword free. The rage inundated him instantly. He slashed through a wing. The queen recoiled, yanking the claw free from his shoulder. The wrath of the magic helped him ignore the pain as he sprang to his feet.

He stabbed with the sword as the beast lunged at him, snapping her jaws. She seemed all wings, teeth, claws, and tail, plunging at him as he scurried backward. Richard stabbed an arm, and the queen drew back in pain. Her tail lashed around, catching him across the middle, throwing him up against the wall. He hacked wildly at the tail, taking off the tip.

The red mriswith queen reared back on her hind feet, under the spiked portcullis. Richard dove for the catch lever and caught it with all his weight. With a squealing clatter, the gate plunged toward the raving beast. The queen twisted as the gate crashed down, just missing her back, but catching a wing, pinning it to the ground. She howled even louder.

Richard started in cold fright when he saw that Kahlan was on the ground—on the other side of the gate. The queen saw her, too, and with a mighty effort, ripped her wing out from under the gate, tearing it into long, ragged shreds.

"Kahlan! Run!"

Groggy, she tried to crawl away, but the beast pounced. It snatched her by a leg, holding her fast.

The queen turned and spewed a fetid odor at him. Richard had no trouble understanding the meaning: revenge.

With mad effort, he pulled at the wheel that lifted the gate. It rose inches at a time. The queen was wriggling down the road, dragging Kahlan by her leg.

Richard released the wheel and, driven by the fury of the magic, swung the sword at the flat bars of the portcullis. Sparks and hot shards of steel smoked through the air. Screaming in rage, he swung the sword again at the iron, ripping another gash through the bars. A third swing and a piece was cut free. He kicked it over and plunged through the opening.

Richard charged down the road toward the retreating red beast. Kahlan clawed at the ground in a desperate attempt to get away. When it reached the bridge, the queen hopped up on the wall at the edge, snarling at him as he came at full speed.

The queen flapped its shredded wings, as if it didn't realize it couldn't fly. Still running, Richard screamed out as it turned, spreading its wings in readiness to leap off the bridge with its prize.

The tail swept across the road as Richard raced onto the bridge. He lopped off a six-foot section. The queen spun, holding Kahlan upside down by her leg like a stick doll. Richard, beyond reason, swung the sword in a blind rage as she snapped at him. Sprayed by the beast's blood, he slashed off the front half of a wing, the bone splintering to white shards under his blade. She lashed her truncated tail at him as she flapped her other mangled wing.

Kahlan screamed as she stretched toward Richard, her fingers spread, just out of reach. He drove the sword into the red belly. A red claw pulled Kahlan away as he tried to snatch her hand. Richard sheared the other wing off at the shoulder. Blood sprayed the air as the raging beast twisted this way and that, trying to get at him. It kept her from her hunger to rip Kahlan apart.

Richard took off another section of tail when it came close enough. As the reeking blood sprayed everywhere, the queen's reactions became sluggish, allowing Richard to inflict still more wounds.

Richard lunged and seized Kahlan's wrist, and she his, as he drove the sword hilt-deep up into the underside of the heaving red chest. It was a mistake.

The mortally wounded mriswith queen had a death grip on

Kahlan's leg. The red beast teetered, and with a nightmarishly slow twist, tumbled off the bridge over the yawning abyss. Kahlan shrieked. Richard tightened his hold on her with all his strength. The pull on his arm as the queen fell slammed his stomach against the wall above the dizzying drop.

Richard swung the sword over the edge and with one powerful stroke sheared the arm that held Kahlan's leg. The red beast spiraled down between the sheer walls that dropped for thousands of feet, to disappear in the distance far below.

Kahlan hung by his hand over the same drop. Blood was running down his arm and over their hands. He could feel her wrist slipping through his grip. His thighs were the only thing keeping him from going over the wall.

With a mighty effort, he lifted her a couple of feet. "Grab the wall with your other hand. I can't hold you. You're slipping."

Kahlan slapped her free hand onto the top of the stone wall, taking some of the weight. He tossed the sword to the road behind and got his other hand under her arm. Richard gritted his teeth and, with her help, pulled her up over the wall and onto the road.

"Get it off!" she cried. "Get it off!"

Richard pried the claws open and extracted her leg. He tossed the red arm over the edge. Kahlan fell into his arms, panting in exhaustion, too weary to speak.

Through the throb of pain, Richard felt the heady warmth of relief. "Why didn't you use your power . . . the lightning?"

"It wouldn't work down inside the Keep, and out here that thing knocked me senseless. Why didn't you use yours—some of that fearful black lightning, like back at the Palace of the Prophets?"

Richard considered the question. "I don't know. I don't know how the gift works. It has something to do with instinct. I can't make it work at will." He stroked a hand down her hair as he closed his eyes. "I wish Zedd were here. He would be able to help me control it—learn to use it. I miss him so."

"I know," she whispered.

Over their labored breathing, he could hear the distant cries of men and the ring of steel. He realized he smelled smoke. The air was hazy with it.

He helped Kahlan up, ignoring the fierce ache in his shoulder, and they rushed down the road to a switchback where there was a view of the city below.

As they stumbled to an abrupt halt at the edge, Kahlan gasped.

In shock, Richard sank to his knees. "Dear spirits," he whispered, "what have I caused."

CHAPTER 53

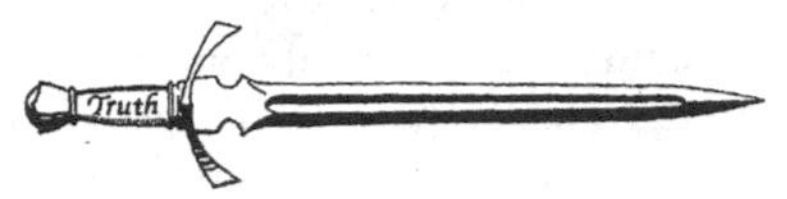

"IT'S LORD RAHL!" VOICES carried the shout back through the horde of D'Haran troops. "Rally! It's Lord Rahl!"

A cry swelled in the late-afternoon air. Thousands of voices rose above the din of battle. Weapons thrust into the smoky air with the roar of the shouts. "Lord Rahl! Lord Rahl! Lord Rahl!"

Grim-faced, Richard marched through the soldiers at the rear of the battle. Wounded, bleeding men staggered to their feet and joined in the throng following him.

Through the haze of acrid smoke, Richard could see down the slope of the streets to the frantic fighting at the van of dark uniformed D'Harans. Beyond, a sea of red flooded into the city, driving them back. Blood of the Fold. To each side and all around, they came, relentless, unstoppable.

"There must be well over a hundred thousand," Kahlan said, seemingly to herself.

Richard had sent a force of a hundred thousand to search for Kahlan. They were weeks away from the city. He had divided the force in Aydindril nearly in two, and sent half away. And now came the Blood of the Fold, to take advantage of his mistake.

But still, there should have been enough D'Harans to hold against that many. Something was deadly wrong.

With a growing crowd of wounded dragging along behind,

Richard reached the rear of what seemed the largest battle. The Blood of the Fold were pressing in from all sides of the city. Flames snapped skyward from Kings Row. In the center of the sweep of dark uniforms stood the white splendor of the Confessors' Palace.

Officers came at a run, their joy at seeing him tempered by what was happening just beyond. The screams from the site of the fighting burned through his nerves.

Richard was surprised to hear the dead calm quality of his own voice. "What's going on? These are D'Haran soldiers. Why are they being driven back? They are not outnumbered. Why are the Blood of the Fold this far into the city?"

The seasoned commander spoke only one word. "Mriswith."

Richard's fists tightened. These men had no defense against mriswith. One mriswith could cut down dozens of men in a matter of minutes. Richard had seen long lines of mriswith enter the sliph—hundreds of them.

The D'Harans may not have been outnumbered at the start, but they were now.

Already, the voices of the spirits were speaking to him, drowning out the screams of mortal pain. He glanced to the dull disc of the sun behind the smoke. Two hours of light left.

Richard's gaze met the eyes of three of the lieutenants. "You, you, and you. Collect whatever size force you need." Without turning, he lifted a thumb behind to gesture toward Kahlan. "Get the Mother Confessor, my queen, to the palace, and protect her."

The look in Richard's eyes made any statement of the mission's gravity absolutely unnecessary, and any warning of the consequences of failure superfluous.

Kahlan cried out a protest. Richard drew his sword.

"Now."

The men bounded to do as bidden, sweeping Kahlan back with them as she screamed at him. Richard didn't look, nor did he hear her words.

He was already lost in the living rage. Magic and death danced dangerously in his eyes. Silent men inched back in a widening circle.

Richard wiped the blade in the blood on his arm to give his sword a taste. The rage twisted tighter.

His head turned, the eyes of death seeking the walking dead.

Through the twin storms of the sword's wrath and his own anger, he heard nothing but the howling fury inside, yet he knew he needed more. In staccato succession he felled all the barriers and loosed all the magic, holding back nothing. He was one with the spirits within, with the magic, with the need. He was the true Seeker, and more.

He was the bringer of death come to life.

And then he was moving, through the men trying to get to the front, through the dark-leather-clad soldiers grunting with determination as they grappled with crimson-caped men in shiny armor who had broken through the lines, through shopkeepers who had taken up swords, through young men of the city with pikes, and boys with cudgels.

As he stalked forward, he cut down the men of the Blood of the Fold only when they tried to bar his way. He was after something more deadly than them.

Richard vaulted up onto an overturned wagon in the center of the melee. Men swarmed around him to keep harm away. His raptor's gaze scanned the scene. Harm was his purpose.

Before him, the sea of red capes inundated the dark shore of dead D'Harans. The numbers of D'Haran dead were appalling, but he was lost in the magic and thought for anything but his enemy was mere dross in the cauldron of his wrath.

Somewhere in the dim recesses of his mind, he cried out at the sight of so much death, but the cry was lost on the winds of his rage.

Richard felt their presence, and then he saw them. Fluid movement, scything into living flesh, reaping a harvest of death. The Blood of the Fold surged in behind them, overwhelming the decimated D'Harans.

Richard brought the Sword of Truth up, touching the crimson blade to his forehead. He gave the whole of himself over.

"Blade," he whispered in supplication, "be true this day."

Bringer of death.

"Dance with me, Death," he murmured. "I am ready."

The Seeker's boots thumped onto the street. Somehow, the instincts of all those who had used the blade before had fused with his own. He wore their knowledge, experience, and skill like a second skin.

He let the magic guide him, but it was driven before the storms of anger, and his will. He turned loose the hunger to kill, and slipped through the lines of men.

Deft as death, his blade found its first mark, and a mriswith went down.

Don't squander your strength killing those others can kill, the spirit voices told him. *Kill only those they can't.*

Richard heeded the voices, and let his inner sense feel the mriswith around him, some concealed in their capes. He danced with death, and death occasionally found them before they saw him coming. He killed without wasted effort or extra thrusts. Each commitment of his blade found flesh.

Richard stalked along the lines, seeking the scaled creatures that led the Blood of the Fold. He felt the heat of the fires as he moved through the streets, hunting. He heard the hisses of surprise as he spun into them. His nostrils filled with the stink of their blood. It became one long blur of fighting.

Still, he knew it wasn't going to be enough. With a feeling of drowning in dread, he knew it wasn't going to be enough. There was only one of him, and if he made the slightest mistake, there wouldn't even be that. It was like trying to wipe out a whole ant colony by stepping on one ant at a time.

Already, *yabree* were coming closer than he had intended to allow. Twice, they sang along his flesh, leaving red tracks. But worse, all around, his men were dying by the hundreds, with the Blood of the Fold merely coming in behind to slaughter the wounded. The fighting stretched on endlessly.

Richard glanced at the sun, and saw that it was halved at the horizon. Night was descending like a shroud over the last gasps of the dying. He knew that, for him, too, there would be no morning.

Richard felt a stinging slice along his side as he spun. A mriswith's head burst apart in a red spray as he caught it with his sword. He was tiring, and they were getting too close. He brought the blade up, ripping open the belly of another. He was deaf to their death howls.

He remembered Kahlan. There was going to be no morning. For him. For her. Death was coming for them like the darkness.

With effort, he forced her from his mind. He couldn't afford the distraction. Turn. Blade up, taking off a claw. Twist, slice to the gut. Spin, blade down on a smooth head. Thrust. Duck. Cut. The voices spoke to him, and he reacted without question or pause.

With choking consternation, he realized that they were being pushed to the center of Aydindril. He turned and looked beyond the large square swept with the turmoil, disorganization, and confusion of the brawl of battle, to see the Confessors' Palace not a half mile away. Soon, the mriswith would break through the lines and pour into the palace.

He heard a loud roar and saw a mass of D'Haran soldiers behind the enemy lines charge into the Blood of the Fold from a side street, turning their attention from the fight at the front. From the other side, a like number poured in, pinching off a large number of crimson-caped men in the wide thoroughfare. The D'Harans hacked into the pocket of the Blood of the Fold, cutting them to pieces.

Richard stilled to a statue when he saw Kahlan leading the charge from the right. She was leading not only D'Haran troops, but men and women of the palace staff. His blood ran cold as he remembered how the people at Ebinissia had joined in the defense of the city at the end.

What was she doing? She was supposed to be at the palace, where it was safe. He could see that while it was a bold move, it was going to be fatal. There were too many of the Blood and she would be trapped in the middle of them.

Before that could happen, she pulled the men back. Richard lopped off the head of a mriswith. Just as he thought she must have retreated to safety, she made another stabbing attack from another street, at a different place in the line.

The crimson-caped men at the front turned to the new threat, only to be set upon from behind. The mriswith blunted the effectiveness of the tactic, and soon sliced into the new front with the same deadly efficiency they had been using all afternoon.

Richard cut a line straight through the mass of crimson capes toward Kahlan. After fighting mriswith, men seemed slow and dull by comparison. Only the distance made it a struggle. His arms were weary, and his strength was flagging.

"Kahlan! What are you doing!" The rage of the magic powered his voice as he snatched her by the arm. "I sent you to the palace where you would be safe!"

She pulled her arm away. In her other hand she held a sword slick with blood. "I will not die cowering in a corner of my home, Richard. I will fight for my life. And don't you yell at me!"

Richard spun when he felt the presence. Kahlan ducked as blood and bone glutted the air.

She turned and shouted orders. Men wheeled to the attack at her word.

"Then we die together, my queen," Richard whispered, not wanting her to hear his resignation.

Richard felt the massing of mriswith as the lines were pushed back to the square. The sense of their presence was too overpowering to pick out individuals. Over the heads of the sea of red capes and polished armor, he could see something green in the distance advancing toward the city. He couldn't make meaning of it.

Richard shoved Kahlan back. Her protest was cut short when he spun into the line of scaled creatures as they became visible right before them. He danced through their charge, cutting them down as fast as he could move.

Through his frenetic onslaught, he saw something else he could make no sense of: spots. He thought it must be that he was so tired he was beginning to see a sky full of spots.

He screamed with rage at a *yabree* that came too close. He lopped off the arm and then the head in quick succession. Another blade came at him and he ducked under it, coming up sword first. He backhanded another with the knife in his other hand. He had to kick the one behind before he had time to yank his sword free.

With cold fury, he realized that the mriswith had finally determined that he was their only threat, and were surrounding him. He could hear Kahlan screaming his name. He could see beady eyes everywhere. There was nothing he could do, and nowhere to run, even if he wanted to. He felt the sting of blades that came too close before he could stop them.

There were too many. Dear spirits, there were just too many.

He didn't even see any soldiers close anymore. He was surrounded by a wall of scales and flashing three-bladed knives. Only the rage of the magic slowed them. He wished that he had told Kahlan he loved her, instead of yelling at her.

Something brown flashed in his side vision. He heard a howl from a mriswith, but it wasn't one he killed. He wondered if confusion was what you felt when you died. He was dizzy from spinning, from swinging his sword, from the bone-jarring impacts.

Something huge dropped from above. Then another. Richard

tried to wipe mriswith blood out of his eyes in an effort to tell what was happening. All around, mriswith howled.

Richard saw wings. Brown wings. Furry arms were flashing in his vision, twisting off heads. Claws rent scales apart. Fangs ripped into necks.

Richard stumbled back as a huge gar thumped to the ground right in front of him, tumbling the mriswith back.

It was Gratch.

Richard blinked as he glanced around. There were gars everywhere. More were coming, up in the air—those were the spots he had seen.

Gratch heaved a ripped mriswith into the Blood of the Fold, and lunged at another. The gars all around tore into them. More dropped from the darkening sky atop mriswith all along the lines. There were glowing green eyes everywhere. The mriswith shrouded themselves in their capes, becoming invisible, but it did them no good; the gars could still find them. They had nowhere to run.

Richard held the sword in both hands, gawking. Gars roared. Mriswith howled. Richard laughed.

Kahlan's arms clamped around him from behind. "I love you," she said in his ear. "I thought I was going to die, and I hadn't told you."

He turned and looked into her wet green eyes. "I love you."

Richard heard shouts over the cries of battle. The green he had seen were men. There were tens of thousands of them, charging into the rear of the Blood of the Fold, pouring in around buildings, crushing the crimson-caped men back. The D'Harans on Richard's side, free of the mriswith, rallied and tore into the Blood with the deadly competence they were known for.

A huge wedge of the men in green cleaved through the Blood of the Fold, coming toward Richard and Kahlan. To each side, dozens of gars set upon mriswith. Gratch flailed into them, ramming them back. Richard climbed up on a fountain to better see what was happening. He took Kahlan's hand and helped her up beside him. Men surged in to protect him, driving the enemy back.

"They're Keltans," Kahlan said. "The men in green uniforms are Keltans."

At the van of the Keltish charge was a man Richard recognized: General Baldwin. When the general saw them on the fountain, he and a small guard peeled away from his main force of men, shouting orders as he departed, and cut a line through the crimson-caped men, their horses trampling men underfoot like autumn leaves. The general hacked at a few with his sword for good measure. He broke through the battle lines and reined in before Richard and Kahlan standing on the fountain.

General Baldwin sheathed his sword and bowed in his saddle, his heavy serge cape, fastened at one shoulder with two buttons, draped to one side, revealing the green silk lining. He came up and clapped a fist to his tan surcoat.

"Lord Rahl," he said with reverence.

He bowed again. "My queen," he said with even more reverence.

Kahlan leaned toward him when he came up, her tone ominous. "Your what?"

Even the man's shiny pate reddened. He bowed again. "My most . . . glorious . . . esteemed queen, and Mother Confessor?"

Before she could speak Richard tugged the back of her shirt. "I told the general here how I had decided to name you the Queen of Kelton."

Her eyes widened. "The queen of . . ."

"Yes," General Baldwin said as he glanced about at the battle. "It kept Kelton together, and our surrender unbroken. Lord Rahl told me of this great honor, that we were to have the Mother Confessor as our queen, just as Galea, showing how he honors us as our neighbors. So I immediately brought a force to Aydindril to help protect Lord Rahl, and our queen, and to join in the battle against the Imperial Order. I didn't want either of you to think we weren't prepared to do our part."

Kahlan finally blinked and straightened. "Thank you, General. Your help came just in time. I am most appreciative."

The general pulled off his long black gauntlets and tucked them through his wide belt. He kissed Kahlan's hand. "If my new queen will excuse me, I must return to my men. We have half our force spread out behind just in case these traitorous bastards try to escape." He blushed again. "Pardon a soldier's language, my queen."

As the general returned to his men, Richard scanned the battle. The gars were searching, looking for more mriswith, and finding only a few. Those didn't last long.

Gratch looked to have grown another foot since Richard had

last seen him, and was now the size of any of the males. He seemed to be directing the search. Richard was dumbfounded, but his joy was tempered by the scale of the carnage before him.

"Queen?" Kahlan said. "You named me Queen of Kelton? The Mother Confessor?"

"It seemed a good idea at the time," he explained. "It seemed the only way to keep Kelton from turning on us."

She appraised him with a small smile. "Very good, Lord Rahl."

As Richard finally sheathed his sword, he saw three spots of red break through the dark leather of D'Haran uniforms. The three Mord-Sith, Agiel in hand, came at a run across the square. Each wore her red leather, but it did a poor job this day of disguising the blood all over them.

"Lord Rahl! Lord Rahl!"

Berdine flew at him like a squirrel flinging itself for a branch. She landed on him, webbing him in arms and legs, knocking him back off the wall and into the fountain full of snowmelt.

She sat up on his stomach. "Lord Rahl! You did it! You took the cape off like I told you! You heard my warning after all!"

She fell on him again, clutching him in red arms. Richard held his breath as he went under. Though the icy water wouldn't have been his choice, he was glad for the excuse to wash off some of the stinking mriswith blood. He gasped for air when she grabbed his shirt in her fist and hauled him up. She sat in his lap, legs around his middle, and hugged him again.

"Berdine," he whispered, "my shoulder is hurt. Please don't squeeze so hard."

"It's nothing," she announced in true Mord-Sith disregard for pain. "We were so worried. When the attack came, we thought we would never see you again. We thought we had failed."

Kahlan cleared her throat. Richard held out an introductory hand. "Kahlan, these are my personal guards, Cara, Raina, and this is Berdine. Ladies, this is Kahlan, my queen."

Berdine, making no attempt to get off his lap, grinned up at Kahlan. "I'm Lord Rahl's favorite."

Kahlan folded her arms as her green-eyed glare darkened.

"Berdine, let me up."

"You still smell like a mriswith." She shoved him back in the water and again hauled him up by his shirt. "That's better." She pulled him closer. "You ever run off like that again without listening to me, I'll do more than give you a bath."

"What is it about you and women and baths?" Kahlan asked in an even tone.

"I don't know." He looked out over the battle still raging, and then back to Berdine's blue eyes. He hugged her with his good arm. "I'm sorry. I should have listened to you. The price of my foolishness was too great."

"Are you all right?" she whispered in his ear.

"Berdine, get off me. Let me up."

She flopped off his lap to the side. "Kolo said that the mriswith were enemy wizards who traded their power for the ability to become invisible."

Richard gave her a hand up. "I nearly did, too."

She stood in the water on her tiptoes and pulled his shirt collar aside, inspecting his neck. She let out a relieved sigh. "It's gone. You're safe. Kolo said how the change came, how their skin began to scale over. He said that that ancestor of yours, Alric, created a force to battle the mriswith." She pointed. "Gars."

"Gars . . . ?"

Berdine nodded. "He gave them the ability to sense mriswith, even when they were invisible. That's what gives the gars' eyes that green glow. Because of this interrelationship of magic all the gars share, those who dealt directly with the wizards accrued dominance over the others, becoming something like the wizards' generals among the gar nation. These intermediary gars were greatly respected by the other gars, and got them to fight alongside the people of the New World against the enemy mriswith, driving them back to the Old World."

Richard stared in astonishment. "What else did he say?"

"I haven't had time to read any more. We've been kind of busy since you left."

"How long?" He stepped out of the fountain and addressed Cara. "How long have I been gone?"

She glanced to the Keep. "Nearly two days. Night before last. Today, at dawn, the sentries came in a lather and said the Blood of the Fold were right on their heels. They attacked shortly after. The fighting has been going on since this morning. At first, it was going well, but then the mriswith . . ." Her voice trailed off.

Kahlan put an arm around his waist to steady him as he spoke.

"I'm sorry, Cara. I should have been here." He stared in a daze at the sea of dead. "This is my fault."

"I killed two," Raina announced without any attempt to mask her pride.

Ulic and Egan came at a run and spun to a stop in defensive positions. "Lord Rahl," Ulic said over his shoulder, "are we ever glad to see you. We heard the cheer, but every time we got to you, you were somewhere else."

"Really?" Cara said, lifting an eyebrow. "We managed."

Ulic rolled his eyes and turned toward the battle.

"Are they always like this?" Kahlan whispered in his ear.

"No," he whispered back. "They're on their best behavior for you."

Richard saw white flags flying among the Blood of the Fold. No one paid them any heed.

"D'Harans give no quarter," Cara explained when she saw where he was looking. "It is to the finish."

Richard hopped down off the fountain. When he strode off, his guards immediately followed.

Kahlan caught up with him before he had taken three strides. "What are you doing, Richard?"

"I'm putting a stop to this."

"You can't do that. We have sworn to kill the Order to a man. You must let it be done. That's what they would have done to us."

"I can't do it, Kahlan. I can't. If we kill them all, then others of the Order will never surrender, knowing it would mean death. If I show them that we will take them prisoner instead of killing them, then they'll be more willing to quit. If they are more willing to quit, we win without losing the lives of so many of our men, and that makes us stronger. Then, we win."

Richard started shouting orders. They were carried through the ranks of his men, and the din of battle slowly began subsiding. The eyes of thousands began turning to him.

"Let them through," he told a commander.

Richard went back to the fountain and stood on the wall, watching the commanders of the Blood of the Fold lead their men to him. All around, D'Harans, bristling steel, stood guard. A corridor opened, and the crimson-caped men stepped forward, glancing from side to side as they came.

An officer halted at their lead before Richard. His voice was hoarse, and subdued. "Will you accept our surrender?"

Richard folded his arms. "Depends. Are you willing to tell me the truth?"

The man glanced about at his quict, bloody men. "Yes, Lord Rahl."

"Who told you to attack the city?"

"The mriswith gave us instructions, and many of us were instructed in our dreams, by the dream walker."

"Do you wish to be free of him?"

They all nodded or spoke up in weak voices. They also readily agreed to telling everything they knew about any plans that they knew of that the dream walker and the Imperial Order had.

Richard was so exhausted, and in such pain, that he could hardly stand. He drew anger from the sword to sustain himself.

"If you wish to surrender and be subjects of D'Haran rule, then go to your knees, and swear loyalty."

In the fading light, accompanied by the groans of the wounded, the remaining Blood of the Fold went to their knees and gave the devotion as they were instructed by the D'Harans who joined in.

In one mass voice that carried through the city, they all bowed heads to the ground and took the oath.

"Master Rahl guide us. Master Rahl teach us. Master Rahl protect us. In your light we thrive. In your mercy we are sheltered. In your wisdom we are humbled. We live only to serve. Our lives are yours."

As the men all tore off their crimson capes, casting them in fires as they were led away to be guarded for now, Kahlan turned to him.

"You have just changed the rules of the war, Richard." She looked out over the carnage. "So many have died already."

"Too many," he whispered as he watched the empty-handed Blood of the Fold marching off into the night, surrounded by the men they had tried to kill. He wondered if he was crazy.

" 'In your mercy we are sheltered,' " Kahlan quoted from the devotion. "Perhaps it is meant to be this way." She put a comforting hand to his back. "I know it somehow feels right."

Not far off, Mistress Sanderholt, holding a bloody meat cleaver, smiled her agreement.

Glowing green eyes gathered in the square. Richard's black

mood brightened when he saw Gratch's gruesome grin. He and Kahlan hopped down and hurried to the gar.

It had never felt so good to be enfolded by those furry arms. Richard laughed with tears in his eyes as he was lifted from the ground.

"I love you, Gratch. I love you so much."

"Grrratch luuug Raaaach aaarg."

Kahlan joined the hug, and then received her own, separate embrace. "I love you, too, Gratch. You saved Richard's life. I owe you everything."

Gratch gurgled with satisfaction as he stroked a claw down her hair.

Richard swished at a fly. "Gratch! You have blood flies!"

Gratch's self-satisfied grin widened. Gars used the flies to help flush out their quarry, but Gratch had never had any before. Richard didn't want to swat Gratch's blood flies, but they were becoming more than annoying. They were stinging his neck.

Gratch bent, scooped a claw through the gore of a dead mriswith, and smeared it across the taut, pink skin of his abdomen. The flies obediently returned to feast. Richard was astonished.

He peered around at all the glowing green eyes watching him. "Gratch, you look like you've had quite an adventure. You gathered all these gars together?" Gratch nodded with a clear look of gar pride. "And they did what you asked?"

Gratch thumped his chest with authority. He turned and grunted. The rest of the gars returned the odd grunt. Gratch smiled, showing his fangs.

"Gratch, where's Zedd?"

The leathery smile withered. The hulking gar sagged a bit as he looked over his shoulder, up at the keep. He turned back, his glowing green eyes dimming a bit as he shook his head sorrowfully.

Richard swallowed back the anguish. "I understand," he whispered. "Did you see him killed?"

Gratch thumped his chest, lifted his fur out atop his head, apparently a sign for Zedd, pointed at the Keep, and put his claws over his eyes—Gratch's sign for mriswith. Through his signs, and Richard's questions, Richard was able to determine that Gratch had brought Zedd to the Keep, there had been a fight with many mriswith, Gratch had seen Zedd lying unmoving on the ground with blood running from his head, and then Gratch could no longer find the old wizard. The gar had then gone in search of help to fight the mriswith and protect Richard. He had worked hard to find the other gars, and to gather them to his purpose.

Richard hugged his friend again. Gratch held him in a long embrace, and then backed away, looking for the other gars.

Richard felt a lump rising in his throat. "Gratch, can you stay?"

Gratch pointed one claw at Richard, another at Kahlan, and then brought them together. He thumped his chest and then pointed behind at another gar. When it came forward to stand beside him, Richard realized it was a female.

"Gratch, you have a love? Like I have Kahlan?"

Gratch grinned and thumped at his chest with both claws.

"And you want to be with the gars," Richard said.

Gratch nodded reluctantly, his smile faltering.

Richard put on his best smile. "I think that's wonderful, my friend. You deserve to be with your love, and your new friends. But you can still visit us. We would love to have you and your friend any time. All of you, in fact. You're all welcome here."

Gratch's smile returned.

"But Gratch, can you do one thing for me? Please? It's important. Can you ask them not to eat people? We won't hunt gars, and you won't eat people. All right?"

Gratch turned to the others, grunting in an odd guttural language that the others understood. They offered grumbling murmurs of their own, and a conversation of sorts seemed to ensue. Gratch's growling words rose in pitch, and he thumped his massive chest—he was at least as big as any of them. They all finally offered a hooting assent. Gratch turned to Richard and nodded.

Kahlan hugged the furry beast again. "Take care of yourself, and come see us when you can. I'm always in your debt, Gratch. I love you. We both do."

After a last embrace with Richard that needed no words, the gars took to wing and vanished into the night.

Richard stood beside Kahlan, surrounded by his guards, his army, and the specter of the dead.

CHAPTER 54

RICHARD AWAKENED WITH A start. Kahlan was curled up with her back to his chest. The wound in his shoulder from the mriswith queen ached. He had let an army surgeon put a poultice on it, and then, too exhausted to stand any longer, he had fallen onto the bed in the guest room he had been using. He hadn't even taken off his boots, and the uncomfortable pain in his hip told him that he still wore the Sword of Truth, and he was lying on it.

Kahlan stirred in his arms, a feeling that swelled him with joy, but then he remembered the thousands of dead, the thousands who were dead because of him, and his joy evaporated.

"Good morning, Lord Rahl," came a cheery voice from above.

He frowned up at Cara and groaned in greeting. Kahlan squinted in the sunlight streaming in the window.

Cara waggled a hand over the two of them. "It works better with your clothes off."

Richard frowned. His voice came as a hoarse croak. "What?"

She seemed mystified by the question. "I believe you will find such things work better without clothes." She put her hands to her hips. "I thought you would know at least that much."

"Cara, what are you doing in here?"

"Ulic wanted to see you, but was afraid to look, so I said I would. For one so large, he can be timid at times."

"He needs to give you lessons." Richard winced as he sat up. "What does he want?"

"He found a body."

Kahlan rubbed her eyes as she sat up. "That shouldn't have been hard."

Cara smiled, but it vanished when Richard noticed it. "He found a body at the bottom of the cliff, below the Keep."

Richard swung his legs over the edge of the bed. "Why didn't you say so."

Kahlan rushed to catch up with him as he charged out in the hall to find Ulic waiting.

"Did you find him? Did you find a body of an old man?"

"No, Lord Rahl. It was the body of a woman."

"A woman! What woman?"

"She was in bad shape, after all this time, but I recognized those gapped teeth and tattered blanket. It was that old woman, Valdora. The one who sold those honey cakes."

Richard rubbed his sore shoulder. "Valdora. How odd. And the little girl, what was her name?"

"Holly. We saw no trace of her. We found no one else, but there's a lot of area to search, and animals could have . . . well, we may never find anything."

Richard nodded, words failing him. He felt the shroud of death all around him.

Cara's voice turned compassionate. "The funeral fires will begin in a while. Do you wish to go?"

"Of course!" He checked his tone when he felt Kahlan's tempering hand on his back. "I must be there. They died because of me."

Cara frowned. "They died because of the Blood of the Fold, and because of the Imperial Order."

"We know, Cara," Kahlan said. "We'll be there just as soon as I see to the poultice on his shoulder and we get cleaned up."

The funeral fires burned for days. Twenty-seven thousand were dead. Richard felt as if the flames carried away his spirits, as well as those of the men who had died. He stayed and said the words along with the others, and by night stood guard over the flames along with the others, until it was done.

From the light of this fire, and into the light. Safe journey to the spirit world.

Richard's shoulder worsened over the next few days, getting swollen, red, and stiff.

His mood was no better.

He walked the halls and occasionally watched the streets from the windows, but talked to few people. Kahlan strolled at his side, offering her comforting presence, remaining quiet unless he spoke. Richard couldn't banish the image of all the dead from his mind. He was haunted by the name the prophecies had given him: the bringer of death.

One day, after his shoulder had at last begun to heal, he sat at the table he used as a desk, staring at nothing. Suddenly there was light. He looked up. Kahlan had come in, and he hadn't even noticed. She had pulled the drapes open to let in the sunlight.

"Richard, I'm starting to worry about you."

"I know, but I can't seem to make myself forget."

"It's right for the mantle of rule to be heavy, Richard, but you can't let it crush you."

"That's easy to say, but it was my fault that all those men died."

Kahlan sat on the table in front of him and with a finger, lifted his chin. "Do you really think that, Richard, or are you just feeling sorry that so many had to die?"

"Kahlan, I was stupid. I just acted. I never thought. If I would have used my head, maybe all those men wouldn't be dead."

"You acted on instinct. You said that that was the way the gift worked with you, sometimes anyway."

"But I—"

"Let's play 'what if.' What if you had done it differently, as you now think you should have?"

"Well, then all those people wouldn't have been killed."

"Really? You're not playing by the rules of 'what if.' Think it through, Richard. What if you had not acted on instinct, and had not gone to the sliph? What would have been the result?"

"Well, let's see." He rubbed her leg. "I don't know, but things would have worked out differently."

"Yes, they would have. You would have been here when the attack came. You would have gone to fight the mriswith in the morning, instead of at the end of the day. You would have been worn down and killed long before the gars arrived at dusk. You would be dead. All these people would have lost their Lord Rahl."

Richard tilted his head up. "That makes sense." He thought about it a moment. "And if I hadn't gone to the Old World, then the Palace of the Prophets would be in Jagang's hands. He would have the prophecies." He stood and went to the window, looking out on the bright spring day. "And no one would have any protection from the dream walker, because I would be dead."

"You've been letting your emotions control your thinking."

Richard came back and took up her hands, truly noticing how radiant she looked. "Wizard's Third Rule: Passion rules reason. Kolo warned that it was insidious. I've been breaking it by thinking I had broken it."

Kahlan slipped her arms around him. "Feeling just a little better, then?"

He put his hands on her waist as he smiled for the first time in days. "You've helped me see. Zedd used to do those kinds of things. I guess I'll just have to count on you to help me."

She hooked her legs around him and pulled him closer. "You had better."

As he gave her a little kiss, and was about to give her a bigger one, the three Mord-Sith marched into the room. Kahlan put her cheek against his. "Do they ever knock?"

"Rarely," Richard whispered back. "They enjoy testing. It's their favorite thing to do. They never tire of it."

Cara, in the lead, came to a halt beside them, looking from one to the other. "Still with the clothes, Lord Rahl?"

"You three look well this morning."

"Yes, we are," Cara said. "And we have business."

"What business?"

"When you have the time, some representatives have arrived in Aydindril, and have requested an audience with the Lord Rahl."

Berdine brandished Kolo's journal. "And I would like to have your help with this. What we already learned has helped us, and there is much more yet that we haven't translated. We have work to do."

"Translate?" Kahlan asked. "I know many languages. What is it?"

"High D'Haran," Berdine said, taking a bite out of a pear in her other hand. "Lord Rahl is getting even better at High D'Haran than me."

"Really," Kahlan said. "I'm impressed. Few people know High D'Haran. It's an extremely difficult language, I'm told."

"We worked on it together." Berdine smiled. "At night."

Richard cleared his throat. "Let's go find out about the representatives." He boosted Kahlan with his hands on her sides and set her on the floor.

Berdine gestured with her pear. "Lord Rahl has very big hands. They fit perfectly over my breasts."

One eyebrow went up over a green eye. "Really."

"Yes," Berdine observed. "He had us all show him our breasts one day."

"Is that right? All of you."

Cara and Raina waited without expression as Berdine nodded. Richard put a hand over his face.

Berdine took another bite of her pear. "But his big hands fit best over my breasts."

Kahlan ambled toward the door. "Well, my breasts aren't as large as yours, Berdine." She slowed as she passed Raina. "I think Raina's hands would fit mine better."

Berdine choked and coughed on her bite of pear as Kahlan strolled from the room. A smile spread on Raina's lips.

Cara burst into a hearty laugh. She clapped Richard on the back as he walked past. "I like her, Lord Rahl. You may keep her."

Richard paused. "Well, thank you, Cara. I'm fortunate to have your approval."

She nodded earnestly. "Yes, you are."

He hurried out of the room, finally catching up with Kahlan down the hall. "How did you know about Berdine and Raina?"

She regarded him with a puzzled frown. "Isn't it obvious, Richard? The look in their eyes? You must have noticed right away, too."

"Well . . ." Richard glanced back down the hall to make sure the women hadn't caught up, yet. "You'll be happy to know that Cara said she likes you, and that I'm allowed to keep you."

Kahlan slipped an arm around his waist. "I like them, too. I doubt you could find guards who would better protect you."

"Is that supposed to be a comfort?"

She smiled as she leaned her head against his shoulder. "It is to me."

Richard changed the subject. "Let's go see what these representatives have come to say. Our future, everyone's future, hinges on this."

Kahlan, wearing her white Mother Confessor's dress, sat silently in her chair, the Mother Confessor's chair, beside Richard, under the painted figure of Magda Searus, the first Mother Confessor, and her wizard, Merritt.

Escorted by a smiling General Baldwin, Representative Garthram of Lifany, Representative Theriault of Herjborgue, and Ambassador Bezancort of Sanderia crossed the expanse of polished marble floor. They all seemed surprised, and pleased, to see the Mother Confessor sitting beside Richard.

General Baldwin bowed. "My queen, Lord Rahl."

Kahlan smiled warmly. "Good day, General Baldwin."

"Gentlemen," Richard said, "I hope all is well in your lands. What have you decided?"

Representative Garthram smoothed his gray beard. "After extensive consultation with the rule at home, and with Galea and Kelton leading the way, we have all decided that the future lies with you, Lord Rahl. We have all brought the surrender documents. Unconditional, as per your request. We wish to join with you, to be part of D'Hara, and under your rule."

The tall Ambassador Bezancort spoke up. "While we are here to surrender, and join with D'Hara, it remains our hope that the Mother Confessor approves."

Kahlan considered the men for a moment. "Our future, not our past, is where we and our children must live. The first Mother Confessor and her wizard did what was best for their people and their time. As the Mother Confessor, now, I and my wizard, Richard, must do what is best for ours. We must forge what we need to fit our world, but our hopes are for peace, as were theirs.

"Our best chance for strength that will insure a lasting peace lies with Lord Rahl. Our new course has been set. My heart and my people go with him. As the Mother Confessor, I am a part of this union, and I welcome you to it."

Richard returned the squeeze of his hand.

"We will continue to have our Mother Confessor," he said. "We need her wisdom and guidance as much as we always have."

A few days later, on a fine spring afternoon, as Richard and Kahlan strolled hand in hand through the streets, checking on the cleanup of the destruction from the battle, and the construction that was already beginning to repair what had been destroyed, Richard had a sudden thought. He turned, feeling the cool breeze and warm sun on his face.

"You know, I've demanded the surrender of the lands of the Midlands, and I don't even know how many there are, or all their names."

"Well, then, I guess I have a lot to teach you," she said. "You'll just have to keep me around."

A smile overcame him. "I need you. Now, and always." He cupped her cheek. "I can't believe we're together, at last." He glanced up at the three women and two men not three paces behind them. "If only we could be alone."

Cara arched an eyebrow. "Is that a hint, Lord Rahl?"

"No, it's an order."

Cara shrugged. "Sorry, but we can't follow that order out here. You need protection. Do you know, Mother Confessor, that we sometimes have to tell him which foot to use next? He sometimes needs us for the simplest of instructions."

Kahlan was overcome with a helpless sigh. Finally, she looked past Cara to the towering men behind. "Ulic, did you see to it that those bolts were installed on the door to our room?"

"Yes, Mother Confessor."

Kahlan smiled. "Good." She turned to Richard. "Shall we go home? I'm getting tired."

"You have to wed him, first," Cara announced. "Lord Rahl's orders. No women allowed into his room, except his wife."

Richard scowled. "I said except Kahlan. I never said wife. I said except Kahlan."

Cara glanced to the Agiel hanging on the thin chain around Kahlan's neck. It was Denna's Agiel. Richard had given it to Kahlan in a place between worlds where Denna had taken them to be together. It had become a sort of amulet—one the three Mord-Sith had never mentioned, but had noticed from the first instant they saw Kahlan. Richard suspected it meant as much to them as it did to him and Kahlan.

Cara's cavalier gaze returned to Richard. "You charged us with protecting the Mother Confessor, Lord Rahl. We are merely protecting our sister's honor."

Kahlan smiled when she saw that Cara had finally managed to nettle him, something she was rarely able to do. Richard took a calming breath. "And a fine job you're doing of it, but don't you worry; by my word, she'll soon be my wife."

Kahlan's fingers idly stroked his back. "We promised the Mud People that we would be wedded in their village, by the Bird Man, in the dress Weselan made for me. That promise to our friends means a great deal to me. Would it be all right with you if we were wedded by the Mud People?"

Before Richard could tell her that it meant as much to him, and was his wish, too, a crowd of children swarmed around them. They pulled at his hands, begging him to come watch, as he had promised.

"What are they talking about?" Kahlan asked as she let out a joyful laugh.

"Ja'La," Richard said. "Here, let me see your Ja'La ball," he said to the children.

When they handed it up, he tossed it in one hand, showing it to her. Kahlan took the ball and turned it around, looking at the gold letter *R* embossed on it.

"What's this?"

"Well, they played with a ball, called a broc, that was so heavy that children were constantly getting hurt with it. I had the seamstresses make up new balls that are light, so all the children can play, not just the strongest ones. It's more a game of skill, now, instead of just brute force."

"What's the *R* for?"

"I told them that anyone willing to use this new kind of ball would get an official Ja'La broc from the palace. The *R* stands for Rahl, to show that it's an official ball. The game was called Ja'La, but since I changed the rules, they call it Ja'La Rahl, now."

"Well," Kahlan said, tossing the ball back to the children, "since Lord Rahl promised, and he always keeps his word . . ."

"Yes!" one boy said. "He promised that if we used his official ball he'd come watch."

Richard glanced to the gathering clouds. "Well, there's a storm coming, but I guess we have time for a game first."

Arm in arm, they followed the gleeful crowd of children up the street.

Richard smiled as he walked. "If only Zedd were with us."

"Do you think he died up at the Keep?"

Richard glanced up the mountain. "He always said that if you accept the possibility, then you make it real. I've decided that until someone proves it otherwise to me, I'm not going to accept his death. I believe in him. I believe he's alive and out there, somewhere, causing someone trouble."

The inn looked to be a cozy place, not like some they had been to, with too much drinking and too much noise. Why people wanted to dance whenever it got dark was beyond him. Somehow, the two seemed to go together, like bees and flowers, or flies and dung. Darkness and dancing.

People sat at a few tables, eating quietly, and one of the tables near the far wall was crowded with a group of older men, smoking pipes, playing a board game, and sipping ale as they engaged in lively conversation. He caught snippets of phrases about the new Lord Rahl.

"You keep quiet," Ann warned, "and let me do the talking."

A friendly-looking couple behind a counter smiled at their approach. The woman's cheeks dimpled.

"Evening, folks."

"Good evening," Ann said. "We would like to inquire about a room. The boy at the stable said you had nice rooms."

"Oh, that we do, ma'am. For you and your . . ."

Ann opened her mouth. Zedd beat her to words. "Brother. Ruben is the name. This is my sister, Elsie. I'm Ruben Rybnik." Zedd flourished a hand. "I'm a cloud reader of some note. Perhaps you've heard of me. Ruben Rybnik, the famous cloud reader."

The woman's jaw moved as if in search of where all her words went. "Well, I . . . well . . . yes, I believe I have."

"There you go," Zedd said, patting Ann on the back. "Nearly everyone's heard of me, Elsie." He leaned on an elbow toward the couple behind the counter. "Elsie thinks I make it up, but then she's been off on that farm, with those poor unfortunates who hear the voices and talk to the walls."

In unison, the two heads swiveled toward Ann.

"I worked there," Ann managed to get out between her clenched teeth. "I worked there, helping the 'poor unfortunates' who were our guests."

"Yes, yes," Zedd said. "And a fine job you did, Elsie. Why they let you go I'll never understand." He turned back to the mute couple. "Since she's out of work, I thought to take her out in the world with me, let her see what life's all about, don't you see."

"Yes," the couple said as one.

"And actually," Zedd said, "we'd prefer two rooms. One for my sister, and one for me." They blinked at him. "She snores," he explained. "I need my sleep." He gestured toward the ceiling. "Cloud reading, you know. Demanding work."

"Well, we have lovely rooms," the woman said, her cheeks dimpling again. "I'm sure you will get a good rest."

Zedd shook a cautionary finger. "The best you have, mind you. Elsie can afford it. Her uncle passed on, left her everything he had, and he was a wealthy man."

The man's brow drew down. "Wouldn't he be your uncle, too?"

"My uncle? Well, yes, he would, but he didn't like me. Little bit of trouble with the old man. He was a morsel eccentric. Wore socks as mittens in the dead of summer. Elsie was his favorite."

"The rooms," Ann growled. She turned and gave him a dark frown. "Ruben needs his sleep. He has a lot of cloud reading to do, and must be at it early in the morning. If he doesn't get his sleep, he gets the oddest burning rash in a ring around his neck."

The woman started around the counter. "Well, let me show you to them, then."

"That wouldn't be roasted duck I smell, would it?"

"Oh, yes," the woman said, turning back. "That's our dinner tonight. Roasted duck with parsnips and onions and gravy, if you've a desire for some."

Zedd inhaled deeply. "My, but it does have a delightful aroma. Takes talent to roast a duck just right, but I can tell by the fragrance that you've gotten it right. No doubt about it."

The woman blushed and giggled. "Well, I am known for my roasted duck."

"It sounds lovely," Ann said. "If you could be so kind, would you send it up to our rooms?"

"Oh, of course. It would be my pleasure."

The woman started them down the hall.

"On second thought," Zedd said, "You go ahead, Elsie, I know how nervous you get to have people watch you eat. I'll take my dinner out here, madam. With a pot of tea, if you don't mind."

Ann turned and shot him a scowl. He could feel the collar at his neck heat. "Don't be long, Ruben. We must get an early start."

Zedd waved a dismissive hand. "Oh, no, my dear. I'll just have my dinner, perhaps a game with these gentlemen, and then be off to bed straightaway. See you in the morning, bright and early, so we can be off to show you the world."

Her glare could have boiled pitch. "Good night, then, Ruben."

Zedd smiled indulgently. "Don't forget to pay the kind woman, and add something extra for her generosity with the large helping of her excellent roasted duck." Zedd craned his neck toward her with a weighty look, his voice thinning. "And don't forget to write in your journal before bed."

She stiffened. "My journal?"

"Yes, the little travel journal you keep. I know how you like to write about your adventures, and you haven't been keeping up to date like you should. I think it's about time you did."

"Yes . . ." she stammered. "I will, then, Ruben."

Once Ann had gone, sending warning glances at him the whole way, the gentlemen at the table, having heard the entire conversation, invited him over. Zedd spread his maroon robes and descended among them.

"Cloud reader, you say?" One asked.

"The very best." Zedd held up a bony finger. "Cloud reader to kings, no less."

Astonished whispers passed around the table.

A man to the side took his pipe from his teeth. "Would you do a cloud reading for us, Master Ruben? We'd all put in and pay you a bit."

Zedd held up a thin hand, as if warding them off. "I'm afraid I couldn't." He waited for the disappointment to build. "I couldn't accept your money. It would be my honor to tell you what the clouds had to say, but I won't take a copper."

Smiles returned. "That's most generous of you, Ruben."

A heavyset man leaned in. "What do the clouds have to say?"

The innkeeper set a steaming plate of roasted duck before him, diverting his attention. "I'll have your tea shortly," she said as she hurried off to the kitchen.

"The clouds had much to say about the winds of change, gentlemen. Dangers and opportunities. About the glorious new Lord Rahl, and the . . . well, let me have a taste of this succulent-looking duck, and I'll be delighted to tell you all about it."

"Dig in, Ruben," another said.

Zedd savored a mouthful, pausing dramatically to sigh with pleasure as the men all watched with rapt attention.

"That would be a mighty strange necklace you wear."

Zedd tapped the collar as he chewed. "They don't make them like this anymore."

Squinting, the man pointed his pipe stem at the collar. "Doesn't seem to have a clasp. Looks to be one piece. How did you get it down over your head?"

Zedd unfastened the collar and held it out for them, working the two halves on the hinge. "Yes it does. See? Mighty fine work, isn't it? A person can't even see the workings because they're so delicate. Master workmanship. Don't see things like this anymore."

"That's what I always say," the man with the pipe said. "You don't see fine workmanship anymore."

Zedd snapped the collar back around his neck. "No, you don't."

"I saw an odd cloud today," a hollow-cheeked man to the other side said. "Strange cloud. Snakelike it was. Wriggled in the sky, sometimes."

Zedd leaned in and lowered his voice. "You saw it, then."

They all leaned in. "What's it mean, Ruben?" one whispered.

He looked from eye to eye. "Some say it's a tracer cloud, hooked on a man by a wizard." Zedd was satisfied by the gasps.

"What for?" the heavyset man asked, the whites of his eyes showing all around.

Zedd made a show of looking about at the other tables before he spoke. "To track him, and know where he goes."

"Wouldn't he see such a cloud, all snakelike and all?"

"There's the trick to it, I'm told," Zedd whispered as he used his fork to demonstrate. "It points down at the man followed, so all he would see is a tiny dot, kind of like looking at the tip of a cane. But those off to the side see the whole of the cane."

The men aahed and leaned back with this news, digesting it as Zedd dug into the roasted duck.

"Do you know about these winds of change?" one finally asked. "And about this new Lord Rahl?"

"Wouldn't be a cloud reader to kings if I didn't." Zedd brandished his fork. "It's a mighty good tale, if you gentlemen have a mind to hear it."

They all leaned in again.

"It all started before, in the ancient war," Zedd began, "when were created the ones called dream walkers."

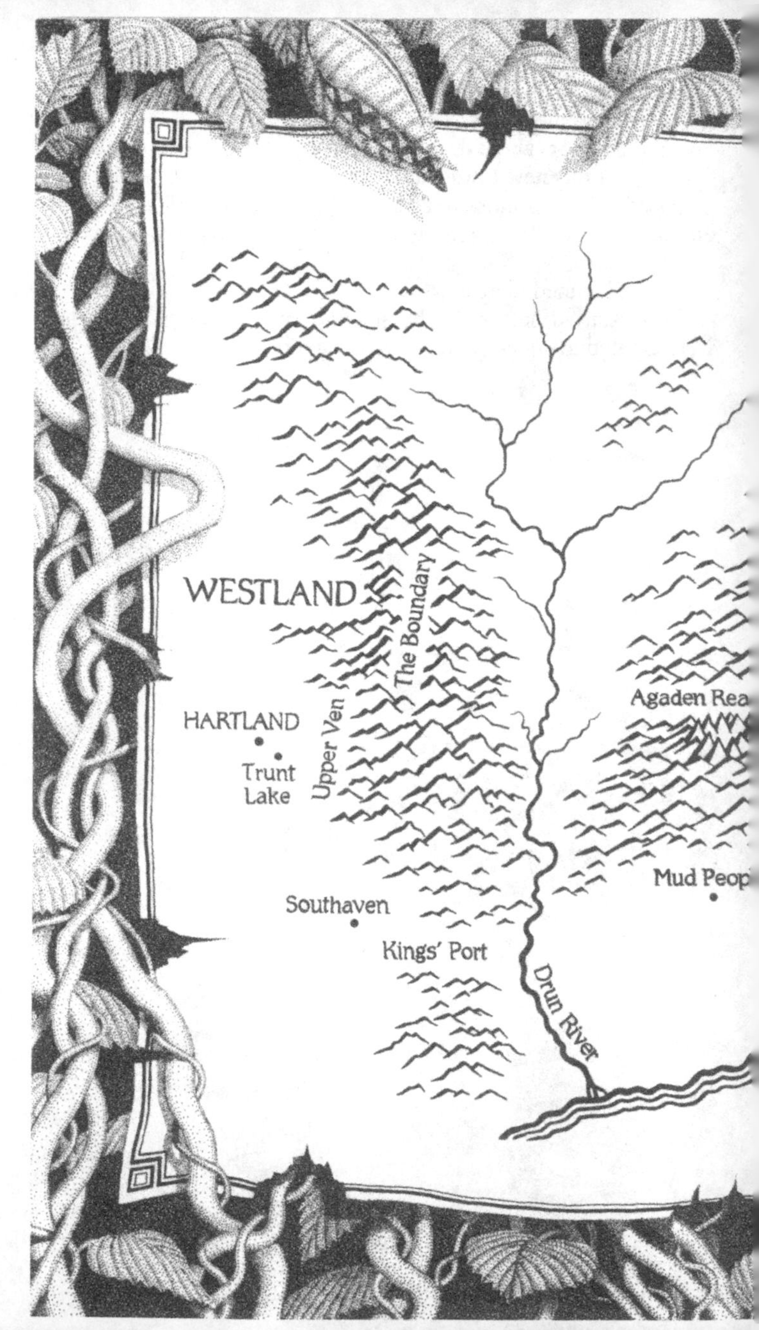

WESTLAND
The Boundary
Upper Ven
HARTLAND
Trunt
Lake
Southaven
Kings' Port
Drun River
Agaden Rea
Mud Peop

ang'Shada Mountains
AYDINDRIL
D'HARA
The Boundary
THE MIDLANDS
PEOPLE'S PALACE
Azrith Plains
TAMARANG
Kern River
THE WILDS
Callisidrin River
THE OLD WORLD
TANIMURA
TERRY GOODKIND